DOUBLE

JEOPARDY

&

THE
CAULDRON

Colin Forbes writes a novel every year. For the past twenty-five years he has earned his living solely as a full-time writer.

He visits all the locations which will appear in a new novel. Forbes says, 'It is essential for me to see for myself where the book will take place. Only in this way can I conjure up the unique atmosphere of the chosen locales.'

He has explored most of Western Europe, the East and West coasts of America, and has made excursions to Africa and Asia. Each new book appears on all major bestseller lists.

Surveys have shown that his readership is divided equally between women and men.

DOUBLE JEOPARDY

&

THE CAULDRON

COLIN FORBES

PAN BOOKS

Double Jeopardy first published 1982 by William Collins Sons & Co. Ltd.
First published by Pan Books 1983
The Cauldron first published 1977 by Macmillan
First published by Pan Books 1998

This omnibus edition published 2004 by Pan Books
an imprint of Pan Macmillan Ltd
Pan Macmillan, 20 New Wharf Road, London N1 9RR
Basingstoke and Oxford
Associated companies throughout the world
www.panmacmillan.com

ISBN 0 330 43914 6

Printed and bound in Great Britain by
Mackays of Chatham plc, Chatham Kent

DOUBLE JEOPARDY

For Jane

Chapter One

Sunday May 24

After the murder it was assumed that Charles Warner – always so vigilant – had let down his guard because of the atmosphere. When he left the harbour at Lindau, Bavaria, and took his powerboat out on to Lake Konstanz it was a sunny, peaceful afternoon.

'And it was a diabolically clever and audacious killing,' Tweed commented to Martel two days later in London.

The powerboat, with Warner as its sole occupant, moved slowly as it passed through the harbour exit, flanked on one side by the stone statue of the Lion of Bavaria; on the other by the towering lighthouse. Conforming to regulations, he sounded his hooter.

A lean, agile man of forty, Warner was wearing a German suit. On the seat beside him lay a Tyrolean hat. For his secret crossing to his landfall on the Swiss shore he had substituted a peaked, nautical cap which merged into the holiday scene.

There was nothing ahead of him on the huge lake to arouse suspicion. In the glare of the afternoon sun a fleet of yachts with coloured sails drifted like toys. Beyond rose the jagged, snowbound peaks of

Liechtenstein and Switzerland. To his right one of the many white steamers which ply the lake disappeared towards the German town of Konstanz.

To his left a group of wind-surfers was using the light breeze to skim over the glassy surface of the water. He counted six of them as they moved across his bows.

'Kindly get out of the Goddamn way,' he muttered as he throttled back his engine.

They were all young, fine physical specimens, clad only in bathing trunks as they propelled their strange craft in an enclosing arc. Two of them were blond. Warner was about half a mile from the shore when he realised they were playing games, circling round to stop him opening up the throttle.

'Go and play elsewhere,' Warner growled.

He had a damned good mind to open up and scare them – but they were so close he might run them down. The tallest blond waved and brought his craft alongside the powerboat. He held the sail steady with his left hand while his right gripped the sheath knife strapped to his thigh. Too late a flicker of alarm alerted the Englishman. The wind-surfer abandoned his sail and jumped into the powerboat. He wielded the blade with speed and lethal efficiency, plunging it into his victim at varying angles.

The other five wind-surfers formed a screen of sails, masking the powerboat from anyone who might be watching them through glasses onshore. And the

Wasserschutzpolizei – Water Police – had a unit and a launch at Lindau.

They maintained the screen while the tall blond completed his butchery. Then he left the powerboat, slipped into the water and upended his own sail. They resumed formation, heading for the deserted shore between Lindau and the Austrian border at the end of the lake.

'Multiple stab wounds – like the work of some maniac...'

Sergeant Dorner of the Water Police stood up from his examination of the body in the drifting powerboat. He looked at the launch with *Polizei* painted in blue letters on the hull drawn up alongside. The youngest policeman aboard who had been watching the examination began to retch over the side. Baptism of fire, Dorner thought.

He frowned as he noticed something gleaming by his foot. When he picked it up and saw what he had found he slipped it quickly into his pocket. A triangular-shaped badge very like the Greek letter *delta*. He glanced down at the body again; it was a pretty grisly mess. He opened the passport extracted from the corpse's jacket together with a wallet.

'He's English. Funny, the wallet is stuffed with money...'

'Maybe those wind-surfers panicked...' From his

high point on the bridge of the launch, Busch, Dorner's deputy and the third man in the team, shielded his eyes and stared east. 'No sign of the bastards. They moved off fast . . .'

'It takes only seconds to snatch a man's wallet,' Dorner persisted. 'This is the strangest killing I've come across . . . Christ!'

Sifting through the contents of the wallet he had found a small card made of plastic rather like a credit card. But this was no credit card Dorner thought grimly as he studied the green and red stripes, the embossed number – which identified the owner – and a five-letter code reference which meant London.

'What's the matter?' Busch called down.

Something in his chief's expression warned him they had found trouble. Dorner slipped the card back inside the wallet and beckoned Busch to leave the bridge and come close to the powerboat. He kept his voice low when Busch faced him over the narrow gap between the two vessels.

'This has to be kept quiet. First we inform the BND at Pullach immediately . . .'

'You mean he's . . .'

'I don't mean anything. But I think there are people in London who will want to know about this before nightfall . . .'

Sergeant Dorner was very silent as he stood on the bridge of the police launch, leaving the handling of the vessel to his subordinate as they approached the harbour of Lindau. Attached by a strong rope, the powerboat with its ghastly cargo was being dragged at the stern, the body carefully concealed by a sheet of canvas.

It was the macabre condition of the corpse's back which worried Dorner, a fact he had not mentioned even to Busch. And the horror of what he had discovered seemed such an appalling contrast to the holiday atmosphere of Lindau where visitors strolled in the sun along the short harbour front.

Keep close watch for group six wind-surfers possibly approaching your shore now. If seen apprehend and hold in close custody. Proceed on basis group armed and dangerous.

This was the top priority signal Dorner had told the young radio operator to send before they began the return trip to Lindau. By then the latest addition to his crew had fortunately recovered from his bout of vomiting. And the signal had been sent to police headquarters at Bregenz on the Austrian shore as well as to Dorner's home base.

'I thought I saw some weird markings carved on his back,' Busch remarked as he sounded the siren prior to entering the harbour. 'Almost like some kind of symbol – but there was so much blood . . .'

'Keep your mind on your job,' Dorner told him tensely.

With the sun blazing down on their necks they entered the small harbour and turned east to the landing-stage where the launch always berthed.

Dorner was most concerned about how to smuggle the body the short distance from harbour to headquarters without anyone seeing it. He need not have worried. The early discovery of Charles Warner's body was already being observed.

The ancient town of Lindau with its medieval buildings, narrow, cobbled streets and even narrower alleys stands on an island at the eastern end of Lake Konstanz. There are two quite separate routes to reach this geographical oddity.

Coming by car you drive over the Seebrücke – the road bridge. Travelling to Lindau by international express from Zürich, you cross a rail embankment further west. The train stops at the Hauptbahnhof perched by the waterfront; it then moves back over the embankment and proceeds on to München.

The pavement artist was located outside the Bayerischer Hof, the most luxurious hotel on Lindau which faces the station exit. From here he could easily observe arrivals by train or boat.

A lean, bony-faced man in his early twenties, he wore a faded windcheater and jeans. The clothes were spotlessly clean. There are few beggars in Germany but those who exist preserve a respectable appearance. Only in this way can they hope to obtain money from passers-by.

His work was a picture of the Forum in Rome drawn in crayon on the stones of the sidewalk, a small cardboard box by its side for coins. At frequent intervals he paused while he walked up and down slowly, hands clasped behind his back.

He was now watching the police launch entering the harbour. As it swung round, broadside on, heading for its berth, he saw the powerboat being towed in its wake. Turning away, he made sure no one was watching him and checked his watch strapped well above the wrist. Then he strolled across the road, pushed open a door and walked into the Hauptbahnhof.

Before he entered the phone booth he checked to make sure no one was coming out of the office marked *Polizei*. Once inside the booth he called the number and waited. From an apartment block in Stuttgart a girl's voice answered.

'Edgar Braun,' he replied.

'This is Klara. I'm just going out so I only have a minute . . .'

'A minute is all it will take . . .' He paused. The agreed opening had confirmed to each the other's identity. 'I thought that you would like to know the expected consignment has arrived . . .'

'So quickly?'

She sounded startled. The man who called himself Braun frowned. It was most unlike the girl to lose her detachment. Whoever's body was inside the powerboat had clearly been found much earlier than expected.

'Are you sure?' she demanded.

7

'Of course I'm sure.' He bridled. 'You want the details?' he suggested nastily.

'That won't be necessary.' Her voice had resumed its normal cold tone. 'Thank you for calling . . .'

'And my fee?' Braun persisted.

'Waiting to be collected at the Post Office in the usual way two days from now. And continue in your present job. Remember, jobs are not so easy to get at the moment . . .'

He was left staring at the phone. The bitch had broken the connection. He shrugged, left the booth and returned to his pitch on the pavement. Braun knew what he had to watch for but beyond phoning a girl called Klara he had never met – and the fact she had a Stuttgart number – he knew nothing about the organisation he was spying for.

In the luxurious penthouse apartment in Stuttgart Klara stared at herself in the dressing-table mirror. An ex-model with a superb figure she was twenty-seven years old. Her sleek black hair was attended to weekly by the city's top hairdresser and there was a small fortune in her wardrobe of clothes.

She had dark, sleepy-looking eyes, fine bone structure and was a chain-smoker. She was hesitating before she picked up the white telephone and called the man who owned the apartment. She lit a fresh cigarette and dialled the number in southern Bavaria.

Inside the moated *schloss* many miles north-east of

Lindau a firm, leathery hand picked up the receiver. On his third finger the man wore a large diamond ring. Beneath his strong jaw he wore a solid gold tie-slide. Attached to his left wrist was a Patek Philippe watch.

'Yes!'

No identification, just the single curt word.

'Klara calling. It is convenient to talk?'

'Yes! You received the fur I sent? Good. Anything else?'

The voice had a gravelly timbre, a hint of impatience that they must go through this identification rigmarole before they could get to the point. Like Klara earlier, he sounded startled when she relayed Braun's message.

'You say the consignment has arrived *already*?'

'Yes. I knew you would be relieved . . .'

The sixty-year-old man she was talking to was not relieved. He concealed his reaction but he was alarmed at the speed with which the police had discovered the body of the Englishman.

The reference to the 'consignment' confirmed that Warner had been liquidated on schedule as planned. The further reference to 'has arrived' told him the corpse was already in police hands. He repeated almost the same words Klara had used to Braun.

'Are you quite certain? It is very quick . . .'

'I wasn't there to witness the collection,' she said, her voice tinged with sarcasm. 'I'm reporting what our observer told me less than five minutes ago . . .'

'Remember who you're talking to,' he told her. He replaced the receiver, took a Havana cigar from a box on his desk, clipped off the end and lit it with a gold lighter.

In her Stuttgart apartment Klara was careful to replace her own receiver before she used the four-letter word. He might share her bed, pay the rent, buy her clothes but he didn't bloody well own her.

She lit a fresh cigarette, studied herself in the mirror and began manipulating an eye pencil. The trouble was Reinhard Dietrich was a millionaire industrialist, a considerable landowner and a well-known politician. And she never let herself forget that she was consorting with one of the most dangerous men in West Germany.

Chapter Two

Tuesday May 26

Tweed sat behind his desk in the first floor office of a house which overlooks Regent's Park in the distance. Through thick-lensed spectacles he gazed at the pile of relics taken by the Lindau Water Police off the dead body of Charles Warner.

The hub of Britain's Secret Service is not – as has been reported – in a concrete building close to Waterloo Station. It is situated inside one of many Georgian buildings in a crescent, most of which are occupied by professional institutions.

The location has a number of advantages. On leaving the building there are different directions one can take. To check whether anyone is following you the simplest route is to walk straight into Regent's Park. In the open parkland it is impossible for a shadow to conceal his presence.

Only a few paces away is the entrance to Regent's Park Underground. Unlike most other stations you descend in a lift to reach the platforms. Again, anyone following has to show himself by stepping into the same lift.

'Pathetic what a man carries about with him,' Tweed remarked.

Keith Martel, the only other occupant in the room, lit a cigarette and wondered whether Tweed was criticising the relics because they offended his sense of order or commenting on the poverty of what a man left behind. He decided it was the latter.

There was about twenty years' difference in the ages of the two men. Martel, tall, well-built, dark-haired and with an air of supreme self-confidence, was twenty-nine. His most prominent feature was his Roman nose. His most outstanding characteristic was insubordination.

He chain-smoked, using a black holder. He spoke German, French and Spanish fluently. He was a first-rate pilot of light aircraft and helicopters. He swam like a fish and hated team sports.

No one knew Tweed's age. Five feet eight inches tall, wiry and with a ramrod back, he had the appearance of an ex-Army major – which he was – and his grey moustache matching his thatch of hair was neatly trimmed. Behind the spectacles his eyes bulged and held a haunted look as though expecting the worst.

'It usually happens – the worst. Count on it,' was his favourite maxim.

Events had an uncanny habit of proving him correct. It was this fact – his reputation for solving problems – and his caustic manner which had persuaded the new head of the department to sidetrack him into the post of Chief of Central Registry. Also the new supremo, Frederick Anthony Howard, had taken an instant dislike to Tweed when they first met in some mysterious past.

'What do you make of it all, Keith?'

Tweed gestured to the possessions of Warner spread in a gap on his desk he had cleared amid tidy piles of dossiers. Martel picked up several slips of paper and tickets extracted from the dead man's wallet.

Warner had been a squirrel, stuffing his wallet with odd items other agents would have thrown away. But Martel knew it was not carelessness: Warner had worked on the basis that if ever anything happened to him while on an assignment he should leave his successor clues.

'What was he doing in Germany?' Martel asked as he examined the collection.

'On loan from me to Erich Stoller of the *Bundesnach-richtendienst*. I owe Erich and he needed an outsider who could pass for a German to infiltrate this Delta outfit in Bavaria – neo-Nazis, as you well know. They cleverly keep just inside the law so they can't be banned.'

The *Bundesnachrichtendienst* – the BND – was the German Federal Secret Service with discreet head-quarters near Münich. There was a dull *clink* as Tweed took something from his pocket and dropped it on the desk. A triangular-shaped silver badge like the Greek letter *delta*.

'That's their latest version of the swastika,' Tweed remarked. 'The badge was found under Warner's body. The killer must have dropped it without realising he'd lost it . . .'

'How *was* he killed?'

'Brutally.' Tweed took off his glasses and leaned back in his swivel chair, settling himself on his favourite cushion. 'The BND pathologist reports that Warner was struck with some kind of knife twenty-five times. Twenty-five! And they completed the job by carving their trademark on his naked back – the Delta symbol.'

'We're relying on that to identify it as a Delta killing?'

'We're relying on an impartial eye-witness – whose name Stoller won't reveal even to me. Some German tourist was sitting on an elevated terrace above the harbour at Lindau . . .'

'Sounds like the Romerschanze,' Martel interjected.

'Of course, I'd forgotten. You know Lindau. Rum-looking sort of place – I checked it up on the map. From the air it must look like a raft linked by a couple of planks to the mainland. As you know, it's an island linked to Bavaria by two bridges . . .'

'One road bridge and a separate rail embankment with a cycle and pedestrian track running alongside the railway.'

'Nice to have an eye for detail,' Tweed commented with a hint of sarcasm. Martel appeared not to notice: the reaction showed Tweed was concealing considerable anxiety.

'As I was saying,' Tweed continued, 'this German tourist using his binoculars watched Warner take his powerboat out on to the lake. He saw a crowd of wind-surfers – six to be precise – get in Warner's way so he had to stop his boat. When they pushed off he saw Warner's boat was drifting – with Warner slumped over the wheel. He thought he must have been taken ill so he immediately contacted the Water Police who berth their launch just below that Romer-what-not terrace . . .' He consulted Stoller's report. 'Chap called Dorner went out to have a look-see . . .'

'And the rest is history – past history, unfortunately.'

'Except that I want you to go out and replace Warner for me,' Tweed said quietly.

Frederick Anthony Howard came into the office without knocking. It would be more accurate to say he *breezed* in. It was the essence of Howard's personality that you dominated a room the moment you entered it.

He was accompanied by Mason, a new recruit. Mason had restless eyes and a lean and hungry look. He said nothing and stood behind his chief like a commissionaire.

'Tweed, I suppose you know we need all *active* personnel mustered for the protection of the PM during her trip to the summit conference in Vienna?'

He invested the word 'active' with a significance which included Martel and specifically excluded Tweed. Florid-faced and with a choleric temper,

Howard was a well-built man of fifty who had an unruly shock of grey hair and a brisk manner. He had a reputation for being a devil with the women, a reputation he relished.

The fact that his wife, Cynthia, lived at their 'small manor' in the country and he rented 'a pied-à-terre' in Knightsbridge could not have been more convenient. Tweed's privately expressed comment had been rather devastating.

'Pied-à-terre? I've been there once. When he has a girl with him it must be standing room only . . .'

'What's all this bumf?' Howard demanded, picking up the wallet from the desk. Martel had palmed the slips of paper he was perusing and slipped them into his pocket as Howard entered the room.

'That *bumf*,' Tweed said grimly, 'happens to be the personal effects of the late Charles Warner. The BND kindly flew them straight to London from München so we can begin our investigation at the earliest moment.'

Having delivered his statement in a calm, cold voice Tweed put on his spectacles. Without them he felt naked, especially in the presence of people like Howard. And he was well aware that wearing the glasses made it impossible to judge his expression.

'Getting touchy in our old age, are we?' Howard enquired lightly, trying to bluff his way through what he now realised had been the height of bad taste.

'The man is dead,' Tweed replied, giving no quarter.

'I don't like it any more than you do.' Howard

16

strolled over to the heavily net-curtained window and gazed through the armoured glass. He clasped both hands in a theatrical pose before making his pronouncement.

'I simply must insist that all active personnel are available to travel aboard the Summit Express from Paris to Vienna one week from today. Tuesday June 2 . . .'

'I do have a calendar,' Tweed commented.

Howard looked pointedly away from Tweed and at Martel who said nothing, his cigarette holder in his mouth – which to Howard was insubordination. He had made it very clear he preferred no one to practise the filthy habit in his presence.

'Well?' he pressed.

Martel stared back at Howard, puffing away, his expression hard and hostile. 'I'm otherwise engaged,' he said eventually, still clenching the holder. Howard turned to Tweed and erupted.

'This is too damned much. I'm taking Martel and attaching him to my protection group. He speaks good German . . .'

'Which is why he's going to Bavaria,' Tweed told him. 'We were suspicious something strange is going on in that part of the world. It looks as though we were right. Otherwise why was Warner killed?'

Howard glanced at Mason who still stood by the door like a commissionaire. Time to assert his authority. '*We?*' he repeated in a supercilious tone. 'May I enquire the identity of "we"?'

17

'Erich Stoller of the BND and myself,' Tweed said tersely. Time to get rid of Howard. 'I have a minute from the Minister – authorising me to investigate the Bavarian enigma and full powers to use my staff in any way I see fit. May I also point out that the route of the Summit Express carrying the four top western leaders to Vienna to meet the Soviet First Secretary passes through Bavaria?'

They were alone again. Howard had stormed out of the office on hearing of the existence of the special ministerial minute. Mason had followed, closing the door carefully behind him.

'He was memorising my appearance,' Martel said.

'Do let's get on. Oh, all right, who was?'

'The new boy, Mason. Who brought him in off the street?'

'Ex-Special Branch, I gather,' Tweed replied. 'And it was Howard who recruited him – interviewed him personally, I heard. I think he'd been angling to join us for a while . . .'

'We don't take people who apply,' Martel snapped.

'We do now, apparently. How are you going to pick up Warner's trail? And since you've had your breakfast your stomach should be strong enough to study these pictures taken by Stoller's man – two show clearly the triangular symbol of the Delta Party carved out of Warner's back . . .'

'Delta being the neo-Nazis,' Martel ruminated as

he studied the glossy blow-ups. 'Delta is run by that millionaire electronics industrialist, Reinhard Dietrich. He's also running for office in the Bavarian state elections which take place . . .'

'On Thursday June 4 – the day after the Summit Express crosses Bavaria,' Tweed interjected. 'Which is something else Howard may have overlooked. You know, Keith, I have the oddest feeling the whole thing interlocks – the Bavarian crossing by the express, the state elections, and the murder of Warner before he could reach us.'

Martel dropped the glossy prints back on the desk and extracted from his pocket the pieces of paper he had secreted while Howard was in the room. He showed Tweed one particular piece of paper.

'I'll start in Zürich to try and find out what got Warner killed.'

'Why Zürich? I did notice a first-class ticket from München by train to Zürich – and another from Lindau to München, but . . .'

'This little scrap of paper. Go on, have a really good look at it.'

Tweed examined it under a magnifying glass. It was some kind of ticket which carried the printed legend *VBZ Zuri . . . Linie*. The words RENNWEG/AUGUST had been punched in purple on the ticket together with the price 0.80.

'From the last time I was in Zürich I'm sure you're holding a tram ticket,' Martel explained. 'A tram whose route takes it along Bahnhofstrasse – Rennweg is a side street running off Bahnhofstrasse. Warner travelled about inside the city. Why? Where to? He never wasted time.'

Tweed nodded agreement, unlocked a drawer and brought out a file. From inside he produced a tiny black notebook and thumbed through the pages. Then he waved the key he had used.

'I suppose you know Howard waits until everyone has gone home in the evening and then prowls – hoping to find something he hasn't been told about? He spends more time spying on his own staff than on the opposition. Still, it will help to keep his hand in . . .'

'You're just about to play your strongest card,' Martel observed. 'You're enjoying the anticipation. Could I now see what you hold in the way of aces?'

'It came with Warner's possessions Stoller flew to me with such commendable speed.' Tweed riffled the pages of the tiny notebook. 'Only I know Warner carried two notebooks – a large one inside his breast pocket, which is missing. Presumably filched by the swine who mutilated him. That was full of meaning-less rubbish. This little fellow he kept in a secret pocket Stoller himself found when he flew to Lindau – or the nearest airstrip – when he heard from Dorner of the Water Police.'

'Am I to be allowed to see it?'

'You have a viper's tongue, Mr Martel.' Tweed handed over the notebook. 'The trouble is the jottings in it don't make sense.'

Martel went through the pages. The references seemed disjointed. *Hauptbahnhof, Münich ... Hauptbahnhof, Zürich ... Delta ... Centralhof ... Bregenz ... Washington, DC, Clint Loomis ... Pullach, BND ... Operation Crocodile.*

'Charles ...'

They had always called him Charles. Warner was the kind of man they would never dream of calling Charlie; he would have resented it.

'Charles,' Martel repeated, 'seems to have been fixated on the main stations – the Hauptbahnhofs in Münich and Zürich. Why? And if the note sequence means anything Delta is somehow linked with Zürich, which is odd, wouldn't you say?'

'Delta is the official neo-Nazi party with candidates standing in the coming Bavarian state elections,' Tweed remarked. 'But it also works underground. Rumour has it Delta cells are operating in north-east Switzerland between St Gallen and the Austrian border. Ferdy Arnold of Swiss counter-espionage is worried ...'

'Enough to give us support?' Martel enquired.

'At arm's length. You know the Swiss – policy of neutrality so they feel they have to be careful ...'

'With that bunch of thugs? Look what they did to Warner. And who is Clint Loomis – Washington, DC?'

'I can't fathom that reference.' Tweed leaned back and swivelled his chair through small arcs. 'Clint is an old friend of mine. *Ex*-CIA. Kicked out by Tim O'Meara, now chief of the Secret Service detachment which will protect the US President aboard the Summit Express to Vienna. Makes no sense . . .'

'Who provides most of the funds for this link-up with the BND if Howard is against it?'

'Erich Stoller of the BND – and he has plenty of money at his disposal. Delta is scaring Bonn . . .'

'So Charles, being the secretive type he was, could have flown on a quick trip to Washington from Münich without your knowing?'

'Yes, I suppose so.' Tweed sounded dubious. 'I don't see why.'

'But we don't see anything yet, do we? Least of all what Warner found out that provoked his cold-blooded murder.' He checked the notebook again. '*Centralhof.* That rings a bell.'

Tweed stirred in his chair and the expression behind his spectacles went blank. Which meant, Martel knew from experience, he was going to be told something he wouldn't like. He lit another cigarette and clamped his teeth on the holder.

'You at least have some help on this thing, Keith,' Tweed said cheerfully, 'Ferdy Arnold put his best operative at the disposal of Warner and that operative may have more to tell you. Outside of his killers, she may have been the last person to see Warner alive . . .'

'*She?*'

'The pronoun denotes a woman. Claire Hofer. Her mother was English, her father Swiss – and one of Ferdy's best men, which is how she came to join the

Swiss Service. She lives at Centralhof 45 in Zürich. Hence the reference, I presume . . .'

'Except that Warner seems to have used his secret notebook for suspect factors . . .'

'You may need all the help you can get . . .'

'All the help I can *trust* . . .'

'She could be a major asset,' Tweed persisted.

'You do realise,' Martel began vehemently, 'that Warner was betrayed by someone who *knew* he was making the crossing to Switzerland – by someone he *trusted*. And tell me again why Stoller asked for outside help.'

'Because he thinks the BND may have been infiltrated. You will find an atmosphere of suspicion everywhere you go. And with the Summit Express leaving Paris at 2335 hours on Tuesday June 2 you have exactly seven days to crack this mystery.'

Chapter Three

Wednesday May 27

Will Mr Keith Martel bound for Geneva please report immediately to the Swissair reception desk . . .

Martel was inside Heathrow on his way to the final departure lounge when the message came over the Tannoy. He went back down the stairs slowly and paused where he could see Swissair. Only when two more passengers had called at the reception desk did he wander over.

The Swissair girl told him he was wanted urgently on the phone and left him as he picked up the receiver, fuming. It was Tweed. His voice held that quality of detached control which meant he was alarmed. They went through the identification routine and then Martel quietly exploded.

'What the hell do you mean broadcasting my name so everyone in the bloody terminal can hear . . .'

'I did change the destination to Geneva. Didn't they . . .'

'They did. Thank you for that small consideration. I now have ten minutes to board my flight . . .'

'My office was bugged – while we were talking yesterday. About Delta, the lot . . .'

24

'Where are you calling from.'

'A phone booth at Baker Street station, of course. You don't imagine I'm such a damned fool as to call from the building, do you? I found the bloody thing purely by chance. The cleaning woman had left a note that my main light bulb had gone. I checked it – the bug was inside the shade . . .'

'So anyone could have overheard our conversation, could have taped it, could know where I'm going and why?'

'I thought you ought to know – before you boarded the plane.'

Tweed sounded genuinely concerned. Unusual for Tweed to display any emotion.

'Thanks,' Martel said shortly. 'I'll keep my eyes open . . .'

'Probably it's the Zürich end you should watch. A reception committee could be waiting for you . . .'

'Thanks a million. I must go now . . .'

The Swissair flight departed on time at 1110 hours. In London it had been 50°F. As they lost height over Switzerland Martel, who had a window seat, watched the saddleback ridge of the Jura mountains which he felt he could reach down and touch. The plane had come in over Basle and headed east for Zürich.

As the machine tilted the most spectacular of views was framed in a window on the other side of the plane, a sunlit panorama of the snowbound Alps.

Martel picked out the savage triangle of the Matter-horn, a shape not unlike Delta's badge. Then they landed.

At Kloten Airport, ten kilometres outside Zürich, a wave of heat enveloped him as he disembarked. 50°F in London; 75°F in Zürich. After Heathrow it seemed unnaturally quiet and orderly. When he had passed through Customs and Passport Control he started looking for trouble.

He was tempted to take the train from the airport's underground station to the Hauptbahnhof, the second location recorded in Warner's notebook. Instead he took a cab to the Baur au Lac.

He was staying at one of the top three hotels in Switzerland and the room tariff would have caused Howard to have apoplexy. But Howard was not paying the expenses. Before Martel left London a large amount of deutschemarks had been telexed to Tweed for the trip from Erich Stoller.

'The Germans are paying, so enjoy yourself,' Tweed had commented. 'They're conscious of the fact that the first man I sent to help is no longer with us . . .'

'And that I may be next?' Martel had replied. 'Still, it's good cover – to stay at the best place in town rather than some grotty little *pension* . . .'

Good cover? He recalled the remark cynically as the cab sped along the two-lane highway into the *centrum* of Zürich. It had been made in Tweed's office which they now knew had been bugged. He could change his hotel – but if the opposition sought him out at the

Baur au Lac it might present him with a golden opportunity.

Just so long as I see them first he thought as he lit a fresh cigarette.

It was good to be back in Zürich, to see the blue trams rumbling along their tracks. The route the driver followed took him down through the underpass, sharp right across the bridge over the river Limmat and into the Bahnhofplatz. Martel stared at the massive bulk of the Hauptbahnhof, wondering again why the place had figured in Warner's notebook.

To his left he caught a glimpse of the tree-lined Bahnhofstrasse, his favourite street in his favourite European city. Here were the great banks with their incredible security systems, their underground vaults stacked with gold bullion. Then they were driving down Talstrasse, the street where the Baur au Lac was situated at the far end facing the lake.

A heavy grey overcast pressed down on the city and, as was so often the case when the temperature was high, the atmosphere was clammy. The cab turned in under an archway and pulled up at the main entrance. The head porter opened his door and Martel counted five Mercedes and one Rolls Royce parked in the concourse. Beyond the entrance the green lawns of the mini-park stretched away towards the lake.

From the airport to hotel he had not been followed. He was quite certain. The fact somehow did not reassure him as he followed the porter inside. The hotel was almost full. On the phone he had accepted a twin-bedded room overlooking the park. When the porter left he checked bedroom and bathroom for hidden microphones and found nothing. He was still not happy.

He went down the staircase after checking his room – avoiding the lift because lifts could be traps. The atmosphere was luxurious, peaceful and disturbingly normal. He strolled over the concourse to where tea and drinks were being served under a canopy near the French Restaurant. He ordered coffee, lit a cigarette and waited, watching the world's élite arrive and depart. He was looking for a shadow.

His appointment with Claire Hofer at her apartment was eight in the evening, an odd hour which he had wondered about. Normally he would have scanned the area in advance but the bugging of Tweed's office changed his tactics. He was good at waiting and he counted on the impatience of the opposition.

By 7.30 he was swimming in coffee and people were starting their evening meal in the nearby restaurant. He suddenly scribbled his signature and room number on the bill, stood up and walked out under the archway. Crossing Talstrasse, he turned left up Bahnhofstrasse away from the lake. He had spotted no one but could not rid himself of a feeling of unease.

Stopping by a machine in the deserted street, he inserted four twenty-centime coins obtained from the

Baur au Lac cashier, took his ticket and waited for one of Zürich's 'sacred cows'. These gleaming trams had total right-of-way over all other traffic – hence the Zürichers' irreverent description.

The ticket gave him a slight twinge. Inside his breast pocket was an envelope which contained the contents of Warner's wallet – including the tram ticket with the destination RENNWEG/AUGUST inscribed. This stop was not far away and the ticket could have been used by Warner when he called on Claire Hofer. A tram glided up the street, streamlined and freshly-painted. Martel climbed aboard and sat down near the exit doors.

From the hotel it would have taken him five minutes to walk to Centralhof 45, Claire Hofer's address. Taking a tram and travelling only one stop he hoped to flush out anyone following him. He played it deviously at the next stop. Standing up, he pressed the black button which would automatically open the double doors when the tram stopped.

The doors opened, he checked his ticket and stared about in a perplexed manner as though uncertain of his destination. People left the tram, came on board. Still he waited. The doors began closing. Martel *moved* . . .

He knew how the tram worked. He stepped down on to the outside footboard just when it began to elevate in conjunction with the closing of the automatic doors. As a safety device, when there is weight on the footboard, the doors remain open – or open again if they are closing. Reaching the sidewalk he paused to light a cigarette, to see if anyone rushed out after him. The doors shut, the tram moved off.

Centralhof is a square enclosed by buildings. One side overlooks Bahnhofstrasse. There are four entrances under archways at the centre of each side of the square – one leading off Bahnhofstrasse – to the interior garden beyond.

Martel crossed the street, walked down Poststrasse, turned right and continued along the third side of the block. Walking under the archway he saw the trees and the fountain he remembered. Nothing had changed. He sat down on a seat.

He had never visited this apartment in Centralhof before – but on an earlier visit he had used exactly the same tactic to entice a shadow to show himself. On that occasion it had worked.

The only sounds in the semi-dark were the chirruping of invisible sparrows in the foliage of the trees, the gentle splash of fountain water. It was impossible to imagine a more peaceful scene. He looked up at the windows masked by net curtains and the silence was almost a sound.

No one had followed him into this oasis of peace. He began to think he had evaded detection. He got up and headed for the archway Tweed had shown him on a street plan which contained the entrance to the apartment.

There was only one name-plate, a bell-push by its side. *C. Hofer.* He pressed the bell and a woman's voice responded through the metal grille of the speak-phone almost immediately. In German – not Swiss-German, which he would not have understood.

'Who is that?'

'Martel.'

He kept his voice low, his mouth close to the grille. The other voice sounded disembodied, filtered through the louvres.

'I have released the catch. I am on the first floor . . .'

He went into a bare hall and the spring-loaded hinge closed the door behind him. An old-fashioned lift with open grille-work enclosing a cage faced him. He ignored it and ran lightly up the staircase to arrive a few seconds before she would expect him.

Height: five feet six inches. Weight: nine stone two pounds. Age: twenty-five. Colour of hair: black. Colour of eyes: deep blue.

This was the description of Hofer Tweed had supplied to Martel in London. It was typical of Ferdy Arnold's consideration and efficiency that he should supply the girl's vital statistics in this terminology: he knew Tweed's detestation of the Common Market and the metric system.

Martel was not armed with any weapon when he reached the first floor. He expected Hofer to supply a hand-gun. A closed door faced him on the deserted landing and he noticed that – blended in with the grain of the highly-varnished woodwork was a spy-hole. At least she took *some* precautions when strangers arrived.

'Welcome to Zürich, Mr Martel. Please come in quickly . . .'

The door had been opened swiftly and the girl examined him as she ushered him inside, closed the door and double-locked it. Martel had stubbed out his cigarette as he waited inside the archway below. He held the black holder between his fingers and studied her without any show of enthusiasm.

She was wearing dark-tinted glasses with the out-size exotic-shaped lenses so many girls affected these days. Her hair *was* very black, her height was about five foot six and he calculated she *would* turn the scales at around nine stone. She was also very attractive and wore a flowered blouse and a pastel-coloured skirt which revealed shapely legs.

'Satisfied?' she demanded in a waspish tone.

'You can't be too careful,' he told her and walked out of the tiny hall into a living-room whose windows overlooked the garden inside Centralhof. His manner was off-hand and he inserted a cigarette and lit it without asking her permission.

'Yes, you may smoke,' she told him.

'Good. It helps my concentration . . .'

He looked round the room which was filled with heavy leather arm-chairs and sofas and the usual weighty sideboard. The German Swiss went in for solid furniture which was probably a reflection of their sturdy character. He thought he knew what Hofer was thinking. *Hell, do I have to work with this bastard?*

'I'm just making some coffee,' she said in a more friendly voice.

'That would be nice . . .'

He went towards the window and changed direction as she vanished through a swing-door into a kitchen. From a quick glimpse it looked expensively equipped. Quietly he turned the handle of a closed door and eased it open, peering inside.

The bedroom. Large double bed. Large dressing-table with a few cosmetic articles neatly arranged. A pair of large double doors which presumably led to a large built-in wardrobe or dressing room. Everything spotless. He left the door half-open.

She had the percolator bubbling away when he walked uninvited into the kitchen. On a wing counter there were plates of half-eaten food, an unwashed glass, unwashed cutlery and a pair of scissors with a piece of sticking-plaster attached to one of the blades. She swung round, her mouth tight.

'Make yourself at home, Martel . . .'

'I always do . . .' He smiled briefly, the cigarette-holder still clenched between his teeth. 'Did Warner sleep here often?'

It threw her. She almost caught the percolator with her hand and knocked the whole thing over. He waited, watching her, smoking his cigarette. She unplugged the percolator, which had stopped bubbling, went to a wall-cupboard and opened it.

'Spring-cleaning – that's when I change things around to stop life getting boring . . .'

She took coffee-cups from another cupboard next to the one she had first opened and Martel was relieved to see they also were large. He drank coffee by the gallon. He said no cream and she poured two cups of black coffee, put them on saucers and looked at him.

'You're in my way . . .'

'Allow me . . .'

He picked up both cups and carried them into the living-room where he placed them on mats on a low table. She followed him, talking as she came through the swing-door.

'You're agile – I can't get through that swing-door with two cups. I have to take them one at a . . .'

He looked up as she stopped in mid-sentence. She was staring through her dark glasses at the half-opened bedroom door. It was impossible to see the expression in her eyes but her mouth compressed into a bleak gash.

'You've been in the bedroom . . .'

'I like to be sure I really am alone with someone . . .'

'You've got a bloody nerve . . .'

She started towards the bedroom but he reached forward, caught her arm and sat her down on the sofa beside him. Still gripping her arm with one hand he reached up towards the outsized tinted glasses. She clawed her other hand and struck at his face with talon-like nails. He had to move fast to grab her wrist to protect himself: she had moved like a whip-lash.

'Martel, I've had you in a big way,' she hissed through perfectly formed teeth. '*If* we are going to work together we have a few things to get straightened out . . .'

'You never answered my question about you and Warner . . .'

He had released her and picked up his cup of coffee, sipping at it while he watched her. She got herself under control very quickly, picking up her own cup before she replied.

'That's one of the things. First, it's none of your damned business. Second, the answer is no – he didn't even make a pass at me in all the time I knew him. It was strictly a business relationship – like ours is going to be . . .'

'Oh, that you can count on, Claire. When did you last see Warner before he was murdered? And I may call you Claire?'

'I suppose so. I last saw Charlie three days before he went off on a trip to Lindau. He was frustrated – said he felt he wasn't getting anywhere . . .'

'With Delta?'

She paused. Martel sat thinking and guessed if she could have read his thoughts they would have surprised her. He was recalling Tweed's comment that the dossiers never lied.

'If the facts conflict with your expectations, always believe the facts,' was a maxim Tweed had hammered into Martel. Hofer had worked out her reply.

'You're referring to their neo-Nazi background?'

'I'm referring to Delta's underground organisation he was tracking.'

Martel's attitude now was one of complete relaxation but inside his nerves were tingling as he forced himself to lean back and cross his legs. Hofer drank more coffee and then stood up. When she had followed him in the kitchen she had brought with her a shoulder bag which she left on a chair behind the sofa close to the window. She went round the back of the sofa, talking while she moved.

'He did leave a notebook with me. There's a lot in it but I'd have remembered any reference to Delta . . .'

Martel was like a coiled spring. There was a faint thumping sound which came from beyond the half-open bedroom door. Hofer continued talking as she undid the clasp of her bag.

'The workmen next door are a nuisance – they're making alterations to the apartment before redecorating. The people cleared out to Tangier until it's all finished . . .'

Martel had chosen the sofa to sit on because it faced a large mirror over the fireplace. There were vases of flowers on the ledge but between them he could watch Hofer behind him. He had made a bloody awful mistake when he was so careful to check that he was not followed to Centralhof. He had got it the wrong way round. The danger had been in front of him, not behind. *The enemy was waiting for his arrival at the apartment . . .*

'I'm sorry if I was uptight when you arrived,' Hofer continued, 'but the news of Charlie's death shook me . . .'

He heard the click, watched her coming up behind him through a gap in the flowers in front of the mirror. He swung round suddenly, grasped Hofer's right hand by the wrist. The hand held an object like a felt-tip pen.

The click had occurred when she pressed something and a blade shot out from inside the handle, a blade unlike any he had ever seen, a blade like a skewer with a needle-thin tip. She had been pushing the needle-point towards the centre of the back of his neck.

He twisted the wrist brutally and she yelped as she dropped the weapon and he hauled her bodily over the back of the sofa and sprawled her along its length. Her skirt was dragged up to her thighs exposing a superb pair of legs. She arched her supple body in a sexual movement, using her free hand to try and pull him down on top of her.

'Bloody cow . . .'

He hit her a hard blow on the side of the jaw and she went limp. Standing up, he undid his leather belt and tightened the adjustable fasteners on either hip. When he bent down to turn her over on her face she suddenly came awake and jabbed two stiffened fingers towards his eyes. He became rougher, gave her a tremendous slap.

'Start struggling and I'll break your Goddamn neck . . .'

For the first time he saw her mouth go slack with fear and she remained passive as he turned her over, pulled the upper part of her body towards him, then used the belt to strap her ankles to her wrists.

It was the most uncomfortable position anyone can be forced into: if she struggled she would suffer excruciating pain. He tightened the belt to the limit of his strength. Soon the circulation would start to go. He left her on the sofa after using his handkerchief as a gag.

'It's not too clean,' he assured her.

Then he walked into the bedroom where the faint thumping was repeating itself. He opened both doors of the built-in wardrobe cupboard and looked down. The dark-haired girl on the floor had been trussed up like a chicken and her mouth was sealed with a band of sticking plaster.

'Hello, Claire Hofer,' he said. 'Thanks for the warning. Now let's make you comfortable. You have got guts . . .'

Chapter Four

Wednesday May 27

Hofer was emerging from the state of shock brought on by her ordeal inside the cupboard. She had cleared up the mess in the kitchen and was making coffee for herself and Martel.

'How did you know that girl was impersonating me?' she asked.

Their prisoner was lying on the living-room floor. Martel had released her from his belt and replaced it with the ropes used to bind up Hofer. Her mouth was sealed with a fresh strip of sticking-plaster Hofer had provided from the kitchen.

'She made a lot of mistakes,' Martel explained. 'Although her physical description fitted the one I had been given she wore dark-tinted glasses – in a room where the light was dim anyway. Now we know why – her eyes are brown . . .'

'There must have been more . . .'

'When I peered into the bedroom your cosmetics were neat and tidy on the dressing-table – one hell of a contrast with the food remains and dirt in here. The bit of sticking-plaster stuck to the scissors intrigued me. She had no visible injury. The normal one is when a woman cuts her hands in the kitchen. There were other things, too . . .'

'Such as?'

'More damning was the fact she didn't know which cupboard held the coffee cups. She denied Warner had ever made a pass at her – he always made one try for an attractive woman. And she called him Charlie. He always insisted on Charles.'

'You really are observant. Coffee in here?'

'No, in the living-room. I have questions to ask our imposter. She also over-reacted to my leaving the bedroom door half-open. Plus her elaborate explanation to cover your thumping the inside of the cupboard. You took a chance there . . .'

'I heard a man's voice and guessed you had arrived. I felt such a fool that I'd let her overpower me I had to warn you. Was she going to kill you?'

They had moved back into the living-room where their prisoner was rolled on her side in front of the fireplace. Martel lowered his voice so she couldn't hear him.

'Was she going to kill me?' He picked up the needle weapon he had earlier rescued from the floor and placed on a table. 'I think so. This ingenious little toy is very like a hypodermic. When I grabbed her she was about to ram it into the back of my neck. Press this button a second time and I'd say it injects the fluid. Let's test her reaction to her own medicine . . .'

Holding the weapon out of sight he knelt on the floor and rolled the girl on her back. With the other hand he took a grip on the plaster and ripped it off her mouth. She screamed. He placed a hand over her lips.

'No more noise. I'm going to ask questions. You're going to answer. Your real name?'

'Go stuff yourself . . .'

'What would happen if I jab this into you and press the button?'

He showed her the needle weapon. He moved the point close to the side of her neck. Her brown eyes glared up at him with a mixture of hatred and apprehension.

'For God's sake, no! *Please* . . .'

'She says *please*,' Martel observed sarcastically. 'And yet she was about to give me the same treatment. Oh, well, here we go . . .'

'Gisela Zobel . . .'

'Where is your home base?'

'Bavaria . . . München. For pity's sake . . .'

'Pity?' Martel glanced up at Hofer who was staring intently, wondering how far he was prepared to go. 'She wouldn't know the meaning of the word, would she?'

'Not from the way she treated me . . .' Hofer responded with deliberate callousness. 'You decide . . .'

She lit a cigarette and the girl on the floor watched her with bulging eyes. Sweat beads were forming on her forehead. Martel moved the needle closer as he asked the question.

'Who do you work for?'

'He will kill me . . .'

'How could he? If you don't give the reply – the right reply – and we have certain information Warner sent by a secret route, you will be dead anyway. That is, unless I'm mistaken about what this instrument you were going to use on me contains. So, once again, here goes . . .'

'Reinhard Dietrich . . .'

Then she fainted from terror – whether from uttering the name or because of Martel's threat to use the weapon he was not sure. He looked into Hofer's deep blue eyes, shrugged and withdrew the needle tip from the proximity of Zobel's neck.

'Get me a cork to protect this damned thing,' he suggested and while she fetched one from the kitchen he gazed at the weapon. He was convinced that the contents injected into the victim would be lethal, that Gisela Zobel *had* planned to kill him. He would hand it to the counter-espionage people: Forensic could then check it.

At ten o'clock night had descended and Martel decided they could safely leave the apartment. Hofer packed a bag and Martel arranged with the police to send a plain-clothes man to the Baur au Lac to pay his bill and collect his suitcase. The bag was now standing in the small hall outside the apartment.

'We take a train to St Gallen,' Martel told the Swiss

girl in the living-room. 'We have to pick up Warner's trail there . . .'

'We have very little to go on,' the girl reminded him. 'Only that he stopped off there on his way here from Bavaria . . .'

'So we make use of what little we have got . . .'

The evening had been packed with activity. Hofer had looked up the number in her pocket diary and Martel had phoned Berne. While he was talking to her boss, Ferdy Arnold, he had studied her in the mirror.

Her description fitted the one provided by Tweed perfectly but he was puzzled by her passive personality. She was a nice girl with long dark hair, a soft voice and graceful movements. Already he liked her. But he had expected someone more dynamic.

The Swiss counter-espionage chief had flown by private plane to Zürich. The atmosphere changed the moment he entered the place. A small, serious-faced man with rimless glasses, Ferdy Arnold resembled a banker. He took immediate decisions.

'We smuggle her out in an ambulance,' he announced, indicating Gisela Zobel who was now propped up in one of the deep arm-chairs. 'She will be taken to a special hospital. She will be kept under heavy guard. She will be intensively interrogated.'

He looked at Martel, ignoring Hofer. 'Phone me at this number at ten in the morning . . .' He scribbled a number on a small pad, tore off the sheet and handed it to the Englishman. 'I've left off the Zürich code in case you lose the paper . . .'

Arnold, smartly dressed in a dark blue suit, looked at Martel with a wry smile. 'It isn't that I don't trust you . . .'

'But one English agent, Warner, was spotted – even posing as a German – so you're playing it to cover all angles. And why do I phone at ten in the morning? Surely you'll only just have started Zobel's daily interrogation . . .'

'On the contrary, we shall just have *finished* since she will be interrogated throughout the night without a break . . .'

Martel was not happy. There was an atmosphere which did not ring true. Something in the relationship between Ferdy Arnold and his 'top operative', Hofer. He was damned if he could detect why he sensed he was being tricked – but his instincts had never let him down yet.

'Come into the bedroom,' Arnold suggested, glancing at Gisela Zobel, who sat motionless watching and listening. 'Keep an eye on her,' he told Hofer. When he had closed the bedroom door he accepted a cigarette from Martel.

'All that I said in there was strictly for Zobel's ears. It can help the breaking-down process if they worry about what is in store for them.'

'She admitted she was working for Reinhard Dietrich,' Martel told him.

'I see.'

Arnold showed no interest in the statement. Martel recalled a remark Tweed had made in London. *At arm's length ... you know the Swiss. Policy of neutrality ...* It was understandable – that the Swiss counter-espionage should not want an open war with a German neo-Nazi movement. Understandable but unhelpful. Arnold was, he suspected, maintaining a watching brief.

'Berne,' Arnold commented, 'is disturbed about rumours that an underground organisation has spread its tentacles into northern Switzerland ...'

'St Gallen?'

'What made you mention that place?' Arnold enquired.

'Because it is one of the chief towns in north-eastern Switzerland,' Martel replied casually. 'I find the choice of the word *delta* interesting – the Rhine delta is located just beyond your border with Austria. The Vorarlberg province ...'

He watched Arnold's reaction closely. One of the references in Warner's tiny notebook had been to *Bregenz*. This was the only port Austria had on its narrow frontage of lake shore at the eastern end of Lake Konstanz.

'We've been in touch with Austrian counter-espion-age,' Arnold commented vaguely. 'Nothing has come of it so far. Berne is sensitive about the recent unpre-cedented student riots here in Zürich. It is suspected they are organised by a secret Delta cell.' He checked his watch and seemed disinclined to linger. 'I must go now.'

He left without saying a word to the girl except for a brief exchange before walking out. Martel frowned as he looked round the living-room. Gisela Zobel had disappeared. Hofer explained before he could ask.

'A team dressed like ambulance men came. They took her away on a stretcher.'

'Arnold doesn't waste much time, does he? By the way, as he was leaving he said something to you. Did you mention that we are on our way to St Gallen?'

'No.' She looked surprised. 'Is something wrong? I'm beginning to know your intonations . . .'

Martel passed it off lightly as he picked up both bags in the hall. 'When you get to know me better you'll realise I often ask random questions. We board one of the trams for the Hauptbahnhof?'

'It will be quicker – the tram goes straight to the station. A number eight. And it's an unobtrusive way of travelling . . .'

'Warner thought that, too . . .'

The brutal assault – the insane shock – commenced as soon as they closed the street door to the apartment and emerged from the archway leading into Bahnhofstrasse. Ten o'clock at night. Illuminated by the street lights, the trees lining one of the most famous thoroughfares in the world cast patches of shadow on the wide pavement. It was very quiet and few people were about.

One essential addition to Martel's equipment since he arrived at the Centralhof apartment was the Colt .45 he now carried in a spring-loaded shoulder holster. Hofer had provided this, taking it from a secret compartment in the floor of the wardrobe cupboard where she had been imprisoned. She had also given him ammunition.

Martel was committing a strictly illegal act carrying the gun but they would cross no frontiers on their way to St Gallen. He had asked her not to mention to Ferdy Arnold the fact that he was now armed. He was not sure why he made this request.

'The ticket machine is over here,' Hofer said and he followed her with the two cases. 'I'll take my own case once we're on the tram.'

He watched her inserting coins. Light from a lamp shone down directly on her. She really was a very beautiful girl and he wondered why she had ever joined the service. He'd try to find out when he knew her better . . .

A tram was coming in the distance from the lake direction so, if it was the right number, it would take them to the top of the street which faced the Hauptbahnhof. That was the reason he stood with a case in each hand, ready to board the tram – which put him at an initial disadvantage.

He was listening to the rumble of the approaching tram, the faint hiss of the traction wires, when the huge six-seater Mercedes appeared and charged like a tank. It came out of nowhere and swung up on to the sidewalk alongside the ticket machine, alongside the girl . . .

The shock hit Martel like a physical blow. Men were pouring out of the Mercedes, men dressed in respectable business suits and wearing dark glasses. He saw two of them grab Hofer, one of them pressing a cloth over the upper part of her face. Beneath the glare of the street light they had another common denominator – a triangular silver badge like the Greek letter *delta* in their coat lapels.

He heard the oncoming tram ringing its warning bell – the car was positioned diagonally, its front on the sidewalk, its rear in the street, blocking the tramline. A second car appeared, a Rolls Royce, and swung across the tramline blocking it completely. The tram's bell continued clanging as the driver jammed on his brakes and stopped a few feet from the Rolls Royce.

Martel had dropped his bags and was moving. The Colt .45 was in his hand as the Rolls turned slightly and swivelled the glare of its undipped headlights full on him. Shielding his eyes with one hand he snapped off two shots. There was a tinkling of glass and both lights died. One of the men from the Mercedes produced an automatic and aimed point-blank at Martel. The Englishman shot him and the gunman sagged back against the Mercedes, blood cascading from his forehead.

Martel ran towards the two men still grappling with Hofer. She had torn the cloth away from her face and in the clammy night air a waft of chloroform reached Martel's nostrils. The first man was turning towards Martel when the Englishman lashed out. The savage kick reached its target – the assailant's knee-cap. He screamed and dropped in a heap. More men appeared from the far side of the Mercedes and now Hofer was screaming at the top of her voice.

Martel found it a nightmare. This was anarchy, violence, kidnapping on the main street in Zürich. Another attacker levelled an automatic at Martel who fired in a reflex movement, still trying to reach the girl. The man clutched at his chest and his hand came away covered in blood as he toppled forward.

More men were appearing – from inside the Rolls. Martel ducked and weaved, never still for a moment, lashing out with the barrel of his Colt, catching one man a terrible blow on the side of his face, raking him from his ear to the tip of his jaw.

The arrival of reinforcements distracted Martel. He was fighting for his life. He went on using the Colt as a club, preserving his remaining bullets. He took refuge with his back to the ticket machine so they could only come at him from the front – and something very hard struck his skull, blurring his vision. As his sight cleared he saw an appalling sight. Hofer was being dragged head first inside the rear of the Mercedes, her legs kicking until another man grabbed her ankles and twisted them viciously over each other. She looked as though she were being sucked inside the maw of a shark.

And now there was smoke. One of them had thrown a smoke bomb – probably several – in the direction of the tram. The street began to fill with fog. A car engine started up. A man grappling with Martel let go and tried to flee. They had Hofer inside the Mercedes. *He had to reach the Mercedes!* As the man ran Martel shot him and he sprawled with a crash on the flagstones.

The Mercedes backed off the sidewalk. The injured and the dead had been collected and taken inside the two cars – except for the man on the flagstones. The Rolls Royce also was moving. With the Mercedes leading both cars sped off up Bahnhofstrasse, then turned left at the Paradeplatz.

It was suddenly very quiet and the stationary tram was still hidden in drifting smoke. Martel slithered in a pool of blood. He stumbled back to the man they had abandoned, the one who had grappled with him.

The body was lying on its face and Martel quickly felt the neck pulse, cursing when he realised the man *was* dead. As he would have been had Hofer not given him the Colt. He shoved the weapon back into the holster, bent down and heaved the man over on his back. Yes, he also wore the silver badge in his coat lapel. Martel ripped it free and dropped it in his pocket.

A ten-second search of the man's pockets revealed

they were empty. No means of identification – except for the badge. He had no doubt all clothing identity such as maker's tabs had been removed. He straightened up and looked around, frustrated and dazed.

The tram was still hidden in the smoke but its silhouette was becoming clearer. No sign of the driver. Sensibly he had remained inside his cab. Martel felt sure he had kept the automatic doors closed to protect his passengers. Nearby was a pathetic sight – two cases standing on the pavement.

At any moment the tram driver was going to emerge from his cab. Martel scraped his shoes back and forth on the edge of the kerb to remove blood from the soles. Then he picked up the two suitcases and left the scene of the nightmare as he heard the distant scream of a patrol-car siren.

The blast from the explosion sent a shock wave down the funnel of Bahnhofstrasse which thumped Martel in the back. He turned down a side street towards the Old Town, taking a roundabout route to the Hauptbahnhof. He didn't think anyone aboard the tram had seen him but a man carrying two suitcases at that hour was conspicuous.

What had caused the explosion he had no idea. He wasn't too interested. At that moment he had three objectives. To hide Hofer's suitcase in a left-luggage locker at the station. Next, to book himself temporarily into a hotel near the station – if he returned to the

Baur au Lac he could walk straight into the arms of the opposition. Finally, to phone Ferdy Arnold's headquarters in Berne.

Martel felt he was on the edge of a whirlpool. He could hardly credit what had happened in Bahnhofstrasse. And Swiss security was renowned for its ruthless efficiency. What the hell had gone so horribly wrong?

When a woman replied to his call to the Berne number Arnold had given him he opened with the identification phrase and she didn't react.

'What was that you said? Who are you calling? You know what time of night it is . . .'

'I'm sorry,' Martel replied. 'I was calling . . .' He repeated the number Arnold had provided him and risked it: after all, Arnold was a common name.

'No one here of that name – you have the wrong number. This is the number you said you were calling but – for the second time – there is no one here of that name. *Good night!*'

Martel sat staring at the receiver and replaced it. He was inside a third-floor bedroom he had booked at the Schweizerhof – which faced the Hauptbahnhof. Hofer's suitcase was parked in one of the station lockers, the key for which he had in his pocket. Why had Ferdy Arnold given him a meaningless phone number when he visited the apartment in Centralhof?

The obvious conclusion was that *he was not the real Ferdy Arnold* – whom Martel had never met.

If this same man had organised the savage onslaught on himself and Hofer it explained his anxiety to leave the apartment urgently. *He had known what was waiting for them outside.* So he had to be well clear of the place when Martel came out with Hofer. But in that case why had Hofer accepted him as Arnold? Martel felt the sensation of being swept inside a whirlpool growing.

Leaving his room, he went down the staircase, again instinctively ignoring the lift. Crossing the street to the station he found a row of phone booths, went inside one and dialled the Ferdy Arnold number Tweed had given him in London.

He *had* realised 'Arnold' had provided a different number, but he had assumed it was a security precaution and Tweed had not been immediately informed of the change. This time the reaction at the Berne number was different. He used the code-phrase, a girl asked him to wait just a moment.

'Who is this?'

The voice was crisp, almost curt, and had a ring of competence, of no nonsense about it. Martel identified himself.

'Where are you calling from?' Arnold demanded.

'That doesn't matter at the moment,' Martel replied. 'I have regretfully to report that your assistant, Claire Hofer, has been kidnapped by Delta . . .'

'You were part of that massacre in Bahnhofstrasse in Zürich?'

'Massacre?'

'Delta – if it was Delta – bungled a major bank raid. A limpet mine was attached to the main door of a certain bank. It detonated and some people alighting from a tram which had been stopped were badly injured. What was that about Claire Hofer? And I'd still like to know where you're calling from . . .'

'Skip that. This call is going through your switchboard . . .'

'That's crazy.' Ferdy Arnold's voice reflected indignation and disbelief. 'Our security . . .'

'You said something about a bungled bank raid.' Martel was bewildered. 'I'm limiting this call to two minutes so talk . . .'

'I've just told you – a bomb, presumably with a quick-acting timer, was attached to the entrance to a bank. It blew the door but no one followed it up. The driver of the tram which was stopped saw nothing because smoke bombs were used . . .'

'What about the Rolls Royce that stopped him by driving across his bows?'

'I don't know anything about that. On the pavement we found a small silver badge shaped like a triangle – or a delta . . .'

'Send out an all points bulletin alarm for Claire Hofer.' Martel was checking the length of the call by the second-hand on his watch. 'I'm very worried about her . . .'

'You can stop worrying.' Arnold paused and there was something in his tone Martel didn't like. 'We know what happened to her – part of the story anyway.'

'Then for Christ's sake tell me – and fast. In the short time we were together I came to like – admire – the girl . . .'

'Her body was discovered floating down the Limmat less than half an hour ago. She had been brutally and professionally tortured before they dumped her in the river. I want you to come in, Martel. I want you to come to an address in Berne . . .'

Arnold stopped speaking. Martel had broken the connection.

Chapter Five

Wednesday May 27

If Arnold had kept the conversation going so his tracers could locate the source of the call Martel was confident he had rung off in time. He was no happier about the real Arnold knowing his whereabouts than he was for the fake Arnold to obtain the same information. And the news of Claire Hofer had hit him hard.

Leaving the booth he walked round the huge Hauptbahnhof, stopping to study the departure board like a man waiting for his train. This great station – along with its counterpart in Münich – had fascinated the murdered Warner. Why?

Martel made a swift inventory of the place. *Gleise* 1–16: sixteen platforms, all of the tracks ending here. The long row of phone booths for communication and, he realised as he strolled round the hushed concourse, numerous exits. There was a *kino* – cinema – *the Cine-Rex*, and a Snack-Buffet.

He walked down one of the broad aisles leading away from the platforms past a large luggage storage counter facing a door marked *Kanton-Polizei*. Two men emerged dressed in blue uniforms with berets, their trousers tucked into boots. They had the look of paratroopers.

He passed *Quick*, a first-class restaurant which provided two more exits and came out into the street. The Hauptbahnhof was a place you could get out of swiftly – a place you could linger inside for a long time unobtrusively. An idea formed at the back of his mind and receded. He crossed two roads and gazed down into the back water of the Limmat river. Dizzying reflections from street lamps danced in the night.

These were the waters which within the past hour had carried the mutilated body of poor Claire Hofer. Martel was not a sentimental man but he decided someone was going to pay for that barbaric act.

Glancing round he noticed the huge greystone bulk of a four-storey building to his right on the Bahnhofquai. The *Stadtpolizei* – police headquarters. The working quarters of a friend, David Nagel, Chief Inspector of Intelligence. He checked his watch. 2245 hours.

While at the Hotel Schweizerhof he had borrowed a rail timetable and found that the last train from the Hauptbahnhof left at 2339, reaching St Gallen at 0049 hours. He had less than one hour to catch that train – to get out of Zürich which was becoming a death-trap.

He entered police headquarters through the double doors in Lindenhofstrasse. The receptionist, a stocky policeman in shirt sleeves, confirmed that Chief

Inspector Nagel was in his office. He asked Martel to fill in a printed form.

'Just tell him I'm here, for God's sake,' Martel snapped. 'If you keep me waiting you won't be popular. This is an emergency.'

'Even so . . .'

'And he's expecting me,' the Englishman lied. 'My name is all he will need . . .'

Within minutes he was inside Nagel's third-floor office overlooking the Limmat. The windows were wide open, letting in dense clammy air. There were the usual heavy net curtains, the usual neon lighting, harsh and uninviting, the usual filing cabinets along one wall.

'I've been hoping you would contact me,' Nagel said when they had shaken hands. 'Tweed called from London and warned me you were coming in. He said you might need help . . .'

'I think I do . . .'

David Nagel was a well-built Swiss with a thick moustache, humorous eyes and a mass of dark hair he kept well-brushed. Some of his colleagues dismissed him as a bit of a dandy whose greatest interest in life was women.

'No, that is my second greatest interest,' he would correct them when they hinted as much. 'My first is my work – which is why I'm not married. What wife could stand the hours I keep? So, being normal, my second greatest interest is . . . Now get the hell out of here.'

Martel liked him. Tweed said he had the most acute brain in the Swiss police and security system – and Intelligence had one foot in both camps. Nagel came straight to the point – as he always did.

'You didn't fill in a form before you came up here, I hope?' He looked worried as he asked the question, and Nagel rarely showed anxiety no matter how critical the situation. 'You were dressed like that?' the Swiss continued, speaking rapidly. 'And not using that blasted cigarette holder . . .'

'No to all your questions – and yes I was wearing these glasses.' Martel removed a pair of horn-rimmed glasses fitted with plain lenses. 'I had to give my bloody name to get through to you. Are you going to nag about that . . .'

'Please, please, Keith . . .!' Nagel held up a restraining hand in a pacific gesture. 'But from your point of view your whereabouts might be best left unknown. Ferdy Arnold's security mob is moving heaven and earth to locate you.'

Martel lit a cigarette and indulged himself in the luxury of employing his holder. He knew that Nagel disliked Arnold, that he had once told Tweed it 'was purely a political appointment'. The Swiss continued talking.

'Your name doesn't matter. When you have gone I shall tell the man at reception you are one of my key informants, that you used a code-name – that officially you never entered these premises. With no written record you will be safe from Arnold's hard men.'

'That's reassuring at any rate . . .' Martel was about to refer to the débâcle in Bahnhofstrasse when Nagel again went on speaking.

'I have a number here you must phone urgently. She called me only ten minutes ago – knowing we are good friends. Despite my reservations about her chief, I like and trust Claire Hofer . . .'

Martel felt himself spinning, the whirlpool whipping him round faster.

Chapter Six

Wednesday May 27

Stunned, Martel's teeth clenched tight on the cigarette-holder. To mask his reaction he took the holder out of his mouth and readjusted the position of cigarette in holder. *She called me only ten minutes ago.*

What the hell was wrong with the timing? Thirty minutes earlier Arnold had told him on the phone that 'less than half an hour ago' her body had been found in the Limmat. That meant Hofer had been found about one hour from this moment. And now Nagel – the most precise Swiss – had clearly stated the call from Claire Hofer had come through 'ten minutes ago'. On the scrap of paper Nagel had handed to him was written a St Gallen phone number.

Nagel would know the girl's voice well. Being Nagel he would have wanted proof of the identity of his caller. *Irrevocable* proof. Martel began to consider whether he could be going out of his mind.

'Something wrong?' Nagel enquired softly.

'Yes, I'm tired.' Martel folded the scrap of paper and put it in his wallet. 'What sort of a night are you having?'

'Routine so far.'

Again Martel was stunned. David Nagel, chief of police Intelligence, *had no knowledge of the traumatic event which had taken place in Bahnhofstrasse.* There was no reason for him to conceal such knowledge – Martel felt certain of this. He had to tread damned carefully.

'Why do you mistrust Ferdy Arnold?' he asked.

'It was a political appointment – not a professional one . . .'

'And why does Claire Hofer – who works for Arnold – call *you* when she has a message for me?'

'Because she knows you and I are close friends.' The Swiss paused. 'I also employed her before she transferred to counter espionage . . .'

'You said you've had a routine night so far,' Martel probed.

'Except for the explosion aboard some tourist's launch out on the lake. Some poor idiot who obviously knew nothing about engines or boats – so he had an accident and lost his life. We did hear the faint boom of the detonation . . .' He pointed towards the open windows behind curtains which hung motionless in the airless night. 'The sound came up the Limmat from the lake . . .'

No, it didn't, Martel thought. It came straight up the funnel of Bahnhofstrasse and then down Urania-strasse, the side street leading towards police head-quarters. He was watching Nagel and the extraordinary thing was he was convinced the Intelligence man was not lying. Someone was trying to cover up the incident, to pretend it had never happened.

'Good to see you, David,' Martel said and stood up. 'And I'll call Claire Hofer soon but there's something I have to attend to, and you don't want to know about it . . .'

'That is a direct line which bypasses the switchboard,' Nagel suggested, pointing to one of three phones on his desk. 'I can leave you on your own . . .'

'It isn't that, David. I'm just short of time.'

'Enjoy yourself while you're in Zürich . . .'

It was 2310 hours when Martel left police headquarters. He had half an hour to catch the 2339 train to St Gallen, but he still had things to deal with. He walked past a patrol car parked outside, a cream Volvo with a red trim. Two uniformed men sat in the front with the windows open. Where the devil had they been when all hell broke loose in nearby Bahnhofstrasse?

And he *had* lied to Nagel he recalled as he hurried back to the Hauptbahnhof. He felt certain he could rely on the Swiss but he had mistrusted the offered phone which passed through no switchboard. He was now gripped by a feeling of insecurity and determined to take no chances.

'Maybe I'm getting paranoid,' he told himself as he slipped inside one of the empty phone booths in the station. These were safe. Again he remembered the dead Warner who apparently had also haunted Hauptbahnhofs. As he dialled the number Nagel had given him he began to sympathise with Charles Warner. Martel himself felt *hunted*.

The receptionist at the Hotel Hecht in St Gallen confirmed that Claire Hofer was staying with them. She asked him to hold while she tried her room. A girl's voice came on the line – decisive, sharp and wary.

'Who is this?'

'Our mutual friend, Nagel, passed on your message and I want you to take certain action very fast. Can you get to an outside payphone? Good. Get there immediately and call me at this number.' He read out the booth number from the dial. 'It's Zürich code,' he added tersely. 'I'm very short of time . . .'

'Goodbye!'

Martel found he was sweating. The atmosphere inside the booth was oppressive. He felt both exposed and trapped in the confined space. The phone rang in an astonishingly short time. He snatched up the receiver. The same voice asked the question crisply.

'Is that . . . ? Please confirm name of our mutual friend . . .'

'Nagel. David Nagel . . .'

'Claire Hofer speaking . . .'

'Again do what I tell you without questioning my judgement – as fast as you can. Pay your bill at the

Hotel Hecht – make up some plausible reason why you have to . . .'

'All right, I'm not stupid! What then?'

'Book in at another hotel in St Gallen. Reserve a room for me. Warn them I'll arrive about one o'clock in the morning . . .'

'You need parking space for a car?'

'No. I'm coming in by train . . .'

'I'll call back in minutes. I have to find accommodation and tell you where to come. Goodbye!'

Martel was left staring at a dead receiver. More precious time was being consumed. But she sounded good, damned good. He had to give her that. The whirlpool was gyrating faster. He felt he had been talking to a ghost. Claire Hofer had just been dragged out of the Limmat – according to Arnold . . .

Despite the growing heat inside the kiosk he inserted a cigarette into his holder, cursed, removed the cigarette and placed it between his lips minus holder. While talking he had turned round with his back to the coin box so he could watch the deserted concourse. He took several deep drags and the phone was ringing a second time. Her voice . . .

'Is that . . .? Good. Our mutual friend . . .'

'Nagel. Martel here . . .'

'I got lucky. Two twin-bedded rooms on the first floor. Hotel Metropol. Faces the station exit. Staring at you as you come out. I'll leave a note at the desk with just my room number inside the envelope. O.K.?'

'Very . . .'
'Goodbye!'

In the next few minutes Martel moved very fast. He bought his rail ticket for St Gallen. At the Hotel Schweizerhof he paid for the room he no longer needed. He did his best to make the cancellation seem normal.

'I'm a consultant – medical – and I'm urgently needed in Basle by a patient . . .' *Consultant* was the word he had filled in on the 'occupation' section of the registration form when he had arrived. The term was impressive and totally vague.

He had not unpacked his bag – a precaution he always took when arriving at a fresh destination – so all he had to do was to shove his shaving kit and toothbrush inside and snap the catches. Running down the stairs – the night clerk would see nothing odd now in his speedy departure – he hurried across to the first of the taxis waiting outside the station.

'I want you to take me to Paradeplatz. Can you then wait a few minutes by the tram stop while I deliver something? Then drive me straight back here?'

'Please get in . . .'

He was using up his last few minutes before the St Gallen train departed but – knowing Zürich and the quietness of the streets at this hour – he believed he could just manage it. *Because he had to check the state of*

Bahnhofstrasse where shots had been fired, blood spilt all over the sidewalk and a bomb detonated against a bank.

He began chatting to the driver. All over the world cabbies are plugged in to a city's grapevine.

'Did you hear that terrific explosion not so long ago? Sounded like a bomb going off.'

'I heard it.' The driver paused as though picking his words with care. 'Rumour is some fool of a tourist blew himself and his boat up on the lake . . .'

'It sounded closer . . .'

Martel left the query mark hanging in the air, wondering why the driver sounded so cautious. They were near Paradeplatz: soon all conversation would cease.

'Sounded closer to me,' the driver agreed. 'I was with a fare in Talstrasse and that was one hell of a bang. Now it could have come up the street from the lake . . .' He paused again. 'Anyway, that's what the police told us.'

'The police?'

'A patrol car stopped at the Hauptbahnhof rank. The driver got out to chat. He told us about this fool tourist blowing himself up on the lake.'

'Someone you knew? The policeman?' Martel asked casually.

'Funny you should say that.' Their eyes met in the rear-view mirror. 'I thought I knew every patrol car policeman in the city. I've been driving this cab for twenty years – but I never met him before . . .'

'Probably a new recruit · fresh out of training school.'

'He was fifty if he was a day. All right if I wait here?'

It suited Martel admirably. The cabbie had parked well inside Paradeplatz – which meant he wouldn't be able to see where Martel went after he turned down Bahnhofstrasse. He lit a fresh cigarette and walked quickly. He was going to catch – or lose – the train by a matter of seconds.

The street was deserted and the only sound was that of his own footfalls on the flagstones. He crossed over to the other side and then stopped in sheer bewilderment. The whirlpool was spinning again.

There was no sign of the bloody incident Martel had witnessed and participated in two hours earlier. And there was no mistaking the location. He could see the archway where he and the girl had come through into Bahnhofstrasse. And there *was* a large and important bank in just the right position – opposite where the tram had been stopped, a bank with double plate-glass doors. But *the glass was intact*.

There was not a sliver of shattered glass in the roadway that Martel could see. The Swiss were good at clearing up messes, at keeping their country neat and tidy – but this was completely insane.

Now he was checking the sidewalk for blood, the blood he had slipped in, the dried blood still staining the soles of his shoes. *The sidewalk was spotless*. He had almost given up when he saw it. The fresh scar marks where bark had been torn and burnt by explosive from a tree. Even the Swiss couldn't grow a new tree in two hours.

Chapter Seven

Thursday May 28

It was just after midnight at the remote *schloss* in the Allgau district of Bavaria. Reinhard Dietrich stood by a window in his library, looking out at the lights reflected in the moat. In one hand he held a glass of Napoleon brandy, in the other a Havana cigar. A buzzer began ringing persistently.

Sitting down behind a huge desk he unlocked a drawer, took out the telephone concealed inside and lifted the receiver. His tone was curt when Erwin Vinz identified himself.

'Blau here,' Dietrich barked. 'Any news?'

'The Englishman has left Zürich. He caught a train departing at 2339 hours from the Hauptbahnhof.' The wording was precise, the voice hoarse. 'Our people just missed getting on board after he jumped inside a compartment . . .'

'*Left Zürich!* What the hell do you mean? What happened at the Centralhof apartment?'

'The operation was not a complete success . . .' Vinz was nervous. Dietrich's mouth tightened. Something had gone wildly wrong.

'Tell me exactly what happened,' he said coldly.

'The girl has taken a permanent holiday and she was unable to tell us anything about her job. We gained the impression she had no information to pass on. You don't have to worry about her . . .'

'But I do have to worry about Martel! Goddamnit, where is he now? Which train?'

'Its final destination was St Gallen . . .'

Dietrich gripped the receiver more firmly, his expression choleric. In clipped, terse sentences he issued instructions, slammed down the receiver and replaced the instrument inside the drawer. He emptied his glass and pressed a bell.

A hunchback padded into the room. His pointed ears were flat against the side of his head so they almost merged with his skull. He wore a green beize overall and smelt of cleaning fluid. His master handed him the glass.

'More brandy! Oscar, Vinz and his special cell bungled the job. It looks as though Martel has arrived in St Gallen, for God's sake . . .'

'We dealt with the previous English,' Oscar reminded him.

Reinhard Dietrich, a man of sixty, had a thatch of thick silver hair and a matching moustache. Six feet tall, he was well-built without an ounce of excess fat. He was dressed in the outfit he preferred when at his country *schloss* – a London-tailored leather jacket and cavalry twill jodphurs tucked inside hand-tooled riding boots. Dietrich looked every inch the man he was as he stood savouring the Havana – one of post-war Germany's richest and most powerful industrialists.

He had entered the electronics field in its infancy, shrewdly judging this to be the product with the greatest development potential. His headquarters was in Stuttgart and he had a second large factory complex at Phoenix, Arizona. He sipped at his refilled glass, watching Oscar's unblinking eyes.

'We shall certainly deal with this fresh meddler from London. Vinz is flooding St Gallen with our people. Martel will be tracked down by nightfall. They have eliminated that Swiss bitch, Claire Hofer.' His voice rose, his florid face reddened. 'Nothing must interfere with Operation Crocodile! On June 3 the Summit Express will be crossing Germany. On June 4 the Bavarian state elections will be held – Delta will sweep into power!'

'And Martel . . .'

'The order is – kill him!'

Martel left the night train at St Gallen confident that no one had followed him. At Zürich he had caught the train seconds before it departed. Once aboard he had waited by the window to see if there were any other last-minute passengers. No one appeared and he made his way through an almost-empty train to a first-class compartment. With an overwhelming sense of relief he sank into a corner seat.

At St Gallen he took his time getting off the train. As he carried his suitcase slowly towards the exit the platform was deserted. There is no more depressing place than a station in the early hours. As Claire Hofer had told him, the Hotel Metropol faced the station.

The night porter confirmed his reservation and Martel asked him the room rate. He counted out banknotes, talking as he did so to distract the man, adding a generous tip to keep him distracted.

'That's payment for two nights – this is for you. I'm so tired I can hardly stand up. I'll register in the morning. Are there any messages for me?' he asked quickly.

'Just this envelope . . .'

It had worked – the delay in filling in the registration form which is obligatory for a guest to complete on arrival at any Swiss hostelry. The form is in triplicate. During the night the police tour the hotels to collect their copy. By not filling in the form immediately Martel had delayed knowledge of his presence in St Gallen by twenty-four hours.

Inside his twin-bedded room he opened the sealed envelope. In a neat feminine script were written the words 'Room 12'. It was the room next to his own. He knocked very lightly on the door and she opened it immediately. She didn't say a word until she had closed and locked it. Over her right hand was draped a towel.

'The mutual friend?'

'David Nagel, for God's sake . . .'

'I saw you from my window which looks across to the station – but you can't blame me for checking . . .'

'I'm sorry. I *want* you to be careful. It's just that I last ate before noon on the plane. I'm tired . . .'

'You look exhausted.' She removed the towel, exposing a 9-mm pistol she had been concealing and which she slipped under her pillow. 'You must be thirsty. It's a hot night. I'm afraid I only have Perrier water . . .'

'I'll take it from the bottle.'

He sank on to the bed furthest from the window and forced himself to study her as he drank. She was the right height, correct weight, and her dark hair was cut with a heavy fringe over her forehead and shoulder length at the back. In the glow from a bedside light her eyes were a deep blue. 'You'll want proof of my identity . . .' He hauled out his passport, gave it to her and finished off the Perrier.

She tried to show him her own identity card but he was so weary he waved it aside. What bloody difference did it make? Delta had put in a substitute – Gisela Zobel – in Zürich. He had rescued another girl – whose description also matched – trussed up in a cupboard at the Centralhof apartment. The whirlpool began spinning in his head again . . .

But this girl *felt* right. It was his last thought before he lay back on the pillow and fell fast asleep.

*

He woke with a sensation of alarm. It was dark, the air heavy like a blanket pressing down. He wasn't sure where he was – so much had happened in so short a period of time. He was lying on his back on a bed. Then he remembered.

He was just relaxing when he experienced a second tremor. He kept his breathing regular. Someone had taken off his tie, undone the top buttons of his shirt, taken off his shoes. What alerted him was the lack of weight under his left armpit. The shoulder holster was still strapped to him but *his Colt had been removed*. He turned his head carefully, not making a sound, and reached out with his right hand. The fingers of another hand touched his own, grasped his hand. A girl's voice whispered before the bedside light came on.

'You're all right. You're in St Gallen at the Hotel Metropol. I'm Claire Hofer. It's four o'clock in the morning so you've only had two hours' sleep . . .'

'I can get by on that.'

Martel was wide awake now, his throat feeling like sandpaper. He sat up and propped the pillow behind him. Claire Hofer was still wearing her pale grey two-piece suit and, like himself, sat propped against a pillow. In the light glow he noticed she had made herself up afresh. No blood-red nail varnish, thank God!

'Your Colt is in your bedside table,' she told him. 'Not very comfortable sleeping with that. The door is double-locked – and as you see I've tipped a chair under the handle . . .'

75

'You seem to have thought of everything . . .'

Martel, who never accepted anyone at face value, set about discovering every facet of Claire Hofer. She was remarkably like the second girl he had encountered in the Zürich apartment, the girl he had rescued – only to let her be kidnapped and . . . Martel found it hard to push the atrocity to the back of his mind.

'What are you thinking about?' she asked.

'This . . .'

He extracted from his jacket pocket the silver Delta badge he had ripped from the lapel of a dead would-be assassin in Bahnhofstrasse. Casually, he tossed it on her bed. She moved away from it as though it were alive, staring at him, her eyes wide with fear.

'Where did you get that?'

She was quick and clever. During the few seconds while she was talking her right hand, which was furthest away from him and in shadow, slipped under her pillow and reappeared holding the 9-mm pistol which she aimed point-blank at his stomach.

'The badge frightens you?' he asked.

'*You* frighten me now. I shan't hesitate to shoot . . .'

'I believe you.'

He was careful to keep his hands folded in his lap, well away from the bedside table drawer. There was no softness in her voice now, in her expression, in the posture of her well-developed body. If he miscalculated the Swiss girl would pull the trigger.

'I took that badge off the body of a man I shot in Bahnhofstrasse last night. They were waiting for us

76

when we came out of the apartment – Delta. None of your men with stocking masks or Balaclava hoods. Men in business suits! And each wearing a badge in his lapel. There was a lot of blood spilt – but an hour later the place was nice and tidy for tomorrow's tourists . . .'

'You said blood was spilt. You said "us" . . .'

'Why didn't *you* keep our appointment at Centralhof?' he snapped.

'Arnold was going to take me off the Delta investigation after Warner's murder – so I went underground. Lisbeth was supposed to bring you here, to make sure you weren't followed. Unlike you, she knows some of Arnold's trackers . . .'

'And she knows Ferdy Arnold himself?'

'No, she has never met him. Why?'

'Let me describe Arnold,' he suggested. 'A thin, wiry man in his late thirties. Brown hair brushed back without a parting. Slate-grey eyes . . .'

'That's not a bit like him . . .'

'I thought so. Someone impersonating him turned up while we were at the apartment. I was even suspicious of Lisbeth because she had to look up his number in her notebook – she should have known that backwards if she had been you. The fake Arnold must have phoned her before I arrived and made some excuse as to why she should use that number if the need arose. Who is . . .' He was very careful still with his use of tenses '. . . the girl who impersonated *you*?'

'Before she got married we both worked for David Nagel in police Intelligence. We once played a joke on him – we dressed in exactly the same clothes and went into his office separately, one after the other within the space of ten minutes. He didn't grasp there was any difference and was furious when we told him. It's no wonder you were fooled.'

She showed her renewed confidence in him by slipping her pistol back under the pillow. Smiling by way of apology, she leaned forward and asked the question he had been dreading.

'Where is Lisbeth? Did she wait in the station here to catch a train back to Zürich? As you'll have gathered, she does look terribly like me – although we aren't twins. You realise she is my sister?'

In London Tweed was still at his desk studying a file when he received the frightening news. Rubbing his eyes, he glanced wistfully at the camp-bed he had had set up 'for the duration' as he termed it. Miss McNeil, his faithful assistant, brought in the signal.

A handsome, erect, grey-haired woman – men in the street turned their heads when she passed them – no one knew her age or even her first name, except Tweed, who had forgotten. She was just McNeil – who was always on hand when needed at any hour of the day or night. She also possessed a shrewd brain, a caustic tongue and an encyclopaedic memory.

'This just came in from Bayreuth . . .'

Bayreuth. Alarm bells began ringing. Tweed unlocked the steel-lined drawer containing his code-book. At the moment the signal read like a perfectly normal business enquiry about the despatch of certain goods.

Bayreuth was in *Bavaria*. Lindau, the last place Charles Warner had set foot in before being murdered, was in Bavaria. Delta, the neo-Nazi Party, had its power base in Bavaria. He busied himself with the decoding, using a piece of thick paper clipped to a metal sheet so there could be no imprint of what he was writing.

'Would you prefer me to leave you alone?' McNeil suggested.

'Of course not! Just let me concentrate, woman . . .'

It was a compliment – that she should be asked to stay, because Tweed felt that when the decoding was completed he might welcome company. She sat down, crossed her shapely legs and watched. It was fortunate that – like Martel – she could manage on two or three hours' sleep. As he finished his task Tweed's expression became blank – which told McNeil a great deal.

'Bad news?'

'The worst, the very worst.'

'You will cope. You always do . . .'

'I'm not the one who has to cope. Manfred has just crossed the border into Bavaria from East Germany. Oh, Christ . . .'

*

Manfred!

Tweed was appalled as he re-read the signal. It had travelled to him along a most devious route he could see in his mind's eye. First, his agent planted inside the Ministry for State Security in Leipzig, East Germany, had radioed the message from his mobile transmitter. The message had then been picked up by Tweed's station in Bayreuth.

From Bayreuth a courier had driven at breakneck speed to the British Embassy in Bonn. There the signal would have been handed personally to the security officer. He, in his turn, had radioed it to Park Crescent. The decoded signal was deadly and un-nerving in its implications.

Manfred today Wednesday May 27 crossed East German border near Hof into West Germany. Ultimate destination unknown.

He handed the signal to McNeil without a word, stood up and went to examine the wall-map of Central Europe he had pinned up when Martel had left for the airport. Tweed was quite familiar with the map. In his head he carried a clear picture of the geography of the whole of western Europe. But he wanted to verify which route Manfred might have taken.

From the Hof area an autobahn ran due south via Nuremberg to the Bavarian capital of München. That was the most likely route. And Warner had spent a lot of time in München, paying special attention to the Hauptbahnhof for some unknown reason. He went back to his swivel chair, adjusted his glasses and sagged into his cushion.

'We don't know much about Manfred, do we?' McNeil ventured.

'We know nothing – and we know too much,' Tweed growled. He tapped a file. 'I must be getting psychic in my old age – I was looking at his dossier when you brought that signal.'

'He's a top East German agent, isn't he? Some query about his nationality and origins. A top-flight assassin – and a first-rate planner. An unusual combination . . .'

'But Carlos is an unusual man,' Tweed said and pushed his spectacles back over his forehead.

'You really think he is Carlos? Nothing has been heard of him for ages . . .'

'The Americans assume so. But there is something very peculiar going on which I don't understand. Delta is the neo-Nazis. Manfred is a free-lance Communist expert on major subversive operations. So who is behind Operation Crocodile – whatever that might be? And *Crocodile* – that reminds me of something I have seen . . .'

'You look really worried. Shall I make coffee?'

Tweed stared at the silent phone on his desk. He spoke half to himself. 'Come in, Martel, for God's sake! I must warn you – before it's too late. You're up against both Nazis and Communists. It's double jeopardy . . .'

*

In a darkened apartment in a large building near München police headquarters in Ettstrasse a gloved hand lifted a telephone. The man wearing nylon gloves was the sole occupant. The only illumination came from a shaded desk light. He dialled a number. It was 4 a.m.

'Who the bloody hell is this? Don't you know the time . . .'

Reinhard Dietrich had been woken at the *schloss* from a deep sleep and his voice reflected his fury. If it was Erwin Vinz again he would blast him to . . .

'Manfred speaking.' The tone of voice was creepily soft and controlled. 'We hear you have a problem and that we find most disturbing.'

Dietrich woke up very quickly, thrown off balance by the identity of the caller, by his words which suggested he knew something about the Zürich débâcle. He sat up in bed and his tone of voice became polite and cooperative.

'Nothing we can't handle, I assure you . . .'

'But in Zürich, it was *mis*handled, so what may we expect next in St Gallen?'

Dietrich, a man accustomed all his life to issuing commands, dreaded the sound of Manfred's sleepy voice. When Manfred had first approached him at his Stuttgart office with his offer to supply arms and uniforms at cut-rate prices he had jumped at the chance. Now he half-regretted the decision – when it was too late.

'You don't have to worry about St Gallen.' He

spoke in a bluff confident tone. 'I have already made arrangements to deal with the situation . . .'

'We are very pleased to hear it. More arms and uniforms are available for immediate collection at the same warehouse. Where and when will you store this consignment?'

Dietrich told him. There was a click and the industrialist realised Manfred had gone off the line. Arrogant bastard! And he detested his caller's habit of using the plural 'we' – as though Dietrich was taking orders from some all-powerful committee. At least more arms were on the way – God knows they had lost enough. How Erich Stoller of the BND tracked down the locations he had no idea.

In Münich Manfred switched off the desk light. Wherever he was staying in the West he always wore gloves – there would be no fingerprints to trace when he left the apartment. There was a thin smile on his face. Operation Crocodile was proceeding according to plan.

In the bedroom at the Hotel Metropol Claire Hofer was enduring a state of delayed shock after Martel told her of Lisbeth's murder. He omitted reference to the fact that she had been tortured. When she reacted she caught him off guard.

'And you let them take her? *Bastard!*' She hit him across the side of the face with the flat of her hand. When she raised her hand a second time he grabbed her wrist and pushed her down on the bed, his face inches from hers as she glared up at him. Their position reminded him of when he had pinned his would-be assassin, Gisela Zobel, down on the sofa in the Centralhof apartment and she had attempted to distract him with sexual games.

But this girl was different. Tough as whipcord, but vulnerable, a vulnerability she covered up with an outwardly controlled manner. The deep blue eyes seemed larger than ever in the light from the bedside lamp. He kissed her gently on the forehead and felt her whipcord muscles relax.

'There were at least a dozen armed Delta soldiers in the assault,' he told her softly, still gripping her wrist. 'They piled out of two cars. I shot three men. I saw them hauling Lisbeth inside a large Mercedes which drove straight off. I blew it . . .'

'A dozen armed men!' Her eyes gazed into his. 'But how could you have saved Lisbeth against such odds? And why did they do this thing – take her away?' Her body had gone limp. He relaxed his grip on her wrist.

'They thought they were taking you . . .'

'Me? Why me?'

'Something big is coming up.' He perched on the edge of her bed and lit a cigarette. 'So Delta is eliminating every agent who might get in their way. First Warner, then the attempt on yourself. I'm their next target. Incidentally, why didn't Warner use the train to get from Lindau to Switzerland – why that business of the boat?'

'He was an ex-Navy man and mistrusted confined spaces – a train could be a trap he'd say. There was nowhere to run. Can't we hit back at these people?'

'We're going to. That's why I'm in St Gallen. There's a rare embroidery museum here, isn't there? The receptionist at the Baur au Lac said so . . .'

'There is.' She was sitting up now, using a hand-mirror and a brush to tidy her dishevelled hair. 'And that's the place Charles used as a rendezvous to meet his contact inside Delta. How do you know about it?'

'We'll come back to that. Do you know how far Warner had gone with his attempt to infiltrate Delta?'

'He had this contact I've just mentioned. I've no idea what he looks like. Charles went to great lengths to protect his identity, but his code-name is Stahl. Incidentally, you've seen the latest news about Delta?'

She reached for a newspaper and handed it to him. It was dated the previous day. The headline jumped out at him and beneath it was the main article.

New Cache of neo-Nazi Arms and Uniforms Found in Allgau.

The text was padded out but the message was simple. Acting on information received the Bavarian police had raided an isolated farmhouse just before dawn and found the arms dump. The farmhouse had shown traces of recent occupation but was deserted at the time of the raid . . .

'That's the seventh Delta arms dump they've found in the past four weeks,' Claire remarked. 'They don't seem to be all that efficient . . .'

'Odd, isn't it?'

'What are you thinking about?' she asked. 'You've got that look again . . .'

He was staring at the wall, recalling his conversation with Tweed. Fragments of that conversation kept beavering away at the back of his mind.

The badge was found under Warner's body. The killer must have dropped it without realising . . . And they computed the job by carving their trademark on his naked back – the Delta Symbol . . .

'I think there's something we're missing – it's just too damned obvious.' He checked his watch. 0430 hours. 'But we can trap the bastards. In the Embroidery Museum here in St Gallen. In less than eight hours from now.'

Chapter Eight

Thursday May 28

'This is what we're talking about – I hope . . .'

They were sitting at a secluded breakfast table in the hotel dining-room. Martel produced from his wallet an orange-coloured ticket and handed it to Claire. The ticket bore a number, several words printed in German and no indication of a town. *Industrie und Gewerbemuseum . . . Eintritt: Fr. 2.50.*

'Warner had that in his own wallet when he was killed,' Martel continued. 'I have my fingers crossed . . .'

'You can uncross them,' she said cheerfully. 'It *is* an entrance ticket to the St Gallen Embroidery Museum. The building is in Vadianstrasse – near the Old Town. Not ten minutes' walk away . . .'

'Look at the back.'

Claire turned over the ticket and saw words written in a script she recognised. Charles Warner's. She was probably looking at the last words he wrote before he had embarked on his fatal boat trip from Lindau.

St. 11.50 May 28.

She looked at Martel and he detected a hint of excitement in her expression as he drank his eighth

cup of coffee. He had already consumed seven crois-
sants, three slices of ham and a large piece of cheese.
He was beginning to feel better.

'May 28 – that's today,' she said and checked her
watch. 'Nine o'clock. *St.* must stand for Stahl. In less
than three hours we shall be talking to him . . .'

'*I* shall be talking to him,' Martel corrected her.

'I thought I was part of the team . . .'

'You told me Warner never let you attend these
meetings. And if whoever turns up sees you he may
take fright . . .'

'He won't recognise *you*,' she persisted stubbornly.

Martel quietly blew up. 'Now listen to me, Claire
Hofer. You're not going to like this but there's no nice
way to get the message across. I work alone – because
then the only person I have to worry about is me. And
me is all I've got – so I worry about me quite a lot.'

'I don't have to come inside the museum . . .'

'I haven't finished yet, so kindly shut up! Ever since
I landed in Zürich nothing has been what it seemed.
At the Centralhof apartment Delta had put in a girl to
take me out. I find another girl in a cupboard – sorry
about this, but it's necessary – and I'm led to think
she's Claire Hofer . . .'

'I told you why we arranged it like that, damn it!'

Her face flushed with rage and her eyes blazed. He
admired her spirit – he might even be able to use it –
but he had to get his point across.

'Next thing,' he went on patiently, 'is a holocaust

in Bahnhofstrasse – and within one hour all signs of it disappear . . .'

'Ferdy Arnold's wash-and-brush-up squad,' she said shortly.

'Come again?'

'You said yourself earlier you thought they had cleaned up the carnage to keep it quiet – to avoid worrying tourists. Arnold has this special team of engineers, glaziers, builders – you name it – standing by in case of a riot or terrorist outrage. They seal off the area temporarily and their motto is "as good as new within thirty minutes". They even have experts who fob off the press with some phoney story if necessary . . .'

'That's what I mean,' Martel said as he buttered another croissant. 'Nothing is what it seems. Delta – for some reason I have yet to fathom – advertises its outrages. Arnold pretends nothing has happened. He even spreads some lying story which fools Nagel of Intelligence. You really expect my meeting with this Stahl will turn out to be straightforward? Damned if I do.'

'And yet you're walking headlong into it?'

'I'll arrive at exactly 11.45. After breakfast you show me the place . . .'

'The rendezvous is 11.50,' she reminded him.

'So I arrive five minutes early and wait to see who does come into that room. Warner could have been followed.'

'He was always extremely careful,' she observed.
'He is now extremely dead . . .'

In Münich the wide avenue of Maximilianstrasse
leads straight as a ruler from Max-Joseph-Platz to the
Bavarian state Parliament on an eminence overlooking
the river Isar. To reach the east bank it passes over
two bridges as it crosses a large island. The body was
found trapped on the brink of one of the giant sluices
below the first bridge.

It was discovered about two hours before Martel
sat down to fortify himself at the Metropol in St
Gallen with a considerable breakfast. A lawyer on his
way to work glanced over the parapet as he crossed
the bridge. In the river a series of giant steps like four
great weirs carried the swift flow of the water. At
each step there is a series of square cement pillars at
intervals. The corpse was folded round one of these
pillars, snagged by chance.

The *Kriminalpolizei* arrived with a doctor to super-
vise retrieval of their evidence when a frogman had
reported the man had been shot in the head. A
preliminary examination was carried out inside an
ambulance by the riverside. Chief-Inspector Kruger
looked at the doctor after a few minutes.

'Surely you can tell me something? I have a pile of
work on my desk a mile high and my wife is beginning to ask questions about my secretary when I
arrive home.'

'Get a less attractive secretary,' the doctor suggested. 'Shot three times in the head. Powder burns visible. Likely time of death – but don't hold me to it – within past twelve hours. And no signs of rope abrasions on the wrists so they didn't tie him up to murder him . . .'

'I can at least check through his clothes for identification? That really is most kind of you, Doctor.'

Kruger searched quickly with expert fingers while his deputy, Weil, carefully said nothing. He could tell from his chief's expression that he was not pleased. He completed the search without producing one single item from the waterlogged body's pockets.

'No means of identification,' Kruger announced. 'That's just what I need. I can see what kind of a day this is going to be . . .'

'His watch,' replied Weil.

He lifted the corpse's left arm which seemed to weigh a ton and unstrapped the watch which had stopped at 0200 hours. He showed Kruger the back plate of the watch which was made of steel and had a single word engraved on it.

'One hell of a lot of help,' commented Kruger.

The word engraved in the plate was *Stahl*.

On their way to the Embroidery Museum Martel and Claire walked arm in arm. It was Martel who had made the suggestion. 'A couple is far less conspicuous,' he commented.

'If you say so . . .'

He bridled. 'Use your head. Two groups may be hunting for us. Delta for me – so they will search for a single man. Arnold's mob for you – so they'll look for a single girl . . .'

'Logical, I suppose,' she said indifferently.

'And never let emotion cloud your judgement. I make it 11.30, fifteen minutes before I have to be inside that museum. That wallplate says Vadianstrasse . . .'

'The Embroidery Museum is at the far end on the left-hand side – and I've decided, I'm coming with you . . .'

'Not inside the place. I'll find somewhere nearby to park you.'

'I'm not a bloody car!' she flared up. She played her part well, hugging his arm and staring up at him with lover's eyes as she hissed the words. 'You're expecting trouble – you brought a silencer for your Colt.'

'I told you – nothing so far has been what it seemed and I have an idea the trend will continue.'

During their walk Martel had observed that St Gallen was located inside a deep notch or gulch. Hemmed in on two sides by vertical hill-slopes, the shopping area had been built on the floor of the gorge. Stepped up on the hillsides, one above another, were large solid-looking villas erected in the previous century.

The weather was again clammy with a heavy

overcast and there was a hint of a storm in the air. Martel walked more slowly as they came closer to the entrance, his eyes scanning the area for signs of danger. He stopped again to look in a shop window but no one followed his example. On the surface the area was clean – only women shoppers, smartly dressed, strolling along the street.

'The police station isn't near, is it?' he murmured.

'As a matter of fact it is. *Stadtpolizei* is at Neugasse 5 – the first turning off to the left from that street over there . . .'

'Great! How far away on foot – walking fast? The Swiss police can walk fast.'

'Less than five minutes – two if they use a car. Why?'

'I like to know where all the pieces on the board are – in case of emergency.'

They had left the shop and walked the full length of the building containing the museum. Claire pointed to where the Old Town started while Martel searched for a convenient café to leave her. They should have allowed more time.

'Looking for somewhere to park the car?' she enquired. 'Well I've found the ideal place – and I can watch the entrance to the museum without anyone seeing me . . .'

She was pointing across the wide street to an orange booth with a black curtain pulled back revealing a metal stool. In large letters over the booth were the words PRONTOPHOT PASSFOTOS.

'I'd better grab the seat before someone else decides they want a passport picture,' she said. 'Good luck. Don't forget to collect me on your way out. I don't want to sit there all day taking my picture – the results are lousy . . .'

Martel took one final look-round. He couldn't rid himself of the feeling something was wrong about the atmosphere. Shrugging his shoulders, he crossed Vadianstrasse, opened the door and went inside.

It was exactly as Claire had described: a wide flight of steps leading up into a large entrance hall. At a ticket window he paid a woman two francs fifty for a ticket like the one he had in his pocket, the one Warner had purchased. While buying it he held a handkerchief over his face and blew his nose incessantly. The woman behind the window would never be able to identify him later.

A notice indicated that the museum was on the first floor. He climbed two longer flights of steps. There was no one else about, the atmosphere was hushed. He could see why Warner had chosen this place and this time for meeting his Delta contact. On the wall outside the front entrance a plate had given the opening hours. *10.00 – 12.00* and *14.00 – 17.00*. When the place closed at midday who else would arrive at 11.50?

To his left along the wide landing were a pair of

double doors leading to the library. Very quietly, his soft-soled shoes making no noise, he walked to the library and tried the door. It was locked. He crossed back over the landing quickly and tried the Embroidery Museum door. It gave way under his pressure. He stepped inside, closed it and scanned the silent room.

The exhibits were in glass cases standing in various positions in a large room with windows overlooking Vadianstrasse. Before he was convinced the place was empty he checked several alcoves. Then he extracted the Colt from his shoulder holster and screwed on the silencer. His watch registered precisely 11.50 when he saw the handle of the door turning slowly.

He watched, fascinated, the Colt held behind his back, as the turning handle completed its revolution and then remained in that position without the door opening. It was a good ten seconds before the door began moving slowly inwards. Martel stepped back out of sight.

Because his hearing was acute he heard the slight click – the release of the door-handle after closing. He controlled his breathing. The silence in the museum room was so complete the patter of a mouse across the wood-block floor would have been heard.

Soon the new arrival, Stahl, would come into view. Was he checking to make sure he was alone? Or did he – as Martel would have done in his place – sense a presence in that silent archive of the ages, the repository of craftwork by people who had died centuries earlier . . . ?

It was a man in a light overcoat and smart trilby. Very like a businessman. Like the men who had flooded out of the Rolls and the Mercedes in Bahnhofstrasse. Under the hat a bleak white bony face. In his lapel a silver triangular badge, the symbol of Delta.

In his right hand he held an object like a felt-tip pen – the needle-blade was already projecting ready for action. The click Martel had assumed to be the door-handle had been the pressing of the button which projected the blade.

When he appeared the bony-faced man was only a few feet from Martel. Stiffening his hand, he lunged forward, the needle-point aimed at Martel's stomach. The Englishman remained exactly where he was, jerked up the Colt and fired twice in rapid succession. The *phut-phut* of the silenced gun sounded unnaturally loud in the hushed atmosphere.

The bony-faced man dropped his hypodermic weapon and reeled backwards. He slammed into one of the display cases, flopped sideways and his head crashed down through the glass lid. As his legs gave way he slithered to the floor, his heels making runnels across the polished surface. A stream of blood gushed from his torn face.

*

Martel left the museum without being seen. As he slipped past the ticket window he glimpsed a woman's back. She was drinking from a cup. The Colt was rammed inside his belt. They closed in less than five minutes. He had to get out on the street. But they were waiting for him out there. Delta.

They had sent in a single man to do the job but they would have people outside as back-up. It was that kind of thorough organisation. Martel had not forgotten the nightmare in Bahnhofstrasse. The audacity, the ferocity. He opened the door and stepped out into Vadianstrasse.

Everything seemed normal. Housewives out shopping, singly or in couples. A man wearing yellow oilskins and a cap, carrying some kind of bag, leaned against a wall on the opposite side. He was trying to light a cigarette: the lighter seemed to be defective.

Claire! He had to protect Claire, to lead them away from her. Already one Hofer – Lisbeth – had been killed. And they were out here somewhere. He could see Claire's legs below the closed curtain inside the photo booth. He began walking.

He timed it carefully. Taking out his holder to make himself conspicuous he inserted a cigarette. He stopped alongside the booth and cupped his hand to use the lighter, to conceal the fact that he was talking. The curtain was open a fraction of an inch. He didn't look towards the booth as he spoke.

'They sent a Delta operative. He's dead inside the

museum. I am giving you an order. Stay there, give me two minutes to lead anyone out here away, then get the hell back to the Metropol and wait till I contact you . . .'

Then he was moving away, heading into the Old Town where the road surfaces were cobbled, the buildings ancient, the shops new. He turned into Neugasse and followed the curve of the street.

Neugasse 5, Claire had said. Police headquarters. Five minutes' walk, two or less by car. He had to pinpoint the opposition and this should give him more time. The bastards could hardly start something in close proximity to a police station. He stopped to look in a window.

He had no idea what the shop sold. He was concentrating on a reflection. The man in yellow oil-skins had stopped on the other side of the narrow street. He was staring into another window, holding a large carrier bag and puffing at his cigarette. His lighter had conveniently worked as soon as Martel began moving.

The Englishman sucked at his holder. Something was wrong. Something more than the fact that it appeared he was being shadowed by Yellow Oil-skins. He resumed his walk. *Stadtpolizei*. Walls a muddy grey roughcast, grey shutters almost merging into the walls. An archway entrance wide enough for a single car. He walked on.

He was approaching an intersection, a more spacious area which, he remembered from the street map Claire had shown him, was the Markt-Gasse. He turned left and stopped to drop his half-smoked cigarette which he stubbed under his heel. The possibility of a coincidence ended. Yellow Oil-skins was looking in yet another shop window. Something was very wrong indeed.

It was too damned obvious: using as a shadow a man clad in an outfit which could be picked out hundreds of yards away. It was as though he were making his presence as conspicuous as possible – to divert Martel's attention from someone else. *The danger was going to come from another quarter.*

He stood on the kerb gazing at a curious spectacle. In the middle of the street stood a small train for children made up of wooden, open-sided coaches with canvas canopies. At the front was a black railway engine with a gold trim and the driver, a man, was operating a whistle to signal imminent departure. Each of the coaches carried four children, two facing each other. A couple of coaches were occupied by mothers sitting with their offspring. The trolley-car train was large enough to carry adults.

Yellow Oil-skins remained staring into a window displaying ladies' underwear, for God's sake! Martel moved quickly, leaving the train still stationary. If there was to be havoc – Zürich-style – it must not happen near those children. Ahead he saw a buff-coloured building which was the Hotel Hecht – where

Claire had originally been staying. Crossing the road, he concentrated his attention on everyone except Yellow Oil-skins.

The attack came from the least-expected quarter at a moment when his alertness was briefly distracted by an astonishing sight. He was walking past the Hecht when he heard a piercing shriek, the train's whistle. It had followed him as it proceeded confidently amid the traffic to pass alongside the Hecht. In the last coach on the side nearest to him sat Claire Hofer.

The seat next to her was occupied by a small girl and two more children faced them. They were all looking away from the Hecht while Claire stared straight at him. Under cover of her handbag, the flap open, she was holding her pistol, the barrel aimed towards him.

He sensed rather than felt someone close to his left. Glancing away from the train he saw a tall woman wearing a dark hat with a veil concealing her face. Her shoulder-bag was supported by her left arm. In her right hand she held a familiar object – the needle-pointed hypodermic weapon.

This was the back-up Yellow Oil-skins had tried so very hard to conceal from him. Martel had a vague memory of seeing this veiled, elegantly-dressed woman in Neugasse and for a second he was taken off guard. He almost put out a hand to ward her off, which would have been his last movement since she would have jabbed the weapon into his hand and injected its contents.

Somewhere close by a car backfired, a sound cut off by the blare of a car's horn. The elegant woman wore a dress with a deep V-cut which exposed a generous portion of her bosom. Another distraction? Then she leaned back against the wall of the hotel. A small hole had appeared in the V of her bosom, as though drilled by a surgeon. The hole began to well redness as she sagged to the ground.

In falling her hat had tipped sideways, removing the veil from her face. Martel forced himself to walk on, threading his way among the morning shoppers. The face now exposed to view was not unfamiliar. It was the dead face of Gisela Zobel.

He saw the train moving on towards an ancient gateway in a wall which had probably once protected the town. Claire was still on board, clasping her closed handbag as she chatted to the girl next to her. The Swiss girl had shot his would-be killer from a moving vehicle. Marksmanship of that order he had never encountered before. And Yellow Oil-skins had now vanished as a crowd began to gather in front of the Hecht, huddled over something lying on the ground.

Chapter 9

Thursday May 28

In her bedroom at the Metropol Claire was shaking with fright. She held herself in check until Martel arrived back a few minutes after she had returned. Now reaction set in and she broke down. He sat on the bed beside her and she pressed her face into his chest and quietly sobbed. He stroked her soft black hair, saying nothing until he felt the tremors easing.

'You disobeyed orders,' he said harshly. 'While you were in the photo booth I told you get to hell back here. The next thing I see is you riding on that kids' train . . .'

'A bloody good job for you I did!' she flared up, then her expression changed to one of consternation. 'Oh, my God – are you saying that woman wasn't trying to kill you – I distinctly saw a knife in her hand . . .'

'It wasn't a knife – it was one of those hypodermic weapons Delta favour. You saved my life,' he went on in his normal blank monotone to help quieten her. 'How the devil did you follow me? I never saw you . . .'

'I wouldn't be much good if you had done,' she snapped back and blew her nose. 'Sorry if I fouled it up.'

'If shooting an assassin accurately from a moving vehicle comes under the heading fouling it up then please make a habit of it.'

'Did I kill her?'

'You killed the bitch,' he said shortly. 'It was Gisela Zobel, the girl who impersonated Lisbeth at Central-hof. There seems to be no end to the ruthless ingenuity of Delta. First they send in a man to keep the appointment inside the museum – a man wearing the Delta symbol in his lapel . . .'

'You left him there – with the badge?'

'Yes. Odd, isn't it, the way they flaunt that badge. Almost as though someone wants to advertise their role as murderers. I am beginning to get an idea about that. Then they have a back-up team. A very obvious man in yellow oil-skins follows me while a very unobvious woman in hat and veil waits her chance to finish me off . . .'

'I spotted both of them through the gap in the booth curtain. That's why I came after you . . .'

'And thank God you did,' Martel replied as he stood up. 'You haven't unpacked your case?'

'You told me not to – so only my toilet things are in the bathroom . . .'

'Pack them. We're catching the first train out of St Gallen.'

'Why? I'm exhausted . . .' she protested.

'You can rest on the train. We're heading east for Bavaria . . .'

'What's the Goddamn rush?'

'The Goddamn rush is the police. They'll soon realise they have two murders on their hands. *Two!* The man I killed in the museum, the woman you shot outside the Hecht. Then they'll be watching every train leaving St Gallen . . .'

Martel concealed one fact from Claire as they sat in a first-class compartment which they had to themselves aboard the Münich express. He was convinced they were moving into the zone of maximum danger – Bavaria. Somewhere in that scenically glorious part of Germany Delta had its headquarters.

Switzerland, the most neutral, stable country in Europe, had almost been a death-trap. But the risks encountered in Zürich and St Gallen were nothing compared with what lay ahead of them.

While waiting for the train in St Gallen station Martel had called Tweed in London. This was one of the many advantages of Switzerland: its superb telephone system enabled you to dial abroad from a payphone where no one could intercept the call.

Martel had used his usual technique when speaking to Tweed – knowing his call would be tape-recorded. He had spoken in a kind of shorthand –

shooting random facts at Tweed, every scrap of information he had picked up. Later Tweed, remote from the battlefield, would try to fit the fragments of data into some kind of pattern.

'Thursday calling,' he said as Tweed came on the line and waited for the answering code identification.

'Two-Eight here . . .'

It was Thursday May 28. Martel used the *day* of the week while Tweed responded with the *date* of the month. Martel began to pour out data.

'Delta very active inside Switzerland . . . agents wear businessmen suits . . . Delta symbol openly displayed in lapels . . . strange lack of cooperation from locals . . . dummy Claire waiting Centralhof tried to kill me . . . arrested by fake Arnold . . . imprisoned Hofer waiting Lisbeth Hofer . . . Claire's twin-like sister . . . Lisbeth kidnapped during bloodbath in Bahnhofstrasse . . . repeat in Bahnhofstrasse . . . Ferdy Arnold later reported her body found in Limmat . . . Nagel denied all knowledge events in Bahnhofstrasse . . . now with genuine Claire Hofer St Gallen . . . leaving immediately with her to investigate scene Warner murder . . . Claire reports Warner made three mentions Operation Crocodile . . . something phoney about Delta neo-Nazis . . . must go . . .'

'Wait!' Tweed's tone was urgent. 'Bayreuth reports Manfred has crossed the border near Hof into West Germany. Manfred – got it?'

'Christ!'

Martel had slammed down the receiver, grabbed his suitcase and run across the platform to the compartment door Claire had left open. Boarding the express, he hauled the door closed behind him as the train began moving east, dumped his case on a seat and sat down.

Even in the early afternoon the third-floor apartment in the sombre Münich apartment block was so dim the occupant had turned on the shaded desk-lamp. He had entered the apartment to find the phone ringing. His gloved hand lifted the receiver.

'Vinz – calling from Lindau . . .'

'We are here,' Manfred replied in his soft, calm voice. 'You are calling to confirm that a successful deal was concluded in St Gallen?'

'Regrettably it was not possible to conclude the deal . . .' Erwin Vinz forced himself to go on. 'Kohler has reported from there . . .'

'And why was the deal not concluded?'

'The opposition's negotiator proved uncooperative . . .' Vinz was sweating, his armpits felt damp. 'And the services of two of our people were terminated . . .'

'T-e-r-m-i-n-a-t-e-d?'

Manfred repeated the word with great deliberation as though he were sure he had misheard. There was a pause and the light from the desk-lamp was reflected in the lenses of the large dark-tinted glasses Manfred wore. In Lindau Vinz made the effort to continue.

'The Englishman is now aboard an express bound for Münich. It is due here in about half an hour . . .'

'So,' Manfred interjected smoothly, 'you have made all preparations to board the express at Lindau to continue negotiations with this gentleman.' Now it was Manfred's turn to pause. 'You do, of course, realise it is imperative you conclude the deal with him before the train reaches München?'

'Everything has been arranged by me personally. I just thought I should check with you . . .'

'Always check with me, Vinz. Always. Then, as a matter of courtesy, you keep Mr Reinhard Dietrich informed . . .'

'I will report progress . . .'

'Passengers have been known to fall out of trains,' Manfred purred. 'You will report *success* . . .'

Cooped up inside his payphone on the Bavarian mainland Erwin Vinz realised the connection had been broken. Swearing, he pushed open the door and hurried away through a drift of grey mist.

The medieval town of Lindau – once an Imperial city – was blotted out in the fog coming in off the lake. The Old Town is a network of cobbled streets and alleyways which at night only the most intrepid venture down. Not that there is normally any danger – Lindau is a most law-abiding place.

Shortly after Manfred received his phone call three cars proceeded over the road bridge and headed for the Hauptbahnhof. The station is another curious feature of Lindau. Main-line expresses on their way from Zürich to Münich make a diversion at this point. The line takes them across the embankment to the west on to the island. They stop at the Hauptbahnhof next to the harbour.

If you alight from an express at Lindau you pass through *Zoll* – the customs and passport control post – because you have crossed the border from Austria into Germany. But boarding a train at Lindau for Münich you do not pass through *Zoll* – since you are already in Germany.

This factor was important to the eight men led by Vinz alighting from the three cars at the Hauptbahnhof. The drivers took the cars away immediately. Dressed like businessmen, two of the eight passengers carried suitcases containing uniforms. These would be donned aboard the Münich express as soon as it began moving out of Lindau.

The uniforms were those of a German State Railways ticket inspector and a German Passport Control official. It was the latter – travelling rapidly through the train and explaining there was a double-check on passports – who expected to locate Keith Martel. The plan was simple. Erwin Vinz, thirty-eight years old, small, thin and with hooded eyelids, was in charge of the execution squad.

Vinz would wear the Passport Control uniform. Vinz would locate the target. If Martel were travelling alone in a compartment it would be invaded when the express was travelling at speed by four men. The outer door would be opened and the Englishman would be hurled from the train. The whole operation, Vinz calculated, would take less than twenty seconds.

If Martel had fellow-passengers in his compartment Vinz would ask him to accompany him because there was a query on his passport. He would be guided to an empty compartment and the same procedure would be followed. Vinz knew that this particular express was always half-empty on this day of the week.

The platform marked for the arrival of the express was deserted as the eight men arrived separately from the concourse. The fog created a hushed atmosphere and the men moved in it like ghosts. Vinz checked his watch. They were in good time. The express was due in twenty minutes.

Chapter Ten

Thursday May 28

'You'll like Lindau, Keith,' Claire said as Martel peered out of the window from the fast-moving express. 'It is one of the most beautiful old towns in Germany . . .'

'I know it.' He had his mind on something else. 'I shall want to contact Erich Stoller of the BND as soon as we can – to let him have a look at this . . .'

Unlocking his case, he produced something rolled up in a handkerchief. A blue, shiny cylinder like a large felt-tip pen. There were two press-buttons: one on the casing, the second at the base.

'I rescued this little Delta toy from the floor of the Embroidery Museum where the killer dropped it. This button half-way along the casing ejects and retracts the needle. I imagine the one at the base injects the poison. Ingenious – you can use the full force of the palm of your hand to operate the injection mechanism. Stoller's forensic people will tell us what fluid it contains . . .'

'That woman I shot outside the Hecht . . .'

'Was going to use the duplicate of this. Intriguing that Reinhard Dietrich runs an electronics complex – which involves fine instrumentation . . .'

'You mean *he* manufactures that horrible thing?'

'Damned sure of it.' He replaced the weapon inside his case and looked again out of the window. Up to now the view had been one of green cultivated fields and rolling hills – one of the most attractive and least-known parts of Switzerland. Well clear of the tourist belt.

The landscape was changing. They were crossing flatlands dimly visible in swirling mist which hid nearby Lake Konstanz. They saw few signs of human habitation and there was something desolate in the atmosphere. Martel concentrated on the view as though he might miss something important.

'This is the Rhine delta, isn't it?' he queried.

'Yes. We cross the river soon just before it runs into the lake.'

Delta. Was there significance in this geographical curiosity at the extreme eastern end of the lake? The southern shore was Swiss except for a weird enclave of land occupied by the German town of Konstanz away to the west. The northern shore was German. But at this eastern tip a few miles of lake frontage was *Austrian.*

Martel adjusted the horn-rimmed spectacles with plain glass he wore to change his appearance. He lit a fresh cigarette, being careful not to use his holder. He seemed to have relapsed into a dream.

'We shall soon be in Lindau,' Claire said exuberantly, trying to drag him out of his dark mood. 'Surely we must find something – it was . . .' Her voice wavered and then she had herself under control. 'It was the last place Warner was seen alive.'

'Except that we are getting off at the stop before – Bregenz in Austria.'

'Why?'

'Bregenz could be important. And it will be the last place Delta will expect us to leave the train . . .'

Hauptbahnhof, München . . . Hauptbahnhof, Zürich . . . Delta . . . Centralhof . . . Bregenz . . . Washington, DC, Clint Loomis . . . Pullach, BND . . . Operation Crocodile.

These were the references the dead Charles Warner had written in the tiny black notebook hidden in a secret pocket, the notebook Erich Stoller of the BND had discovered on the body and flown to Tweed in London.

Bregenz.

As the express slowed down Claire caught a glimpse of Lake Konstanz through the corridor windows – a sheet of calm grey water. The express stopped and when Martel opened the door at the end of the coach he found no platform – they stepped down on to the track. He dumped his suitcase, took Claire's and held her elbow while she descended the steep drop. She shivered as she picked up her case and they made their way across rail tracks to the station, an old single-storey building.

'You shivered . . .'

'It's the mist,' she said shortly.

A cold clammy dampness moistened her face and she felt it penetrating her light raincoat. She had lied. It *was* the mist partly – but mainly it was the atmosphere created by the drifts of greyish vapour. You saw things, then they were gone.

Behind Bregenz looms the massive heights of the Pfänder, a ridge whose sides are densely forested. As they crossed to the station Claire saw a gap appear in the mist pall exposing the dripping wall of limestone, then it too was gone. There was no ticket barrier to pass through – tickets had been checked aboard the express. They deposited their cases in the self-locking metal compartments for luggage and walked into Bregenz.

The place seemed deserted, as though it were a Sunday. A line of old block-like buildings faced the station. Martel paused, puffing his cigarette as he glanced round searching for anything out of place. Claire gazed at him.

'Those glasses make you look studious – they change your whole personality. And you're walking more ponderously. You're just like a chameleon. Incidentally, what are we going to do here?'

He extracted two photos of Charles Warner obtained from Tweed before leaving Park Crescent and handed her one of the prints. She looked at the picture of the man she had worked with for over six months, the man who had been brutally murdered on the lake behind them – only a short distance from where they stood.

'The story is we're looking for a friend – Warner,' Martel told her. 'His wife is seriously ill and we think he's somewhere here. We'll buy a street map, divide up the place into sections – then meet up at an agreed place in two hours' time . . .'

'It sounds a hopeless task,' she commented when they were studying a street plan bought at a kiosk.

'Warner was here – he made a reference to the place in his notebook. Concentrate on anywhere selling cigarettes – he smoked like a chimney. He had a strong personality, made an impression on anyone he talked to. Now, we'll decide which district each of us is going to tackle. Half this job is legwork . . .'

In the Münich apartment the phone began ringing and Manfred, who was expecting the call, picked up the receiver with his gloved hand. It was Erwin Vinz. Manfred, a teetotaller, poured Perrier water as he listened intently.

'I am speaking from Münich Hauptbahnhof,' Vinz began after giving the identification code. 'I got off the train a few minutes ago . . .'

Manfred knew immediately something was wrong. Vinz was rambling, reluctant to come to the point. Manfred introduced into the conversation his often-used ploy.

'Excellent! We assume all went well. Appointment kept and deal concluded!

'The Englishman was not on the train. There is no

doubt – I can vouch for the fact personally. *If* he got aboard at St Gallen he must have got off at Romanshorn or St Margarethen in Switzerland.'

'Kohler saw him closing the compartment door after he boarded the express at St Gallen . . .'

Manfred's voice was gentle and delicate, concealing his livid rage. Vinz's insolence in emphasising *If* cast doubt on Kohler's competence. Not that Manfred cared a damn about Kohler – but Vinz was trying to shift the blame and that he would not tolerate.

'Kohler would have known,' Manfred continued, 'if our friend left the train while it was moving through Switzerland . . .' Manfred saw no reason to explain that Kohler would have had men with a clear description of Keith Martel waiting at each Swiss stop. He continued to make Vinz sweat.

'Your sector began at the Swiss border. You got on the train at Lindau . . .'

'The bastard must have got off at Bregenz,' Vinz interjected. 'It was the only place left uncovered . . .'

'Left uncovered by *you* . . .'

Bregenz! Manfred's hand gripped the receiver tightly. The one town he did not want Martel poking around in was Bregenz. He felt like screaming at Vinz, but the sensitivity of the situation must at all costs be hidden.

'I can have a team in Bregenz in one hour,' Vinz volunteered, disturbed by the silence at the other end of the line.

'We would like your team to keep its appointment

with the client in half an hour. I hold you personally responsible for bringing about a successful conclusion to this transaction . . .'

Inside the payphone at Münich Hauptbahnhof Vinz swore again. Once more Manfred had abruptly terminated the conversation. And now he had to fly his bloody team back from Münich to the airstrip nearest Bregenz. This time they had to eliminate the Englishman.

In London Tweed had left his office for his flat in Maida Vale after receiving the St Gallen call from Martel. Mason, Howard's new deputy, had tried to delay him. Looking leaner and hungrier than ever, he arrived as Tweed was leaving.

'The chief would like to see you in his office, sir. He says it is extremely urgent . . .'

'It always is – to him. I'll see him when I get back.'

Tweed took a cab to the flat. He also took Miss McNeil and she carried the Martel tape concealed in a hold-all. While in the cab he asked his question.

'That new recruit, Mason. Is he any good at anything?'

'He'd make a good bodyguard,' McNeil replied in her crisp Scots accent. 'He's an expert at judo, karate. A marksman with handguns. Special Branch were happy for Howard to take him.'

'Why?'

McNeil had a finely-tuned ear on the grapevine. Probably due to her gift for listening with attentive concentration and unlimited patience.

'He was too physical – always resorted to heavy handling of any suspect at the drop of a hat. A lot of hats – and clangers – were dropped, I gather.'

At the flat McNeil played back the tape of Martel's conversation on the machine kept there permanently, making notes in neat loops and curls. She had offered to make the tea but Tweed insisted only he could make it the way he liked it. You would imagine he had been a lifetime bachelor, McNeil thought, as she went on making her notes. Tweed arrived with the tray of tea as the tape came to the end of the recording.

The block of flats Tweed lived in was self-service. He had a Sicilian woman who came in to clean the place and often complained she was 'illiterate in three languages'. There was a restaurant on the ground floor. Here Tweed, now on his own, led a self-contained existence. He poured the tea as he asked the question.

'Anything strike you about Martel's data?'

'Two things. Delta seems to be acting in a frenzy – as though they're working against a deadline. *Bloodbath*. That's strong language from Martel in a report. And another reference – *something phoney about Delta neo-Nazis*. I don't understand what he's driving at . . .'

'McNeil, you're a treasure. You always spot the salient facts. Makes me feel redundant. I'm pretty sure the deadline is June 2 when the Summit Express leaves Paris – because by morning it will be crossing Bavaria . . .'

'You're thinking about the Bavarian state elections?'

'Exactly. Three main parties are competing for power – to take over the state government. Dietrich's Delta – the neo-Nazis – the government party under Chancellor Kurt Langer, and the left-wing lot under Tofler, the alleged ex-Communist. If something dramatic happens on June 3, the day before the election, it might swing the election result – into Tofler's hands. For the West it would be a major disaster.'

'What dramatic event could happen?'

'I only wish I knew.' Tweed sipped his tea. 'I'm convinced Delta has some secret plan – hence the frenzy to eliminate anyone digging into their affairs.'

'What about the reference to *something phoney*?'

McNeil sat quite still, watching Tweed gazing owlishly through his spectacles into the distance. He was, she knew, capable of sudden flashes of intuition – a leap into the future he divined from just the sort of ragbag of facts Martel had provided.

'It has the feel of a separate cell operating secretly inside Delta,' Tweed said slowly. 'That's the only explanation for some of their actions which seem to be designed to ensure they *lose* the election . . .'

'Now you've *lost* me,' McNeil commented tartly.

*

'Where *have* you two been?'

Howard was waiting for them when McNeil and Tweed returned to the latter's office. Standing stiff-backed he had the window behind him – so his own face was in shadow while the new arrivals were caught in the full glare of the light from the curved window. He clasped his hands over his stomach which was decorated with the double loop of a gold watch-chain.

Very militant in mood as well as stance, Tweed observed as he sat behind his desk. He knew the type only too well. An inferiority complex as large as Everest – so they compensated by periodic assertions of authority just to make sure they still held it.

'Went for a walk in Regent's Park,' Tweed lied blandly.

'You're working on a problem?' Howard pounced.

The SIS chief was in a nervous state of mind, McNeil decided. She was carrying the empty hold-all inside which she had smuggled out Martel's tape to the flat in Maida Vale.

'What's inside that hold-all?' Howard demanded.

'Cheese sandwiches – Cheddar, if you must know,' Tweed interjected. 'It's better than the Cheshire – more flavour . . .'

'Could you very kindly find something to do elsewhere?' Howard asked McNeil, who promptly left the room, still carrying the hold-all.

'Have you heard from Keith Martel?' Howard barked as soon as they were alone.

'I thought you were concentrating on security for the PM on her trip to the forthcoming Summit Conference in Vienna. So why interest yourself in Martel . . .'

'It's a waste of personnel. Just when I need every man . . .'

'So you told me. If you want it on record send me a minute and I can show it to the Minister.' Tweed perched his glasses on the end of his nose and peered over the rims at his visitor, a mannerism which he knew infuriated Howard. 'By the way, I suppose the normal people are in charge of security for the others – the Presidents of America and France, and the German Chancellor?'

'Tim O'Meara in Washington, Alain Flandres in Paris and Erich Stoller in Bonn. Does it really concern you?'

'Not really. I just wondered if all my old friends were still in their jobs.' Tweed looked at his chief. 'These days so many get the chop just when they least expect it . . .'

Howard left the room, his mouth tight, his stride almost that of an officer route-marching. He would be incensed for days over the exchange which had taken place – and would therefore keep well away from Tweed, which was what the latter intended. McNeil peered round the door.

'Has he gone?'

'Yes, my dear, the British lion has roared. It is now safe to return.' He opened a copy of *The Times* atlas.

'Crocodile – I'm sure the meaning of that codeword is under my nose . . .'

Erwin Vinz took his execution squad back into the new search area – Bregenz – by the fastest possible route. Flying from a private airstrip outside Münich he landed his men at another airstrip close to Lindau. From here the eight men piled into three waiting cars and were driven at speed to the border and Bregenz beyond. It was three o'clock when they pulled up in front of the station.

'I think Martel got off the train here,' Vinz told the two men in the rear of his car. 'He may well still be in Bregenz. You stay here. The rest of us will quarter the town and drive round until we locate him . . .'

'And if we do see him board a train?' one of the two men asked as he alighted from the car.

'He has a fatal accident, of course!' Vinz was irritated by the man's stupidity. 'Whatever happens he must not reach Münich . . .'

Vinz held a brief conference with the other five men. 'There are twenty thousand deutschemarks for the man who locates Martel. You have his description. You tell people he escaped from a home for the mentally disturbed, that he is dangerous. Rendezvous here two hours from now. Turn over this backwater!'

*

121

Martel picked up the spoor Charles Warner had left behind in Bregenz at his twelfth attempt. The contact was a bookseller, an Austrian in his early forties with a shop at the end of Kaiserstrasse. Outside was the pedestrian underpass where Martel had arranged to meet Claire in half an hour's time. He told his tale, showed Warner's photo and the reaction was positive.

'I know your friend. Grief seems to be his companion . . .'

'Grief?' Martel queried cautiously and waited.

'Yes. His closest friend died here while on a visit. It was during the French military occupation of the Vorarlberg and the Tyrol after the war. His friend was buried here so he thought he would pay his respects.'

'I see . . .'

Martel did not see at all and was careful to say as little as possible. The bookseller broke off to serve a customer and then continued.

'There are two Catholic cemeteries in Bregenz and one Protestant. This man's friend had a curious religious history. Born a Protestant, he was converted to the Catholic faith. Later he appeared to lose his faith. Under the peculiar circumstances the man who came into my shop asked for the location of all three cemeteries. I showed them to him on a street map.'

'How recent was his visit to you?'

'Less than a week ago. Last Saturday . . .'

'Can you sell me a street map and mark the three cemeteries?'

The bookseller fetched a map and ringed the areas. 'There is the Blumenstrasse, the Vorkloster – both are Catholic. And here is the Protestant burial-ground . . .'

Claire was waiting when Martel descended the steps into the otherwise deserted subway. She stood gazing at a scene behind an illuminated window set into the wall. The glass protected relics of an archaeological dig which had unearthed the ancient Roman town which once stood on the site of present-day Bregenz.

'Spooky, isn't it?' Claire remarked and gave a little shudder. 'All that time ago. And today in this mist the whole place seems creepy – and I haven't found a trace of Warner . . .'

'Last Saturday he was standing not a hundred feet from where we are standing now . . .'

She listened while he summed up his interview with the helpful bookseller. As he completed his résumé she was frowning. 'I'm not grasping the significance . . .'

'Join the club – except that one thing's almost frighteningly certain. He was here last Saturday. Sunday he's murdered out on the lake. Whatever he found in Bregenz probably triggered off that murder . . .'

'But how long ago was the French military occupation of Austria, for God's sake? This goes back to just after the war . . .'

'Not necessarily. The Allied occupation of Austria ended May 15 1955 – so whatever Warner dug up could have happened close to that date . . .'

'It's still over a quarter of a century ago,' she objected, 'so what could have happened then that's relevant to today?'

'Damned if I know – that's what we have to find out. That yarn Warner spun about his closest friend dying here was eye-wash, but he had his teeth into something. The period – the time of the French occupation might mean something . . .'

'So how do we find out, where do we start?'

'We hire a car first at a place I saw near here. Then we visit the three cemeteries Warner was enquiring about. The secret has to lie in one of them. Literally . . .'

Erwin Vinz walked into the bookseller's shop in Kaiserstrasse. Despite his later arrival in Bregenz he had, without knowing, an advantage over Martel: six men were scouring the town. He spoke first to a girl assistant and asked for the manager. She went upstairs to find the proprietor who had talked to Martel.

'I'd better go down and see this man myself,' the bookseller decided.

On the ground floor he listened while Vinz told his story. The verbal description Vinz gave was graphic. Take away the glasses and add a cigarette holder and the bookseller recognised that this man was describing his earlier visitor. The Austrian studied Vinz and was careful not to interrupt.

'You say that this man has escaped from a mental asylum?' he enquired eventually.

'Yes. A very violent patient. Unfortunately he can give the impression he is completely normal and this makes him even more dangerous. You have seen this man?'

Chapter Eleven

Thursday May 28

In Gottes Frieden Alois Stohr 1930–1953

In God We Trust ... Inside the mist-bound cemetery known as the Blumenstrasse three people stared at the headstone. Martel and Claire were bewildered. Alois Stohr? The name meant nothing to either of them. Martel turned to the gravedigger who had brought them to this spot. Again he showed him Warner's photo.

'Look, you're quite certain this was the man who asked to see this particular grave?'

The old gravedigger wore an ancient cap and his moustache dripped moisture globules from the grey vapour swirling amid the headstones. So far as Martel could see – which was not very far – they were the only visitors. It was not a day to encourage sentimental journeys.

'This is the man.'

The gravedigger, Martel noted, spoke with the same conviction of recognition as had the bookseller when viewing the photo. And he had identified Warner previously before Martel gave him a sheaf of schilling notes.

'When did he come here?' Martel asked.

'Last week. Saturday.'

The same story that the bookseller had told. It was maddening. Martel no longer had any doubt that Charles Warner had visited this particular grave only a short time before he was murdered. But where was the link-up – what made Alois Stohr so important he must remain undisturbed at all cost?

'Did he say anything else, anything at all?' Martel demanded.

'Simply asked me to show him the grave of Alois Stohr . . .'

Watching on the sidelines Claire had an overpowering impression the gravedigger was withdrawing into his shell under the impact of Martel's interrogation. The Englishman continued.

'Did he give the date of Stohr's death?'

'Only said it was near the end of the French occupation . . .'

Warner had used a similar phrase while talking to the bookseller in Kaiserstrasse. *It was during the French military occupation* . . . Why pinpoint the time like that instead of giving an approximate year?

Claire had remained silent, studying the gravedigger, and she spoke suddenly, her voice confident as though she knew the reply and was interested only in confirmation.

'Who else visits this grave?'

'I don't know as I should talk about such things,' the old boy said after a long pause. Martel almost held his breath: Claire, by a flash of intuition, had put her finger on something they would otherwise not have been told. She kept up the pressure.

'My friend gave you a generous sum so we expect complete frankness. Who comes here?'

'I don't know her name. She comes every week. Always on a Wednesday and always at eight in the morning. She lays a bunch of flowers, waits a few minutes and then goes . . .'

'How does she get here?' Claire persisted. 'By car? By cab?'

'She comes in a cab – and keeps it waiting till she leaves . . .'

'Her description? Colour of hair? Her age – roughly. How is she dressed? Modestly? Expensively?'

The barrage of questions reinforced the grave-digger's obvious reluctance to say more. He handed Warner's photo back to Martel and picked up his shovel, prior to departure.

'Expensive – her clothes . . .'

'Colour of hair?' Claire went on relentlessly.

'Can't say – she always wears a head-scarf . . .'

'And you passed on the same information to the man in this photo when he came here?' Martel asked.

The gravedigger, shouldering his shovel like a soldier, was moving away, vanishing into the mist shrouding the headstones. His voice came back like that of a ghost.

'Yes. And I think he found out where she lived.

While she was here I saw him talking to her cab-driver. Money exchanged hands . . .'

Have you seen this man?

The bookseller who had talked to Martel adjusted his glasses and gazed at Erwin Vinz. He took his time before replying.

'You have some form of identification?' he enquired.

'You *have* seen the escaped patient then?' Vinz pressed eagerly. 'As to identification – we're not police, we don't carry cards . . .'

'Your description means nothing to me. I have never had anyone in my shop remotely resembling this man. If you will excuse me, I have a shop to run . . .'

He watched Vinz leave, shoulders hunched, his mouth a thin line. He climbed into a car outside, said something to the driver and the vehicle disappeared. The girl assistant spoke tentatively.

'I thought we did have a man in here earlier . . .'

'You think that man who just called had anything to do with an asylum?' There was a note of contempt in the Austrian's voice.

'For one thing he was a German so he would have approached the authorities if his story were true . . .'

'You think he was . . .'

'Lying in his teeth. You have just met a neo-Nazi – I can smell the breed, to say nothing of the badge he

129

flaunts in his coat lapel. If he returns, tell me and I will call the police . . .'

The sun had burnt off the mist and it was now a brilliant afternoon. When Vinz arrived and left two men to watch the railway station there remained a team of six – including himself – and he had divided them up into pairs. Each couple took one of the three cars to explore the district allocated to them.

One couple was driving up Gallus-strasse, a prosperous residential area, while Vinz was making his abortive visit to the bookshop. Vinz's men had just enquired at yet another hotel and again drawn a blank. The car descending Gallus-strasse towards them contained Martel and Claire. Both vehicles moved at a sedate pace as they closed the gap between them.

Vinz's men, in a BMW, were keeping down their speed so they could check the sidewalks for any sign of Martel. Behind the wheel of the Audi they had hired, Claire drove slowly through the unfamiliar district while Martel, beside her, gave directions as he studied the town plan.

'At the bottom – to avoid going past the railway station – we turn . . .'

'Oh, my God! Keith – inside that BMW coming towards us. I saw the sun flash off something shiny in the lapel of that man beside the driver, I'm sure it's a badge. It's Delta . . .'

'Don't speed up, don't look at them, don't change anything – just keep going as you are doing . . .'

'They'll have your description . . .'

'Good luck to them!'

Inside the BMW the man in the front passenger seat carried a Luger inside his shoulder holster. He studied the two people in the oncoming Audi. It was second nature for him to overlook no-one. Imprinted in his memory was the detailed description of Martel every member of the squad had been provided with.

Gallus-strasse was exceptionally quiet at this hour. Claire was suddenly aware she was gripping the wheel tightly and forced herself to relax – *not to look at the BMW driver who had lowered his window which would allow his passenger to fire at her point-blank.*

'Steady now . . .'

Martel spoke softly, his lips scarcely moving as he studied the street map spread out on his lap. The two cars, still slow-moving, drew level. The passenger inside the BMW stared hard at the man next to the girl driver. Then the cars were moving away from each other.

'Something about that Audi?' asked the man behind the wheel.

'Just checking. Not a bit like him . . .'

At the bottom of Gallus-strasse Martel directed Claire to keep them away from the lake front – and the railway station. She gave a sigh of relief.

'Not to worry,' he remarked. 'I wonder how they got here while we were still in town . . .'

'They were Delta . . .'

'I saw the badges out of the corner of my eye as they passed us. In any case, I was prepared . . .' He lifted a corner of the street plan and she saw his right hand gripping the butt of his .45 Colt. 'Any sign of hostile action and I could have blown them both away. There was no one else about. And how did you expect them to recognise me?'

She glanced at him. He wore a Tyrolean hat with a feather in the band purchased while she arranged the hire of the Audi. Clamped between his teeth was a large, ugly-looking pipe he had bought in another shop. On the bridge of his Roman nose perched horn-rimmed glasses. The transformation from his normal hatless appearance with cigarette-holder at jaunty angle was total.

'God,' she said, 'I'm a fool not to have your confidence . . .'

'Your reaction was correct,' he rapped back. 'The day you're not nervous in a situation like that is likely to be your last. Now, let's head for the border and the whirlpool – Lindau.'

In the late afternoon Vinz phoned Reinhard Dietrich from Bregenz. He was exhausted. So were his men. By phoning the *schloss* he also avoided reporting to the man he most feared. Manfred.

'Vinz speaking. We were asked to undertake a commission . . .'

'I know.' Dietrich sounded irritable. 'I was informed by the agent who placed the commission. I take it you have earned your keep?'

In the payphone near Bregenz station Vinz gazed out at the dense fog rolling in from the lake. 'From the beginning it was an impossible task,' he said. 'We ran ourselves into the ground. The Englishman is not here . . .'

'What! He must have got off that express at Bregenz. Don't you see – he chose that stop because he guessed the competition might be waiting for him at Lindau. And Bregenz is a small town . . .'

'Not all that small,' Vinz snapped. He was so tired he answered back. 'The layout is complex – and the fog has returned. The whole place is blotted out . . .'

'Get back here at once! All of you! We'll discuss our next move the moment you arrive. And don't stop anywhere for a drink or anything to eat . . .'

'We haven't eaten all day . . .'

'I should bloody well hope not! Straight back here! You understand?'

Dietrich slammed down the receiver. He was red in the face. He ran his hands through his silver hair and gazed round the library. Vinz would never know his outburst had been promoted not by rage but by *fear*. He rang for Oscar and when the hunchback arrived told him to pour a large brandy.

'They haven't found the Englishman,' he said savagely.

'He must be clever. The first spy, Warner, was

clever – but he revealed himself in due course. This new Englishman will make the same mistake . . .' He handed the brandy to Dietrich who took a large gulp and shook his head.

'He eludes every trap. He has been on the continent less than two days and is getting closer to Bavaria, to Operation Crocodile, every moment. In six days' time the Summit Express will be crossing Bavaria!'

'So we have six days to find him,' Oscar said reassuringly, refilling his master's glass.

'God in heaven, Oscar! Don't you see you can turn that round? *He has six days to find us!*'

Close to the main entrance to Dietrich's walled estate there was a small forest by the roadside. The entrance was guarded by wrought-iron gates and a sentry lodge. It was early evening when a large bird swooped over the gates and all hell broke loose.

Behind the gates ferocious German shepherd dogs appeared, huge brutes which leapt at the gates, barking and snarling, eager to tear any intruder to pieces.

Inside a Mercedes parked out of sight on the edge of the trees. Erich Stoller, chief of the BND, listened to the sound of the dogs, his slim hands lightly tapping the wheel. Forty-three years old, Stoller was six feet tall and very thin, his face lean and sensitive.

His chief assistant, Otto Wilde, sat beside him clasping a cine-camera equipped with a telephoto lens. Small and plump, Wilde was terrified of fierce dogs. He glanced at his chief.

'Supposing they open the gates . . .'

'Oh, we can deal with that.' Stoller opened the glove compartment, extracted the gas-pistol nestling inside and handed it to his companion. 'A whiff of tear-gas up their nostrils should discourage their ardour . . .'

'They know we're here – they have picked up our scent . . .'

'Nonsense! They were startled by that large bird which swooped past the entrance. When we develop your film it will be interesting to see if any old friends are present. I think I recognised one – the driver of the first car . . .'

Parked out of sight they had witnessed the recent return to the *schloss* of a cavalcade of three cars. Erwin Vinz had been driving the leading vehicle. What Vinz did not know was that when they pulled up at the entrance – waiting while the dogs were locked up in their compound – Otto Wilde had been busy with his camera.

This was Stoller's first visit to the area of the *schloss* owned by Dietrich. By chance Vinz's team, returning from its fruitless search for Keith Martel, arrived while the BND chief was surveying the target area. Stoller was persisting in his efforts to locate Delta's main base.

'I'm convinced, Otto,' he remarked as he reached

for the ignition, 'that Delta could have its head-quarters here.'

'Why?'

'Because it is the home of Reinhard Dietrich who has put himself forward in the state elections as the next Minister-President of Bavaria, because you say the estate is vast . . .'

'I showed you on the map. Look at the distance we drove round the perimeter to get here . . .'

'So, it could fit. You can't see the *schloss* from any point from the road. It is remote, secluded – ideal for concealing a horde of rabble-rousers. And God knows they are rousing – look at the riots recently. Almost as bad as in England . . .'

'They're opening the gates!'

Stoller had started the engine and was already driving into the open and on to the road leading past the entrance to the *schloss*. It was the direct route to München and Stoller was not prepared to go the other way for some millionaire thug who employed killer dogs.

'Raise your window,' he ordered Wilde, using one hand to shut his own. The dogs were out in the road, rushing towards the unmarked police car. Faces appeared at either window, fangs bared, mouths slavering, the heads huge, paws clawing desperately to get beyond the glass to ravage the men inside. Stoller put his foot down.

The car leapt forward. Two of the beasts appeared briefly in front of the radiator. The occupants felt the

thuds of speeding metal colliding with animal bodies.
Then they were hurtling past the open gates where
men were pouring out led by a tall, well-built blond
giant. Wilde looked back.

'They're going to follow us in a car . . .'

'That damned bird started it,' Stoller said calmly.
'The dogs kicked up, Dietrich's guards became suspicious – and sent out the hounds. Did you notice the
blond Adonis who appeared to be their leader? That
was Werner Hagen – a keen wind-surfer. We have to
evade them – on no account must they know they're
under surveillance . . .'

'Evade them? How?'

They moved at manic speed round bends in the
country road and Wilde braced himself. He was
almost as terrified of Stoller's driving as he was of
fierce dogs: his chief had the reputation of being the
fastest driver in Bavaria. Stoller gave a fresh order.

'When I stop at the next intersection stay in the car
– and get well down out of sight. I'll need the gas-
pistol – I'm going to block the road. Look, this will
do . . .'

Wilde glanced over his shoulder and saw only
deserted roadway. Stoller had gained a temporary
lead – but Wilde knew the road ahead would be
empty and for miles there were long straight sections.
It couldn't be done . . .

Ahead a farm-track led off to the right. Stoller
jammed on the brakes. There was a screech of rubber
and he turned through ninety degrees, ending up a

short distance along the track. Wilde was saved from being hurled through the windscreen by Stoller's insistence that he always wore his seat-belt. It was not over yet.

Stoller was now backing rapidly until his vehicle blocked the road. Grabbing the gas-pistol handed to him by Wilde who was already hunching himself below window level, he left the car, slamming the door shut. He ran towards a large tree near the roadside and hid behind the massive trunk.

The pursuing car – driven by Werner Hagen with two men accompanying him – came round a nearby bend. Hagen found himself confronted by a Mercedes broadside on and which appeared to be empty. He braked, stopped, reached for the gun under his armpit and told the two men to wait in the car.

Leaving his door open he looked cautiously round while the man in the back lowered his window to see what was going on. Stoller used the tree trunk to steady himself, aimed the gas-pistol and pulled the trigger. The missile exploded on the driver's seat – a bull's eye which spread fumes in all directions, smothering Hagen who dropped his gun and staggered, coughing, unable to see anything.

The man in the front passenger seat was choking, his vision blurred. In a matter of seconds Stoller reloaded and took fresh aim. The second missile passed through the open rear window and exploded in the rear of the car. Stoller ran back to his own vehicle.

Minutes later he was miles away, driving along one of the endless stretches with no sign of any other vehicle in his rear-view mirror. Wilde saw that his chief was frowning.

'You pulled that off beautifully. Why the scowl?'

'I was thinking about Martel. Tweed warned me he was coming – but he's a loner . . .'

'So, like Warner, no cooperation?'

'On the contrary, he'll contact me when he needs me. Excellent judgement. I just wonder where he is at this moment . . .'

Chapter Twelve

Thursday May 28

Martel drove the hired Audi across the road bridge linking the mainland of Bavaria with the island of Lindau. He no longer wore the Tyrolean hat nor was he smoking the pipe used to disguise his appearance in Bregenz.

Hatless, his profile prominent with its strong Roman nose, the Englishman smoked a cigarette in his holder at a jaunty angle. It was as though he wished to draw attention to his arrival to any watchers who might be stationed in Lindau.

'What do you think you are doing?' Claire had demanded when he discarded his disguise as soon as they had crossed the border into Germany.

'Showing the British flag,' replied Martel. 'If I had a Union Jack pennant I'd be flying it . . .'

'Delta will spot us soon enough . . .'

'Sooner, I hope.'

'You're setting yourself up as a target?' she protested. 'You must be mad – have you forgotten Zürich, St Gallen . . .'

'The point is I have remembered them – and we're working to a time limit. You said the Bayerischer Hof is the top hotel on the island?'

'Yes, and it's next to the Hauptbahnhof . . .'

'Then we must rig it so it looks as though you've arrived on your own by train. We'll register separately, eat separately in the dining-room. We don't know each other. That way you can guard my back. And put on those dark glasses which transform your appearance . . .'

'Would sir like anything else?'

'Yes, guide me to the hotel,' he said. 'This place is a rabbit warren and I've forgotten the burrows. Use the map.'

They had a taste of the beauty of the island when they drove over the bridge and past a green park which ran to the lake edge. The mist had lifted temporarily and the sun was a luminous glow. She checked the map and gave directions. Within minutes she laid a hand on his arm.

'We're almost there. Better drop me here. Turn left at the end. The Bayerischer Hof is on your left, the Hauptbahnhof on your right, the harbour straight ahead. Where do we meet?'

'At the terrace elevated above the harbour, the Romerschanze – the place where a tourist looking through binoculars witnessed the killing of Warner without realising it . . .'

She left the vehicle, carrying her suitcase. Only two or three tourists were in this quiet section of the old street but she took no chances, calling out in German.

'Thank you so much for the lift. Now I shall catch my train.'

'My pleasure . . .'

The pavement artist, Braun, spotted Martel as soon as he drove round the corner.

Today Braun's picture drawn in crayon on the flag-stones was an impression of the amphitheatre at Verona. The small cardboard box for coins lay beside the picture. Again wearing a windcheater and jeans he was patrolling back and forth, hands clasped behind his back as though taking a rest from his labours.

He was actually watching the exit doors from the Hauptbahnhof. A main-line express from Switzerland was due. He turned round at the precise moment Keith Martel appeared and recognised him immediately. It was no great feat of observation.

Thick black hair, early thirties, tall, well-built, clean-shaven, prominent Semitic-like nose, habitually smokes cigarettes in holder at slanting angle . . .

The pavement artist was so thrown off-balance by Martel's sudden appearance, by the accuracy of the description provided, that he almost stopped in mid-stride – which would have been a blunder since it might have drawn the target's attention to himself. He strolled on as the Audi passed him and he heard it pull up. He sneaked a glance over his shoulder so he would be able to recognise the Englishman *from behind*.

'I wonder, you curious sod . . .'

Martel muttered the words to himself as he stared in his wing mirror, still seated behind the wheel. It had been a reflex action – to make one final check before he got out of the car with his suitcase. The swift glance of the pavement artist over his shoulder showed clearly in the mirror.

He got out of the car and saw the mist beginning to roll in from the lake, invading the harbour. He walked inside the hotel's spacious, well-furnished reception hall and up a few steps to the desk. The girl behind the counter was helpful and brisk. Yes, they had an excellent double bedroom on the third floor overlooking the lake. Certainly it would be acceptable for him to pay for his room in advance as he might have to make a sudden departure on business.

'And if you would fill in the registration form, sir?'

The conversation had been carried on in English – Martel was booking in under his own name and nationality. Under the heading *Occupation* he wrote *Consultant*.

Escorted upstairs in the lift by the porter, he was shown into a huge room with a large bathroom. Martel liked to travel well and Erich Stoller was paying. As soon as he was alone he went to the side window which, as he expected, overlooked the Hauptbahnhof and hotel entrance. He saw Claire coming out of the station.

Her performance had been a model of skilled evasion. Wearing her dark glasses and a head-scarf, she had crossed the road immediately Martel had

143

turned the corner. The pavement artist had not even seen her. He was not *looking* for a girl, only a man, Martel . . .

Once inside the Hauptbahnhof Claire had waited for someone else to walk out. A couple staying at the hotel had gone across to check the timetable board. Claire emerged with them, having heard a brief snatch of their conversation in German.

'I'm looking for the Bayerischer Hof,' she said to the elderly man who was beside her. It was his wife beyond who answered.

'My dear, it is just across the road. We're staying there ourselves. You'll find it an excellent hotel . . .'

'Let me have your case,' the German said and took it, grasping the handle.

It was perfect cover for anyone who might be watching. Claire appeared to belong to the couple who had gone to the Hauptbahnhof to meet her. The pavement artist never even noticed her as the trio vanished inside the hotel entrance.

From the open third floor window in his bedroom Martel stared at the sidewalk immediately below where his car was still parked. The pavement artist held a tiny notepad in the palm of his hand and he was noting down the vehicle's registration number.

Seen from street level, the pavement artist's action was carried out with such skill no one noticed what he was doing. He never gave a thought to the possibility that he might be observed from above.

'Got you, you bastard . . .'

Martel muttered the words as he ran to his case, snapped open the locks and pulled out from under neatly folded clothes a small instrument. He shoved it inside his jacket pocket, left the room and descended in the waiting lift.

At ground floor level he ignored Claire who was completing the registration form after reserving a single room with bath. Walking to the exit, Martel peered out and strolled into the street. As he expected, the pavement artist was casually crossing the road on his way to the Hauptbahnhof.

The watcher had to have some quick means of communication with his employers – what could be more convenient than the public telephone booths he would undoubtedly find inside? The double doors closed in Martel's face as the pavement artist entered ahead of him. The Englishman pushed a door open slowly and walked into a large booking-hall. The row of phone booths was to his left.

The pavement artist had entered a booth in the middle of the row, the only one now occupied. Martel paused. Shoving his hand into his jacket pocket he waited until his quarry picked up the receiver and commenced dialling. Then Martel entered the booth to the right and slammed the door shut.

The noise attracted the pavement artist's attention. Out of the corner of his eyes, his head bent over a notebook he appeared to be consulting, Martel sensed the man's shocked disbelief. For the next few seconds he held his breath. It was a question of psychology.

The pavement artist turned his back on Martel and continued making his call. It was the reaction Martel had prayed for. The man was *not* a top-flight professional. Had Martel been in his place he would have continued dialling the first figures which came into his head, listened for a moment as though getting the wrong signal, slammed down the receiver and left the booth.

He knew exactly what had happened instead. Startled to find his target in the next booth, the man had experienced seconds of indecision. *But because he had started dialling – and because he was certain Martel could not possibly suspect him* – he continued what he had been doing.

Martel raised his own receiver with one hand while the other performed a quite different action. Extracting the instrument taken from his suitcase, he pressed the rubber sucker at waist-level on the glass window separating his booth from the next one. He then inserted the hearing-aid in place, using his upper left forearm to conceal the wire from the sucker to the earpiece.

The Englishman was gambling on the second-rate calibre of the pavement artist – that he would keep his back to Martel to hide his features. The instrument was working perfectly. Every word of the conversation in the next booth was transmitted to him with great clarity.

'Is that Stuttgart . . .'

Martel memorised the number, although unable to hear the other end of the conversation.

'Edgar Braun speaking,' the pavement artist said formally. 'Is that Klara . . .'

'*Cretin!* You have already made *two* mistakes!' the girl told him venomously. 'No number or name at this end to be transmitted. You want someone to keep an appointment with you?'

'S-orry . . .' Braun mumbled the words. He had been badly thrown off balance by Martel's sudden appearance in the next booth. His fervent wish now was that he had broken off the call – but he dare not do that at this stage because Klara would guess something was wrong, that he had blundered. The only thing was to press on.

'The second consignment you were expecting has arrived,' Braun continued. 'It has been delivered safely to the Hotel Bayerischer Hof a few minutes ago . . .'

'Where exactly is that?' Klara demanded, her tone icy.

'Facing both Hauptbahnhof and harbour. The following car registration number is linked with the consignment . . . I stay on duty?'

'Yes! We shall react at once. And I shall have to report your indiscretion . . .'

'Please . . .'

But the Stuttgart connection had gone dead. Behind Braun's back Martel had pulled the rubber sucker from the glass, hauled the earpiece free and thrust the whole contraption in his jacket pocket. The change in Braun's tone had warned him the conversation was ending.

Martel performed a pantomime as Braun sneaked out of the booth without a glance in his direction. He spoke loudly in English about nothing into the receiver. When Braun disappeared through the exit he left the booth. He now had solid data for Stoller to check.

Inside the luxurious tenth-floor apartment in a building less than a mile from the headquarters of Dietrich GmbH, Klara Beck slammed down the receiver. Tearing open a fresh pack with nails painted like red talons she lit her forty-first cigarette of the day.

'Braun must be losing his marbles,' she said to herself.

The cigarette was necessary to calm her nerves – and her voice – before she phoned Reinhard Dietrich. Although sexually attractive she knew it was her outward coolness which most appealed to the Bavarian millionaire, which made her his mistress. Her apparent calm in all situations was such a contrast to Dietrich's choleric temperament – and to that of his whining wife.

Taking several deep drags, she expelled smoke from her lungs, her bosom heaving with the relaxation afforded by the nicotine. It was time to make the call.

She dialled the number of the *schloss*. Dietrich himself answered.

'Yes!'

Just the single, curt word.

'Klara calling. It is convenient to talk?'

'Yes! You received the emerald ring? Good!'

They had performed the ritual of positive identification. During alternate calls Dietrich would refer to sending her a fur or some item of jewellery – which secretly infuriated her since few of these desirable gifts were ever given to her. She hurried on.

'The second consignment has been delivered. I have just heard – it has arrived at the Hotel Bayerischer Hof in Lindau . . .'

'Meet me there this evening!' Dietrich responded instantly. 'Get the executive jet to fly you to the airstrip nearest Lindau. Then take a hired car. A room will be reserved for you. Your help may be needed . . .'

'There is a car registration number. Here it is . . .'

Dietrich repeated the number and broke the connection without a goodbye. Klara Beck replaced the receiver slowly, preserving her self-control. Despite her annoyance she was impressed. She had just told Dietrich in an oblique manner that Keith Martel – the man they had scoured Switzerland, Austria and Bavaria to track down – had been located. Dietrich had reacted decisively to the news, taking only seconds to plan his next move.

One phrase intrigued her. *Your help may be*

needed ... It conjured up one possibility – Dietrich was considering asking her to seduce Martel. She went into the bedroom, slipped out of her dress, the only item of clothing she was wearing in the clammy atmosphere, and studied her full-bodied nude form in a full-length mirror.

It could be fun – playing with the Englishman. Before – at the appropriate moment – she rammed the needle between his ribs and pressed the button which released the lethal injection.

At the *schloss* Dietrich had ordered Oscar to bring one of his packed suitcases for an overnight stay. A series of cases were packed and unpacked daily by the attentive Oscar.

There were cases for a short trip, cases for more prolonged journeys, cases for hot climates and cases for countries like Norway in the depths of winter. The system meant Dietrich was ready for departure anywhere at a moment's notice. On the intercom he summoned Erwin Vinz who had recently returned with his team from Bregenz. He did not mince his words.

'Someone else has done the job for you! A woman at that! I am leaving at once for the Bayerischer Hof in Lindau – Martel has just arrived there. Choose your best men, follow me and book in at the same hotel . . .'

'This time we should get him . . .' Vinz began.

'This time you will get him, for God's sake! Before

morning – he will be tired after his recent activities . . .'

'Peter has the car waiting,' reported Oscar who had returned with a Gucci suitcase.

Wearing a suit of Savile Row country tweeds Dietrich left the library, crossed the large hall and Oscar held open one of the two huge entrance doors. Dietrich ran down the steps and climbed into the rear of a black, six-seater Mercedes. The uniformed chauffeur closed the door as his master pressed a button and lowered the window to give the order.

'Lindau. Drive like hell . . .!'

Inside Lindau Hauptbahnhof Martel paused outside the phone booth, inserted a cigarette into his holder and lit it. Braun had vanished through the exit doors but Martel waited to see whether the German was smarter than he appeared to be – whether he would dodge back into the station to check up on the Englishman. He did not reappear.

Martel strolled towards the exit doors, opened one a fraction and peered out. On the sidewalk outside the Bayerischer Hof, Braun was on his knees with his back towards Martel, adding to his drawing. The Englishman walked out and got inside one of the taxis waiting under a huge tree.

'The Post Office,' he said. 'Quickly, please – before it closes.'

'It is no distance . . .'

'So you get a good tip for taking me there . . .'

At the post office Martel explained he wanted to call London and gave the girl behind the counter the Park Crescent number. He was gambling that Tweed was waiting for his call. Within two minutes the girl directed him to a booth.

'Thursday calling,' he said quickly as Tweed came on the line.

'Two-Eight here . . .' the familiar voice replied.

Martel began pouring out data to be fed into the recording machine.

'*Warner seen in Bregenz . . . visited cemetery, grave of Alois Stohr . . . headstone 1930–1953 . . . references to time of French occupation . . . expensively dressed woman, identity unknown, visits grave each Wednesday morning . . . Warner contacted her . . . Delta active everywhere . . . two men in car in Bregenz . . .*'

'Did they see either of you?' Tweed interrupted urgently.

'*We sighted them . . . no reverse sighting . . . now staying Bayerischer Hof Lindau . . . Delta watcher pavement artist Braun sighted and reported me – repeat me . . . Stoller should check Stuttgart phone number . . . Stuttgart contact woman named Klara . . . closing down . . .*'

'Wait! Wait! Damn! He's rung off . . .'

Tweed replaced the receiver and stared at McNeil who switched off the recording machine. A very thrifty, Scots type, McNeil. Tweed was certain she had never taken a taxi in her whole life. Buses and the Underground were her sole means of transportation.

'The maniac is setting himself up as bait to flush Delta into the open,' he snapped. 'I know him . . .'

'He's a loner. He gets results,' McNeil said placidly.

'He's in the zone of maximum danger,' Tweed replied grimly. 'Get me Stoller on the phone. Quickly, please. I sense an emergency.'

Chapter Thirteen

Thursday May 28

The signal had been arranged between Martel and Claire before they made separate entrances into the magnificent dining-room as though strangers. The Englishman had a single table next to a picture window which looked out on to the fog-bound harbour.

The signal was that if anyone significant entered the dining-room while they ate their separate meals Claire would light a cigarette. In the middle of her dessert she was doing just that, lighting a cigarette.

A most dominant personality had made his entrance – and he came into the room in precisely this fashion, like an accomplished actor making his entrance on stage. There was a sudden hush in the conversation: eyes turned and stared towards the entrance. The new arrival paused and surveyed the people at their tables.

He ran a hand through his thick, silver-coloured hair, tugged gently at his moustache, his ice-blue eyes sweeping the assembled guests. Other eyes dropped as they met his gaze. His skin was tanned and leathery. He had changed into an immaculate blue bird's-eye lounge suit.

The maître d'hôtel escorted Reinhard Dietrich to another window table at the opposite end of the room from Martel. And since his arrival there had been a subtle change in the atmosphere. The conversation was now carried on in murmurs. Handsome women glanced at the table where the millionaire sat, which amused Martel.

There's no glamour like a lot of money, he thought.

Two or three minutes after Claire had vacated her table he left the room. Wandering along a wide corridor he found her standing at the reception desk, waiting her turn while a fresh arrival – (an attractive brunette in her late twenties with a full-bodied figure) was completing the registration form.

The reception hall opened out into a well-furnished and spacious lounge area with comfortable armchairs. Martel chose one of these chairs, settled himself and picked up a magazine. He inserted a cigarette into his holder, lit it and waited.

The attractive new guest had gone up in the lift to her room with the porter. Claire was asking the receptionist about train times to Kempten – the first thing which came into her head. The receptionist was being very helpful, checking a rail timetable and noting times on a slip of paper.

'Thank you.' She turned away and then turned back. 'I thought I recognised the girl who just arrived. She stays here often?'

'Her first visit as far as I know, Madame . . .'

Claire had her handbag open, slipping the piece of

paper inside as she wandered into the lounge area. As she passed Martel's armchair she deliberately tipped her bag and the contents spilt over the floor. Her 9-mm pistol remained safely inside the special zipped-up compartment.

'Let me help you,' Martel said, gathering up objects.

'I'm so sorry . . .'

Their heads were close together. The receptionist was a distance from where Martel sat. They carried on their brief conversation in whispers.

'That girl who just arrived,' Claire told him. 'I saw the name on the registration form. *Klara* Beck – from *Stuttgart* . . .'

'The hyenas are gathering. And the man in the dining-room who arrived as though he owned the damned world – Reinhard Dietrich?'

'Yes – I've seen pictures in the paper . . .'

The spilt contents had been collected up. Claire, who had been crouching with her knees bent, her back to the receptionist, stood up and raised her voice.

'That really was most kind of you – and most clumsy of me . . .'

Claire wandered to the far side of the room and chose a chair where she could see everything and had her back to the wall. She opened her handbag, unzipped the compartment, slid out the pistol and left it inside the bag where she could reach it swiftly. She had just completed this precaution when Erwin Vinz and his associate, Rolf Gross, walked into the reception hall, each carrying a small case.

Claire *froze* – then slid the gun out of her handbag and covered it on her lap with a newspaper. *Rolf Gross had been the driver of the Delta car they had encountered in Gallus-strasse in Bregenz.*

Both men glanced into the lounge area as they crossed to the steps leading to the reception counter. Claire thought Gross stared at Martel who was reading a newspaper and smoking a cigarette in his holder. Vinz appeared to notice nothing and neither man showed any interest in the girl at the back of the room.

Slipping the gun inside her handbag, she closed it, stood up and wandered over to the reception desk where both men were filling in their registration forms. She waited patiently, looking at a picture on the wall.

'We require two single rooms with baths,' Vinz said in the tone of voice used for addressing serfs. 'If you haven't singles, two doubles will do. And we want dinner . . .'

'I have two single rooms . . .' The receptionist was not looking at Vinz although his tone of voice remained polite. 'And I would suggest you hurry to the dining-room which stops serving . . .'

'Inform them of our arrival! We both require steaks, plenty of potatoes. The steaks rare – and a very good bottle of red wine. We'll be down as soon as *we* are ready . . .'

'Understood, sir. The porter here will show you your rooms.'

With obvious relief he turned to Claire with a smile. She asked for a street plan of Lindau and he explained that a section of the Old Town was a 'walking-only' zone. At that moment Reinhard Dietrich, smoking a large cigar, came down the corridor from the dining-room. Continuing past the reception desk he marched into the lounge and eased his bulk into the armchair next to Martel.

'Reinhard Dietrich at your service. You are English?'

Martel looked at the leathery hand extended in greeting, made a movement as though about to clasp the hand – and ignored it, inserting a fresh cigarette in his holder.

Dietrich overlooked the insult. His extended hand grasped the glass of cognac a waiter had just placed on the table, making it appear that had been his original intention. He raised the glass.

'Yes,' said Martel.

'I beg your pardon?'

'Yes, I am English.'

'Oh, of course! Taking a holiday in our beautiful Bavaria?'

Martel turned and looked straight at the industrialist, switching to German, which momentarily threw him off balance.

'You are a Nazi. They need wiping off the face of the earth.'

'Unless we inherit the earth,' Dietrich replied

harshly. 'In the coming state election someone has to make sure Tofler does not win. How would you enjoy a Communist controlling the largest state in Germany – geographically speaking? The West's main bulwark against the Soviets would be shattered . . .'

'I could never see the difference. Both are inhuman dictatorships. Both rule through secret police – KGB or Gestapo. They are interchangeable – as are the systems. I prefer Chancellor Langer's party. And now, if you will excuse me . . .'

'Take a cigar with you – they are Havanas . . .'

'From Cuba?' Martel was standing, his expression ironical as he stared down at the German. 'Thank you – but I smoke only cigarettes. It has been most illuminating meeting you. Goodnight.'

It has been most illuminating meeting you . . . The words disturbed Dietrich because he sensed a hidden meaning. He watched the Englishman stroll to the lift, his eyes narrowed as he recalled the conversation word for word, trying to decide whether he had made a slip.

A girl who had been talking to the receptionist had reached the lift first and was entering it when Martel called out, asking her in German, please could she hold it? The lift ascended out of sight with both passengers aboard.

The third floor landing was deserted as Martel escorted Claire out of the lift. Unlocking the door of his own room, he ushered her inside, closed the door and gripped her arm. She remained quite still in the darkness while Martel checked the bathroom. He then closed all the curtains and turned on the bedside lights which gave out a shaded glow. She began reporting at once.

'I worked the same trick when those two were-wolves arrived. I saw their registration forms and the one who seems to be boss is Erwin Vinz. His sidekick – the driver of the car in Bregenz . . .'

'I know . . .'

'He goes under the name Rolf Gross. Both regis-tered as coming from München . . .'

'Which is probably a lie. They're trained killers. Things are developing as I hoped – but faster than I expected. The enemy is here in force. My guess is Dietrich is here to see they don't botch the job of eliminating me as they did in Zürich, St Gallen and Bregenz. Vinz and Gross do the job. Klara Beck provides back-up . . .'

'She's a reptile,' Claire commented savagely. 'You should watch out for her – *the others* may be diver-sions. And why did you set out to provoke Dietrich? I heard every word both of you said – it was like a duel . . .'

'It was a duel. He was weighing me up – I was doing the same with him. I thought he was a stiff-necked has-been, but he's no fool. He believes in what he's doing. He's ruthless and he's decisive. We have to be very careful . . .'

'He might take action tonight?'

'No – because he's staying at the hotel. He won't risk being present when his dirty tricks squad goes into action. We'll still take precautions. You stay here for the night and we'll take turns – one sleeping, one in a chair with a gun handy.'

'And tomorrow?'

'First thing we approach this Sergeant Dorner of the Lindau Water Police – the man who brought in Warner's body.'

'And the second thing?' she asked, watching him closely.

'Lay a trap for Delta.'

'I'm still not happy about tonight,' she persisted. 'In this hotel we have two men who are almost certainly killers – and one woman who is pure poison. You said Dietrich was decisive – I've the strongest feeling he'll move faster than you expect . . .'

Chapter Fourteen

Thursday May 28

At eleven o'clock at night Martel realised Claire had been right. He had underestimated Reinhard Dietrich. The bedroom was in darkness, he was taking the first turn on guard and Claire was lying on the bed fast asleep. He heard sounds of activity at the entrance to the hotel.

Pulling aside the curtain over the side window he looked down. Below, outside the hotel entrance, a black, six-seater Mercedes was parked by the kerb, its engine gently ticking. A uniformed chauffeur stood by the rear door in the mist, a mist blurring the street lights which were vague haloes in the drifting vapour. A familiar figure emerged from the hotel, the rear door was opened and Reinhard Dietrich climbed inside.

Within a minute the large vehicle had driven away and a hushed silence descended. From the harbour direction came the mournful moan of gulls, like the sirens of ships at sea destined never to reach a port. A distant foghorn sighed. And there was a third sound – the creak of a door opening or closing from the Hauptbahnhof.

He moved to his suitcase, felt inside, extracted a light raincoat and slipped it on. The bedsprings stirred and Claire called out, no more than a whisper.

'Something has happened, Keith?'

He went over to the bed where she lay fully dressed and placed a reassuring hand on her shoulder. He could smell the faint aroma of perfume. What was it about women that never made them forget their personal impact when they were exhausted – when they were living on their nerves?

'You were right,' he said. 'Dietrich has tricked us. He gave the impression he was staying the night and now he has left in a chauffeur-driven limousine. Something is going to happen . . .'

'What do we do?' she asked calmly.

'One trump card is they don't know there are two of us – they think I'm on my own . . .'

'So?'

'Slip back to your own room – be careful no one sees you.'

'And what are you going to be doing?'

'Contacting the local police. It's late but I want to talk with Sergeant Dorner. My guess is he's the only man in Lindau we can trust . . .'

'You're going out in this fog? It is still foggy?'

'Thicker than ever. Which is helpful. More difficult for anyone to see me leaving and where I go. It's only a short distance – you showed me on the map . . .'

'I'm coming with you!' She sat up in bed and felt for her shoes on the floor. 'I can watch your back . . .'

'Go to your room before I belt you . . .'

'You are a very stupid man and I don't like you much. Bloody well take care . . .'

He waited until she had gone before venturing out. And he had deliberately not mentioned the creaking door. If she had known about that he would never have got rid of her.

The atmosphere of menace hit Martel the moment he walked out into the night. Mist globules settled on his face. The damp chill penetrated his thin coat. He could just make out the bulk of the Hauptbahnhof as he turned right and headed for Ludwigstrasse, a narrow, cobbled street which was the direct route to police headquarters.

There was no one visible but he heard it again, the sound he had detected from his bedroom window three floors up – the creak of one of the station doors being opened. He was careful not to glance in that direction as he turned right again and proceeded along the centre of Ludwigstrasse – as far away as possible from the darkened alcoves of doorway recesses.

His rubber-soled shoes made no sound on the cobbles although he had to place his feet firmly on their surface – the street was slimy with dampness. He wore his grey-coloured raincoat, which merged with the atmosphere, unbuttoned. Anyone grabbing him would find themselves holding only the fabric of the coat. And he had easy access to the Colt in his shoulder holster. He stopped.

The sound of the foghorn out on the lake. But his acute hearing had caught a second sound – the whispering slither of a padded sleeve moving against a coat, something like Gannex material. Behind him.

The watcher waiting inside the Hauptbahnhof had heard nothing, he was convinced. But even in the mist he could have seen Martel's silhouette outlined for a few seconds against the glow of lights in the lounge as he left the hotel.

He stood motionless in a shadowed area and the whispering stopped. Somewhere behind him his follower realised that Martel had also paused. The trouble was the bastards probably knew every inch of Lindau. *Their* problem was they could not be sure of his destination.

He started walking again suddenly, sensing there were several men somewhere in the mist. There would be several: Delta operated in strength. He had not forgotten Zürich where men had poured out of the two cars. He had been counting side-turnings and came to a street light, a milky globe supported by a wall-bracket. *Krummgasse*.

Martel had no option. To reach the main street, Maximilianstrasse, he had to leave the dubious safety of the narrow Ludwigstrasse and make his way along the even narrower alley of Krummgasse. Moving away from the blurred glow of the light he stared into the well of darkness. Once he negotiated Krummgasse he was within shouting distance of the police station.

Behind him he heard again the slither of sleeve against cloth. They were moving in. Reinhard Dietrich would be miles away – his previous presence totally unlinked with the murder of a second Englishman in the Lindau area. Martel went inside Krummgasse – taking longer strides to confuse the man behind him, accustomed to his earlier, slower pace.

Martel's vision was exceptional and he was peering ahead. For the moment he had out-distanced the follower behind. He stopped again and heard no whispering slither. His tactic was to get to the more open Maximilianstrasse and then sprint for police head-quarters. *Ahead of him* he heard the squeak of a shoe.

The mouse in the trap. Himself. A man – men? – coming up behind. And the enemy also in front just when he was close to the end of Krummgasse. Delta had planned well. The moment he entered Ludwig-strasse they had guessed his destination – or assumed the one place he must never be allowed to reach. The police station.

So at the end of each alley leading from Ludwig-strasse to the parallel street, Maximilianstrasse, they had positioned a soldier. The squeaking shoe suggested the man in front was advancing down Krummgasse towards him, closing the pincer move-ment. Martel darted into the shadowed recess of a doorway and prayed that Squeaky Shoe would arrive quickly.

Something solid emerged from the swirling mist, right hand projected forward like a fencer about to lunge. With his left hand Martel extracted a Swiss five-franc coin from his pocket and tossed it across the street. *Clunk!*

In the hushed silence the sound was surprisingly loud and the man, who seemed familiar – something about his marionette-like movements – stopped next to the Englishman's doorway, glancing the other way. There was still no repetition of the slither – so the follower behind was a distance away. Martel moved.

The man sensed danger, turned and held his right hand ready to ram it forward. The barrel of Martel's Colt crashed down on the would-be assassin's head with tremendous force. Martel felt the barrel hammer through a hat, strike the skull and reverberate off it. The attacker slumped and lay in a twisted heap on the cobbles like a pile of old clothes.

Martel ran. Reaching the end of the alley he turned right and by the glow of a street lantern read the legend *Stadtpolizei* on a wall-plate. The entrance was round the corner in Bismarckplatz. He shoved open the door and stopped in front of a counter behind which a startled policeman gazed at him.

He slammed down a piece of plastic like a credit card on to the counter and slipped the Colt back inside its holster as the policeman surreptitiously unbuttoned his hip holster. Still short of breath, he gasped out the words.

'Sergeant Dorner! And bloody quick! If he's at home get him out of bed. There's my identification. And send a couple of men to Krummgasse. There should be a body for them to trip over . . .'

'We've had an alert out for you, Martel – they should have seen you when you crossed the Bavarian border . . .'

Martel was impressed by Sergeant Dorner. A short, burly man in his early forties, he had sandy hair, shrewd grey eyes with a hint of humour, and a general air of a man who knew what he was doing, a man not frightened to take decisions.

Martel was seated across a table from the police officer on the second floor of the building overlooking Bismarckplatz, drinking a cup of strong coffee. It was very good coffee.

They had found the body lying in Krummgasse, the body Martel had identified as Rolf Gross, the second man who had arrived late at the Bayerischer Hof. They had found more than that. Underneath the corpse – Martel's powerful blow had split Gross's skull – was lying what Dorner called a 'flick hypodermic'. He held up the weapon with the needle projecting inside a plastic bag.

'You were lucky,' Dorner commented. 'And this clears you. The fingerprint boys checked Gross's against those on the handle. It must look like a felt-tip pen before this button is pressed and the needle shoots out. Forensic were dragged out of bed to tell me what it contains . . .'

'And what is inside it?'

'Potassium cyanide in solution. It's the kind of weapon you'd expect the Soviets to have dreamt up . . .'

'Maybe they did . . .'

'But these people are Delta – neo-Nazis. I've never seen any weapon like it before . . .'

'I have. It's a Delta special,' Martel replied with grim humour. 'So how do you account for the fact that neo-Nazis are using it?'

'I don't,' Dorner admitted. 'Nothing makes sense about what is going on. We're finding the caches of their weapons and uniforms with Delta badges too easily . . .'

'*Too easily?*'

'Yes. Erich Stoller of the BND is on his way here. I got him out of bed, too . . .' Dorner lowered his voice. 'When Stoller flew here after Warner's body was found he told me he has an informant who regularly passes on the location of these arms dumps. Always in an uninhabited place – an abandoned farm building, an empty villa.'

'In other words you get the arms, the uniforms – the *news* in the press – but you never grab a single person?'

'Weird, isn't it?' Dorner stood up and lit a cheroot,

staring out of the window he had closed against the mist. 'We get no individual, no record of a property owner we can trace. Just as we've been unable to locate any colleague of Gross's . . .'

'I told you Erwin Vinz is staying at the Bayerischer Hof . . .'

'Paid for his room and left ten minutes before my men got there. Said an urgent business message had called him away. I've put my best man on guard outside Claire Hofer's room dressed as a porter, he's whiling away the night cleaning shoes.'

'Thanks.' Martel, almost dropping from lack of sleep, was beginning to approve of Sergeant Dorner more and more. 'And as I told you, Reinhard Dietrich was staying at the same hotel . . .'

'Not *staying*,' Dorner corrected him. 'He arrives in that bloody great Mercedes, has a leisurely dinner, a chat with you – and then leaves. What do I charge him with? Eating too large a dinner and smoking Havana cigars?' He eased his large buttock on to the edge of his desk. 'Bloody frustrating . . .'

'So we set a trap – make them an offer they can't refuse.'

Dorner took the cheroot out of his mouth and frowned. 'Just what are you proposing?'

It took Martel one hour, the arrival of Erich Stoller, eight cups of coffee and four cheroots to obtain their backing for his plan.

Chapter Fifteen

Friday May 29

Claire reports Warner made three mentions Operation Crocodile . . .

While Martel was finally catching up on his sleep at the Bayerischer Hof after the key meeting with Stoller and Dorner, Tweed – in his Maida Vale flat – was playing the same section of the tape-recording of Martel's report from St Gallen over and over. It was the fifth time he had listened to the recording, he was alone and tired.

During the day there had been another row with Howard who was about to fly to Paris. There he was attending a meeting of the four security chiefs responsible for the security of the VIPs who – in only five days' time – would start their journey from Paris aboard the Summit Express bound for Vienna.

The British Prime Minister would fly to Charles de Gaulle Airport and from there would be driven direct to the Gare de l'Est. At about the same time the French President's motorcade would be on its way to the same destination.

The head of the French Secret Service in control of security for his President was Alain Flandres, an old friend of Tweed's. And the American President, flying the Atlantic direct to Orly Airport in Air Force One, would be driven from there at high speed to join the others.

The security chief – head of the American Secret Service – responsible for his chief of state was Tim O'Meara, a man Tweed had met only once. It was a recent appointment. The fourth VIP – Chancellor Kurt Langer of West Germany – was scheduled to board the express the following morning at München. Erich Stoller of the BND would lose sleep watching over his master.

'Why this bloody train lark?' Tweed had asked Howard during the confrontation in his office. 'They could all fly direct to Vienna to meet the Soviet First Secretary. It would be a damned sight safer . . .'

'The French President,' Howard had explained tersely. 'Hates flying. The excuse given is they'll all take the opportunity to coordinate policy at leisure before the train reaches Vienna. I do need every man possible and Martel . . .'

'What's the route?'

'The direct one,' Howard had replied stiffly. He implied Tweed's knowledge of geography was limited. 'Paris to Strasbourg . . .'

'Ulm, Stuttgart, München, Salzburg – then Vienna . . .'

'Then why ask?' Howard rasped.

'To check no diversion is planned . . .'

'Why the hell should there be one?'

'You tell me,' Tweed had replied, watching with some satisfaction as Howard stormed out of the office.

But Howard had cause to worry, Tweed thought later in the early hours in his flat. *The Times* atlas was open in front of him with the double-page spread of Plate 64 – South-West Germany including the northern tip of Switzerland. On it he followed a large section of the route from Strasbourg across Bavaria to Salzburg.

Operation Crocodile . . .

What the hell could that be? He took off his glasses, rubbing his eyes. Without them everything – including the map – was blurred. You saw everything in simplified shapes. He raised a hand to close the atlas and then stopped, rigid, like a man unable to move. *He could see the crocodile!*

In the morning after breakfast Martel made an elaborate pantomime about hiring a launch from a man in Lindau harbour – the same harbour from which Charles Warner, also in a hired launch, started out on his last journey.

There was a lot of waving of hands. There were discussions about the merits of one vessel compared with another. There was debate as to how long he wanted to hire the craft for. Finally, there was lengthy argument about the price.

From a distance two women watched this carefully staged charade. Perched on a seat on the Romerschanze terrace overlooking the harbour, Claire played the role of tourist. And Martel had warned her again there must be no sign to tell a watcher that they knew each other.

She swivelled her field-glasses at apparent random. Lake Konstanz was living up to its unpredictable reputation. Fogbound the previous evening, the new day was crystal clear with a vault of Mediterranean-like sky. To the south across the placid lake was a superb panorama of snow-tipped mountain peaks including the Three Sisters of Liechtenstein. A handful of tourists trudging round the waterfront added to the peaceful scene.

Klara Beck, also equipped with binoculars, sat on a seat on the front with the hotel behind her. She had not been forgotten by Martel who had reported her presence to Sergeant Dorner and Stoller the previous night.

'My men report Klara Beck is apparently staying the night at the hotel,' Dorner relayed to Martel after receiving a phone call.

'That I would expect,' Martel had commented.

'Why, may I ask?' enquired Stoller.

'Because Delta don't realise I know she belongs to them. She's had no contact with Dietrich since she arrived, no contact with Erwin Vinz or Rolf Gross – so she's the ideal person to leave behind as a spy. And in the morning I can use her . . .'

Martel was using Beck now, Claire decided as she trained her lenses on the girl. Like Claire, Beck was using her binoculars and they were aimed in the direction of Martel.

'I think, dear, you're going to move soon,' Claire said to herself.

She left her seat, strolled down the steps to the harbour front and wandered slowly towards the hotel in the warming glow of the sun. Her timing was perfect. She was close to Beck's seat when the German girl got up and began walking rapidly back towards the Bayerischer Hof entrance. On the mole Martel had just ostentatiously shaken hands with the man he was hiring the launch from.

But when she turned the corner it was not the hotel Beck headed for. Instead she crossed the road, passed under the large tree where taxis waited and disappeared inside the Hauptbahnhof. Her shadow followed.

Pushing open a door, Claire glanced to her left and saw what she had expected. Beck was inside one of the telephone booths, making a call. Claire drifted over to a bookstall and started to look at paperbacks. The new development worried her.

Inside the phone booth Beck dialled a local number, cradled the receiver on her shoulder and looked towards the station exit. No one was there. At the other end of the line a man's voice responded as though waiting for her call.

'Hagen here . . .'

'Werner, this is Klara . . .'

'We are ready. Any joy?'

'The goods are aboard a grey launch. Departure imminent . . .'

She broke the connection and left the station, crossing over to the hotel at a leisurely pace, drinking in the delight of the sun's warmth. On the steps she paused close to a pavement artist as he began drawing a fresh picture, taking out her cigarette pack.

'Watch for the police bringing back that grey launch,' she murmured.

She lit the cigarette and went into the lounge. She had just triggered off the execution of the second Englishman.

Sergeant Dorner was not looking where he was going as he walked down Ludwigstrasse towards the harbour. He crashed into the girl and would have knocked her over except for his swift grab round her shoulders with both hands. Claire Hofer, who had timed her arrival as agreed earlier, stood quite still. Dorner, wearing civilian clothes, spoke loudly.

'I do apologise. My own clumsy fault . . .' His voice dropped, his lips scarcely moved. 'Everything is organised. Fifteen minutes from now the island is sealed . . .'

Dorner left Claire who walked rapidly after checking her watch. Minutes – seconds – counted if the trap were to be successfully sprung. She turned down a short cut to the harbour front. Martel was aboard his launch, reached by climbing down a steep ladder attached to the side of the mole.

Claire glanced to her right, saw the pavement artist, Braun, as he strolled into view, hands clasped behind his back. Taking a brilliant red head-scarf out of her shoulder-bag she wrapped the covering round her head.

Aboard the launch Martel saw the flash of brilliant red cloth – the signal that everyone was in position. He caught a glimpse of Sergeant Dorner strolling round the harbour to where the large police launch was berthed. Lighting a cigarette he watched Claire out of the corner of his eye. She was hurrying now towards the open-air bathing-pool walled off from the lake below the Romerschanze terrace.

Reaching the pool, she used the entrance ticket purchased earlier and entered one of the changing cubicles. With the door locked she stripped off her synthetic jersey dress, revealing the bikini she wore underneath. Slipping the rolled-up dress and her pistol inside a water-proof bag, she attached the bag to her wrist with a leather thong.

She left the shoulder-bag which was now empty inside the cubicle, locked the door, checked her water-proof watch and walked along the outer wall. At that time of day there was hardly anyone about. She dived off the wall into the lake.

*

Slipping loose the mooring rope, Martel went inside the cramped wheel-house of the launch and checked his watch – which earlier he had synchronised with Claire and Sergeant Dorner. Two minutes to go. He inserted a cigarette into his holder and lit it.

The only lingering traces of the mist which had shrouded Lake Konstanz the previous day covered the Austrian shore. The forecast promised a warm sunny day. It was a major factor Martel had taken into account when finalising his plan with Dorner and Stoller. And at this moment the BND chief was controlling operations from an office at *Stadtpolizei*.

Martel was careful not to look towards the eastern side of the harbour. Moored to its berth by the Lion Mole lay the two-decker launch of the Water Police commanded by Sergeant Dorner. The German was already below-decks, changing into official uniform after slipping aboard unnoticed. Martel double-checked his watch, took a deep breath and began to leave harbour.

Inside his office at *Stadtpolizei* Erich Stoller stood looking out of the window into the main street. It was just another day for the townspeople. Tourists sat at tables outside Hauser's drinking coffee and consuming cream cakes. Behind him on a heavy table were the transceiver and its operator – the key to Stoller's control.

With the use of the transceiver he could instantly communicate with police cars discreetly stationed near the road bridge, with other vehicles strategically placed on the mainland near the end of the rail embankment.

The transceiver also kept him in direct touch with Sergeant Dorner aboard the police launch still berthed in the harbour. A signal came over the transceiver.

'Siefried is riding . . .'

Dorner had reported that Martel was on his way.

At a remote point on the misty shore five wind-surfers ran down the shallow beach to board their waiting craft. They were stationed midway between Lindau and the Austrian town of Bregenz. Their leader, Werner Hagen, a six-foot blond giant, was running towards them, gesturing at the lake. He had been waiting by a telephone inside a deserted warehouse, waiting for the call from Klara Beck.

'He's leaving Lindau harbour,' he shouted as he ran to his own sail. 'A grey launch. Martel alone is aboard . . .'

They wore swimming trunks as they manoeuvred their sails into the gentle breeze. Round each man's wrist was a belt from which hung a sheath encasing a large throwing knife. A silver triangle, the Delta symbol, was attached to the side of their trunks. The team of executioners, led by Werner Hagen, headed for a position about half a mile outside Lindau harbour.

*

'Thank God I found you – it was difficult in this mist . . .'

Claire leaned against the hull of the launch where Martel had hauled her aboard. With her legs stretched out and her bosom heaving with the recent effort she let Martel untie the leather thong and place the waterproof bag beside her.

The launch was stationary. Martel had taken it out through the harbour exit moving slowly, sounding his siren – according to regulations for ships entering or leaving – for longer than necessary to help Claire locate him. A wind was blowing up, making a low whining sound which got on Claire's nerves.

'You think they'll come?' she asked.

'Damned sure of it . . .'

She extracted from the bag her dress and the 9-mm pistol. He looked at the dress and picked it up to take it inside the wheelhouse. 'This won't be much good for you to wear . . .' He came out checking the action of his .45 Colt and slipped it back inside the shoulder holster.

'It's synthetic jersey cloth,' she told him. 'I chose it since it's practically crease-proof . . .'

She broke off, realising his attention was elsewhere. He still had the engine switched off as he peered eastward into the grey, thinning mist. The light wind was dispersing it slowly.

'You think they're coming from over there?' Claire asked.

'It's the shortest distance from a shoreline where

they're least likely to be detected. In a minute you put on this face-mask – if one of them gets away I don't want you recognised . . .'

'And that thing?' She pointed to a bulky instrument on the small chart-table in the wheelhouse. 'Is it radar?'

'It's a tape-recorded signal which does two things – it signals Stoller at his headquarters when I press a button – warning him we're under attack. It also sends out a continuous signal which Dorner in his police launch can pick up to home in on where we are.'

'You worked this out pretty well,' Claire commented.

'Because from the Warner killing I know we're up against a first-class brain who thinks out *his* plans well . . .'

'Reinhard Dietrich?'

'No. An international anarchist called Manfred.' Martel was inside the wheelhouse, about to start up the engine. 'And I should never have agreed to your coming . . .'

'But you did!'

'So put on your face-mask and shut up,' he told her brusquely, then fired the engine.

The mist had cleared in the west where the vast waters of the lake stretched away like an oil blue sheet. On the eastern mole of Lindau harbour the Lion of Bavaria was a massive silhouette as they got under way.

Claire had adjusted the face-mask and after checking her pistol tucked the weapon inside the top of her pants. Martel's instructions – given to her earlier in his room at the hotel – had been precise.

'If they come – as they came for Warner – I need one man alive so I can work on him. After what they did to Warner, the rest can drown . . .'

Martel kept down the launch's speed, heading out direct across the lake towards the distant Rhine delta. That, he was convinced, was the lonely country where Warner had intended to make his landfall.

One thing bothered him. The grey pall to the east between the launch and the Austrian shoreline was persisting. How could anyone moving in from that direction locate him? And if they did they would be on top of the launch almost before he saw them. Looking again towards Austria he saw movement in the mist.

Werner Hagen gripped his sail with one hand while he checked the compact device attached to the mast. It was a miniature radar set designed at Dietrich's electronics factory in Arizona. Martel's launch showed clearly on the screen.

He's following Warner's route, Hagen thought.

He made a gesture to the other five wind-surfers who were closer together than would be their normal tactic: it was vital they did not lose sight of each other.

The gesture told them the target had been sighted. And the mist was lifting as they glided across the rippled waters of the lake.

Hagen timed it nicely, keeping one eye on the radar screen, the other on the dispersing wall of vapour ahead. He held on to the sail with his left hand and dropped his right, unsheathing the razor-edge knife which had carved out of Warner's back the crude outline of Delta's symbol. Then he saw the launch, made a fresh gesture and the team curved in a semi-circle to force Martel to stop.

It happened too fast for comfort. One moment the views from the wheelhouse showed a vague disturbance in the wall of mist, shapes which could have been a mirage. Then six wind-surfers appeared, three of them steering their sails across the course Martel was following, compelling him to stop the engine.

'They're here,' he yelled to Claire and pushed the signal button.

'I've seen them!'

She knelt with her back to the wheelhouse, holding the pistol out of sight, gripping the butt with both hands.

'They're under attack!'

Crouched inside the wheelhouse of the police

launch Sergeant Dorner watched the winking bleep which had suddenly appeared on his specially adapted radar screen. Standing up in full view, he switched on the powerful engine which flared with a roar.

Dorner knew that at this moment there would be no lake steamer approaching the entrance but he obeyed regulations, sounding his siren as the launch rushed from its berth – the mooring rope had been surreptitiously slipped free when he sneaked on board.

Parallel to the exit, he stopped the forward rush and swung his wheel well over, turning the craft through ninety degrees, thrashing up a wake which transformed the harbour into a turmoil of waves and froth. With his bow aimed between the two moles he opened the throttle, his siren screaming non-stop. The launch shot forward as he increased speed, checking the blip on his screen.

'Get me there in time,' Dorner prayed.

Klara Beck had decided not to leave the excitement to Braun so she had occupied the same seat on the front. Confident, now that she had made her vital telephone call, she had been relaxing and gazing round like a tourist. The sudden departure of the police launch appalled her.

She hurried along the promenade, dashed across the street and into the Hauptbahnhof. She was halfway to the row of telephone booths when she stopped. Across the window of each booth a gummed sticker carried the legend Out of Order. A uniformed policeman strolled up to her and she fought down a moment of panic.

'You wished to use the phone?' he enquired.

'They can't *all* be out of order,' she protested.

'The notice is clear enough,' he replied less politely. 'They are working on the fault now.'

'Thank you . . .'

She made herself walk out of the Hauptbahnhof slowly. Her pace quickened as she went across to the Bayerischer Hof. Once in her room she picked up the receiver to dial a number. A girl's voice came on the line.

'I am very sorry but there is a temporary breakdown in the phone system. Would you like to give me a number and I will call you as soon as . . .'

'It's not important . . .'

Exerting her exceptional self-control Klara Beck put down the receiver and lit a cigarette. God, would she be blamed for not warning Dietrich. What the bloody hell was going on?

'Cut all the lines to the mainland . . .'

At the police station Erich Stoller gave the order immediately he received Martel's signal. In the same room with him a policeman sat with the phone to his ear – the line held open to the exchange where

185

they were waiting for precisely this order. The turning of three switches isolated Lindau island from all telephonic communication with the outside world.

On hearing the order a second policeman left the room and ran to the radio-control office. A signal went out to patrol-cars strategically placed in advance. The road bridge to the mainland was blocked. Other patrol-cars appeared at the mainland end of the rail embankment, closing off the cycle track and footpath.

A 'fault' developed in the signal box controlling rail traffic to Lindau, stopping all trains. Only a man with Stoller's authority could have achieved this result. Now his main worry was what might be happening out on the lake.

Werner Hagen was supremely confident as he led his team of wind-surfers to encircle and engulf the launch. The element of surprise was everything. The blond giant was the first to reach the port side of the stationary launch and he placed one bare foot over the side prior to temporarily abandoning his sail. His right hand held the large-bladed knife ready for the first lunge.

He was surprised to see a girl, her features concealed behind a face-mask, and then he was otherwise occupied. Martel came out of the wheelhouse wielding a boat-hook. He had guessed Hagen was the leader – it was written all over him.

The swing of the boat-hook ended as it struck Hagen a vicious blow at the side of the head. He sprawled full-length inside the launch, lifting his head in time to meet the carefully calculated thud of Martel's gun barrel. He collapsed unconscious.

A second man was coming aboard, knife in hand, when Claire aimed her pistol and shot him three times in the chest. Blood spurted and formed a pool below the deck-planks. Martel looked round and summed up the situation. Four killers left. Three still forming a crescent round his bow, another coming up behind the stern. He heaved Claire's target overboard, dashed back inside the wheelhouse and opened up full throttle.

The trio blocking his passage could not react in time. The launch moved too suddenly, too fast. One moment it was stationary, then it was a projectile hurtling towards them, its bow smashing their frail craft, weathered wood hammering into pliable flesh.

One man, giving a final scream, was literally keel-hauled as the launch beat his already-broken body to pulp. The other two men lay floating close together in a patch of lake which suddenly became red, their bodies crumpled like the relics of their sails.

'There's the man behind us,' Claire called out.

Martel was already taking appropriate action as he put the engine into reverse and moved backwards at speed, steering by glancing over his shoulder. The stern of the launch struck the surviving killer, he fell and the propeller passed over him.

'We'll run for it,' he told Claire. 'I think I see Dorner on the way . . .'

Chapter Sixteen

Friday May 29

It was a sunny, hot, sweaty day in Paris when Howard flew in to Charles de Gaulle. He was attending the conference to finalise security aboard the Summit Express. Typically he travelled alone. Typically he wore country tweeds.

From the airport a car sent by Alain Flandres drove him to No. 11, rue des Saussaies, official headquarters of the Sûreté. This narrow, twisting street, only a few minutes' walk from the Elysée, is rarely noticed by tourists. Inside an archway uniformed policemen watch the entrance.

Flandres often chose the complex of sombre old buildings for a clandestine meeting. The place was well-guarded, there was much coming and going by plain-clothes detectives – so the arrival of three civilians in separate cars was unlikely to attract attention. The head of the French Secret Service was waiting to greet Howard in a second-floor room equipped with a table, chairs and little else.

'Good to see you, Alain,' Howard said tersely.

'I am delighted to welcome you to Paris, my friend,'

Flandres replied enthusiastically as he shook hands and turned to a man already seated at the table.

'You know Tim O'Meara, of course? Just in from Washington . . .'

'We had the pleasure of meeting once,' the American interjected. He shook hands without rising from his chair and resumed smoking his cigar.

They sat round the highly polished table while Flandres poured drinks. Howard fiddled with the new pad and pencil in front of him, sitting stiff-backed. O'Meara did not improve on further acquaintance he was thinking. Heavily built, in his early fifties, the American had a large head, was clean-shaven, wore rimless glasses and exuded self-confidence. He did not behave as the 'new boy'.

The fact was Tim O'Meara had only been chief of the American Secret Service detachment which guarded his President for a year. In his loud check sports jacket – he also was obviously playing the tourist – he settled his bulk in his chair as though he had been a member of the club for a decade.

As he poured the drinks Alain Flandres observed all this with a hint of Gallic amusement. Short and of slim build, Flandres was impeccably dressed in a lounge suit despite the heat. Also in his early fifties, the Frenchman's features were finely chiselled and he sported a trim, pencil-style moustache the same colour as his well-brushed dark hair.

'Erich Stoller from Germany is due any moment,'

he announced as he settled in his own chair and lifted his glass. 'Gentlemen – welcome!'

He sipped at his cognac, noted that Howard took a big gulp while O'Meara swallowed half his glass of neat Scotch. There was tension under the surface, Flandres observed. This was a gathering of nervous men. Who was the catalyst?

The door opened and Erich Stoller was ushered into the room. His tall, thin figure was in extreme contrast to the other three, as was his manner. He tended to listen, to say very little. He apologised for his late arrival.

'An unexpected problem required my urgent attention . . .'

He left it at that. It was mid-afternoon and he had no wish to reveal that in the morning he had been in Lindau, sealing off the island while Martel took his launch on to the lake. He'd had the devil of a rush to reach Paris – involving a helicopter flight to München airport where a plane had waited for him.

'Only some beer,' he told Flandres, sitting bolt upright in his chair. An excellent psychologist, he proceeded to throw Howard completely off Martel's scent by irritating him. 'And how is my friend, Tweed?' he enquired. 'I expected to see him here . . .'

'Tweed is home-based these days,' Howard said curtly, his face very bony. 'Getting on in years, you know . . .'

'Really? I thought you were both the same age,' Stoller remarked blandly and drank some beer.

'This isn't his territory,' Howard snapped. 'Maybe we can get on with the subject which brought us to Paris?'

'But, of course!' Flandres agreed, even more amused by this exchange. 'I have the route of the Summit Express . . .' He proceeded to unroll a large-scale map of Northern Europe with the route marked in red. He sat back in his chair and lit a cigarette watching the others study the sheet.

Alain Flandres, whose handsome features and easy charm proved so irresistible to women, also had a flair for the dramatic. He made the remark casually and three heads bent over the map jerked up.

'A sighting of Carlos – Manfred – call him what you like, was reported in London this morning – in Piccadilly to be precise . . .'

'*Manfred!* How the hell do *you* know what's happening in London? And will someone tell me whether he really is Carlos?'

It was Howard who had exploded. Flandres noted he was edgier than he had realised. Why, he wondered? In a casual tone of voice the Frenchman explained.

'A girl operative of mine, Renée Duval, is working at the French Embassy for the moment. This telex just came in from her with an extract from your midday paper.' While Howard read the strip the Frenchman handed him, Erich Stoller commented on Carlos.

'Carlos has no known base. Manfred has no known

base. No one is sure of the real appearance of Carlos. The same applies to Manfred. Carlos has been known to take temporary refuge behind the Iron Curtain – as has Manfred. Both are independents who cooperate with the KGB only when it suits them . . .'

'So there *are* two of them?' Howard broke in.

'Or,' O'Meara intervened in his gravelly voice, 'has Carlos *invented* two of them – if so, which is the real one? You omitted, Erich, to add that both men – *if* two exist – are brilliant assassins.'

Flandres studied the American more closely. That is a most telling point you have made, my friend, he was thinking. Howard coloured with annoyance at Stoller's next question.

'Could you be more precise about this sighting in London? How was he dressed? Why was he recognised so easily?'

'His usual "uniform",' Howard murmured reluctantly. 'Windcheater, jeans, his dark beret and very large tinted glasses.'

'Can you elaborate on this incident?' the German persisted.

'He was recognised by a policeman patrolling on foot. Carlos – if it was Carlos – vanished up Swallow Street leading to Regent Street. The policeman pursued him and lost him in the crowds. Later, one of the assistants in Austin Reed, a nearby man's outfitter, found on a chair the windcheater with the beret and glasses on top. Underneath the windcheater was a loaded .38 Smith & Wesson . . .'

'A *patrolling* policeman,' Stoller continued. 'He was walking up and down a particular section of this street?'

'I imagine so, yes. Probably keeping an eye open for IRA suspects. Where is all this leading to?' Howard demanded.

'Someone dressed in this manner could have made sure the policeman did see him and then disappeared?'

'I suppose so, although I hardly see the point . . .'

O'Meara relit his cigar. 'A Havana,' he explained. 'I have to get through this box before I return to the States where, as you must know, they are contraband.'

Stoller, after his unusual burst of conversation, lapsed into silence and Flandres had the eerie impression the German was studying one particular person. But he could not identify which man had for some unknown reason aroused the BND chief's interest.

They proceeded with the main business in hand – planning security for their respective political heads attending the Vienna Summit. The rail journey was broken down into sectors. The division into sectors was marked on the map.

Paris to Strasbourg – French. From Strasbourg via Stuttgart and München to Salzburg – German. The last stage, Salzburg to Vienna – American, with nominal cooperation from the Austrians. Alain Flandres, in sparkling good humour, did most of the talking.

Howard was allocated a 'mobile' role – his team

would cover all three sectors. Flandres went over his sector in detail, pointing out potential danger points from terrorist attack – embankments, bridges. O'Meara, puffing his cigar, decided the Frenchman knew his job.

Then it was Erich Stoller's turn and again O'Meara was impressed. The German paused as he reached a certain point on the map and was silent for a short time. Something in his manner heightened the tension inside the airless room as he prodded with his finger.

'Here the express crosses into Bavaria. There is a certain instability in this area. It is unfortunate the state elections take place the day after the train crosses this sector . . .'

'The neo-Nazi business? Delta?' Howard enquired.

'Tofler,' O'Meara said with great conviction. 'His support is growing with each fresh discovery of more Delta arms and uniforms. And Tofler is a near-Communist. His programme includes plans for detaching Bavaria from West Germany and making it a "neutral" province or state like Austria. That would smash NATO and hand Western Europe to the Soviets on a platter . . .'

'Chancellor Langer is fully aware of the problem,' Stoller said quietly. 'His advisers tell him Tofler will not win . . .'

Flandres arranged for excellent food and drink to be brought in and they continued going over the route until late in the evening. The Frenchman sipped at his glass of wine as he looked round at his colleagues, all of whom were now in shirt-sleeves. The evening was warm and clammy. The bombshell fell after he made his remark.

'I am beginning to think, gentlemen, that the main requirement for our job is stamina . . .'

He broke off as an armed guard entered the room and handed him a message. He read it, frowned and looked at Howard. 'This says the British ambassador is outside with an urgent signal which he must pass to you at once.'

'The *Ambassador*?' Howard was shaken but nothing showed in his expression. 'You mean he has sent a messenger . . .'

'I mean the Ambassador in person,' Flandres said firmly. 'And I understand he wishes to hand you the signal himself while you are present at this meeting.'

'Please ask him to come in,' Howard requested the guard.

A tall distinguished man with a white moustache entered the room holding a folded slip of paper. Everyone stood, brief introductions took place, and Sir Henry Crawford handed the folded slip to Howard.

'Came direct to me, Anthony – in my personal code. No one except myself knows about it. It was accompanied by a request that I came here myself. Reasonable enough – when you read the contents.' He looked round the room. 'A pleasure to meet you all and now, if you will excuse me . . .'

Howard had unfolded the slip and read it several

times before he sat down and gazed round the table. His expression was unfathomable but the atmosphere had changed. The Englishman spoke quietly, without a trace of emotion.

'This signal is from Tweed in London. He makes an assertion – I emphasise he gives no clue as to his source. Only the gravity of the assertion compels me to pass it on to you under such circumstances . . .'

'If Tweed makes an assertion,' Flandres commented, 'then we can be sure he has grounds for doing so. The more serious the assertion the less likely he is to reveal the source. It might endanger the informant's life . . .'

'Quite so.' Howard was aware that his armpits were stained with dampness. He cleared his throat, glanced at each man and read out the contents of the signal.

Reliable source has just reported unknown assassin will attempt to eliminate one – repeat one – of four VIPs aboard Summit Express. No indication yet as to which of four will be target. Tweed.

Chapter Seventeen

Friday May 29

On the morning of the day when the four security chiefs met in Paris for their afternoon conference, Martel's launch headed for a remote landing-stage on the eastern shore of Lake Konstanz.

Werner Hagen, sole survivor of the wind-surfer execution squad, lay helpless in the bottom of the launch. His mouth was gagged, wrists, knees and ankles were bound with strong rope and a band of cloth was tied round his eyes. All he could hear was the chugging of the engine, all he could feel was the compression of the ropes and the glow of the sun on his face.

Inside the wheelhouse Martel steered the craft closer to their objective, guided by Claire who stood alongside him. The mist had dispersed, the shoreline was clear, and he slowed down until they were almost drifting as he scanned the deserted stony beach, the crumbling relic of a wooden landing-stage.

'You're sure we won't run into someone – campers, people like that,' he checked as the momentum carried them forward in a glide.

'Stop fussing,' she chided. 'I told you – I know this

area. I used to meet Warner here when he came down from Münich. And last night I parked the hired Audi among those trees before I walked to the nearest railway station to catch a train back to Lindau.'

'I don't see the Audi . . .'

'You're not bloody meant to see it!' she exploded. 'When are you going to give me credit for being able to cope on my own? You know your trouble, Martel?'

'If I don't do a job myself I start worrying about it . . .'

'Right! So have a little faith. And – before you ask me – I do know the way to that old water-mill I mentioned, which is another place where Warner and I used to meet. Although why we're driving there I don't understand . . .'

'To interrogate Blond Boy . . .'

He had carried Werner Hagen to the car and dumped him on the floor in the rear, folding him up like a huge doll so no part of him protruded above window level. Then he had relaxed while Claire took the wheel and drove them some distance to another crumbling relic – the water-mill, located at a remote spot in the Bavarian countryside.

Everything was exactly as Claire had described it. There was no way of guessing the purpose the mill had once served – but the huge wheel still turned ponderously as foaming water from the rapids behind the structure revolved the wheel. Martel studied the wheel, watching the blades dip below the surface before they emerged dripping to commence another revolution.

'Yes,' he decided, 'it will work . . .'

'What will work?'

'My new version of the old Chinese water torture. Blond Boy has to talk . . .'

It took their combined strength to manhandle the German into the required position. Before they started Martel told Claire to don her face-mask again. 'To scare the living daylights out of him he has to *see* – which means removing his blindfold. Tuck your hair up inside the back of your mask. You're wearing the slacks left in the car – he'll think you're a man . . .'

With her face-mask adjusted she helped Martel as he stood on the platform above the slow-turning wheel. They spread-eagled Hagen over a part of the wheel clear of the water and moved rapidly – whipping more rope round his recently-freed ankles and attaching them to one of the huge blades.

To make it worse, Martel had laid the German with his head downwards so it submerged under the water first while the upper part of his body was still above the surface. It took them ten minutes to secure Hagen's splayed body to the wheel and then the blindfold was removed. He glared with hatred at Martel and then a look of doubt crossed his handsome face as he caught sight of the sinister figure of Claire.

Standing very erect, wearing Martel's jacket to

conceal her bosom, she stared through the face-mask at the German with her arms crossed, her pistol in her right hand. She looked the epitome of a professional executioner.

Then the wheel dipped again and Hagen took a deep breath for when he went under the water. The trouble was the slow revolution of the wheel kept him submerged for longer than he could hold his breath. He surfaced spluttering water, his lungs heaving. He knew there was a limit to the period of time he could survive the ordeal.

There was another factor Hagen found increasingly difficult to combat. The circular rotation was disorientating and he was becoming dizzy. His great fear was he would lose consciousness, taking in a great draught of water while submerged.

Martel made a gesture that they retreated from the platform to the river bank. He inserted a cigarette into his holder and lit it as the wheel continued its endless revolutions. Away from the shade of the water-mill the sun beat down on them out of a sky like brass.

'We can talk now without him hearing us,' he remarked. 'He is, of course, slowly drowning . . .'

'Let him,' Claire said calmly, her face-mask eased up clear of her mouth. 'He's probably the one who carved up Charles . . .'

'The female of the species . . .'

'How long are you going to leave him?' she enquired.

'Until I gauge his resistance is broken. When we release him he has to talk immediately. I just hope he knows something . . .'

They waited until Hagen was on the verge of losing consciousness, until he was swallowing huge quantities of water each time he went under. Claire readjusted her face-mask and they ran to the platform. They had the devil of a job freeing Hagen: constant immersion in water had made the ropes impossible to untie. Martel used a knife he kept inside a sheath strapped to his left leg.

When he carried the water-logged man to the river bank Martel had to work on him, kneading his body to eject water. Claire sat on a rock a short distance away, her pistol aimed at the German. The first question Martel fired was an inspired guess.

'Who are you?'

'Reinhard Dietrich's nephew and heir . . .'

Only the face-mask concealed Claire's astonishment at the reply. They had hit pure gold. She remained still and menacing as Martel continued the interrogation.

'Name?'

'Werner Hagen – you know these things . . .'

'Just answer the questions.' He waited while Hagen coughed and cleared his lungs. 'What is the Delta deadline for Operation Crocodile?'

'June 3 – the day before the election . . .' He paused and Claire sensed his powers of resistance were returning. She raised her pistol in her right hand, used her left arm as a balance and took deliberate aim.

'Oh God, stop him!' Hagen pleaded with Martel. 'I'm answering your questions. I want out of the whole bloody business. Something's wrong. Vinz's . . .'

'You said June 3. You were going to add something,' Martel prodded.

'The key is the Summit Express will be moving across Bavaria . . .'

'All this we know,' Martel lied. 'Warner got the information to London.' He puffed at his cigarette to let his statement sink in. 'I simply want confirmation from you about Delta's flashpoint for June 3 . . .'

'You know that!' The surprise was apparent in Hagen's tone. He was still in a state of disorientation.

'So why not tell us what is worrying you – something to do with the Summit Express? Yes?'

'One of the four western leaders aboard is going to be assassinated . . .'

The statement sent Martel into a state of shock although nothing in his expression betrayed the reaction. His teeth clenched on the holder a fraction tighter and he continued the interrogation.

'Who is the target?'

'I don't know! *God in heaven, I really don't know . . .!*'

Hagen's shout – caused by Martel's glance towards the revolving wheel – was convincing.

'How do you know any of this? You – a mere lad,' Martel jibed, 'but a murderous thug at that . . .'

'Because I'm Reinhard Dietrich's nephew!' Hagen flared. 'I'm regarded as his son, the son his wife never provided. He confides in me . . .'

'You said earlier "I want out of the whole bloody business. Something's wrong." Don't think about it! Tell me quickly – what is wrong?'

'I'm not sure I know,' Hagen replied sulkily.

'I'm waiting for a reply,' Martel reminded him. 'The trouble is, I'm not a patient man.'

'My uncle is supposed to take over Bavaria in the coming election. The people are turning to us because they fear the party of Tofler, the Bolshevik.' He was recovering rapidly, sitting with a frown on his face. 'But as soon as we build up a store of uniforms and arms for the militia to be formed when we win, the BND discover them – as though someone is informing the BND . . .'

'And who is going to assassinate one of the western leaders?'

Martel threw the question at him. Hagen stood up slowly. 'I have the cramp . . .' He bent down and massaged the calf of his left leg, then straightened up, flexing his hands.

'I told you I'm not a patient man,' Martel snapped.

'The assassin – again I swear I do not know his identity – is one of the four security chiefs supposed to be guarding the western leaders . . .'

*

The reply threw Martel completely off guard for the fraction of a second. It was all Hagen needed. He rushed forward, aiming a blow at Claire which knocked her off the rock she had perched on. She could have pulled the trigger but knew Martel wanted the German alive.

Hagen's headlong-rush was intended to carry him to cover behind the water-mill before either captor could react. It carried him forward as he intended but he stumbled over a protruding outcrop of rock close to the water-mill.

He screamed, hands outstretched to save himself. Claire heard the horrid sound of his skull striking one of the descending metal blades and the scream faded to a gurgle. He lay motionless, head and shoulders in the river. A gush of blood welled, mingling with the peaceful sound of tumbling water.

Claire ran forward, steadied herself on the slope and checked Hagen's neck pulse as Martel came up behind her. Standing up she looked at the Englishman, shaking her head.

'He's dead. What do we do now?'

'Get him back to civilisation and contact Stoller or Dorner at once. I have to find a safe phone to call Tweed.'

They reached police headquarters in Lindau with the body concealed in the back of the car under Martel's raincoat. Dorner gave them the news without preamble.

'Erich Stoller left a message strictly for your ears – he flew to Paris for a security conference. I will make arrangements about Hagen – Stoller will want him sent by special ambulance to a morgue in Münich. As to making a phone call to London which can't be intercepted, the answer is the Post Office . . .'

Dorner drove them there himself. They were closing the doors when the German gently pushed them open and escorted his two companions inside.

A few words from Dorner persuaded the switchboard operator to call the London number. Martel first tried the Maida Vale flat and was relieved when he heard Tweed's voice which sounded weary. The voice changed pitch when Tweed realised who was calling. He activated the recording machine, rushed through the identification procedure and spoke before Martel could say any more.

'Operation *Crocodile*, Keith. You're standing in the middle of it. Look at a map of southern Germany through half-closed eyes – concentrate on the shape of Lake Konstanz. The damned thing is just like a crocodile – jaws open to the west with the two inlets, Uberlingersee and Untersee . . .'

'That confirms my data – something is scheduled to happen in Bavaria. Reinhard Dietrich's nephew, Werner Hagen, talked before he left us permanently . . .'

Crouched over the table in his flat Tweed gripped

the receiver more tightly. Events were piling on top of each other – always the most delicate and dangerous phase in an operation. He listened as Martel continued.

'One of the four VIPs aboard the Summit Express is scheduled for assassination on the train. Do you read me . . .'

'Of course I do.' Tweed's voice and manner had never been calmer. 'Give them numbers – starting geographically from west to east. Which number is the target . . .'

'Informant didn't know . . .'

'At least we're alerted. Aboard the train – I've got that. Identity of assassin?'

The question Martel was dreading. Would Tweed think he had gone off his rocker? He took a deep breath, thankful that Dorner had stayed with the switchboard operator so no one could overhear this call.

'I'm convinced – and so is my colleague – that this next bit of information provided by Hagen is genuine. You have to trust my judgement . . .'

'Get on with it, man . . .'

'The killer is one of the four security chiefs who will be guarding the VIPs. And, before you ask, not a damned clue as to who is the rotten apple. I'd better get off the line, hadn't I?'

'I consider that a sensible suggestion . . .'

*

Tweed had the devil of a time, almost the worst few hours he could remember. He found a cab quickly to take him to Park Crescent, but then his problems were only beginning. That supercilious careerist, Howard, had flown to the security meeting in Paris without telling anyone where the conference was being held. Supercilious *careerist*? It suddenly occurred to him that Howard was one of the four prime suspects ...

Never averse to using unorthodox methods, Tweed was careful to follow protocol on this occasion. He knew Sir Henry Crawford, the British Ambassador in Paris, but his first move was to call a friend at the Foreign Office.

'... an emergency,' Tweed explained. 'I have to send a signal and it must reach the Ambassador within two hours ...'

'Why not phone the Embassy first to make sure he will be there to receive the message,' his friend had suggested.

Had Tweed put forward this suggestion he had no doubt it would have been stiffly rejected as a breach of protocol – but it was all right providing the idea came from the Foreign Office.

He made the call, spoke to the Ambassador, who assured him there was no problem. He would wait for the arrival of Tweed's coded signal and, since the matter was so delicate, deliver the decoded message himself.

'Yes,' he concluded, 'I do know where the conference you are concerned with is taking place ...'

Crawford was cordial – and discreetly uninforma-
tive as to where the conference was being held. It was
the reaction Tweed had anticipated. He took another
cab to meet his contact at the Foreign Office.

'I have spoken to Sir William Crawford,' he
announced when he was seated in an uncomfortable
armchair. This statement formed a bridge between the
Ambassador in Paris and his contact – across which
the contact was compelled to walk.

'What is the message?' the other man in the room
enquired.

'It was agreed I should present that in isolation to
the cipher clerk on duty. I hope you don't mind?'

Tweed was at his meekest, most concerned with
not offending the august institution inside whose
portals he had been privileged to enter. This was
unusual – for someone outside the Foreign Office to
use its private code. Tweed employed the weapon of
silence, adjusting his glasses while the other decided
whether he could see any way out. He couldn't.

'Come with me,' he said, a chilly note infusing his
tone.

Ten minutes later the signal was on its way to
Paris. Other than Tweed, the only person who knew
its contents was the cipher clerk. *He* would reveal it
to no one. Tweed sighed with relief as he hailed yet
another cab in Whitehall, gave the Park Crescent
address and sank back into the seat.

Low cunning had won the day. The Ambassador
himself would know the contents – should any wit-

ness ever be needed that the signal had been sent. And the Ambassador was personally delivering the message to Howard *in the conference room*. That would force Howard to read out the warning to the other three security chiefs.

'I wish I could be there to study their faces when that message is read out,' Tweed reflected as the cab proceeded up Charing Cross Road. 'One of those four men will be shaken to the core . . .'

'It could be any one of the four. You'll have to track through their dossiers back over the years . . .'

Tweed gave the instruction to McNeil as they strolled together in Regent's Park after the clammy heat of the day. It was still light, the trees were in full foliage, the grass had a springy rebound which Tweed loved. Everything was perfect – except for the time-fuse problem he must solve.

'O'Meara, Stoller and Flandres . . .'

'Don't forget Howard,' Tweed said quickly.

'What am I looking for?' McNeil enquired with a note of sharp exasperation.

'A *gap*.' Tweed paused under a tree and surveyed the expanse of green. 'A gap in the life – in the records – of one of those four trusted men. Maybe as little as two months. Time unaccounted for. He will have been trained behind the Iron Curtain – I'm sure of that. This man was planted a long time ago . . .'

'Checking Howard's dossier will be tricky . . .'

'You'll need cover – a reason why you're consulting all these files from Central Registry. I'll think of something . . .'

He resumed his walk, his shoulders hunched, a faraway look in his eyes. 'The funny thing, McNeil, is I'm certain we've already been given a clue – damned if I can put my finger on it . . .'

'Tim O'Meara won't be any easier than Howard to check – he's only been head of the President's Secret Service detachment for a year.'

'Which is why I'm taking Concorde to Washington tomorrow if I can get a seat. I know somebody there who might help. He doesn't like O'Meara. A little prejudice opens many doors . . .'

'Howard will want to know why,' she warned. 'The expense of the Concorde ticket will be recorded by Accounts . . .'

'No, it won't. I'll buy the ticket out of my own pocket. There is still something left from my uncle's legacy. I'll be away before Howard returns. Tell him I've had a recurrence of my asthma – that I went down to my Devon cottage . . .'

'He'll try and contact you . . .'

'About my signal via the Ambassador?' Tweed was amused. 'I've no doubt when he returns his first job will be to storm into my office. Make it vague – about my trip to the cottage. I felt I just had to get out of London. It will all fit,' he remarked with an owlish expression. 'He'll think I'm dodging him for a few days. He'll never dream I've crossed the Atlantic.'

McNeil stared straight ahead. 'Don't look round – Mason is behind us. He's pretending to take that damned dog of his for a walk . . .'

Tweed paused, took off his glasses, polished them and held them up as though checking his lenses. Reflected in the spectacles was the image of Howard's lean and hungry-looking deputy recently recruited from Special Branch. He also had stopped by a convenient tree which his Scottie at the end of a leash was investigating.

'I prefer the dog to the man,' Tweed commented as he replaced his glasses and started walking again. 'Add him to the list. If anyone can find the vital discrepancy in the dossiers you can . . .'

Howard had reserved a room for the night at the discreet and well-appointed Hôtel de France et Choiseul in rue St Honoré. While he waited for his guest he put in a call to Park Crescent. When the night duty operator answered he identified himself and continued the conversation.

'I want a word with Tweed,' he said brusquely.

'Just a moment, sir. I will put you through to his office.'

Howard checked his watch which registered 2245 hours. He was disturbed: Tweed was still inside Park Crescent when the building would be empty. It was later than he had realised when he made the call. He had another surprise when McNeil's voice came on the line. He spoke quickly to warn her it was an open line.

'I'm talking from my hotel room. I'd like an urgent word with Tweed . . .'

'I'm afraid Mr Tweed has been taken ill. Nothing serious – a bad attack of asthma. He's gone down to the country for a few days . . .'

'It's not possible to get him on the phone?'

'I'm afraid not, sir. When can we expect you back?'

'Impossible to say. Goodnight!'

Howard ended the call on a stiff note: he never liked questions about his future movements. Sitting on his bed he frowned while he recalled the conversation. That was an odd departure from McNeil's normal behaviour – asking a question she knew he would disapprove of.

In the Park Crescent office Miss McNeil smiled as she replaced the receiver. She had been confident the final question would get Howard off the line before he probed too deeply. She returned to her examination of the dossier in front of her. It carried a red star – top classification – on the cover, and a name. Frederick Anthony Howard.

In the Paris bedroom Howard was pacing impatiently when there was an irregular knocking on his locked door, the signal he had agreed with Alain Flandres. Despite the signal he extracted from his case the 7.65-mm automatic Flandres had loaned him and slipped it inside his pocket before opening the door. Flandres walked into the room.

'*Chez Benoit, mon ami!*'

The slim, springy Flandres was a tonic; always optimistic, his personality fizzed. He walked round the room smiling, his dark eyes everywhere.

'Chez What?' Howard enquired.

'Benoit! Benoit! They serve some of the best food in all of Paris. The last serving is at 9.30 in the evening – but for me *le patron* makes the exception. The Police Prefect often eats there. You are ready? Good . . .'

Flandres had a cab waiting at the entrance to the hotel. The journey took no more than ten minutes and the Englishman, sunk in thought, remained silent. Normally voluble, Flandres also said nothing but he studied his companion until they arrived and were ushered to a table. They were examining the menu when Flandres made his remark.

'My telex from London about the Carlos sighting this morning in Piccadilly has disturbed you? You wonder who he went there to meet? You were in London this morning?'

Howard closed the menu. 'What the bloody hell are you driving at, Alain?' he asked quietly.

'I have offended you?' Flandres was astonished. 'Always it is the same – I talk too much! And Renée Duval, the girl who sent me the telex – I have withdrawn her from London. She was only on routine assignment. Now, the really important subject is what we are to select for dinner . . .'

Flandres chattered on, steering the conversation

away from the topic of the telex. He was now convinced something else was disturbing the Englishman, something he was carefully concealing from his French opposite number.

Chapter Eighteen

Saturday May 30

Washington, DC, Clint Loomis . . .

The extract from the secret notebook discovered on
Warner's dead body had linked up with nothing so
far, Tweed reflected.

Concorde landed on schedule at Dulles Airport.
Tweed was not among the first passengers to alight,
nor among the last. He did not believe in disguises
but before disembarking he removed his glasses. This
simple act transformed his appearance.

Clint Loomis was waiting outside. He ushered him
straight into a nondescript blue sedan. The American,
in his late fifties, had not changed since their last
meeting. Serious-faced, his dark eyes penetrating
and acutely observant, he wore an open-necked blue
shirt and pale grey slacks. His hair had thinned
somewhat.

'We can say "Hello" when we get there,' he
remarked as he drove away from Dulles. 'Maybe
you'd better take off your jacket . . .'

The sun was blazing, the humidity was appalling.
It was like travelling inside a ship's boiler room.

'Is it always like this in May?' Tweed enquired as he wrestled himself out of his jacket, turned to cast it on the seat behind and looked through the rear window, studying the traffic.

'In Washington nothing is "always",' Loomis replied. 'In the US of A we're a restless lot – so we change the weather when we can't think of anything else to change. We'll talk when we get there – and no names. O.K.?'

'The car could be bugged?'

'They're bugging everything these days – even clapped-out old CIA personnel. Just to keep someone in a job. You have to file a report to show the boss you're still in business.'

'Why the rush at the airport? My bag slung on the back seat . . .'

'We could be followed, that's why. By the time we get where we're going we'll shake any tail . . .'

'Like arriving in Moscow,' Tweed said drily.

The signposts told him they were heading for Alexandria. Tweed looked through the rear window again and Loomis glanced at him with a frown of irritation.

'We're *not* being followed if that's what's bothering you . . .'

'When we get to a place where you can stop, could I take the wheel for awhile, Clint?'

'Sure. If that's the way you feel . . .'

This was one of the many things Tweed liked about Loomis – if he trusted you he never asked questions.

217

He did whatever you requested and waited for explanations.

Later, as they stood outside the car prior to changing places, the Englishman glanced back up the highway. A green car had also pulled in to the side and one of the two male occupants got out to lift the bonnet. A blue car cruised past which also contained two men – neither of them spared the stationary sedan a glance, Tweed observed. He got in behind the wheel and began driving.

'What make is that green car behind us – the one behind the truck? You'll see it as we go round this curve . . .'

'A Chevvy,' Loomis replied. 'It pulled up when we did . . .'

'I know. And that blue car ahead of us – which was cruising and is now picking up speed to keep ahead. They have a sandwich on us, Clint. Those two cars have been with us since we left Dulles. They keep changing places – one in front, one behind . . .'

'Jesus Christ! I must be losing my grip . . .'

'Just the fresh eye,' Tweed assured him. 'Better lose our friends one at a time, don't you think?'

They were coming up to traffic lights at an intersection and the green Chevvy was still one vehicle behind them when Tweed performed. To his right was one of those damned great trailer trucks which transported half of America's freight coast to coast. He rammed his foot down . . .

'*Look out – the lights . . .!*' Loomis yelled.

There was a scream of rubber as Tweed shot forward like a torpedo. He swerved crazily to avoid the trailer which was coming out with the lights in its favour. A second scream – of airbrakes being jammed on. Loomis looked back and then at Tweed who had returned to his correct lane. To the American he looked so bloody unruffled.

'You nearly got us killed back there . . .'

'I don't see the green Chevvy any more,' Tweed commented with a glance in his rear view mirror.

'Like hell you don't – it just rammed its snout into the side of that trailer. It was overtaking as you hit the lights . . .'

'To change places with the blue job ahead of us. Now . . .' Tweed tapped his fingers on the wheel. '. . . we lose him and we're on our own, which will be more comfortable . . .'

'Not the same way. *Please!* I thought you Brits were sober, law-abiding types. You realise what would have happened had a patrol-car been nearby . . .'

'There wasn't one. I checked.'

The meeting place was a white power cruiser moored to a buoy on the Potomac river. Tweed had followed signposts to Fredericksburg and then, guided by Loomis, turned off down a minor road to the east. By now he had lost the blue car in an equally hair-raising performance which had ended in their tail skidding off the highway. It was very quiet and deserted as

Tweed switched off the engine, climbed out and savoured the breeze coming off the water.

'That's yours?' he asked, pointing at the cruiser.

'Bought it with my – severance pay, don't you call it? – when I left the Company. Plus a bank loan I'm damned if I'll ever pay off. It gives me safety – I hope...'

'Safety?'

Tweed concealed his sense of shock. His trip to Washington was developing in a way he had never expected. First they had been followed from Dulles by an outfit which had money at its disposal. It cost a lot of dollars to employ *four* men to do a shadow job. And ever since he had arrived Clint Loomis, retired from the CIA, had shown signs of nervousness.

'The Company doesn't like people who leave it alive.'

Loomis was dragging a rubber dinghy equipped with an out-board which had been hidden among a clump of grasses down to the river's edge. He gave a lop-sided grin as the craft floated and he gestured to his visitor to get aboard. 'I suppose it comes from all those dumbos who got out and wrote books, revealing all as the publishers' blurbs say.'

'You're writing a book?' Tweed asked as he settled gingerly inside the vessel and Loomis started up the out-board.

'Not me,' Loomis said with a shake of his head. 'And when we get to the *Oasis* ...' He pointed towards the power cruiser, '. . . that's when we shake hands.'

'If you say so,' Tweed replied.

They crossed the smooth stretch of water and Loomis slowed the engine to a crawl as the hull loomed up. Aboard the *Oasis* a huge Alsatian dog appeared, running up and down the deck, barking its head off. Then it stopped at the head of the boarding ladder and stared down, jaws open, exposing teeth which reminded Tweed of a shark.

'Now we shake hands,' Loomis explained. 'That shows him you're a friend and you don't get chewed up.'

'I see,' said Tweed, careful to make a ceremony of the display of friendship. The dog backed off as he mounted the ladder without too much confidence while Loomis tied up the dinghy and followed him on deck.

'Over the side!' Loomis ordered.

The dog dived in, swimming all round the boat until it completed one circuit. Loomis stretched over the side down the ladder, hooked a hand in the dog's collar and hauled it aboard as the animal pawed and scrambled up the rungs. It stood on the deck and shook itself all over Tweed.

'Shows he likes you,' Loomis said. 'We'd better go below now that everything is safe. A beer?'

'That would be nice,' Tweed agreed, following his host down the companionway where the American handed him a towel to dry himself. He was beginning to have serious doubts as to whether he had been wise to cross the Atlantic.

'What was all that business about the dog?' he enquired.

'The swim in the river?' The American settled himself back on a bunk, his legs stretched out, his ankles crossed. For the first time he seemed genuinely relaxed. 'Waldo has been trained to sniff out explosives. So, we get back and find him alone on deck. Conclusion? No intruders *aboard* the cruiser – or one of two things would have happened. Waldo would be dead – or a man's body would be lying around with his throat torn out. O.K.?'

Tweed shuddered inwardly and drank more beer, 'O.K.,' he said.

'Next point. Waldo is trained to stay aboard no matter what. So the opposition uses frogmen who attach limpet mines with trembler or timer devices to the hull – devices which detonate with the vibration of a grown man's weight walking on deck. I send Waldo overboard and he swims round once without a pause. Conclusion? If there were mines Waldo would be yelping, kicking up one hell of a row when he gets the sniff of high-explosives. Now we know we're clean . . .'

'What a way to live. How long has this been going on? And who is going to attach the limpet mines?'

'A gun hired by Tim O'Meara who kicked my ass out of the Company when he was Director of Operations – before he transferred to become boss of the Secret Service.'

'And why would O'Meara do that?'

'Because I know he embezzled two hundred thousand dollars allocated for running guns into Afghanistan.'

In his München apartment Manfred concentrated on the long-distance call. His main concern was to detect any trace of strain in the voice of his caller. Code-names only had been used.

'Tweed knows there is a selected target,' the voice reported.

'He has identified the target?'

Manfred asked the question immediately, his voice calm, almost bored, but the news was hitting him like a hammerblow. He might have guessed that in the end it would be Tweed who ferreted out the truth. God damn his soul!

'No,' the voice replied. 'Only that there is one. You might wish to take some action.'

'Thank you for informing me,' Manfred replied neutrally. 'And please call me tomorrow. Same time . . .'

Replacing the receiver, Manfred swore foully and then comforted himself with the thought that he had detected no breaking of nerve in the voice of the man who had called him. Checking in a small notebook, he began dialling a London number.

223

This incident took place on the day before Tweed departed for Washington, late in the evening on the day the four security chiefs attended the conference at the Sûreté building in Paris.

Tweed realised he had walked into a nightmare. The question he couldn't answer to his own satisfaction was whether Clint Loomis was paranoid, suffering from a persecution complex which made him see enemies everywhere. Hence the obsession with security aboard the *Oasis*.

Against that he had to weigh the fact that they *had* been followed by four unknown men in two cars when they left Dulles Airport. It was Loomis who changed the subject – much to Tweed's relief.

'Charles Warner came to see me two weeks ago – he was interested in O'Meara. Have you also flown to the States just to talk to me? I'd find that hard to believe . . .'

'Believe it!' Tweed's manner was suddenly abrupt. 'When O'Meara was CIA Director of Operations he manipulated your retirement?'

'Bet your sweet life . . .'

'You know his history. What is that history?'

'He was an operative in the field early on. I was the man back home who checked his reports . . .'

'After a period of duty at Langley he was stationed in West Berlin for several years? Correct?' Tweed queried.

'Correct. I don't see where you're leading, Tweed. That always worries me . . .'

'*Trust me!*' The Englishman's manner had a quiet, persuasive authority. He had to keep Loomis talking, to concentrate his mind on one topic. O'Meara's track record. 'You say you checked his reports from West Berlin. He speaks German?'

'Fluently. He can pass for a native . . .'

'Did he go under cover – into East Berlin?'

'That was strictly forbidden.' There was a very positive note in Loomis' reply. 'It was written into his directive . . .'

'Anyone else with him in this unit?'

'A guy called Lou Carson. He was subordinate to O'Meara . . .'

'And all the time O'Meara was in West Berlin you're convinced he obeyed the directive – under no circumstances to go over the Wall?'

He was watching Loomis closely. The American had swung his legs off the bunk and was opening another can of beer. Tweed shook his head, his eyes fixed on Loomis who was staring into the distance.

'Maybe that was when the bastard first started to dislike me,' he said eventually.

Tweed sat quite still. He had experienced this before with interrogations – you *sensed* when pure chance had played into your lap. There was a time to speak, a time to preserve silence.

Loomis stood up and stared through a porthole across the peaceful waters. The craft rocked gently, scarcely moving. Tweed looked round the neat cabin. The American kept a tidy ship. He had kept a tidy desk at Langley, Tweed recalled – which was where he should still be. Loomis started talking.

'This particular unit in West Berlin was just these two guys – keeping tabs on the East German espionage set-up. It was one time Carlos was reported as being in East Berlin . . .'

'Really?'

'We had a system of identification codes,' Loomis continued, 'so I always knew when a signal came from O'Meara and when it was from Lou Carson – without either man knowing the other had his personal call-sign. We started playing it pretty close to the chest after the débâcle . . .'

'Let me get this clear. Each man had his own identification signal so you knew who was sending a report. But both O'Meara and Carson thought the system applied only to them – not to the other?'

'You've got it. You know, Tweed, you get a feeling when something is wrong. Signals were coming through from O'Meara but the wording didn't sound like O'Meara – although they carried his sign. So I hopped on a plane and arrived in West Berlin unannounced. Lou Carson was pretty embarrassed. I'd caught him with his pants down. He was on his own . . .'

'And where was O'Meara?'

'He surfaced two days later. Swore he had gone underground to another base for a couple of months because our normal one had been blown to the East German security people . . .'

'You believed him?' Tweed pressed.

'No, but that was only a gut feeling. You don't go to the Director with gut feelings. He likes solid evidence . . .'

'How had O'Meara got round the identification system?'

'Simple – he'd handed Lou Carson his identification log book so Lou could send messages and it would look as though they came from O'Meara. Carson cooperated because O'Meara told him to . . .'

'What happened next?' Tweed asked while Loomis was still wound up.

'Both men were recalled to Washington and others took their place. O'Meara had done a good job in West Berlin, he knew the right people, he can charm the birds out of the trees. Before I know it, he's promoted over my head and he's sending me to Bahrain with two hundred thousand dollars in a case aboard a special flight . . .'

'You said he embezzled the money.'

'Let me finish, for Christ's sake! When the people with the guns for Afghanistan checked the money I handed over they said it was counterfeit. They had a bright Indian who had worked for currency printers . . .'

'The counterfeit was good enough to deceive you?'

'I'd have accepted it without question. O'Meara had the case locked in his office safe, he took it out and handed it to me. He levered me out of the

Company over that incident,' Loomis blazed. 'They let me go quietly because there had been too many scandals and they were worried about their image . . .'

'O'Meara just cleaned you out? No one else?'

'Lou Carson went. There were others. He was bringing in his own people. When he'd wrecked half-a-dozen lives he joins the Secret Service and walks away from the wreckage. There are guys like that everywhere . . .'

'It happens – but it's not pleasant,' Tweed murmured, then he changed the subject. Best to leave a pleasant atmosphere behind when he boarded Concorde for London the following day.

The second long-distance call to Manfred came duly at the agreed hour the following day while Tweed was aboard the *Oasis*. It was Manfred who opened the conversation.

'You have nothing to worry about. Tweed is in Washington.'

'The devil he is! How do you know that?'

'Because I have people everywhere. The problem is a small one. Measures have already been taken to deal with it . . .'

'You mean you're going to have Tweed . . .'

'*Enough!* And the answer to your question is no. It would be bad policy. Crocodile will proceed on schedule. Now I must go – I have matters to attend to . . .'

It would be bad policy ... Manfred stood quite still, staring into space. He had not been quite frank with his caller, but Manfred was often anything but frank. He was certainly not going to admit that the killing of Tweed would be an extremely difficult operation. The Englishman was equipped with a sixth sense where danger was concerned.

Instead there was a better way of dealing with the problem. He picked up the phone again to call a Washington number.

It was Sunday May 31. Tweed had spent the night aboard *Oasis* – which the American had moved to a fresh mooring. This action confirmed the nervousness Tweed had detected on his arrival.

'Never stay in the same place for long,' Loomis remarked as he tied up the cruiser to a fresh buoy. 'And always move after dark without lights.'

'Illegal, isn't it?' Tweed enquired. 'To sail without navigation lights?'

'Bet your sweet life it is ...'

Over a meal which the American cooked in the galley they talked about old times. Loomis remarked he had heard Tweed was being held in reserve for 'the time when Howard trips over his big feet. Then they bring you back to clean up the mess. No, don't protest,' he admonished, waving his spatula, 'my grapevine is good.'

Just prior to his departure for Dulles, it was Tweed

who noticed two incidents which disturbed him. He was on deck with his suitcase, waiting for Loomis to climb down the ladder into the dinghy, when he observed movement onshore.

'Loan me your field-glasses, Clint,' he called out.

Something in his guest's tone made Loomis react quickly. Tweed raised the glasses to his eyes, adjusted the focus and studied the shoreline briefly. Then he handed them back, his lips compressed.

'Bird-watching?' Loomis enquired.

'There were two men in the trees over there. One of them had a camera with a telephoto lens – bloody great piece of equipment. I think he was photographing the *Oasis* . . .'

'Probably just a camera nut. They shoot anything.'

They had climbed down into the dinghy and the dog, Waldo, stood at the top of the ladder keening, when a helicopter appeared, flying from the Chesapeake Bay direction down the centre of the channel. As they left the cruiser Tweed craned his neck to get a look at the machine.

'That's the third time that chopper has over-flown us since I arrived,' Tweed commented.

'You see them all the time in this part of the world. Coastguard machines, private jobs . . .'

Loomis was concentrating on steering the dinghy to where they had parked his car. Tweed, hunched in the stern, continued staring up at the helicopter. The sun was reflecting off the plexiglas, making it impossible to see inside the pilot's cabin.

'I think it was the same machine each time,' he insisted.

Loomis was unconcerned. 'It's O.K. – we left Waldo on board.'

At Dulles they repeated their performance of the previous day – wasting no time. Tweed got out of the car and walked rapidly into the building without a glance back. Behind him he heard Loomis already driving away.

Aboard Concorde after lift-off it seemed to Tweed he might never have visited America – it had all happened so quickly. He was so absorbed in his thoughts he never noticed when they passed through the sound barrier. Fragments of conversation with Loomis drifted back into his mind.

. . . O'Meara . . . surfaced two days later . . . he had gone underground to another base . . . a couple of months . . . he'd handed Lou Carson his identification log book . . .

Tweed began to feel drowsy. He closed his eyes and fell asleep. It was the steep angle of descent which woke him. They were landing at London Airport. It had all been a dream. He had never been away at all. When he arrived at Park Crescent McNeil's expression prepared him for the shock.

Chapter Nineteen

Sunday May 31

Clint Loomis parked his car in a different place when he returned from Dulles alone. He knew every inch of the shoreline on both banks and this time he chose an abandoned shed at the end of a dirt track to house the vehicle. Then he started the long walk back to where the out-board was concealed.

It was another brilliant sunny day and the heat beat down on the back of his neck as he dragged the dinghy to the water's edge, got inside and fired the motor. In the distance the cruiser *Oasis* was gleaming, the sun reflecting off the highly-polished brass. For a moment he was reminded of Tweed when he heard the sound of a helicopter and saw the machine disappearing in the direction of Chesapeake Bay. Then he concentrated on navigating his small craft.

Waldo was waiting for him, barking his head off at the top of the ladder. As he was tying up the dinghy Loomis vaguely noticed a second power cruiser rather like his own heading on a course towards him from Chesapeake Bay. He went through the same security precaution – tipping Waldo overboard and waiting while the dog swam round the boat before hauling him aboard.

The odd thing was Waldo only displayed signs of agitation when he was back on deck. He was shaking himself dry – and Loomis grinned as he recalled how Tweed had taken the brunt of the water the previous day – when the dog stopped, still dripping. His body tensed, his ears lay flat, his teeth were bared and he stood rigid while he emitted a slow, drawn-out snarl.

'What's the matter, boy? Tweed got you nervy . . .'

Loomis followed the direction of Waldo's stare and his expression changed. Waldo was gazing at the oncoming cruiser which, unless it changed course, would pass close by them on its way upriver. Loomis could see no sign of anyone on board, which was odd. You would expect someone on deck on such a glorious day. He ran down into the cabin.

In a locked cupboard the ex-CIA man kept a small armoury. Opening it, he looked at the machine-pistol, the double-barrelled shotgun, the three hand-guns. He chose the shotgun.

It was like a ghost ship, the oncoming cruiser, Loomis thought as he came up on deck. Tinted glass in the wheelhouse windows which masked the presence of men who *must* be inside. Damnit, one man must be at the wheel. Chugging slowly and ominously, a cloth over the side concealing the name painted on its bow, it closed with *Oasis*.

Waldo was a coiled spring, hairs bristling, the softness of the growl from deep in his throat infinitely

more menacing than his normal barking. Loomis
glanced round to see if help was near at hand. Only a
vast expanse of empty water greeted him.

He crouched low, his shotgun out of sight. If this
was trouble one blast through the wheelhouse
window was liable to take out anyone inside. The
helmsman certainly – which meant the vessel would
no longer stay on its remorseless course.

It was due to pass within yards on the port side,
the side where Loomis waited. The hell of it was he
couldn't initiate any action in case they were peaceful
sailors going about their lawful occasions as the Brits
would phrase it. The thought made him wish he had
Tweed on board. He had a feeling Tweed would not
just have sat and waited. But what the hell else could
he do?

Stand up and address them through his loudhailer? And present someone with a perfect target.
Already he was working on the premise that the
approaching cruiser was hostile – without one shred
of evidence. Yes! Waldo was evidence – his reaction
to the vessel was unusually violent . . .

They set about the task in a way Loomis had not
foreseen. They were almost alongside *Oasis* when a
flutter of dark, pineapple-shaped missiles sailed
across the water separating the two vessels and
landed in various places. On deck. On the foredeck.
At the foot of the companionway. *Grenades!* Jesus
Christ . . .!

They had slightly different time fuses. One landed

underneath Waldo and detonated on impact. The dog disintegrated into a flying mass of bloody meat and bone, smearing the woodwork. Loomis went crazy. He stood up.

'Bastards!'

His shotgun was levelled point-blank at the tinted glass of the other vessel but before he could pull the trigger a grenade which had landed just behind him exploded. All feeling suddenly left his legs and he found himself floating backwards, falling down the companionway. He landed at the bottom just as one of the grenades which had ended up in the cabin also detonated. It sliced away half his head.

A boathook grappled *Oasis's* side when ten separate explosions had been counted. The man holding it wore a frogman's suit. The engine of the killer cruiser had been stopped and another man, also wearing a frogman's suit, leapt nimbly aboard holding a submachine gun.

He took only two minutes to search *Oasis*, to note that Loomis was dead, that no one else was hiding aboard. Then with the same agile movements he returned to his own cruiser, the engine started up and the vessel set on a new course which took it far away from *Oasis* as swiftly as possible.

In the burning-glass blue of the sky the pilot of a helicopter turned his machine and headed it away from Washington. Over his radio he spoke one word repeatedly.

Extinction . . . extinction . . . extinction . . .

Chapter Twenty

Sunday May 31

The headquarters of *Bundesnachrichtendienst* – the BND, the German Federal Intelligence Service located at Pullach – is six miles south of München. Erich Stoller's nerve centre was surrounded by a wall of trees and an inner wall comprising an electrified fence. Stoller, with his dry humour, referred to it as 'my own Berlin Wall'. He had just made this remark over coffee to Martel.

Tweed, due to catch the 13.05 flight back to London, was still fast asleep aboard the *Oasis* owing to the difference in the time zones. They sat in Stoller's office inside a single-storey concrete blockhouse of a building. Through the armour plate-glass window a stretch of bare earth showed where armed guards patrolled. Beyond was the electrified fence and beyond that dense pine trees. It was another hot morning and the temperature was rising rapidly.

'I spent four years in Wiesbaden with the Kriminalpolizei,' the German told Martel. 'Then I transferred to the BND.'

'And after that?'

Martel watched Stoller's dark eyes as he drank

some more of the strong coffee, his manner relaxed, his voice expressing friendly interest.

'A year here and then two inside the Zone . . .' Stoller's tone became sombre at the recollection of his time in East Germany. 'You know what it's like – going underground. It felt like ten years. Every hour of your waking day on the alert, every waking minute expecting a hand to drop on your shoulder. And you don't sleep too well,' he concluded with a wry smile. 'I thought you knew about that period . . .'

'Tweed doesn't tell me everything,' Martel lied easily. 'How long have you been back in civilisation?'

'Four years – if you can call Bavaria civilisation just at the moment. The riots are getting worse. The neo-Nazis march, the left-wing people counter-march, the two lots meet – and *Boom!*'

'The state government elections in a few days should solve all that,' Martel suggested.

'If Langer's moderates win. The trouble is Dietrich's party and the frequent discovery of Delta arms dumps may drive people into Tofler's left-wing bear-hug. Then he'll set up Bavaria as some kind of so-called Free State – detached from the Federal Republic . . .'

'You don't really believe that, Erich . . .'

'I do believe you've just been subjecting me to some kind of personal interrogation and I'm wondering why.'

Martel swore inwardly. He'd had to take the risk Stoller would catch on. Maybe he'd been stupid to try the experiment – facing a fellow-professional. He set out to repair the damage.

'Why so edgy? If we're to work together I like to know about a man. Maybe I can provide you with my career sheet . . .'

'Sorry!' Stoller raised a hand and smiled his slow, deliberate smile. The German did everything deliberately. He even sipped his coffee as though testing for a suspect ingredient.

'I am edgy,' he went on. 'You would be if you faced a crucial election – just when the Summit Express is crossing your territory with the West's top leaders aboard. My responsibility is the sector from Strasbourg through to Salzburg . . .'

'And the German Chancellor?'

'Kurt Langer boards the train at Münich Hauptbahnhof – but I still have the other three to guard through the night from Strasbourg.'

'You sound as though you expect trouble,' Martel suggested.

'I do.' Stoller stood up behind his desk. 'Shall we collect your friend, Claire Hofer, and drive to Münich?'

'Can I make one phone call to London before I leave?'

'I'll go and entertain Miss Hofer. No, no! You may prefer to talk in private.' Standing up, Martel reflected, the German was an imposing figure; not the sort of man you would expect to survive behind the Iron Curtain for two years.

'I will be in the canteen where we left her while we talked,' Stoller informed him. 'Just ask the operator for your number, press the red button and you're on scrambler . . .'

While he waited for the Park Crescent number Martel studied a wall-map of Bavaria. It showed where caches of Delta arms and uniforms had been found. Flags indicated the discovery dates.

He found it strange that the rate of success was accelerating. No wonder the polls were showing increasing support for Tofler's party as Election Day approached. Each discovery increased the voters' fear of a Delta win. The phone rang and he heard McNeil at the other end of the line. He asked her to supply 'photos of the four principals . . .'

'Tweed is out of London,' she told him quickly. 'He asked me to give you a message, Keith. Tomorrow, Monday, catch the first available flight to Heathrow where you will be met. You can give me the flight number? Good. And the ETA? Bring a passport picture of Miss Hofer. As soon as the meeting is over you fly back to Bavaria. Time is running out . . .'

'Don't I know it,' Martel replied.

It was a hot Sunday morning in Paris.

Howard had stayed in the city at the urging of Alain Flandres for a further discussion with O'Meara about security precautions aboard the Summit Express. The train was due to leave the Gare de l'Est late Tuesday evening, June 2 – only three days hence.

Despite Howard's protestations Flandres had insisted he would personally drive his British opposite number to Charles de Gaulle Airport to catch his London flight. Howard had a shock when he stepped out of the lift with his bag into the reception hall of the Hôtel de France et Choiseul ready for his departure.

'Tim is flying to London with you,' the Frenchman announced.

'Decided I'd call at the Embassy there and check out certain unfinished business, then fly back here for *Der Tag*,' O'Meara explained. 'It will give us a chance to get better acquainted . . .'

Howard said nothing as he contemplated the two men, contrasting their styles. They were opposites – the slim, elegantly dressed Alain, every hair in place, his movements nimble and precise, and the large American in his check sports jacket who exuded aggressive self-confidence.

'I have to pay my bill,' Howard said and walked to the counter. His eyes scanned the guests seated in the lounge area. A slim, fair-haired girl, fashionably dressed and with her superb legs crossed, sat reading a copy of *Vogue*. A blue Vuiton suitcase stood by her chair and she glanced up briefly as Howard passed her.

It took only a few moments to settle the bill, he lifted his case, went back to the entrance and Flandres led the way to where a blue Citroën was parked. He opened the rear door and Howard was forced to join O'Meara in the back. As the car left the kerb the fair-haired girl with the Vuiton case emerged and climbed inside a waiting cab.

During the journey the Englishman encouraged O'Meara to talk and maintained an almost uninter-rupted silence. Without appearing to do so he was watching Alain behind the wheel who frequently glanced in his rear-view mirror. Howard gained the impression they were being followed.

He was on the verge of asking the Frenchman if he had spotted a tail when something made him keep quiet. At de Gaulle Alain accompanied them to the barrier and bade them an effusive farewell.

'. . . until we meet again here in Paris aboard the Summit Express,' he murmured.

He watched as the two men stood on the escalator carrying them up inside a transparent tube elevated at a steep angle. A fair-haired girl passed him carrying a Vuiton case followed by a small, stocky man wear-ing a trilby. The tails were in position. Renée Duval would report on all Howard's movements and con-tacts. Georges Lepas would perform the same oper-ation on O'Meara. Alain Flandres was a professional, his favourite maxim *trust no one – particularly those close to you.*

Because something was wrong . . .

*

241

München Hauptbahnhof. The location Charles Warner had haunted on his visits to the Bavarian state capital. Martel and Claire had asked Stoller to drop them at the Four Seasons Hotel in the centre of the city. As soon as the German had departed Martel picked up both bags and shook his head at the hotel porter.

'We're not staying here . . .'

They walked a short distance before Martel hailed a cab and gave an address close to the Hauptbahnhof. After he had paid the fare they separated, each carrying their own bag. When they entered the vast station there was nothing to indicate they knew each other. Claire followed Martel at a distance, thankful for the pistol concealed in her handbag.

Both got rid of their cases in self-locking storage compartments and Martel began his search. Why had Warner found this place – and its alter ego in Zürich – important enough to record in his notebook? Knowing it would help identify him to any watcher, he strolled into the Sunday turmoil with his cigarette-holder at a jaunty angle. Behind him Claire checked for shadows. They were now in the middle of the spider's web.

Erwin Vinz felt desperate – which he knew was bad because a mood could cause him to make a mistake. After two fiascos in Lindau – Gross's unsuccessful attempt to kill Martel in the fog followed by the elimination of the wind-surfer execution squad – Reinhard Dietrich had flown into a fury in his Münich penthouse apartment.

'You had Martel! You had him in the palm of your hand in Lindau. What happens? Gross is killed by Martel while you stand by! Are you degenerating into some kind of amateur? If so, there is always a remedy . . .'

'I do have a plan . . .' Vinz began.

'Wonderful! Just as you had a plan at Lindau! I hope you also realise I hold you partly responsible for my nephew, Werner's demise?' He paused, choking on his emotion. The news had come over the phone from Erich Stoller of all people, the Intelligence creep Dietrich loathed. Vinz made a great effort.

'I am sure that Martel will surface in Münich. He is likely to come in by train. He uses trains a lot. He travelled to St Gallen from Zürich by train. He left St Gallen aboard the Münich express last Thursday . . .'

'And you lost him,' Dietrich broke in sarcastically.

'I have crammed Münich Hauptbahnhof with our soldiers,' Vinz persisted. 'They have his description. The station is so overcrowded an accident can occur and no one will notice. A man falls off a platform under a train . . .'

'Dangerous,' Dietrich said thoughtfully as he lit a cigar, 'to draw attention to the Hauptbahnhof . . .'

'Only if the Englishman realises its significance – only if he survives to pass on the information . . .'

'Kill him!' Dietrich crashed his fist on the desk, his face red with fury. *'Kill him for Werner! Now – get out . . .'*

The Hauptbahnhof was an inferno: the noise, the chaos incredible. Martel was caught up in the mob of passengers hurrying for trains, getting out of the city for a Sunday break. Expresses arriving, departing . . .

Saarbruecken, Bremen, Frankfurt, Zuerich, Dortmund, Wuerzburg . . . The destination boards carried the names of cities all over Europe. Under the tall roof in the cavern below were platforms 11 to 26. A sign pointed to an adjoining *second* station – the Starnberger. There was even a third station for platforms 1 to 10.

Wartesaal, a huge waiting room. Rows of telephone booths. A cafeteria. *Kino* – a cinema open from 0900 to 2100 hours, entrance six deutschemarks, for which sum you could sit there all day and in the evening. A score of different exits – including one to the complex U-Bahn system.

Martel was like a sponge, soaking up data, smoking his cigarette, strolling among the hustling, shoving crowds. At the back of his mind an idea was forming. Warner had noted down this rendezvous of strangers as important. Was the reason staring him in the face?

The noise was appalling, trapped by the overhang of the roof, the noise of voices, trampling feet, Tannoys booming. An assault on the nerves. The heat, again trapped inside the cavern by the roof, was exhausting – the clammy humidity, the sweat of God knew how many hurrying passengers.

Patiently, her handbag under her left arm, her right hand close to the flap and the pistol inside, Claire Hofer appeared to drift into the whirlpool as she doggedly followed the Englishman. Then she saw him. *Erwin Vinz* . . .

She was sure the killer would not recognise her. When he came into the reception hall of the Bayer-ischer Hof late in the evening he had not even glanced at her. But she had been trained never to make easy assumptions. From her handbag she took a pair of tinted glasses and slipped them on. She had to warn Martel.

Keith Martel's attention was absorbed by something else. He had the uncanny feeling that he was sur-rounded by hostile forces, that amid the surging crowd was a more compact, organised detachment of men. Then he saw a man wearing a Delta symbol in his lapel, a man waiting by the barrier where the Münich Express from Zürich was gliding to a halt.

More people poured off the platform into the station. Martel pretended to study a timetable board while he watched the man. One of the disembarking passengers showed his ticket but retained it – so it was a *return*. It happened in seconds – showing the ticket, the shaking of hands with the waiting Delta man and then they walked into the cafeteria. The new arrival also wore a silver triangle in his lapel.

'Erwin Vinz is here. Wearing the same clothes as in Lindau. He is standing by a loaded trolley behind you – he's seen you . . .'

Claire Hofer gently rubbed the side of her face to conceal the movement of her lips as she stood alongside Martel, also appearing to consult the timetable.

'Watch *yourself*,' he warned. 'I think the place is crawling with Delta types. Two have just gone into the cafeteria . . .'

He left her and she remained for a few moments studying the times and scribbling them in her pocket notebook. When she turned round Martel was disappearing inside the cafeteria. Erwin Vinz had spoken to a man she had only a brief glimpse of: she had an impression of tanned skin, large sun-goggles and the man vanished towards the exit.

Inside the cafeteria Martel ordered a cup of coffee, paid for it and selected a table close to one of the doors to the concourse. He sat in a chair with his back to the wall. The two Delta men were absorbed in conversation. The recent arrival from the express handed to his companion a thick envelope which disappeared inside the companion's breast pocket.

A glance, the briefest lifting of eyes in Martel's direction by the man who had waited at the barrier, warned the Englishman he had walked into a trap.

*

They crowded round the nearest exit, blocking his escape route – five well-built men wearing Tyrolean hats and carrying beer steins. One of them sat down at his table as Martel grasped the pepper pot. The man put his stein on the table, reached inside his pocket and produced a notebook which he laid on the table. He had not looked once in Martel's direction.

He put his hand in his pocket again and it reappeared holding a felt-tipped pen. He held it below the level of the table, pressed a button and the needle shot out into the action position. Martel ripped off the top of the pepper pot and tossed the contents into his eyes. He screamed – and his scream coincided with a louder sound. The explosion of shots fired from a pistol.

Martel jumped up and pushed over the table, tipping the killer opposite and his chair sprawling to the floor. The men round the door were stumbling against each other and their faces registered stark fear. They were desperate to get away from the door they had been blocking a moment earlier.

'This way out!'

Martel had a brief vision of Claire standing in the doorway, the pistol she had fired three times gripped in both hands and aimed at the Delta men. Her earlier shots had gone over their heads. Martel ran forward, using the stiffened side of his hand to chop down a man who made an attempt to stop him.

Then he was outside. Claire had rammed the pistol inside her handbag and he gripped her by the arm, hustling her across the concourse. Behind them they left a scene of confusion and shouted curses as frightened customers panicked and struggled to leave the place.

'U-Bahn!'

Martel shouted the words close to Claire's ear as he continued moving her fast among the crowds, elbowing people out of his way, forcing a swift passage towards the main exit and the escalator to the U-Bahn system.

'Tickets . . .' Claire reminded him.

'I bought a couple earlier when I was prowling round – to give us a line of retreat . . .'

Before entering the U-Bahn it is necessary to buy a ticket which you insert into an automatic punching machine and then descend the escalator. Still moving rapidly, still gripping her arm, he headed for the U-Bahn entrance, weaving in and out among the passengers.

He was careful now not to force his way through, to merge into the background. They had a short head-start; the U-Bahn must swallow them up before the Delta men inside the Hauptbahnhof arrived. They reached the machines, punched their tickets, went below and arrived on a platform as a train was pulling in.

As it moved out Martel was certain no one had followed them on to the train. He looked at Claire sitting beside him. She removed her dark glasses. Her forehead was glistening with beads of sweat – but other people in the coach sat in shirt-sleeves and mopped their own foreheads. She looked back at him uncertainly.

'We go straight to the Clausen,' he told her quietly. 'It's a small hotel in a side street. We can go back for our bags later – much later.'

'Was it all worth it?' she asked.

'You tell me. I know now why the Hauptbahnhofs are important.'

The Sunday Concorde flight from Washington departed 1305 hours local time and arrived at Heathrow at 2155 hours local time. The cab deposited Tweed at Park Crescent – where McNeil, forewarned by his call from Dulles – was waiting for him in his office. The clock on the wall registered thirty minutes before midnight.

'The news has just come over the telex.'

McNeil made no attempt to soften the shock she knew Tweed would receive. The one thing her chief detested was any kind of fuss.

'What news?' he enquired.

'Your old friend, Clint Loomis, has been murdered . . .'

She handed the telex to Tweed and sat down, her notebook at the ready. She doodled while she waited, carefully not looking at Tweed who sank into his swivel chair and eased his buttocks into the old cushion. He read the signal three times.

Ex-CIA agent Clint Loomis killed by unknown assassins this day . . . aboard power cruiser Oasis . . . attorney fishing witnessed second cruiser sail alongside . . . grenade attack killed Loomis and the guard dog . . . FBI investigating with full cooperation CIA . . .

'That damned helicopter,' Tweed muttered. 'He wouldn't take any notice . . .'

'I beg your pardon?' McNeil queried.

'Sorry, just thinking aloud.' His voice became crisper, he sat up erect in his chair as he pushed the telex strip back across his desk. 'Put that in the shredder. No one else is to see it. Any word from Martel?'

'He phoned me from Bavaria. He's coming in early tomorrow and I have booked the necessary hotel accommodation at Heathrow. He has given me the flight details so you can meet him there.'

Tweed swivelled in his chair and gazed at the blinds which were closed over the windows. They were as blank as his thoughts. He was very worried.

'Things are coming to a head,' McNeil suggested.

'And only two days to solve the insoluble. The Summit Express leaves the Gare de l'Est in exactly forty-eight hours' time.' He swivelled back to face her. 'You've been going through all the dossiers. No hope, I suppose . . .'

'There is something,' McNeil replied.

The call from Washington came through just before midnight and Manfred was asleep in his Münich apartment. He switched on the bedside light, slipped on his gloves and picked up the receiver. The identification procedure was concluded and the American-sounding voice gave its message briefly.

'Loomis' contract has been terminated. We decided not to renew it . . .'

'Thank you . . .'

Manfred replaced the receiver, got out of bed and began padding round the room. All was going well. Nothing could now stop Crocodile. The big killing would be carried out on schedule.

Chapter Twenty-One

Monday June 1

'We have the rest of today and part of Tuesday before the Summit Express leaves Paris for Vienna tomorrow night,' Tweed said.

'And in those few hours,' Martel commented, 'we have to identify the target out of the four western leaders. And we have to track down the security chief who is the rotten apple – again from four potential candidates . . .'

At the London Airport Hotel McNeil had reserved three bedrooms – all in different names. The accommodation would only be used for the short time while Tweed conferred with Martel, but this would not seem strange: it was common practice among international business executives.

They were ensconced in the middle room. Earlier Tweed had checked the rooms on either side to make sure they were empty. Martel was inserting a cigarette in his holder after his comment. He had arrived a short time ago on a flight from Münich. Once they had talked he would fly straight back to Germany.

'Any ideas?' Martel asked. 'Does the Loomis murder tell us anything?'

'It is pretty certain that after my signal was read out in Paris to the security conference by the British Ambassador one of the four security chiefs present reacted. He had me followed to London Airport when I boarded Concorde. There just wasn't sufficient time to kill Loomis *before* I talked to him . . .'

'What about Alain Flandres? His earlier history is pretty thin in the files. Then there's O'Meara – that absence from his West Berlin base for two months Loomis told you about. It could have been spent in East Berlin.'

'That is my reading of the situation . . .'

'Except that I have another candidate – Erich Stoller of BND. He spent two *years* under cover in what he called "The Zone".'

'I didn't know that,' replied Tweed. Intrigued, he leaned forward over the coffee table. 'You dug up this fact?'

'No, he volunteered it, implied you knew about it. He also knew I was interrogating him, but on the surface it hasn't affected his cooperation . . .'

'I didn't know, but Erich is clever,' Tweed leaned against the back of his chair and stared at the ceiling. 'He may be pre-empting the possibility we'd find out in his dossier. So we have two possibles – O'Meara and Stoller. And after we've finished here I'm flying to Paris to meet Alain. I want his version of his past.'

'And Howard?'

'The least likely.' Tweed took off his glasses and

rubbed his eyes. Martel noticed traces of fatigue. 'I don't like him,' he continued, 'but that's irrelevant. We're looking for a traitor who has practised his trade of treason for years . . .'

'So you're ignoring Howard?'

Without replying Tweed burrowed inside a briefcase he had propped against the side of his chair. Extracting the photocopy of a file he handed it to Martel. On the front was the security classification, file reference number and three words. *Frederick Anthony Howard*.

Martel began skip-reading as Tweed explained. 'We have McNeil to thank for that. How she got the original out of Central Registry and made that photocopy I'll never know. I think she has a duplicate key to the dossier cabinet . . .'

'Christ!' Martel looked up, stupefied at the thought of the risk McNeil was running. 'She's never told you that?'

'No,' Tweed said quietly. 'That is her way and I don't ask her questions. Have you come to it yet?'

'Come to what?'

'Page 12. Several years ago Howard spent a tour of duty with the Paris Embassy as Intelligence Officer. While he was there he took a spell of leave – six weeks. In *Vienna*.'

'Normal leave?'

'No, sick leave. He was on the edge of a nervous breakdown – "mental exhaustion" is the phrase used by the quack. The medical report is there. He was away January to February. Think of the Austrian climate. Damned funny place to go for sick leave . . .'

'If he knows Vienna that will help him protect the PM.'

'That's another odd note,' Tweed commented. 'He's never made a single mention of the fact as far as I know.'

Martel handed back the photocopy and sat puffing his cigarette. Tweed produced an envelope with four glossy prints. 'You wanted photographs of Flandres, O'Meara, Howard and Stoller . . .' Martel put the envelope in his pocket, stubbed out his cigarette and spoke with great vigour.

'Time is so short we have to put maximum pressure on all four security chiefs – in the hope that the unknown assassin makes a wrong move. We stir up the cauldron . . .'

'How?'

'By telling each of them on the quiet the part we left out. I can deal with Stoller – you'll have to pass the word on to Howard, Alain and O'Meara . . .'

'What word?'

'That the same unimpeachable source which told us one of the Western leaders is marked for assassination aboard the express also told you that the killer is among the four security chiefs.'

From an inside pocket Tweed extracted a card protected by a plastic folder and gave it to his companion.

Martel studied the card, which carried his photograph, as Tweed explained while he wandered restlessly round the room. So far he had not reacted to the audacious suggestion Martel had put forward.

'Keith, we shan't meet again before the Summit Express leaves the Gare de l'Est tomorrow night. That card enables you to board the train at any point en route. No one can stop you – not even Howard . . .'

Permission to board . . . every facility to be given to the bearer, Keith Martel . . . specific permission to carry any weapon . . .

Across his photograph was inscribed the neat and very legible signature of the Prime Minister. She had counter-signed the reference to weapons. Martel stared at Tweed.

'In God's name, how did you get this?'

'I approached her directly through the Minister. I spent half an hour with her. I told her one of the four security chiefs may be an assassin . . .'

'She must have loved that . . .'

'Took it very calmly,' Tweed replied. 'She even said she would feel perfectly safe in *our* hands. She went through your dossier while I was there. Incidentally, you brought a good passport picture of Claire Hofer with you? Good. Do you trust her?'

'With my life – I *have* done already. *Twice* . . .'

'Give me her photo.'

Tweed sat down at the table, produced a second card, a duplicate of Martel's but without the photo or signatures. Taking a tube of adhesive from his pocket, Tweed carefully affixed Claire's photo in position. He then extracted a pen Martel had not seen before and proceeded with great care and skill to forge the PM's signature twice. He looked at Martel over his glasses.

'I have her permission – and she loaned me her pen to do the job. Here is Miss Hofer's card. One thing I must remember to do above all else.'

'What's that?'

'Return the PM her pen. She'll give me hell if I forget. One thing more is exercising my mind – before we go. *Manfred . . .*'

'What his next move will be, you mean?'

'I know,' Tweed replied. 'I have duelled with him long-distance before and I should know by now how his mind works. Sit in his chair for a moment. He has been informed that we know one of the four western leaders is marked down for assassination. When we reveal to the security chiefs that one of them is the assassin he will react – he may already have put into action the next phase of his strategy . . .'

'Which is?'

'*Smokescreens*. To conceal the identity of the killer he will try to divert our suspicions to the wrong man. He will aim for the maximum confusion in our minds – simply put, so we don't know where the hell we are. And we have no time at all left to locate the guilty man.'

'You agree my idea, then,' Martel said and stood up, checking his watch.

'Yes. We tell the security chiefs one of them is a phoney. And then watch all hell break loose . . .'

Reinhard Dietrich was in a state of controlled fury as he drove the Mercedes 450 SEL from his apartment to the underground garage which Manfred had designated as the meeting place. On the phone it had almost been in the nature of a summons for Dietrich to come immediately – alone and with just sufficient time to get there.

Inside the deserted underground garage Manfred sat behind the wheel of his BMW hired under a fictitious name with false papers. He had deliberately arrived early and positioned himself so his car would face Dietrich's on arrival. He heard Dietrich coming, driving on the brake.

The garage was dimly lit and Manfred timed it perfectly. As the millionaire appeared driving towards him he turned on his light full power. The unexpected glare blinded the industrialist who threw up a hand to shield his eyes and cursed as he reduced speed and pulled up alongside the BMW. Manfred promptly turned off his lights, which further confused Dietrich's vision.

He saw a vague image of a man wearing a dark beret, the face turned towards him concealed behind large sun-goggles. Switching off his motor he lowered the window. Manfred was already talking as the window purred open.

'If you lose the election you go ahead with the *putsch* as planned. Your men in full uniform. You march on München – make it as much a replica of Hitler's 1923 march on München as you can.'

'Hitler didn't succeed,' Dietrich pointed out. 'He ended up in Landsberg Prison . . .'

'Where is the new weapons dump?' Manfred interjected. 'I see . . .' He paused. 'We are so close to zero hour you should use armed guards to protect the place this time. That is all . . .'

'*Wait!*'

Manfred had not even heard the plea. He was driving out of the garage, his red tail-lights disappearing round a corner. Dietrich swore again, took out a cigar and lit it. The arrangement was he should wait two minutes before he also left.

Arriving back at München Airport, Martel took a cab to the corner of a side street in the city. Waiting until the cab had gone, he walked the last four hundred yards to the Hotel Clausen where the Swiss girl was staying. He was relieved to find Claire safe in her room.

'I've been busy while you were away,' she announced. 'I spent a lot of time at the Hauptbahnhof . . .'

'That was foolhardy – you could have been spotted . . .'

'When will you learn I'm not stupid?' she flared

up. 'I change my clothes before each visit. A trouser suit in the morning, a skirt and blouse with dark glasses after lunch . . .'

'Sorry.' Martel dropped his brief-case on the bed and stretched his arms. 'I'm tensed up. The Summit Express leaves Paris tomorrow night and we're no nearer knowing who the target is, let alone the assassin . . .'

'The dossiers that woman in London is checking? She has found nothing?'

'It could be Flandres, Howard, O'Meara – even Erich Stoller. Any one of them. But she's persisting. The Hauptbahnhof . . .'

'You never told me what *you* had noticed after we ran for it,' she reminded him.

'Your impressions first.'

He slipped off his shoes, lay on the bed and propped his back on the bedboard. While she talked he smoked and watched her, thinking how fresh and appetising she looked. He felt a limp, sweaty, mess: the humidity in München was growing worse.

'The Hauptbahnhof here,' she began, 'and probably in Zürich – for the same reasons – is the *mobile* headquarters of Delta. Which explains why Stoller has never managed to locate their main base. The *schloss* Dietrich has in the country is a blind . . .'

'Go on.'

'It makes an ideal headquarters because of all the facilities. It is always crowded. So a meeting between two men – or several – is unlikely to be noticed. Couriers come in on trains, deliver their messages – and depart on other trains. They never actually go into München! How am I doing?'

'Promising. Do go on.'

'You observed one of those meetings – the man off the Zürich Express. Plenty of meeting-places – far less risky than any so-called safe houses which might be located and watched. The cafeteria, the cinema, and so on. They even have fool-proof communications which can be used with the certainty no call will ever be intercepted. The payphones.'

'I think you've got it,' Martel agreed. 'But suppose they are spotted?'

'Look at the number of exits available. They can even rush on to a train just leaving. Remember how we escaped – by diving down into the U-Bahn . . .'

'That's what I think Warner worked out – all you've been saying. And it explains his reference to the Hauptbahnhofs in his little notebook.'

'I did observe one thing which worried me,' Claire went on. 'I saw men coming in on different trains, tough-looking customers who all made for the self-locking luggage containers. They had *keys to the lockers* and collected large, floppy bags – the kind you use to conceal automatic weapons. Then they walked out into the city . . .'

Martel whipped his legs off the bed and frowned in concentration. 'You mean Dietrich is sending in an élite force – probably placing them in hotels close to strategic targets like the TV station, the central telephone exchange – all the key centres of control?'

'That was my guess . . .'

'We should contact Stoller,' Martel was pacing the room. 'The trouble is we don't know whether the assassin we're trying to pinpoint is Stoller. If he is, he'll thank us – and do nothing.'

'Can't we do one damned thing?' Claire protested.

'We can try . . .'

'Alain,' Tweed said quietly, 'we know one of the four passengers aboard the Summit Express leaving for Vienna tomorrow night is the target for an assassin . . .'

'We must certainly assume that, my friend,' Flandres replied.

They were eating dinner in a small restaurant at the end of a court off rue St Honoré. *Le patron* had escorted them to a table in a secluded corner where they were able to converse without being overheard. It was an exclusive place and the food was excellent. Alain was in the most exuberant of moods.

'What I am going to tell you is completely confidential – just between the two of us – and because we have known each other all these years. How long is it?' Tweed ruminated.

'Since 1953 when I left the Army – I was Military Intelligence, you recall? I then joined the Direction de la Surveillance du Territoire. An orphan, I have spent all my adult life engaged in the traffic of secrets. A strange pastime.' Flandres sipped at his wine glass. 'I do not like your Frederick Anthony Howard,' he said suddenly. 'He is not sympathetic – like a man who fears to say much in case he reveals more than he wishes to . . .'

'I find that impression interesting, Alain.' Tweed spoke in all sincerity: he greatly respected the Frenchman's acumen. 'And you chose Military Intelligence when you joined the Army?'

Flandres laughed, a vibrant laugh. 'My God, no! My whole life has been a series of absurd accidents. Military Intelligence chose me! Can you imagine it? Two weeks after I put on uniform I am commissioned overnight – and all because of two accidents! My predecessor got drunk, fell out of a window and broke his neck! And my second language was German – because I had been born in Alsace. So I am attached to General Dumas' staff as Intelligence officer since at that moment he was advancing through Bavaria. Absurd!'

'And later you were demobilised . . .'

'That is so. I return to Paris. My only trump card is a commendation from Gen. Dumas. I show this to the DST and to my utter astonishment they take me on. Even the commendation is an accident. Dumas mixed up the documents! He intended it for a quite different officer! It is a mad world. Now, what were you going to tell me? Something amusing, I hope?'

'Anything but amusing, I fear . . .'

Tweed looked round the small restaurant, shook his head as *le patron* caught his eye and moved towards them. He was not happy about what he had to say – and he was enjoying a pleasant evening with his old friend.

'This is a message from a dead man – I prefer not to identify him. I believe he told the truth but I cannot prove it. He reported that the assassin who will kill one of the western leaders aboard the Summit Express is – one of the four security chiefs charged with their protection.'

'That is a really terrifying prospect,' Flandres replied slowly. He sipped more wine, his dark eyes pensive 'Is there any clue as to which of the four is the guilty man?'

'None whatsoever . . .'

'It could even be me? That is what you are thinking?'

'I have an open mind on the subject – some people might say my mind is blank . . .'

'That is something I cannot believe. You will have ideas. You will have investigated. How long have you known this?'

Flandres was in one of his rare solemn moods. But his surface temperament had always been mercurial. Only those who knew him well realised he was possibly the most astute security chief in the West.

'For the last few days,' Tweed replied. 'I have told

no one else – not even Howard. Officially I'm not concerned with this Summit Conference . . .'

'And unofficially?'

'I root around,' Tweed replied vaguely.

'In Europe? In America?'

'In my mind. I do have a prime suspect. There was, shall we say, an incident? It could point in one direction only. It needs further checking. As regards the Summit Express, let no one board that train without impeccable credentials,' Tweed warned.

'I shall lose a little sleep,' Flandres assured him. 'I am not entirely happy that the train leaves the Gare de l'Est at 11.35 at night and that it will still be dark when it crosses the frontier into Germany.'

'I understand it is the normal train with a section of coaches sealed off from the rest of the express for our illustrious passengers? Plus their own restaurant . . .'

'That is so. Which means there are six stops before the express reaches München. There Chancellor Langer boards the train . . .'

Flandres threw up both hands in a gesture of frustration. 'All because my own President will not get into a plane – so the others agree, seeing it as a chance to confer during the journey so they present a united front to the Soviet leadership in Vienna.'

'Well, you can't alter that, so let's talk about something more congenial . . .'

For the rest of the meal Flandres was his normal

ebullient self, a tribute to his exceptional self-control. But Tweed thought he could see in the Frenchman's eyes an unspoken question. Who was the Englishman's prime suspect?

The caller gave the code-name Franz to the operator at Stoller's Pullach headquarters and said he would ring off in twenty seconds if he was not put through without delay. It was late on Monday evening but the BND chief was waiting hopefully in his office.

'Erich Stoller here . . .'

'Franz speaking again. I have more information for you – the location of the largest arms dump yet. This time it will be protected by Delta men . . .'

'Let me get a notepad, I'll only be a moment . . .'

'*Stop!* I know that trick! Make your notes afterwards. Wait until the dump has been built up – organise your raid for tomorrow, the day before the election. The location of the dump is . . .'

Having provided Stoller with the information Reinhard Dietrich had given him earlier in the underground garage, Manfred replaced the receiver.

Chapter Twenty-Two

Tuesday June 2

FREISTAAT BAYERN!
TOFLER! TOFLER!! TOFLER!!!
FREE STATE OF BAVARIA! TOFLER . . .

The banners and posters had appeared overnight and were everywhere. Small planes flew over the cities cascading thousands of leaflets bearing the same message. Two days before the election Bavaria seethed in a turmoil.

There were marches by Delta men wearing peaked caps, brown shirts and trousers tucked into jackboots. They sported armbands carrying the Delta symbol.

There were counter-marches by Tofler's supporters waving banners and dressed in civilian clothes – each cavalcade preceded by small groups of teen-age girls carrying flowers – which made it tricky for the police to intervene for fear of hurting the girls.

Münich was like a cauldron with motorists shrieking their horns as planes above fluttered leaflets like confetti. Standing by a window in the office reserved for him at police headquarters Erich Stoller's expression was grim as he spoke to Martel who stood beside him.

'It's getting out of control. And the news tomorrow that we've seized the biggest Delta arms dump yet isn't going to help . . .'

'Your informant again?' enquired Claire who stood behind the two men. 'There has to be an informant for you to have traced so many weapon caches recently . . .'

'Yes, Franz phoned me again . . .'

'*Franz?*'

'The code-name for my informant.' Stoller made a gesture of impotence. 'I really have no idea who he is – but every time we react to his brief messages we find a fresh dump . . .'

'The timing is interesting,' Martel commented. 'This business of the arms dumps has been rising to a crescendo – and the climax, oddly enough – will coincide with the Summit Express crossing the Bavarian sector. There is, incidentally, an item of news I should pass on to you. Just before Werner Hagen caused his own death at the water-mill he made an alarming statement.'

'What was that?' Stoller asked quietly as he went to the table and poured more coffee.

'He alleged – and both Claire and I believed him – that . . .' He swung round and stared at the German as he completed his sentence. '. . . the assassin who will kill one of the western leaders aboard the train is one of the four security chiefs assigned to protect those leaders . . .'

A hush descended on the large room. Claire remained quite still, sensing the rise in tension. Stoller paused in the act of pouring coffee. Four sparrows settled on the window-ledge outside, which struck Claire as very strange. *Four.* There were four security men involved.

'Did – you – say – Hagen?' asked Stoller, spacing his words.

'Yes.'

'He said that just before he died?'

'Yes.'

'Which means you withheld this information for three days?'

'Yes.'

The two men faced each other like fierce dogs squaring up for battle. Stoller had gone very pale, his long arms close to his body. Martel watched the German as he lit a fresh cigarette. He asked the question casually.

'What was it like – your two years under cover in what you still call The Zone? That length of time must be something of a record – to survive undetected . . .'

'And what does that mean?' Stoller asked very quietly.

'Simply that my main job is to identify the rotten apple in the barrel – O'Meara, Flandres, Howard – or yourself. And the train is leaving Paris tonight. You're going to find the atmosphere aboard rather electric. Think of it, Erich, all four of you looking over your shoulders . . .'

'Why take Hagen's word?'

'Because my job is to tell when a man is lying – and I believe Hagen was telling the truth.'

'Would you think me rude if I asked you to leave? And at least you won't be on board the train . . .'

'Why the hell did you do that to Stoller? God knows he's helped us,' Claire raged.

They had returned to the Hotel Clausen and Martel was sitting on her bed while she stormed round the room. The Swiss girl was in a furious temper. She sat down in front of the dressing-table and began brushing her hair vigorously.

'We're letting them all know at the last moment. It's the plan Tweed and I cooked up when I met him at London Airport. It will throw the killer off balance, may cause him to make a slip . . .'

'They'll *all* know? Is that a good idea?'

'They'll be watching each other.'

'As you said, the atmosphere will be diabolical. One thing's for sure – you've made an enemy of Stoller . . .'

'Only if he's guilty . . .'

She swung round on her stool and glared. 'For

God's sake remember what you said to him. We can't go near him again.'

'You think we're marooned?'

'Aren't we?' she challenged.

They were waiting for Tweed in his office after his return flight from Paris. Seated behind her desk, McNeil half-closed her eyes to warn her boss. Big Trouble.

'This is Tim O'Meara,' Howard began very stiffly, introducing the large American who remained by the window to avoid shaking hands with Tweed. 'Someone took this photograph while you were on board Clint Loomis' power cruiser on the Potomac . . .'

Tweed took the glossy print and examined it carefully. It was a blow-up which had been produced with great skill, doubtless in the CIA laboratories at Langley. The print provided a clear reproduction of Tweed who was squinting as though gazing into the sun.

'Well?' Howard demanded.

'How did you come by this photo? It is important that I know.'

Previously Tweed had given O'Meara one brief glance on entering his office. The question was now addressed to him. Howard went purple at Tweed's reaction.

'By God, you're going to regret this . . .'

'No,' Tweed corrected him briskly, '*you* are going to regret this if my question is not answered. I happened to notice when the photo was being taken.' He looked direct at O'Meara again. 'I need to know how you obtained this picture . . .'

'Delivered by messenger to Langley,' O'Meara said brusquely. 'I gather the messenger was held at the gate – normal procedure. He said he had been called by phone, told to go to the reception desk of a Washington hotel where an envelope would be waiting with my name on it. Another envelope contained the delivery fee and a fat tip.'

'You believe this?'

'We checked out his story, for Christ's sake,' the American snapped. 'Who took the picture we haven't a snowflake in hell's idea. It was obviously taken with . . .'

'A telephoto lens – then your technicians produced this remarkable blow-up. There was a message with the print and negative?'

'Yes,' said O'Meara, unconsciously confirming Tweed's query as to whether both print and negative had been delivered. 'It said that I might like to know an Englishman called Tweed had been aboard the Oasis before the unfortunate aftermath. All this stuff was flown to me top priority by Langley.'

'Manfred,' Tweed murmured.

'What was that?' Howard pounced.

'*Manfred!* He arranged it – the taking of the picture after he had had Loomis and myself followed from

Dulles. He's playing his usual tactic – sowing confusion prior to launching Crocodile . . .

Tweed then proceeded to play his own diversionary tactic before Howard could interrogate him about the Washington trip. Unlocking a desk drawer he lifted out three articles and placed them neatly on his desk top. A .38 Smith & Wesson Special. A black beret. A pair of large tinted sun-goggles. He added to the collection a dark blue windcheater.

'The interesting question,' Tweed remarked, 'is who was in London last Friday morning when Manfred-Carlos was in Piccadilly?'

'We were in Paris for the security meeting. I caught the noon plane,' said O'Meara.

'I was on the 10 a.m. flight . . .'

Like the American, Howard answered quickly, then stopped in mid-sentence. In a matter of seconds Tweed had reversed the roles, had become the inquisitor instead of the accused. He followed up his advantage before Howard could explode.

'That doesn't exonerate either of you. The wearer of these garments, the owner of the gun was seen by a policeman in Piccadilly at nine o'clock in the morning. As you know, shortly afterwards this little collection was found on a chair in the man's shop, Austin Reed. My question really is *who* did this mysterious man who vanished so quickly come to London to meet . . .'

He broke off as the door opened and Howard's deputy, Mason, came into the room. He was closing the door when Tweed spoke abruptly.

'Not now, Mason. And next time, knock first. It is customary.'

'But I was invited to attend . . .'

'You are now invited to leave immediately.'

Mason stared at Howard who looked away towards the window. He wet his lips as though about to say more when he caught Tweed's gaze. It was bleak and intimidating and Mason suddenly realised no one was coming to his aid. With a mumbled apology he left the room.

'Did you invite him?' Tweed asked Howard sharply.

'Not really . . .' Howard seemed as relieved as anyone to see the back of Mason at this juncture. 'He is, of course, my deputy . . .'

'Who has yet to work his passage,' Tweed replied caustically. 'Returning to the subject of this strange incident in Piccadilly, Special Branch – at my request – handed these items to their Forensic boffins for urgent analysis. No manufacturer's labels, of course. The beret is from Guyana, the windcheater and goggles from Venezuela next door. Origin of the gun untraceable. Does their report suggest anything?'

'South America,' O'Meara said grimly. 'Carlos again?'

'Except that it is rather obvious,' Tweed pointed out. 'And we are getting too many obvious signals. I'm looking for something not obvious . . .'

'What the devil do you mean?' demanded Howard who had recovered his normal balance. 'And what has this to do with our over-riding concern – the Summit Express?'

'It's a question of timing.' Tweed was still addressing O'Meara. 'You should read a little more history. In the early part of 1919, when Germany was falling apart, a Soviet republic was established in Bavaria – so there is a precedent for Operation Crocodile. Luckily the so-called people's government was destroyed by the remnants of the German Army and the Freikorps. Look at the map . . .'

Tweed opened *The Times* atlas and showed them Lake Konstanz and how its shape was like that of a crocodile with its jaws agape.

'That is the significance of Crocodile – it denotes the locale of the conspiracy. Bavaria is their immediate target. The plan is to set up a neutral government under this creature, Tofler – who has Communist links. Bavaria has a narrow section of the Konstanz shore – and reports had reached me that a secret factory in Czechoslovakia is building motor torpedo-boats . . .'

'But Czechoslovakia has no coastline,' the American protested.

'So when Tofler takes over, the torpedo-boats are sent by road aboard giant trailers and launched into Lake Konstanz. Only a few would be needed to dominate the Rhine delta – even to help a campaign later to seize the Vorarlberg province from Austria . . .'

'I find this sinister,' O'Meara muttered.

'A typically audacious Manfred plan,' Tweed assured him. 'To detach Bavaria from the rest of the Federal Republic and then one-third of the land mass of Western Germany is severed from the main bulwark against Soviet Russia. The stakes in Crocodile are enormous . . .'

'You could be dramatising the situation,' O'Meara suggested.

'No, he isn't,' Howard agreed, to Tweed's surprise. 'If by some twist of political events Bavaria were detached from the Federal Republic the Soviets have conquered Western Europe. It is a scenario we have feared for years – not that I dreamt Bavaria would be the key the Kremlin would turn to unlock Western Europe . . .'

'This crap about a Soviet Republic in 1919 . . .' O'Meara broke in aggressively.

'Is history,' Howard confirmed. 'It existed for a short time. Now I want to know the source of your information,' he told Tweed firmly.

'Werner Hagen, the recently deceased nephew of Reinhard Dietrich. What neither of you know,' he continued poker-faced, 'is that he also revealed that the assassin is one of the four security chiefs attached to the train . . .'

Howard recovered from the shock first. His expression froze and he walked round the side of the desk to stare down at Tweed. His tone was clipped.

'For this I will have you thrown out of the Service.'

'If I'm wrong, you might manage it,' Tweed agreed. 'But if I am right you will have questions to answer at the highest level . . .'

'The guy's crazy!' O'Meara burst out. 'First he gets involved in the Clint Loomis killing. Now he comes across with this lunatic accusation . . .'

'Alain Flandres is taking it very seriously,' Tweed observed. 'I met him in Paris only yesterday . . .'

'You did what!'

Howard was almost apoplectic. He thrust both hands inside his jacket pockets to regain control. Tweed gazed back at Howard over the rims of his glasses as his chief spoke with great deliberation.

'You have no authority to involve yourself in any way in the security of the Summit Express. You have grossly exceeded your brief and will be held answerable for this dereliction of duty . . .'

'Washington will hear of this, buddy,' snapped O'Meara. 'They will be interested to hear a senior British agent has made this accusation about their security chief . . .'

'I said one of the four security chiefs,' Tweed reminded him.

'There are precedents. Remember Chancellor Willy Brandt's closest aide, Guenter Guillaume, turned out to be a Soviet plant – which destroyed Brandt. Now I believe they have planted someone else.' He looked at Howard. The assassin could have been recruited many years ago. I rather think he was. You had better be extremely careful from the moment you board that train tonight . . .'

Chapter Twenty-Three

Tuesday June 2

Name: Alain Dominique Flandres. **Nationality:**
French. **Date of birth:** January 18 1928. **Place of
birth:** Strasbourg

Tweed, alone again in his office with McNeil, studied
the file she had handed him. Alain's personal description followed – his height, weight, colour of eyes,
colour of hair. It matched the file's subject. He settled
himself more comfortably in his chair to peruse the
life history.

Career record: Escaped to England, April 1944.
Commissioned as lieutenant in Free French Forces.
Appointed to Military Intelligence due to fluency
in German. At war's end transferred to staff of
Gen. Dumas for French occupation of Vorarlberg
and the Tyrol. Demobilised and returned to
France, May 1953. Immediately joined Direction de
la Surveillance du Territoire. Transferred to Secret
Service in charge of special unit guarding
President, July 1980.

Tweed finished reading the file and drank more tea
while he ran over the details again. 'What about his
marital status?' he asked.

McNeil replied from memory. 'He married Lucille
Durand, daughter of a textile manufacturer from Lille
in . . .'

'That's enough,' Tweed interjected. 'What about
the dirt?' he enquired with an expression of distaste.
'The yellow sheet – an appropriate colour for the
things we record about people's lives. But sometimes
that's where the clue lies . . .'

'Seven different mistresses so far . . .' McNeil was
consulting a yellow flimsy. 'You want the erotic
details?'

'No. Were all his women French?'

'The names look French to me. Who next?'

'O'Meara,' Tweed hunched forward in the chair,
his eyes screwed up in concentration. 'This file will be
meagre, I presume?'

'Here it is.' She handed him a slim dossier. 'And,
as you say, meagre . . .'

Name: Timothy Patrick O'Meara. **Nationality:**
American. **Date of birth:** August 3 1930. **Place of
birth:** New York City.

Career record: Served with Cryptoanalysis Section,
CIA, Langley, 1960–1965. Assigned other duties,
1965–1972. Served with West Berlin station under
Controller, Clint Loomis, 1972–1974. A two-man

unit; other member (junior) Lou Carson. While in
Berlin had affair with 18-year-old German girl,
Klara Beck. On return to US promoted to Assistant
Director of Operations, Langley. Transferred to
Secret Service on . . .

Tweed stopped reading. 'He's married?' he enquired.

'Yes.' McNeil produced another yellow flimsy. 'He
did rather well. Nancy Margaret Chase, educated
Vassar and all that implies. Daughter of a powerful
Philadelphia banker. What they call "the quiet money".'

'His first and only wife?'

'Yes. The yellow sheet hints his father-in-law's
connections with the White House helped his rapid
rise. O'Meara carries lots of clout. His next move may
be to stand for the Senate . . .'

'The yellow sheet says that?'

'No, McNeil says that. And you still haven't
explained why you lit fires under Howard and
O'Meara this morning . . .'

'Just trying to arrange the key pieces on the board
prior to the opening moves in the game. Again, I'm
fighting Manfred long-distance – and already the
bastard is breathing down my neck.'

'And your rogue piece – Martel? I wonder what
he's up to?'

'I'm going to pay a call on Reinhard Dietrich at his
schloss,' Martel informed Stoller, who greeted him

with apologies on his return to police headquarters in Münich.

'You are completely mad,' the German protested.

'There's something very peculiar going on,' Martel continued. 'I suspect that – unknown to Dietrich – Erwin Vinz is operating a secret cell inside Delta, a cell controlled directly by the East Germans, which means ultimately by the Soviets. Dietrich is being manipulated, conned – and I think I can raise doubts in his mind. That could upset the whole Crocodile apple cart at the last moment – and with the Summit Express leaving Paris tonight *this* is the last moment . . .'

The tall German wandered over to the window with an expressionless face. 'What makes you come up with this bizarre theory – what is it based on?'

'Four attempts on my life so far, for God's sake. In Zürich, two in St Gallen and one off Lindau. In every damned instance the killers wore Delta symbols – the worst type of publicity for Dietrich's movement. They even *left* a badge under Warner's dead body – because that didn't get there by accident.'

'How are you going to handle it?' Stoller enquired.

'I have phoned Dietrich who apparently had just returned to the *schloss*. I'm going as a foreign correspondent. Dietrich wallows in publicity . . .'

'And what paper are you pretending to represent?'

'*The Times* of London. I always carry credentials confirming my status as a reporter. I have one for *Die Welt* . . .'

'In your own name?'

'No, as Philip Johnson – who exists . . .'

He broke off as the phone rang. Stoller answered it, listened for a moment, spoke a few words and handed the receiver to the Englishman. 'It's for you – from London . . .'

At the other end of the line Tweed chose his words carefully. It was quite possible the call was being secretly recorded for Stoller to play back to himself later.

'Keith, a courier – carrying diplomatic immunity – is bringing you certain records for you to peruse in the hope that something will point the finger. The courier is my assistant. She will be arriving aboard an evening flight at München Airport. Have someone meet her. The flight details are . . .'

'Thank you,' Martel said. 'And goodbye . . .'

'I still think you are mad,' Stoller repeated as Martel replaced the receiver. 'You could get yourself killed visiting Dietrich at that *schloss*.'

The Englishman glanced at Claire who had remained silent during their conversation. 'At least you can't say I don't inform you of my movements on your patch, Erich. I'm driving down to Dietrich's place at once.'

'Don't delay . . .' Stoller paused. 'Late tonight I have to fly to Bonn . . .'

'I didn't understand what went on in Stoller's office,' Claire said later when they were leaving the outskirts of Münich with Martel behind the wheel of his hired Audi. 'I had a feeling that signals were being exchanged . . .'

'He was just showing he was sorry for his earlier outburst. And Tweed is sending in a courier with the dossiers on the evening flight to Münich. We're clutching at every last straw we can lay our hands on.'

'Why tell Stoller about your suspicions about Vinz and his secret cell? If it is Stoller who is guilty . . .'

'Then his reaction – or lack of it – will tell me something. Incidentally, Reinhard was most cordial when Philip Johnson of *The Times* phoned. He's looking forward to seeing me.'

'That's what worries me,' Claire replied.

'You say this British reporter who calls himself Philip Johnson has an appointment at the *schloss*? At what time? Dietrich, why did you agree to see this man?'

In the Münich apartment Manfred's gloved hand held the receiver tightly as he waited for the reply. It was pure chance that he had called the *schloss*, that the millionaire had then volunteered this information.

'Because I am convinced he is Martel, the man responsible for the murder of my nephew . . .'

'Why?'

'Because I checked immediately with *The Times* in London.' A note of exasperation had crept into Dietrich's voice. Manfred questioned every decision he took. 'They confirmed they have no correspondent of that name based in Bavaria . . .'

'No correspondent of that name on their staff?'

'I didn't say that!' Dietrich rapped back. 'They do have a man with that name on their staff, he is a foreign correspondent – but at the moment he is in Paris. This man who called himself Johnson is driving here this afternoon by the direct route from Münich in a blue Audi. Any more data you require?'

'Be very careful what you say . . .'

Once beyond the outskirts of Münich Manfred drove his BMW like a maniac. The sniperscope rifle was concealed inside a zipped-up golf-bag on the seat beside him. His features were concealed behind an outsize pair of dark-tinted glasses. His hair was hidden by a soft hat pulled well down over his forehead.

He braked about half a mile from the main entrance to the Dietrich estate. His phenomenal memory had not let him down. Yes, the gate in the wall was there. And beyond it stood a ramshackle farm-cart abandoned long ago and which he remembered from his secret meeting with Erwin Vinz by the roadside.

The geography, also, was right for his purpose. Beyond the gate a field rose up steeply to a ridge surmounted by an outcrop of rock. An excellent firing-point. Getting out of the BMW, he opened the gate, lifted the shafts of the cart and heaved to get it moving.

Manfred possessed extraordinary physical strength. He had once broken the neck of a man weighing twenty stone. He hauled the cart into the road where he positioned it carefully. He could have blocked the road completely – but this would have been bad psychology.

If you are quick-witted, confronted by a barrier you turn your car swiftly on the grass verge and drive like hell back the way you have come. So he used the cart to block the road partially – to force an oncoming vehicle to *slow to a crawl* and negotiate the obstacle.

It also provided against the contingency that the wrong car could arrive first and the occupants might get out and shift the cart. As the cart was positioned they would simply drive slowly round it. He next hid the BMW inside the field behind a clump of trees, not forgetting to close the gate. His target would notice little details like that.

Five minutes later, confident from what Dietrich had told him on the phone that he had arrived first, Manfred settled himself in place behind the rocky outcrop and peered through the gun's 'scope. In the crosshairs the road came up so he felt he could reach out to touch it. Then he heard the sound of an approaching car. Martel's blue Audi came into sight.

*

'I still don't like this idea of visiting Dietrich,' Claire said as she sat beside Martel in the Audi. 'But, oh, this must be one of the most beautiful places in the world.'

According to the map Martel had studied earlier they were within two miles of the main entrance to the *schloss*. All around them the sweeping uplands of Bavaria were green in the blazing sun. At the summit of limestone ridges which reared up like precipices clumps of fir trees huddled. They had not passed another vehicle for some time.

'*You* are not going to visit Dietrich,' Martel told her. 'Before we get there I'm leaving you with the car while I walk the rest of the way. If I haven't reappeared in one hour you drive like hell to München and report to Stoller . . .'

'I'm not frightened. I'm coming with you . . .'

'Which means if I run into trouble there's no one available to fetch help . . .'

'*Damn you, Keith Martel!* That's blackmail . . .'

'That's right. Now what, I wonder, is this?'

'It's a farm-cart someone has left in the road. You can drive round it along the verge.'

Martel was driving at fifty miles an hour when he first spotted the obstacle. He began to reduce speed, agreeing with Claire that to get past the obstruction he would have to edge his way round it along the grass verge. He looked in his rear-view mirror, expecting to see one or more cars coming up behind him. The mirror showed an endless stretch of deserted road.

He looked to his right and saw a vast field running away to the foot of an upland. He looked to his left and saw ahead, close to the farm-cart, a closed gate. Beyond the gate the land rose steeply, ending in a rocky escarpment which loomed over the road. He scanned the escarpment, reducing his speed further so that he would be moving at less than ten miles an hour as he nosed his way round the ancient cart.

The escarpment was deserted. Claire followed his gaze, shading her eyes against the glare of the sun. The escarpment had a serrated edge like a huge knife with large notches. In one of the notches she saw movement. She pressed her back hard against the seat as she shouted.

'There's someone up there . . .!'

In the crosshairs of Manfred's 'scope the windscreen of the blue Audi was huge. The sun was in an ideal position – shining from behind his shoulder. He took the first pressure on the trigger. The Englishman's features were clear – even the cigarette-holder at a jaunty angle. The girl beside him wore dark glasses, making identification impossible. It didn't matter. The car was crawling . . .

'Hold on tight!'

Martel yelled the warning as he did the opposite to what instinct dictated – to reverse and turn on the verge. He rammed his foot through the floor. The Audi surged forward. The farm-cart rushed towards them. Claire blenched. The accident would be appalling. There was a sound of shattering glass.

Martel heard the whine of the high-powered bullet wing past the back of his neck. He kept his foot down, skidded as he swerved round the cart, regained control, drove off the verge and down the clear stretch beyond the cart.

Missed! On the ridge Manfred was stupefied. It was unprecedented. Following his normal cautious policy – which had enabled him to survive so long – he left the area immediately and drove back to München.

Chapter Twenty-Four

Tuesday June 2

Name: Frederick Anthony Howard. **Nationality:**
British. **Date of birth:** October 12 1933. **Place of
birth:** Chelsea, London.

Career record: Joined Foreign Office, June 1958 . . .
Appointed to Intelligence Section, May 1962 . . .
Transferred to Paris Embassy, May 1974 as
Intelligence Officer . . . Owing to pressure of work
took six weeks' special leave, January 1978 . . .
Appointed head of SIS, May 1980.

Studying the dossiers once again with McNeil in his
Maida Vale flat, Tweed skip read Howard's details. In
any case he knew them from memory. He handed the
dossier back.

'Anything?' she asked.

'I don't know. I'm intrigued by that special sick
leave he took while in Paris and which he spent in
Vienna. Intrigued because he has never mentioned the
fact . . .'

'You'd have expected him to?'

'I'm not sure.' Tweed took off his glasses and chewed on the end of one of the frame supports. 'Despite his apparent extrovert personality if you listen to him carefully he is highly vocal but says little.'

'A natural diplomat?'

'Now you're being cynical,' Tweed admonished. 'But the Vienna incident reminds me of someone . . .'

'Who?'

'Kim Philby.' Tweed replaced his glasses. 'It was in Vienna that Philby was first contaminated by the plague – by a woman. So that leaves only Erich Stoller, thank God – I'm beginning to see double. Drag out his file and we'll see what we have there . . .'

At the entrance to Reinhard Dietrich's *schloss* the noise was ear-splitting, the source of the noise terrifying. A pack of German shepherd dogs snarled and leapt towards Martel, restrained only by the leashes held by the guards. The Englishman immediately recognised Erwin Vinz. The German walked forward and stopped close to the visitor.

'Yes?' he enquired, his slate-grey eyes studying Martel.

'Philip Johnson of *The Times*. Mr Dietrich expects me . . .'

'Why do you arrive on foot?' Vinz demanded.

'Because my bloody car broke down a couple of miles back. You think I'd walk all the way from

Münich? And I'm late for my interview – so could we stop wasting time?'

'Credentials?'

Vinz extended a hand and took the press card Martel handed him. Somewhere high in the warmth of the azure sky there was the distant murmur of a helicopter. It reminded Martel of the humming of a bee. Vinz returned the card.

'We will drive to the *schloss* . . .'

He led the way to the large wrought-iron gates which were opened and then closed behind them with the dogs and their handlers on the inside. The guards were dressed in civilian clothes and wore Delta symbols in their lapels.

Vinz climbed in behind the wheel of a Land-Rover-type vehicle and gestured for Martel to occupy the front passenger seat. When they were moving Martel glanced back and saw the rear seats were occupied by two burly guards.

He lit a cigarette and made a display of checking his watch. As he did so he looked surreptitiously into the blue vault of the sky over Bavaria. The tiny shape of a helicopter was receding into a speck.

It was a good five minutes' drive through parkland dotted with a variety of trees before they turned a corner in the curving drive and the *schloss* appeared. It was not reassuring – a grey-stone walled edifice like a small fortress complete with moat, drawbridge and raised portcullis gate in the arched entrance.

Vinz slowed down as they bumped over the

wooden drawbridge, crossing the wide moat of green water. They passed under the archway and the main building came into view, enclosing a cobbled court-yard. At the top of a flight of steps a man and a woman waited to greet their visitor.

Reinhard Dietrich wore his favourite country garb, riding clothes and breeches tucked into gleaming boots. In his right hand he held a cigar. His ice-cold eyes stared at Martel as he dismounted from the vehicle, but it was the woman who gave the English-man a shock.

Dark-haired and sleek, she was dressed in a trouser suit with her jacket open exposing her full figure. There was a half-smile on the finely chiselled face, a smile with a hint of triumph. Klara Beck was obviously pleased to see their guest.

They led him inside the open doors of the *schloss* into a vast hall with a highly polished floor scattered with priceless Persian rugs. Vinz and his two henchmen had produced Luger pistols and escorted him across the hall into a large library overlooking the moat.

Martel was faintly amused at this display of weaponry – somehow it symbolised the poor imitation of Hitler's bodyguard Dietrich was aping – and the reaction helped to quell the cold fear growing at the pit of his stomach. He had not anticipated Klara Beck.

'Stay with us, Vinz – just to ensure our guest preserves his manners.' Dietrich gestured with the cigar he had lit. 'The other two can go dig the garden...'

Wary of Vinz's Luger, Martel took out his pack slowly, inserted a cigarette in his holder and lit it. He sat down in a leather, button-backed chair in front of a huge Empire desk. An ash-tray of Steuben crystal was filled with cigar butts.

'You may sit down, Martel,' Dietrich said sarcastically. 'We can dispense with the charade of Philip Johnson, I suggest...'

'We all seem to be making ourselves at home...'

Martel gestured to Klara Beck who had perched herself on the arm of his chair. She crossed her legs and even the trousers could not disguise their excellent shape. Taking off her jacket, she revealed more of her superb breasts. Dietrich glared at her, went behind his desk and sank heavily into his chair, his voice harsh when he addressed his visitor.

'What suicidal motive drove you to come here? And don't tell me that if you're not away from the *schloss* in half an hour Stoller and his minions will rush to the rescue. I read the papers. The BND commissar is flying to Bonn – doubtless to escape the humiliation of witnessing my victory at the polls...'

'Your *defeat*...'

Martel was watching Beck as he spoke and caught the flicker of surprise in her dark eyes. *Surprise* – not alarm or disbelief. Dietrich exploded.

'You bloody amateur! What do you know of politics

in Germany? I hope you don't imagine you will leave this place alive? Where is the witness to prove you were ever inside the grounds, let alone the *schloss*? Why the hell did you come here . . .'

'To tell you that you are being conned, Dietrich,' Martel replied harshly. He ground out his half-smoked cigarette in the ash-tray and lit another. 'You have been manipulated. Right from the start you've been a pawn in a game you were never equipped to play . . .'

The atmosphere in the library had changed. Martel could sense the change and, resting against the back of his chair, he was watching everyone in the room under the guise of an attitude of nonchalance. He could *feel* Beck's nervous reaction, the tensing of her muscles which subtly shifted the chair leather.

Vinz reacted differently. He tried to freeze his emotions but he shifted nervously from one foot to the other. Dietrich, who was no fool, noticed the movement. He frowned but concentrated his ire on Martel.

'Bloody hell! What are you talking about . . .'

'I'm talking about your betrayal,' Martel continued in the same even tone. 'Betrayal by someone you trusted. Why does Stoller keep locating the Delta arms dumps so easily and swiftly? He has an informant – that is the only answer . . .'

Vinz took a step forward and waved the Luger. 'You are asking for a mouthful of broken teeth . . .'

He got no further. Dietrich stood up and moved

round his desk with surprising agility. With the back of his hand he struck Vinz across the face. The German stood very still as Dietrich stormed.

'Shut your trap! Who do you think is in charge here? Get out of this room and go fishing!'

Martel waited until Vinz had left and then went on speaking. 'Ask yourself the question, Dietrich. Is there one other person only who knows the location of the dumps? If so, that has to be Stoller's informant. Maybe a series of anonymous phone calls? If you are wondering why, every newspaper headline reporting discovery of another dump swings the polls a few points more against you. I say you are being manipulated by a mastermind . . .'

There was a flurry of activity. The door into the library burst open and one of the guards rushed in. Dietrich glared at the intruder.

'What is it, Karl?'

'The gate. They have just phoned through. A convoy of cars is approaching the entrance – they think it is the police . . .'

Dietrich stood considering the news for a few seconds, staring at Martel. Then he barked out an order and two more men appeared from the hall through the open door.

'Put him in the cellar – he can shout his head off down there and no one will hear him. Search him first . . .'

He moved across to a bookcase and removed a volume. Behind it was a button which he pressed. A section slid back with a purr of hydraulics, an addition to the *schloss* no doubt built by his Stuttgart technicians. Martel carefully did not look at Beck as he extracted the smoked cigarette from his holder and stubbed out the butt in the messy ash-tray.

'On your feet!'

Karl had spoken and his Luger was aimed point-blank. Beyond the dark well exposed by the secret door Martel could see a staircase curving down out of sight. He followed one of the guards across the shag carpet as Karl gestured with his gun, walking slowly. The muzzle was rammed into his back. As he stepped through the opening he heard Klara Beck speak urgently.

'Empty that ash-tray – it contains his cigarette stubs . . .'

Trust lovely Klara not to overlook any little detail, the bitch. A smell of damp, of mustiness rose to meet him as he descended the spiral with the guard in front and Karl behind. Dietrich called out a final threat.

'Later you will talk – or we open the moat sluices and you drown slowly in that pit . . .'

At the bottom of the steps a doorway led into a stone-walled cellar. Karl thrust a hand against the small of his back and shoved him forward. He lost his balance, sprawled full-length on the floor. When he stood up he was alone and the door was closed and locked.

*

The BND motorcade, comprising three six-seater black Mercedes crammed with armed men in civilian clothes, pulled up in a semi-circle round the entrance gates. The chief guard inside panicked and gave an order.

'Release the dogs!'

The gates were opened and the pack of unleashed dogs rushed out, jaws agape, snarling as they leapt at the cars. Beside the driver in the lead car sat Erich Stoller. He gave the command at once.

'Shoot those beasts . . .'

A window was lowered, a machine-pistol appeared and a fusillade rattled. The vicious animals stopped, some in mid-leap as the hail of bullets swept over them. Within seconds every dog lay inert in the roadway. Stoller stepped out followed by two men.

'Cut the communications in the gatehouse,' he ordered.

The two men ran forward and inside the building as one of the guards held the phone to his ear calling the *schloss*. One man grabbed him. The second ripped the instrument from the wall. Shaken, the guard still protested.

'That's illegal . . .'

'You're under arrest. Charge – obstructing the authorities in the performance of their duty . . .'

Outside another guard was shouting at Stoller. 'You will pay for this – killing the dogs . . .'

'I noticed one of them was foaming at the mouth,' Stoller told him. 'I suspect rabies. Tests will be carried out.' He returned to his car and spoke to the driver. 'Burn rubber to reach the *schloss* . . .'

The motorcade swept up the curving drive, spinning round corners. One minute after leaving the entrance Stoller saw ahead the walls of the *schloss*.

'Keep up the speed – they may try to lower the portcullis . . .'

He was right – as they approached the drawbridge the hydraulically operated portcullis began to move down. All three cars swept through the archway and the gate closed behind them. At the top of a flight of steps stood Reinhard Dietrich, hands on his hips. Stoller, followed by his men, jumped out and ran up the flight.

'You cannot enter,' Dietrich told him. 'And when I am elected you will be booted out of Bavaria . . .'

'This warrant . . .' Stoller waved the document under Dietrich's nose '. . . signed by the Minister-President, allows me to do what I like – tear down the place stone by stone should it be necessary. Are you going to invite us in or attempt obstruction?'

Dietrich turned away and walked back into the hall followed by Stoller. Inside the industrialist began moving towards a room on the left. Stoller noticed a door to the right which was half-open. He made for it and entered a large library. An attractive dark-haired woman holding a glass sat on a sofa and looked at him over the rim as she drank.

'Your name?' Stoller demanded.

'This is outrageous!' Dietrich had hurried after

Stoller and was standing behind a huge desk. 'I shall complain to the Minister-President . . .'

'There is the phone.' Stoller turned to the woman again and his manner became polite. 'We have full powers of search. Could you please give me your name . . .'

'Don't answer,' Dietrich told her, reaching for a cigar.

'Klara Beck,' the woman replied and smiled. 'I am Mr Dietrich's secretary and personal assistant. Is there any other way in which I can help you?'

'You can let me know the present whereabouts of an Englishman who called here within the past hour. His name is Philip Johnson . . .'

Klara Beck. One of the names Stoller had checked out when Martel had reported the conversation he had eavesdropped on in the phone booth at Lindau Hauptbahnhof. The Stuttgart number had been traced to a penthouse apartment owned by Dietrich GmbH. There was also an interesting file on Beck which went back to her early days in Berlin.

'I have been working in my office upstairs and just came down to the library before you arrived,' Beck replied. 'I have never heard of anyone by that name . . .'

'You live here at the *schloss*?'

'What bloody impertinence . . .!' Dietrich exploded from behind his desk.

Stoller ignored the industrialist, concentrating his whole attention on examining the room and questioning Beck. His men were at this moment searching the rest of the *schloss*. Dietrich knew this, yet he had left Erwin Vinz to keep an eye on them. He seemed most reluctant to leave the library, which convinced Stoller he was in the right room.

'I have an apartment in Stuttgart,' Beck replied as she took out a pack of cigarettes and inserted one between her lips. Stoller leant close to her with his lighter and ignited the cigarette. As he did so she watched him with her large eyes and there was a hint of invitation. A dangerous woman.

'It is a company apartment,' she went on. 'One of the advantages of working for the owner.' Her eyes again met Stoller's directly. 'And I'm very good at all aspects of my job.'

'I'm sure you are.'

Stoller bowed courteously, then resumed his slow stroll round the room. The ash-tray on the desk had recently been hastily cleaned. There were smear-marks of ash round its interior. He looked up as one of his men entered the room followed by a colleague.

'Anything so far, Peter?' Stoller enquired.

The man shook his head and Stoller told both of them to wait with him in the library. He noticed Dietrich was beginning to enjoy his cigar, to relax in his chair.

'Who has told you this fantastic story about this mythical person being anywhere near my home?'

'The aerial camera – plus the co-pilot's field-glasses. The film taken will, when developed, provide the evidence. We used special film which shows the exact date and time pictures are taken – one of the products of your company, I believe?'

'Camera? Pilot? Have you gone mad?'

'A helicopter tracked Johnson up to the *schloss* – with a cine-camera recording the incident as I have just explained. What cigarettes do you smoke, Mr Dietrich? The brand, I mean.'

'I only smoke cigars – Havanas.' Dietrich was mystified by the turn events were taking and shifted restlessly in his chair.

'And Miss Beck smokes *Blend* – as I noticed when she took out her pack . . .'

Stoller was walking along the line of bookcases. He stopped and stooped to pick up a cigarette stub half-hidden in the shag carpet at the foot of a bookcase. He showed everyone the stub which he had spotted a few minutes earlier.

'Interesting. Dietrich – on his own admission – smokes cigars. Miss Beck smokes *Blend*. This stub is *Silk Cut* – a British cigarette. It was lying at the base of this bookcase. I find it hard to surmise how it comes to be there – unless it was dropped when someone walked through a solid wall. Or is the wall so solid . . .' He began taking out volumes from the shelves and dropping them on the floor. To speed up the process he swept whole sections of the calf-bound volumes on to the carpet as he nodded to his two men. They produced Walther automatics and held them ready for use. Enraged, Dietrich strode round his desk.

'Those volumes are priceless . . .'

'Then show me where the catch is which releases the concealed door.'

'You are mad . . .!'

Dietrich stopped speaking as another half-dozen books went on the floor and Stoller gazed at a red button set in a plastic frame which had just been exposed. He pressed the button and a section of bookcase slid back revealing the spiral staircase beyond.

'Peter,' he ordered, 'go and see what is down there. Should you meet any resistance use your gun.' He glanced round the room. 'I doubt if I have to remind anyone terrorist kidnapping is punishable by long terms of imprisonment . . .'

'I was upstairs helping Klara,' Dietrich began.

'Was he, Miss Beck?' Stoller enquired. 'Be careful how you reply since criminal proceedings may be involved.'

'I'm confused . . .' Beck started choking on her cigarette but was saved from saying more by the appearance of Martel brushing dirt from his sleeve. There was dried blood on his knuckles where his hands had hit the cellar flagstones. Peter came into the room behind him and spoke to Stoller.

'He was imprisoned in a cellar like a pig-pen but they left the key on the outside of the door – it saved shooting off the lock.'

'Well, Dietrich?' Stoller asked.

'He is an imposter . . . I was sure he was an assassin

sent to kill me . . . After he made an appointment I phoned *The Times* in London . . . They told me Johnson is in Paris . . . I have many enemies . . .'

The Delta leader was talking like a machine-gun, gesturing to indicate his alarm, the words tumbling out as he struggled forcefully to make his story sound plausible enough to make Stoller doubt the wisdom of preferring charges. It was Martel who guided Stoller to a decision.

'I suggest we get to hell out of this den of nauseating clowns. The atmosphere here smells even fouler than it did in that filthy cellar . . .'

The three BND cars reached the exit, turned past the heap of dog corpses lying in the road and headed back towards München.

'In a minute,' Stoller said to Martel, 'we come to where I left Claire Hofer parked in your Audi – where you left her. She recognised me and blasted hell out of her horn to stop us. Then she blasted more hell out of me to hurry to the *schloss*. That girl likes you,' Stoller commented with a sideways glance.

'I'll bear it in mind – and thanks for keeping tabs on me with the chopper – and for battering your way into the fortress . . .'

'Why did you visit Dietrich?' the German asked.

'To set the enemy at each other's throats. To convince him he is being betrayed, which I believe is the truth. It may throw a last-minute spanner in the works

of Operation Crocodile. And God knows we're close
to the last minute . . .'

Claire made her remark as Martel drove them in the
Audi back to München. Stoller's motorcade had long
since vanished as he hurried to reach the airport to
catch his flight to Bonn.

'I assume we cancel out Erich Stoller now as a
possible assassin?'

'Why?'

'For God's sake because he rescued you from the
clutches of that swine, Dietrich . . .'

'And what will be the prime objective of the
security chief who is the secret assassin?' Martel
enquired.

'I don't follow you,' she said with a note of
irritation.

'To act in a way that will convince Tweed and me
that he is not the man we're looking for.'

'You can't mean Erich Stoller is still on the list.'

'Yes. He is no more cleared than the others. Let's
hope those records we're collecting from München
Airport do tell us who we're looking for.'

Chapter Twenty-Five

Tuesday June 2: 1400–2200 hours

Name: Erich Heinz Stoller. **Nationality:** German.
Date of birth: June 17 1950. **Place of birth:** Haar,
Münich.

Career record: Served with Kriminalpolizei,
Wiesbaden, 1970–1974 . . . Transferred to BND,
1974 . . . served as undercover agent inside East
Germany, 1975–1977 . . . Appointed chief, BND,
1978 . . .

Tweed again skip-read the file McNeil had handed
him. Examining dossiers produced this reaction: the
more you tackled the faster you absorbed them.
Tweed pushed the file back across the desk to McNeil.
He rubbed his eyes and yawned before asking the
question.

'What do you think of Stoller? You never met him
– which can be an advantage. His personality doesn't
intrude, you concentrate on the facts.'

'He's by far the youngest of the four – in his early
thirties. Isn't that unusual – to become chief of the
BND at his age?'

'Chancellor Langer personally promoted him over the heads of God knows how many more senior candidates. He has a reputation for being brilliant . . .'

'I detect a "but" in your inflection,' McNeil observed.

'Well, he did spend two years behind the Iron Curtain . . .'

'But you said he was brilliant . . .'

'So we start going round in circles again.' Tweed frowned and leaned forward to tap the neat pile of folders McNeil had arranged. 'I'm convinced that in one of those folders is the answer — a fact pointing straight at the guilty man. It's at the back of my mind but I'm damned if I can bring it to the surface.'

'Maybe Martel will spot it when he reads the copies I'm taking with me to Münich this evening . . .'

'It worries me, McNeil,' Tweed said quietly, 'you're breaking all the regulations by taking even copies of those dossiers out of the country . . .'

'I'll be covered by my diplomatic immunity pass. Martel will meet me as soon as I get off the plane. Nothing can happen while I'm in the first-class section of the plane. I'm quite looking forward to the trip . . .'

'I'm having you escorted to Münich with an armed guard,' Tweed decided. He reached for the phone, dialled a number, gave brief instructions and listened. 'He'll be here in half an hour,' he told McNeil as he replaced the phone. 'It will be Mason — he says he's the only one available.'

'At least he will be company on the flight.'

Tweed looked at her and marvelled. Some of these

middle-aged English women were extraordinary. They undertook the most dangerous missions as though they were taking a trip to Penzance. He watched as she packed the copy files in a special security briefcase. Her own small bag had been packed hours ago.

'You're not to chain that thing to your wrist,' he told her.

'Why not? I'm doing this job.' She spoke sharply as she locked the case, extended the chain from the handle and clamped the cuff of steel round her wrist, snapping shut the automatic lock. Both knew why he had said that.

Tweed would sooner lose the case rather than subject McNeil to a frightful ordeal – and instances had been known where attackers used the simple method of obtaining such a case. They chopped the hand off at the wrist.

1800 hours, the American Embassy, Grosvenor Square. In a second-floor office Tim O'Meara stood holding his executive case while his deputy, James Landis, listened on the phone, said yes and no, and then replaced the receiver.

'Well?' O'Meara demanded impatiently.

'Air Force One is on schedule over the Atlantic. It will touch down at Orly in good time for the President to be driven direct to the Gare de l'Est and the Summit Express . . .'

'Then let's get to hell out of here so we're at Orly ourselves in good time . . .'

'A curious report came in about a half-hour back, sir – concerning the investigation into the murder of Clint Loomis on the Potomac. Apparently a nosey international operator in Washington listened in on a call which came through from . . .'

'I said *come on!*' O'Meara blazed, cutting off his deputy in mid-sentence.

1800 hours, Elysée Palace, Paris. In the courtyard outside the main entrance and behind the grille gates leading to the street Alain Flandres watched the anti-bomb squad going over a gleaming black Citroën. In a few hours this car would transport the French President to the Gare de l'Est.

As always, Flandres could not keep still – nor trust anyone except himself. As two men directed a mirror at the end of a long handle underneath the car he stood to one side and watched the mirror image.

'Hold it there a moment!'

He stared at the reflection and then called out to a leather-clad man nearby. 'Get underneath this car and check every square centimetre. The mirror could miss something . . .'

He ran up the steps inside the Elysée and went to the operations room where an armed guard opened the door. Two men were hunched over powerful transceivers while the third, a cryptographer, checked decoded signals. He looked up as Flandres came into the room and tried to hand his chief a sheaf of messages.

'Just tell me what they say, my friend! Why should I ruin my eyes when you are paid to ruin your own?'

There were grins at the sally and the tense atmosphere lightened with Flandres' arrival. It was part of his technique to defuse any heightening of tension. Calm men took calm decisions.

'The American President lands at Orly at 2300 hours . . .'

'Which leaves exactly one half-hour to drive him from airport to train. We had better close off the route – they will drive like hell. It is the Americans' idea of security. A demonstration by Mr Tim O'Meara of his efficiency! Long live the Yanks!'

'The British Prime Minister will land in her special flight at Charles de Gaulle at 2200 hours . . .'

'Characteristic of the lady – to allow sufficient time but not so much that she wastes any. A model passenger!'

'The German Chancellor is scheduled to board the express at Münich Hauptbahnhof at 0933 tomorrow morning . . .'

'That I know – it has long been planned . . .'

'But there is an odd signal from Bonn I do not understand,' the cryptographer told him. 'We are particularly requested to stand by in the communications room aboard the Summit Express for an urgent message from Bonn during the night.'

'That is all?'

'Yes.'

Flandres left the room, walking slowly along the corridor. The Bonn signal was a new, last-minute development which he could not understand – and because he did not comprehend its significance it worried him.

1800 hours, The Chancellery, Bonn. Erich Stoller left the study of Chancellor Langer in the modern building on the southern outskirts of the small town which overlooks the Rhine. The tall, thin German wore an expression of satisfaction: his dash by private jet from Münich had been worthwhile.

During the flight Stoller had wondered whether he could manage it: Langer was notoriously unpredictable, a highly intelligent leader with a will of his own. And it had taken only ten minutes' conversation to persuade the Chancellor.

Stoller had sent off the coded signal – prepared in advance – while he was still in Langer's study, the signal to control H.Q. at the Elysée in Paris. Alain Flandres would by now, he hoped, have received this first signal. It was the second signal, timed to be sent later when the train was on its way, that was vital.

'I have pulled it off,' Stoller said to himself. 'The plan is working . . .'

*

1800 hours, Heathrow Airport. Flight LH 037 took off for München on schedule, climbing steeply into the clear blue evening sky, leaving behind a vapour trail which dispersed very slowly. Two passengers had come aboard and settled themselves in the first-class section at the last moment. Special arrangements had been made in advance to receive the couple.

Neither McNeil, carrying her brief-case locked to her wrist with a metal hand-cuff and chain, nor her companion, Mason – who carried a Smith & Wesson .38 in a shoulder holster – passed through normal channels. Once identified, they were hustled to an office with a sign outside. *Positively No Admittance.*

They remained inside the locked office until a phone call to the uniformed police officer sharing the room informed them all other passengers were aboard. They ran down the covered way leading into the aircraft where stewardesses waited to escort them to reserved seats.

'Isn't it nice to be VIPs?' McNeil whispered as she sipped her champagne and the plane continued its non-stop ascent.

'All in a day's work,' Mason replied, his expression blank.

1930 hours, Heathrow Airport. Flight BE 026 departed for Paris on schedule. Tweed – who was deliberately travelling economy class – had a difficult job timing his boarding of the flight. As he knew from McNeil's private intelligence service, Howard was travelling on the same flight, but first class.

Tweed, therefore, entered the final departure lounge just as the last-but-one passenger disappeared down the ramp. The steward on duty beckoned frantically.

'The flight is just departing!'

'So I'm just in time,' Tweed responded as he rushed down the ramp. Damnit, he had paid for his ticket.

As the stewardess ushered him aboard he glanced into the first-class section on his left. The back of Howard's head was just visible. Fortunately when disembarkation took place the custom was to let off first-class passengers ahead of the plebs. Tweed chose a seat he hated, a seat at the rear of the plane. He detested flying.

He sank into his seat and after take-off forced himself to gaze out of the porthole window. In the evening sunlight the full glory of Windsor Castle revolved below. For Queen and Country. A bit old-fashioned these days, but Tweed never bothered about what impression he might create on the rest of the world.

Flight LH 037 had crossed the German border when Mason excused himself to McNeil. 'I want to send a message to Martel confirming we are aboard this flight – the pilot can radio it for me . . .'

'But he's expecting us,' McNeil reminded him.

'Expecting is not the same thing as knowing we caught the plane. With what you're carrying we can't take any chances . . .'

He made his way towards the pilot's cabin and was stopped by a stewardess. He took out his identity card and gave it to her.

'Show this to the pilot. I have to send an urgent radio signal. The pilot knows we are aboard . . .'

After a short delay he was shown into the cabin and the door was locked behind him. Mason introduced himself and then turned to the wireless operator. The pilot nodded that it was all right and the agent asked for a pad to write the message. It was addressed to a Münich telephone number.

'The signature is a code-name,' he explained as the operator read the wording. Mason nodded his thanks to the pilot and left the cabin as the operator began transmitting.

Telephone number Münich . . . McNeil and I aboard Flight LH 037 from London. ETA . . . Please arrange reception committee. Gustav.

In the Münich apartment a gloved hand picked up the phone as soon as it began to ring. The operator checked that she had the correct number and then began to transmit the message.

'"McNeil and I aboard Flight LH 037 . . ."'

'Thank you,' said Manfred, 'I have that correctly. Goodbye.'

The gloved hand broke the connection, lifted the receiver again and dialled a München number. It was answered by Erwin Vinz whose voice changed when he realised the identity of the caller.

'You will take a team of men to the airport . . .'

Manfred's instructions were precise, although masked in everyday conversation. When the call was completed he checked his watch. It was convenient that the airport was close to the city – Vinz's execution squad would be in position by the time Flight 037 had touched down.

And Mason, who was still over twenty thousand feet up, would have been appalled had he known the instructions.

'Kill them both – the man as well as the woman . . .'

Martel stood by a bookstall inside the exit area at München Airport, apparently studying a paperback. He also appeared to be on his own, which was not the case. At the other side of the large hall Claire, wearing dark glasses, stood with a small suitcase at her feet like a passenger.

The arrival of Flight LH 037 from London had been announced over the Tannoy. Passengers who had disembarked were hurrying across the hall for cabs and the airport bus. Martel scanned the small crowd and saw McNeil, carrying a briefcase in one hand, a suitcase in the other. He also saw Mason alongside her.

'Tell you what,' Mason was saying to her, 'I'll just dash over to that kiosk and get a pack of cigarettes – you go and grab a cab and then we shan't have to wait . . .'

'But we're being met . . .' McNeil shrugged. Mason was gone. Martel saw the separation and frowned. He dropped the paperback, picked it up and quickly returned it to the revolving rack. Claire was waiting for the signal and now she recognised McNeil from the description Martel had given her.

She also knew something was wrong. The dropping of the paperback had warned her. Had Martel simply returned the book to its rack it would have been no more than a recognition signal. Inside her handbag she gripped the 9-mm pistol. McNeil, an erect, slim woman, headed for the exit.

A man dressed in the uniform of a Lufthansa pilot standing near the exit produced a Luger equipped with a silencer from a briefcase. Erwin Vinz, carrying a light raincoat folded loosely over his arm, walked into the hall, dropped the raincoat and aimed the machine-pistol the garment had concealed.

'*McNeil, drop flat!*' Martel yelled.

It was remarkable: Claire was amazed. The middle-aged Englishwoman fell forward, dropped her suit-case, used her hands to cushion the shock of the fall and lay quite still, hugging the floor.

Martel pointed the Colt .45 snatched from his shoulder holster and aimed at the most dangerous target – Vinz and his machine-pistol. He fired rapidly.

Three heavy slugs hammered with tremendous power into Vinz's chest, hurling him backwards. His shirt crimsoned as he crashed to the floor, still clutching the weapon. He had not fired a single shot.

The Lufthansa 'pilot' aimed his Luger point-blank at his agreed target – Mason, who stood near a cigarette machine. Two bullets struck Mason who fell forward against the machine, clawing at it as he sagged to the ground. Claire aimed, steadying her pistol over her left arm. It was remarkable shooting – clear across the hall. Two bullets hit the killer and he toppled forward.

'McNeil, stay flat!' Martel yelled again.

Three men apparently waiting for passengers had produced hand-guns.

Martel had just shot Vinz ... Claire was firing at the 'pilot' ... The three new Delta professionals were aiming their weapons at the still-prostrate form of McNeil ... There was panic spreading among the other passengers ... A woman screamed and went on screaming and screaming ...

A steady drum-fire of fresh shooting filled the hall and Martel watched in amazement as all three Delta assassins fell to the floor. Men in civilian clothes appeared from different parts of the hall armed with Walther automatics. One of them came up to Martel, an identity card held up in his left hand.

'BND, Mr Martel. Josef Gubitz at your service. The others you see are my men.'

'How the hell did you know . . .?'

'The plane's pilot transmitted the message the Englishman on the passenger list named Mason had sent, transmitted it to Stoller as instructed.'

'Who instructed him?'

'A man called Tweed in London. Any signals sent by Mason from the aircraft to be immediately transmitted to us. Stoller reacted from Bonn by sending us here. It was kind of complicated . . .' The German, a small, well-dressed man, looked over his shoulder at the carnage in the hall. '. . . but it worked.'

'Thank God for that – and thank you.'

Claire was helping McNeil to her feet who was looking down at her grazed knees as Martel joined them. She looked at Martel. 'You know something? My nylons are ruined. Do you think I could indent for a new pair?'

Martel, Claire and McNeil were sitting in the Englishman's room at the Hotel Clausen. The two women drank tea as Martel checked the four photocopy dossiers McNeil had brought him. McNeil sat in an armchair next to Claire and placed her cup on the table. The Swiss girl was marvelling at her placidity.

'That tea you poured me was just right,' McNeil announced. 'It was nice and strong – just a dash of milk and no sugar. You can't beat a cup of tea after a bit of a dust-up.' She paused. 'Mason tried to get me killed, didn't he?'

'Yes,' said Martel. 'And they wiped him out because by now he had served his treacherous purpose. I'm certain he bugged Tweed's office. I'm equally sure he dressed up in the windcheater, beret and sun-goggles, made sure he was spotted by a policeman in Piccadilly and then took off his things – probably in a lavatory – and left them with the gun on a chair in Austin Reed's . . .'

'Why?' Claire asked.

'To confuse us. Manfred was never within hundreds of miles of London. And it must have been Mason who followed Tweed to London Airport before he boarded Concorde – then reported it back to Manfred. It's odd Howard ever took on a man like that . . .'

McNeil was watching Martel who had closed the last file. 'Do they tell you anything?' she asked. 'Tweed gave the impression he couldn't find anything but I believe it's there . . .'

Martel took a sheet of the hotel notepaper, scribbled something on it and showed it to McNeil. She read what was on it, tore the sheet into small pieces, got up and walked across to the toilet. They heard her flush the loo and she came out and sat down again.

'Well?' Martel enquired.

'I thought so, too,' McNeil replied. 'You can't trust Tweed, of course – he keeps so much to himself. The trouble will be proving it . . .'

'So we leave you here until it's all over with

Stoller's armed guard on the door. Claire has some
distance to travel – and I'm heading for a different
destination. What scares me is we have so little
time . . .'

Chapter Twenty-Six

Tuesday June 2: 2030–2335 hours

Charles de Gaulle Airport, 2030 hours. Flight BE 026 landed on schedule. Howard was among the first passengers to disembark. His special pass took him straight through Customs and Immigration and Alain Flandres was waiting for him with a large Citroën.

'This is what I call service,' Howard remarked as they settled back in the rear and the chauffeur-driven car glided away.

'We pride ourselves on our organisation,' Flandres replied with a cynical smile. 'Since the change of government we have little else to pride ourselves on.'

'As bad as that?' Howard glanced sharply at his companion who, as always, was the soul of relaxation. 'Is everything proceeding according to plan?'

'There is something I do not understand – and in the situation we are faced with incomprehensible things disturb me. I have had a signal from Bonn warning us to expect an urgent communication from Germany during the night. Stoller is not at Pullach . . .'

'Well, that's his problem . . .' Howard dismissed the whole thing with a curt wave of his hand.

'It might be our problem as well,' Flandres responded.

Under Flandres' instructions French security forces at both Orly and Charles de Gaulle were checking all arrivals for known faces. But they missed one person who came in on Flight LH 323 from München via Frankfurt. The aircraft landed at Charles de Gaulle at 2215 hours and the passenger, who had travelled first class, passed through the security checks unchallenged.

Elegantly clad in a black Givenchy dress and wearing a string of pearls, she also wore a hat with a veil. Porters carried her Gucci luggage to a waiting chauffeur-driven limousine. She raised her veil briefly for Passport Control.

'I wonder how many ingots of gold she is sitting on in the Bahnhofstrasse,' the Passport official murmured to a colleague after he had returned Irma Romer her Swiss passport and she moved away.

'I wouldn't mind having her sitting on me,' his colleague replied. 'She *is* a beauty . . .'

Settling herself in the spacious rear of the car the woman with the veil spoke to the chauffeur as the car was driven away from the airport.

'Emil, we have one hour before the train leaves – so you must drive slowly, kill some time. I must board the Summit Express five minutes before it departs.'

'My instructions were clear, Madame,' Emil replied. 'There will be no problem.'

'There *must* be no problem.'

Having issued this injunction, Klara Beck crossed her long legs and relaxed. It had been a rush to drive from the Bavarian *schloss* to catch the plane at Münich but she was sure she had successfully eluded the man who had tried to follow her. That would be Stoller's doing, of course.

'Stick Stoller,' she thought inelegantly and checked the time by her diamond-studded watch.

Gare de l'Est, 2300 hours. The twelve-coach express stood in the station. At the front the giant locomotive which would haul its precious cargo gleamed under the lights. It had been polished and polished again like a jewel. The chief engine-driver, Jacques Foriot, was the most experienced driver in the whole of France. He stood checking his array of dials and controls and then peered out of his cab.

The first six coaches immediately behind the engine were reserved for the train's illustrious passengers. The Prime Minister of Great Britain, typically, had arrived first. She had gone to bed without delay in Voiture One, the coach attached to the locomotive.

Voiture Two would be occupied by the French President who was at this moment climbing aboard after his swift ride from the Elysée. Alain Flandres stood on the platform, his eyes everywhere as the short, stocky President mounted the steps and disappeared inside. Flandres let out an audible sigh of relief.

'One more worry off my mind,' he remarked to his deputy, Pierre Buzier, a giant of a man with a bushy moustache who towered over his chief. 'And now one more worry on my mind,' Flandres continued with a shrug of his shoulders.

'But he is safe now,' Buzier reassured him. 'It was the drive from the Elysée that bothered us . . .'

'And you imagine that the next seven hundred-mile ride across Europe does not worry me, my friend?' He squeezed Buzier's huge arm and smiled cynically. 'It will be a long night – followed by a long day . . .'

The makeup of the express had been the subject of considerable study and much discussion by the security staff at the Elysée to ensure maximum safety. Voiture Three was reserved for the American President who was expected to arrive from Orly at the last moment. And Voiture Four would be the preserve of Chancellor Langer when he boarded the train at München at 9.33 a.m. on the following morning.

Behind these four coaches was attached the communications coach which carried some of the most sophisticated equipment available. One section was devoted entirely to a link between the train and the White House in Washington. The president would be accompanied, as he was everywhere, by an official carrying the black box – the sinister device for signalling a nuclear alert in varying stages of urgency.

Flandres and his technicians had devoted a great deal of energy to equipping this coach, cooperating with the Americans who had installed their own devices.

As though to counter the austere purpose of this coach, the one behind was taken up by the restaurant car for the exclusive use of the western leaders. It was expected that during daylight hours they would confer at length while they hammered out a united policy before facing the Soviet leader in Vienna.

'I want more men on this barrier,' Flandres ordered as he passed through the second barrier temporarily erected on the platform, a barrier sealing off the VIP section at the front from the rest of the express.

'Surely we have enough men already,' Buzier protested.

'For practical purposes, yes,' Flandres agreed. 'For public relations' purposes, no. The Americans are great believers in numbers. Bring ten more men from outside the station. That should impress them, should it not, Pierre?' Again he smiled cynically.

'If you say so . . .'

'I know O'Meara. If I am not mistaken I can hear the approach of the great man . . .'

'The American President?'

'No – O'Meara! Accompanied by the President!'

*

Beyond the second barrier was the rest of the train, the public section which comprised another six coaches. Two for first-class passengers (one a sleeping-car), three for second-class and, at the rear of the express, the public restaurant.

As he passed them alone – Buzier had hurried ahead to gather up ten more men – Flandres glanced at each window. Most of the blinds in the sleeping-car were closed but the station pulsated with a sense of expectancy. As he continued towards the main ticket barrier the little Frenchman scanned the other windows and eager faces stared back. He stopped to request that a window be closed. Until the train was moving the order was all windows must remain shut.

In the corridors on the other side of the express armed men of the French security services stood at intervals. At the main barrier he saw Howard waiting and pursed his lips. Having seen his own charge safely aboard, the Englishman was going to be present when the President of the United States arrived.

The distant sirens shrieking like banshees came closer. He must feel at home, Flandres reflected. He himself had been kept awake when he visited America by the hellish wail of patrol cars dashing through the night.

'He's only just on time,' Howard commented as Flandres reached the barrier. 'Why is it that Americans have to arrive at the very last minute?'

'Because they see no point in waiting. What they accomplish with the time saved is another matter . . .'

As the Frenchman had anticipated, O'Meara made a great performance of the arrival. When the motorcade swept into the station the American security chief leapt from the leading vehicle almost before it had stopped. Several men, their coats open at the front, followed him as he glared up the platform. The President rather spoilt the effect.

'I want men facing every window before the President moves up the platform,' O'Meara demanded.

'If they're going to take a pot-shot at me, Tim, they're going to,' said the President who stepped out from his car looking as cool and unaffected as a clerk walking home from work. 'And your remark is hardly a great compliment to M. Flandres . . .' He extended a hand. 'It is Alain Flandres, isn't it?'

'A pleasure to see you again, Mr President . . .'

They shook hands while O'Meara moved restlessly and gestured for the American Secret Service men to form a circle round Flandres and the President. 'Washington, two years ago – am I right?' the President said.

'You have a remarkable memory . . .'

There was tension as the procession of men made their way along the platform, so many alert to danger which might come from any quarter – and the potential target was the most powerful leader in the western world. Flandres was disturbed and felt he must speak.

'I don't like being hemmed in like this . . .'

The President, smiling and amenable, stopped. 'Tim, I think we must allow Alain to command the security operation. This, after all, is his territory.'

'More space, please!' Flandres spoke curtly to O'Meara. 'We must have a clear field of fire in an emergency . . .'

At the foot of the steps leading up into his coach the President lingered to speak again to the Frenchman. 'I just want you to know that I feel perfectly safe in your capable hands. And now, if you'll excuse me, I like an early night's sleep . . .'

Three minutes from departure time two unexpected events occurred. A chauffeur-driven limousine drove into the station and an elegant woman alighted and presented her ticket while the chauffeur brought her bags. The ticket collector noted that she had a sleeping compartment reserved. At the same time the Passport controller – brought to check the identity of all ordinary passengers – noted she was Swiss.

'You had better hurry, Madame,' the collector advised. 'The train departs in three minutes.'

Further down the platform at the second barrier Howard watched the elegant woman walking gracefully towards him while her chauffeur carried her luggage. She disappeared inside the sleeping-car and Howard turned to his deputy, Peter Haines, a short, wiry man.

'I wouldn't mind joining that one in her bunk,' he observed and climbed aboard the train.

The ticket collector was closing the barrier when a cab drew up.

A compact figure wearing glasses and a rumpled

hat who had paid the fare earlier got out. He ran towards the barrier, carrying a small case.

He had his ticket ready and a plastic card which he presented to the Passport official. The latter glanced in surprise at the card which bore a photograph of its owner and then turned to hold up his hand to the guard indicating that the train must wait.

The late arrival moved rapidly down the platform to the second barrier opposite which Howard was standing in the open doorway to get a last-minute breath of fresh air. As he saw the passenger his face went rigid and he stepped down on to the platform.

'Tweed! I don't know what the hell you are doing here but I'm forbidding you to board this train . . .'

'I don't think you have the power.' Tweed showed his card with green and red stripes running across it diagonally. 'And you are holding up the train . . .'

'Say, what the devil goes on here?'

O'Meara had appeared behind Howard. Now Flandres stepped down from the other end of the coach and ran along the platform to join them. O'Meara peered over Howard's shoulder.

'Jesus Christ! She signed the pass herself!'

'This is outrageous!' Howard exploded. 'I was not informed . . .'

'You were not informed for security reasons,' Tweed replied. 'If you are worried, why not wake up the lady and check? But I doubt whether she will appreciate the interruption . . .'

'Get aboard, my friend.' Alain Flandres had grasped Tweed's arm and was ushering him up the steps. 'You are most welcome.'

Tweed waited in the corridor as Flandres waved his hand towards the guard, climbed the steps and closed the door.

'Alain, there is one I would like checked as a matter of top priority. At the barrier the Passport controller told me the lady who came on board at the last moment is travelling on a Swiss passport, that her name is Irma Romer. Can you use the communications set-up to radio her details to Ferdy Arnold in Berne? Ask him to confirm whether their people have issued Irma Romer with a passport – that she does in fact exist . . .'

'Why bother about her?' Howard demanded.

'Because her car was parked in a side street for some time before it drove into the station. I arrived earlier myself, you see . . .'

The train was moving now, the huge wheels of the locomotive revolving faster as the Summit Express emerged from under the canopy of the Gare de l'Est and headed east on its historic journey for its final destination, Vienna. Seven hundred miles away.

Chapter Twenty-Seven

Wednesday June 3: 0100–0810 hours

'Has anything unusual happened yet, Haines?' Tweed asked.

'Unusual?' Howard's deputy enquired cautiously. At one o'clock in the morning he had a haggard look.

'Unexpected, then.'

They were sitting at one end of the communications coach where two bunks had been installed for security chiefs off duty. Haines glanced towards the far end of the coach where the three security chiefs were gathered round the teleprinter.

The express was ninety minutes away from Paris, moving at over eighty miles an hour as it thundered through the dark. The coach swayed round a curve. No one felt like sleep.

'I'd sooner you addressed that question to Howard,' said Haines.

'I'm addressing it to you.' Tweed reached towards his pocket as he continued. 'Perhaps you are unaware of my authority?'

'There was something, sir,' Haines began hastily. 'While he was at the Elysée Flandres had a message from Bonn warning us to await an urgent signal aboard the express. Stoller has disappeared . . .'

'Disappeared?'

'Yes. We don't know where to communicate with him. The secrecy of the whole business is worrying Flandres . . .' He looked again at the far end of the coach. 'I think something is coming through on the teleprinter.'

It was Howard, beginning to look strangely dishevelled, who came with the telex strip which he waved at Tweed with an expression of satisfaction.

'Signal from Ferdy Arnold in reply to your query. The Swiss can be damned quick. Irma Romer was issued with a passport four years ago. Widow of an industrial magnate – engineering. She's travelling outside the country somewhere in Europe. So can we now forget about your paranoid aberrations?'

'Can I see the telex, please?'

'I've just read the damned thing out to you!' Howard threw the strip into Tweed's lap. 'Admit it,' he snapped, 'it's a wild goose chase.' He turned and stepped on the right foot of O'Meara who had come up behind him. 'Do you have to follow me everywhere?' Howard demanded.

'People apologise when they bump into me,' O'Meara rasped.

Tweed watched the two men over his spectacles. Already they were getting on each other's nerves – because under the surface there was a terrible suspicion that one of the security chiefs was the enemy.

And with the windows closed tightly for the sake of the communication experts the atmosphere was growing torrid. Something had gone wrong with the air-conditioning.

Flandres, who had witnessed what was happening, came rapidly to their end of the coach. 'Gentlemen, we have the most nerve-wracking assignment any of us has probably faced – let us face it calmly and help each other . . .'

'What I'd like to know,' O'Meara demanded, 'is who is in charge of British security – Tweed or Howard . . .'

'I would say Alain is in supreme control for the moment,' Tweed said quickly. 'We are passing across French territory . . .'

'Still nobody answers my Goddamn question,' O'Meara persisted.

Tweed read through the Berne signal and looked at Howard. 'You left out a bit, didn't you? Arnold ends his message with the words *further details to follow as soon as available.*'

'What further details do we need?' asked Howard wearily.

'Her full description,' Tweed replied.

Nobody slept inside the communications coach as the express sped on through the night. The atmosphere grew worse as the air became more clammy and oppressive. Conditions were not improved by the cigar O'Meara smoked as he lay half-sprawled in the lower bunk.

Tweed moved away and sat in a swivel chair screwed to the floor, his head slumped forward, apparently asleep. But he was aware of everything going on as the thump-thump of the train's wheels continued its hypnotic rhythm. The factor he found most disturbing was Stoller's disappearance.

They had arranged a duty roster for one security chief to patrol the corridors of the four coaches where the VIPs were presumably asleep. This was at Flandres' suggestion despite the armed guards from each contingent occupying the corridors of their respective coaches. At the moment Flandres himself was on duty.

The Bonn signal arrived at the ungodly hour of 0431 – after the express had left Strasbourg and ten minutes before they were due at Kehl on the German border. Tweed sat up in his chair because he saw the cypher clerk decoding the signal which had arrived. He held out his hand as the clerk walked towards O'Meara who appeared to be asleep.

'I'll take it . . .'

'What the hell is it now?' O'Meara suddenly demanded.

The American – who had obviously not been asleep – was stripped to his shirt-sleeves, exposing the holstered gun strapped under his left arm. He leaned over Tweed's shoulder and the Englishman caught a whiff of stale sweat from his armpits. Howard, who had just entered the coach, joined them as all three men perused the signal.

'Christ Almighty, what is going on?' O'Meara growled and lit a fresh cigar. Howard's reaction was a tightening of the muscles of his jaw, Tweed noted.

Urgent change of schedule. Chancellor Langer will board Summit Express at Kehl, not München. Repeat Kehl not München. Stoller.

'It's a nightmare,' Howard said. 'What does it mean?'

There were pouches under his eyes betraying his fatigue. The underlying strain of mutual suspicion and mistrust was beginning to take its toll on the three security chiefs. Flandres had now joined them and was mopping moisture off his forehead with a silk handkerchief. The atmosphere was becoming claustrophobic. Each man was conscious of being cooped up inside a confined space he could not escape. Only Tweed seemed relaxed as they re-examined the signal.

'He has given us less than ten minutes' warning. It's just not good enough. What *does* it mean?' Howard repeated.

'It appears to mean,' Tweed suggested, 'that Stoller is using his considerable ingenuity to protect his leader. That is,' he added, 'assuming Chancellor Langer is the assassin's target . . .'

He was watching the three men as he spoke, searching for a clue in his blunt reference to the assassin. The American chewed at his cigar and spilt ash down his front.

'You're not making sense,' he complained irritably.

'The timetable of the western leaders for their journey to Vienna has been widely publicised,' Tweed explained patiently. 'Including the fact that Langer was scheduled to board the train at München when he had made his brief speech outside the Hauptbahnhof. By coming aboard much earlier this unexpected change may throw the unknown assassin off balance.' He stared round the trio hovering over him. 'It *has* already thrown you off balance . . .'

'You're assuming Langer is the target,' Howard pointed out.

'True,' Tweed agreed. 'The target may already be on board. I am not sure . . .'

'Just as you're not sure of any of us,' Flandres said amiably.

'True again. And the train is slowing down – we are at Kehl. So the fourth suspect, Stoller, should join the happy band . . .'

There was a further surprise when the express drew into Kehl and Flandres opened the door of Voiture Four to find Chancellor Kurt Langer staring up at him, his lean face wearing an expression of amusement. Like the French security chief, the German spoke fluent English and, wearing his well-cut business suit, could have passed for an Englishman.

'Alain Flandres, how pleasant to see you again. I trust my early arrival did not get you out of bed?'

'None of us have had much sleep . . .'

Flandres ushered the Chancellor quickly aboard into the corridor and away from the open doorway. He peered briefly out into the early morning. The gloomy platform, glowing with sepulchral lamps, was lined with BND men facing *away* from the express. Flandres frowned and turned to speak to the Chancellor.

'Where is Erich Stoller, Chancellor? Surely he is accompanying you?'

'I have no idea where he is,' Langer answered affably. 'He is as elusive as a lark. The train can leave when you are ready – I go this way? Thank you . . .'

Flandres signalled to the guard and closed the door. The train began to move again, picking up speed, the coaches swaying slightly as they started to cross Germany, heading for Bavaria. Flandres wasted no time making sure Langer was comfortable: the Chancellor was notorious for his dislike of fuss. He hurried back into the foetid atmosphere of the communications coach where the others sat waiting for him.

'Stoller did not come aboard,' he announced. 'And Langer tells me he has no idea as to his present whereabouts . . .'

'That's crazy,' O'Meara protested.

'It could also be very serious,' said Tweed.

His remark did nothing to lighten the highly nervous mood which had now spread to the communications technicians. Howard left the coach to take up his duty roster, glaring at Tweed as he passed him hunched in his swivel chair.

The early hours when morale is at its lowest crawled and no one spoke unless it was absolutely unavoidable. Friendly cooperation had long since given way to raw-edged nerves and outbursts of irritation over trivia. Only Tweed remained detached and watchful – like a man awaiting an event he has foreseen and which is inevitable.

When they had at last settled down into some kind of neutral silence the second signal came in from Berne.

Subject: Irma Romer. **Height:** 5ft. 4 ins. **Weight:** 120 lbs. **Colour of eyes:** Brown. **Age:** 64. **Married:** to industrialist, Axel Romer, 34 Years. **Destination:** Lisbon. Arnold, Berne.

The second signal promised from Berne reached the communications car of the Summit Express as it was pulling into Ulm Hauptbahnhof at 0805 hours. Tweed automatically converted the details from the metric system as he read the message and passed it to Howard.

'The elegantly-dressed woman who came aboard at the last moment at Paris,' he commented. 'The one you said was of no significance. The description doesn't tally in one single detail . . .'

'We had better go to the sleeper coach at once,'

Flandres said. 'With armed guards,' he added. He looked at Tweed. 'Coming?'

The two men passed through the restaurant coach where breakfast was being laid for the four western leaders to the end door which was kept permanently locked, sealing off the coaches occupied by the public. A guard unlocked the door and Flandres, followed by Tweed, hurried along the corridor of the sleeping car.

'Come with us,' Flandres ordered two of the guards standing in the corridor. 'Have your weapons ready. Good, there is the attendant . . .'

The uniformed attendant in charge of the sleeper was making the morning coffee and looked up in some trepidation as Flandres began questioning him. He then explained that the passenger, Irma Romer, had left the express at Stuttgart after complaining that she felt unwell.

Stuttgart . . . The timetable details flashed into Tweed's mind. *Arrive 0651; Depart 0703*. A twelve-minute stop, the longest of the whole trip except for Münich. Flandres looked at Tweed and made a gesture along the corridor.

'So, once again you are right, my friend. We should examine her compartment?'

'Yes,' said Tweed.

The attendant opened the door which he had locked after the passenger had left. Tweed stepped inside followed by Flandres. The Englishman raised the wash-basin lid.

'The soap is untouched. She hardly used the place . . .'

'The bed has not been slept in,' Flandres pointed out. 'So she sat up all night . . .'

'Waiting until she reached Stuttgart,' Tweed said thoughtfully. 'I don't like this, Alain, I don't like it at all. Why should she book a sleeper, spend the night in it from Paris to Stuttgart and then get off? This business of feeling ill is nonsense.'

'Well, she is off the train – and we are moving again, thank God. I hate these stops. Let us go back and check with Howard and our American colleague . . .'

It was only a two-minute stop at Ulm. An essential element in the overall security was that at each stop one of the security chiefs climbed down on to the platform to check who was leaving or boarding the public section of the train. As they made their way back through the restaurant car Tweed asked his question.

'Who was watching the platform at Stuttgart?'

'O'Meara volunteered for the job . . .'

'And he wouldn't recognise Irma Romer,' Tweed remarked. 'He has never seen her.'

'And there was a fair amount of activity at Stuttgart. It will remain a mystery . . .'

In the first-class day coach a woman passenger sat reading a copy of American *Vogue*. Her hair had a tinted rinse and she wore horn-rimmed glasses which were also tinted. She was dressed in an American trouser suit and perched on the luggage rack above her was a case with a bright tartan cover.

She was travelling on an American passport in the name of Pamela Davis and her occupation was given as journalist. Taking out a pack of *Lucky Strike* she lit a fresh cigarette. By her side the ash-tray was crammed with half-smoked butts – but on top in view were fully-smoked stubs.

After complaining to the sleeping-car attendant of feeling ill, Reinhard Dietrich's mistress, Klara Beck, had got off the express at Stuttgart carrying her large Gucci suitcase. It was, she knew, a twelve-minute stop. She made her way to the ladies' room.

She had changed into the trouser suit behind a locked toilet door. She had used a hand-mirror to adjust carefully the rinsed wig which concealed her dark hair. Inside the large Gucci suitcase were some expensive clothes but it was mainly occupied by a smaller, tartan-covered case.

She had used a steel nail-file to force the locks on the Gucci. When it was found it would be assumed it had been stolen, certain contents taken and then abandoned in the toilet. There was no way the suitcase could be linked with its owner.

She had put on the tinted glasses, filled her new handbag with the contents of the one she had carried earlier, and substituted the Pamela Davis American passport for the Irma Romer Swiss passport. In her handbag was a fresh ticket purchased in advance from Stuttgart to Vienna. The transformation was now complete.

Klara Beck had overlooked nothing. Her actions had neutralised any check which she felt pretty sure would be made on the occupants of the sleeping-car. She was now ready for the final stage of the operation.

Normally Tweed would have been standing on the platform at Ulm during the two-minute stop – and Tweed was the man capable of recognising Claire Hofer. Martel had not only given him a verbal description of the Swiss girl during their meeting at Heathrow; he had backed this up with the passport photo attached to the special card. Instead it was Howard who checked passenger movement.

Claire was waiting on the platform when the Summit Express came in. She carried a small suitcase and her handbag. And she wore a pair of glasses with plain lenses which gave her a studious air. When the train stopped she approached the entrance to the first-class coach and showed her ticket to the waiting official.

'And your passport, Madame – or some other form of identity,' another uniformed official requested.

Claire produced her Swiss passport and this immediately satisfied the German. She climbed aboard and began moving along the corridor glancing into each compartment. The first one with only a single passenger was occupied by a tall man wearing lederhosen – the leather garb seen so often in Bavaria. His hat was tipped over his eyes and he appeared to be asleep.

She went inside, closed the door and heaved her case up on to the rack. The fact that it was a smoker had influenced her choice. And she wanted a quiet compartment so she could think. Inside the next compartment – only a few feet further along the corridor – sat another lone passenger, a woman carrying a passport in the name of Pamela Davis.

'What a pleasant surprise, Miss Hofer . . .'

She nearly jumped out of her skin. Her hand slid to the flap of her handbag which contained the 9-mm pistol. The tall man tipped back his hat as he spoke softly.

'No need for protection. I'm quite harmless,' he continued.

Stupefied, she stared as Erich Stoller stared back at her. The express began moving east again. It was exactly 8.07 a.m.

Chapter Twenty-Eight

Wednesday June 3: 0800–0845 hours

'The Blumenstrasse cemetery. I haven't much time . . .' Martel told the Bregenz cab driver.

'Where you're going they have all the time in the world . . .'

The cab-driver's response was typically Austrian, taking life as it came – and went. But Martel's urgency communicated itself to him and he drove away from the solid wall of buildings along the lakeside at speed.

The Englishman made an effort to contain his impatience. Away to the north the Summit Express was speeding across Germany and, if on schedule, was approaching Ulm. At the eastern end of Lake Konstanz a grey drizzle blotted out the mountains. Through the open window moisture drifted in and settled on his face.

Arriving at the entrance to the cemetery, he paid the fare, added a generous tip and told the driver to wait. Then he plunged into the sea of headstones, his eyes scanning the maze. It was such a long shot – a remark made to him by a gravedigger when he had last been in Bregenz.

But it was the right day. He checked his watch. It was also the right time. 8 a.m.

'She comes every week without fail,' the grave-digger had told him. 'Always on the Wednesday and always at eight in the morning when no one else is about . . .'

Martel buttoned up the collar of his raincoat against the rain. The only sound was the low whine of a wind. Clouds like grey smoke were so low you felt you could reach up and touch them.

As the mist parted occasionally there were brief glimpses of the forest on the precipitous Pfänder mountain. Then he saw behind a headstone the crouched form of the gravedigger. He was levering his spade, adding to a mound of freshly dug earth.

'Back again, sir.'

The old man had straightened up and turned. His moustache dripped moisture and his cap was soggy. He regarded Martel's expression of surprise with amusement.

'You didn't startle me. Saw you coming soon as you entered the Friedhof. Thank you kindly, sir . . .'

He pocketed the sheaf of Austrian banknotes Martel had earlier counted from his wallet, then leaned on his shovel. Martel had one hand clenched behind his back, the nails digging into his palm to conceal his frustration. It was no good asking direct questions immediately: that was not the way of the Vorarlberg.

'You work in all weathers?' Martel enquired.

'They don't wait for you on this job . . .' The grave-digger then surprised him. 'Looking for that woman who comes here each week? She's just coming through the main gate. Don't turn round – the slightest change of atmosphere disturbs her . . .'

Martel waited and then glanced over his shoulder. Beyond the pallisade of large headstones a woman wearing a red head-scarf was walking briskly. She wore a fur coat and carried a spray of flowers as she headed in a diagonal direction away from them.

'She's not short of a schilling,' the gravedigger whispered to Martel. 'Saw her in town once – my wife said that fur is sable.'

'Whereabouts in Bregenz?'

'Coming out of a house in Gallus-strasse. Now's your chance.'

The woman was crouched with her back to them laying the flowers on a grave. Stooping low, Martel ran among the maze of headstones which reminded him of huge chess-pieces.

His rubber-soled shoes made no sound as he came up behind her and stopped. It was the same grave. *In Gottes Frieden. Alois Stohr. 1930–1953.* The woman stood up, turned and saw him.

'Dear God!'

Panic! A slim, shapely hand clutched at her mouth as she stifled a scream. Large luminous eyes stared at Martel in sheer fright. A reaction which was hardly justified. Startled – yes, Martel would have expected that. But her reaction was too extreme – like that of

346

someone whose dreadful secret had been discovered. He spoke in German.

'I have to ask you certain questions . . .'

'Questions?'

'Police.' He produced the special pass which gave him access to the Summit Express and showed her only a glimpse. Documents were designed to delude the innocent. 'Security from Vienna . . .'

'Vienna!'

'I need information on Alois Stohr – as he is called on the headstone . . .'

Afterwards he could never have explained why instinctively he chose this approach – only another trained interrogator would have understood. 'Seventh sense,' Tweed would have commented tersely.

'Why do you say that?' There was a quaver in the woman's voice. She would be in her late forties, Martel estimated. Still a very handsome woman. She must have been a beauty at eighteen, say. In 1953 when Alois Stohr was buried. 'I come here to put flowers on the grave of an old friend,' she went on.

'A friend who died nearly thirty years ago? You come here each week after all this time? To recall the memory of a *friend*? The man who died in 1953 when the Vorarlberg was under occupation . . .' The words poured out of Martel in a torrent as he aimed blind, hoping to strike a sensitive spot. He went on, saying the first thing which came into his head. '. . . occupation by Frènch troops – that is, French officers and Moroccan other ranks . . .'

347

He stopped.

He *had* struck home – he could tell by the brief flicker of alarm in her eyes which vanished as swiftly as it appeared. Martel felt he had a lousy job to carry out but there was no other way.

'You know then?' she asked quietly.

'I am here,' he replied simply. One wrong word would lose her.

'I keep a taxi waiting . . .' She stooped and gathered up the loose cellophane wrappings in which she had brought the flowers. The cellophane was printed with the name of a florist and was moist with the mist. 'You want to come back with me?' she continued quietly, her voice soft and weary. 'Here . . .' she gestured at their surroundings. '. . . is hardly the place.'

'Of course . . .'

Her taxi was waiting behind his own at the gate, the drivers chatting together. Martel paid off his own driver and climbed into the back beside the woman who gave an address in Gallus-strasse.

The bookseller Martel had talked to on his previous visit had informed him it was one of the wealthier residential districts. As they drove away Martel recalled a remark the gravedigger had made about the woman. *Not short of a schilling.* It was all beginning to make hideous sense.

The four-storey villa in Gallus-strasse had cream-washed walls, brown shutters and was a square, solid edifice. Eight steps led up to the front door. Alongside the door were eight names, each with its own bell-push. There was a speakphone grille. One of the names, Martel noticed as she unlocked the door, was Christine Brack.

She had an expensively furnished apartment on the second floor. When she offered to make coffee he refused – he was desperately short of time. She removed the head-scarf, the sable coat, and underneath she was wearing a dark dress with a mandarin collar. As he had expected, she had an excellent figure.

Sitting down on a chair close to his own and facing him, she used both hands to shake loose long black hair. She was a very attractive woman.

'I suppose I have been waiting for you to arrive all my life – ever since it started . . .'

'May I smoke?' Martel asked.

'Please do. You can give me one . . .'

Was it a reaction to the state of extreme tension affecting him? He felt a wild desire to pick her up and carry her to the bed he could see through a half-open door. She followed his glance and crossed her shapely legs.

'Will the money stop now?' she asked. 'Not that I really care. It has felt like blood money all these years. And going to the Post Office to collect the envelope seemed undignified. Does that make sense, Mr . . .?'

'Stolz, Ernst Stolz . . .'

'You know, of course, I still retain my maiden name, Brack?'

'Yes, and I understand the blood money feeling,' Martel probed cautiously. 'Although I think you are wrong . . .'

'We were deeply in love, Mr Stolz. When the accident happened we had just got married . . .'

'It was an accident?'

He was – to use another of Tweed's phrases – creeping over thin ice. She looked startled.

'But of course. My husband was driving the American jeep alone on a dangerous road in the Bregenzer-wald and it was winter. He skidded over a precipice . . .'

'Who confirmed it was an accident?'

Perplexity mingled with suspicion in her expression as Martel struggled to draw her into the web of revelation. 'The two security men who brought me the news,' she replied.

'They wore civilian clothes? Had you ever seen them before? Do you speak French?'

'In the name of God what are you suggesting?' she demanded.

'It would help if you answered the questions . . .'

'*Yes!* They wore civilian clothes. *No!* I had never seen them before. And *no*! I do not speak French . . .'

'So, from the way they spoke, you would not be certain whether these two men were really French – because naturally you conversed in German?'

'That is correct. They explained to me how important it was for my husband's death to remain a secret – he was part of a long-term anti-Soviet operation. They said I owed it to his memory that his work should continue – probably for many years. They told me that his real rank was much higher than the one he had borne – that of lieutenant – and that each month I would therefore receive via the post a generous sum of money as a pension. From the amount I get he must have been a colonel at least . . .'

'What about the burial? Who identified the body?'

'I did, of course! In a private mortuary in the mountains. He had broken his neck but there were few other injuries.'

'And who was buried in the grave? Alois Stohr?'

'My husband, of course . . .' Christine Brack was shaking. 'He was buried under a different name because the long-term anti-Soviet operation depended on pretending he was still alive. They told me he would have wanted me to agree to the deception . . .'

They had committed two murders, Martel reflected. The man whose neck had been broken – and some poor devil of an Austrian whose body had probably been weighted and dumped in the nearby lake. It had been vital to kill and remove the unknown Stohr because of the death certificate regulations and so on – when all they had needed was his name.

Christine Brack, too, would have been killed except for one snag. A third murder might have loaded the dice against the conspirators. Instead they had told her black lies and provided money. He was now at the crux of the whole business. As he reached into his coat pocket for the envelope he realised his palm was moist.

'I want you to look at these photographs and tell me if you recognise anyone. Prepare yourself for a shock. These photos were taken recently.'

Martel waited, concealing a sensation of turmoil. Everything depended on what Christine Brack said during the next minute. She spread out the glossy prints on her lap and then uttered a little exclamation. Her expression was frozen as she held out one photograph.

'That is my husband, Mr Stolz. Older yes, but that is him. I have been dwelling under some terrible illusion for thirty years. What does it mean . . .?'

'You are quite sure?'

'I am certain. Incidentally, I will now tell you another man came to see me recently but I told him very little.' Martel realised she was referring to Charles Warner as she returned the photographs to him.

'That is not your husband,' Martel said gently. 'It simply looks very like him. And you have been living under no illusion – your husband did die thirty years ago.' He stood up. 'You may well be under observation and in grave danger now I have called. Can you pack a bag in five minutes and come with me to a place of safety for a few days?'

Shock made her amenable and she agreed to his

suggestion. Also she was a woman able to pack in five minutes.

Martel hurried her down Gallus-strasse to the lake front where he found a cab and told the driver to take them to a nearby airstrip. The pilot who had flown him from Münich was waiting with his plane.

'I have to be in Münich so I reach the Hauptbahnhof by 9.30 at the latest. And first I have to drop this lady at a hotel . . .'

'We're going to have to move,' the pilot warned.

'Then *move!*'

As they settled into the plane Martel prayed to God that he would not be too late. It had certainly been *German* 'security' men who had fooled Christine Brack all those years ago. And he now knew for certain the identity of the assassin.

Chapter Twenty-Nine

Wednesday June 3, Münich

The arrival of Erich Stoller in the communications coach after the express had left Ulm caused a sensation. Howard was furious and did not resort to diplomatic language.

'Where the hell have you been? You realise the three of us – O'Meara, Flandres and myself – had to assume the responsibility for the safety of your own Chancellor . . .'

'Who is where at this moment?' Stoller broke in.

'Still locked in Compartment 12. The others are impatient for their breakfast but felt they had to wait until he emerged . . .'

'Follow me,' the German suggested. 'And surely you mean the *four* of you?' He glanced at Tweed who remained oddly silent. 'So, had someone hurled a bomb through the window of Compartment 12, you feel it would have been due to my negligence?'

'That's how I see it,' O'Meara replied.

They were following the German who led the way from the communications coach to Voiture Four. He stopped outside Compartment 16 and raised his hand to rap on the door.

'Wrong damned compartment,' Howard snapped.

Stoller rapped on the door with an irregular tattoo and it opened from the inside. Framed in the doorway stood Chancellor Kurt Langer, fully dressed and smoking one of his inevitable cigarettes. He wore a fresh business suit and an enquiring look.

'Time for breakfast, gentlemen? The others must be ready for a good German meal. May I rouse them myself so I can officially welcome them on German soil?'

O'Meara, Howard and Flandres – who had come hurrying up behind Tweed – were stunned into respectful and bewildered silence. They stood aside as Langer, chatting amiably, returned with his fellow-leaders and escorted them to the restaurant car. When they were alone Howard exploded.

'Stoller, you owe us an explanation . . .'

'He owes us nothing,' Tweed intervened. 'We are now in Germany and he can take whatever action he likes. But he may wish to tell us the latest score. Something in the public section of the train worries you, Erich?'

'It was all arranged with the Chancellor in advance when I flew to Bonn,' Stoller told them as they returned to the communications car. 'I boarded the express secretly at Kehl as a passenger while the Chancellor distracted your attention . . .'

'But why?' Howard demanded.

'Because,' Tweed again intervened, 'he sensed there is danger in the public section. I suspect he checked every passenger while pretending to be one of them . . .'

'Correct,' Stoller agreed.

'And,' Tweed continued, 'I imagine you checked the sleeper?'

'Again, correct.' The BND chief permitted himself a wintry smile. 'For the sleeping-car I donned a uniform and examined credentials soon after the train left Stuttgart at 7.03 when they would have had a good night's rest. I found something curious – a woman left the train at Stuttgart, said she was feeling unwell. I'm unhappy about her . . .'

'All of us are,' Tweed replied and explained the mysterious disappearance of Irma Romer who had proved to be an imposter.

A subtle change had come over the relationship between the security chiefs since Stoller's arrival. Before his appearance the personality of Alain Flandres had dominated the group. Now, without seeming to, Tweed had assumed authority.

'I'm going along to the breakfast car to make sure all is well while they breakfast,' Howard suggested. 'Want to join me, Tim?'

Tweed said he would stay with Erich. Stoller waited until they were alone and guided Tweed to the end of the communications coach out of earshot of the technicians. He sat on one of the bunks and lit a cheroot. Tweed thought he looked badly in need of sleep. The German kept his voice low.

'Claire Hofer, Martel's Swiss assistant, came aboard

at Ulm – she's by herself in the first-class coach. It worried me . . .'

'I'll go and see her in a minute,' Tweed replied.

'You know where Martel is? He's gone missing.'

'No idea. I think you have something on your mind . . .'

'I know who is the target for the assassin – it's staring us in the face,' Stoller asserted.

'I agree. But you tell me – and why you think so.'

'My own Chancellor. The state election in Bavaria is knife-edged – with Tofler, the Kremlin's creature, using the neo-Nazis to frighten the electorate into voting for him. So, what would be the effect of the assassination of Langer today?'

'Panic. A potential landslide for Tofler, leading ultimately to Bavaria becoming a Soviet republic – as it briefly was in 1919.'

'So we agree,' said Stoller. 'And you know where I'm convinced the assassination attempt will take place?'

'Go on . . .' Tweed was watching Stoller through half-closed eyes.

'München. He insists on making a brief speech outside the Hauptbahnhof during the stop there and I can't dissuade him. Have you made any progress in locating the assassin?' he asked casually.

'No,' lied Tweed. 'But I'm going along to have a quiet word in her compartment with Claire Hofer. Did you bring any of those new alarm devices your boffins invented?'

'Half-a-dozen were put aboard. I'll get you one . . .'

Stoller walked to the far end of the coach and returned with a rectangular plastic box he carried by a handle. 'This is The Wailer. It's designed to look like a powerful torch – but if you press this button a siren starts up. All hell breaks loose.'

Tweed picked up the 'torch' and made his way along the speeding express through the restaurant. The four western leaders were eating breakfast and the American President, as relaxed as ever, had just cracked a joke which was making his companions laugh. As Tweed passed their table the PM looked up and smiled at him.

Tweed walked on, showing the guards his pass, and moved into the first-class coach. He heard the door being locked behind him and nodded at the two guards outside. Walking slowly along the corridor, he glanced into each compartment.

The one before Claire's was occupied by a single woman wearing what the Americans called a pant suit. He noticed she had a tartan-covered suitcase on the rack and she was smoking as she stared out of the window. He wasted no words as he sat down beside Claire Hofer and showed the pass with his photograph.

'Miss Hofer, my name is Tweed. Keith Martel will have told you about me. Where is he?'

She examined the pass carefully before returning it. 'He flew to Bregenz in Austria late yesterday evening. He ordered me to board this train at Ulm.'

'Bregenz? Then I was right. But we need *proof*. Where will he board the express?'

'At München – he was flying back this morning. I just hope that he makes it . . .'

'He has to make it. The target is Langer. The attempt will be made at München. There is a thirteen-minute stop. Langer insists on making a speech outside the Hauptbahnhof – in front of a vast crowd. The assassin has to be identified and exposed before Langer mounts that podium . . .'

'Which means Martel must be on the platform and ready to board the express instantly . . .'

'I don't like the split-second timing,' Tweed confessed. 'And now I must go . . .' He tapped the plastic box, explaining how the device worked. 'Don't forget The Wailer. You see anything wrong, you press the button . . .'

Alone again in the compartment, Claire was beset with anxiety. What could she possibly hope to see that was wrong?

'For Christ's sake, move faster! I've paid you enough,' Martel rapped at the cab-driver. 'Use the side-streets . . .'

'The traffic – the one-way system . . .'

The driver lifted both hands briefly off the wheel to indicate his own frustration. München was jammed with cars. People on foot were streaming towards the Hauptbahnhof to hear Langer's speech. And

Christine Brack was now safely ensconced in the Hotel Clausen.

They passed the river Isar where it debouched into an intricate system of sluices. Martel remembered the rendezvous a man called Stahl never kept at the Embroidery Museum in St Gallen. Stoller had later told him of the body found trapped in one of the sluices, a body whose only identification had been a wrist-watch engraved with the word *Stahl*. Then the memory was gone.

Martel contemplated getting out and running the rest of the way. Then he saw they were passing the Four Seasons Hotel. Too far yet. He would never make swift progress through this mob of Langer supporters.

He checked his watch again in an obvious gesture which the driver saw in his rear-view mirror. It was 9.23 a.m. The Summit Express was due to arrive at the station in exactly ten minutes' time. The turmoil following the Chancellor's assassination would be appalling. It could easily sway the election into Tofler's hands.

Like Tweed, Martel had worked out that the target was the German leader. And now he knew the identity of the assassin – but only he could confront the killer and prove his identity. He stared in the rear-view mirror and met the driver's eyes.

'Here I can try a side-street,' the man said. 'It could save a few minutes . . .'

A few minutes. They could make all the difference

360

to the future of western Europe – of the whole of the West.

Manfred's nylon-clad hand lifted the receiver the moment the instrument began ringing. He was aware he was gripping the receiver tightly. His packed case stood by the apartment door.

'Ewald Portz speaking,' a voice said. 'I am in position . . .'

'Watch your timing – it must be perfect . . .'

'We have gone over it a score of times,' Portz snapped.

'Then just remember – this is not a rehearsal . . .'

In a phone booth at München Hauptbahnhof Portz, a short, stocky man in his thirties, glared at the phone he was still holding. The line had gone dead. The bastard had rung off.

Inside the apartment Manfred picked up his case and kept on his gloves while he opened the outer door, closed and locked it. Only then did he remove the gloves and stuff them in his pocket. The main thing was that Portz – the *decoy* – was ready and in position. Armed with a pistol loaded with blanks he had to aim and fire at the Chancellor at the same moment as the real assassin. Then he would run like hell in the confusion, making himself prominent as he disappeared inside the U-Bahn.

This tactic should divert attention from the real assassin who, once he had done the job, would make his way to the adjoining Starnberger Hof, the station for trains to the mountains. Then he would travel only a few stops before he left the train, was met by a waiting car and driven to a nearby airstrip.

Getting behind the wheel of his car parked at the kerb, Manfred adjusted his spectacles and drove off to the underground garage for his final meeting with Reinhard Dietrich.

It was hopeless. The traffic was getting worse the nearer they came to the Hauptbahnhof. Martel rapped on the window, gesturing to the driver to stop. He had the money for the fare – in addition to the earlier tip – ready in his hand as he leapt out.

'You will catch your train?' the driver enquired.

'This is the one train in the world I *have* to catch . . .'

Martel disappeared and the driver shook his head. What a statement. The English, they were all mad. Perhaps that was why they had won the war?

Martel barged his way through the crowd, elbowing aside men who shouted after him as he plunged on through the milling mob. He could see the Hauptbahnhof now. It was 9.31 a.m. Only two more minutes before the Summit Express arrived – before the Chancellor, noted for his briskness, left the train and made his way to the specially-constructed podium Martel could see. He forced a path round the edge of the jostling mass.

Reaching the road in front of the Hauptbahnhof he encountered a fresh problem but he was ready for it. In his left hand he held the special pass which allowed him to board the express. The new problem was police guards who held back the crowd. He shouted at the top of his voice.

'*Polizei!* Make way! Polizei . . . !'

'Stop . . . !'

A uniformed policeman drew his Walther from his holster as Martel dashed past him and across the open space. He zigzagged, risking a bullet in the back. The voice called out with greater urgency.

'Halt or I fire . . . !'

Only at this critical juncture did he have some luck. He recognised a man in civilian clothes as one of Stoller's aides – and the aide recognised Martel. He raised a bullhorn and bellowed the order to the policeman.

'Hold your fire! Let this man through . . . !'

Martel dashed past him and the station entrance was ahead with more sightseers behind a cordon of police waiting for a glimpse of the Chancellor. Beyond he saw the locomotive of the express just stopping. He ran on . . .

As the express slowed to a halt Klara Beck was walking through the corridor towards the exit, carrying her tartan-covered suitcase. She did not even glance into Claire Hofer's compartment. Something about the way she moved made Claire study the woman.

Lindau! Claire had seen Beck arrive in the reception hall of the Bayerischer Hof. From the elevated terrace above the harbour she had observed Beck walking rapidly towards the Hauptbahnhof – Klara Beck!

Claire stood up, grabbed The Wailer and left the compartment, following the woman in the trouser suit. When she reached the exit the door was open and Beck stepped down on to the platform.

Half-way along the coach Beck paused, stood the case on the platform, twisted the handle through a one hundred and eighty degree arc and walked on, leaving the case. Alain Flandres had descended from the restaurant car and glanced quickly round as though looking for something suspicious. Then he walked swiftly through the ticket barrier to the side of the station. Chancellor Langer had left the train and waved a hand, acknowledging the crescendo of cheering.

Claire dropped The Wailer on the platform and pressed the button. She nearly jumped out of her shoes as a hellish wailing sound like a police siren blasted out, its high pitch penetrating the cheers. Langer paused uncertainly. Stoller appeared beside him, a gun in his hand, followed by O'Meara. Beck glanced back and recognised Claire.

There was a searing flash of light as the magnesium flares packed inside the paper-thin walls of the tartan-covered case exploded. It was the five-second moment of distraction the assassin was waiting for. Ewald Portz raised his pistol and began firing the blank shots. Martel appeared behind him, the Colt .45 in his hand. He gripped the butt with both hands and elevated the muzzle.

At the side of the station Alain Flandres aimed his Luger equipped with a silencer point-blank at Langer. Martel swivelled his weapon and snapped off three rapid shots. The bullets missed the Frenchman but ricochetted all round him. He ran for the entrance to the Starnberger Hof station and disappeared.

Klara Beck was on the verge of pulling the trigger of her pistol pointed at Claire when Stoller fired once. Beck stooped forward, the pistol falling from her hand, and sagged to the ground.

O'Meara had produced his .38 Smith & Wesson and took deliberate aim at Portz. After firing his blanks the German was fleeing towards the U-Bahn. The American's bullets slammed into his back and he sprawled on the concrete, leaving behind a smear of red as he lay inert.

As Alain Flandres ran on to the platform a train was just leaving the Starnberger Hof. The timing had been vital. He grabbed a door-handle and heaved it open. A train guard shouted at him as Martel came round the corner. Flandres had heaved himself up on to the step and was about to hurl himself inside the compartment. Martel fired twice and both bullets rammed into the target's back.

The train was gathering speed as he hovered, half-inside the compartment and half on the step. He stayed poised like a figure frozen in a tableau. Then his body jack-knifed, toppled backwards into space and hit the platform like a sack of cement. He was dead when Martel reached him.

Chapter Thirty

Wednesday June 3

'The Soviets – using East Germans as proxies – replaced a young French lieutenant in the Army of Occupation in Bregenz with their own man thirty years ago,' Martel said and accepted a cigarette from the German Chancellor who sat opposite him in the restaurant car of the Summit Express.

The train had left München and was heading east for Salzburg and Vienna. Martel was not in the least embarrassed by his audience which included his own Prime Minister, the American and French Presidents, together with Tweed, Stoller, O'Meara and Howard. He just felt unutterably weary.

'How did they manage that deception?' Langer asked.

'By a process of elimination, I assume. Everyone has a double. I happen to know you have your own for security reasons – and never use him. They had a man – my guess would be an Armenian – and he looked very much like the real Alain Flandres. They undoubtedly scoured the French forces in the Vorarlberg, the Tyrol and Vienna searching for their double. Poor Alain was made to order.'

'In what way?' Langer pressed. 'And drink some more cognac . . .'

'The real Flandres was an orphan. No one back in France knew him well. He was being demobilised and planned to join the Direction de la Surveillance du Territoire – an outfit where everyone would be a stranger. Damn it, Chancellor – if you don't mind my recalling the episode – Chancellor Willy Brandt was compelled to resign when his chief aide, Guenter Guillaume, turned out to be a KGB agent. An even more difficult plant than Alain Flandres.'

'You're right,' Langer agreed. 'And I am most grateful that you saved my life. But how did you detect Flandres?'

'It's a tragic story. We had a previous agent, Charles Warner, who was murdered. In his notebook was an intriguing reference to Bregenz. I showed Warner's photo round the town and that led me to a cemetery – to a grave still visited by the woman who married the real Flandres just before he was murdered . . .'

'She knew about the impersonation?' Langer queried.

'The East Germans fooled her, kidded her up with a story so her dead husband was buried under another name. They had to do that if the fake Alain Flandres was going back to France to infiltrate the security services . . .'

'We were not very clever,' interjected the French President.

'Every security outfit has been penetrated at some time – even the KGB overlooked Col. Oleg Penkovsky. We worked on a process of elimination . . .'

'What exactly do you mean by that?' Howard demanded.

'Let Mr Martel continue,' the PM reprimanded Howard sharply.

'It looked like O'Meara at one time,' Martel said, staring at the American. 'When Tweed visited Clint Loomis to check up your background Loomis ended up dead . . .'

'Hell, I'm not taking that . . .'

'You are taking that – and whatever else comes,' the President of the US told him mildly.

'As I was saying, Loomis ended up dead. But that was to point us in the wrong direction – Manfred's doing, we suspected. Plus a missing two months when you were in West Berlin and absent from your base.' Martel tactfully omitted to mention that O'Meara had spent time with the now-deceased Klara Beck.

'You, sir,' Martel switched his gaze to Howard, 'posed a problem. While attached to the Paris Embassy you spent six weeks' leave in Vienna. You've made no mention of this fact since this operation started – even though Vienna is our destination.'

'Purely personal reasons,' Howard responded stiffly and lapsed into silence.

'Then there was Erich Stoller.' Martel glanced at Tweed. 'You might like to go on . . .'

'Erich was the obvious suspect,' Tweed began

briskly. 'He had spent two years underground inside East Germany. Plenty of time for him to be trained by the state security people in Leipzig or East Berlin. *Too* obvious. Had he gone over to the other side, after a year or so they'd have faked an imminent exposure which made him dash back across the border. That would have built up a nice credit balance of trust. The fact he was there two years proved he was just damned good at his job.'

'So we came to Alain Flandres,' Martel explained. 'Likeable, lively Alain who seemed above suspicion. Until it occurred to us that his early background was the vaguest of all four security chiefs. And now, if you don't mind, I'd like to snatch a little sleep. I'm getting off at Salzburg . . .'

'I shall also get off there,' said Tweed.

'Well,' Howard broke in boisterously. 'I think you can safely leave security for the rest of the journey in our hands . . .'

'Now that *they* have located the assassin,' the PM interjected cuttingly.

Manfred received his first warning when he drove into the underground garage to keep his rendezvous with Reinhard Dietrich. To his surprise he saw Dietrich's Mercedes had already arrived – although it was strictly understood that Manfred would be there first.

He checked his watch. No, he was not late –

Dietrich was early. In the deserted cavern Manfred swung his car in a semi-circle and backed rapidly to position his vehicle alongside the six-seater Mercedes. He used one hand on the wheel while the other opened the automatic window and then grasped from the seat beside him a Luger with the silencer screwed on the barrel. When he switched off his motor he realised Dietrich had kept his own engine ticking over.

'You are early,' he called out. 'Another mistake – I trust you do appreciate the whole manoeuvre has failed?'

'Entirely due to you,' the millionaire replied.

Dietrich was sitting in the automatic car with the gear in drive, the hand-brake off – and only his pressure on the foot-brake preventing the car moving forward. The front passenger window was open, his right hand gripped a Walther pistol, his left hand a metallic sphere, and the passenger door was not closed.

'Your meaning?' Manfred asked quietly. 'Because Langer was not assassinated his party will win?'

'That, of course. But it is not pleasant to grasp that I have been tricked from the beginning. You supplied the arms to Delta, I told you every time the location of the dumps. You, alone – and myself – had this information. Stoller must have been delighted as you relayed the locations to him. You are a bloody Bolshevik . . .'

Both men reacted at almost the same moment.

Manfred raised the Luger and fired twice. *Phut-phut*. Dietrich had used his right foot to kick the door open wide as he leant forward and aimed the Walther. He was too late.

Manfred's bullets thumped into his chest and he slumped sideways over the passenger seat. His hand holding the large sphere lost its grip and, unseen by Manfred, the 'rolling' bomb thumped on to the concrete floor and disappeared beneath Manfred's car.

The new device designed by Dietrich's boffins in the secret research section of his Stuttgart factory was like a massive grenade. The button Dietrich had been holding depressed was released, the device activated and timed to detonate in five seconds. Dietrich's foot slipped from the foot-brake and the Mercedes glided forward.

Manfred turned on the ignition at the very moment the rolling bomb exploded with tremendous power. Compressed between concrete floor and chassis, the blast soared upwards and *elevated* the car. The sound was deafening, the ruination total. Afterwards they were never able to find enough of Manfred to make any kind of identification possible. He was literally blown to pieces.

The three of them – Martel, Tweed and Claire Hofer – stood on the platform at Salzburg Hauptbahnhof watching the end of the rear coach grow smaller as the Summit Express headed on the last lap for Vienna.

'I'm flying back home,' Tweed announced. 'I shan't expect you for three weeks, Keith.' He glanced at Claire. 'I expect I can keep Howard at bay until you return . . .'

They watched the compact figure of Tweed striding briskly away, his shoulders erect, looking from side to side, still observing all that was going on around him. Martel turned to Claire who spoke first.

'He'd make a marvellous chief of your SIS. He's so amazingly cool under pressure. When he came to give me The Wailer just before the train reached Münich the tension must have been terrific. You would have thought he was on holiday.'

'Talking about holidays, you're going back to Berne to report?'

'Yes . . .'

'On the other hand there's no rush, surely? I'm going to pick up Christine Brack from the Hotel Clausen to take her back to Bregenz. I want her to know the man who impersonated her husband is dead – psychologically it may close a long, painful chapter in her life. Bregenz is on the way back to St Gallen. Didn't you find the Metropol a comfortable hotel?'

'I think I'm going to find it even more comfortable this time,' she replied, linking her arm inside his.

THE
CAULDRON

FOR SUZANNE

Author's Note

All the characters portrayed are creatures of the author's imagination and bear no relationship to any living person.

The same applies to all residences whether located in Cornwall or California. Again, they are invented out of the author's imagination.

Prologue

Paula Grey tensed as she saw the floating body crest a huge wave, carried close inshore across the Pacific Ocean like a surfer lying on its back in the lonely moonlight.

She had started on a night-time walk from the luxurious Californian Spanish Bay Hotel, down the boardwalks between the deserted golf links which swept away on either side. Depressed, because she had discovered nothing suspicious about Vincent Bernard Moloch, billionaire owner of the world's largest conglomerate, AMBECO – the mission Tweed had sent her on from London – she had decided to walk to clear her mind.

It was cold in July at this time of night and the storm building up from the ocean chilled her, despite her heavy blue jeans and woollen sweater and windbreaker. Another giant wave lifted the sinister body near the shore. She calculated it would hit the coast at Octopus Cove.

Glancing round, she unzipped the windbreaker and grasped the .32 Browning tucked inside the top of her jeans. As she hurried down to the raging sea the roar of the boiling water became deafening. It hurled itself against craggy rocks, throwing up great bursts of surf.

The body was very close to the rocks she scrambled down, her clothes soaked with the ferocious surf. Her fear of the ocean's turmoil vanished as she watched the corpse thrown inside a deep gulch into shallow water.

Reaching down she grasped an ice-cold hand and saw it was the body of a woman.

Before the next wave could smash it against the rocks she hauled the dead woman upwards and out of the relentless ocean. In the moonlight she had a clear view of the woman's face, dark hair plastered against the skull, the body clad in a white dress clinging to her above the stomach. Round the left wrist she had used to haul her out Paula saw an ugly red abrasion. She looked at the right wrist and round it was a torn rope. Blood had earlier seeped from a large wound on the head and congealed. That was when Paula heard engines coming towards her at speed from the sea.

Looking up, she saw three large rubber dinghies powered by outboard motors racing towards Octopus Cove. Each craft contained a number of men, heads hooded and holding what appeared to be assault rifles. The lead dinghy had one of the largest men she had ever seen. Standing up, despite the savage swell, he held on to the side with one hand and removed his hood with the other. He was staring straight at her, a man with thick dark hair and a Roman nose. Paula crouched down, shifted the heavy corpse closer to the side of a rock and then ran, still crouching.

She started up the boardwalk, a series of parallel wooden planks, then turned off it onto the golf course. Some sixth sense warned her to find a hiding place. Her sodden trainers squelched as she ran across the trim grass of the rolling links. Where to hide, for God's sake? Stay cool.

She was well clear of the boardwalk when she literally ran into a hideaway – a large bunker of sand. Flopping down inside it, she wrenched out the Browning automatic she had shoved back down inside her jeans while hauling out the body of the woman. Cautiously she wriggled her way up to the rim of the bunker, looked over the top down to Octopus Cove.

Clouds were beginning to drift over the moon but Paula now saw about half a mile offshore the silhouette of a huge luxury yacht. Stationary, swaying with the swell of the rising storm, she estimated it must be almost three hundred feet long. Above the main control cabin was a cluster of radar equipment and a Comsat dish, so it had communications via a satellite. No lights. Not even a starboard light. Very weird.

Hooded figures from the dinghies were scrambling ashore at Octopus Cove in wetsuits. Several bent down to where the corpse lay, lifted it, began carrying it through the turmoil of the wild ocean towards a dinghy. The giant with black hair stared round the golf links, made a sweeping gesture with his left hand. Six men, gripping their automatic rifles, advanced over the links, spread out. They were coming for her.

Lying deep inside the bunker in her soaking clothes, she heard the clumping feet of men prowling close to her. She kept her eyes on the rim where they would appear, the Browning clasped in both hands. Now and then their voices, some English, some American, came to her clearly.

'She has to be somewhere around here.'

'Buddy boy, she sure is. No time for her to reach the hotel. We'd have seen her . . .'

Later another couple came much closer to the bunker.

'Joel will spit in our faces if we don't get her.'

'No names, Loud Mouth. Keep searching . . .'

By the illuminated hands of her wristwatch Paula knew she had lain in the bunker for an hour when she heard a distant sound of engines starting up. Gun in her

3

right hand, she crawled to the rim, peered over. The three dinghies were leaving Octopus Cove, heading back to their mother ship, the long silhouette rocking from side to side. Then the moon was blotted out by dark clouds and she lost sight of them.

She scanned the links to make sure she was alone, knowing it could be a trap. They might have left one man behind to watch out for her. Only when she felt sure no one was about did Paula wearily plod back up the boardwalk to Spanish Bay Hotel, which overlooked the links and the Pacific beyond. Thanking heaven she had slipped out unseen from her magnificent ground floor suite, she slid back the tall glass windows, stepped inside, closed, locked them. She forced herself to draw the curtains, felt her way to the door to the splendidly equipped bathroom, closed that door and switched on the lights.

Placing the Browning on the edge of the jacuzzi, Paula stripped off, stepped into the shower stall, and, still shivering, turned on the shower to hot. The glass was steamed up when she eventually left the shower, ignored the sodden clothes on the floor, towelled herself, went through another door past gleaming washbasins and into the large room with its double bed. Putting on pyjamas, she perched on the edge of the bed and drank hot coffee from a thermos she always had refilled by Roy's, the restaurant in the hotel.

Feeling able to cope, she dialled Tweed's number in London at Park Crescent, headquarters of the SIS. She had checked the time. 3 a.m. California was eight hours behind Britain, so it would be 11 a.m. London time.

'Monica, Paula here. Urgent I speak to him.'

'Hang on, he's here . . .'

'Good to hear from you, Paula,' the familiar voice opened tersely. 'Anything to report?'

4

'No. The company is in excellent shape. I have . . . nothing . . . to tell you.'

'Better catch the next plane home, then. Looking forward to seeing you.'

'Cheerio for now . . .'

Paula put down the phone and felt a burst of relief. There had been two coded messages in the way she had phrased her call. Use of the word *excellent* had told Tweed something was wrong. Plus her deliberate pause before *nothing*.

She tumbled into bed, feeling so far from home. Monterey, the pleasant town near Spanish Bay, together with Carmel, close by, were among the most peaceful parts of the States she had visited. At least on the surface. And until her recent ordeal.

Her head buried in the pillow she had an image of the mysterious yacht she had seen out at sea. Maybe in the morning she could wheedle out of the Harbormaster at Monterey the name of the vessel. Exhausted, she fell into a deep sleep.

It was a brilliant sunny afternoon, temperature a perfect 70°, when Paula left the yellow cab which dropped her near Monterey harbour. A large anchorage protected by enclosing jetties, it was full of shipping. Fishing craft were moored close to Coast Guard vessels at the southern end of the big harbour. Several expensive power cruisers bobbed gently by their pontoons.

'There's plenty of money round here,' Paula said to herself.

The cab driver had pointed out to her the Harbormaster's office. As she walked towards the building Paula blessed the fact that last night's storm had stayed out at sea. Had it come inland she would have had a much worse experience. Now the sky was a blue dome. In the distance beyond Monterey brown hills, scorched by the sun, rose to meet the blue.

She was near the building when she saw a stocky man leaving with an unbalanced walk. She paused by a restaurant with awnings where a man in whites was brushing the area outside.

'Excuse me, but is that person who has just left that building the Harbormaster?'

'Like your English accent.' The man smiled pleasantly. 'He is standing in for the Harbormaster, who returned from his vacation a few minutes ago.' He lowered his voice. 'That guy is Chuck Floorstone. Between the two of us he spends too much time lifting a glass. Done that myself. Been there. Now Coke is my drink.'

'Very sensible. Thank you.'

She hurried after the stocky figure whose T-shirt was hanging out over baggy trousers. She caught up with him at the moment he was entering a bar. Paula pushed in front of him, then apologized.

'I really am sorry.'

'No need, pretty lady. You on your own? I am. Buy you a drink.'

'Thank you. That would be nice.'

Chuck Floorstone guided her to a quiet table in a corner by a window overlooking the exit from the harbour. At that hour they were almost the only customers. Paula had asked for a glass of Chardonnay. Floorstone had shuffled to the far end of the bar so she couldn't hear what he was asking for. She had made herself very presentable for this hoped-for talk. She wore a form-fitting white silk blouse, high at the collar, and a blue skirt which hung just below her knees.

Floorstone was eyeing her as he shuffled back, spilling her wine over the rim of her glass. He saw a slim woman in her thirties, her dark well-brushed hair almost touching her shoulders. She had a good figure and shapely legs and the bone structure of her strong face expressed character. Her intelligent grey-blue eyes studied him as he approached, placed the wine in front of her, slumped into the next seat.

'We could hit the town, pretty lady.'

'Somebody told me you had an important job,' she replied.

'I'm the Harbormaster here.'

His weather-beaten face, lined with the tell-tale red veins of the hardened drinker, grinned with self-importance, exposing bad teeth. Paula smiled, glanced out of the window, stopped herself stiffening. A huge luxury yacht was heading out of the harbour, a vessel with a complex of radar apparatus above the main control cabin with a Comsat dish.

'What's that vessel?' she asked.

'That little rowboat belongs to Vincent Bernard Moloch. Owns half the world. The Big Boy.'

'Really? What's it called?'

'*Venetia V* . . .' Floorstone was slurring his words and he realized it. 'V . . . e . . . n . . . e . . . t . . . i . . . a . . . Five,' he repeated carefully. 'Word is it's headed for Baja California in Mexico.' Taking another large gulp of his own drink, he leaned towards her. 'Moloch plays it close to the chest. My guess is it's headed for the Panama Canal, then through it into the Atlantic.'

'It's been here for a while?' she asked casually.

'Naah. Came in early morning, refuelled, now it's off again. You never know with Moloch. You're not drinking.'

'I'm a slow drinker.' Paula was suspicious about the ingredients of her glass, which tasted too potent. 'Is this Moloch character on board the *Venetia V*?'

'Naah. His bully boy, Joel Brand, is the boss on this trip.'

7

Paula kept her face expressionless at the mention of the name. 'Bully boy?'

'Yeah. A Brit. An ugly customer. Does all Moloch's dirty work. Now about us going on the town?'

'This Joel Brand is just the skipper of the yacht?'

'Naah. He's Moloch's right arm. Was in the Navy. The Brit Navy. Now about . . .'

'What are you drinking?'

'Bourbon and soda. Need a freshener. Get you one. Back in a minute.' He waved a warning finger. 'Don't walk out on me.'

Paula watched him staggering back to the bar, slipped on her shoulder bag, quietly left the bar. She had already packed, paid her bill at Spanish Bay, hired a car to take her the two-hour drive to San Francisco International and had reserved a first-class seat.

As she rode back in a cab to the hotel she wished Bob Newman was with her. She could have found out more from Floorstone, but she had found out enough. Now for the endless eleven-hour night flight back to Heathrow. Not a trip she relished, even though Tweed was generous in allowing her to travel first class.

On the drive north to San Francisco she was haunted by the image of the dead woman's face, the woman she had dragged out of the sea. Who was she?

Several weeks later she was in Cornwall with Bob Newman, sent there by Tweed with clear instructions.

Tweed had briefed them in his first-floor office at Park Crescent with its windows looking towards Regent's Park. A man of medium height and build, middle-aged, clean-shaven and wearing horn-rimmed glasses, he was someone you could pass in the street without noticing. This appearance had served him well as Deputy Director of the SIS.

Paula had sat at her desk in a corner of the large room, and close to the door Monica was ensconced behind her own desk, equipped with a press-button phone linked to the phone on Tweed's otherwise clear desk. She also had the latest fax machine and other sophisticated equipment.

Monica, a woman of uncertain age, with her grey hair tied in a bun, had been Tweed's assistant for years and was totally loyal and discreet. The fourth occupant of the room was Bob Newman, world-famous foreign corre-spondent who had long ago been vetted for security and intelligence work.

Newman was a well-built man in his forties, also clean-shaven, fair-haired, with a half-smile and a sense of humour which had appealed to many women. He sat with his arms folded, turned his head as someone tapped on the door and entered. Marler had arrived late as usual.

'Mornin', everyone. See the clan has gathered,' he drawled in his upper-crust voice. 'Something big brewing?'

He took up his normal position, leaning against a wall as he lit a king-size cigarette. Slimly built, in his late thirties, he was a snappy dresser – and the best marksman with a rifle in Western Europe. Tweed nodded to him and began speaking, leaning forward, his voice quiet but expressing great force of character.

'Paula returned from California several weeks ago after a three-week stay in the Monterey–Carmel area. She went to dig up any data she could on Vincent Bernard Moloch. She'll tell you in a minute about that trip so you, Marler, are up to date. Moloch has a large mansion out in the Cornish wilderness way behind Falmouth. I want you, Paula, to go down there with Bob and Marler to investigate Moloch. I've booked separate rooms for all of you at a very nice country hotel, Nansidwell, near a village called Mawnan Smith. I know the proprietor, a very likeable chap . . .'

'He doesn't know who you really are, I presume?' chimed in Paula.

'Of course not. I used our usual cover story – General & Cumbria Assurance. We investigate suspected insurance swindles on a large scale.'

'Isn't three people a large team even for that?' Marler enquired.

'I've told you that you'll occupy separate rooms. You'll eat at separate tables. You don't know each other. I got several friends at Special Branch to call the hotel to book in you and Bob. They phoned about the reservations on different days. I booked in Paula.' He switched his gaze to her. 'The doctor has said you're suffering from a state of complete exhaustion. Convalescent leave.'

'Try to look exhausted,' Marler chaffed her. 'Make a real effort.'

'If I may continue,' Tweed said sharply. 'Moloch's mansion is called Mullion Towers. It's near a nowhere place called Stithians.'

'What I'd like to know,' Marler suggested, 'is why is this chap Moloch the target?'

'He may not be,' Tweed said cryptically. 'But his outfit AMBECO is so enormous – plus the fact he's in touch with certain Arabs – that it's worrying not only London but also Washington. He worries me – the amount of power he has set about accumulating.'

'And what is AMBECO?' Marler persisted. 'Heard of it but no idea what it does.'

'*A*,' began Tweed, 'is for Armaments. *M* is for Machine tools. *B* is for Banking. *E* is for Electronics. *C* is for Chemicals, could be biological. *O* is for Oil.'

'Tricky combination,' Newman intervened. 'Armaments – and chemicals. Sounds like advanced weapon systems. Don't like the sound of Mr Moloch.'

'Actually,' Tweed went on, 'Moloch's main interest at

10

present is in electronics. He wants to dominate the world systems in communications.'

'He'll get stiff competition from Bill Gates of Microsoft in Seattle,' Newman observed.

'Maybe. Now, Paula, tell everyone about your experiences in California.'

They listened intently as she gave a precise report. She concluded with an encounter she'd had while staying at Spanish Bay.

'A very attractive English redhead called Vanessa Richmond kept trying to make friends with me. I was suspicious and evaded her. Another woman, an American, told me she was nicknamed by the locals "Vanity" Richmond. I think it was a jealous remark.' She turned to Tweed. 'Tell me,' she said insistently, 'isn't there something more menacing about this Moloch? What you *have* told us doesn't seem to me to justify the major effort we're making to track him.'

'You have enough information for the moment,' Tweed replied abruptly. He smiled to soften the impact. 'Now off you all go and enjoy yourself in Cornwall.' He stood up, his tone serious. 'But regard this as a dangerous mission . . .'

They travelled fast to Cornwall. Each had had a case packed for instant departure from Park Crescent. Newman left first in his beloved Mercedes 280E. He was passing Stonehenge when he saw Marler coming up behind him in his Saab. Later Paula appeared in her Ford Fiesta.

She was in an impish mood. When they reached a deserted dual carriageway she rammed her foot down, overtook Marler, then Newman. Grinning to himself, Newman slowed down and she disappeared from sight.

Still on the dual carriageway, Paula frowned as she spotted a blue Volvo roaring up behind her. The driver, alone at the wheel, was a brunette wearing large sunglasses. Paula felt sure she had seen her shortly after leaving Park Crescent. And a very similar-looking girl had been aboard her flight back from San Francisco.

'Interested in me, honey?' she said to herself, reverting to American phraseology.

She kept moving, maintaining her speed. Sunglasses dropped back but stayed within sight as Paula by-passed Exeter, crossed Bodmin Moor. By the time she had reached Nansidwell Country Hotel Sunglasses had disappeared.

The proprietor himself greeted her warmly but respectfully. She was shown to her room on the first floor which overlooked the parklike gardens, descending in lawn plateaux, the grass perfectly mown, and with a semi-distant view of the sea looking like an azure lake under brilliant sunshine. A tanker and a large freighter were waiting for permission to berth outside Falmouth harbour.

After a long soaking bath she dressed for dinner, went down the impressively wide staircase, saw Bob Newman was standing near the entrance inside one of two comfortable lounges. He smiled as though greeting an attractive stranger.

'Good evening. This is a lovely hotel. Have you been here long? Oh, I'm Bob Newman.'

'Paula Grey. No, I just arrived today. I gather dinner is 7.30 p.m. onwards.'

'It's only 6.30. I was just going for a look round outside. If you'd care to join me in my first exploration? Or maybe you'd sooner be on your own?'

'No, let's explore together. You're a birdwatcher? Those binoculars looped round your neck.'

12

'They're only for viewing distant points.'

Their conversation had been for the benefit of a couple sitting on a couch with drinks who were obviously taking in every word. As they wandered out of the main entrance, heading for the terrace at the rear of the hotel, Marler's Saab appeared at the end of the rhododendron-lined drive, swung at speed in a sharp circle to occupy a vacant space close to Paula's car. He never gave as much as a glance in their direction.

Paula froze. Parked next to Newman's Mercedes was a blue Volvo. During the journey she had never been able to see the registration number of the car driven by Sunglasses. 'There are a lot of Volvos in the world. Stop getting so jittery,' she told herself. She and Newman wandered on round a corner onto a pebble path in front of the topmost grassy terrace. Here they had the same sweeping panoramic view Paula had from her bedroom window.

'What do you do for a living – if it isn't too personal a question?' she asked.

'Oh, I'm a foreign correspondent.'

They were now talking for the benefit for another couple with drinks before dinner who sat perched on a banquette seat by an open window.

'Really?' Paula continued. 'I vaguely seem to have heard the name,' she teased him.

'I'm surprised. I've written the odd piece for one or two newspapers.'

She glanced out to sea and froze again, this time with a real sense of shock. The tanker had vanished. In its place was anchored a very large luxury yacht, a complex of radar above the main control bridge – and a Comsat dish. She had now seen a similar vessel starboard-on – once off Octopus Cove and again leaving the harbour at Monterey.

She walked further along the path, then across the grass, and stood by a small wall decorated with various plants. Newman strolled after her.

'Bob,' she whispered, 'that looks exactly like the yacht I saw standing offshore when that woman's body floated in to Octopus Cove.'

'That seems pretty unlikely.' Newman raised his binoculars, focused them on the vessel. 'It would be an extraordinary coincidence if you were right. Don't believe in them – coincidences.'

'So it's a different ship.'

'There are a few people in the world who could afford a toy like that. Must be almost three hundred feet long. Mind you, Tweed has many ways of finding out things. And you could have been right when you suggested he was holding back information.'

'So what is the name of the damned thing?'

'Tweed did know what he was doing. The name of that floating gold vault is *Venetia V*.'

As ordered, they occupied separate tables in the spacious and comfortable dining room which overlooked the gardens. Marler, typically, had manoeuvred it so he sat by himself at a corner table at the rear of the room with his back to the wall.

The meal was excellent, served by three girls who, Paula gathered by talking to them, were all local. As she ate, never glancing at Newman, conscious of Marler's presence a couple of tables behind her, she thought about what a beautiful building Nansidwell was.

Built of grey stone, covered here and there with creeper, it had deep windows with mullioned panes. A house with great presence. The proprietor had told her it had once been a private residence. Paula looked out of the window as dusk fell, making the rolling hills sloping down towards it from the south look like velvet. Gazing out to sea, she saw the brilliant glow of lights aboard the *Venetia V* and felt a chill despite its appearance of a luxury cruise liner.

She was eating her dessert when she had another shock. The door to the dining room opened and a woman walked in and sat at a table by herself close to Newman. A brunette, she wore tinted glasses, a blue designer dress, low-cut below the neck, which hugged her very good figure. Seen in profile she seemed very familiar to Paula and her mind flashed back to the woman at Spanish Bay who had attempted to get to know her.

God! Paula thought, I'm sure that's Vanity Richmond. But she was a glamorous redhead in California.

Leaving the dining room, Newman signalled to Marler, who – characteristically – was engaged in deep conversation in one of the lounges with an attractive woman. Marler had a gift for amusing conversation and his companion was almost choking with laughter.

Waiting outside in the dark, Newman suddenly found Paula alongside him.

'What's going on?' she asked. 'I saw you signal Marler.'

'I'm taking him with me down a secret path to a cove by the sea the proprietor told me about. I want a closer look at that ship.'

'I'll come with you.'

'No, you won't. The three of us together would give the game away if we were seen.'

'It isn't that. You think it might be dangerous.'

'All right. Tweed put me in command of this team. So I am ordering you to stay in your bedroom.'

'Bossy so-and-so!'

She was going back inside when she returned quickly after checking no one had seen her.

'I'm sorry, Bob. I shouldn't have said that. I know you're in charge. I'll stay in my bedroom. Be careful.'

'Aren't I always?'

'No, you're not.'

She gave his arm an affectionate squeeze and went inside. A few minutes later Marler strolled out, smoking a king-size.

'Get rid of that,' Newman told him.

Marler bent down to stub out the cigarette while Newman told him about his plan. Taking out an empty packet, Marler slid the dead cigarette inside to leave no traces. Newman went on talking in a low voice.

'I'm carrying a .38 Smith & Wesson in my hip holster. What about you?'

'My faithful Walther automatic is hugging me. Look, there's a back way out just past my ground-floor room. I'll meet you at the other end of the house. That way no one sees us together if you stroll along the terrace . . .'

The narrow pathway down to the sea, sunk below high hedges on either side, descended steeply. With their eyes tuned to the darkness Newman and Marler avoided tripping over a spider-like pattern of tree roots. The trees enclosed them on both sides and created an atmosphere of imminent danger.

The path twisted and turned, always shielded by hedges growing on banks high up. It was silent as they walked rapidly down and down until they reached the small cove. No one was about. The only sound was the swish of the incoming tide, then a foghorn began to boom eerily as a mist rolled in.

'Just what we needed,' Newman commented.

'Someone is swimming in towards us,' said Marler. 'I think it's a woman. Quite a way out and I think they're tiring. I'd better strip off and go out.'

'Wait a minute.'

Newman was focusing his binoculars. He gazed through them for several minutes, then lowered them from his eyes.

'She's got her second wind, is swimming strongly. And she is heading for this cove. What was that?'

'That,' said Marler, 'was undoubtedly the crack of a rifle shot. But she's still coming. Even a top rifleman won't hit her from that distance. They must be firing from that *Venetia V* ship you told me about on the way down the path.'

The swimmer came on with powerful strokes. No more shots. The mist had blotted out the ship. Newman and Marler were waiting for her when she reached the end of a concrete ramp. As she tried to crawl ashore they lifted her gently and carried her, choking, to the path, where they laid her down.

The woman, hair flat against her well-shaped head, was clad in a swimming costume. She reached up with one hand to pull Newman closer to her, her grip on his arm surprisingly strong. He bent close to listen to what she was trying to say.

'Quack ... Quack ... Prof. Benyon ... Quack ...'

Then her head slumped back and she was still. They tried every known means to bring her back to life. Eventually, exhausted, Newman stood up, shook his head.

'No good, Marler. She's dead. No pulse. Nothing. She took in too much water during the swim, would be my guess.'

'We'd better report it ...'

'And have the police on our backs for God knows how long? Tweed wouldn't like that. This is going to seem obscene but it has to be done.'

He took out the camera he always carried, stood close to the poor woman and took three flash pictures. With a sigh he left the cove, led the way back up the path towards the hotel.

'I'm going to make an anonymous phone call to the police in Truro when we get back,' he told Marler. 'Driving through that nice village of Mawnan Smith I noticed a public phone box.'

'Why Truro? Falmouth is closer.'

'Because then the police won't associate the call as coming from anywhere near here. At the same time I'll call Tweed, get him to send a courier straight down to pick up the film in my camera. The boffins in the Engine Room basement at Park Crescent can develop and print the pics I took. At the same time I'll ask Monica to report it to Truro.'

'Sounds sensible. We don't want anyone else seeing what you photographed. We tell Paula?'

'Not yet.'

When he eventually returned to Nansidwell after making his phone call Newman had a word with the proprietor.

'I've got a courier coming down from London with some urgent documents. He could arrive early in the morning. Mind if I sleep in my clothes on a couch near the front door?'

'You'll end up with a crick in your neck,' the proprietor joked. 'Of course I don't mind. I'll show you how the special lock on the front door works.'

The sturdy, tough Harry Butler arrived at 3 a.m. He had approached discreetly, cutting out the engine of his motorcycle when he saw the entrance to Nansidwell. He freewheeled down the drive and Newman, who was restless, had the door open when Butler arrived.

Stepping outside, Newman saw the precautions Butler had taken: he wore a dispatch rider's outfit and the invented name of a courier service was attached to his machine. He took the camera Newman handed him, holding his helmet in the other hand. He kept his voice down.

'Tweed is sending me back with prints as soon as the Engine Room lads have done their stuff. I should be here again while you're eating breakfast.'

'Three hundred miles there, another three back – that's a tough ride, Harry.'

'I've done more. The photographic team has been alerted to wait for me. We're speed merchants, Bob. I'd better get cracking . . .'

Newman crept back to his room after locking up. He had a leisurely bath, and slipping his revolver under his pillow, fell fast asleep. He woke at 7 a.m. – Newman could get by on four hours' sleep. He stayed in his room to avoid any risk of being conspicuous and entered the dining room at 9 a.m. Paula was at her own table, finishing off a full English breakfast. He marvelled at how slim she remained – she always ate large meals when she could. He thought how attractive she looked, wearing a pale blue T-shirt, white linen trousers and white pumps.

As he sat down the brunette was about to leave her table, still wearing tinted glasses. He estimated her height at five foot six against his own five feet nine and again she wore an outfit which showed off her figure to full advantage. She sat down again when she saw him, poured herself more coffee. He was careful not to catch her eye.

Newman had just ordered his own full English breakfast when one of the serving girls came over and bent down to whisper.

'There's a courier outside who has asked for you. He insisted he must see you personally. Don't worry about your breakfast. I'll wait until you get back ...'

Butler, still in courier kit, was waiting for him in the large courtyard a distance from the hotel. This time he kept his helmet on. Smart, Newman thought as he went over to him – Butler had realized at this hour guests would be about. Handing him a large cardboard-backed envelope with nothing on the outside to indicate its source, Butler raised his helmet, began talking in a low voice.

'Tweed's instructions are for you to stay down here. All of you. I have to back you up. I've left my case at the Meudon Hotel just down the road. Tweed may arrive here himself – on the pretext of keeping Paula company. He said it's important we check Mullion Towers, Moloch's place out in the wilds.'

Newman said nothing as, with his back to the hotel, he carefully unsealed the envelope and withdrew three large glossy prints. The face of the dead swimmer had come out even better than he had hoped for. He slid them back as Butler went on talking.

'You'll see I've removed the courier sticker from the machine. If you need me, call the Meudon. I'm registered as Butler. Don't do anything I wouldn't do.'

'That gives me unlimited scope for any risky enterprise,' Newman joshed him. 'And thank you, Harry. You look amazingly fresh after your long trips.'

'Who needs sleep?'

Butler pulled down his helmet, turned to his machine, and when Newman swung round the attractive brunette was coming out. He acknowledged her briefly, went back inside.

Paula was sitting by herself, legs neatly crossed as she appeared to be absorbed in a magazine. Newman paused by her side, pointed to something in the magazine.

'We need to meet. All three of us. But not obviously. Inside this place.'

'My room,' she said promptly. 'It's large. I'll leave the door unlocked . . .'

Marler stood in the other lounge, staring out of the window at *Venetia V*, still floating outside the entrance to Falmouth harbour. His acute hearing had caught the lowered voices. He swung round and there was no one else in the lounge as Newman approached him, the envelope tucked under his arm.

'Meeting in Paula's room. The door will be unlocked. You slip in after a few minutes.'

'Understood. Paula has just left the other lounge . . .'

Ten minutes later Newman and Marler had joined Paula in her spacious room on the first floor. She had already prepared for their conversation – the small radio she always took with her on trips was playing classical music and she had turned on both bathtaps and left the bathroom door open. More than enough to scramble what they said if someone was trying to eavesdrop.

'Harry Butler is staying at Meudon Hotel just down the road,' Newman began. 'Under his own name. Tweed himself may come here suddenly. If he does, he'll know you, Paula, but none of the rest of us.'

'What's happening?' Paula interjected. 'Tweed sounds to be assembling a powerful force in this area.'

'Do let me finish,' Newman requested. 'The main target for us is Moloch's mansion, Mullion Towers. I've checked it on the map. It's right in the wilderness so far as I can tell.'

'So he's very concerned about Moloch,' Paula mused.

'If you'll just let me proceed,' Newman told her with mock severity.

'I'm a mute,' Paula replied and put her hand across her mouth. 'Do go on – and on and on.'

21

Newman then told her of his experience with Marler the previous night, when they had brought the woman swimmer out of the water. Paula was startled, appalled.

'This is a repeat performance of what I experienced back at Octopus Cove. It's amazing.'

'It's significant,' Newman agreed. 'Considering *Venetia V* was present on both occasions. I'm convinced now the reason Tweed sent us down here was he knew that ship was heading for Falmouth, was due to reach here very soon.'

He then picked up the envelope he had dropped on Paula's bed. Taking out the three prints he held them in his hand.

'These are pics of the woman who came out of the sea at the bottom of the path Marler and I walked down. They're good shots. She was dead when I took them.'

'You left her there?' asked Paula.

'No alternative. Tweed doesn't want us tangled up with the police. I called Truro police station anonymously so she wouldn't lie there all night.'

He spread the prints out on the bed. Paula and Marler stood up, went to the end of the bed. As she stared down at them Paula almost let out a small scream. Controlling herself, she gazed at the photos as though hypnotized. Newman sensed her shock.

'What's wrong?'

'This is the *same* woman I hauled out at Octopus Cove – but she was dead. Dead! So how can she have come ashore here? Six thousand miles away from California. I *know* it's the same woman. Oh, God, what is going on?'

1

Inside his office at Mullion Towers a small neat man in his late forties sat behind his desk. His expression was hypnotic, his eyes pale and penetrating, and he radiated an air of power. The world would have expected this man to occupy a large palatial room furnished with expensive carpets and antiques. Instead, the room had no carpet on the wooden floor, his desk and swivel chair were inexpensive furniture, the pictures on the walls were prints of Monet paintings and in one corner stood two massive metal filing cabinets. A carver chair stood on the other side of his desk and in another corner was a massive safe with two combination locks. Its base was sunk into concrete and it was equipped with a series of sophisticated alarms. Anyone even touching the safe would have set off a flashing light in the Guard House situated on the ground floor below the office.

Vincent Bernard Moloch was studying a map of California with strange irregular lines running from the south up through the state, past Silicon Valley, the home of the electronics industry in America, and on to San Francisco. As someone started to open the door he folded the map quickly, clasped his hands on the desk.

'You wanted to see me?' Joel Brand asked truculently as he entered the room.

'We need to talk,' Moloch said in a quiet mild tone. 'Do please take a seat.'

He observed his visitor through gold-rimmed spectacles, missing nothing. Brand's shaggy dark hair was ruffled, he wore an open-necked T-shirt, its half-sleeves exposing thick hairy arms, blue denims and boots with metal studs in the toecaps. He sat back in the carver and waited.

'How did that woman come to be aboard the *Venetia*?' Moloch asked quietly.

'Must have stowed away while the ship was in Monterey harbour. She appeared with a bag of clothes when we were leaving the Panama Canal, heading out into the Caribbean bound for here.'

'So what happened next?'

'Nothing much while we were at sea. What did you expect was going to happen?'

Brand's manner was resentful, as though he disliked being interrogated. Moloch's tone remained mild, his intelligent face showing no reaction as he spoke again.

'Joel, when I ask a question I do not expect to have another question as a reply. Give me details.'

'She was given a cabin. I wasn't sure how to handle her. Then she appears in the dining room, a real sexy chick and dressed up to the nines. She was very pleasant, joked with me and the others a lot. I couldn't make out what was going on.'

'You searched her suitcase?'

'Yes, if you must know . . .'

'I must know. Please continue.'

'Found she'd hung up most of her stuff in the wardrobe. In the case I found her handbag with her passport. I took that. Oh, there was also a swimsuit.'

'Didn't that make you wonder?'

'Why should it? Most days she'd take a dip in the swimming pool.'

'She was clever. I'm not sure it was so clever to remove her passport. She'd know you'd searched.'

'That gave her identity.' Brand took out a pack of cigarettes, lit one. 'I suppose I can smoke in the holy of holies?'

'You know I don't smoke. Would you be so good as to kill that?'

Brand savagely stubbed out the cigarette in an ashtray Moloch had produced from his drawer. He made a great performance of it, screwing the cigarette round and round. Moloch leant back in his chair, arms folded.

'Joel, what happened when the *Venetia* had anchored outside Falmouth harbour?'

'I've told you . . .'

'Please tell me again. It's important.'

'It was evening. I was strolling round the deck to make sure everything was shipshape and Bristol fashion. Then I saw her – wearing her swimsuit and poised to dive over the side. I ran forward to stop her but got there too late except I thumped her.'

'Thumped her, Joel?'

'Yes, bloody well thumped her on the back with this.' He clenched his huge fist. 'But she was already diving off the deck.'

'You injured her?'

'Didn't look like it. She was swimming like a fish towards the shore. I had to run to my cabin to get my rifle. When I got back on deck she was miles away and a mist blurred her. I fired one shot. Don't think I hit. Then the mist closed in round the ship.'

'You didn't send out powerboats or dinghies after her?'

'How the hell could I?' Brand blustered. 'That mist was like a fog. We wouldn't have known where to start looking.'

'You fired a shot?'

'I just told you.'

'I think that was unwise. It could have been heard if a small yacht was about. So she must have reached the shore and is now somewhere in Britain. This is very serious. We have one of the most formidable men in the world on our track. Tweed . . .'

There was a stunned silence while Brand absorbed what Moloch had said. Eventually the big man reacted.

'You've told me about this Tweed. How the hell does he come into the picture? You must be wrong.'

'I'm never wrong.' Moloch smiled without humour. 'I've made it my business to learn about that secretive outfit. People he knows in the States talked to me too much. While you were sailing to Monterey, Tweed's right arm, a woman called Paula Grey, was staying at Spanish Bay. I'm quite certain she wasn't there on holiday. She had been sent by Tweed to nose around about what I was up to.'

'How can you be sure?' Brand demanded obstinately.

'Because I check anything which has a whiff of suspicion. While you were crossing the Atlantic I had some of my people from my headquarters near Big Sur trawl around the harbour at Monterey. A first-class woman detective enquired all over the harbour. Eventually she came up with gold.'

'Gold? What gold?'

'She played up to a drunken man called Floorstone who had been standing in as harbour master. He told her about meeting an attractive dark-haired English girl. She was very interested in the *Venetia* when you left Monterey harbour – wanted to know if I was aboard. The detective got a description of her and it fits with descriptions I have of Paula Grey. Also I have another source of information about Grey's stay at Spanish Bay. There's no doubt that Tweed is on our track.'

'So maybe we should liquidate this Paula Grey. And Tweed.'

Moloch froze. He leaned forward, his expression grim, his ice-blue eyes glittering.

'Are you out of your skull? First, these people are world professionals . . .'

'That guy – whoever he is – you call The Accountant could do the job . . .'

Moloch said nothing. He stared at Brand, went on staring at Brand, his body motionless. The big man stared back at the ice-cold eyes and he was frightened. He cleared his throat.

'OK. Maybe I was out of order.'

'You were out of your mind.' Moloch's voice was as cold as his eyes, he sat like a grim waxwork. After a long pause he spoke again, slowly, with great deliberation and precision.

'You *are* out of your mind. Tweed is SIS. Paula Grey is SIS. We evade them. If I ever catch you within a mile of either of them I'll terminate your employment. Permanently,' he added.

'Understood,' Brand said tersely. 'May I go now?'

'I think that would be a good idea. But you stay on the premises for the moment. Call Penhale aboard the *Venetia*. Tell him he's in command of the ship for the moment.'

'Penhale is useless . . .'

'Penhale is one of the best skippers afloat. I would much appreciate your carrying out my request.'

'If you say so. Oh, here are some balance sheets your pet accountant, Geach, prepared for you. Don't trust that guy one little bit.'

'You don't have to trust him. I do,' replied Moloch reaching for the sheaf of papers Brand had placed on his desk. 'One more thing – if my stepmother, Mrs Benyon, calls from California I'm not here.'

At Park Crescent Tweed looked up as Howard, the Director, walked into his office with a lordly air. He saw Monica pull a wry face. Howard was immaculately dressed in his latest Chester Barrie suit from Harrods. He also wore a new pink shirt and a Chanel tie. Ignoring Monica, he sat down in a leather armchair near Tweed's desk. Crossing his long legs – Howard was six feet tall – he carefully adjusted the crease in his trousers.

'How goes the battle?' he enquired.

'Which battle?' Tweed flashed back.

'Well, actually, I was thinking of this investigation into the eminent VB. That's what his close associates call Vincent Bernard Moloch.'

'We know. Monica discovered that during her researches on him.'

'Good for Monica,' Howard replied without a glance in her direction. 'The Prime Minister is panting for news.'

'Let him pant until I'm good and ready – which I am not at this moment. Monica is in the middle of building up a profile on VB.'

'Taking the devil of a long time . . .'

'No, it isn't. Monica was up till three this morning, calling contacts in the States.'

'We need a little action on this one . . .'

'We're getting plenty of that.' Tweed held up a hand. 'No, don't ask for details. You need a complete report.'

Howard ran a finger over his pink, plump, clean-shaven face. Checking the shave, Tweed noted. Was he starting to go out with girl friends again? He doubted it – Howard's wife, Cynthia, had forced him to close down

28

his London flat, to come home to his house in Ascot every night.

'Suppose I must be content with the little you've given me,' remarked Howard. 'But no one is indispensable.'

'I hope you include yourself in that observation,' Tweed said tartly.

'Just a joke, old chap,' Howard concluded, standing up to leave. 'Carry on the good work, Monica,' he went on as he opened the door. 'Late hours are good for you.'

Monica raised both eyebrows and said nothing until he was gone. Then she stood up and exploded.

'Some joke. You could get his job tomorrow. I know you get on well with the PM, that he admires you. May I open another window? Can't stand his aftershave.'

'Of course. I don't want his job. And he's useful with a glass in his hand, attending Russian, et cetera diplomatic receptions. Now tell me.'

'VB is the Mystery Man. I've had a frightful job building up his profile. He doesn't like publicity. Here we go. First, his right-hand man is a brute called Joel Brand – here is a photo of him. Supposed to have been in the Navy. The Admiralty report they have never heard of him. Next, Brand isn't his real name. He is an Armenian – real name Varouj Kerkorian. Likes to play the rough type. But he has brains – so many Armenians have. He attended the Harvard School of Business and got an MBA. Master of Business Administration, however little that stands for these days. Returned to Britain and became a smuggler of contraband across the North Sea . . .'

'Hold it there. Was he ever convicted?'

'No, too slippery. But Customs and Excise are convinced he ran a big ring. He goes from girl friend to girl friend once he's got what he's after. Rather like changing his clothes. He once nearly killed a man in the Hamburg Reeperbahn.'

'Sounds more and more unsavoury. A womanizer and a thug.'

'A good description of Mr Brand. Again he got off scot-free. The German police couldn't even charge him with attempted murder – witnesses were intimidated and refused to testify. Supposed to be thirty-eight years old, but being Armenian that's impossible to check.'

'Why would someone like Moloch employ such a man? I gather outwardly VB is sophisticated and refined.'

'From what I can gather from people who have known him Mr Brand is a kind of Dr Jekyll and Mr Hyde. I've described the Hyde. On other occasions he can be charming and good company – especially with women. But with men, too, if he wants to. He's attended receptions here and in the States on Moloch's behalf. VB keeps in the background. I'm still getting more data coming in on Brand.'

'What about the all-powerful Moloch? What's his nationality?'

'All-powerful is the key to Moloch. He knows some of the richest men in the world – as you know they form a kind of club. Moloch is the richest. His original nationality is a mystery. I think he arrived in this country as a youth supposedly from what was Czechoslovakia, now the Czech Republic. He came here as a student, qualified as an accountant, then pushed off to America. There he built up an electronics company in California. Other outfits combined, eliminated him as a competitor, wiped him out.'

'He must love America,' Tweed commented.

'The word is he hates it after what happened to him. But he keeps his real feelings to himself. He then set about building up AMBECO into the biggest conglomerate in the world. Borrowed money from a bank, immediately paid back the loan when he was successful to keep his independence. He works like a Trojan, needs very little sleep.'

'Personality?'

'I'm told he can be a real charmer – far more so than Brand. I can't find a photograph of him anywhere but I'm persisting. He objects to having his picture taken. He has plants all over the States, here in the North, in Germany and France and Holland. He has one in Saudi Arabia.'

'The Arab connection.'

'Exactly. He's fluent in Arabic, German, French, Italian, Spanish, and English, of course. My informant on that score told me he was self-taught. He has a first-rate brain . . .'

'Married?'

'Never. At least so far I haven't traced a wife. VB has a succession of girl friends – all of them so-called upper-class types. There have been seven of them so far. They have all disappeared.'

'Disappeared? What on earth do you mean?'

'What I said. They vanish without trace. They are supposed to have gone off travelling with money VB supplied them with but they've never been seen since. I spoke to Cord Dillon, your American opposite number at the CIA in Langley. The wealthy father of one of the girls, Julia Sanchez, called Cord from Philadelphia. Cord, as a favour, checked out her movements. The records show a return ticket to London, and a girl who looked like Julia did board the flight, then she vanished. A flight from San Francisco.'

'Were these girl friends VB's confidantes, I wonder?'

'I gather they may have been. Cord is equally worried about the amount of power Moloch has accumulated. He has certain key senators in his pocket. Money roars.'

'It certainly does.' Tweed looked thoughtful. 'Any chance of obtaining a photo of this Julia Sanchez?'

31

'Yes. The father in Philadelphia supplied Cord with several. At my request Cord has sent one to you by Federal Express. Should arrive tomorrow.'

'Does this Armenian Varouj Kerkorian – or Joel Brand as he now calls himself – jealously guard his position as Moloch's deputy?'

Monica looked surprised at this unexpected question. She gazed at Tweed, smiled wrily.

'You do have a sixth sense. One of the things I left out was that Brand can't stand anyone else getting close to VB.'

'Where is VB's main base?'

'I asked Cord that question. VB has a huge house near Big Sur south of Carmel. It's called Black Ridge, overlooks the Pacific, is heavily guarded. Savage dogs, searchlights, an electric wire on top of a wall round the place. You name any form of advanced security and he's got it.'

'What about his fabulous ship, *Venetia V*?'

'Well, as I told you the other day, it sailed from Monterey some time ago. My contact at Lloyd's said it was supposed to be bound for Baja California in Mexico, then it changed its destination to Falmouth . . .'

'Yes, I remember.'

'Which I suppose is why you sent that large team down to Cornwall . . .'

'Yes. I omitted telling them about the ship to see how they reacted spontaneously. And, of course, Paula had phoned some of that information to me from San Francisco airport before she boarded her flight to return here. Now, about the contact at Lloyd's.'

'He said it was the most expensive and sophisticated private vessel in the world – especially as regards communications.'

'Must have cost a packet – but Moloch's resources appear to be unlimited. That's it so far?'

'Not quite. Living in a big house near Mission Ranch, just on the southern fringes of Carmel, is Moloch's grim-looking stepmother, Mrs Benyon.'

'Why grim-looking? How do you know?'

'Because I obtained a recent picture of her from a photo library.' Monica stood up, produced a large print from her desk drawer, laid it in front of Tweed. 'That's her.'

Tweed gazed at the picture. It showed Mrs Benyon sitting in a chair like a throne. She was grotesquely fat, had two plump jowls, hawklike eyes which stared straight at Tweed. She reminded him of a Buddha and he didn't like the look of her. Her mouth was pouched venomously and her thick grey hair hung to her wide shoulders. Even in a photo she exuded an air of command, a woman who expected everyone to obey her slightest whim. He handed the photograph back to Monica.

'How old is the dear lady?'

'That I haven't found out. But she has a son who works for Moloch. He's called Ethan Benyon, and is a seismologist.'

'What is VB doing with seismology?'

'No idea. It's another factor that worries Cord Dillon. He wouldn't say why so I didn't press him. I'm still digging, but what do you think of it all so far?'

'I don't like it. Especially that item about VB's seven girl friends vanishing without trace. Sounds sinister. I may have to go down to Cornwall very soon. With Harry Butler's partner, Pete Nield.'

'The eagles gather.'

She had just spoken when the phone rang. Tweed grabbed it before Monica could reach it. Newman's voice came clearly over the line.

'Bob reporting in.'

33

'Tweed here.'

'I'm making a brief call over a safe line. Local call box. We're on our way to take a close look at Mullion Towers.'

'Be careful. Monica found out from Jim Corcoran, Chief of Security at Heathrow, that Moloch arrived from the States a few days ago, then took off again after refuelling for Newquay airport. That's close to Stithians. So the great man is probably in residence. Could be very dangerous – proceed with great caution . . .'

2

Emerging from the phone box, Newman jumped behind the wheel of his Mercedes with Paula by his side. As he left the small village of Mawnan Smith, with its thatched cottages, the Red Lion pub and a square with the local shops, another car took off behind him. Marler followed in his Saab, his Armalite rifle concealed on the floor. Ahead of Newman, Butler led the way on his Harley-Davidson motorbike. Everyone knew where they were going, the route they were taking to Mullion Towers.

'I always feel like royalty when we ride like this,' Paula commented. 'A motorcycle outrider ahead and Marler guarding our rear.'

'You're more worthwhile than some royalty I could mention,' Newman replied and grinned roguishly at her.

'Thank you, kind sir,' she replied mockingly.

'Any time, Princess.'

'Seriously, Bob, do you think this is going to be a quiet trip?'

'I doubt it. From what you told us about your experience in Monterey – and that woman, Vanity Richmond, who tried to make friends with you – I suspect Moloch knows more about us than is comfortable. I've told Butler and Marler we're on maximum alert.'

'I looked again at that map you showed us and it seemed pretty remote country where Moloch has his mansion. I'll bet there's not much traffic out there, that any there is will be noticed. And we're a ruddy convoy.'

'So let's see how the king of the castle reacts to having visitors. Moloch himself is probably there.'

'What makes you say that?'

'While I was collecting my case at Park Crescent Monica warned me the great man flew from San Francisco in his Lear jet to Heathrow, refuelled, then flew on to Newquay airport. From there it's just a short car drive to this place Stithians.'

'So this could be exciting. I've got my Browning inside my shoulder bag.'

'Good. My advice is prepare for fireworks . . .'

Driving through open countryside they went straight over a crossroads down a lane signposted *Stithians*. They had entered a typical Cornish lane, the banked hedges of ferns and gorse closing in on both sides. Topping the crest of a hill they had a panoramic view – great sweeps of rolling land with few trees, stretching away into the far distance towards high ridges silhouetted against an azure sky. The sun beat down and the inside of the car became an oven, even with all the windows open.

'It's getting a bit hot and airless,' Paula remarked.

'A bit!' exclaimed Newman. 'It's torrid, tropical. My shirt is already sticking to my back.'

The lane twisted and turned while Paula forced herself to concentrate on the open map in her lap. They turned along a more major road for a short distance, then swung off along an even narrower lane again signposted

Stithians. Paula braced herself as Newman squeezed the car between the enclosing banks. After a while they turned again into another similar lane sign posted *Stithians Dam*.

'A dam out here?' Paula queried. 'That's strange.'

'There's a reservoir below where I expect Mullion Towers is. Hence, probably a dam . . .'

They passed through Stithians, no more than a hamlet of granite-walled cottages with grey slate roofs. There was not a soul about: even a few whitewashed houses failed to lighten the gloom of the place. They passed a children's playground with swings and Paula stared. 'What future can children expect here when they grow up?' she wondered aloud.

'No future at all down here . . .'

He stopped speaking as he slowed, turned a corner and below them a large deep dam barred off a large stretch of still water, the reservoir. Turning off the engine, Newman got out, put on his jacket reluctantly, but he had to conceal the hip holster holding the Smith & Wesson. Taking hold of a pair of binoculars from the back seat, he looped them round his neck, walked down towards the dam.

Paula walked alongside him, tense because of the dam and the heavy sultry silence. They had passed no traffic during the whole trip and the area round the dam was equally deserted. Newman stopped, raised his binoculars, focused them.

'That has to be Mullion Towers – on top of the ridge.'

'Are you sure?' Paula queried. 'It looks a horrible place.'

'Pretty sure – it has towers at each corner with gargoyles. The windows are mullion-paned. What else is there round here that could be it?'

Glancing back, Paula saw Marler had pulled up a

distance behind the Merc. He was standing on the far side of the Saab, crouching down. She guessed he was checking the action of the Armalite rifle. Butler had hidden his machine close to a wall. Paula looked towards the remote mansion and was appalled.

The long savage ridge the house was perched on stretched a mile down towards them, hideously arid, not a tree or shrub on its barren slope. Newman scanned the house inch by inch. Built of granite the hulk was three storeys high and higher than any of the towers rose a mast with a complex of radio aerials and a Comsat dish. Just like the set-up aboard the *Venetia*. That convinced him they had found their objective.

'That's Mullion Towers,' he said.

'The whole area is a wilderness,' Paula commented without enthusiasm. 'Might be a flaming desert.'

Newman had started walking down the steep slope to the dam and Paula walked by his side. There was something eerie about the silent dam which unsettled her.

'It's a wilderness,' Newman agreed. 'Not another sign of human habitation. Just the place a secretive billionaire would favour.'

Thigh-high rails, painted a hideous blue, almost purple, lined each side of the walkway spanning the top of the dam. Low gates at either end of the walkway appeared to be locked. They reached a tall railed gate with a notice warning them to proceed no further. The dam loomed above them.

Looking up, Newman measured the distance from the walk to the bottom of the dam where the wall sloped outwards. Anyone falling over from near the centre would never survive the drop.

Now the unnerving silence was broken by the low surge of water passing under the dam. The silence was further broken by another more penetrating sound – the engine of a helicopter. They looked up and saw a helicopter circling above them a few hundred feet up.

'Had we better hide if we can?' Paula suggested.

'Nowhere to hide. Just walk back with me quietly to the car like a couple of tourists.'

'It might be a helicopter from that big RAF training airfield at Culdrose,' Paula surmised as they continued walking back to the car. 'Our hotel proprietor told us.'

'Could be.'

'But you don't think so,' she insisted.

'Well, when I was down at that cove with Marler I had a chance to scan the *Venetia*. Aft of the main control cabin was a helipad. Perched on it was a similar machine to that one circling above us.'

'Then they might know we're coming.'

'They *will* know we're coming. The chopper will radio a warning to the communications complex Moloch has on top of his mansion.'

'Should we go on? I'm game, but if they're expecting us . . .'

'Let's see what equipment Marler has brought with him. And Harry always carries his tool kit. There's a high wall round the place with wire on top, probably electrified.'

'Welcome all,' Marler greeted them cheerfully as he shoved something back into the rear of the car.

'That's a telescopic ladder, isn't it?' Newman asked.

'Just that. From what I heard of Moloch he'll have this little cottage with a wall round it.'

'He has.'

'And, Harry,' Newman went on as Butler approached them, 'it has a wall with a wire, probably electrified.'

'Child's play,' Butler assured him.

'Then we go on up to that architectural masterpiece?' Paula suggested.

'Tweed wanted us to check out the place. What Tweed wants, Tweed gets.'

Joel Brand put down the earphones after receiving the coded message from the pilot of the chopper. He hurried down to Moloch's office. Moloch was again studying the map of California with strange wriggly lines. He looked up as Brand burst in with his usual unceremonious manner. Moloch passed the map to him after tearing it into four pieces.

'Put that through the shredder. It must be destroyed.'

Brand stuffed the pieces impatiently in the pocket of his denims, sat down in the carver, bolt upright. Moloch clasped his finely shaped hands and leant back.

'Why don't you calm down, Brand, before you tell me what's on your mind?'

'Because it's a friggin' emergency. Intruders are coming this way in force . . .'

'What intruders? Please be more specific.'

'I had a radio message from the chopper from the *Venetia*, which watches over this place. Prior to that, in the radio room upstairs I'd been watching them myself through field glasses. Down by the dam. There was a heavily built guy who looked tough – not that I can't handle that type,' he added aggressively. 'He was with a nice-looking chick, dark haired – hair tied back with a ribbon. Had on a T-shirt and white trousers. Then . . .'

'Just a moment,' Moloch reached into a drawer, took out a photograph taken secretly in California. He pushed the print across the desk. 'That wouldn't be this girl?'

'Spitting image. A good looker. In this pic she doesn't have her hair tied back, but it's her. No doubt about it . . .'

'This is bad news.' Moloch replaced the photo inside

his drawer. 'This is Tweed's lot. Tweed,' he repeated. 'He has moved fast.'

'Tweed isn't Superman . . .'

'Keep quiet. You don't know what you're talking about. Just the two of them?'

'No! At least four. One is a slim guy wearing a linen suit. Looks like a toff. Then there's a bruiser on a motorbike. They've left the dam and they're heading up the road towards us. I've alerted the boys. They're carrying shotguns. Before you blow your top, farmers are often carrying shotguns – to clear their fields of vermin.'

'Let me think – these people have to be handled carefully, especially as Paula Grey, Tweed's right arm, is with them. She . . .'

'The chick's Tweed's girl friend?' Brand sneered.

'No, she is not.' Moloch slapped the palm of his hand on the desk and it sounded like a pistol shot. 'You listen to me. Tweed is a very ethical man. Not that you would ever understand a man like that, but I respect him as a man, as a very formidable opponent. The dogs are to be brought in and chained up in their kennels. That's an order. Try to deal with the situation with *finesse* . . .'

'*Finesse*?'

'*Finesse*. You probably think that's a French pastry. It means tread carefully. Now get the hell out of my sight . . .'

Brand, who despite his rough exterior was a good strategist, left Moloch's office, ran up the stairs to the communications room. He had left the radio op. stationed behind his very modern set.

'We're under siege. Send a coded message to the chopper to fly straight back to the *Venetia*. He's giving the game away that we know intruders are on their way here. Do it yesterday . . .'

He ran back down the staircase to the back door to check his guards patrolling the grounds. He was passing the litter bin when he remembered the instruction Moloch had given him.

'Frig the shredder,' he muttered to himself.

Pulling out the four pieces of paper, he screwed them up, lifted the plastic lid, dropped the pieces on top of a load of rubbish. Then he ran round the house, met his most reliable thug, Gene Lessinger.

'Call in all the dogs quickly. Shove them in the kennels. All except one. You keep Brute on a leash and take him round the place constantly. Dangerous intruders coming . . .'

Gene, a lean, bony-faced man with a hideous scar down his right cheek, grinned. His favourite weapon was a knife and he had one tucked inside a sheath suspended from his leather belt.

'When they see Brute they'll run for it.'

'That would be my guess. Get moving . . .'

Brute was the largest and fiercest of the Dobermanns which prowled the grounds. Brand felt pleased with himself as he continued running round the estate to contact his other guards.

'VB used the word "dogs",' he said to himself. 'He didn't say anything about one dog. And I'm in charge of security in this mob. So come on, Grey and Co. We have an interesting reception party waiting for you.'

Ahead of the small convoy Butler rode his machine along the narrow lane leading uphill towards the strange mansion. He rode slowly now and stopped abruptly as he topped the crest of a hill. Switching off the motor, he freewheeled the bike back a few feet, then held up a hand to stop the Merc. and the Saab.

Newman stopped his car, jumped out and ran to meet Butler with Paula at his heels.

'We're very close,' he warned them. 'Just over that top you can see the house perched on the ridge.'

'Good,' said Newman as Marler joined them. 'Let's take a peek.'

Earlier Newman had outlined a plan with the others. It was based on what he had observed when he had carefully scanned the mansion through his binoculars from near the dam. Marler had added his own suggestions. They walked to the top until they could see. Paula shuddered inwardly at the view.

The ridge which Mullion Towers was perched on looked even bleaker close up. Nothing grew on the long sharp slope descending from the ridge towards the reservoir and the dam far below them now. The slope seemed to consist of dust which, in the scorching sunlight, had a strange, almost yellowish colour.

'Could be the Sahara,' she commented. 'I never realized Cornwall inland could be so uninviting. So different from near the sea with its nice beaches and coves and intriguing creeks.'

Following Newman's example, they were lying alongside each other in the road, their heads peering over the top. Newman again scanned the Gothic-like horror called Mullion Towers, then he handed the binoculars to Marler.

'What do you think of the creeper up the side of the place?'

'Just what I need, I think. I'll only know when I see it close up, but it looks as though it's grown there for years. The stems are thick and gnarled. The plan is going to work, I'm sure – just so long as I reach that creeper unobserved.'

'What is that long knotted rope attached to your telescopic ladder for?' Paula asked.

'All will be clear when we get there. Guards with shotguns are patrolling – but they seem to be concentrating on the front of the house. One has a somewhat unfriendly-looking Dobermann. I'll worry about the little canine.'

'Let's get on with it,' Newman said, sliding backwards before he stood up. 'Interesting the way that chopper has disappeared. I think they recalled it to lull us into a false mood of self-confidence. Assume the worst possible case – that they know we're coming . . .'

At Park Crescent Tweed sat behind his desk, very still as he gazed towards the windows. Monica knew he was worrying about what was happening in Cornwall. He checked his watch again as the phone rang. Monica answered it. She frowned, repeated her question several times.

'Who is this speaking?'

Then she pressed the secrecy button and called across to Tweed.

'Someone with a strangely hoarse voice insists on speaking to you. They're using the name Waltz.'

'I'll take the call. Tweed here.'

'You should know that while Paula was in Monterey a Vanity Richmond secretly took several pictures of her. I followed her and she sent a package by Federal Express to somewhere in Cornwall. That is all for now.'

'Thank you.' Tweed put down the phone and looked grim. He was still staring out of the window when he told Monica what the caller had said.

'Who is Waltz?' she asked.

'An informant who was present in Monterey at the same time as Paula. It is, of course, a code name.'

'It's not good news.'

'At this juncture it most certainly isn't. I wish I'd had that call yesterday. It means that if our team is spotted approaching Mullion Towers someone may recognize Paula – and know who they are.'

'Oh, my Lord, doesn't that mean the whole enterprise could end in a frightful disaster?'

'Newman can handle any situation, but it doesn't help our finding out what Moloch is up to – I have no doubt he is up to something pretty major. If only we could find out the identity of that girl who was washed ashore at Octopus Cove – and the identity of the same woman who jumped ship off Cornwall.'

'Cord's picture of Julia Sanchez, the girl from Philadelphia who disappeared, and who was Moloch's friend, should arrive at any moment. It might help.'

'It might – and it might not.'

Tweed checked his watch again. 'I reckon from the time Bob called me, from the distance to Stithians on the map, he and his team should just be about ready to assault Mullion Towers – may already be doing so.'

3

Marler led the way back to his Saab, asking the others to come with him. He opened the back door of his car and inside Paula saw a large canvas bag on top of the telescopic ladder.

'I know you're all equipped with weapons,' he said crisply, 'but you may well need extra defences. That bag contains them. Father Christmas is about to give you his toys.'

Diving inside, he opened the large bag, produced a small device like a grenade, handed one to Paula.

'That's the new type of smoke bomb. Press the button on the top and hurl the thing. It will not only fog the enemy, it gives off an acrid smell which will put them out of action for thirty minutes. They then recover quickly. Here are two for you, Paula, two for you, Bob.'

'You've come well prepared,' Paula commented as she examined the device quickly and put it inside her shoulder bag.

'Wait, there's more . . .'

'We're starting a small war,' Paula joked.

'It may well be that,' Marler replied.

He handed her a grenade with a pin. This she recognized as he spoke.

'Stun grenade. You've practised with it down at the training centre in Send. As you know, when it explodes near your opponent the deafening explosion puts *him* out of the picture for long enough for us to get away. Here's another, Paula.'

He gave two more to Newman and Butler, then stood away, closed the door quietly. He lit a king-size.

'I'd say we're ready to take on a whole army of thugs – which we must assume is what's waiting for us. You all know where I'll be. What are we waiting for?'

'For you to shut up,' Newman told him with a grin.

The convoy then took off, driving at speed, again with Butler in the lead. Well behind him, Newman followed in the Merc. with Paula alongside him and Marler bringing up the rear a distance behind them.

They sped down a hill and then up a much steeper, higher incline. At the top of the ridge they passed the closed high wrought-iron gates leading down a long drive to Mullion Towers. The tactic was to confuse the enemy – by driving at speed it appeared they were on their way elsewhere. Only Butler had stopped just beyond the gates, hiding his machine in a hedge.

He took a grenade out of the satchel Marler had given

him before they left Nansidwell Country Hotel and waited. Crouching in the hedge, he watched both the entrance gates and the crest of the road where it crossed the ridge.

A few minutes later Marler appeared, carrying his telescopic ladder, with his Armalite slung over one shoulder, and ran back down the hill, shielded from view of the house by the high granite wall. By the time he came close to Butler, the latter had studied the wire along the top of the wall. Newman and Paula appeared, running after Marler. All wore soft-soled shoes and ran silently. When Marler stopped a hundred yards or so from Butler, he signalled and the operation began. A dog was snarling somewhere close to the mansion.

Butler emerged, hurled the grenade expertly so it landed at the foot of the gates. It detonated, blew the locked gates open. The guards would assume it was a frontal attack straight up the drive.

'Can you eliminate that electric wire?' Marler snapped at Butler.

'I told you. Child's play. Get the ruddy ladder up against the wall. We haven't got all day.'

Marler swiftly pulled out the sections of the metal ladder to their fullest extent, propped it against the wall at a point where it turned at a right angle behind the house. Shinning up, he glanced over the wire. Two guards, armed with shotguns, one holding a huge Dobermann on a leash, ran past near the house, half-hidden by Ali Baba pots containing large shrubs. They were heading for the front. Marler heard a loud voice calling out.

'Mass on either side of the front gate – that's where the bastards are coming through.'

Marler smiled to himself: the plan was working. He shinned down again and Butler climbed the ladder, a leather tool kit slung from his side. Marler had placed the ladder at precisely the point he had indicated.

A master electrode was supporting the wire through an iron ring covered with rubber. Taking a tube from his kit, Butler squeezed out a thick, glue-like liquid over the whole electrode and part of the wire on either side. Then he pulled out a pair of secateurs, clipped the wire on both sides where it was covered with the liquid. The entire electric wire was now out of operation and no alarm would sound inside the house. He descended the ladder to where Marler waited with Paula and Newman.

'Wire's out . . .'

He had hardly spoken when Marler shot up the ladder, again peered over. No one in sight. He uncoiled the knotted rope with a weight on the end attached to the top of the ladder, lowered it over the far side of the wall after wrapping it several times round the iron ring embedded into the stone. This was their escape route.

Climbing rapidly down the rope, he crouched low, running from one Ali Baba pot to another until, unseen, he reached the side wall of the house covered with creeper. He tested the strength of the creeper, tugging it with one hand. Satisfied that it was strong enough, he clawed his way up the creeper with the skill of a cat burglar.

Reaching the gutter, he clambered over it on to the flat roof of the mansion. Further on it had a tiled slope but here were several massive chimney stacks. Still crouching he ran across to the front of the house, shielded from view by another chimney stack. He had the Armalite in his hands as he peered over. He had a bird's-eye view of the scene in front of the house, men with shotguns a short way back from the entrance, directed by a black-haired giant waving his hands, ordering them to spread out.

Marler ran back to the side of the house, lifted his head, saw Newman's head waiting at the top of the

47

ladder. He waved his hand once, then ran back to his viewing point. The assault was about to begin.

Newman descended the knotted rope, followed by Paula and Butler. Paula, shoulder bag close to her, held her Browning as Newman led the way towards the front. Both had weapons concealed behind their backs. Butler stayed behind to guard their escape route, his hand inside a small canvas satchel.

Newman's approach was peaceable and he had a smile on his face as he arrived at the front. Brand was the first one to spot him. Not expecting anyone to take him in the rear, his first reaction was one of surprise. Newman called out to him genially.

'Excuse me, is this Mullion Towers? If so I'd like a word with the owner, Mr Moloch.'

'About what?' Brand demanded, playing for time.

'I'd have to explain that to Mr Moloch himself. It's kind of personal,' Newman explained amiably.

'So is this,' Brand replied and aimed his shotgun straight at Newman. 'How did you get in?'

'Through the back way. The front gate looked a shambles. Couldn't just drive in there.'

'You're trespassing. Tell me who you are or I'm shooting.'

Paula aimed her Browning at Brand's stomach. She held the weapon in an unwavering grip, her voice like a whiplash.

'Pull the trigger and I'll blow your stomach open.'

Brand swung his shotgun so the muzzle was aimed at Paula. He grinned as though confident he held the upper hand. Paula continued aiming the gun at his stomach.

'Pull the trigger,' she repeated, 'and my finger will fire as a reflex action. You'll still end up with your stomach blasted open.'

Again Brand looked taken aback. It was the last reaction he had expected from a mere woman. He hesitated, then gave a braying laugh, throwing down his shotgun. With an evil grin he advanced towards Newman, hand held out. As he did so Newman slipped his revolver into his holster. Brand grinned again.

'That's right. A man like you doesn't need a toy pistol. Shake hands with the devil and we can talk . . .'

As he came close his left hand bunched into a huge fist, came forward with lightning speed. He grazed Newman's jaw with enough force to send him falling over on his back. Still grinning, Brand lifted a boot with metal studs on the toecap to give his opponent a brutal kick in the side which would have broken ribs. Paula stood back, her Browning aimed at other men who were advancing.

Newman moved even more swiftly, both hands gripping Brand's ankle, twisting it savagely. The large man yelped, lost his balance as Newman jumped to his feet. Bending down, he took hold of Brand's shaggy hair, pulled at it and when the giant instinctively jerked back Newman shoved the head down with great force. It connected with one of the paving stones of a path crossing the thin lawn. The noise sounded like a hammer crashing into the stone and Brand lay still.

Other men were continuing to advance, shotguns aimed despite Paula's Browning, and they knew she couldn't cover all of them. Then a series of shots rang out, each shot landing just in front of each advancing man. They stood stock-still, in a state of shock, wondering where the shooting was coming from as Marler continued to pick off one man after another, always firing just in front of him. Newman had just dealt with Brand when Paula called out a warning.

'To your right, Bob!'

Newman swung round. Gene was walking slowly

towards him from the side of the mansion, holding Brute on a leash. He released the dog, which leapt towards Newman who had no time to reach for his revolver. Brute was leaping into the air, aiming for Newman's throat, when he stopped, for a moment suspended in mid-air as the bullet penetrated his skull – the bullet from Marler's Armalite. As the animal flopped, Gene came rushing towards Newman, a long stiletto-like knife in his hand.

Newman stood very still, hands on his hips. Again no time to reach for the Smith & Wesson. He called out to Gene in a calm voice.

'Before you stick that in me could I take a few puffs at a last cigarette?'

'Smoke away. It will be your last chance on this earth.'

Newman carefully withdrew a packet from his pocket with a lighter. He lit the cigarette while Gene gloated at Newman, taking deep drags. Scared to death, Gene told himself with sadistic glee. The cigarette end was glowing strongly when Newman glanced behind Gene.

'Take him, Ed,' he called out.

Gene felt compelled to glance over his shoulder. In that moment of distraction Newman plunged the cigarette end down onto the hand holding the knife. Gene screamed with pain, dropped the knife. Newman's right knee rammed into his attacker's groin and Gene yelled, crumpled forward. Snatching his revolver from the holster, Newman brought the barrel down on Gene's exposed skull. The would-be killer collapsed.

Chaos broke out as Paula hurled her stun grenade. Three men fell unconscious to the ground. She threw a smoke grenade into the middle of the remaining opponents and they were lost, coughing, their eyes streaming inside the dense fog. From somewhere inside the smoke a series of shots was fired at them. Newman recognized the weapon as an automatic rifle. One of the guards had, he guessed, dropped to the ground, closed

50

his eyes and was shooting at random in the hope of getting a hit.

'Time to move out,' he told Paula. 'Get back over the ladder. Now!'

He glanced up at the parapet of the flat roof and saw Marler peering down, waiting for an enemy to emerge from the fog. Newman gestured to him to come down immediately, to make for the ladder. Then he moved a few paces closer to where Butler stood on guard while Paula climbed the knotted rope, and disappeared over the top of the wall with the agility of an acrobat.

Marler, Armalite slung over his shoulder, was clawing his way down the ancient creeper. Newman waited, watched him, his Smith & Wesson in his hand. Marler reached the ground, dropping the last few feet. An automatic rifle, Newman was thinking. These thugs were professionals.

As Marler stood up he saw a plastic bin for litter at the corner of the house. He ran to it, prised off the lid. A load of rubbish. Then he saw a screwed-up ball of paper, grabbed it, shoved it inside a pocket as he rammed the lid back on.

'What the hell did you think you were doing?' demanded Newman as Marler ran up to him.

'Never know what you can pick up . . .'

'Get up the rope. *Move!*'

As Marler shot up the knotted rope, vanished, Newman took a few steps closer to the escape route. He would be the last man out. Ordering Butler to leave, he kept his eye on the fog, which was thinning. A guard appeared, a handkerchief wrapped round his mouth, tight-fitting goggles over his eyes. He was holding an automatic rifle which he aimed at Newman, who dodged sideways. He hurled a stun grenade at the guard, followed that up with another smoke grenade. The guard was falling when smoke enveloped him.

Newman climbed the rope, heaved himself over the wall, then hauled up the rope, used a knife to cut it free from the iron ring it was twisted tightly round now, dropped the whole rope to where Marler, waiting, swiftly coiled it. The moment Newman was off the ladder they telescoped it and Marler ran with it to his Saab.

When Newman reached the Merc. he found Paula behind the wheel, the engine running, ready to take off the moment Newman was aboard in the front passenger seat. Ahead of them Butler revved up his machine, shot down the hill. As he was passing the damaged gates he threw another stun grenade, sped on.

The Merc. followed him at high speed with the Saab behind them. Newman wiped sweat off his brow.

'Exciting enough for you?'

'We've been there before,' she replied calmly. 'In similar situations. Do you think we achieved anything?'

'We'll have put the wind up Moloch. Which I'm sure was Tweed's idea. Someone was gazing down at us from a side window when we left. It could have been the emperor himself, I suppose. Anyone following us?'

'Only Marler,' she replied after another swift glance in the rear-view mirror. 'Back to Nansidwell, I suppose? Good job Moloch doesn't know where we're staying.'

'I wouldn't count on that.'

Moloch had witnessed the entire operation. Standing by the window of his first-floor office, hands clasped behind his back, he had heard the first grenade which damaged the gates. As he watched Brand assemble his large force of guards near the gate he guessed it was a diversion, that the attack would come from elsewhere. Still, Brand usually knew what he was doing.

Later he left his office quickly, went along a corridor to a room with a side window. He was in time to see

Newman put out of action the guard with the automatic rifle, saw him climbing up the rope, haul it out of sight, disappear.

'A very well-organized operation,' he said to himself. 'I have underestimated Tweed. We'll have to close in on him.'

4

Howard burst into Tweed's office, looking worried. As he sat in the armchair he shot his cuffs, revealing a pair of gold cuff links, each like a flower with petals. Monica shuddered inwardly behind her desk – not the style of links a man should wear.

'The PM's getting worked up about Vincent Bernard Moloch,' Howard began in his lofty voice.

'I know,' replied Tweed. 'He called me this afternoon.'

'You mean he called you first?' Howard demanded indignantly. 'I'm supposed to be running the show.'

'Then complain to the PM.'

'You know I can't do that. He wants to get his priorities right. Anyway, VB has bought up a key electronics plant in the Thames Valley. You know that's our version of Silicon Valley in California.'

'I know.'

'You mean you know about the Thames Valley?'

'I mean I know VB has bought up that plant. He's already put in hand plans for doubling its size and capacity.'

'May I ask how *you* know all this?'

'I have a contact in the area I can't name. I was informed earlier under a seal of secrecy,' Tweed said firmly.

'What is infuriating – worrying – the PM is that VB

already has several important members of Parliament on his payroll. The usual racket – they're called consultants. He thinks Moloch is getting too powerful.'

'He is. What do you want me to do? Go out and shoot him?'

'Might be a good idea,' Howard replied in a rare flash of humour. 'How is your investigation proceeding?'

'It's proceeding. When I have something positive you'll be the first to know.'

'I would hope so . . .'

Howard stood up, left the room. Monica raised her eyes to heaven. Tweed grinned at her.

'I'm going to say it,' Monica insisted. 'That man is a pain. I notice you tell him as little as possible.'

'Well, I do know that when he's had three double whiskies at his club he can get talkative. What do you think of the call I had from Newman?'

Newman had called him from the phone box in Mawnan Smith on his way back from Mullion Towers. Monica frowned.

'Sounds to me as though he cleverly outmanoeuvred a pretty tough bunch. What was the object of the exercise?'

'To unsettle Moloch, to show him we're on his track. In that mood he may make a wrong move. I'm interested in that paperwork Marler took from the litter bin. A map of California with strange lines on it.'

'Is that why you sent Pete Nield haring down to Nansidwell?'

'Yes,' Tweed responded. 'He's bringing the map straight back with him. I want to see that for myself. Oh, by the way, did you find out any more about the Buddha, Mrs Benyon, VB's stepmother – and her son, Ethan?'

'Mrs Benyon has a small amount of stock in the private company controlling VB's empire. The rumour is she's always going on at VB about giving her more stock, that she'd like a bigger say in the conglomerate.'

'Fits in with that photo you showed me. What else?'

'Her son, Ethan, seems a strange character. He hates his mother, who bullies him when she can. He doesn't live with her – he's living at Black Ridge, VB's HQ down the coast from Carmel and near Big Sur. They say he's brilliant at his work . . .'

'What exactly is his work?'

'He's a seismologist – you know, an expert on earthquakes. And that's all I know. Except when he was a student over here, his colleagues thought he had a screw loose. I can only suppose because he's a typical boffin, wrapped up in what he does.'

'Interesting.' Tweed had a faraway look.

'Interesting? Why?'

'Because certain fragments of the puzzle are beginning to fit into the whole picture. Vaguely. I could be wrong.'

'Incidentally, while you were out this morning the photo of Julia Sanchez arrived from Cord Dillon by Federal Express. The girl friend of VB's who vanished into nowhere along with the other six. Here it is.'

She laid it on his desk and Tweed looked at the photo of a very attractive brunette. She had a firm chin, suggesting character, and laughing eyes. The type of girl who would be fun. Tweed guessed her age at early thirties.

'Nothing like the woman Newman pulled ashore down in Cornwall, the one Paula swore was the same woman she hauled out of the sea at Octopus Cove in California. Here is the Identikit pic. Paula worked out with our artist in the Engine Room,' Monica pointed out.

Tweed glanced at the drawing Paula had worked on with the artist. He knew she was very good at recalling individual features. Even before studying it closely he had realized there was no resemblance to Julia Sanchez.

Another dead end – they had encountered so many over the years.

'Not a bit like her,' he agreed. 'Better phone Cord and bring him up to date . . .'

He was interrupted by the phone ringing. Monica answered it, told Tweed Cord Dillon was on the phone.

'Hello, Cord. Tweed here.'

'Hi! Tell me something; do I sound cheerful, as though I've just heard good news?'

'You do . . .'

'Which shows I can bluff my way during any crisis.'

'What crisis?'

'The President. I was summoned to see him in the Oval Office. He was storming. Moloch has now built up so much power in the House of Representatives – and in the Senate – the President thinks he could swing the next election any way Moloch wants it to go. I tried to tell him he was exaggerating – but he wouldn't have it. I've been told to find out what VB is up to. I ask you – I've just found out Moloch has crossed the Atlantic in his Lear jet, is now in England somewhere . . .'

'He has. I know exactly where he is.'

'Do me a favour, friend. Get me some data on what he's doing – and why. Your people are experts at that sort of thing and I can't get anything on him from over here. I know I'll get another summons to the White House soon. The whole of Washington is in a panic. They're saying Moloch is a winner in controlling the levers of power . . .'

'Cord, leave it to me. I'm already launching a major operation tracking this man. When I have something positive I'll call you. In fact the operation is well under way.'

'Maybe I'll sleep better tonight. My thanks.'

Tweed told Monica what the American had said. She pursed her lips.

'You didn't tell him the PM also is in a dither for the same reasons.'

'Deliberately. Why upset him more? So this one amazing man, VB, is able to cause tremors of anxiety in both London and Washington. Tremors,' he repeated thoughtfully.

'I'm continuing to check out Vanity Richmond,' Monica told him. 'I used a reliable contact in San Francisco. They tried to locate a Vanessa Richmond through the DMV, Department of Motor Vehicles, TRW, the credit-rating bureau, the IRS, Internal Revenue Service, the Immigration Department for registered aliens – foreigners with residential permits to live in the States – and a Social Security number. They came up with a blank everywhere. Vanessa Richmond is a woman with no identity.'

'Most mysterious,' commented Tweed.

'I'm more than halfway trying to find her over here but I'm registering more blanks.'

'When Newman phoned me his report on the Mullion Towers assault he then put Paula on the line. She says there's a woman staying on her own at Nansidwell who looks exactly like Vanity. But in California she was a redhead. The woman at Nansidwell is a brunette.'

'She's wearing a wig. Or maybe she's dyed her hair.' Monica said quickly.

'That thought had occurred to me. I'll have a chat with the lady when I arrive at Nansidwell. You booked me a room?'

'Of course. Starting tonight. Shouldn't you be driving off soon?'

'I'm waiting for Pete Nield to arrive back with that paper Marler grabbed out of VB's dustbin. He should be here soon.'

Half an hour later Nield arrived, having driven all the way to Cornwall and back again. Monica thought he looked surprisingly fresh. He handed Tweed a cardboard-backed envelope.

'Marler said what he found was torn into four pieces. He's assembled it with sellotape into the original document.'

'Don't you need a drink of something after that trip?' suggested Monica.

'I could do with a jug of water and some of that sweetened coffee you make so well, please?' Nield requested with a smile. 'I was parched during the last lap. Heat inside my car was like a furnace. I had a bottle of water but that soon went.'

'Sit down, Pete,' Tweed told him. 'I want to talk to you in a minute.'

Tweed was studying the document Marler had skilfully reassembled. It was a map of California with a series of five squiggly lines running from south to north through the state. Each had a name written in tiny letters at the bottom of the sheet. He immediately recognized the notorious San Andreas earthquake fault. What puzzled him was another line running close to the coast, named the San Moreno fault.

When Monica returned with refreshments for Nield, including a plate of sugary buns, Tweed waited until he had drunk all the liquid, consumed all the buns. Pete Nield, Harry Butler's partner, could have hardly been less like the rough-tongued, burly Butler. Of slim build, in his late thirties, he dressed smartly, had an intelligent face with a neat moustache under his strong nose.

'Monica,' Tweed called out, 'could you see if you can get Professor Weatherby on the phone?'

'The top seismologist in this country?'

'Yes. Tom Weatherby.'

A few minutes later Monica nodded to Tweed, who picked up his phone. The familiar voice with its Scots burr greeted him jokily.

'Tweed? Thought you'd joined the government.'

'Perish the thought. Tom, this is asking a bit much but could I drive over to see you now? Only be there a few minutes but it's urgent.'

'When isn't it when you come to bring me a riddle? See you as soon as you arrive here . . .'

Tweed went to a cupboard, brought out a case always kept for immediate departure. He also carried out Pete Nield's, handed it to him.

'We're off to Cornwall. First we have to call on Weatherby.'

'Pete has just been all the way down there and back,' Monica protested.

'Pete is ready to go back again,' Nield assured her.

'I'll drive,' said Tweed. 'You can reach me at Nansidwell,' he told Monica. 'While I'm gone you're in charge. And tell Howard you don't know where I've gone if he asks – which he will . . .'

They drove to a large house in the Holland Park district of London first. Weatherby opened the front door, ushered them inside as soon as they arrived. He took them into a spacious, comfortably furnished living room with a large desk against one wall, asked them what they would like to drink. Both visitors asked for coffee.

Weatherby, in his seventies, was like an amiable gnome. He had greying hair and a wide, high forehead. Of medium height, he had a puckish grin and greeted Tweed warmly. Nield thought he looked like a brain box.

'Now, what problem have you brought me?' he asked Tweed when he had served coffee. He had a glass of whisky, which he sipped. 'Some situation you hope I can decipher?'

'Yes, exactly that.'

Tweed handed him the map of California Marler had rescued. Weatherby opened it out, stared at it for several minutes. He looked up at Tweed.

'May I ask where you obtained this?'

'Sorry, Tom, that's confidential.'

'I do recognize the tiny script at the bottom which has different names on it. The man who built up this map is short-sighted. I knew him. Ethan Benyon. He studied seismology under me.'

'That's a coincidence,' Tweed replied.

'Not really. Seismologists comprise a small club, communicate their findings to each other. If it doesn't sound immodest Ethan came to me because he believed I was the best in Western Europe. An absurd exaggeration. It was several years ago. He was a brilliant student. Shy, quiet, but he had a natural affinity for the subject.'

'You know where he is now?'

'No idea. Although if this map is recent it looks as though he's in California. He is so short-sighted he wears those pebble glasses. He was particularly interested in the VAN method for predicting earthquakes.'

'What is that?' asked Tweed.

'Difficult to explain. In a few words, it was invented by three Greek professors. They worked out this VAN method which uses a series of strategically placed stations to register natural electrical currents which occur close to the Earth's surface. These currents are initiated by the Earth's magnetic field. The stations are equipped with sensors buried in the ground a distance apart. They're linked with a conducting wire to a voltage amplifier and a chart recorder. Are you with me so far?'

'I think so,' said Tweed.

'More than I am,' Nield commented quietly.

'The chart recorders can detect a signal which invariably precedes an earthquake. For a long time seismologists generally thought it was nonsense, but now they acknowledge the VAN system works – at least some do. I do know the Americans are still sceptical. Ethan had an original mind.'

'In what way?'

'He was deeply interested in the real cause of earthquakes, in whether they could be controlled. I found some of his ideas disturbing, but he is a maverick. Never communicates any findings to his fellow scientists. He has nothing to do with them.'

'That map tells you nothing else?'

'Well, it puzzles me. There's one line I do not understand, the one marked the San Moreno fault. Its route, along the Pacific coast, inland, and then back near the coast, is one I have never heard of. It worries me – I'm not sure why. Would you object to my making a photocopy of it?'

'No, so long as no one else sees it.'

'You did say it was confidential,' Weatherby reminded him, and grinned amiably.

'Go ahead. Then we must leave.'

'I understand. You're like a dragonfly, always dashing hither and thither. Excuse me . . .'

He was back in a few minutes, handed back the original to Tweed. Thanking him for his help, Tweed left the house, got behind the wheel of his Ford Sierra with Nield beside him and headed for Cornwall.

'Did that help?' Nield asked as they left the outskirts of London and Tweed pressed his foot down.

'I'm not sure. It echoed a mad theory I have at the back of my mind. Probably all wrong. Maybe we'll have better luck in Cornwall.'

'Maybe we'll have more excitement. Marler told me about their firefight at Mullion Towers. Let's hope things are hotting up.'

'Just so long as we don't run into a furnace.'

5

'It was a complete and total shambles,' Moloch told Brand as they sat in his office. 'From start to finish they out-manoeuvred you. Call yourself a security expert? You're a rank amateur.'

'They took us by surprise,' Brand mumbled.

'Which means their tactics were infinitely superior to yours. Did you put that paper I gave you through the shredder?'

'Yes,' lied Brand. 'I've reorganized all our defences . . .'

'We're not on the defensive now. We're going on the offensive against Tweed.'

'Great idea.'

'Shut up. I'll take over the planning now. You take the whole team, check every hotel in the area – Truro, Falmouth, Mylor. You're locating where Paula Grey is staying. Apart from Tweed, she's the only name we have in that top-flight outfit at the moment. The opposition has to have a base in the area – they wouldn't have driven all the way from London to launch their attack. What are you sitting there for? Get off your backside. Get moving.'

'We're on our way . . .'

'I also want powerboats sent out from the *Venetia* – to explore the rivers and creeks. You can take command of that part of the operation. Don't come back until you have found them.'

'On my way,' Brand said hastily as he reached the door. 'But that means there will be no guards here . . .'

'Moron! You don't expect them to return the same day, do you?'

'Good thinking . . .'

'Someone round here has to think. And don't overlook the small villages. Explore Mawnan Smith and Mawnan. There are some good hotels in that area.'

'Will do. And I could check whether Tweed is staying down here . . .'

'Idiot! Tweed will be in London, planning Lord knows what. He's the last man on earth you'd find down here. Now, for God's sake, *go.*'

Moloch waited until he had watched from his window a cavalcade of cars leave. The damaged gates had been removed and he made a mental note to check whether Brand had ordered new and stronger gates. He then sat down at his desk and from memory pressed the buttons of a number in California. It was 6 p.m. in England so it would be 10 a.m. in California. He was calling Black Ridge and asked to be put through to Ethan Benyon.

'Ethan? This is VB. How is the project going? When will you be ready?'

'It goes well,' answered an English voice, quiet and subdued. 'I should be ready in a few weeks. It will work.'

'Good. Try and speed everything up. Is the offshore drilling ship operation going well?'

'Ahead of schedule.'

'Have there been any suspicions voiced about it?'

'No, Mr Moloch. Everyone is convinced it's a research ship drilling for specimen cores off the seabed.'

'Good.' He paused. 'Ethan, you sound depressed.'

'It's Mother. She's just moved to a house near Big Sur on the coast. I have to visit her. She's making my life a misery. She even threatened to beat me.'

'I see. Ethan, don't let her take your mind off your work. I'll deal with the old horror . . .'

'Please, Mr Moloch, don't do that. She'll take it out on me something terrible.'

'No, she won't. I have an ace card I can play to make her behave like a civilized human being. Keep up the good work. And thank you for your dedication.'

'It's my life's work . . .'

Moloch put down the phone. Standing up, he wandered round his office, hands clasped behind his back. He hated his stepmother. Lord knew why his father had ever married the creature. And she had driven him into an early grave.

His mouth was tight when he sat again behind his desk and called Mrs Benyon.

'Arabella?' he enquired. 'Vincent Bernard here.'

'What the hell do you want?' a raspy growling English voice demanded. 'And it's time I had more stock in AMBECO.'

'I've been talking to Ethan. You've been treating him very badly – even brutally. I won't have any more of that. Do you understand?'

'And what are you going to do about it?' she sneered.

'I can always take back the stock you already hold.'

'You friggin' well can't.'

'I suggest you study the attorney's agreement I had drawn up. It clearly states that at any time I can recall the stock and you have to return it.'

'You swine.'

'Compliments will get you nowhere. I'm ordering you to treat your son decently. You wouldn't like someone to put a bomb under your new house, I presume?'

'You wouldn't dare.'

Her voice became horrendous, but under the unbridled rage Moloch detected a note of fear. That was the only thing which made her control her evil temper. He put down the phone without replying. It worried him that Mrs Benyon was now so close to Black Ridge. He didn't want to order the guards to refuse her admittance to his headquarters. If he did so she would spread the story and the locals in Carmel and Monterey might wonder what was really going on inside the place – the last thing he needed at this critical time.

Tweed had driven more than halfway to Cornwall when Nield insisted on doing his stint behind the wheel. In the front passenger seat Tweed promptly fell asleep. He had the knack of closing his eyes and immediately falling into a deep sleep. Much later Nield warned Tweed.

'We're nearly there,' he said as he nudged Tweed, who woke, instantly alert.

'Nearly where? Isn't this the road up to Nansidwell?'

'Yes. How do you know?'

'I was once down here on another problem. I toured the whole area, stayed at Nansidwell. Hadn't I better take the wheel, drop you off at the entrance to the Meudon, where Butler is staying? Monica booked you a room there.'

'I know. Good idea . . .'

They changed places and Tweed drove along a country road which passed a long marshy area below them. Nield told Tweed what he had done earlier.

'I called Paula on the mobile phone, told her you would be arriving within fifteen minutes. Then I called Harry, warned him I was about to arrive.'

'You were careful what you said, I assume. No names.'

'Of course.'

Tweed disliked mobile phones. There has been too many instances of marauders listening in, recording conversations. He dropped off Nield with his case a short distance from Meudon. Butler had transport – he had hired a car and reported the fact earlier to Monica.

Tweed drove down the curving drive to Nansidwell, prepared to meet the proprietor, who knew him as Chief Claims Investigator of General & Cumbria Assurance. When he entered the lounge the first person he saw was Paula, who came up and hugged him because no one else was about.

'Trouble?' Tweed asked quietly as he registered in the open book on a desk.

'Someone interesting you should meet. But you must be tired after your long day.'

'Let's get on with it as soon as I've had a quick bath in my room.'

A pleasant man appeared, relieved him of his case and led him to his room. Paula tapped on his door as he finished dressing again after his bath. He let her in and she put down a tray of tea and scones. Tweed had changed from his London business suit into more casual wear.

'Thank you – this is most welcome,' he said as she poured a cup of tea. 'Driving down, the car was like a hothouse. Seems pretty warm here.'

'It's been torrid since we got here. I'm ready to take you to see this person if you really want to. I can warn them here we'll be a bit late for dinner.'

She was wearing a short black dress, a short jacket with a string of pearls and black suede pumps. He thought she looked very chic and said so.

'Who is this person?' he asked in a lowered voice.

'Maurice Prendergast. I met him when I was driving into Mawnan Smith. Nearly knocked down his wire-haired terrier, which appeared suddenly. I saved it with an emergency stop and apologized, and he was very grateful. So grateful he invited me to tea at his house. He'd left his car parked in the village.'

'What happened next?' Tweed enquired with an odd smile.

'He got in his car and led the way to his house overlooking a creek. Actually, it's a two-storey thatched cottage. He gave me tea, which he prepared himself.'

'No one else there? You took a chance.'

'I had my Browning in the special pocket inside my shoulder bag. And I'd already assessed him as a very nice man.'

'Some of the most famous murderers were nice-looking men,' Tweed chaffed her. 'Learn anything about him?'

'He said he'd had a good job in London – then he went on to say he got out of London before London got him. I told him I was with an insurance company and he smiled strangely. I still don't understand that particular reaction. I had the funny feeling I'd seen him somewhere before.'

'He'd seen *you* before,' Tweed told her at last.

Paula stared at him. Then she burst out laughing and playfully punched his arm.

'You devil. Letting me chatter on without saying anything. Who is he?'

'Maurice Prendergast, ex-Special Branch officer. You saw him a couple of years ago when I was driving with him by my side in London. You caught only a glimpse of me – I certainly didn't think you'd seen him. And I was driving fast. He's just one reason why I'm down here – to see him. He can tell me what's going on round here. A strange coincidence you two should meet.'

'Not really. He told me he took three long walks a day with his dog round this area. I think he's a very lonely man. His wife died about a year ago . . .'

'I didn't realize that. Knowing him, he'll be pretty down.'

'He doesn't show it. He's very cheerful, jokey. Made only a brief reference to it and changed the subject.'

'Maurice would do that. He's good at bluffing, at concealing his feelings from the outside world. We'd better go and see him now.'

'I'll drive – it's a tricky route,' Paula suggested. 'We're going to a place called Porth Navas on the Helford River – but it looks like a creek higher up. Daphne du Maurier country – at least she lived there in her earliest days.'

'I'll drive, you navigate,' Tweed said firmly. 'I had a nap on the way down while Pete took the wheel. I'm fresh as the proverbial daisy. I wonder what Maurice will have to tell us . . .'

Leaving the hotel, they walked past Bob Newman, sitting in a chair in one of the lounges. Tweed strolled past him as though they'd never met before and Newman hardly glanced up from a magazine he was reading.

Paula guided Tweed into Mawnan Smith, where they turned left in a sharp fork past the Red Lion. Later they entered a narrow lane, the high banks of hedgerows on both sides barely giving room for the car and no room at all for two vehicles to pass each other. Tweed made his comment as they descended a steep hill.

'I know these Cornish lanes – they're like rabbit warrens. All right for a visit but who would want to live here?'

'At the bottom where the road levels out you have to take a very sharp turn to the left and proceed along the edge of the creek. Apparently a very interesting character runs an oyster farm at the point where the road comes to a dead end.'

'Oysters!' Tweed said with relish. 'I'm going to enjoy myself down here.'

'Yuck,' said Paula in a tone of disgust. 'Some people have perverted tastes.'

'Just look the other way when I'm eating them. Here we go.'

A truck was coming in the opposite direction. Here and there they had passed setbacks in the hedges but the previous one was way behind them.

'Now we play a game of poker,' Tweed said with enthusiasm. 'We stop here, see what he does, let him work it out.'

After a minute of deadlock the truck driver began reversing until he reached a passing place. He waited until Tweed drove slowly past, acknowledging the truck driver's courtesy with the wave of a hand.

'There's the bottom of the creek,' Paula warned. 'Where you turn along the creek. And I was wrong saying it was on the Helford River. This is one of several creeks which run back from the Helford.'

Tweed swung the car round at a steep angle, found himself driving along a narrow road perched on the edge of the creek to their right. Again only space for one car. To their left at the edge of the road were pleasant two-storey old houses with whitewashed walls, each nearly touching its neighbour. Several boats were moored in the creek. Paula stopped him as he reached a larger building with an open space for parking cars.

'This is the Yacht Club,' she explained. 'They'll think we're having dinner here. It's only a short walk back to Prendergast's place . . .'

The Ark, with white rough-cast walls and a thatched roof, seemed to Tweed to be built into the side of a cliff. He and Paula mounted three stone steps to a heavy wooden door equipped with a spyhole. Tweed was lifting the heavy anchor-shaped knocker when the door opened.

'Saw you pass the house,' Prendergast told them in his cultured voice. 'Long time no see, as they say. Come in and relax.'

He greeted Tweed warmly, shaking his hand with a firm grip. Tweed followed Paula into a large long room with a low beamed ceiling and a big inglenook fireplace at one end. The furniture was Jacobean with a sturdy dining table. There was a small modern kitchen at the other end. He felt immediately at home as Prendergast pulled up an armchair for Paula close to the fireplace.

'Why The Ark?' Tweed enquired as he sat in another chair.

'Because some strange animals – of the human variety – have come here. You've come to Porth Navas, a refugee colony. What can I serve you both for drinks?'

After he had provided drinks Prendergast sat on a leather seat by the inglenook where he could see both of them. He raised his glass of whisky.

'Cheers! Thought you'd be arriving on my doorstep, Tweed.'

'What made you think so?'

'Sixth sense. And when Paula appears Tweed can't be far behind. If you're hunting you've come to the right place.'

'Why did you call Porth Navas a refugee colony?' Tweed enquired.

'Because so many down in this part of the world have fled from London, which they nickname the Inferno. They found the pressure of modern life too much. Really they're almost expatriates, the type you find abroad. Often they are – or have become – boaty types. Live for messing about in boats, having an evening get-together at the local pub.'

Tweed nodded. He had been studying their host. Maurice Prendergast was six feet tall, in his late thirties, had a strong, clean-shaven face with a long nose, a firm mouth and a rugged jaw. Fair-haired, his eyes were a deceptive sleepy-looking blue, his movements apparently slow and he appeared to be smiling all the time, a humorous smile. He was a handsome man, far too young to be buried in this faraway creek.

'You said if I was hunting I'd come to the right place,' Tweed remarked. 'Why did you say that?'

'Money. People take off from their normal lives, settle here and find they can't really afford to have retired, so to speak. Some are willing to take on any kind of dirty work if the payment is right.'

'What type of dirty work?' Paula asked.

'A very powerful man who has a big house beyond Stithians uses certain people round here as spies. They are paid large sums in cash – so no tax to the Inland Revenue. Their job is to report back to him any strangers appearing in the area. He'll know you are here.'

'How on earth will he know that?' Paula persisted.

'Because when you were driving slowly along the road past my house you were photographed from a boat in the creek.'

'How do you know that?' Paula was alarmed about Tweed, who could be the number one target.

'Because from a window I saw Adrian Penkastle aiming his camera at you. Not only has he photographed you but I'm sure he has now phoned your description to his paymaster. That's the system they use. Rather effective.'

'Tell us something about this Adrian Penkastle,' Tweed suggested.

'Oh, he was an executive in a big advertising agency in London. He got kicked out of his job for insulting a top client of the agency. He was drunk as a lord at the time. He knocks back brandies as though they are water.

In the late evening he floats back from the Yacht Club along the road outside – floats on alcohol. Thinks he's a bit of a toff.' He jumped up from his seat.

'I saw him from this window . . .' He paused. 'I don't believe it. Here he comes . . .'

They all stood by the window, which was masked with heavy net curtains. They saw a portly man with a slow tread, a round head with grey hair and a red face. He carried himself with an air of self-importance and was looking at Prendergast's cottage as he continued along the road with a duck-like waddle.

Penkastle was clad in a white shirt and white flannels and had a nautical cap perched on the back of his head at a rakish angle. Paula, in an impish mood, ran to the front door, opened it, ran down the steps and clasped him with both hands on his fat shoulders. She was grinning as he stared at her, stopped by her sudden arrival.

'Adrian,' she gushed, 'thank you so much for taking my picture. You really are a scream. Don't forget the name of the house I came out of. He'll want to know that. It's called The Ark.'

'The A . . . r . . . k?' He was slurring his words. 'Why is it called that?'

'Adrian,' she went on, still clasping his shoulders. 'It is called that because so many animals – the human type – are wandering round here. Just like you're wandering. A bit unsteady, are we? Still, a few drinks never did any harm . . .'

'Don't know what . . . you're talking about,' he mumbled.

'Surely you remember me?' she went on, grinning again. 'That night at the pub when I danced on the table and you couldn't take your eyes off my legs. Oh, come on, Adrian – you must remember that.'

'S'pose I must. Which pub was that?'

'Oh, come on, Adrian.' She shook him. 'You know

which pub. You do remember me dancing on the table. You loved it. So stop being so shy.'

'I do remember,' he mumbled again, slurring his words more than ever. 'You were great ... great ... great.' He leaned towards her, spoke confidentially. 'I've had a couple ...'

'Adrian, you've just drunk the Yacht Club dry. So stop trying to kid me. How many did you have?'

'Lost count ...'

'Adrian, you've already taken my picture once. How about a close-up. I'll lift my skirt a bit for you. Let's do it now. You've got your camera ...'

Penkastle did have his camera, slung from a strap over his back where it hung out of sight. As he tried to get hold of it with shaky hands Paula moved. She grabbed hold of the camera, swinging the loop over his head.

'There,' she went on after a quick glance at it. 'You still have plenty of film. Take six shots and you'll get a good one of me ... Whoops!'

She had let the camera slide out of her hand. It plunged over the edge of the road down into the water of the creek. Penkastle stared down to where it had vanished with a doleful look on his fat face.

'That ... was extensive ...'

'Expensive? Oh, dear. Still, I'm sure you have plenty more at home. What fun we're having. We always have fun, don't we, Adrian?'

'Yes. Yes. Yes. We do ...'

'Excuse me now. I've got to dash back for my drink – only my fifth this afternoon. Mind you don't fall into the creek.' She swivelled him round so he was facing the way he had come. 'Now, back to the Yacht Club – don't forget to have one on me. Lovely to see you again, Adrian ...'

As she went back inside the house, closed the door, Maurice was saying something to Tweed.

'Wasn't that a bit dangerous?'

Tweed was laughing. He shook his head while Paula joined them.

'What a wonderful performance, Paula. No, Maurice, I want to rattle the man who is Adrian's employer. He'll wonder what our tactics are when Adrian sobers up and reports to him. And Paula lost the camera.'

'It did have the three shots in it,' Paula told them. 'I checked the number just before I let it slip into the drink.'

'Talking about drink,' Tweed said, peering out of the window, 'Adrian is duck-waddling back to the Yacht Club for a refill. Duck-waddling. Quack! Quack!' he went on, joining in the fun with Paula to show how much he approved of her swift tactic. Then he looked thoughtful. 'Quack,' he repeated in a very different tone. 'I think I've got it.'

'Let's all sit down again,' Prendergast suggested. 'The man you're talking about is Vincent Bernard Moloch out at Mullion Towers beyond Stithians? I thought so. I can tell you quite a lot about him that isn't generally known.'

6

Moloch was eating a meagre meal in his office when the phone rang. He always ate frugally and this never seemed to affect his endless capacity for work.

'Hello,' he said.

'Penkastle here, Mr Carson. Adrian. You know ... Adrian.'

Moloch pursed his lips. His caller was obviously the worse for drink. He hadn't known Penkastle imbibed heavily when Brand recruited him as an informer. He had been given Moloch's ex-directory number and told to report to a Mr Carson.

'Yes,' Moloch said. 'You have news?'

'Paula Grey, the girl Joel gave me a pic. of, is visiting a man in Porth Navas. Ex-Special Branch type . . . Maurice Prender . . . gast.'

He was having trouble pronouncing names. Now Prendergast came across clearly.

'Go on,' Moloch said patiently.

'I took photographs of her with another man when they were driving along the road by the creek to the Yacht Club . . .'

'Where are you now?'

'Yacht . . . Club.'

'Give me the address of this Prendergast.'

'Funny name. The Ark. Halfway down the road along the creek at Porth Navas . . .'

'How do you know this Maurice Prendergast is ex-Special Branch?'

He was firing questions at Penkastle, who was slurring his words. Moloch needed the information while this drunk could still answer questions.

'Doesn't make any secret of the fact. Says he got fed up with the work and decided to get away from it all.'

'Did he now?' Moloch paused. 'You said you took pictures of two people in a car – Paula Grey and a man. Describe them as best you can . . .'

Penkastle managed a description of Paula, which satisfied Moloch he had identified her. The description of the man driving the car was vague, blurred. Moloch never gave a thought that this might be Tweed.

'Give the film with the photos to Joel. I'll arrange for him to call on you. Return to your house there.'

'Can't do that. You see . . .'

Penkastle then described the scene outside The Ark when Paula had accosted him and, later, dropped his camera in the creek. Moloch listened with growing amazement and alarm. Paula Grey appeared to have had no worries about being recognized. He admired the way she had got rid of the camera.

'Is that all?' he asked eventually.

'Yes. The camera was expensive . . .'

'I'm sure it was. Now go straight back to your house and wait for Joel to call on you with new instructions. You understand?'

'Yes. Got a headache. Good idea.'

Moloch sat at his desk for several minutes, tapping his pen, then doodling on a pad. The opposition was getting on his nerves. What was Tweed up to? He hated unknown factors and Tweed was certainly the greatest unknown one he'd ever come across in a ruthless career.

Tearing off a sheet from the pad, he wrote a long message to Brand. The gist of it was to give Prendergast's details and address, and the order to intimidate him. He then added a fresh order that Penkastle was unreliable and he must be dealt a lesson.

The wording was obscure but he knew Brand would understand it. He took it to the communications room, handed it to the radio op. on duty.

'Send that to Joel Brand – aboard the *Venetia*. Immediately.'

By this time Brand had boarded the *Venetia*. He had decided the most interesting part of the mission to locate Paula Grey was to join the powerboat fleet exploring the many creeks. Climbing down a ladder over the side, he paused as one of the crew called out.

'Urgent message for you, Mr Brand, from the Chief.'

Brand read it, grinned to himself. This assignment should be fun. The idea of eliminating Penkastle and this Maurice Prendergast, whoever he might be, appealed to him. He screwed up the message, jammed it inside the pocket of his well-worn denims, pulled down his oilskin jacket – rather warm considering the blazing sun but waterproof – and adjusted his nautical cap. The way he was clad made him look like one of the boaty types who, at this time of the year, pottered about in the creeks.

Three tough-looking men were already aboard the powerboat, two with automatic rifles, one at the wheel. Brand pulled him away, taking command as he prepared to start the engine.

'Well, my hearties,' his voice boomed, 'we're heading for the Helford River. On a hunting expedition. You may have to use your knife, Gene,' he went on, addressing the bony-faced man whose hand Newman had burned with his cigarette.

'It will be a pleasure,' Gene replied as the powerboat took off.

Inside his cottage at Porth Navas Prendergast was telling Tweed and Paula what he knew about Moloch.

'I've just had news that one of the leading electronics plants in the Thames Valley was destroyed totally by a bomb during the night. A lot of talk about the IRA but I don't believe a word of it.'

'You think it was Moloch's work?' enquired Tweed.

'Darned sure it was. He's recently bought one of the best electronics companies in that area. The firm which has gone up in smoke would have been one of his main competitors. He didn't get to the summit in the States by playing Tiddlywinks.'

'He does have an armaments company, which could well include manufacture of explosives.'

'Exactly my thinking. Back where I work – worked – it's known his main expansion at the moment is in electronics.'

'Freudian slip,' Tweed observed, quoting his own

words back at him. ' "Work" – and then "worked". You're not retired at all, are you, Maurice? Coming down here is just cover, isn't it? It puts you within driving distance of his HQ at Mullion Towers.'

Prendergast paused, no particular expression on his face. Paula smiled, prodded him verbally.

'Come on, Maurice. We don't swallow a story like that so easily. Give.'

'Let's just say,' Prendergast told her slowly, 'that I personally think it would have been better if our two outfits combined on certain operations. That does not necessarily mean my bosses would agree with me.'

'A positive answer to my question,' Paula commented and smiled at him.

'Any more data on VB?' Tweed asked.

'His chief of staff is a real villain called Joel Brand. So big and tough-looking you might think he hasn't a lot going on in the upper storey in the way of brains. That would be to seriously underestimate him. Moloch hasn't chosen him for his role without knowing what he's doing. And a clever woman called Vanity Richmond – of all names – is on his payroll. Pretty close to him, I gather.'

'Really?' said Tweed.

'I met her in Monterey,' Paula broke in with more enthusiasm than Tweed had shown. 'She tried to get next to me but I fended her off. I was suspicious.'

'With good reason,' Prendergast told her. 'It took us months to spot her when she was over here some time ago, staying at Mullion Towers.'

'She's here now, I'm sure,' Paula continued. 'A woman just like her is staying at our hotel, the Nansidwell. The trouble is she was a flaming redhead . . .'

'Good description,' Prendergast agreed. 'And attractive, I thought, when I watched her wandering in the grounds.'

'But now this woman at Nansidwell, who ignores me, is a brunette.'

'So she's wearing a dark wig,' Prendergast said laconically. 'You're not often wrong, Paula. What's she up to at your hotel?'

'For one thing she's trying to hook Bob Newman, but he isn't playing. At least so far,' she added. 'But Bob does take his time before he moves.'

'Talking about moving,' Prendergast stood up, 'since you were spotted by that Penkastle idiot, the news has probably been passed to Moloch by now that you're here. I suggest you give me the keys to your car. I'll drive it back to Nansidwell after dark.'

'And how do you suggest we get all the way back?' Paula demanded. 'Hoof it? It's miles – most of the way uphill.'

'I've got a better plan. You can be away from here in no time – and not a soul will know you've even left.'

'How?' asked Tweed bluntly.

'We'll travel in my large dinghy – it has a powerful outboard motor. We go down the creek, heading for Durgan where a friend of mine has a car. He'll loan it to me and I'll drive you to Nansidwell – no distance at all. I leave the dinghy at Durgan, drive back there, then take the dinghy to get back here. Simple.'

'Where exactly is Durgan?' Tweed enquired.

'Further down the Helford River . . .'

While Prendergast locked up the place Paula noticed the uneasy look on Tweed's face. He was a very bad sailor and hated any kind of floating craft. She dived into her capacious shoulder bag containing the two smoke bombs Marler had handed to her when they returned to the hotel from Mullion Towers.

She brought out the strip of Dramamine she always

carried, handed one of the anti-seasickness pills to Tweed. He hastily swallowed it, washing it down with the rest of his orange juice as Prendergast returned.

'Tally ho!' he called out cheerfully. 'Here we go – sailing the Spanish Main . . .'

Outside, wearing gumboots, he climbed down a small flight of steps, hauled in a large dinghy. Waiting until Paula and Tweed were seated, he started the engine. The sun had dropped behind the forested hills on the far side of the creek and it was cool and fresh on the water.

'Lovely day for a trip,' Prendergast called out, full of zest.

'Isn't it,' replied Tweed in a dull voice.

They cruised down the creek and entered the much wider Helford River, and soon Paula saw the open sea at its mouth. Woods came down to the water's edge and Prendergast was moving into the centre of the river when Paula saw a large powerboat speeding up the river towards them. At the wheel reared up a large man with black hair. She tensed as he raised a pair of glasses with one hand, focused towards them. She immediately recognized Joel Brand. Lowering the field glasses, he gripped the wheel with both hands and the powerboat's prow lifted out of the water as he roared towards them.

'Brand is in that powerboat!' she shouted to Prendergast. 'He's going to run us down!'

'He's got more speed than we have,' Prendergast warned.

Paula took out a smoke bomb from her shoulder bag, sat tensely as the powerboat, looking like a mechanical shark, tore down on them. Prendergast was desperately trying to reach the shore but she knew he would never make it. Tweed leaned close to Paula.

'Have you another of those things? If so, I'd like one.'

She gazed at him dubiously. She felt sure he couldn't

hit a barn door from six feet away. Reluctantly, she took out the second smoke bomb, handed it to him. He sat calmly, watching the approaching craft which would cut the dinghy to shreds.

'I'll manoeuvre out of his way when he's very close – if I can,' Prendergast shouted back.

The roar of the powerboat's engine became deafening. It seemed to loom above them as at the last minute Prendergast steered his dinghy with great skill in a different direction. The powerboat was within yards of them when Tweed hoisted his arm, hurled his smoke bomb. It landed inside the powerboat.

Paula, who had been good at rounders while at school, threw her smoke bomb a second later. It landed in the water. Tweed's bomb had detonated. A cloud of dense acrid smoke enveloped the craft, which suddenly went crazy. At the wheel Brand was blinded, coughing his guts out, his right hand still on the wheel, his left rubbing his eyes. The powerboat zigzagged madly across the river, following no logical course, heading for a steep bank where rocks protruded. Some instinct made Brand slow the engine, then cut it out. The powerboat stopped just before it smashed into the rocks, drifted, the smoke still rising from it.

'Durgan, here we come!' Prendergast shouted, making no attempt to conceal the relief in his voice.

'Where did you learn to throw like that?' Paula asked Tweed.

'Long ago I played cricket,' he told her. 'Actually I was a bit of a bowler.'

7

Tweed entered the lounge at Nansidwell while Paula stayed outside to chat to Prendergast whom she'd taken a liking to. In the right-hand lounge he saw Vanity Richmond, who sat down next to Newman, perched on a banquette in front of the windows overlooking the garden.

She's decided to forget about her black wig to see if her real appearance will get Newman going, he thought.

Which was exactly what had happened. She crossed her shapely legs, wore a very short skirt so he could admire them. Tweed had disappeared to his room as she opened the conversation.

'I hope you don't mind my joining you,' she began, 'but I gather we're both alone. You're Robert Newman. Am I right?'

'You are.'

'The famous international foreign correspondent. But I haven't seen any of your pungent articles in the top papers or magazines for a long time. You always had your photo at the top, which is how I recognize you.'

'I haven't written any recently . . .'

He looked up as the pleasant waiter came up to them and smiled.

'Would you like an aperitif?'

'Might go down rather well.' He turned to his new companion with a guarded smile. 'What would you like to drink?'

'A large dry Martini, please.'

'I'll have Scotch and water,' said Newman.

'I'm Vanity Richmond,' the very attractive redhead said.

'And I thought you were a brunette.'

'No wonder.' She laughed. 'I was in a dark mood so I wore a black wig. Now I'm beginning to enjoy myself in this lovely hotel I decided to be myself.'

'And who is myself?' Newman probed.

'Oh, I'm a PA to an industrialist. I travel a lot with him, see the world. He needs a lot of personal attention but I don't mind. The pay is good, the travel free.'

'Which industrialist?' Newman persisted.

'Oh, you'd never have heard of him. He maintains a modest profile . . .'

'Where do you travel to?' Newman went on, gazing at her greenish eyes.

'My,' she chided him with a smile on her full red lips, 'is this an interrogation? Oh, of course, you're a top journalist. It must be second nature for you to question people.'

'I'm interested in you.'

'That's a nice compliment.'

She inched closer to him along the banquette until their thighs were touching. Waiting until the drinks had been served, she lifted her glass, clinked it against Newman's.

'Here's to an interesting friendship.'

'I'll drink to that,' replied Newman, thinking she was coming on pretty strong.

'Why haven't you written for quite a while?' she asked, turning his own guns on him. 'I remember you wrote a great international bestseller, *Kruger: The Computer Which Failed*. I suppose that set you up for life financially?'

'Which comes under the heading of a very personal question,' he rapped back.

'Sorry, I'm notorious for not being very diplomatic.'

'I have noticed that failing.'

Newman's manner had suddenly become more

distant. He had never liked women who approached him openly. His response threw her off balance. Looking at her, he could see how men would find her attractive – she exuded allure. Not a word he preferred but it seemed to fit. She choked down the rest of her drink, looked at him, smiled warmly.

'Could I have another?'

'Of course.'

He gestured to the waiter, ordered more drinks, including a Scotch for himself, this time a double without water. Newman was very good at pretending to be slightly drunk while his brain was still in high gear. He had fooled a lot of people with the tactic. He asked the question quickly before she recovered her poise.

'You didn't answer my question – where do you travel to with this anonymous industrialist?'

'All over the place.' She paused and Newman read her mind. She was trying to decide whether to be more frank. A minute later she went on. 'The main destination,' she said with an air of defiance, 'is California. Near San Francisco . . .'

'Go there often? Spend a lot of time there?'

'So, so. Yes!' Her eyes flashed. He'd got under her skin and there was a trace of arrogance. 'I do spend quite a bit of time in California. That's because my boss does. I enjoy travel . . .'

'So your boss is an American?'

'I didn't say that. Candidly, I'm not sure where the hell he came from, nor do I care. As I told you, the pay is good. Is that enough background information for you, Bob? Oh, goody, here are the drinks.'

She swallowed half her Martini, paused then drank more. Newman had noticed at dinner that she had a large capacity for liquor. He drank his Scotch quickly, then ordered a repeat of the drinks without consulting her. Vanity recrossed her legs, leaned closer.

84

'I like generous men.'

'I imagine you've met a lot of them.'

He was lisping a trifle as he spoke, giving the impression the liquor was starting to take effect on him.

'What the devil does that mean?' she demanded coldly.

'Shimply that an attractive woman like you is bound to have well-off men after you. Makes sense, I'd have thought.'

'Oh, I see what you mean. That's quite a compliment, Bob.'

'Not really, just stating a fact.'

The third round of drinks had been served. They were consuming them when Tweed appeared, walking into the lounge, sat down with his back to them and started reading a magazine explaining the delights of Cornwall. Newman knew that although he wasn't close he could hear every word. Vanity took no notice of him.

'What do you do with your life, Bob?' she continued. 'Are you married?'

'I was once.' Newman's expression became grim. 'My wife was murdered horribly in the Baltic area. I hunted down the killer.'

'I'm so sorry I raised the subject.' Her hand rested on his leg. 'What happened to the killer? Or maybe you'd sooner not talk about it.'

'He fell over a cliff.'

Newman drank more whisky, occasionally slurring his words. His mind was still quite clear. Vanity changed the subject.

'So what do you do, Bob? I'm sure a man like you couldn't just sit around all day.'

'Now and then I contribute articles to certain international papers and magazines – under a different name,' he lied easily. 'So they involve making trips abroad to find out what is really going on.'

'You're a wanderer.'

'You could call me that.' He laughed. 'I wander into the strangest of places. Like here. You must have noticed that huge luxurious yacht standing off Falmouth harbour. It even has a helipad with a chopper sitting on it. Someone told me the owner was a man called Vincent Bernard Moloch.'

He was watching Vanity closely now. Her face froze for a moment, then she dived inside her Hermès handbag, brought out a tiny lace-edged handkerchief. Hermès, Newman was thinking. I'll bet that little item cost not a penny less than five thousand pounds. Her boss pays her very well for her services, whatever they might be.

'How did you find that out?' she asked.

Wrong question, Newman was thinking, but nothing showed of his reaction.

'A chap in a pub told me. Half Falmouth seems to know,' he lied again. 'They say he's the richest man in the world. With a job like that floating out there he must be.'

'Then, with all your experience of the world, you must know something about this man,' she suggested.

'Not a lot.' He finished his drink. 'In any case he's not news, so I'm not interested. I think they're ready for dinner. Care to join me at my table?'

'I'd love that.'

Tweed watched them vanish towards the dining room and smiled to himself. Newman wasn't wasting much time. And he'd handled a tricky situation with his usual skill.

Paula wandered down the staircase, intending to go into dinner. She was wearing an ivory gabardine trouser suit with a cream silk blouse, her latest addition to her wardrobe. The proprietor greeted her cheerfully, commented on how smart she looked. Paula smiled, thanked him, noticed over his shoulder that Vanity Richmond was standing in the entrance, obviously about to go outside for a breath of fresh air.

Vanity was feeling inside her handbag, brought out a compact mobile phone, disappeared round a corner into the courtyard. Paula strolled after her, pausing before she went into the courtyard. Taking a few steps further she saw Vanity huddled against the wall of the building, the mobile phone close to her ear. With her acute sense of hearing Paula could hear every word Vanity said.

'You know who this is, VB. Calling from Nansidwell. I had a long conversation with a one-time foreign correspondent called Robert Newman . . .

'What was that you said? Yes, Newman is staying here. No, I have no reason to suspect him so far. But he told me half Falmouth knows you're here . . .

'How does he know? He heard someone talking in a pub . . .

'Did I hear you correctly? You're flying to Newquay on the chopper? Where to? Didn't catch that . . .

'You're flying on to Heathrow and then to San Francisco in the jet? Surely I should be coming with you . . .

'No? Stay here for the moment and check up on what is going on? Make sure a lot of people see me during the whole evening? Why on earth . . .

'None of my business. Sorry . . .

'Yes, when you send for me I'll board a flight at Heathrow, phoning you from the airport . . .

'OK. Safe flight . . .

Paula was walking into the dining room when she saw Vanity reappear at the entrance. In the dining room she was surprised to see Bob Newman sitting at his usual table, but now it was laid for two people. Tweed was occupying a table not far away, already ordering his meal.

Paula was escorted to her own table and sat down in a tense state. The sooner she warned Tweed that Moloch was on his way back to the States the better. The trouble was she couldn't work out a way of telling him in that crowded room without risking being overheard. Writing a message and handing it to one of the serving girls to take to him was equally dangerous.

At that moment Vanity entered the room, walked straight to Newman's table. He stood up, pulled out a chair for her and they were immediately engaged in animated conversation. And now Paula knew the woman *was* Vanity Richmond. She had the same head of flaming red hair as she'd had when she approached Paula in faraway Monterey. She had been wearing a dark wig – but why had she discarded it?

Paula ordered automatically, her mind racing. Vanity's presence ruled out any chance of her approaching Tweed during dinner. And what about the business of Moloch obviously warning Vanity to be seen during the whole evening? It had a sinister ring which she found disturbing.

Adrian Penkastle rented a tiny one-storey whitewashed cottage at the edge of the creek. Rather the worse for wear after his second bout of drinking at the Yacht Club, he was staggering round his small room, searching in vain for a bottle, when he heard the knock on his door.

'Who the hell can that be at this hour?' he mumbled to himself.

When he eventually managed to unlock the front door he found Joel Brand standing outside. His visitor wore seaman's clothes and a nautical cap pulled well down over his shaggy hair. Joel grinned, waved a bottle of whisky in his gloved hand. He took his gumboots off and entered the house in his socks.

'Got another job for you, Adrian. Big money for this one.'

Joel waved a fistful of twenty-pound notes with his other hand. Penkastle gazed at the money, stood back to let Brand enter. Closing the door, Brand looked round at the primitive furniture which included a large wooden table.

'Let's sit down,' he said cheerfully. 'Bring up a couple of chairs and I'll tell you all about it.'

Penkastle hurried into his minute kitchen-scullery and came back with two greasy glasses. He sat down opposite the big man, who poured a large slug of whisky into his host's glass, then the same amount into his own. Raising his glass, he toasted Penkastle.

'Here's to a long and prosperous life.'

'I'll drink, to that,' Adrian mumbled.

He watched Brand stuff the sheaf of banknotes into one of his pockets. He could only vaguely estimate the amount but it seemed to him Brand was carrying something like five hundred pounds.

'Have a refresher,' Brand urged and poured more whisky into Penkastle's glass. 'You're about to get into the big-time stuff, Adrian. Pays a fortune. In cash, of course.' He winked. 'Don't want the Inland Revenue taking a large cut do we?'

'Prefer cash.'

He stumbled over the first word, drank some more, put down his glass. Brand promptly refilled it. Propping his elbows on the table – Adrian was worried about falling off the chair, which would not make a good impression.

'Tell me about the job. What have I to do this time?'

'You know a guy called Maurice Prendergast? Lives on the other side of the creek.'

'Yes,' Adrian replied eagerly. 'I can tell you the name of his house. Place called The Ark.'

'You have to record his every movement. You have a car, haven't you?'

'An old banger, but it goes.'

'Has Prendergast seen it?'

'I'm sure he hasn't.'

'Then if he takes off you can follow him, report his movements.' Brand drank a little more and Adrian took another large gulp. His head was swimming. 'You report who he meets – where and when. Got it?' Brand asked.

'Yes. I'll drive my car round to his side of the creek, park it at the Yacht Club. Then if he drives off I can be after him . . .'

'We'll also want pictures of him. You can take those, I imagine, from that little boat you use to cross the creek.'

'That's no problem . . .'

'You'll have to spend a lot of hours on this one. That means keeping a watch on his house at night. He might try to slip away well after dark.'

'I can manage that.'

Take photographs of Prendergast, Adrian was thinking. He had lost his camera in the creek – or rather that clumsy woman had dropped it in the water. But with the money Brand was going to give him he could buy a cheap one – which would leave plenty over for trips to pubs.

'You're not drinking,' Brand observed.

'Down the hatch.'

As Adrian lifted his glass Brand raised his own, stood up, swallowed the contents. He grinned at Penkastle, went round to where he was sitting, put an arm round his shoulder.

'Adrian, stand up. I want to show you something from the door. Something which will help you observe Maurice Prendergast.'

Adrian made a supreme effort. Placing both hands flat on the table, he forced himself upright, turned carefully to follow his guest. Brand lifted his pullover, pulled out a stiletto-like knife, rammed it into Adrian's chest at just the right point, avoiding ribs. He shoved the knife upwards with great force. Adrian opened his mouth, gurgled as Brand, using great strength, managed to haul out the knife. He was helped when Adrian fell backwards, hitting a wooden skirting board with the back of his skull.

'Good riddance to bad rubbish,' Brand said aloud.

He wiped the knife clean on the clothes of the dead form lying at his feet, returned it to the concealed sheath. He picked up his own glass, opened the front door, peered out. No one in sight. He put on his gumboots.

It took him less than a minute to step into the dinghy powered by an outboard, to start the motor. He guided it until he reached the powerboat waiting for him by the bank of the Helford River. Gene, who had loaned him the knife, started up the engine.

In mid-river Brand threw the whisky glass overboard, then the knife. A powerboat going up the creek would have attracted attention. Now, with the dinghy attached to its stern, the powerboat began speeding back towards the *Venetia*.

8

'Yes, Ethan. Since it is unusual for you to call me I am hoping this is good news,' said Moloch, leaning forward over the desk in his office at Mullion Towers.

'The operation is well advanced,' Ethan's subdued voice informed him. 'I know it will work. In a matter of weeks or maybe much sooner.'

'And the explosive test? Xenobium.'

He said the last word quickly. There was a pause and Moloch gripped the phone more tightly.

'Successful. More powerful even than we expected.'

'Good. Thank you for keeping me in touch . . .'

It was this phone call which decided him to return to the States immediately. He contacted Vanity Richmond on her mobile. Then he phoned the *Venetia*, ordered the pilot to fly the chopper to Mullion Towers to pick him up and take him on to Newquay airport where the jet was waiting. His final call was to the pilot of the jet.

He had deliberately let no one else know his destination – except for Vanity Richmond. Typically, he wanted to arrive at his main HQ at Black Ridge in California unexpectedly. It was a method he frequently used – partly to keep his movements secret, partly to see what had been going on in his absence. He trusted no one completely.

In the dining room at Nansidwell Paula had glanced several times at Newman's table. His conversation with Vanity appeared to be going well, but knowing Newman so long Paula detected something guarded about his manner. He's not swallowing all her guff, she thought as she left the room.

She found Tweed drinking coffee in one of the lounges and signalled to him, then walked out into the courtyard. Tweed finished his coffee, stood up, stretched, left the other guests and wandered out as though he felt like some fresh air.

'I overheard Vanity Richmond using her mobile phone out here . . .' she began.

Tweed listened as she relayed the gist of what had been said. His expression didn't change as they continued walking up the bush-lined drive out of sight of the hotel and along a side road.

'This is important news,' he said eventually. 'You did well to catch all that. It could be sinister – the fact that he told Vanity to stay in sight of people all evening. I don't like the implications of that one bit. Also the fact that he's suddenly taking off for the States. Do you fancy a stroll into Mawnan Smith? Good. I think I'd better use the phone box Newman used – I need to inform Cord Dillon of this development.'

They turned round, took the road direct into the village. It was a very warm night and Tweed took off his jacket as they quickened their pace.

'Bob seems to have struck up a friendship with that Vanity woman,' Paula observed.

'I know. Bob is playing a wily game. She'll be like putty in his hands. He'll get more out of her than she will ever get out of him. He knows she's Moloch's confidante. I did get the chance to tell him while you were having a bath and changing.'

'Thank Heaven he's clued up.'

'No woman has ever fooled Bob Newman – at least not for long . . .'

Paula waited outside the box in the village while Tweed made his call via the international operator. He always carried plenty of change for emergencies like this. It would be 5 p.m. in Langley, he calculated, waiting for the call to go through. Dillon's time zone was five hours behind London's.

'Cord, Tweed here. I've just heard VB is flying back to the States – to California. He may take off tomorrow morning. I suspect something momentous is imminent. I gather it was probably a quick decision.'

'Got it. OK. I know his transatlantic flights system. He flies to New York, gets the Lear jet refuelled, then flies nonstop to California. I'll have a man waiting at Kennedy in New York, another one at San Francisco International. That way we can track him.'

'I'm asking Monica to call Jim Corcoran, a friend and Security Chief at Heathrow. He'll be able to tell when VB is leaving Britain. She'll call you.'

'That would help. Washington is in a growing panic over VB, the power he has built up in the heart of government over here. They can't do anything about it – unless someone can catch him out in a big scam, something horrendously illegal. He has, of course, a whole battery of top attorneys.'

'Anything else?'

'Something I forgot to tell you. He has erected a series of dome-shaped buildings on the hills overlooking the Pacific – all the way from south of LA and north via Big Sur. They're supposed to be observatories, the most modern in the world.'

'Didn't know he was interested in astronomy,' commented Tweed. 'They sound like eyesores. It's a wonder they were sanctioned in that beautiful scenic section of the coast.'

'He's been clever again. Each one is painted a colour to merge it within the surrounding countryside. They all have a view of the ocean.'

'Very strange. Can't you have them checked?'

'Me? You're joking. He did invite certain scientists to visit several on different days a while ago. Each had a giant telescope inside it.'

'I still find the idea of those buildings strange, even sinister.'

'You've got a reason for saying that?'

'No. Just a feeling,' Tweed said vaguely. 'Take care.'

'You do just that. You're dealing with a man who can get away with just about anything. Maybe even murder. Look at how seven of his girl friends vanished off the face of the planet.'

'I have a theory about that. No, I won't burden you with it. Rather too bizarre. Keep in touch . . .'

Tweed then phoned Monica, gave her instructions

about calling Jim Corcoran. He came out, told Paula on their way back about his conversations. She checked her watch.

'It's much later than I thought. It was a leisurely dinner and your calls took up more time.'

'I had to wait until they found Cord.'

Later, when they wandered down the drive to Nansidwell, Paula went ahead, rushed back to warn Tweed to wait out of sight. She returned to the hotel where two police cars were stationed in the courtyard, their lights flashing as though they'd forgotten to turn them off – or the occupants had been in a hurry.

She approached the entrance slowly, peered inside, and a woman guest she'd chatted to rushed up to her.

'There's been a murder. Everyone is excited – some are annoyed at being kept up out of bed . . .'

Paula had glanced over her shoulder. She saw a tall lanky man with a neat moustache in civilian clothes talking to Newman. She froze, got a grip on herself.

'Who was murdered?' she asked quietly.

'I don't know . . .'

'Excuse me, I need a breath of fresh air. Had a long drive in the car.'

She found Tweed calmly waiting at the entrance to the long drive. He knew from her expression that something serious had happened.

'What is it?'

'There's been a murder. Don't know who, where. Two police cars outside the entrance. Inside someone you know and will be pleased to see – I don't think – is questioning Bob. Your old sparring partner, Chief Inspector Roy Buchanan. Of all people – this distance from New Scotland Yard . . .'

'You and I have just been for a walk after a large meal – into Mawnan Smith and back. No mention of my phone calls,' Tweed said briskly. 'We'll go in now. If Roy is in sight I'll go straight up to him . . .'

Buchanan was still questioning Newman, sitting down now on a couch in the lounge he'd had cleared. The other guests were crammed into the other lounge and looked not best pleased. Extra chairs had been taken in for them and Buchanan's assistant, the wooden-faced Sergeant Warden, was watching over them. Buchanan looked up as Tweed and Paula walked across to him.

'Long time no see,' Tweed said cheerfully. 'Down here for the sea breezes?'

'Hardly.' Buchanan's long lean face had a bleak expression. He turned to Newman. 'That will be all for now. I may wish to see you later. You may go.'

'I'm staying right here,' Newman informed him.

'This is a very serious matter. I wish to talk to Tweed and Miss Grey.'

'Are you charging me?' Newman demanded.

'Of course not.'

'Then I can stay where I want to. Like here.'

Buchanan sighed. Tweed was bringing two chairs, one for Paula, the other for himself. He placed them close to the two men on the couch, they sat down and Buchanan started speaking in a lowered voice to avoid guests in the other lounge hearing him.

'Do you know a man called Adrian Penkastle?'

'Who is he?' Tweed asked.

'A man who lived on his own in a tiny house at Porth Navas. On the edge of the creek.'

'What's he done?' Tweed asked.

'He got himself murdered in his own house early this evening. That's a guesstimate on the part of the doctor who examined the corpse. A pathologist is on his way down from London. We'll know the time of death better when he has carried out the autopsy in Truro.'

'Go on.'

'Tweed, it's no use denying you know him. We have a witness who described a woman who apparently accosted Penkastle on the road on the other side of the creek. The description fits Miss Grey perfectly—'

'I did encounter a portly man at Porth Navas who was drunk,' Paula broke in. 'I tried to talk some sense into him. I was worried he'd topple into the creek. Tweed has never met him,' she went on, talking rapidly. 'I'd never seen him before.'

'How drunk was he?'

'He was pretty far gone.'

'So you did your good deed for the day,' Buchanan remarked ironically.

'That's enough of that, Roy,' Tweed interjected. 'Sarcasm is the lowest form of wit. Dr Johnson coined that phrase, at least I think it was him. If you want to continue talking to Paula mind your manners.'

Buchanan flushed at the rebuke. Tweed had provoked him deliberately and he watched the policeman fighting for self-control. Tweed decided to switch the direction the interrogation was taking.

'Would you be willing to tell us how Adrian Penkastle was murdered?'

'Professionally,' Buchanan replied after a pause. 'He was stabbed to the heart, probably with some stiletto-like instrument, maybe a knife. He was very drunk at the time. The room smelt of whisky fumes.'

Newman folded his arms, still sitting next to Buchanan. It was his only reaction to what he was recalling – the thug with the knife at Mullion Towers whose hand he had burned with his cigarette end. His knife had been a stiletto type.

'Let's go into the dining room, which is empty. We can talk more easily there,' Buchanan suggested.

He stood up, had a brief word with Sergeant Warden, then led the way into the dining room, choosing a table well away from the windows. They all sat down. Buchanan's manner was more relaxed as he stretched his long legs under the table and crossed them at the ankles. Tweed instantly became even more alert. He knew the detective well.

'I wish you'd be franker with me, Tweed,' he said amiably.

'Franker?' Tweed queried.

'Oh, come on. I checked the hotel register. You're here with Paula and Newman. Somewhere floating around here is Marler. I've had policemen checking the nearby hotels. Harry Butler and Pete Nield are staying at the Meudon down the road. That's a very heavy team force you've assembled, so why are you all in this neck of woods?'

'On a mission. I can't reveal the details to you – you know we operate in secrecy.'

'Could it have something to do with the presence of Vincent Bernard Moloch at Mullion Towers?'

Tweed was inwardly taken aback. So the anxiety about Moloch in London was so great a senior detective had been flown down – when what appeared to be on the surface a random murder had occurred. He countered with his own question.

'May I ask how you got down to Cornwall so quickly? I gather the murder of this man, Penkastle, took place early in the evening. His body must have been discovered quickly.'

'It was. A drinking partner of Penkastle's called at his house at a time which must have been soon after the murder was committed. He phoned up police headquarters in Truro, a town the caller knows well.'

'But why should the murder of a man who, so far as I can gather, and with respect, had little importance in the world, cause someone like you to be sent down here at the double?'

'Well . . .' Buchanan paused again, then took the plunge. 'The Commissioner ordered me down here.'

Again, without showing it, Tweed was taken aback. A top-flight man like the Commissioner. That meant he had probably consulted the PM immediately. It was not only in Washington that panic was spreading.

'You haven't told me how you got here so quickly,' Tweed reminded him.

'Police car with sirens screaming to Heathrow. A plane laid on to fly me to Newquay airport. Another police car waiting there to bring me here – that is, first to the scene of the crime while the Yard had a team of men phoning up to check hotel registers. They hit Nansidwell and I find you and your lot here.'

'So what is the connection between the murdered Penkastle and this Moloch – if there is one?'

'We don't know – yet. What I'm going to say is confidential.' He looked round the table and smiled without humour. 'I believe I can trust the discretion of everyone here.'

'We can't have our hands tied in our present mission in any way,' Tweed warned. 'So we cannot regard whatever you propose saying as confidential.'

'I see.' It was Buchanan's turn to be taken aback. He said nothing for almost a minute, then shrugged. 'What I can tell you is we know certain people residing in this part of Cornwall form part of an intelligence service for Moloch. I can't under the circumstances give your names – but that is why a murder committed in this area interests us.'

It was then that Tweed caught on. The so-called drinking partner of Penkastle's, who had found the body, was Maurice Prendergast. This explained the news reaching London so swiftly. Prendergast would immediately have informed his superiors at Special Branch. They had passed on the news to the Commissioner. Typically, Special Branch had wanted to stay in the background.

I wonder if it was Maurice who reported Paula's presence in the area, Tweed thought. I'll ask him point-blank as soon as I can see him again.

'If you'll excuse us,' he said aloud, 'I think we would all like to get to bed.'

'As you wish, but I may want to ask Miss Grey a few more questions at a later date. On her own.'

'Certainly not,' snapped Tweed. 'If you attempt a ploy like that I'll be in touch with the PM in minutes.'

'She was at the scene of the crime . . .'

'She damned well was not,' Paula burst out. 'She merely encountered a drunken man and tried to save him from drowning in the creek.'

'I won't put up with false accusations of that sort,' Tweed rapped back.

'Perhaps you misunderstood what I said . . .' Buchanan began.

Tweed was already on his feet, in a pretended rage. He gestured to the others.

'We've had enough of this. We're going to get some sleep. Good night . . .'

Paula and Newman followed Tweed out of the dining room. Outside, in the small deserted hallway by a compact bar, Newman took Tweed by the arm, led him halfway up the staircase, checked to see they were alone.

'If you agree, I propose to go back and give Buchanan Joel Brand's name discreetly.'

'Good idea. That will stir up more trouble for VB . . .'

Newman returned to the dining room to find Buchanan still sitting at the table by himself. He had a brooding look, as though trying to solve something which bothered him. He looked up, greeted Newman amiably.

'Back again, Bob. Would you please tell Tweed I apologize to Paula Grey for what I said? I've been up twenty-four hours nonstop.'

'I will do that.' Newman leaned on the table opposite the detective, lowered his voice. 'We can give you one name you ought to investigate. Joel Brand. He's probably aboard the *Venetia* standing out there off Falmouth harbour.'

'What about him?'

'I'm just giving you a name . . .'

Newman left the room, letting Buchanan digest the name.

Aboard the *Venetia* Joel Brand was pacing his stateroom. He only looked more cheerful when he heard the chopper coming in to land on the helipad. It had already transported Moloch to Newquay airport. Picking up his case, he turned to Gene Lessinger, who had earlier thrown the sheath which had contained the murder knife into the sea after weighting it.

'Gene, I'm leaving now in the chopper. It's flying me to Plymouth airport. I'll catch the first available ferry to Roscoff in Brittany.'

'Does our French organization know you're coming?'

'The top man over there does. He's arranging for a car to wait for me. I'll be driven to Paris. Once there I'll board the first Air France flight to the States. VB sent me his instructions from the jet after it took off from Newquay airport.'

'I have a job to do here first,' Gene reminded him.

'To deal with Maurice Prendergast, supposedly retired from Special Branch.'

'I'll use the same method you did with that drunk, Adrian?'

'Why not? It is a good trademark to put the wind up anyone tracking us. Be careful with Prendergast. He's a pro.'

'I've worked that out. Then I leave the country?'

'Yes, by the same route I'm taking. I'll get off now. My instinct tells me trouble is on the way . . .'

When Brand was sitting in the chopper as it took off he saw a police boat approaching the *Venetia*. He gave it a casual wave and laughed coarsely.

'Tomorrow I'm going to visit Maurice,' Tweed told his team, assembled in Paula's large room. Marler had joined them after making himself scarce when he saw the police cars arriving.

'Something funny about that ship, *Venetia*,' called out Paula, standing by the window with the binoculars Marler had loaned her. 'It looks so jolly and inviting with all its lights sparkling. Like a cruise ship.'

'What's funny about it?' asked Newman as she handed him the binoculars.

'Focus on the foredeck. There are some pretty large objects covered in canvas. Strikes me they're something VB doesn't want anyone to know he's got aboard.'

'You're right,' Newman agreed after studying the vessel. 'I can't imagine what they could be, yet they remind me of something.'

He lowered the glasses, frowning, then recalled Tweed's remark.

'If you're going to visit Prendergast I suggest an armed team comes with you.'

'I wanted to make it a quiet visit,' Tweed objected. 'I'll phone him before I go. I memorized his number when we were inside his house.'

'An armed team is coming with you,' Newman insisted.

'That poor little man, Adrian Penkastle,' Paula mused. 'He was such a harmless person. Just drank far too much.'

'Which is probably why he's dead,' Newman said grimly.

'Well, let's hope we find Maurice Prendergast alive,' Marler commented.

9

It was going to be a long night. Tweed was restless, had taken a bath, then got dressed again. He was pacing up and down his room when he heard a tapping on the door. He opened it cautiously, his foot against it. Two in the morning was a curious time for anyone to come calling.

'Can I come in? I saw the light under your door,' Paula said.

'Of course.' After letting her in he relocked the door. Paula was wearing a navy blue suit. 'Why aren't you in bed and asleep?' he asked.

'I might ask you the same question,' she told him as she sat down in a chair.

'Too much to puzzle over.'

'I thought so – from your faraway expression when you went up to bed. What's troubling you?'

'The mystery of the same woman coming ashore near Monterey in distant California – the same woman who came ashore here. And in both cases the *Venetia* was nearby out at sea.'

'I suppose it was the same woman? I did feel sure it was.'

'I checked Newman's pictures of the one he tried to

rescue here with the Identikit picture you helped create of the Monterey woman. They looked exactly the same to me.'

'Nice to know I'm not going barmy.'

'That remark is nonsense – although I could understand it.'

Tweed stood up, began pacing again as he spoke. Walking always helped him to keep his brain in high gear.

'The same woman comes ashore on the coasts of two different continents. At an interval of several weeks, which is the time it took the *Venetia* to sail from Monterey to Falmouth. So the only answer is we're not thinking clearly. It can't be the same woman . . .'

He suddenly paused. Watching him, Paula saw a certain look cross his face. She recognized it. An idea which had been swimming deep in his mind had surfaced. He swung round and stared at her.

'*Twins!* That explains the extraordinary likeness between the two women . . .'

Paula sat dumbfounded. She was wondering why the idea had never occurred to her. She shook her head to clear it, stared again as Tweed went on talking.

'That's what we should be looking for – on both sides of the Atlantic. Twins. It narrows the field enormously. We'll let Cord know when we can. And Monica can start checking over here.'

'Checking in what way?'

'To see if twin women were associated with VB in any way at any time. Just a minute, when the *Venetia* docked at Monterey, then left quickly, we know VB wasn't aboard. That drunken harbour master told you that.'

'What's the significance of that?'

'Joel Brand was aboard – you saw him come ashore with a team of thugs at Octopus Cove. And VB was probably at Mullion Towers when Newman found the woman who swam in to the cove below us. Brand could have been aboard again. Which fits in with another bizarre theory I've pondered.'

'What's that?'

'The disappearance of seven of VB's close girl friends who have never been found.'

'I don't quite follow that.'

'I won't bother to explain now – I could be wrong.'

'Do you know,' Paula said with a smile, 'that when you go mysterious with me you can be the most irritating of men?'

But Tweed hardly heard her. He went on talking, his brain racing.

'The next urgent problem is Maurice Prendergast. I'm sure he is the new target – after Penkastle. I'm going to call him now, tell him we're on our way to see him.'

'At this hour? It's nearly two in the morning.'

'Like me, Maurice works through the night when he has to. He'll be up . . .'

Tweed was careful not to use names when he got through to Prendergast, but the latter recognized his voice. He was indeed up working and said he'd be very glad to see them. He used the phrase, 'Yourself and your right arm, presumably? Good . . .'

'Newman will be furious,' Paula warned. 'He said that you needed an armed escort.'

'I don't want one. Bob will be fast asleep. We'll slip out quietly through the back way. I know how to unlock the door. I checked it earlier . . .'

They drove off quietly up the drive, heading for Mawnan Smith and the 'rabbit warren' lane which led down to Porth Navas. They had just left when another car took off after them. The police cars had driven away earlier.

Gene Lessinger was on his way by car to Porth Navas. He had decided to deal with Prendergast. While aboard the *Venetia* he had grown nervous with Brand gone, safely on his way. The police launch which had put men on to the ship had given up the search for Joel Brand, convinced he had escaped in the helicopter they had seen leaving the vessel before their arrival.

But having police on the ship had made Gene feel that he'd better get on with the job, then fly to Plymouth to wait for the ferry to Roscoff. Before leaving the ship he had sent a message to France, warning them he was coming. Going ashore to the wharf where two cars were always standing by, he used the key he had taken with him to start up one of them.

He was well on his way to Porth Navas, using a map Brand had left him. He drove slowly down the narrow road which led to his destination. He didn't like the narrowness of the road, particularly at night. Following Brand's detailed instructions, he parked the car at the bottom of the hill, started walking along the road perched above the creek.

In a sheath strapped to his belt he carried a fresh stiletto knife. In his right hand he was holding a small container from which he had removed the lid as soon as he had parked his car.

Tweed had parked the car inside the Yacht Club so as not to block the road. Walking back along the deserted and silent road, Paula noticed the tide was out. What had earlier been a channel of water was now a bed of mud, slimy ooze in the moonlight.

106

'I wouldn't like to live here,' she remarked. 'Look at the creek now. A great sight to view from your window.'

'Not very inviting,' Tweed agreed. 'And that is what it will look like for hours. Every time the tide recedes you're staring at a mud bath. When I was down here the last time I noticed that. Up at a place called Mylor. It lasted all the time I was in the house I was visiting. In a pub an estate agent told me a lot of his London clients purchased property in summer. They spent a year there and came to him again – to sell. Funny, there are no lights in Maurice's place, The Ark.'

'Very weird,' said Paula. 'He knew we were coming. Lord, has something happened?'

'I hope not,' Tweed replied grimly, quickening his pace. 'I just hope we haven't arrived too late . . .'

They approached the darkened house. No other residence along the road had lights on, but it was the darkness of The Ark which held their gaze. Paula had her Browning in her hand as they came to the steps leading up to the front door. The silence hanging over the creek was beginning to unnerve her.

Tweed checked the windows masked by net curtains. No sign anywhere of the inner curtains being closed. He went up the steps with Paula beside him, paused, uncertain whether to raise the heavy anchor-shaped knocker or not.

The door opened slowly and Prendergast stood there with a warm smile. He gestured for them to enter.

'Welcome, both of you. And you look so worried,' he said to Paula and kissed her on the cheek before shutting the door.

'Wait just a moment,' he went on, 'and I'll close all the curtains. Sorry if I startled you, but I decided to take precautions. I saw you through the net curtains when you were close to the house. What would you like to drink?'

'I think I could do with a small whisky,' Paula replied.

'I'll have one, too,' Tweed said, surprising Paula, who knew he rarely drank.

'We believe you are the next target for whoever murdered Adrian Penkastle,' Tweed told him after taking a sip of his drink. 'You most certainly are wise to be on guard.'

'I knew you'd arrived,' their host remarked. 'I saw you driving your car slowly along to where you could park.'

'Who killed Penkastle?'

'Tweed, you expect miracles. I have no idea. I found the body only yesterday evening when I drove to see what Adrian was up to.'

'And reported it back to your superiors.'

'I told you I was retired.'

'Cock and bull story. Or rather, a cover story. You're as active as ever you were,' Tweed hammered at him.

'If you say so.'

'I would also like to know whether you reported that Paula was present here last night – that she met Penkastle when she ran outside.' Tweed leaned forward. 'Now I expect the truth.'

Prendergast paused. He didn't look at Paula, who was staring straight at him. He gave a shrug of resignation.

'I'm afraid that was exactly what I did. I had to convince my superiors I was giving them the full data. You may not believe this, but I was trying to get into their thick heads that you were ahead of them in the game, that they should damned well cooperate with you. I feel very strongly about that.'

'I believe you,' Tweed said quietly.

'And I apologize without reservation to you,' Prendergast said, turning to Paula. 'If you hate my guts I wouldn't blame you.'

'I don't hate your guts, Maurice,' Paula told him. 'But you ought to know that I was interrogated by one of the Yard's top men, Roy Buchanan. He'd flown straight down here after your superiors had – obviously – reported what you had told them to the Commissioner.'

'Oh, my God!' Prendergast was clearly appalled. 'I have made a complete balls-up. I should never have told them about you. But I never dreamt the wets would pass it on to anyone – let alone the Commissioner.'

'They want to maintain a low profile,' said Tweed. 'Now, I'll ask you again, who do you think killed Penkastle?'

'One of Vincent Bernard Moloch's thugs,' Prendergast replied instantly.

'Maybe. But we don't know it was on Moloch's orders. Not yet, anyway.'

Tweed felt relieved. He had smoked out Prendergast, a very efficient officer in Special Branch, into the open. They now had a strong ally, which might come in very useful at some stage.

Their host offered them more to drink. Both refused and Prendergast was pouring himself a refresher when there was a knock on the door. Paula looked at Tweed, dived her right hand inside the special pocket inside her shoulder bag, gripped the Browning. Prendergast seemed least disturbed.

'That will be Charlie. Local character who stays up half the night. An insomniac. He comes about this time for a brief chat. Harmless . . .'

Before Tweed could stop him, Prendergast had reached the door, opened it.

'Urgent message from London, Mr Prendergast.'

'How did you get down here?'

'Motorcycle. I'm a courier.'

As he said this, Gene threw the contents of the open can of pepper into Prendergast's eyes. Prendergast flung a hand up, instinctively took a step back into the room. Gene followed him, the stiletto in his right hand, ready to plunge into his target's chest.

Holding her Browning by the barrel, Paula reached Gene, brought down the butt on his wrist. At the last moment Gene let his wrist drop to minimize the force of the blow. Realizing he was outnumbered, he grasped Paula in an armlock round the neck. His right hand still gripped the knife which he held against her throat.

'Get back, you friggin' lot,' he screamed, 'or she gets her throat slit ear to ear. You drop the friggin' gun or get your head cut off,' he ordered Paula.

She had no option – she dropped the Browning. Tweed had reached Gene a second too late, his right hand stiffened to administer a blow to the bridge of his nose which would have killed him. He watched as Gene dragged Paula to the open door, carefully down the steps, along the road towards where his car was parked.

Tweed followed grimly, keeping his steps in pace with Gene's car. Prendergast was still in his kitchen, trying to clear his eyes of pepper although he knew what was going on.

Along the road Tweed was keeping up the macabre death march. He was careful to stay a good twelve paces behind Gene, who kept glancing backwards and then forwards to where his car was waiting. Tweed had picked up Paula's Browning and held it by his side. Gene screamed at him.

'Stop following me or I'll rip her throat to pieces.'

Tweed made no immediate reply. He just continued to march forward, maintaining his distance from Gene and Paula, powerless in Gene's tight grip, only too aware of the cold steel touching her throat. Tweed kept silent, guessing that this would rattle the thug more than anything.

Suddenly they heard the sound of a car approaching. It stopped. Behind the wheel of the Merc. Newman switched on his lights full beam. They silhouetted Gene with his captive. Newman stared in horror. He turned off the engine but kept his lights on.

'Turn out those friggin' lights or this woman has a red circle round her throat . . .'

'Bob,' Tweed called out, his voice calm, 'do as he says. He has a knife at Paula's throat.'

Newman obeyed the order instantly. By his side Marler, his Armalite rifle across his lap, calculated whether he could hit Gene with one quick shot. He realized he couldn't – Paula was too close to her captor.

'Tell him to back that car off the road,' screamed Gene.

'Do what he says, Bob,' Tweed ordered.

Newman began reversing his car onto the main road and then waited, feeling helpless. Tweed had half-closed his eyes when he'd heard the car coming so he was not affected by the glare, nor by the lights going off. He continued his slow, deliberate march, gun still by his side.

'Stop following me,' screeched Gene, continuing to move closer to his car. 'Or she gets it.'

'If – you – harm – her – in – in – any – way,' Tweed said very slowly in a cold voice, 'I will shoot you first in one kneecap, then in the other kneecap – and then between the legs. Or perhaps you're not at all interested in women.'

There was something terrifying in the way Tweed delivered his message. Even in her frightened state Paula thought she had never heard before Tweed speak in such a steely voice.

His voice had the same effect on Gene, and Paula felt his grip tremble, then tighten on her. Tweed seemed to have turned into Nemesis, stalking his prey with a ferocity which chilled Gene. He kept her moving, but was continually glancing back at Tweed's almost casual tread.

'She'll be dead,' Gene called out in a desperate tone.

'You'll be crippled for the rest of your life,' responded Tweed in the same cold, deliberate voice.

'Just stop walking after me,' called out Gene, almost hysterically, 'if you want your girl friend alive.'

Tweed continued walking, still maintaining the same distance between himself and Gene who was now dragging Paula along the road. He had almost reached his car. He planned to take Paula with him as a hostage.

She suddenly sagged against him and Gene swore. She had fainted, was a dead weight he had to try and haul along with him. She had sagged backwards against him, and for a short time her throat was clear of his knife. Still twenty yards from the end of the creek – and his parked car – he tried to tighten his grip but he was startled by how heavily she seemed to weigh. Her eyes closed, she was pressed against his body as he turned again to check how close Tweed was from him.

A shot rang out, the bullet penetrating the back of Gene's skull. With Paula's head now lowered to his chest she was in no danger of being hit. Gene's head jerked under the impact of the bullet. The knife fell from his nerveless hand. He lost his grip on Paula, who dropped to the ground, her eyes wide open.

Gene staggered on the edge of the creek. His dead body toppled over the edge, fell heavily into the muddy creek. Tweed stood still, watching the mud engulf the body until it sank out of sight.

Shakily, Paula climbed to her feet with no trace of the faint, which she had faked. Marler appeared, holding his Armalite rifle. He had slipped out of Newman's car swiftly at a moment when Gene had looked back at

Tweed. Positioning himself behind the wall of a house, he had focused his sniperscope on his target, firing once when the back of Gene's head was exposed.

He walked towards Paula, who braced her legs, ran to him and hugged him.

'Thank you. You saved my life.'

'You saved your own life,' Marler drawled offhandedly. 'By pretending to faint you gave me the one chance I needed to fire a safe shot. Look, someone has stumbled out of the only house with lights on.'

Paula swung round. Prendergast was standing in the road, a hand to his eyes as he peered along the road, trying to see what had happened. She ran to him, took him by the arm, guided him inside to minister to his eyes. She was glad of something practical to do to blot out the horror of her recent experience.

Tweed was staring down at the bed of mud where Gene had disappeared. Newman and Marler joined him.

'I think it will be a long time before that surfaces – if ever,' Tweed remarked.

'And the tide is surging up the creek,' Newman observed. 'What happened? I was petrified – couldn't do a thing.'

Tweed explained tersely the series of events.

'And what are you both doing down here?' he asked. 'Arriving in the nick of time,' he commented, glancing at Marler.

'We were talking outside behind my car in the courtyard,' Newman told him. 'We saw you leaving with Paula and decided to follow. I told you that you needed an armed escort.'

'I should have listened to you. I'm very grateful to both of you. Bob, because you took the decision. Marler because of your superb shooting.'

'Oh, I've had more difficult shots than that.' He looked along the road. 'And it appears that no one heard it.'

'And the body in the mud is really disappearing without any trace,' Newman pointed out.

Tweed looked down. The surge of the tide was slower as it reached the end of the creek but water now flowed over where Gene's body had fallen. He shrugged without a hint of regret.

10

Tweed was driving back to London by himself. The previous night he had instructed Newman while they still stood in the road by the creek at Porth Navas.

'I'm going back to London tomorrow.' He checked his watch. 'Or, rather, today. It's well after midnight. You stay here with Paula and Marler. First thing, Bob, is find out who is controlling the network of watchers VB has established down here. Special Branch can take whoever you unmask into custody.'

'And the second thing?'

'Enjoy yourself with your friend Vanity Richmond.'

Marler smiled drily. Newman looked annoyed and made no reply, which intrigued Tweed.

'Wait for me here,' Tweed then ordered. 'I'm going along to see how Paula is getting on with Prendergast.'

He found Prendergast laid out on a couch with poultices over his eyes. Paula explained.

'He won't go to a hospital so I've managed. I washed out his eyes thoroughly with water. The poultices I created out of two of his handkerchiefs, soaking them in cold water.'

'I'm OK,' Prendergast broke in after removing one of the handkerchiefs. 'I can see you clearly – you've got a serious expression on your face.'

Tweed then took Paula outside and repeated what he had told Newman and Marler. Returning to where they were waiting, he listened while Marler explained what he was going to do.

'The thug came in his own car. I checked it after I'd shot him and he'd left the ignition key in the lock. So, wearing gloves, I'll drive it some distance from here and abandon it in an isolated field – after I've immobilized the engine. Newman picks me up in the Merc. afterwards.'

'Good idea,' Tweed agreed. 'One thing more, Bob, I'm leaving Butler and Nield with you as back-up . . .'

All this was going through Tweed's mind as he made swift progress along the A30. Again he was intrigued as he remembered the expression on Newman's face when he told him to enjoy himself with Vanity Richmond.

'I think he's falling for her,' he said to himself. 'If so, what does it matter? Newman has his head screwed on and she'll never get anything secret out of him.'

He also suspected that Paula liked the look of Maurice. I may have two romances on my hands, he ruminated. But both of them need some relaxation from the tension they have endured.

Arriving at Park Crescent, the first person he met was Howard, who followed him into his office. As Howard sat down he again automatically shot his cuffs. Monica noticed he was still wearing the absurd cuff links, each shaped like a flower.

'Well, how goes the battle?' Howard enquired genially.

'Not so well at this stage,' Tweed replied from behind his desk, determined to get rid of him. 'Special Branch have got into the act. Don't ask for details.'

'Special Branch!' Howard was outraged, his plump face even pinker. 'What the hell has it to do with them? We were asked to investigate VB. By the PM himself.'

'I know. Somehow they've caught on to him all on their own.' He paused. 'I suppose you may have mentioned it casually at your club.'

'You don't think I'm to be trusted?' Howard jumped up, looking more pink-faced than ever. 'I'll expect an apology for that suggestion. In your own time,' he snapped. On this note he stalked out of the room.

'You really upset him,' Monica said with a smile.

'I intended to. There's too much to get moving without him cluttering up my time. Have you anything to tell me?'

'Yes. A report on Vanity Richmond. You're not going to like it . . . Not one little bit of it . . .'

'I phoned Cord Dillon,' Monica began. 'At first he didn't want to say anything, but I told him she was here – therefore under British jurisdiction. That's when he got lurid about what he'd discovered about her.'

'Lurid?'

'I thought so. She's British, her father was, but her mother was French. Which might explain her career so far. If you can call it a career. Cord has nicknamed her The Butterfly.'

'Why?'

'Let me go on. She's attractive to men and she's lived off that. She's moved from one man to another in the States. All of them worth a packet of money . . .'

'Just a minute. Is she married – or has she been? Any children?'

'No to both questions. She's very vain, which is why she's come to be called Vanity – instead of Vanessa, her real Christian name. Money seems to be her god. Her

116

latest conquest is VB, who is susceptible to really attractive women. All this – except the VB bit – is rumour. But Cord said it was hard to pin her down. He can't explain how I couldn't trace her through that detective who used every known method of tracking someone down. No Social Security number, et cetera – in spite of the fact that she's spent a few years in the States.'

'Sounds interesting,' Tweed commented.

'Sounds like a manhunter,' Monica said indignantly.

She watched Tweed, who was staring out of the window where the sun was blazing. The office was very warm despite the ceiling fans turned on. Tweed was thinking about Moloch.

'Have you heard what I said?' demanded Monica acidly.

'I heard every word,' he assured her, still gazing out of the window.

'You don't seem very shocked.'

'Different people live different lives,' he replied.

'She sounds to me to be a predator,' Monica went on with feeling.

'I told you – different people live different lives. I know you were brought up with a strict code of ethics – which is only one reason why you're here all the time. Another reason is your loyalty to me, your capacity for working incredibly long hours . . .'

'Flattery will get you nowhere,' she told him.

'Mrs Benyon, VB's stepmother,' he said. 'And her son, Ethan. I need to know every tiny bit of information you can squeeze out about those two.'

'I'm working on it.'

'And VB's movements . . .'

'Jim Corcoran told me he left Heathrow in the middle of the night, bound for New York. Should be there by now. While the jet was being refuelled VB got out, walked about to stretch his legs. Corcoran had a camera, took several long-distance shots. I got a courier to send them fast. The Engine Room developed and printed them in record time. Here they are.'

'He's quite a small man,' Tweed commented as he studied the pictures.

'So was Napoleon,' she reminded him. 'Perhaps he has a bust of Napoleon at his Black Ridge headquarters.'

'I doubt it.' Tweed was examining the photos with a magnifying glass. 'He doesn't look as though he has an inflated ego to me. What makes this man tick, is the question I keep asking myself. I'd like to meet him sometime.'

'You probably will. I'm sure he knows about you.'

'Can't waste any more time.' He handed back the photos to her. 'Those are probably worth a fortune to a newspaper. He's rarely been photographed. That electronics factory that was blown to pieces in the Thames Valley – it was our most advanced plant, I gather?'

'Yes, it was. No casualties because the bomb went off at night. All the staff had gone home. Even the guards were uninjured – they were patrolling a fence at a distance away.'

'Significant. Now, we must build up a head of steam – I am launching a major offensive against Vincent Bernard Moloch . . .'

Chief Inspector Roy Buchanan was startled to be summoned back to the Yard from Cornwall and told to visit Tweed on a matter of utmost urgency.

'This is a new one for me,' he said to Sergeant Warden as he drove to Park Crescent. 'I usually have to force my way into the place.'

'Perhaps you scared him down in Cornwall,' Warden suggested in his normal monotone.

'Scared Tweed? Are you out of your mind? Here we

are. I'm going to ask if he wants to see me alone. If so, you watch the car.'

'See you alone?' Warden sounded resentful. 'You mean without me as a witness?'

'I mean exactly that . . .'

So it turned out. After a brief chat with Tweed on the phone in the entrance hall, Buchanan sent Warden back to the car, mounted the stairs. Monica was waiting for him with the door open. She stood aside to let him enter, then closed the door from the outside and went upstairs.

'Just the two of us?' Buchanan asked. 'I've never known Monica not be here.'

'Just the two of us,' Tweed agreed. 'Do sit down, and thank you for responding to my message so quickly.'

'I was mystified,' Buchanan admitted.

'I have information for you but it must remain confidential – one of the sources must remain anonymous.'

'When I wanted to give you confidential information down at Nansidwell you refused to have your hands tied.'

'That is quite correct.'

'So why should I agree?'

Buchanan, who normally sprawled in a chair, legs crossed at the ankles, during an interrogation, now sat upright in the carver chair placed for him. His manner was direct but far more friendly.

'Because if you don't agree I can't give you data which might affect two murders.'

'Then it's your duty . . .'

'I said *might*,' Tweed repeated.

'All right, I'll take a chance. Just between you and me.'

'Someone I know who is now abroad,' Tweed said smoothly, 'rescued a woman swimming in from the *Venetia*. They pulled her out of the water but the poor woman died. From exhaustion. Possibly. They took three

119

pictures of her, sent them to me. Her picture is the very image of another woman who Paula hauled ashore dead in California weeks ago. She did an Identikit of the Monterey woman. Look for yourself. The photos are the woman in Cornwall, the photocopy is Paula's Identikit picture.'

He opened the envelope on his desk, spread everything out in front of Buchanan. The detective's face stiffened when he looked at the photos. He paused for several minutes before he spoke.

'These photos are the pictures of a dead woman we found in a cove below Nansidwell. We had an anonymous call. Would that have come from this anonymous character who is now somewhere abroad?'

'I was told a call had been made to a local police station.'

'Truro.'

'I see,' was Tweed's only reaction.

'We kept this discovery quiet.' Buchanan pointed to the photos of the dead woman. 'The pathologist who examined her said she had a heavy bruise on her back. We're treating it as a suspicious death.'

'One more thing,' Tweed added, 'Moloch's floating cruise palace, the *Venetia*, was offshore when Paula hauled out the corpse from the Pacific near Monterey, six thousand miles or so from here. The *Venetia* was standing off Falmouth harbour when the body of the girl in the photos came ashore.'

'Vincent Bernard Moloch,' Buchanan said, half to himself. 'I don't understand this. Both women look exactly alike. Your story doesn't hold water.'

'It does if you assume they were twins. I worked that one out for myself. You're looking for twins, Roy. I'd like that photo splashed across every newspaper in the land. *Do You Know This Woman?*'

'I could arrange that,' Buchanan agreed. 'Just the sort of headline the press loves these days. I'll have to consult certain people. May I mention your name?'

'Certainly not. Under no circumstances.'

'I thought you'd say that. You'll be kept out of it – purely because of your position.'

'And,' Tweed said firmly, 'because I've helped you. Not that you've said anything yet.'

'I do appreciate your cooperation. Really I do. Any chance of identifying who took the photos? Even just for my personal information, if necessary.'

'No chance at all. Roy, you'd never identify one of your personal informants. Come off it.'

'I take your point. May I take all the photos?'

'Of course – they're copies.'

'Twins.' Buchanan stood up. 'It was clever of you to think of that. I may incorporate that in the carefully edited story we hand out to the newspapers. I think this justifies a press conference. I'd better get back now.'

They shook hands before he left. As soon as he had gone Tweed rang for Monica on his intercom.

Tweed brought Monica up to date on his conversation with the Scotland Yard man. She listened, memorizing every word.

'Do you think he'll do it?' she asked eventually. 'I mean will he give the story to the press?'

'I'm sure he will. He has no alternative. This means I've struck the first blow – only the first – in the offensive I'm launching against VB.'

'I don't follow you.'

'The tactic is to do everything possible to disturb VB. That picture of the dead woman who was dragged out of the sea in Cornwall is going to be splashed all over the newspapers. VB – and Joel Brand – will soon hear of it. That will alarm someone. And disturbed people make a fatal mistake – when they are unnerved.'

'It might work,' Monica agreed.

'It *will* work,' said Tweed with great force. 'I also want copies of those photos – and the Identikit Paula helped to create of the Pacific victim – sent post-haste to Cord Dillon.'

'Why? If I may ask?'

'You just did. I'm going to phone Cord later, tell him to do the same thing in California. To get those pictures into the papers over there – the *San Francisco Chronicle*, the *Los Angeles Times* and the local Monterey newspaper. Someone has to recognize those twins.'

'You are getting the pot boiling. You sound strangely ferocious.'

'I am ferocious. After the way that thug treated Paula. And what I've told you to do is only the tip of the iceberg. I'm going to attack VB from every possible angle. Get it moving, Monica . . .'

11

In Cornwall Newman had spent time with Vanity Richmond. They had walked along a side road at the end of the hotel drive, had turned off it along a narrow rough lane, little more than a path, signposted *Rosemullion*. Vanity had suggested the walk.

'The proprietor of Nansidwell told me about this track,' she explained. 'Apparently it leads to a wonderful view of the sea and hardly anyone ever finds it.'

They were walking along a section where hedges lining high banks enclosed it. She looked at him sideways, her eyes half-closed as she made the remark. Her expression almost hypnotized him. He smiled, thinking how attractive she was. Her greenish eyes and the enticing look she had given him made him want to grab hold of her in a passionate embrace. He resisted the temptation.

'You strike me as a very lonely man,' she went on.

'Not really,' he lied.

It was quite a while since he'd had a girl friend. His time had been taken up with working for Tweed, an activity he enjoyed. Now he was beginning to wonder whether he was getting any fun out of life.

'Have you got a girl friend?' she asked.

'Not at the moment. I've been very busy.'

'And yet you haven't written many articles the way you did at one time. You do seem very reserved.'

'The morning isn't my best time. I'm rather an owl. I wake up, get going later in the day.'

'Oh, come on, Bob. No need to look so serious. You need some relaxation. Cornwall is the place where people relax. What a lovely flower.'

She reached up, picked a flower from the hedge, handed it to him with a ravishing smile.

'Put it in my hair for me,' she requested, turning her back on him.

He carefully inserted the flower, told Vanity it suited her. She swung round slowly. When picking the flower she had gone on tiptoe, revealing her shapely legs. While she was picking the flower, still reaching up to the hedge, she turned, gave him an up-from-under look. He had found it entrancing. Now she was close to him with no smile on her full lips. Her eyes stared into his, as though reading his mind.

'Old slow-coach,' she said softly.

He leaned forward to kiss her, touched her lips, and then she backed away from him and resumed her walk. His mind was racing, imagining what they could experience together. So why was the faint danger signal buzzing in his brain? Why did he suspect she had practised all these different expressions in front of a mirror – testing which would be the most desirable to a man? And why did he wonder if she was wearing contact lenses to give her eyes a greenish look?

'Race you to the cliff-top,' she called out over her shoulder and began running down the track, fleet of foot.

He let her get there first, running behind her. She had flopped down on the cliff summit. He sat down close to her and she moved herself away from him several feet. The heat beat down on them and soon Newman was aware that his shirt was pasted against his damp back.

'What a lovely spot,' she remarked, glancing sideways at him quickly, then gazing out to sea again.

'It's so very peaceful,' he agreed, stopping himself from moving next to her so their bodies touched.

Was she playing hard to get? he mused. Her look had again aroused his deep interest. What sort of game was she playing? *Playing?* It crossed his mind that she reminded him of a playgirl, constantly anxious that men would notice her. He dismissed the thought as nonsense, but still the danger signal was reverberating at the back of his mind.

They sat in the heat and watched the azure sea, the *Venetia*, still at anchor, distant yachts like white exclamation marks on the blue water. Vanity suddenly jumped up.

'Time to go,' she said in a cold voice.

Newman was having trouble keeping up with her swift changes of mood. He talked to her part of the way along the track and then gave it up. She had not replied once. He decided he had had enough for the moment. He spoke as they reached the hotel.

'I have to go out,' he said, walking towards his Merc.

'Where are you off to?' she asked, following him.

124

Her manner had mellowed and she was smiling at him. He smiled back quickly, unlocked the car, got behind the wheel. She leaned in the window he had lowered to get some fresh air inside the car – the interior was like an oven.

'Bob, can I come with you?'

'Sorry. It's a business appointment.'

'You're not mad with me?' She gave him her most inviting smile.

'Why should I be?'

He smiled briefly back at her, switched on the engine. She leaned across him, turned it off. Then she stood back, arms by her side.

'I'll see you for dinner here, then.'

Saying which, she marched off into the hotel without a backward glance. He switched on the engine again and drove off. He had a long job to do. An urgent one.

Newman was 'trawling' the pubs. He had earlier assembled Paula, Marler, Butler and Nield in their cars a distance from the hotel in the side lane beyond the drive which led to a dead end.

With the aid of a map he had drawn up his plan. Each member of the team had an area to cover and would call at every pub in it. He gave Paula the hotels.

'Your job,' he told them, 'is to find out if there is a local man with considerable influence in this part of Cornwall. I'm looking for someone who might control the network VB has established. You all have mobile phones – I hid mine from Tweed.'

'He doesn't trust the things,' Paula broke in. 'And I happen to think he's right.'

'Listen to me. If anyone finds such a person they simply call me and say, "Spot on." That way I'll know someone has got lucky. I'll inform the rest of you with the same message. If I'm the one who has tracked our target, all of you come back here. Park at intervals along the road. Very little traffic comes down here. If I've hit a potential target I'll call you all and say, "Spot on, as you said." The last three words tell you I've located what we are looking for.'

He had distributed maps to all of them showing their respective search areas. His own area was Porth Navas, the Helford River, and inland beyond. He adopted the same technique in every pub he visited.

After ordering a glass of French dry white wine he struck up a conversation with one of the locals. He drank very little of the wine, taking it with him at a certain stage to the toilet where he emptied it in a cubicle.

He had got nowhere with his casual conversations when he found himself in an inland village, Constantine. He sat next to a grizzled old inhabitant, had the same blank result. He asked the question when he was on the verge of leaving.

'Is there any other pub in the area where I can get something to eat? They don't serve food here.'

'Try the Trengilly Wartha Inn,' the old boy suggested. 'Go up top of hill . . .'

He gave Newman exact instructions, which was fortunate because he nearly drove past the side road outside the large village. A notice indicated it was five hundred yards to the pub. Newman grinned wrily. Cornish distances seem to differ from everywhere else in Britain.

'It's only thirty minutes,' he had been told many times when checking how far away somewhere was. He drove down a treelined lane, the trees forming an archway over the road. Again he nearly drove past his destination. A steep drive led up to the inn, a cream-washed building with a glassed-in room near the entrance.

The only place he could park his car among the other vehicles was in the sun. When he climbed out it blazed down on him like a blowtorch. He went inside, found it was full of cricketers, dressed in white flannel trousers and shirts rolled up to the elbows.

There was a jolly atmosphere and at the bar Newman deliberately ordered beer; it was something he never drank but it merged him into the crowd, standing with his jacket over his arm and tieless. He also ordered food. It was 2 p.m. – in the heat of the day.

'Cheers!' he said to a youngish chap who had just raised his own glass.

'Tom Hetherington,' the red-faced youngster replied.

'Bob Newman.'

'Your face looks familiar. Not the foreign correspondent chappie, are you?'

'I'm afraid so,' Newman responded with a grin. 'And I'm trying to find someone around here high enough up to give me information.'

'A bigwig? That would be Colonel Arbuthnot Grenville at The Grange. You might get near him. I wouldn't. He's as snooty as hell. Thinks he's Lord of the Manor and all that.'

'Arbuthnot Grenville? Sounds a funny name.'

'Suits His Lordship, as you'll find out – if you ever meet him. Spends the summers here and then hikes off to California for the winters. Nice work, if you can get it, but how he manages it beats me. The Grange is mortgaged up to the hilt.'

'How do you know all this if you've never met him?'

'Talk of the town – or rather the village – down here. I know it sounds like gossip, but he makes the mistake of quarrelling with servants, then sacking them. Servants can be nosy. They get their own back on him by spreading the dirt.'

'You said he wintered in California. Any idea where?'

'Place called Monterey. I looked it up on the map. It's south of San Francisco. You're thinking of trying to interview him? He won't see anyone except by appointment. At least that's what I hear. You're not thinking of living down here?'

'No. You live here?' Newman asked.

'Damned if I would. Join the runaways? Not on your life. I just come down here for the cricket for a month or so. I'm a stockbroker.'

'Sounds as though the idea of living here appals you. And you made a reference to runaways.'

'I wouldn't live here if you gave me a house. Lively as it is – if you have friends – down here in summer, it goes dead as a doornail from October on. Yes, I did call them runaways, didn't I? They've run from the routine of doing a daily job. Some weird types round here.'

'I hope you'll excuse me while I sit down and eat. Do you know how to get to The Grange?'

Hetherington reached over the counter, picked up the pad the barman used to write out orders, swiftly drew a map, starting from where they were.

'As you'll see,' he went on, showing Newman the sketch map, 'his place is well outside Constantine. You'll see it from the road – only house around there, a granite job with tall chimneys. Mind you don't miss the turning I've marked with a cross.'

'I'm very grateful for your help,' Newman said with a smile.

'Any time.' Hetherington grinned. 'I'd love it if I read an article you'd written on him. He hates publicity, keeps a low profile. But I have a feeling you could bluff your way in. See you . . .'

Newman ate his meal quickly, forgetting the second glass of beer he'd acquired when he'd bought a round for Hetherington. Leaving the inn, he walked out into torrid heat. The car was like a furnace. He lowered all the

128

windows, opened the sunroof to its fullest extent and drove off, his jacket neatly folded by his side.

He stopped in a leafy lane, used his mobile phone, calling Paula first.

'Spot on, as you said.'

He spoke the last three words to her slowly, indicating he had probably found his target. Then he repeated the performance to the rest of his team and drove on. The sun glared in his eyes when he left the lane. Lowering the visor was no help – the sun was in high orbit and it persisted in glowing at him as he sat and roasted.

In the middle of nowhere The Grange suddenly came into view. He had met no traffic on the side road and now he stopped, then stared. An aerial mast projecting above one of the chimneys was slowly telescoping downwards out of sight.

'So, he has a secret and probably sophisticated communications system,' Newman said to himself. 'Interesting – especially for a man who sounds short of money.'

Newman drove on until he reached the entrance to a drive. Wrought-iron gates closed. A speakphone in one of the stone pillars complemented the high stone wall surrounding the property. Reminded him of Mullion Towers.

He got out of the car, pressed the button on the speakphone.

'Who is it?' a voice demanded. Abrupt.

'Robert Newman. To see Colonel Arbuthnot Grenville.'

He imagined the owner liked the use of 'colonel'. There was a pause.

'What is your occupation.'

'Foreign correspondent,' he replied laconically.

'How many articles have you written recently?'

'Not many. Not since I wrote *Kruger: The Computer Which Failed.*'

'Made you a packet, didn't it?'

'I get by.'

'The gates will open. Drive up to the main entrance.'

The conversation ended. Newman smiled to himself as he went back to his car. He had seen a flash of sunlight off something in a first-floor window. Grenville had been studying him through field glasses while he spoke. But he felt sure it was because he was known as being a rich man since he wrote the book which interested Grenville. Money spoke volumes.

He drove slowly down the drive after the electronically operated gates had opened. In his rear-view mirror he saw them closing behind him. A careful man, Grenville. Newman observed everything during his progress up to the house.

No guard dogs. No sign of guards patrolling the grounds. Grenville, he suspected, was a man of very limited means.

Probably just able to keep this place going, he was thinking. Flower beds neglected. The lawn Californian brown, due to the scorching summer, plus the lack of gardeners to water it. Yet Cornwall had the highest unemployment rate in the country. Should be easy to get help.

The white paint on the window frames and ledges was peeling off. The pillars supporting the large entrance porch were cracked. No sign of maintenance anywhere. And yet he could afford a very expensive telescopic aerial and, presumably, the accompanying costly communications system. Unless someone else had paid for that?

Parking his car, he climbed four stone steps to the double entrance doors made of heavy wood and iron-studded. The right side opened and a tall, slim man stood framed in the doorway.

'Enter, Newman.'

Newman entered, walked into a large hall with a woodblock floor which hadn't seen polish for a long time.

The door was locked behind him while he waited. His host, back stiff as a ramrod, showed him into a large sitting room furnished with couches and coffee tables.

'Sit *there*,' he ordered.

Newman glanced at his host and sat *there*.

'Time for a sundowner,' the colonel declared. 'Whisky your tipple?'

'The sun hasn't gone down,' Newman pointed out.

'Bloody thing should have done. Whisky your tipple?' he repeated.

'That will do fine.'

Newman studied Grenville while his host went to a cocktail cabinet, the best piece of furniture in the room. Grenville would be about sixty, he estimated. He had grey hair brushed neatly back over his head, a trim grey moustache, quick movements. Under bushy brows his ice-blue eyes missed very little, and his hawklike nose gave him an air of command. Despite a touch of arrogance in his manner there was a wry twist to his mouth which suggested to Newman he had a cynical sense of humour.

'Cheers!' he said after handing a glass to his guest.

'Cheers!' said Newman. 'I haven't seen anyone else since I arrived. Surely you don't live here alone?'

'Why shouldn't I?' asked Grenville a trifle aggressively as he sat on another couch facing Newman. 'A so-called housekeeper – local woman – comes in three times a week. Cooks for me, leaves meals for the intervening days and keeps the place in order. But you didn't call here to ask me about my domestic arrangements.'

'I just happened to be in the area and heard you were its most dominant resident.'

'Just as you happened to be in Oklahoma City and wrote the truth before anyone else – that it was not foreign terrorists who were responsible.'

'I'm intrigued by the unusual mixture of people down here who are exiles from other parts of Britain.'

'Exiles?'

'That was the word I used.'

'Suppose you're referring to the types who've fled to here from the great metropolis, London.'

'Yes.'

'I find it curious myself,' Grenville said evasively.

'And there has been a strange murder down here. At Porth Navas. An inhabitant called Adrian Penkastle. Stabbed to death in his home.'

'Heard about that.' He took his time trimming the end off a cigar, lighting it. 'So that's why you're on the prowl?'

'Interesting that the *Venetia* was – still is – standing offshore at the time of the murder. I heard in a pub today that one of the locals in Porth Navas heard a powerboat taking off at speed down the Helford River soon after Penkastle was murdered. He was sailing back along the river at the time – the local I'm referring to.'

Grenville watched Newman, listening but saying nothing as he puffed on his cigar. Newman went on, making up the next bit.

'Another local in his boat near the mouth of the Helford watched the powerboat speed back to the *Venetia*. I've reported this to the police.'

'A most public-spirited action,' Grenville commented.

'You've heard of Vincent Bernard Moloch?' Newman continued.

'Vaguely. Where is all this leading? I'm confused.'

'You don't strike me as a man who is ever confused. The *Venetia* belongs to Moloch. Or VB, as he is often called.'

'I see. Why are you telling me all this?'

'Because you are the man with most influence in this part of the world. You know everything that's going on here.'

Grenville smiled in a most engaging way. His whole

hawklike face lit up when he smiled. Then he chuckled as he tapped the ash from his cigar into a glass bowl.

'This is very comical, Newman. You credit me with being Master of the Universe – a title which I understand originated in America. You have elevated me to a status which I don't deserve. True I hold the occasional party at the Yacht Club in Porth Navas, but that hardly justifies your description of me. Think I'll just have another whisky on the strength of what you've just said. You'll join me?'

'Thank you, but no. I'm driving.'

'Frankly, I'm mystified why you came to me. But I will say I enjoy your company. Do enlighten me. You are intriguing me no end.'

He said this while helping himself to another drink at the cabinet. When he turned round, still smiling, Newman had the thought that he was a handsome man when he dropped his military style upper-crust manner. Someone who would be attractive to the ladies and probably treat them with a natural courtesy.

'Well, Newman, why choose to come to me?'

He had returned to his couch. He raised his glass and sipped at the contents. His observant eyes watched his guest over the rim of his glass.

'I told you,' Newman persisted. 'You are the well-known figure round here. Seemed the obvious person to come to as I'm trying to get to know this unusual community.'

'Makes me sound like a father figure.' Grenville chuckled again. 'But I do know that there are people who dislike me. "That old fool of a colonel living in the big house which is falling round his ears."'

'Others seem to like you,' Newman went on, using his imagination. 'Otherwise they wouldn't come to your parties at the Yacht Club.'

'Really?' Grenville smiled again. 'Supply free nosh

and booze and you can get plenty of feet under the table.'
He sipped more of his drink. 'Living alone here is – well,
a lonely business. So now and again I mix with some of
the locals. You . . .' he pointed the cigar at Newman, 'are
invited to my next party. May I ask where you're
staying?'

'At Nansidwell Country Hotel, Mawnan,' Newman
replied promptly.

'I know the proprietor. Nice chap. I also knew Adrian
Penkastle,' he said suddenly. 'I was shocked to hear of
his murder.'

'Knew him well?' Newman enquired quietly.

'Only casually. I know he drank a little too much.
That he was short of money – what the Americans call a
loser. Don't agree. He could be very amusing, was a
clever mimic. Had us all rolling in the aisles.'

'Sounds likeable.'

'He is – was.'

'Did you ever meet Moloch?' Newman asked without
warning.

'Heavens, no. I gather no one ever does. Keeps very
much to himself – or so I was told in Falmouth. Got a
great barn of a place somewhere out in the wilds.'

Newman checked his watch, stood up. His host
immediately stood with him.

'You're not off yet? Stay a little longer. I'm enjoying
our conversation.'

'So am I, but I must leave now. We can always meet
again sometime.'

'Make that a promise . . .'

Grenville escorted him not only to the front door but
out to his car. In the distance the gates were beginning to
open. Grenville must have touched a concealed button.

'Safe journey,' he called out, waving him off.

* * *

134

On his way back Newman's mind was in a whirl. He couldn't make out Colonel Grenville. On the one hand there had been the moment when he saw the aerial telescoping. Then his host had made several references to America. On the other hand he seemed a very British character with a personality which was attractive. And he'd made no secret of the fact that he'd known Adrian Penkastle.

Arriving in Mawnan Smith, Newman parked the car. He used the phone box to call Tweed.

'Suggest you check someone living near Constantine. Spelt as it sounds. Lives at The Grange. A Colonel Arbuthnot Grenville. Did you get the name?'

'Yes. Thank you . . .'

In his office at Park Crescent Tweed looked across at Monica. He paused and she waited. She knew he was taking a decision.

'Monica, don't feel left out of this. No one else in the team knows it. I have an agent operating none of you know about. If I get struck by lightning the name and details are in my safe, to which you have a key, inside an envelope marked Personal and Quite Confidential.'

'I wish you wouldn't talk like that.'

'We're in a dangerous business. I'm taking the precaution to protect totally the person concerned. They are very important in this battle with VB.'

12

The first person Newman met on returning to Nansidwell was Vanity Richmond. He had already met the rest of his team in the side road, had told them what he had found.

'Maybe we could talk about it later,' Paula suggested.

'We are going to do that . . .'

Paula had driven back first to the hotel in case anyone associated her with Newman. Newman followed her fifteen minutes later, parked, saw Vanity wandering round the courtyard, wearing a black, sheathlike and form-fitting dress for dinner.

'Welcome back, Bob,' she said, greeting him with a smile. 'Had a successful trip?'

'More than I'd hoped for. Care for an aperitif in the lounge when I've had a bath and changed?'

'Let's leave that for dinner. You know I don't drink a lot . . .'

Which was true, he thought as he strolled through the empty hotel. She was very careful how much she drank. Unseen, he slipped upstairs to Paula's room. He walked in, closed the door, saw her sitting on the edge of the bed, staring out to sea.

'In one pub,' she began, 'I found your favourite brand of cigarettes. Catch.' She threw the pack and he caught it, thanking her. 'Now give,' she went on.

He sat down in a chair, noting she had turned on her radio and the taps in the bathroom to scramble their conversation. She listened intently, her eyes never leaving his face.

'So, that's it,' he concluded. 'I thought I'd found my target but now I'm not so sure.'

'If he is the controller of VB's spy network down here it's strange he told you he knew Adrian Penkastle.'

'That occurred to me. Unless he's very clever and thought I'd found out already – in which case it would be smart to admit it.'

'I suppose you could be right,' she said, dubiously. 'But from your description of him I'd guess he'd take a chance if that were the case – and not mention it.'

'I'm in a muddle about Grenville,' Newman confessed. 'On the other hand that cricket chap in the pub told me that Grenville spends his winters in Monterey.'

136

'Yes, that is odd. You didn't say anything to him about that?'

'Any more probing on my part would have appeared rude, if he's on the level. If he isn't it would have made him suspicious of me. Tweed is checking him out. Through a contact at the Ministry of Defence, I imagine.'

'Pity I hadn't been there. A woman's intuition tells her a lot about a man. I suppose you couldn't fix it so I meet him?'

'If he holds one of his parties at the Yacht Club before we leave I'll take you along.'

'That will make Vanity jealous,' she chaffed him.

'Don't see why,' he commented a trifle stiffly .

'Oh, come on. You two are getting on like a house on fire.'

'Maybe.'

'You need to relax, have some fun. She looks like fun to me.'

'And yet she tried to get to know you out in Monterey. You were suspicious of her then. Now she turns up here. Department of strange coincidence. I wasn't born yesterday.'

'I know you weren't. I was pulling your leg, Bob.' She turned serious. 'I think there's something very strange about her. Maybe by getting pally with her you can find out what she's up to – because she's up to something.'

'So at last you've caught on to what I'm doing. Time for me to get ready for dinner. Now you're in the picture . . .'

But am I? Paula wondered after he had left. Why do I feel that Vanity is fooling him?

In California Moloch got out of his chauffeur-driven stretch Lincoln Continental and paused. Anyone watching him would have assumed he was admiring the view over the blue Pacific from Highway One, south of Carmel. Waves curled in, broke against the rocks far below, threw up puffs of white surf. The coast stretched away in both directions with hills climbing steeply behind the highway.

Moloch was staring up at the new house near Big Sur Mrs Benyon had moved into recently. Perched alone on a ridge, overlooking the ocean, he thought it a crazy structure. The grey-tiled roof sloped down like a ski slope. Porthole windows had been inserted into the roof and the ground-floor windows were triangles of glass.

'More like Walt Disney,' he said to himself as he climbed a series of zigzag steps, also triangular in shape. 'So how does she get down here – when she's supposed to need a couple of sticks to waddle across a room?'

Granted there was a Alpine drive up to the house, but he knew she liked to walk down to the sea. Ethan's cream Cadillac was parked outside the house. Returning to Black Ridge he had been told Ethan had been summoned to see his mother.

In his hand he held a key to the front door. Over the phone from his jet he had ordered Martinez, the guard master, to make a copy of the key. Ethan always left his jacket hanging over a chair. It had been easy for Martinez to extract the key and take an impression while Ethan was hundreds of feet below in the tunnel beneath Black Ridge.

Reaching the house, he noticed the wide terrace was paved with stones carrying weird cabbalistic designs. The old dear had a liking for the occult. His thin lips curled as he looked at the front of the house. Even the heavy wooden front door was a huge triangle.

'Californian architecture,' he sneered to himself.

Inserting the key quietly, he turned it, opened it carefully, closed it once inside. He immediately heard a raised voice, guttural and thick. It came from a room to his right in the curving hall where the door was open.

'Ethan, you'll do as you're told or I'll beat the hell out of you.'

'But, Mother, I can't do that. VB would be furious . . .'

He waited for a moment in the doorway where his grossly fat stepmother sat in a thronelike chair. Ethan stood before her like a frightened schoolboy, tall and thin, with bushy grey hair falling over his high forehead. Mrs Benyon raised one of two sticks she held in her hands, struck him with a savage blow on the arm. She was lifting the other stick to administer further punishment when Moloch walked into the circular room.

He moved quickly. Seizing the raised stick, he broke it in two across his knee. Casting the remnants into a blazing log fire, he grabbed the second stick, broke it, threw it on the fire.

'Vincent!' she screamed at him. 'Now I can't move. You bastard.'

Her heavy jowls were trembling with rage. She sat in the chair which was large, but only just contained her great ugly body. Her eyes, just visible above heavy pouched flesh, glared murderously at her stepson.

'Go back to Black Ridge immediately, Ethan,' Moloch said calmly. 'You are paid a very large salary and I expect you to earn it. If your mother summons you again while you are working, come straight to me.'

Ethan, his hands trembling, left them alone. Moloch waited until he heard the Cadillac drive away. Then he turned to Mrs Benyon, who sat still glaring.

'Please listen to me. You have an evil temper. You treat Ethan, who is over forty, like a child. He has a brilliant brain . . .'

'Which you are exploiting. Bastard!' she repeated venomously.

139

'Since I can't reason with you,' he went on quietly, 'I have to tell you. If there is another repetition of this uncivilized behaviour I shall withdraw all your stock from AMBECO. You know that I can.'

'I'll trip you up some way, Vincent. See if I don't.'

'Oh, that's another thing. You talked your way into Black Ridge past Martinez while I was away. You were poking around, trying to get into my office. Do that again and your stock goes down the drain. Don't think I won't.'

He moved away from her, bent down to warm his hands at the fire. At 4 p.m. or so in this part of California, however warm the day, the temperature dropped suddenly, became chilly. He was leaving the room when she called out to him.

'Vincent! You have left me a cripple without my sticks.' She pointed two open fingers at him, like the points of open scissors. 'I have put the evil eye on you. Get out of my house!'

He made a little bow, smiled, looking directly at her.

'It will be a pleasure to do so. You appear to have lost your British manners.'

Once out of sight in the curving hall, he opened the door, slammed it shut from the inside, pressed himself against the wall. He heard the creak as she left her chair. Tiptoeing back to the entrance to the room he saw her hurrying briskly to the front window to observe him leaving. No sign of any handicap or infirmity, as he had long suspected. He peered into the room.

'Some cripple . . .'

On that remark he left the house before she could reply. Skipping nimbly down the idiotic steps, he never once looked back.

'How on earth did my late father marry such an ape?' he muttered aloud.

* * *

At four in the afternoon in California it was midnight in Cornwall. After dinner Newman had received a phone call from Colonel Grenville.

'My dear chap, I've organized a party at short notice. At a yacht club in Port Navas. Not the one near the end of the creek, another one – at the beginning of the road on the other side of the creek. I am very much hoping you will join us. There will be music and a small dance floor.'

'Thank you. I accept your kind invitation. May I also bring two ladies?'

'You like one in reserve, do you?' Grenville joked. 'I would be most happy – I just hope they are attractive. If you know them they must be. Midnight suit you? Good. I like early morning parties . . .'

Newman had been thinking of Vanity and Paula. When he told the latter she reacted at once.

'I'll phone up Maurice Prendergast and ask him? He had a bad time when we were last there.'

'Why not?' Newman grinned. 'And you had the nerve to pull my leg about Vanity.'

'Well, Maurice is rather handsome,' she replied. 'I hope Grenville won't mind.'

'The more the merrier is his motto, I suspect.'

He hurried into the lounge to tell Vanity. She rushed to her room to have plenty of time to fix herself up for the party.

At Park Crescent Tweed was working late. Monica, behind her desk, had often noticed that as the tempo of an activity began to accelerate one sign was that Tweed worked later and later into the night.

He phoned a contact at the MoD, apologized for the late call, then spoke rapidly.

'Arthur, I'm involved in an important investigation

here and abroad. It would help me if you could tell me something about the career of a certain Colonel Arbuthnot Grenville, now retired presumably, living in Cornwall.'

'Can't tell you a lot about him.'

'Then tell me a bit,' Tweed urged.

'Left the Army ten years ago.'

'Why?'

'Can't really go into that. Sorry. I always try to help when I can.'

'The investigation I'm involved in is sanctioned by the PM. So I need you to tell me everything.'

'You know, Tweed, we can't give out confidential information . . .'

'You have before. I've helped you recently. You owe me,' he snapped.

'Sorry, I've gone as far as I can. Hope this isn't the end of our cooperation at times in the future.'

'Of course not. Goodbye . . .'

Monica was careful not to look at Tweed, not to say one word. She knew his moods well, although he was rarely gloomy or lacking a buoyant attitude.

'I'll phone Special Branch now,' he announced. 'See if they're more forthcoming. No. I'll get the number . . .'

'Freddie,' he said after reaching his contact, 'can you tell me the true role of an ex-officer of yours? A man called Maurice Prendergast, now living down in Cornwall?'

'Oh, that's easy,' Freddie replied glibly. 'He retired about two years ago.'

'Are you sure about that?' Tweed pressed.

'Yes,' Freddie replied – after a pause. 'What's your interest in him?'

'I'm not sure. Yet. I think you could be covering up something.'

'Prendergast retired a couple of years ago,' Freddie insisted.

'He had enough money to do that? At his age?'

'I believe he was left a legacy by an uncle. Not enough to see him through for the rest of his life, I'd have thought. Still, it was his decision.'

'*Why* did he retire?' Tweed probed.

'Found the pressure of his work was becoming intolerable.'

'That's strange. I met him several times. He has the stamina of an ox.'

'The most unexpected people crack,' Freddie replied. 'I'm sure you've experienced that.'

'Not with people like Maurice Prendergast.'

'Well, it did. That's all I have on him. Ancient history.'

'Thank you,' said Tweed. 'Thank you very much.'

He stood up after putting down the phone. He began pacing round the office, polishing his glasses on his handkerchief. Most people could not have guessed something was wrong, but Monica knew better. He put on his glasses, stood by the window, gazing out at the darkness. Both ceiling fans were turning but it was still warm. He swung round.

'I'm wondering if the PM is in such a dither he's asked us to investigate Moloch – but also put Special Branch and the MoD on his track on the quiet. No, that's just too unlikely.'

'What's going on, then?' Monica wondered.

'Darned if I know. Perhaps—'

Whatever he was going to say was lost as the phone rang. Monica picked it up, asked the caller to repeat the name. She pressed the security button.

'It's that hoarse-voiced person called Waltz again.'

'I'll take it. Monica, could you make me a pot of strong coffee while I take this call?'

She gave him an odd look, left the room. Only then did Tweed start talking on the phone. He had a long conversation while she was away. Mostly he listened, then he asked a few questions and listened intently again. He had just finished the call when Monica returned. She poured him a cup without sugar or milk.

'Black as sin,' she remarked.

'There's a lot of it about,' he responded, drinking half the cup. 'A lot of sin.'

He stood up, resumed pacing round the office, hands clasped behind his back. After a while he paused, made his comment, then resumed pacing.

'I'm beginning to wonder if I'm using the wrong person as an agent. If I am, it could turn out to be a major disaster.'

He then went on pacing slowly, his eyes glazed as he concentrated on something which was deeply troubling him. Monica knew all the signs. He was weighing up his options, balancing one against the other. She also knew he would suddenly make up his mind and erupt into action. Again he was interrupted by the phone ringing.

'No peace for the wicked,' said Monica and answered the phone. 'It's Professor Weatherby, the seismologist.'

'Yes, Weatherby,' Tweed said, now sitting behind his desk.

'Tweed, I was clearing out some old files. I found one compiled by Ethan Benyon while he was with me. He must have left it behind. I found the contents disturbing, highly disturbing. If you could come over I'll explain what I've discovered.'

'Would now be too soon? No? I'm on my way . . .'

Telling Monica to hold the fort, that he was rushing to see Weatherby, Tweed slipped into his jacket and left.

'I wonder who Waltz is?' Monica said to herself.

* * *

The Yacht Club building where Grenville was holding his impetuously arranged party was an old two-storey place with rough-cast walls painted white. As Newman parked his Merc., with Vanity alongside him, he saw Maurice's car pull up behind him. Beside him sat Paula. They could hear dance music floating out of the building into the warm night.

Earlier Paula had phoned Maurice, inviting him to join her at the party. He'd agreed immediately.

'I'll drive over and collect you. No, I positively insist . . .'

It gave Paula a pang when she glanced down the road alongside the creek. That was where she had dashed out to intercept Adrian Penkastle. If she hadn't done he'd have presumably continued his way to some pub. And she had an idea that when he was too far gone some landlords would let him stay the night. Had that happened he would probably still be alive.

'A penny for your thoughts,' said Maurice.

'I was just thinking how good the music sounds.' She looped her arm through his. 'We're going to enjoy the party.'

'We will if I have anything to do with it . . .'

Grenville, a good host, was waiting for them with the door open. Inside couples were sitting at tables drinking. Others were dancing on the floor. Everyone seemed to be having a good time.'

'Colonel,' Newman began, 'this is a friend of mine. Vanity Richmond.'

'Wish she was my friend,' Grenville greeted her jovially, taking two glasses of champagne off a sideboard and handing them to his guests.

'And behind me,' Newman went on, turning round, 'is Paula, another friend.'

'Greedy!' Grenville chuckled. 'Don't think you can monopolize them both for the whole night.'

'And this is Paula's escort, Maurice Prendergast . . .'

Reaching for another glass of champagne, Grenville's hand froze. The gesture lasted hardly a second but Newman noticed his host's expression had stiffened, then he was his normal affable self.

'Welcome, Paula. I insist we have a dance together later.' He switched his gaze back to her companion. 'Welcome, Prendergast. Hope you don't mind my pinching her off you during the party.'

'It's a free country,' Prendergast answered with a smile.

They sat down together at a side table for four. Seafood was served – generous portions of crab and lobster. Newman wondered how Grenville afforded this lavish fare. The moment the food was demolished Newman invited Vanity to dance, took her on the floor. Maurice suggested to Paula they follow suit.

'Do you mind if we wait a minute? I'd like to digest my enormous helping.'

Which wasn't her real reason. She wanted to watch Newman dancing with Vanity. Her blazing red mane picked her out from all the other couples, and she was a very good dancer. She pulled Newman closer to her as they moved round the floor. She rested her pointed chin on his shoulder, her hair touching his face. He was saying something which caused her to burst into laughter.

'Those two are getting on well together,' Maurice said.

'They certainly seem to be,' Paula agreed.

Glancing round the room, she estimated there were about a hundred people present. A mixture of young and middle-aged. Many had the look of the 'exiles' Newman had mentioned to her in her room. Maurice guided Paula onto the floor as Newman returned with Vanity.

'I'll get you another glass of champagne,' Newman suggested.

'I think I'll wait awhile. Who are you looking at so so closely?' she asked.

'No one in particular,' he lied.

Opposite him, at a table on the far side of the room, Colonel Grenville was staring fixedly at Prendergast. His eyes reminded Newman of twin gun barrels. He was so intent on watching this particular guest that the ash at the end of his cigar toppled down his smart blue suit. He appeared not to notice what had happened.

As they danced, Prendergast cast the occasional glance in his host's direction, then looked away quickly. What the devil was going on? Newman was puzzled. Vanity drew his attention to the band – five youngsters perched on a dais at the end of the room.

'They're quite good,' she commented. 'And they're playing a mixture of the old and the new. I rather think Grenville instructed them to do that – something to please his mix of guests and ages. He's a very good organizer.'

'And amazingly quick,' Newman remarked. 'He must have been phoning up all over the place this afternoon.'

'Why do you say that?'

'Because of the late hour when he called me to invite me. I don't think I was an afterthought.'

'Can't imagine you'd be that with anyone – especially a woman.'

Newman was cursing himself inwardly. He had nearly slipped up badly because he'd seen Grenville only that afternoon, a fact he was concealing. The trouble was, he knew, his mind was full of Vanity.

Later Grenville danced a quick-step with both women in turn. Newman noted he was surprisingly agile on his feet, more like a man of forty.

The party went on into the early morning hours. At 3 a.m. Newman suggested they left. Grenville was a little too cordial when he said 'goodbye' to Prendergast, a fact which Newman observed with interest.

They returned to Nansidwell. Prendergast wanted to drive Paula back but she insisted that was ridiculous since Newman could take her in the Merc.

'I would have thought you'd at least let me do that for you,' Prendergast said forcefully.

'Well, I won't,' she told him. 'We've had a lovely time. Don't spoil it.'

'You're the one who's spoiling it.'

Newman had stood nearby, saying nothing. Paula had to work this one out for herself. He was glad he'd escorted Vanity inside his car with the windows closed against the night chill. At least she couldn't hear this conversation, which was on the verge of turning ugly.

'Thank you for a most pleasant evening – or early morning – Maurice,' she said firmly. 'I'm going back now with Bob. Good night.'

She omitted to kiss him on the cheek, walked briskly to the Merc., got inside the back, shut the door.

'Good night, Maurice,' Newman said.

'Have you two got something going between you?'

'Good night, Maurice,' Newman repeated.

He walked swiftly back to the Merc. He had to get away from Maurice before he slammed him one on the jaw. On the way back there was very little conversation. Paula was seething inwardly. Vanity was sleepy after her late night.

Arriving at Nansidwell, Newman found a message from Tweed waiting for him.

Phone me urgently as soon as you return. In the usual way.

He showed the message to Paula as soon as Vanity had gone to bed. She read it, handed it back to him.

'He means call him from the phone box in Mawnan Smith,' she said.

'I can do that myself now. Maybe you'd sooner get off to your room?'

'Like hell. I'm coming with you. I want to know what's going on. And after that absurd conversation with Maurice I'm very alert.'

13

Tweed was away so long after leaving to talk to Weatherby that Monica began to worry. She was relieved when he returned well after midnight. Then she saw the expression on his face. He sat down behind his desk, looking grim.

'Something wrong?' she enquired.

'Something is very wrong. After listening to Weatherby I think my bizarre theory as to what is going on with Moloch was right. It's horrendous.'

'You'd sooner not give me any details?'

'Not at the moment. I have to work out what to do. I suppose there haven't been any developments?'

'Yes, there have. I managed to get hold of our contact in Paris, Loriot. He said he'd phone me back and later he did. It's about Vanity Richmond.'

'Yes?'

'She was reported earlier to have an English father and a French mother. Loriot found out she did indeed have a French mother. Now deceased. Vanity was born in Grenoble. She's thirty-eight. Her father was an attaché at the British Embassy in Paris. When he was moved back to Britain her French mother came with him, bringing Vanity with her, who was then ten years old.'

'I see.'

'There's something else. Cord Dillon phoned me from

Langley. Joel Brand, Moloch's so-called second-in-command, passed through San Francisco International airport. Cord's man at the airport followed him to Black Ridge . . .'

'So-called? Is that your phrase?'

'No, it's Dillon's. He says it's not clear which of the two men – Moloch or Brand – is running AMBECO.'

'Curious. Very. What is really interesting is that Brand is now back in California. Which again fits in with the theory I've built up as to what is planned.'

For once the phone ran when Tweed wasn't pacing his office. Monica took the call, told Tweed it was Newman on the line.

'Tweed here . . .'

He listened while Newman gave him a terse report on the events at the Yacht Club. He mentioned Colonel Grenville's reaction to the arrival of Maurice Prendergast.

'Thank you,' said Tweed. 'Warn everyone to be ready for instant departure from Cornwall. Play it canny. Only partly pack your cases. When I tell you to come back, you come back fast. All of you. Hope you enjoyed the party. What you've told me may be important. Goodbye . . .'

He began making notes on a pad in his swift, strong handwriting. It took him a while to complete his list. Then he handed the pad to Monica after tearing off the sheet he'd written on.

'First thing, shred that pad. I don't want Howard snooping round, finding it and tracing the impressions of what I've written.'

His manner was brisk despite the late hour. Everything about him told Monica he had decided what to do. Action was about to erupt.

'And the next thing?' she enquired after shredding the pad.

'Call British Airways at Heathrow. Book open tickets, return, for a flight to San Francisco. Undated,' he emphasized. 'First-class tickets for Paula and me. Club class for Newman, Marler, Butler and Nield. That way they can lose themselves in the crowd. Tell them each passenger is travelling separately.'

'So it's California,' she remarked. 'You've broken the logjam.'

'Pity Philip Cardon wasn't still with us. He'd have come in useful when we do visit California.'

'Where is Philip?' she asked. 'Where did he go when he took extended leave?'

'I've no idea where he is now. We may never see him again. He's roaming the world. Like The Wandering Jew. That's a novel written by someone long ago called Jew Süss. I may have got the title a bit wrong – and the name of the author.'

'So he never really settled down?'

'Can you wonder at it? After what he went through?'

The newspapers broke the story that following morning. At his desk Tweed studied a national newspaper, only one of many which carried the story.

Twin Girls Murdered? Have You Seen Them? The headline was splashed across the front page. A story followed about two women who had been dragged out of the sea, dead, six thousand miles and several weeks apart from the discovery of one to the finding of the other. Two large pictures. One of the twin in California. The other of the twin in Cornwall. Another paper carried the headline *International Twin Murder?* Tweed passed the first newspaper to Monica.

'Buchanan has done a good job. Pulled out all the stops. That's going to rattle VB in his cage, shake the living daylights out of him. The timing couldn't be more perfect.'

'You think Moloch will react?'

'Someone will. Somewhere. I'm hoping we'll get a person who knows who they are coming forward. Here or maybe in California.'

'Why in California?'

'You know I asked you in the middle of the night to collect copies of the newspapers as they came off the presses?'

'I could hardly forget. I was up half the night.'

'At least I packed you off afterwards to get some sleep. I told you not to come in until this afternoon.'

'I can get by on a few hours, as you know. How much shut-eye did you get?'

'None,' admitted Tweed. 'I had a shower here and a change of clothes. After I'd sent copies to Cord Dillon and called him. At my request the RAF had a jet standing by at Heathrow to fly them to the States. I had to get the PM's backing to arrange that.'

'So when do they arrive?' Monica asked.

'Should be there now,' Tweed said, after checking his watch. 'They travelled in one of the RAF's superjets.'

'We really are moving. How will Cord get them to the West Coast?'

'By the same superjet. They may already have hit California. One of Cord's men in San Francisco is delivering them anonymously to Moloch's doorstep.'

It was late afternoon in Britain and early in the morning in California when Cord Dillon phoned Tweed.

'We've hit the button,' Dillon opened. 'Your papers arrived OK, have just been delivered to the big man. But more important, the story is splashed all over the *LA Times*, the *San Francisco Chronicle* – and the *Monterey Herald*. Now I'm waiting some guy who knew these chicks to holler that he knew them, who they are.'

152

'You're moving fast,' Tweed commented. 'How did you manage that?'

'I have contacts,' Dillon replied vaguely. 'We wired the three papers in California with the photo of the woman who came ashore in California and the Identikit you sent of the other one who was washed in on the coast of Cornwall. Someone, somewhere, has to react.'

'I hope so . . .'

Unknown to both Tweed and Dillon, someone had already reacted. An American, a partner in Standish Investigations, a private detective agency, was staring at the pictures in disbelief and growing horror.

Linda Standish was working on a homicide case under cover. She had obtained a job in a dress shop in Carmel at the princely sum of ten dollars an hour. There were no customers in the shop as she stood and rapidly read the story. She made up her mind immediately. Her boss was not pleased when she told him.

'I'm sorry, but I'm resigning, Leon . . .'

'Resigning? You've only been here a week. You can't do this to me.'

'My father's on a visit to London,' she lied glibly. 'I had a call just before you came in. He's been taken seriously ill.'

'You didn't tell me your father was going to London.'

'You don't tell me your private affairs,' she snapped.

'Don't expect you're going to get another week's pay.'

'Keep your pay!'

She was out of the shop and inside her parked car before Leon could think of a comeback. From a phone booth she called her father in Santa Barbara, told him only what she had told Leon, warning him to back her up by getting his girl friend to answer all calls, to say he was away in London. She was careful not to upset him by telling him the truth. He didn't take the papers or

153

watch the TV. He had an aversion to any form of news and his girl friend was as dumb as they come.

Next she phoned British Airways, booked a seat on the night flight to London, using her credit card. Then she called her partner in San Francisco, explained the situation.

'Ed, send one of the girls on the staff to try and get the job in that dress shop. Guy's called Leon.'

'You were getting somewhere with the Armstrong homicide?'

'Not a thing so far. I have to fly. Literally . . .'

Finally, she called the number at Black Ridge, asked to speak to Mr Moloch. She was put straight through to him.

'Linda here. I have to fly to London. My father's ill. Sounds serious. While I'm there I hope to pick up a clue about your missing girl friends.'

'I'll increase the fee to one hundred thousand dollars,' he replied instantly. 'If you trace them. But you don't reveal any information to anyone. Bring it straight to me. Me alone.'

'You told me that before. I have to rush to catch the plane.'

She then started the two-hour drive to San Francisco, pushing over the speed limit. It was going to be a close thing to catch that flight. All the time, at the back of her mind, she was thinking, One hundred thousand dollars is a load of money.

She caught the flight by the skin of her teeth, settled into her seat in Club Class. An expensive trip. Normally she'd have travelled Coach, or what the Brits called Tourist. But she needed time to think to get over the shock.

She knew she could have contacted the police in California, but they had so much crime on their hands she didn't think they'd give the case the attention she was determined to get. Her first move would be to call New Scotland Yard.

Linda drank the champagne the hostess had served while she checked the newspaper. The guy who appeared to be running the case was a Chief Inspector Buchanan. She'd call him. Frig the jet lag.

The following morning Buchanan called Tweed as he was looking again at the map of California Professor Weatherby had given him.

'Tweed, we may have a reaction to the stories in the papers. A Linda Standish has called me. Just said she had information on the missing twins. Wouldn't talk on the phone. Since you started all this would you like to interview her? She's American. I have the feeling you might learn more.'

'Where is this Linda Standish?'

'I'll give you a number. She's staying at some hotel down in Bayswater. Here's the phone number . . . And you'll keep me in touch?'

'Closely. But who am I supposed to be?'

'I hope you don't mind, but I gave her your name. I could have asked you first but I sensed she's highly strung, so didn't want to lose her. You're a chief claims investigator, your usual cover. I told her there could be an insurance angle.'

'I'll call her. And thank you . . .'

Tweed knew this was Buchanan's way of repaying him for his cooperation. Also, he suspected Buchanan realized that he could at times be intimidating. He called the number and asked Standish if she would meet him at Brown's Hotel. She agreed immediately, said she knew London well.

He arrived at Brown's at eleven o'clock, fifteen minutes early, but the concierge told him Miss Standish was waiting for him in the lounge. Accompanying Tweed, he pointed out the American who sat drinking coffee.

Tweed studied Linda Standish quickly as he walked towards her. She would be about five foot seven, was slim, had straight brown hair and a plain face. Rimless glasses were perched on her long nose and she wore a white blouse, high at the neck and with long sleeves. Her legs were clad in beige trousers and on her feet she wore white trainers.

'Miss Standish? I am Tweed.'

'Do sit down, Mr Tweed.'

He settled himself into a comfortable chair opposite and close to her. She stared at him and he knew she was assessing him. He waited patiently while she drank the rest of her coffee. She put the cup down and he tried to help her.

'I understand from Chief Inspector Buchanan that you have information about the missing twin ladies.'

'They were my sisters . . .'

Tears appeared in her eyes. She turned her head away and produced a handkerchief. Tweed was careful not to look at her. Instead he refilled her cup from the pot.

'Thank you,' she said and blew her nose. Her American accent was the softer type sometimes found in California. 'Sorry to make a fool of myself.'

'It's the jet lag,' he said kindly. 'I gather you have just come off the plane recently. A ten-and-a-half-hour flight can be a strain.'

'You are very kind.' She got a grip on herself. 'They were my sisters,' she repeated more firmly. 'Julie was the woman who died in California, Cheryl in Cornwall. They were thirty years old. Unlike me, they were both very attractive.'

She paused. Tweed estimated Linda Standish would

be in her mid-thirties. She was twisting the handkerchief between her hands, realized it, stuffed it inside her shoulder bag.

'Do you know when they disappeared?' he asked gently.

'Yes. Several weeks ago. Both of them about the same time. They were working for a very powerful man. Vincent Bernard Moloch.'

'Working for him. In what capacity? I need all the data.'

'I understand. I'm a private investigator. I work from Carmel. My junior partner covers San Francisco. Ed Keller.'

'I appreciate this is very difficult for you.'

Tweed now understood why she had weighed him up at first with her shrewd grey-blue eyes. It was part of her job to assess people quickly. He thought her intelligent. Probably good at her job – she could enter a roomful of people and no one would notice her, a valuable quality in her profession.

'I saw their pictures in the paper yesterday. I tried to trace their movements but they had just vanished.'

'I need to know in what capacity they worked for Moloch,' he repeated quietly.

'They were his confidantes and lovers.'

'I see. Did you go to see him?'

'Of course. He appeared puzzled and embarrassed. He couldn't understand where they had gone.'

'You said they were both his lovers?' he probed delicately.

'Not at the same time. It was Cheryl first. He can be very charming. She was furious when he turned his attentions to Julie, but she stayed on his payroll. He was a generous man where women were concerned.'

'What do you suspect happened to them?'

'I have no idea, Mr Tweed. There is not a lot of money

in our family. I've had to educate myself. My sisters were inclined to rely on their looks to get by.'

'It's not unknown,' Tweed remarked.

'They could have worked for their living. That's what I did. Instead they floated about looking for rich men.'

There was a note of bitterness. Tweed wondered whether Linda had been jealous of the easy route her sisters had taken. Then he decided he was wrong as she went on.

'Cheryl and Julie both had brains. They could have used them in a different way. I kept warning them but they took no notice of me. I was the elder, bossy sister.'

'They both lived in quarters given them by Moloch?'

'No, not at first. They shared a small flat in Carmel – in one of the tiny courtyards difficult to find. Then Moloch hired Cheryl after meeting her at a party and she moved to his huge mansion at Black Ridge. That's near Big Sur. You may have heard of it.'

'I know the area.'

'Later Julie called to see her sister and Moloch offered her a job. My twin sisters always dressed alike and it was difficult for anyone to identify which was which – except for me. I sometimes wonder if Moloch one evening mistook Julie for Cheryl, so it could have been by accident that he turned to her.' Linda hesitated. 'My sisters liked to play tricks on men, one pretending she was the other. Then their playfulness backfired on Cheryl.'

'Do you know anything about Moloch's early career?'

'Yes. Cheryl told me – he confided in her. When he came to the States from Belgium as a young man he was clever. He built up from nothing a successful electronics business. Other companies combined to ruin him, to put him out of business as a competitor. He had to start all over again. He struck me as a man with tremendous energy. He devotes his life to enlarging AMBECO, works

158

through the night and needs very little sleep. He's like a man obsessed.'

Tweed felt his brain jerk slightly. She had just given him another large piece of the jigsaw which slotted into place. He felt no elation. The grim theory he had slowly worked out was too horrific for him to feel pleased.

'You have no idea at all as to who was responsible for their deaths?' he enquired.

'It could be The Accountant.'

'Who?'

'In my business we hear a lot on the grapevine. There is a strong rumour that an assassin called The Accountant has killed several people. He works meticulously, always prepares the ground carefully for an assassination. We have no idea who he – or she – is.'

'I have heard that rumour.' He paused. Linda was showing signs that jet lag was at last catching up with her. 'You've been very helpful. Talking is very tiring after a long flight.'

'Yes, it is. I think I'd better go back to my hotel and get some sleep. How can I get in touch with you, Mr Tweed?'

He produced from his wallet one of the cards carrying his name as Chief Claims Investigator for General & Cumbria Assurance. He wrote the phone number on the back, handed it to her.

'If I'm not in and you want to tell me something please give my assistant, Monica, the details. She has worked for me for years and is discreet and completely trustworthy.'

'Thank you – and for your sympathy.'

'I don't remember giving you any.'

'The way you've talked to me – and not said more than you had to about my sisters. I like your approach. I suppose you were never a private investigator?'

159

'No.' He smiled. 'That is a profession I have never engaged in. Would you please call me if you are thinking of returning to the States?'

'Promise.'

'Then I'll get you a taxi to take you back to your hotel.'

She sat very still. Again he waited patiently. He sensed she was deciding whether to say something. She lowered her voice, despite the fact that they were the only people in the lounge.

'When Moloch came to the States from Belgium, before he set up the company which his rivals used tough methods to smash, he was an accountant.'

14

Returning immediately to Park Crescent, Tweed phoned Buchanan to give his report.

'Roy, Linda Standish is a private investigator in Carmel . . .'

Buchanan heard him out without a single interruption. Tweed gave every single detail of the conversation from memory. Across the office Monica was recording what he said.

'That's it,' Tweed concluded.

'Doesn't take us a lot further,' Buchanan commented. 'But at least we know the identity of the victims. And again it all goes back to Moloch.'

'Possibly. I think it takes us a great deal further.'

'You do? How?'

'It fits in with a theory I have evolved. No, I can't let you know yet. I could be wrong.'

'That's right. Go cryptic on me. Well, thanks for the

data. I'll inform the press that someone came forward, identified them by their names, which I'll give out.'

'Good idea . . .'

On that note Tweed ended their conversation. Monica smiled wrily.

'Nice to know I'm not the only one who finds you play it close to the chest. Oh, I've been on the phone again to my contact in the States. Moloch does have an accountant.'

'Has he got a name?' Tweed asked quickly.

'I was about to tell you. A man called Byron Landis. He works at Black Ridge, lives on the premises.'

'Interesting. I wonder how VB is reacting to the newspaper stories?'

At Black Ridge Joel Brand entered VB's office at three in the morning. The small man behind the desk was talking to Byron Landis, his accountant, after studying certain balance sheets. He was known for his attention to detail. No one could be employed in his vast organization without being thoroughly vetted by the Intelligence Bureau he had set up. No one earning fifty thousand dollars or more could be taken on the payroll before Moloch had personally interviewed them.

'So you see, Mr President . . .' Landis began.

'I've told you before never to address me in that way. It sounds so stuffy.'

'Sorry, but anyone in your position in America – even in a smaller outfit – is called by his title.'

'I am only in America physically, not mentally. I am a European, a Belgian. Now, get on with it, Landis.'

'I was only going to remark that, as you see, we have cut costs considerably. Except in the Armaments and explosives companies, which you vetoed for cost-cutting.'

'I've already seen that.'

Byron Landis was a small plump man in his forties. He had a bald head, wore steel-rimmed spectacles and had a precise manner. Joel Brand, who stood waiting impatiently with a sheaf of newspapers under his arm, called Landis Old Fussy. The staff working under Landis would not have agreed with the description. They knew him as a hard man. Landis also had a strange walk – he moved slowly with both feet turned outwards in a duck waddle.

'That's all, Byron,' Moloch said. 'Joel is bursting with impatience as usual.'

Brand was wearing an expensive lightweight business suit, a shirt buttoned down at the collar, a tie featuring a crocodile with jaws open and smart shoes. Newman would hardly have recognized him – his shaggy hair was neatly trimmed and brushed and, despite his tough face, certain women found him irresistible. Moloch liked his staff to dress well on duty at Black Ridge.

'You're not going to like this,' Brand said aggressively, sitting in the chair opposite to Moloch.

'Why not let me decide that for myself?'

'Well, take a look.' He shoved the *San Francisco Chronicle* and the *Monterey Herald* across the desk. 'Now the world knows what happened to Cheryl and Julie Standish.'

'And so do I.'

Moloch, a quick reader, had scanned the stories, looked at the photos. Then he checked the date of both newspapers.

'How did these get here so quickly?'

'Guy from our office in San Francisco always gets the paper from their office soon as it's printed, before it hits the streets. He flew down here to Monterey airport, had the smarts to call in at the *Herald*.'

'I like my people to use their heads,' Moloch replied in the same mild tone.

'Jesus! Thought you'd be cracked out of your mind. And there's more to come. London knows, too. This stuff was delivered through our mailbox. Don't know why the alarm didn't go off.'

'Because, Joel, we had monitors to neutralize the alarm stolen from our factory in Des Moines. You really must keep yourself up to date.'

'I'll check it out.'

'You should have done that already.'

'What about the Standish sisters?' Brand wanted to know.

'I'm horrified,' Moloch said quietly. 'Sounds to me like the work of The Accountant. When are you going to track that killer down? You've been working on it long enough.'

'He's shadowy. Moves like a ghost. But you still don't seem to realize the press are going to be down on us like an avalanche. They *did* work here – those two sisters.'

'So phone Des Moines. Get them to fly two more monitors to us immediately. In the meantime, open the gates to no one we don't want to see. Also instruct the telephone operator not to put anyone through to me unless he knows them. And send Ethan to me.'

'Ethan went home.'

'Home? He sleeps here.'

'Mrs Benyon phoned, told him to go to her house.'

'I see.'

Moloch was on his feet, he gave his orders as he slipped on a heavy astrakhan-collared coat.

'Tell Martinez to get the car ready to drive me to my stepmother's house. In future the operator is to accept no more calls from Mrs Benyon. If he slips up he will be fired immediately.'

'Martinez?' Brand sounded surprised. 'He's the chief of the guards, not your chauffeur.'

'Do as I tell you,' Moloch snapped. 'We may have to carry Ethan out of the house . . .'

This time Moloch instructed his driver to take the Lincoln Continental straight up to the house quietly. He got out, shivered. Even in California the night air is chilly. He let himself in through the triangular front door, again with his key. Again he heard Mrs Benyon's raised voice as Martinez followed him inside.

'Ethan, damn you! I said you sleep here from now on. Not under the constant surveillance of my dictatorial stepson,' she screeched.

Dictatorial? Moloch smiled grimly to himself. If anyone was dictatorial it was his detested stepmother. Walking into the room, he paused. Mrs Benyon, so intent on cursing her son, hadn't seen him enter. She was once more equipped with her two unnecessary walking sticks as she went on.

'Ethan, do what I say this moment. Your room is already prepared. Go up to it.'

'Mother, I can't . . .'

'You will obey me!' she screamed at him.

Moloch had had enough. He walked swiftly forward, snatched both sticks out of her hands. He repeated his previous performance, breaking them, hurling the shattered pieces into the fire.

She jumped up, ran forward as he turned, grasped him round the throat. He reached up to remove the hands as she screamed at him.

'I'll strangle you, you bastard!'

It was just the reaction he had hoped to provoke. Glancing at Ethan as he removed her hands, he saw the look of amazement on his face. A look replaced by an expression of fury.

'Mother,' he shouted, 'all this time you've fooled me – to intimidate me. I'll kill you for this . . .'

He walked out of the room as his stepmother stood still, uncertain what to do. She stared at her stepson with loathing.

'I know what you're up to at Black Ridge. You did that deliberately, curse you!' She stabbed two fingers towards his eyes. 'I'll sabotage what you are up to. If it's the last thing I do, I'll ruin you. Did you hear me? I'll ruin you . . .'

She was talking to herself. Moloch had left the room, gesturing to Martinez to follow him. Inside the car he gave him his instructions.

'Put guards on the house. Make sure she doesn't leave the place. Let her take walks on the terrace to get some fresh air. Make sure she has plenty of food. She can prepare it herself from now on. Stop the maid from entering the house in the morning. Give her a thousand dollars, tell her Mrs Benyon has hired someone else . . .'

Ethan had driven on ahead to Black Ridge. Moloch found him in his room. He was sitting on the edge of his bed, staring into the distance.

'Get some sleep,' Moloch advised. 'It will not seem so bad in the morning.'

'I'll kill her . . .'

'Concentrate on your important work tomorrow. You are a remarkable scientist. The project must continue at top speed. Have a bath, it will calm you down.'

'I will kill her . . .'

These were the last words from him Moloch heard that night as he closed the door and went back to his office. Settling behind his desk, he felt relieved. At long last he had destroyed Mrs Benyon's hideous hold over Ethan.

From a window high up in an unlit room a man had watched Moloch's departure, his later return. The accountant, Byron Landis, closed the curtains, switched on the light in his room.

At 4 a.m., the darkest hour in California, it was noon in Cornwall. By arrangement, Paula pulled up her car alongside Newman's Merc. in the square at Mawnan Smith, where the shops were lined along two sides. Newman was sitting in his front passenger seat with the window open as she lowered hers.

'What did you think of Grenville?' he asked her.

'I couldn't see anything strange or suspect about him,' she replied. 'At first I thought he was the typical Colonel Blimp type. But when I danced with him he was charming and amusing. I also found him more intelligent than I had expected.'

'I suppose you could be right.'

'You do sound dubious, Bob.'

'That cricketer chap I met in a pub near Constantine told me Grenville spends his winters in Monterey.'

'Probably a lot of people would like to spend their winters in California – if they could afford it.'

'Now you've hit the nail on the head. His home, The Grange, shows all the signs of a man hard put to keep up the place. Neglected garden. The outside hasn't seen a coat of paint in years. The furniture inside is old and shabby. What did you think of Maurice Prendergast?' he asked suddenly.

'Different kettle of fish. Seemed decent enough when I met him at his house. But after the dance he turned very nasty. You heard what he said about us – implying that we were having an affair.'

'He'd had a lot to drink. Maybe he just fancies you.'

'Like Vanity seems to fancy you?' she asked quietly. 'I would be interested to hear what you think about her.'

'She thinks a lot of herself, no doubt about that. But she's very controlled. Despite her swift changes of mood she's never shown any sign of losing her temper. Vanity Richmond is very cool.'

'I'd agree with you there. Extremely cool. But my woman's instinct tells me she's up to something, that she isn't all that she seems. Something's just struck me about Grenville. If he's short of money how could he afford to throw that party? Must have cost him a packet.'

'Maybe someone else paid for it . . .'

'I'm going to see that detective, the private investigator, Linda Standish, after dinner,' Tweed told Monica. 'At Brown's Hotel again.'

'Has something happened?' she asked.

'I don't think she told me this morning everything she knew. Something a bit mysterious about her. A gut feeling.'

'Your gut feelings have always been right so far . . .'

Tweed carried his jacket. The heat in the London streets was making them feel like airless canyons. He wondered when the heatwave would break as he hailed a taxi.

Linda Standish was already on her way to Brown's inside another cab. She liked to arrive earlier than an appointment – it was part of her technique to catch people off guard.

She was wondering whether to tell Tweed that VB had hired her to find her missing twins. But he had promised her the sum of a hundred thousand dollars. Better keep quiet, she thought to herself. Tweed, the insurance man, might provide information which would help her to earn the huge bonus – a sum she had never seen in her life.

She was seated in the same chair in the lounge at Brown's, drinking coffee, when Tweed came over to her. He shook her hand, sat down facing her, ordered coffee for himself. He kept quiet until the coffee had been served. He had often found that people couldn't stand silence, that they felt they had to say something. Standish was no exception.

'Have you found out who killed my sisters? And I meant to ask you, is there an insurance angle? By which I mean were they heavily insured in case of death?'

'No to the first question. As to the other two I can't be sure yet.'

He was smiling ironically to himself. He had no doubt the murder of Cheryl and Julie Standish had come as a shock to Linda. But it was intriguing that she had asked if they were insured. Had they been, she was obviously hoping, she would be the beneficiary. What a strange mixture human nature was – and how often under the surface there was greed. Money roared, as he had said himself not so long ago.

'Tell me . . .' he began. 'I have found out that VB, as he's so often known, has a right-hand man, a deputy if you like. A man called Joel Brand.' Tweed was watching Linda closely and saw her eyes flicker. She was not immune to his casual manner. 'You've heard of him?'

'Yes. Both Cheryl and Julie mentioned him.'

'In what way? Did they dislike him?'

'Not so far as I could tell. Both said he was polite and courteous to them.'

'Did he ever come on to either of them – make a play for them?'

'Oh, no. Nothing like that.'

'Did either of them talk to you about what VB was doing?'

'No.' Linda was emphatic. 'Both were very tight-lipped when I brought up that subject. I think that was part of their contract – that they revealed nothing of what they heard or saw at Black Ridge. And he paid them very well. I don't know how much, but they started appearing in more expensive clothes.'

'Surely they must have said something. After all, you were their sister.'

'Not a thing.'

'And did you get any impression of the relationship between VB and Joel Brand from them? I mean who wielded the power?'

'Brand was in charge of most operations, I gathered. But it was VB who took all the decisions. Brand carried them out. To that extent I suppose, he had power.'

'Was there any member of VB's staff either Cheryl or Julie disliked?' Tweed enquired.

'Yes. They both detested his accountant, Byron Landis.'

'May I ask why they detested this man?'

'Of course you may. He treated them as intruders. VB would send one of them to fetch certain documents from Landis. He always insisted on taking the documents to VB himself as though they were spies.'

'Curious.' Tweed drank more coffee, sat back in the chair in his most relaxed manner. 'I appreciate your answering my questions so frankly. Oh, surely VB hired a private investigator to try and trace your sisters?'

Linda Standish had responded to all his previous questions immediately but now she paused. What had been a gentle interrogation stalled. She lifted a hand, smoothed down her straight brown hair.

'Why would he do that?' she eventually asked.

Wrong reply. She should have said she certainly hoped he had – or something like that.

'An obvious move, I'd have thought,' Tweed remarked.

'Well, if he did . . .' Linda had recovered her poise, 'I certainly never heard about it.'

Tweed ended the interview, making a sympathetic remark. He offered to get her a taxi but she said she preferred a walk in the glorious weather.

In his taxi on the way back to Park Crescent Tweed felt he had accomplished something. Standish had lied. Why? Had VB hired her? And if she would lie about that had she lied to him about something else?

15

Returning to Park Crescent, the front door was opened by George, the security guard and one-time police sergeant employed by Tweed for years. A short, nimble man with a strong jaw, he put a finger to his lips, whispered.

'You have a visitor in the waiting room. Chief Inspector Buchanan. Monica said to warn you, Mr Tweed.'

'Thank you, George . . .'

Tweed opened the door, peered inside where Buchanan was glancing at the latest newspapers. Tweed greeted him, invited him upstairs.

'I know now what it's like,' Buchanan joked as he entered Tweed's office, 'to be held in a prison cell. The door to that room is self-locking.'

'We have to take precautions. Something to drink, Roy? Tea? Coffee?'

'Not this time.' He looked across at Monica as he sat down. 'Although I know Monica makes excellent coffee. Where have you been, Tweed?'

'Out to have my hair cut, if you must know.'

'They did a good job. Makes you look younger.'

'Thank Heaven for small mercies. What brings you here, Roy?'

'Colorado Junction, that American electronics plant in the Thames Valley which was destroyed by a bomb. No casualties. A businessman who lives opposite it has been away for a few days. He called me, said someone was watching the plant twenty-four hours a day before the bomb went off. He thinks the watcher was checking the routine of everyone who worked there.'

'So?'

'No casualties,' Buchanan repeated. 'The workforce was mostly British. Our technical people with the Bomb Squad report it was detonated by radio from a distance.'

'So?' Tweed said again.

'It looks as though whoever blew it up was anxious there should be no casualties. Not often that a bomber takes all that trouble.'

'Or the man who ordered the plant's destruction, you're thinking?'

'Now you're ahead of me. Have you any idea who is responsible?' Buchahan asked.

'Could be anyone.'

'Could it be Vincent Bernard Moloch?' Buchanan suggested.

'Your guess is as good as mine.'

'When you get that poker-faced look I know you're concealing something.'

'That comes from staring at myself in the hairdresser's mirror. I dislike getting a haircut. It's a bore.'

'A clever reply,' Buchanan responded. 'And I suppose you personally never knew of Adrian Penkastle? A drunk stabbed to death in Cornwall. Place called Porth Navas.'

'Yes, I know about that,' Tweed said promptly, to Buchanan's surprise.

'He's admitted he knows something,' Buchanan said with mock severity, glancing at Monica.

'If he knows he'll tell you,' Monica said pertly.

'If it suits him. Mind telling me, Tweed, how do you know about him? There's been nothing in the papers. We've kept it quiet.'

'Newman told me. He was down in that area. All the locals were chattering about it in the pubs. It isn't all that often they have a murder to gossip about, I imagine.'

'An interesting fact has emerged.'

Buchanan had produced a map, spread it out over Tweed's empty desk. As he did so Paula walked in with a suitcase. She smiled at Buchanan.

'You were there,' Buchanan accused her. 'So was Tweed.'

'Find Tweed, you sometimes find me there too.' Dumping her suitcase in a cupboard, she ran her fingers through her dark hair. 'Where is there?' she asked.

'Here.' Buchanan pointed to the map and Paula came over to look. 'At Porth Navas. You know the place, Miss Grey?'

'Yes.' She smiled inwardly at Buchanan's frowning reaction to her instant cooperation. 'I went to a dance with Bob Newman. Organized by the local squire, Colonel Grenville.'

'I see.' Buchanan sighed. 'We're talking about Adrian Penkastle.'

'The man who was murdered. So was everyone at the dance. Talking about Penkastle.'

'Well,' Buchanan turned to Tweed while Paula studied the map, 'we find out Penkastle often took a walk along this road by the side of the creek. Then he vanished. My bet is he was visiting someone. The question is who?'

'Got an answer?' Paula asked him cheerily.

'I hoped either you or Tweed might know the answer.'

'There are a number of houses along that road,' Paula told him. 'Why not send someone down to check each one.'

'I have done just that,' Buchanan said grimly. 'Thought I might get a short cut by coming to see you.'

'Don't look at me,' replied Paula.

'And don't look at me,' Tweed added.

'Now you've gone dumb on me.'

'No, we haven't,' Paula told him. 'We've been chattering away to you. Don't frown so often – gives you wrinkles in your forehead.'

'You have no information to give me at all, then?'

'Yes, I have. I've just returned from a holiday in Cornwall. The weather was wonderful. But you know that, Chief Inspector. You were down there yourself.'

'I've never heard of anyone here taking a holiday.' Buchanan grumbled as he folded up the map.

'Oh, I have a good boss,' Paula informed him merrily. 'He thinks we all need a refresher now and again.'

'Which is why the lot of you trooped off down there.' He stood up. 'Pull the other leg, it's got bells on.'

'Don't see any bells,' Paula replied.

'And Tweed hasn't said a word.'

Buchanan prepared to leave. He stared round the office with a dissatisfied expression. 'This place is like a bank vault.'

'Have to keep the money somewhere.'

'Tweed still hasn't said a word.'

'Don't know how I'd have got in a word edgeways with all of you chirping away like magpies. I'll see you down, Roy,' Tweed offered.

'Don't bother. I should know the way by now.' His tone became ironic. 'Thank you all for your cooperation.'

* * *

'That was pretty amusing,' Paula said after Buchanan had gone. 'He expected us to deny we knew Porth Navas – or to refuse to answer.'

'You're right,' Tweed agreed. 'That was bright of you to mention the dance.'

'The trouble is it raises a more serious question. Who was Adrian Penkastle going to see? From Buchanan's description of the dead man's movements he could easily have been visiting Maurice Prendergast at The Ark frequently. Why?'

'That's a wild assumption,' Tweed objected.

'I noticed that when we were there Maurice, after watching us approach, left the net curtain over the right-hand window half open. Could have been a signal to Penkastle not to call – that he had other visitors.'

'Another wild assumption.'

'May I ask,' intervened Monica, sensing a row brewing up, 'why Paula has returned so suddenly? I didn't know anything about it.'

'You were out of the room when I called her at Nansidwell,' Tweed explained. 'I'm going to withdraw the whole team – one by one – so there won't be any sign they're together. We don't know who is watching that hotel. I'm getting to know how VB operates. Wherever he is he has unlikely people employed as spies, to see what's going on. Probably has another network in the Carmel area. Either of you make any sense of this?'

He produced a map of California he had brought back with him from Professor Weatherby. It had more squiggly lines on it curving up from southern California to the north. At the bottom was a signature in tiny script. *Ethan Benyon.*

Paula and Monica stood on either side of him as he spread it out on his desk.

'This map,' he informed them, 'was extracted from an old file by Weatherby, who was having a clear-out.

Unknown to him, Ethan was working on a highly original project. I won't give you details – except that Weatherby is now alarmed. There were other papers in the file but he let me bring this map away.'

'Doesn't mean a thing to me,' Monica commented after examining the map.

'Me neither,' Paula said.

'I draw your attention to the line marked "San Moreno fault". Ignore the notorious San Andreas fault which wrecked San Francisco in 1906.'

'I've never heard of it,' Paula admitted.

'Few people have. I suspect Ethan discovered it. Also notice that large red line in the ocean near Big Sur.'

'What is it?' Paula asked.

'I have a vague idea, but too vague at the moment to go into. I need to know if some kind of vessel is operating off Big Sur. I've got it. Standish could tell me . . .'

He explained to Paula who Linda Standish was, gave her a brief update on his conversations with the American private investigator.

'Well, now we know who they were – and that they were twins,' Paula remarked. 'No wonder they looked so alike. I'd begun to think I was losing my grip. And Standish has linked her sisters with Moloch.'

'Which might not be the end of the story,' Tweed said.

'What does that mean?'

'That I'm keeping all my options open.'

'Now he's going cryptic on us,' Monica grumbled and returned to her desk.

Tweed refolded the map, locked it away in a drawer. He looked at Paula.

'What does AMBECO stand for?'

'A for Armaments, M for Machine tools, B for Banking, E for Electronics—'

'Stop there,' Tweed interjected. 'Think again about the

map I showed you, and about the report on Moloch compiled by Monica, especially what happened to him when he first arrived in America.'

'Sorry, I'm all at sea.'

'Monica . . .' Tweed switched his attention to her. 'Newman and Marler must come back to London, so get hold of one of them. Tell them an emergency is imminent, that they're to return instanter.'

Newman was lying in long grass by the side of the road close to The Grange, gazing through field glasses. He reported what he saw to Marler, at his side, who had the monocular he favoured, to check he wasn't missing anything.'

'We've struck oil. Colonel Grenville is carrying suit-cases out to where his car is parked. He's on the verge of leaving.'

'By air,' Marler informed him. 'His luggage is fes-tooned with British Airways labels. Can't read the destination.'

'And he's in a hurry. That chap's fit. He's hurtling in and out of the hall like a rocket. Golf bag too. He's off somewhere abroad where there are golf courses.'

'Could be anywhere . . .' Marler paused. 'Don't move – to our right there's another watcher. Up a tree with binoculars. Move your head very slowly.'

Newman did what Marler had suggested. He stared. Up the stunted oak, not high enough to see them hidden in the grass, was Maurice Prendergast.

He also was gazing at The Grange, watching Gren-ville's hurried arrangements for departure. His car, turned to move off in the opposite direction, at the foot of a steep hill, had to have arrived a while after Newman and Marler had commenced their vigil. Why hadn't they heard him coming? Then Newman got it – crafty Maurice must have freewheeled down the hill with his engine turned off.

As he watched he saw Maurice suddenly shin down, run to his car, dive inside, start up the engine and drive off and out of sight. Marler nudged him.

'Time to go. Grenville is locking his front door . . .'

They both ran down the high-hedged side road. Newman blessed his foresight in parking the Merc. in a field out of sight. He jumped in behind the wheel and Marler joined him in the front passenger seat, then picked shreds of grass off his immaculate linen suit. Even in an emergency he was always careful about his appearance.

They were driving off towards Constantine before Grenville had started down towards his exit, using his monitor to open the electronically controlled gates. Newman pondered the situation as the Merc. vanished over the crest of the hill.

'I'd like to have followed Grenville, find out where he's off to.'

'We can't.' Marler lit a king-size. 'We haven't paid our bill or picked up our cases from Nansidwell.'

'I'll call Tweed from that phone box in Mawnan Smith. Weird that Prendergast was watching him too . . .'

Newman was leaving his room after checking his watch. He had arranged for Marler to leave fifteen minutes after him. During his call to Park Crescent he had been given Tweed's latest instructions by Monica before he spoke to Tweed, reporting the latest developments.

He was paying his bill in one of the lounges, accepted the receipt, was on his own for a moment, when Vanity touched his arm.

'Running out on me, Bob?'

'Just had a tip about a big story about to break in London,' he replied quickly.

177

'But you've stopped writing,' she said shrewdly.

'I'm bored. I feel like going back to work for a while. It's been great knowing you.'

'I'm leaving too. Couldn't we drive back together? It only takes me ten minutes to pack.'

'I've heard that one before.'

'Time me . . .'

'I'm sorry, but I have to leave now.'

'Bob,' she touched his arm again, 'take me out for a drink at the Lanesborough this evening.'

He looked at her and she was giving him her most appealing smile, the high colour in her cheeks glowing, as were her eyes. He felt a sense of passion for her.

'Eight o'clock at the Lanesborough suit you?'

'I'll be there. Drive carefully.'

She kissed him lightly on the mouth and was gone. He cursed himself as he hurried to his car. But he was also aware he felt excited at the prospect of not losing touch with her.

He was well on his way along the A30 when, in his rear-view mirror, he saw Vanity's car coming along the dual carriageway like a thunderbolt. She swept past him, exceeding the speed limit, waved a hand and streaked into the distance.

Behind him now, a few hundred yards away, was Marler in his Saab. Newman waited until he reached a parking area, signalled, drove in and stopped. Marler pulled in behind him, jumped out and leaned in his window.

'Vanity left shortly after you did. She's an expert tracker behind the wheel of a car. She kept just out of sight of you when she caught you up for quite a while.'

'So she can pack in ten minutes,' Newman commented. 'I've an idea she'll be waiting for me further along, waiting to follow me to see where I go. If necessary

I'll give her the slip in London. Let's get back on the road. I think Tweed is almost ready to go somewhere . . .'

He proved to be right. Passing another lay-by later he saw her parked inside it. She had the engine running and moved out after him as soon as he had passed. Newman was annoyed – he omitted to wave to her. In the distance behind her Marler followed in his Saab.

Reaching London, which he knew like the back of his hand, Newman chose a roundabout route to reach Park Crescent. Seeing a one-way street where traffic could only come in the opposite direction, he took a chance. Turning into it he saw in his mirror Vanity following at a distance of about twenty yards. As he reached the end to emerge into a street of two-way traffic he saw a van approaching him.

The driver honked his horn. Newman took no notice. As he drove on he saw the van enter the street, blocking Vanity's further progress. She was nowhere in sight when he arrived at Park Crescent.

'Very strange,' Tweed remarked as Newman, his case by his side, sat in the armchair and told him of the incident. 'Maybe she was worried you wouldn't turn up at the Lanesborough.'

'I doubt that.'

'Did you get her address? Where she's staying?'

'No. I didn't really think to ask for it – and she never brought up the subject . . .'

Marler, carrying his own suitcase, walked in. He gave a little salute to Monica, who liked him. Then he grinned at Newman.

'You gave her the slip cleverly. She had to back all the way down that one-way street. I tried to follow her but a traffic jam got in the way.'

'I'm going back to my flat.' Newman stood up. 'For a bath and a change of clothes. Where do you think Grenville is off to?'

'We'll find out. You've had a long drive. Go home – both of you,' ordered Tweed.

He waited until the two men had left before looking across at Paula.

'Can't understand why Bob didn't try to get her address. Most men would have done.'

'It's clearer than your glasses, which need cleaning. The dust in this heatwave gets everywhere. Bob is in a whirl about the glamorous Vanity – but he doesn't completely trust her, I'm sure. So, he's waiting to see what happens at the Lanesborough.'

'Monica,' said Tweed, 'after Newman phoned us from Cornwall did you get in touch with Jim Corcoran at Heathrow about Grenville and Maurice Prendergast?'

'Yes, I did. He's promised to call me back. And I called the hotel where Linda Standish was staying.'

'Was?'

'That's what I said. They told me she had checked out and left no forwarding address.'

'I see. I'm calling Corcoran at Heathrow.'

He got the Security Chief's special number himself. Jim Corcoran answered the phone immediately.

'Tweed here.'

'Just about to call Monica. Tried British Airways first and struck gold. Told them it was part of an inquiry into a drug ring, heaven help me. Colonel Arbuthnot Grenville is booked to travel First Class on Flight BA 287 to San Francisco. Departs here 1330. Arrives San Francisco 1625, local time, of course. Maurice Prendergast is booked on the same flight – but Club Class. You owe me.'

'I suppose you'd go mad if I asked you to check on a Linda Standish? She might just be aboard the same flight.'

'Stark raving mad. Why do I do these things for you?'

'Because I do things for you from time to time, Jim.'

'I'll come back to you. No, can you hang on a few minutes? I may be able to check – Linda Standish, you said? – that over the phone . . .'

During the few minutes he had to wait Tweed put his hand over the phone, told Paula and Monica what he had found out, then Corcoran was back on the line.

'Linda Standish *is* on the same flight. Club Class. She made the reservation by phone this morning and they just managed to fit her in aboard the plane. Tweed, could you give me a breather now? The airport is buzzing at this time of the year.'

'I'll do my very best. And thank you so much.'

'It was nothing. I am joking . . .'

Tweed put down the phone, told them what he had just heard. Paula was the first to react.

'Isn't it strange they're all on the same flight?'

'It's strange that they're all in such a hurry to reach California. A pattern is building up. It's only recently that Moloch flew back to the same place. A cauldron is bubbling over there.'

'A cauldron?' Paula queried.

'There are many cauldrons seething in the world today but this one is a monster . . .'

16

'The body of Julia Sanchez, daughter of that Philadelphia millionaire I told you about, has been found. Garrotted. Head nearly severed from the body. Guy who did it smeared his trademark on her body in her own blood. Letters AC,' said Cord Dillon.

'Sounds ugly,' Tweed replied.

The call from the Deputy Director of the CIA had

come in the middle of the night. Tweed had again been studying Ethan Benyon's map – comparing it with a detailed map of California.

'So now we've discovered three of Moloch's missing girl friends,' the American went on. 'We only have to find another garrotted and we know we have a serial killer on our hands.'

'AC,' Tweed repeated. 'The Accountant?'

'I'd bet money on it.'

'But didn't Sanchez disappear a while ago? How is the body so well preserved that you have all this data?'

'It was hidden in an alcove in an abandoned mercury mine not too far from Big Sur. It's ice cold down there – like a huge refrigerator. So the body was sufficiently intact to get the information I've given you.'

'There's a curious inconsistency, Cord. Two of the girl friends, Cheryl and Julie Standish, were washed ashore here and in California. Neither was garrotted.'

'I understand the *Venetia* was offshore when both incidents took place. Would the murderer have garrotted them?'

'I suppose not. No, you've got a point.'

'Other people who stood in Moloch's way have been found garrotted – always with the trademark AC painted on their bodies in their own blood. I wish to God we could trace The Accountant. He uses wire to kill his victims – probably with a wooden handle at either end. Maybe he uses the handles afterwards to mark his victims with their own blood.'

'Sounds like a sadist as well as a killer.'

'I agree,' the American said. 'We're searching all the old mercury mines in that area – that is, the local police are. I'll keep you informed.'

'Whoever it is must be attractive to women,' Tweed commented. 'That's the only way he could get them to go with him to a quiet place where he can commit his murders.'

'Don't know why that point didn't occur to me. Might give us a vague lead.'

'Check out Moloch's accountant, Byron Landis,' Tweed suggested.

'A bit obvious, I'd say.'

'A clever man might use the obvious. Keep in touch. Thanks for calling . . .'

Tweed told Paula and Monica what he had heard. He had just finished when Newman came into the office. Tweed stared at him.

'You were supposed to get some sleep.'

'I've had enough. I didn't want to lose touch with what's going on.'

Tweed repeated what he had just told Paula and Monica. Paula was gazing at Newman, who was wearing a smart grey pin-striped suit. He was also freshly shaved.

'So the bodies are beginning to come to light,' Newman observed grimly.

'How did you enjoy your meeting at the Lanesborough with Vanity?' Paula asked.

'I enjoyed it. She was great fun – a first-rate companion. Dressed to kill.'

'An unfortunate phrase,' Tweed remarked.

'Why? All right – in view of what you've told me about this Julia Sanchez, I suppose it was. Still, there's something odd. I couldn't get her address out of her. She said she was changing hotels and would call me at my flat when she got settled in. I didn't go for that.'

'Anything else odd about her, Bob?' Paula asked, watching him closely.

'She asked me about the article I'm researching. Told her this story to explain why I was leaving Cornwall suddenly – I said it was an exposé on one of the world's richest men. She went quiet and then changed the subject.'

'She's VB's personal assistant,' Tweed said quietly.

'Now he tells me!' He waved a hand at the others. 'Tweed is still playing it close to the chest . . .'

'I thought you'd find out more if you didn't know who she was,' Tweed explained.

'Thanks. Well, I guessed it could be him. A big business man who travels the world, she once described him as. She goes with him almost everywhere. Otherwise I got nothing out of her.'

Paula was relieved. She could tell Newman was fond of Vanity, but his brain was still moving in high gear. Tweed then told Newman about Maurice, Grenville, and Linda Standish.

'A mysterious woman,' he remarked as he concluded.

'What do you think she's up to?' Newman asked. 'Strange she should just walk out on you – then catch the same flight as those two. What's she up to?' he repeated.

'I think her search for the killer of her sisters is genuine. But she also has some other secret motive. I'm worried about her.'

'Why?'

'She's obsessed in her determination to track down the killer. She might take one risk too many.'

'She sounds like a professional,' Paula remarked.

'But there's an emotional element involved. It can muddle the judgement. Call it a sixth sense.'

'I've found out something about her, as you suggested,' Monica broke in. 'She lives in an apartment on Junipero Street, Carmel. Not too far from a police station. It's difficult to find – inside a small courtyard.'

She handed him a card with Standish's address. Tweed took out his map of Carmel from a drawer. He studied it, put the card in his wallet.

'I know that area. How did you get that information?

All I got from her was her office address. She palmed it to me when we shook hands. Very careful person, Linda Standish.'

'I called the big private investigation agency in San Francisco we've used before. The man I spoke to knew about her. I imagine that outfit knows every agency in the city.'

'Tell me something,' Newman said as Marler walked in. 'As I arrived I saw Harry Butler's car parked outside. What's going on?'

'I recalled Butler and Nield so I have everyone here close at hand. We're all going to California. I'm waiting for a signal.'

'What signal?' Paula asked.

'I don't know – but I will when I get it.'

'Don't try to push Tweed,' Marler drawled. 'My guess is we're due to depart soon.'

'Then maybe you'd all make sure you have your bags packed for a journey,' Tweed ordered. 'A warm weather climate . . .'

Luis Martinez, guard master at Black Ridge, had flown to London, as ordered. After leaving his suitcase, filled with old clothes bought second hand, at a hotel near the BBC, he went back to his hired car. He drove at once to a position from where he could watch Park Crescent.

He wasn't sure of the house he should watch but that did not bother him. He had all his equipment on the seat beside him. A Panama hat, which fitted in with the hot weather, a grey beret, photos of Robert Newman obtained from a picture library in San Francisco – and a small pair of field glasses. At the moment he wore the Panama hat, a T-shirt and a pair of denims.

His orders were precise, given to him before he had left Black Ridge.

'Here's a map of London. Fly there at once. Park Crescent is marked with a cross. We don't know which house the SIS is located in so watch them all. Here are pictures of the foreign correspondent, Robert Newman. He's the only one we know who is mixed up in this dangerous outfit. Watch for Newman to come out with a bag. I think he'll be flying over here soon. Track him to the airport, find out which flight he's coming on. Phone the flight details to me here. Then come back . . .'

A five foot six man with a tanned skin, Martinez was in his thirties. His strong face was long and lean and he sported a neat black moustache, matching the colour of his hair. Attractive to a certain type of woman, he smiled a lot, showing perfect white teeth. He had a cruel mouth.

Raising the field glasses, he checked a man leaving one of the buildings curving round the crescent. Nothing like Newman. He settled down to wait. He was a patient man and planned to change not only his clothes every day, but also his hired car, complaining the previous one was faulty.

When Linda Standish alighted from her flight at San Francisco International, had passed quickly through Immigration and Customs, she found the car she had hired waiting for her. She drove down the coast road, relieved to be back in California with its wonderful scenery. Before leaving the airport she had phoned Moloch to warn him she was coming.

It was a two-hour drive to Monterey but she had slept on the plane to counter jet lag. She passed through Monterey and Carmel and continued along Highway One. It was dark now and, leaving Carmel behind, lights from isolated houses on the steep hillsides to her left glittered like glowing eyes.

Near Big Sur Linda Standish pressed the horn five times and the electronically operated gates opened. She drove on up an endless steep drive to Black Ridge. Arriving, she was shown in by Joel Brand to the vast palatial room overlooking the ocean where Moloch received visitors. As Brand left Moloch came into the room, sat down on a leather couch opposite her.

'Yes?' he said.

'I met an insurance man called Tweed—'

'You met Tweed?' he interjected in surprise.

'Yes. Scotland Yard advised me to see him at Brown's Hotel.'

'Describe him.'

'I'll do my best. It's difficult to give you a picture. He's rather ordinary – or looks so, until you talk to him. I'd say he has a first-class brain . . .'

She did her best but Moloch found her description of Tweed vague. He asked her to do better but she explained again he wasn't a man you'd easily notice.

'A person you wouldn't easily notice,' he repeated. 'He sounds like a masculine version of yourself, if you don't mind my saying so.'

She did mind, but remarked that it helped in the job she had. Moloch stared at Joel, who was still standing in the room. He had returned after giving orders to the guards.

'I'll call you when I want you.' He turned his attention back to Standish.

'Tell me about your conversation with Tweed.'

He listened carefully. She had total recall and repeated every word of what had been said between herself and Tweed. The only part she left out was that she'd told Tweed that Moloch had trained as an accountant before coming to the States.

'I hope you don't mind my telling him about your

relationships with Cheryl and Julie,' she said nearing the end of her report. 'But as one of my sisters was murdered off Cornwall and Tweed is in Britain—'

'Don't mind at all,' Moloch broke in. 'I'm as anxious as you are to find and punish the killer.'

'Were you on board the *Venetia* at any time while it was anchored off Falmouth?' she asked suddenly.

'A strange question,' he responded with a bleak smile.

'I only asked you,' she went on hastily, 'because if you had been you could have told me who else was on board when my sister was murdered.'

'I take your point. I wish I could help you, but I can't. You said Tweed gave you a card with his particulars. I'd like to see that, please.'

She produced the card from her shoulder bag. Moloch looked at the front. Chief Claims Investigator. General & Cumbria Assurance. No address. Turning the card over he memorized the phone number, handed the card back to her.

'You said that he advised you if you wanted to contact him to ask for Monica if he was out. Who do you think this Monica is?'

'I suppose she serves the same role to him as Vanity Richmond does for you.'

He stared at her. She gazed back without a flicker of her eyes. He wondered if she had implied that Vanity was his mistress, in which case she was wrong. He decided she had made no such suggestion.

'So the visit to London was worth while,' he said calmly.

'I'd say it sure was. Now we know we have the police on both sides of the Atlantic working for us. I spoke to Chief Inspector Buchanan over the phone – he sounds high-ranking. And he took the trouble to put me on to Tweed who, I guess, works closely with him. That's all for the moment.'

'Thank you. Here's a percentage of the fee I promised.'

He handed her an envelope containing the money in hundred-dollar bills, stood up and walked out.

Joel reappeared to let her out. Contrasting with his normal outfit of a T-shirt and denims, he wore a smart business suit, a clean shirt and an expensive silk tie. He took hold of her arm.

'I know you don't like me . . .'

'I've never said or indicated that.'

'OK. But just remember this. Working for VB is no fun. It's a tough job I hold. I'll leave you here – the automatic front door is unlocked and so are the main gates. Drive carefully.'

Linda was off balance. She had never seen this side of Joel Brand. In a daze she continued down the long hall and Byron Landis hurried to catch up with her. He was also well-dressed, carrying an overcoat. He smiled as he came beside her and for the first time since she'd met him he struck her as pleasant, almost attractive.

'Excuse me, Linda,' he said as they continued towards the front door, 'but if you're driving back to Carmel could you take me there? My car has broken down.'

'Of course I could,' she said, after a brief hesitation.

'He just wants to save gas,' Joel's voice echoed down the hall.

She glanced over her shoulder. Brand was standing in the hall some distance back and had obviously heard every word.

'Don't judge everyone by yourself, Joel,' she joked.

Brand grinned, disappeared through a doorway. Outside the huge front door she unlocked her car, invited Landis to sit in the front passenger seat. The accountant had not taken kindly to Joel's remark – she could tell this from his stiff expression.

He soon mellowed as she drove them along the coast road, swinging round the bends with practised ease and as he began talking he became surprisingly amiable.

'There are ten thousand dollars in that envelope VB gave you. Ten per cent of the total payment if you crack the case. Must be difficult for you – trying to find out who killed your own sisters. I don't think VB should have given you the job.'

'Why not, Mr Landis?'

'Byron, please. Because there's too much emotional involvement for you. Let's talk about something else.'

'OK.'

'I need some relaxation from studying figures all day long. Some accountants say the figures talk to them. They don't say one damned thing to me. Think I chose the wrong profession. A lot of people do that. But the job pays well, so I'm stuck with it. No complaints.'

'You're married?' she enquired.

'I was. She took off with a millionaire. Wasn't just the money. He could make her laugh, amuse her. Still, I guess the money also helped. I'm not complaining. She wanted the high life, something I couldn't give her. I'm a loser. I accept that fact.'

'No, you're not, Byron.'

'I'm not a winner. That's for sure.'

'You're in the middle,' she told him. 'Not a bad place to be.'

They chatted for the rest of the drive, Byron cracked a few jokes which made her chuckle. She dropped him in the middle of Carmel.

'Have fun, Byron,' she called out.

'I intend to . . .'

Standish drove round the corner, parked. Locking her car, she hurried back to the courtyard Landis had disappeared into. Before leaving her car she had put on sunglasses, even though it was dark. She had also changed her green windcheater to a grey one she always kept in the car.

The transformation in her appearance was startling. The courtyard, one of many such maze-like areas in Carmel, was illuminated by old-fashioned lanterns. She walked across the cobbles, checking the apartments above the shops, all closed. No lights anywhere. Puzzled, she moved deeper into the yard and along a narrow alley.

She could hear modern dance music and light flooded out of a doorway at the end of the alley. Over it a flashing sign proclaimed *El Soro's*. Could Byron have possibly gone to visit a night club? she wondered. Paying the entrance fee, she wandered in, sat down on a chair behind other rows of chairs occupied by young and middle-aged couples. Often a middle-aged man sat by the side of a teenage girl. Then she stared.

Byron was on the dance floor, holding an attractive twenty-something. Fascinated, Standish watched his action, his feet moving expertly. When the music stopped briefly he switched to another girl. Standish paid the waitress for the glass of wine she had ordered. Plenty of other women were wearing sunglasses, so she didn't feel conspicuous.

She watched Byron changing partners frequently. He could dance so well he had no trouble choosing any partner. He also had great stamina, never leaving the dance floor. Standish watched for a while longer, then left.

Running back to her car, she moved it round the corner, parked it where she could watch the exit from the alley. She was interested in seeing what type Byron took away with him. She smoked a rare cigarette while she waited.

Eventually a Yellow Cab pulled up. Byron emerged alone, climbed into the cab, settled himself in the rear seat and it took off. Standish drove home to her apartment on Junipero. While she made pancakes for her meal her brain was racing.

'I thought I knew these people. Joel Brand now with his smile and friendliness. Byron Landis, the dry-as-dust accountant, so I'd thought, he goes out dancing. Really I don't know these people at all . . .'

At the end of the following day it was dark and Linda Standish was working late on her tax forms for the IRS. She hated forms and she hated tax returns, but the job had to be done. When the figures began to swim before her eyes she decided she'd get a breath of the chill night air.

She was out walking the deserted streets when a grey Audi pulled up alongside her. Vanity Richmond was behind the wheel.

'Hi!' she called out. 'How goes the grim work?'

'Grim work is what I call it.' She knew Vanity was referring to the hunt for her sisters' killers but didn't feel like talking about it. 'The IRS,' she said as Vanity climbed out of the car to chat. 'Tax returns. Stuff them. Haven't seen you recently.'

'I'm just off the flight from London. On my way to the prison and the treadmill.'

'The prison?' Linda queried.

'That's what I call Black Ridge. It's the atmosphere.'

'And the treadmill?'

'Perhaps I'm going too far.' Vanity laughed, raised a hand to push back her red mane. 'VB never stops working – like a hamster on a treadmill. Mind you, I admire his industry. I think I'd better get back. Why don't we have dinner soon? I'll give you a call . . .'

She slipped back into the Audi and roared off into the night. Vanity had high colour and despite her long flight she had seemed very alert. Linda felt she had now had a break from work and returned to her apartment.

Half an hour later, as she pored over the figures, her door from outside opened and she looked up, surprised to see who had entered.

'Hi!' she said. 'There's a pot of coffee, freshly made – pour yourself a cup and I'll be right with you.'

The visitor moved towards the stove, then suddenly slipped behind Linda. Using a razor sharp wire with wooden handles at either end the visitor whipped it round Linda's neck. Linda had no time to call out as the wire ripped through her vocal cords. She uttered a muffled gurgle as the wire was pulled tighter. Tighter. Tighter. She slumped forward over her tax forms in a pool of blood.

17

When it was 10 p.m. in California it was 6 a.m. the following morning in London. Tweed had risen from the camp bed he had slept in at his office, was showered, shaved and fully dressed when Monica arrived. She looked at the camp bed Tweed had folded up and was putting away in a cupboard.

'So it's action stations,' she observed.

Paula arrived a moment later. She observed that Tweed was freshly shaved, looked at Monica.

'He slept here all night?'

'He did.'

'May I ask why you two have arrived here so early?' asked Tweed.

'Because of that call from Jim Corcoran at Heathrow late yesterday evening,' Paula told him.

'I see.'

In response to Tweed's phoning Jim Corcoran he had heard later from the security chief at Heathrow. The call had been terse.

'Tweed? As you requested I checked the flight to San Francisco. The passenger list shows a Vanity Richmond boarded BA 287, departing here 1330, arriving San Francisco at 1625, local time. Travelled First Class. OK? I must go now . . .'

Tweed had told Paula, Monica and Newman, who had called in to see if there were any fresh developments. Paula had reacted at once.

'Is that the signal you were waiting for?'

'I'm not sure. It does mean that all the main players in this grim game have now arrived in California – including the suspects.' He counted them off on his fingers. 'First, Vincent Bernard Moloch. I suspect Joel Brand is with him – although there's no trace of him passing through Heathrow, but he could have taken a ferry to Brussels or Paris and flown on from either city.'

'Doesn't the Sabena flight from Brussels, bound for the States, stop over at Heathrow?' Paula had queried.

'It does, but if Brand was already aboard it wouldn't show up on the computer. Next, Grenville and Maurice, we know, took the flight to San Francisco earlier. Also on board was Linda Standish. Now Vanity Richmond has gone the same route, yesterday afternoon. We'll wait a little longer,' he had told them . . .

'Have you had any coffee?' Paula asked.

'No. I was just about to make it.'

'I'll attend to that,' Monica told him.

'And I'll drive to that café cab drivers use,' Paula decided. 'I'll bring us breakfast.'

'I could do with some,' said Newman who had just entered the room. 'Better get some for Marler, who is on his way.'

'How do you know that?' Tweed wanted to know.

'Because I phoned him before I left my flat. He was already up. That sudden departure of Vanity worried me, and I told Marler.'

'She hasn't treated you very well, Bob,' Paula commented. 'Dashing off to California like that and not even phoning you.'

'I agree. But she probably received an urgent message from our friend VB to return at once.'

'That's exactly what I think happened,' Tweed interjected. 'I think he's marshalling his top people for some major move. Monica, have we provisional bookings aboard the next flight to San Francisco?'

'I've been booking them every day, then transferring them to the following day.'

'Go on doing that. Alert Butler and Nield. They're to be ready for instant departure . . .'

There were two weirdly shaped high-rise buildings in the business district of San Francisco. One was the famous Trans-America building, shaped like a tall slim pyramid. The other was the AMBECO building, shaped like a giant cone, circular all the way round and tapering to a point at its summit. Both were among the marvels of the city, their exteriors often viewed by tourists.

The AMBECO building had a curious 'defect' near its topmost point. Normally invisible to the outside world, a giant alcove was cut into it, masked by a huge sliding door. Inside the alcove was a helipad with a chopper always ready to take off at a moment's notice.

Like the Trans-America pyramid, the AMBECO building was perched on massive rollers. The idea was that if an earthquake struck the city both edifices would 'roll' to counter the tremors. In his circular office near the summit – all the offices were circular – Moloch was studying the latest maps Ethan had produced for him.

He was particularly interested in one area of northern California. The phone started ringing, a low squeak.

'Yes,' he said.

'More trouble with Ethan,' Joel reported from Black Ridge. 'Mrs Benyon is ill. Ethan is insisting he has to go and see her.'

'Keep him at Black Ridge,' Moloch said instantly. 'And call my doctor. Tell him to go to Black Ridge and to wait for me. I'm on my way . . .'

Moloch dealt with every problem in this way. Decisive, he could make up his mind in seconds. He called his chief assistant, gave him a string of orders. Within five minutes he was aboard the helicopter. The giant door slid upwards, the rotors of the helicopter were whirling, the machine was slowly elevated to within yards of the lofty roof, then it moved out, flew across San Francisco to the south.

The pilot was already in touch with the control tower at the airport. Moloch had top priority for a flight. The machine proceeded south, passed over Monterey and Carmel, was soon landing on the helipad behind the grotesque mansion, Black Ridge. Joel was waiting as Moloch alighted.

'I have the car waiting. The doctor is inside with Ethan. Shall I come with you?'

'No, stay in control here. Tighten security. A major project is about to be launched.'

The stretch Lincoln Continental with amber-tinted windows was waiting for him. He got inside next to the driver, told him to drive to Mrs Benyon's home at once. Looking round he saw in the rearmost seats the doctor sitting next to Ethan, his lean face twisted with anxiety.

'There's nothing wrong with Mrs Benyon,' Moloch informed the doctor. 'She's just a psychopath, a mild case.'

'She may be very sick,' Ethan protested.

'I doubt it. The doctor will confirm . . .'

Moloch was first out of the limo when it pulled up at the top of the drive. Using his key, he walked into the living room, followed by Ethan and the doctor. In her thronelike chair Mrs Benyon sat sagged back, gripping her two sticks.

'I'm unwell,' she started in a low voice. 'The guards are frightening me.'

'The doctor is going to check you out.'

'Don't want a doctor,' Mrs Benyon protested, her voice stronger.

Moloch left Ethan and the doctor alone with Mrs Benyon. Standing in the hall out of sight, he could hear every word that was said. After fifteen minutes the doctor reappeared, closely followed by Ethan, who had a stubborn look.

'Is there somewhere we can talk quietly?' the doctor suggested.

'In here.'

Moloch took them into a large study which had a triangular-shaped fireplace. The walls were tiled with weird coloured mosaics. He closed the door.

'She's generally in good shape,' the doctor began. 'Her pulse rate is a little fast. I've given her pills for that.'

'She's frightened of the guards,' Ethan burst out. 'She feels trapped, that the walls are closing in on her.'

'That's true,' the doctor agreed. 'Psychologically, they are bad for her. They make her nervous – which probably explains the fast pulse rate. I strongly urge you to remove them.'

'They're to protect her,' Moloch argued.

'They're having the opposite effect.'

'The bloody guards have to be sent away or I'm staying with her,' Ethan burst out again.

'Then I'll remove them at once,' Moloch replied.

It was a reluctant decision, but he couldn't have Ethan

upset at this stage of the operation. He walked out of the house, ordered the guards to return immediately to Black Ridge, then was driven back to the mansion with the doctor and Ethan in the rear seat.

At the house Mrs Benyon approached the window overlooking Highway One cautiously, without the aid of sticks. She sneered to herself as she watched the limo vanish while the guards walked away down the drive.

'You're a stupid bastard, Vincent,' she said aloud. 'I'm going to ruin you.'

She went to a drawer, took out the pills she had used to increase her pulse rate, threw them on the blazing log fire. A sea mist was floating in from the Pacific, the temperature had dropped and she felt cold.

'I need someone I can tell things to,' she said, again aloud.

At Park Crescent there was a tense waiting period. Such pauses always tested nerves. Marler was standing against a wall, thinking as he smoked another king-size. Newman recrossed his legs in the armchair, trying to concentrate on reading a newspaper. Tweed seemed most at ease, reading again a report Professor Weatherby had sent by special messenger on notes he had just found in an old file, notes made by Ethan.

'I was just thinking of Cornwall,' Paula said to break the heavy silence. 'Most people who go on holiday walk along the rugged cliff-tops, which are magnificent. Or spend their time sitting in the beautiful coves. But these are the fringes of Cornwall. When you get inland it's a grim desert, a wilderness.'

'True,' said Tweed automatically.

'I went into Falmouth,' Paula continued. 'It's built in a kind of valley. Up the steep sides as you enter there are row upon row of terraced houses piled up at different levels. I noticed some strange types in the streets – rather primitive. More like a backward tribe.'

'They're from the remote villages outside,' Newman said, not looking up from his paper. 'I suspect in a few of those villages families interbreed.'

'Cornwall does go back centuries,' Paula agreed. 'But for a holiday the coast and the quaint villages by the sea are wonderful. I think . . .'

It was noon when she was interrupted by the phone call from Langley. Monica immediately transferred the call to Tweed.

'Cord here,' Dillon opened, 'we have another murder. This time in the middle of Carmel. Woman called Linda Standish. Garrotted. Head almost torn off her neck. A private dick. I'm in contact with the local police and they called me.'

'Any idea when the murder took place?' Tweed enquired.

'I got the Medical Examiner out of bed – pathologist to you – and he estimates between 9 p.m. and 11 p.m., California time. He said he had to wait for the autopsy, but if he had to guess, about 10 p.m. It's our serial killer, The Accountant, again.'

'You're sure?'

'Well, the victim had the letters AC painted on her bare back in her own blood. That's it.'

'That's enough. Thanks, Cord.'

Tweed told his team what had happened. No one said anything – they were waiting for Tweed to continue, which he did.

'We just have time to board the flight for San Francisco. Monica, phone British Airways. Confirm all our seats. We're leaving now.'

'Trouble is we arrive there unarmed,' Newman remarked.

'I'll fix that within a couple of hours of getting there,'

Marler said. 'Weapons are easy to obtain in the States. Too easy. But I have a contact in San Francisco who can supply guns that the police can never trace. That will be my first port of call.'

'Our first port of call is Heathrow,' Tweed told them as he fetched his suitcase from a cupboard. 'The battle has started . . .'

Luis Martinez had earlier become bored watching Park Crescent from his parked car. Now he was excited. People were arriving very early at the same building. First, a cleaning woman, well dressed. He had seen Monica.

A dark-haired woman with glossy hair arrived next. Martinez had no idea his field glasses were focused on Paula, but he thought the human scenery was improving no end. Then he hit the jackpot – he immediately recognized Newman from the photos by his side.

Later a slim man wearing a linen suit walked into the same building. Martinez had no idea he was looking at Marler, but the number of people arriving so early told him he had hit the target. Newman's arrival confirmed he was in the right place. He settled down to wait, keeping a close eye on the Merc. Newman had driven up in, now parked by the kerb.

Butler and Nield arrived in Tweed's office soon after Marler. Tweed told them briefly that The Accountant had killed again, that this time the victim was Linda Standish.

'The sooner we track down this serial killer the better,' he remarked. 'He is obviously a skilled operator.'

'He?' Paula queried. 'Why does everyone assume it is a man? Why not a woman?'

There was silence in the room. Tweed looked thoughtful as Paula went on.

'You're all hooked on the idea that it is a man who can charm women. But a lot of women make friends with other women – or even talk to a strange one. The victims would all have been off guard with a woman.'

'You've got a point,' Newman agreed.

'We're leaving now,' Tweed snapped. 'Or we miss the plane. We'll take your Merc., Bob. Paula, Marler and I will go with you. Harry, you take the Ford Fiesta and bring Pete with you. Monica, warn Cord Dillon which flight we're coming on. You know the hotel in San Francisco where we're staying so . . .'

'I should do. I've just reserved rooms for all of you.'

'I meant to say contact me there with any development here. Tell Howard where we've gone, but don't tell Roy Buchanan – unless an emergency arises. Well, everyone, what are you waiting for?'

Monica wished them luck. She watched them leave, full of foreboding.

With Newman behind the wheel they made good time to the airport. Tweed sat beside him while Paula travelled with Marler in the back, and behind them Butler followed, driving with equal skill. They were close to Heathrow when Newman spoke.

'We've been followed all the way from Park Crescent.'

'I know,' said Tweed, who had glanced frequently in the wing mirror. 'He's been watching the office for days in a parked car. He changes his clothes. Today he's wearing a cap. But he always sits behind the wheel of his car in a certain way.'

'Doesn't that mean Moloch will know we're coming?' Paula asked anxiously.

'I hope so.' Tweed sounded cheerful. 'I want him to know I'm on my way. Rattle his cage a bit more.'

'He could have a reception committee waiting for us when we arrive at San Francisco,' Newman warned.

'I've taken out insurance against that happening. Stop worrying. It's battle stations from now on,' he said with enthusiasm. 'Makes a change from being trapped behind my desk. And here is Heathrow.'

They parked the cars in 'Long Stay' and just managed to catch the plane in time. Tweed gave Paula the window seat in First Class while the others were scattered about in Club. Paula gazed out of the window after it had taken off. She caught a glimpse of the curving Thames and then they were heading due north across the middle of England.

'I wonder if I'll ever see this again,' she said to herself.

18

Martinez had watched them as they checked in their luggage. He had no idea that they were aware of his presence. The moment they disappeared through the Fast Track he called Moloch.

'Luis here. They have boarded Flight BA 287 for San Francisco. It arrives there 4.25 p.m., California time.'

'Who are they?' Moloch enquired from his small office at Black Ridge.

'Newman for one. There were five others, including a woman. The rest were men.'

'Give me descriptions.'

'Well . . .' Martinez paused – he was not good on description. 'There was a man smaller than Newman, well-built, he wore horn-rimmed glasses.'

For a moment Moloch thought he was describing Tweed, but Linda Standish had not mentioned horn-rimmed glasses. Had she left out this important item for some reason?

'Describe the woman,' Moloch urged.

'A sexy piece. Dark hair. That's all I can say about her. Oh, she had good legs.'

'We'll recognize her at once,' Moloch said ironically. 'I want you to catch tomorrow's flight to San Francisco – then proceed straight here to Black Ridge. Thank you for calling me . . .'

He repeated the conversation to Joel Brand, sitting upright in the chair opposite him. Brand's reaction was swift and typical.

'We could take out the lot soon after they leave the airport. I'll organize—'

'You'll do nothing of the sort,' Moloch snapped. 'You can have them followed so we know what they're up to. But your idea is insane. You don't know who you're dealing with.'

'I can deal with anyone,' Brand said impetuously, 'run any organization.'

'Such as AMBECO?' Moloch enquired softly.

His pale eyes stared at Brand's, who dropped his gaze. It always worried him when Moloch looked at him like that. He realized he had blundered badly.

'Of course not,' he said quickly. 'It would be far too big a job for me.'

'Don't forget that, Joel. Now, arrange to have our visitors followed. And try, for once, to use some discretion . . .'

Brand was fuming as he left the office. He had his own way of dealing with the opposition. Sitting down behind his huge desk in his own spacious office, he put a silk handkerchief over the phone. Checking a number, he dialled and asked to be put through to the Chief of Customs at San Francisco International.

'Your name,' a rough voice demanded.

'You don't need that. This is a tip off . . .'

'Give me your name . . .'

'I have info from London. Flight BA 287 coming in this afternoon. Two guys called Tweed and Newman. They're carrying a big dope haul. Heroin . . .'

He rang off before anything more could be said. Then he lit a large cigar, feeling very pleased with himself. Moloch wasn't tough enough to run this outfit. He finished his cigar while he thought out his next move.

He next called the AMBECO building in San Francisco. He told the operator who he was, told her to put him through to Gary Kaplan.

'Gary, this is Joel. Get together a tough team of seven men. Dress them in business suits so they don't look conspicuous. Hold them at the building till I arrive. I'm flying there. Got it? You better had . . .'

Stubbing out his cigar, he left the mansion after calling to the pilot to be ready to fly him to the AMBECO building. The rotors were whirling as he climbed aboard the chopper sitting on the helipad behind the mansion.

California hit Tweed soon after the plane had landed. He had arrived at Customs to be confronted by an American built like a quarterback. The big man spread his huge hands on the counter and stared without speaking for awhile. Then he spoke, his manner aggressive.

'I've been waiting for you, Mr Tweed – and for you, Newman. Unlock your bags.'

'They are unlocked.'

'OK. So first I'll go through your bags, then you'll be strip-searched. Behind screens, of course,' he rasped unpleasantly. 'Maybe you've brought something nasty into the US of A.'

'I'd like to speak to the Chief Customs Officer.'

'You're looking at him, buddy.'

Newman noticed a small, heavily built man with black hair brushed over his high forehead and an olive skin who was pushing his way past the passengers leaving Customs. The small man had twinkling dark eyes. He reached the counter where Tweed was standing. Producing a small folder, he thrust it forward. It looked to Newman like a familiar identity card.

'David Alvarez,' he said, looking at the Customs man. 'I'm from Washington. Leave the next seven passengers alone – including the lady.'

'What the hell—' the Customs man began.

'Look at my folder, you big ape. Want me to report your insulting behaviour to distinguished visitors? Report it to Washington?'

The Customs man looked at the folder. His whole manner changed. He became apologetic, almost fawning. Alvarez dismissed his words with a glare, then turned to Tweed.

'Please follow me with your bags. And your friends should also come with me. I am sorry you were treated in such a manner. Someone obviously gave Customs a fake tip off that you were carrying drugs or something. Who knows?'

In the concourse he showed his folder to Tweed and Newman. It gave his name, photograph and other information.

'CIA,' Newman said quietly.

'Yes, but documents can be faked. There's a phone over there where you can call Cord Dillon.'

'I don't think that will be necessary,' Tweed decided. 'We have the cooperation of the San Francisco Police

205

Department,' said Alvarez. 'Police cars are waiting outside to take you to your hotel. I hope you won't mind the screaming sirens, the flashing lights. They will avoid your being tailed to your hotel – the cars will take a roundabout route.'

'You seem to have everything well organized. How do you know which hotel we're staying at?' Tweed asked.

'A lady from your London office spoke to Mr Dillon, who asked her . . .'

Tweed had already realized that, although he spoke perfect English, Alvarez was Spanish – which was obvious from his name and the olive-coloured skin. He liked the man immediately.

They were being escorted to the exit when Tweed noticed several men in business suits grappling with uniformed police. The businessmen were being handcuffed, taken away, and handled none too gently. He nodded his head towards the commotion.

'What's going on over there?'

'We've had the AMBECO building under surveillance. Several known tough characters came out of it, got into cars, drove here. We think they had hostile intentions where you were concerned. We've had them arrested.' He smiled in an engaging way. 'We'll think up some charges to hold them on. They have bad records . . .'

The journey from the airport, a thirty-minute drive to the city, was a nightmare for Paula, who was suffering from jet lag. The police car she was travelling in with Tweed kept its hideous siren screaming nonstop and the flashing lights on the roof bothered her eyes. The driving was pretty hectic, the car swinging round bends at top speed, jerking to a halt suddenly as they reached an intersection where a truck was crossing.

'This isn't Spanish Bay,' she said to herself, recalling

the hotel outside Monterey where she had stayed on her previous trip. 'If this is the real America it's hell . . .'

Alvarez sat in front of Tweed, next to the police driver. Behind them in another police car, siren also screaming, lights flashing, Newman, Marler, Butler and Nield were crammed. Their luggage followed in a third police car.

The momentum was maintained as they entered the city, zigzagging across it so far as Tweed could tell. Alvarez glanced back at Paula and smiled.

'Impressed?'

'Very impressed,' she managed to shout.

Eventually they climbed one of the many steep streets, stopped at the summit outside their hotel. Alvarez hustled them inside, saying he'd take care of their bags. They registered, he escorted them to their rooms, told Tweed he would be staying too and gave his room number.

'Alone at last,' Paula said and sank on to the edge of the bed.

'At least it's a pretty luxurious room,' Tweed remarked as he poured her a glass of water. 'Don't drink it all at once. Half a glass, then the rest later.'

'Thank you.' She did as she was told. 'Welcome to the USA. That business at the airport with that brute of a Customs man. Who do you think was responsible? Moloch?'

'Perhaps.'

'What do you mean?'

'Didn't seem like his style. I'm beginning to get to know that man.'

'Isn't this the hotel where there's a fantastic view from the roof?'

'It is. Drink some more water. Then I'll refill your glass.'

After two glasses of water Paula began to feel better. Her cases had already been brought to the large room before their arrival. At least American staff were efficient. A large bottle of champagne poked its top out of a silver ice bucket. Intrigued, she went across, read the card. *From David A. Have a great time.*

'It's from Alvarez,' she said. 'I do like him.'

'He's a nice chap – and a real professional,' Tweed agreed.

'I'd like to go up to the roof to see the view. Give me ten minutes to clean up. Don't leave the room.'

An unusual request for Paula to make, Tweed reflected when she had closed the bathroom door, carrying new clothes she had swiftly extracted from one of her cases. Jet lag – plus the scene at the airport and the mad drive – had shaken her.

Tweed could have done with a bath himself, but he had freshened himself up during the long eleven-hour flight.

Paula came out of the bathroom in less than ten minutes. She had a new outfit on, had applied fresh make-up and looked a whole lot better. Most women would have taken half an hour, Tweed thought. He had heard the shower running.

'Ready for duty, sir. For the roof view.'

She gave a little curtsey. Her powers of recuperation were remarkable. There was a tapping on the door and Tweed opened it cautiously. Newman, in a new suit, stood outside with Marler behind him.

'Come in,' Tweed invited.

'How are you, Paula, now?' Marler enquired.

'We're going up to the roof to see this famous view. See if it's as good as it's cracked up to be.'

'We'll come with you,' Newman said.

The rooftop area was empty and they had the place to themselves, which surprised Tweed. A moment later Alvarez appeared beside him, as if by magic. He was holding a small pair of field glasses.

'We get the best view from over here,' the American said. 'Really knocks you out.'

'Your English is very English, if you see what I mean,' Tweed told him. 'You even have the phrases.'

'Should have. I worked for two years at the London station. Had a ball in Britain. Everyone is so polite. There it is, the fabulous AMBECO building.'

Paula almost gasped. The view was panoramic. She gazed at the world-famous Golden Gate Bridge, spanning the entrance from the sea into the bay. She pointed it out to Alvarez.

He focused his high-power glasses, handed them to Paula and said, 'Look at the AMBECO building. There's an office near the summit. The window's open. A man is working at a desk. Can you see him?'

She found the window quickly. It seemed to come up and hit her. Inside she saw the man in his rolled-up shirtsleeves, his large head bent over papers. He seemed to be studying them with great concentration. She avoided letting out a gasp of surprise.

'That's Joel Brand,' she said.

'The lady wins the jackpot.'

Paula's mind had flashed back to the firefight at Mullion Towers in faraway Cornwall. The man she was looking at had led the team they had tangled with after scrambling over the wall surrounding Moloch's mansion.

She handed the glasses to Tweed. He studied the man behind the desk, memorizing his appearance. It was the first time he had seen this man who sat at Moloch's right hand. He passed on the glasses to Newman.

'Works hard,' was Tweed's only comment.

'You have to if you're employed by Moloch. Rumour has it that Moloch himself gets by on four hours' sleep a night – he works like a man obsessed.'

'Obsessed people are dangerous. I understand he has

a stepmother, a Mrs Benyon. You may not know anything about her.'

'I know everything about VB that it's possible to know,' Alvarez replied. 'Mrs Benyon moved recently to a house called The Apex. I can show you where it is on a map if you wish to visit her. The place is near Big Sur – and near Black Ridge, VB's headquarters outside the city. You can't miss Black Ridge . . .'

Alvarez took a map of northern California from his pocket, marked clearly the positions of the two houses with a cross, handed it to Tweed, who thanked him.

'Strange we have the roof to ourselves,' Tweed remarked.

'There is a big convention in town – many guests will be there.'

'If that's Joel Brand,' Newman said grimly, peering through the glasses, 'I'd like to meet him some time.'

'Have a care,' said Alvarez, using one of the quaint English phrases he had picked up. 'He's tough.' He looked at Newman. 'But then you look pretty tough – you have to be to survive some of the outlandish places you've been to. I was an avid reader of your articles when you were writing them.'

The phone on the table rang. Alvarez picked it up, spoke a few words, turned to Tweed.

'It's for you. Someone called Monica.'

'Tweed here.'

'I know you're at a hotel.' Monica paused and Tweed knew she was going to code whatever she had to tell him.

'That ship is still standing off the coast over here. I phoned my friend and he said it had reported that in due course it was bound for a cruise in the eastern Mediterranean. I'd like to be on it. It may even cruise off the Lebanon. Who knows? I'd better book my ticket.'

'Do that,' Tweed replied. 'The weather over here is like it is there. Very hot.'

'Not like here any more. The heatwave broke a few hours after you left. It's raining. Enjoy your holiday . . .'

Tweed immediately translated what Monica had reported to him – that the *Venetia* was standing by for a trip to the Lebanon.

'The Arab connection,' Alvarez said quietly. 'That is what Washington fears most. Moloch has a palatial house up in the mountains behind Beirut.'

'The escape route after the event,' Tweed replied.

'What event?'

'I hope to Heaven I'm wrong, so I won't talk about it now. What I think everyone would like is dinner.'

'I'll be in the dining room,' Alvarez assured him. 'But you probably won't see me.'

'If I want to visit Mrs Benyon I suppose I should phone to make an appointment?'

'Not necessary. She's always there. Just drop in on her, take her by surprise.'

'And on the way I'd like to look at the apartment where Linda Standish was murdered. I met her in London. Could that be arranged?'

'Easily. I know the detective from police headquarters down there who is in charge of the case. Guy called Jeff Anderson. Want to see him tomorrow? If so, what time?'

'It's a two-hour drive from here, I understand. Do you think he could meet me at 12.30 p.m.? I have the address and know where the apartment is. You'll have to find out if it's convenient to Anderson.'

'I'll make it convenient . . .'

Marler did not attend the dinner in the restaurant. He had disappeared after a word with Newman. When he returned to the hotel he was carrying a large holdall. He found Tweed's team, including Butler and Nield, sitting in the spacious room occupied by Paula.

She had slept for two hours after dinner and by midnight she was lively and fresh. She was sitting by a partly opened window when Newman let in Marler, carrying his heavy holdall. She was surprised at how alert Marler looked.

'Have you had anything to eat?' she asked.

'I had a bite or two at an all-night place. I've been to see an arms dealer – got his name long ago from someone I know in Strasbourg . . .'

He broke off as there was another tapping on the door and he shoved the holdall in a cupboard containing Paula's clothes. Newman opened the door and Alvarez walked in, gave everybody a smile showing his gleaming teeth. He was holding an envelope. He looked at Marler.

'Just returned from police headquarters. I've got papers for your armoury. Had to pull rank.'

'Armoury?' Paula queried.

Marler retrieved his holdall, took out a .32 Browning automatic, which he handed to Paula. Alvarez watched, gave her a sheet of paper from his envelope.

'That entitles you to carry the weapon, plus the extra ammo Marler has given you.'

Next Marler produced two Walther P38 automatics with magazines, handed one each to Butler and Nield. Alvarez gave them papers. Newman was glad to see a .38 Smith & Wesson, his favourite weapon, which Marler handed him as Alvarez gave him his sheet of paper. Paula was puzzled by the link-up between the two men.

'When was all this arranged?' she enquired.

'While you were going into dinner,' Alvarez told her. 'Marler gave me a list of weapons needed. While he obtained them I chased over to police HQ to get the permits.' He looked at Tweed. 'You weren't included on the list.'

'I never carry a gun.'

'Marler,' Alvarez went on, 'here's your paper for your own weapon. You must be a marksman.'

'The best in Western Europe,' Tweed told him.

'And, Marler,' Alvarez went on with his smile, 'have you got anything in that bag which you haven't shown me?'

'You said we were up against a tough mob.'

'The toughest.'

'Then you don't need to know what else I've got.'

'OK. You're responsible people. I'm going now but I'll have men patrolling this corridor outside all night long. We changed your reservations so you'd all be on the same floor. The management have been informed you are important people, that the orders come from Washington. Good night to all of you. Sleep well . . .'

When he had gone and the door was locked Marler dived again into his holdall. He brought out grenades, handed two to Paula and more to the others.

'Stun grenades?' Paula enquired.

'No, explosive grenades. You heard what Alvarez said – we are up against the toughest. And you all get smoke grenades. I like them.'

Finally, he brought out his own familiar weapon, a dismantled Armalite rifle with a sniperscope. He stroked it and drawled, 'Can't go far wrong with this.'

'And,' Newman interjected, 'I've hired two cars. A Mercedes and a BMW.'

'You don't worry about the expense, do you?' Tweed chaffed him.

'This is America,' Newman reminded him. 'Image is everything.'

'Then I think we all should get some sleep,' Tweed announced, heading for the door. 'Tomorrow we move into enemy territory.'

19

During the night Alvarez had summoned certain expert technicians. With Newman's earlier consent they had worked all night on the Mercedes and the BMW in a sealed-off underground garage. By midmorning the two cars and their occupants were close to Monterey.

Earlier, as they drove along the coast road south from San Francisco, Tweed realized he had forgotten how scenic the journey was. To their right, on a brilliantly sunny morning, a calm Pacific sparkled like mercury, reflecting the sunlight. They passed deserted beaches and small capes.

To their left rose a shallow slope with only here and there a wooden cabin which was someone's home. Apart from these occasional buildings there were no signs of habitation. In a lay-by Newman demonstrated the technical work added to the Merc. at Alvarez's suggestion.

Tweed stood with Paula while Newman pressed buttons in a neat black box attached to the dashboard. Two large aerials emerged from the roof, then splayed out at their summits a neat spider's web of wires. He pressed another button and a small cylinder appeared from a squat box on the roof. They had just got back in the car when a raucous horn began to shriek, on-off-on-off. It resembled a police car siren. Paula clapped her hands to her ears and Newman switched it off.

'What's all that about?' asked Tweed.

'Yes, what's going on?' Paula called out from the back seat.

She sat next to Marler, who had assembled his Armalite and laid it on the floor with the sniperscope attached.

They were driving along the freeway again as Newman explained.

'See the microphone hidden under the dashboard? With that I can communicate not only with Alvarez – but the same message goes straight through to Cord Dillon at Langley. It's one of the most powerful transmitters in the world – through that aerial which I withdrew after elevating it. The siren is psychological, liable to attract any police car within miles. Incidentally, any request for help I send is sent out over another waveband – the one used by police cars.'

'Alvarez is taking no chances,' Tweed observed. 'I hadn't noticed any of this equipment on the roof.'

'You weren't supposed to.'

'I see Butler and Nield are keeping close behind us,' remarked Tweed after a glance in the wing mirror.

'That's the idea. And now we are approaching a large town.'

'It's Monterey. I remember the route to Junipero in Carmel. Follow my directions from now on . . .'

Newman, knowing Tweed had a photographic memory for locations, did exactly as he was told. They passed through long stretches of pine forest, bypassing most of Monterey, then entered Carmel. Tweed gave another instruction.

'Carmel, like so many American towns, is built on the grid system,' he remarked. 'Avenues run down to the sea, streets cross them at right angles. We're on Junipero. Park where you can.'

He took out Alvarez's map to check further. Getting out of the car, he was followed by Paula who asked if she could come with him to the Standish apartment.

'Yes. You might be useful. A woman can tell a lot about another woman's living quarters.'

'This is an interesting town,' she said. 'What a lot of art and curio shops.'

'The place lives off them.'

Tweed soon found the entrance to the small courtyard where Linda Standish had lived. It was hidden away, a narrow entrance leading to a wider cobbled yard surrounded by two-storey buildings. Built mostly of wood, they looked old and each one was in a different architectural style. Paula detected Spanish influence in the railed balconies on the first floors. Hanging baskets of flowers were everywhere.

They were early but a stocky man in a pale lightweight suit came forward to meet them. He had a clean-shaven face, his hair was trimmed short and he looked to be in his thirties. He had a stern expression.

'Who are you?' he demanded.

'I might ask you the same question,' Tweed responded sharply.

'Detective Jeff Anderson.'

'Hello, I'm Tweed. Do you mind if my assistant, Paula, comes with me to the Standish apartment?'

'Not at all.' Anderson cast an admiring glance at Paula without a trace of forwardness. 'Can I see some identification?' he asked.

Tweed produced his passport. Anderson examined it carefully, then returned it. His manner mellowed.

'Welcome to Carmel. Although this is not a pleasant introduction.'

'I've been here before. Can we see Linda Standish's apartment?'

'This way . . .'

Anderson led them across to a corner of the courtyard. He was climbing a staircase with wrought-iron railings when Paula called up to him.

'Excuse me. But is this courtyard well illuminated at night?'

'No. Just by those lanterns you see.'

They had ducked under a tape barring off the staircase and a uniformed policeman stood at the entrance to an alley where he could watch. His gun butt protruded from a leather holster. Anderson opened the studded wooden door with a key, led them inside.

The apartment consisted of one large room with a desk and a chair. There were bloodstains on the chair and on the floor behind it. Anderson pointed to the chair, to papers scattered across the table, also showing signs of dried bloodstains.

'We reckon she was working on her IRS returns when she was garrotted from behind.'

'Was the door open?' asked Tweed.

'Yes it was.'

'And you think she was sitting in the chair when the murder took place?'

'She sure was.'

'Then that suggests she knew her killer. Otherwise she'd have stood up if a stranger had entered. She was a private investigator – had she a weapon?'

'Yes. A Colt, loaded, in that drawer to her right.'

'Again it suggests someone she knew, someone she had no reason to fear when the visitor entered. Look at the distance from the door to her desk. And I noticed the door has a loud squeak when you opened it. She had plenty of time to get the gun out – unless she knew her killer and had no reason to fear him.'

'Or her?' Paula suggested.

Anderson stared at Tweed. He rocked backwards and forwards on his heels.

'Who are you? They said you were insurance. You talk like a policeman – the shrewd questions you asked.'

'He was once the youngest superintendent in Homicide at Scotland Yard,' Paula said quietly.

'That explains it. Now, to get back to business. As you

217

see, all the drawers have been pulled out and emptied on the floor. Except for the drawer with the gun. I guess that he decided to leave that alone.'

'Or she did,' Paula insisted.

'We're talking about a serial killer called The Accountant,' Anderson said bluntly.

'I know we are,' Paula snapped back. 'And in Europe there have been several cases of professional women assassins operating successfully. You think America is some special place?'

'I suppose you could be right,' Anderson said doubtfully.

'This place is a wreck,' Tweed observed. 'Obviously the killer was searching frantically for something, maybe for some clue which pointed in his – or her – direction.'

'We thought that. Every piece of paper has been examined. I guess he found what he was looking for.'

'I wonder,' Paula said.

She looked round carefully. Where would a woman hide something she didn't want found? she was thinking. Where would I have hidden it? There was something in her manner which made Anderson keep quiet as he watched her. She stood in the same spot, slowly gazing at every item of furniture.

Then she walked forward to a very tall filing cabinet where the drawers had been burst open. Going up on tiptoe, she felt with her hands along the dusty top of the cabinet. Her fingers contacted a folder. She eased it forward, lifted it down, opened it. There was a sheet of paper inside with names listed in neat handwriting. It was headed *Suspects*.

After glancing at it, she handed the sheet to Tweed. Anderson peered over his shoulder at the names.

Vincent Bernard Moloch. Joel Brand. Luis Martinez. Byron Landis. Vanity Richmond.

'You men didn't find this,' Tweed said, handing the sheet to Anderson.

'No, they damned well didn't.' He looked at Paula. 'Sorry if I was a bit rough with you.'

'Think nothing of it.'

'I'm pretty sure the killer is on that list,' Tweed observed. 'I gathered from Linda Standish in London that she'd been on the case for a while.'

He stopped speaking as the uniformed policeman from the alley came into the room. He spoke respectfully to Anderson.

'Sorry to interrupt you, but there's a guy who tried to get under the tape and come up the staircase. He's waiting in the courtyard. Wouldn't give me a name.'

'Send him up – after you've checked him for weapons.'

A minute later a bald man with steel-rimmed glasses entered the room. He stared at the three people who were looking back at him.

'I'm Byron Landis,' he said. 'What the hell goes on here?'

'Please sit down, Mr Landis,' Anderson said with exaggerated politeness. 'I'm Detective Anderson.'

'Detective? Where is Ms Standish?' he asked as he sat down.

'In the morgue,' Anderson threw at him.

Watching him, Paula saw no change of expression on Landis's face at the news. But that could be put down to shock.

'What do you mean?' he said eventually.

'I mean,' Anderson said, leaning over him, 'that someone came to her office in the evening and damned near sliced her head off with a garrotte. You knew her?'

'Slightly.'

'So slightly you called on her now? She was your girl friend,' he hammered away, making it a statement.

'She was not,' Landis protested, his manner tougher now. 'That's an outrageous suggestion. I resent it.'

'He resents it,' Anderson sneered, addressing Tweed. 'So maybe I ought to apologize to him.' He put his face close to Landis's. 'And yet you were both seen two nights ago at a nearby discotheque. We have witnesses. You're lying.'

'I was at a disco,' Landis admitted, 'two nights ago. But I was not with Linda . . .'

'So, it's Linda now, is it? On intimate terms with Linda, were we?'

'I've just told you I wasn't,' snapped Landis, who had now recovered his poise. 'And I'd appreciate your moving your face away from mine . . .'

'It will be a pleasure. You've got bad breath. Oh, by the way, where were you two days ago? In the early evening?'

'Doing my job at Black Ridge.'

At the mention of Black Ridge, Anderson's attitude changed. He became quieter, stood well away from Landis, staring down at him.

'Have you some identification?'

'Driving licence.'

Landis slapped it down on the desk. He saw the red stains. His manner had become aggressive.

'What are those red marks?'

'Bloodstains.'

Landis hastily removed his licence, which was resting on one of them, and placed it on a part of the desk without any stains. Anderson examined it, handed it back.

'I may want to interview you again, Mr Landis.'

'You know where to find me.' He looked at Tweed

and Paula as he stood up. 'I don't know who you are but you saw what I was put through. I'm leaving now. Anderson, you said your name was,' he ended, looking at the detective before leaving.

When they were alone Paula stared round again at the cheap furnishings. She supposed private investigators didn't have the money to make the room more comfortable.

'What a place to die in,' she said. 'And so horribly. The poor woman.'

'It happens.' Anderson was all business. 'Mr Tweed, normally I'd have had an assistant to witness what was said. I hope you're not thinking of leaving the States for a while – I might need both of you for back-up. Where are you staying?'

'The Spanish Bay Hotel,' Tweed answered promptly. 'Give me your particulars in case I want to get in touch with you.'

He took the card Anderson produced from his wallet, slipped it inside his own.

'We have to go now,' he said firmly. 'Another appointment.'

Saying which, he departed with Paula. They were approaching the car when Paula made her remarks.

'Anderson never thanked me for finding that list, which could be vital in his investigation. And did you notice how Byron Landis walks? He has a duck-waddle.'

'Yes, I did notice . . .' Tweed seemed sunk in thought. Then he stopped. Paula glanced at him, saw a certain expression on his face.

'What's the matter?' she asked as Newman got out of the nearby Merc.

'Quack. Quack. Those were the words the Standish sister who was dragged from the sea in Cornwall used. I know now what she meant. I was right, Heaven help us. A cauldron of monstrous magnitude is about to explode.

We must hurry and interview Mrs Benyon. She might be able to tell us something . . .'

With the BMW behind them, Newman drove beyond Carmel along the most magnificent coastal road in the world. Highway One followed the very brink of the Pacific, perched about a hundred or two feet above it. Paula gazed, fascinated by the serene ocean on their right, the high near mountain-like hills climbing steeply to her left.

As they proceeded south the highway swung round curving bends, some of them right-angled, some with steel barriers to protect motorists from going over the edge, some without any barriers at all. Newman estimated they were now about five hundred feet above the ocean. Some drop if they went over.

'This is spectacular,' Paula enthused. 'I've never seen anything like it.'

'I remember it from a visit a few years ago,' said Tweed. 'I agree it's unique. And we have it all to ourselves.'

Which was true. To Paula's surprise they had encountered hardly any other traffic in either direction. Ahead and below them a series of deserted coves with beaches were tucked under the cliffs. No sign of anyone.

She switched her gaze from the ocean sparkling in the sun out of a clear sky to the hills dropping almost precipitously above the highway. Rounded hill after rounded hill rolled away into the distance. Bleached by the sun, they had a piebald appearance.

Here and there she caught sight of a strange isolated house clinging to the hillside high up. She found the architecture weird. Every form of contorted shape seemed to have been used to make an expensive-looking dwelling unique. Roofs dropped at a sheer angle above spacious terraces built of stone. Tweed saw her looking up.

'Millionaire stuff,' he remarked. 'Each one trying to outdo the other. An American characteristic. If you've got the dollars, then show them. Look at that one near the summit – it has copper-sheathed chimneys.'

'And a huge swimming pool.'

'Oh, yes. Always a swimming pool, often of marble and with a fantastic shape. I've been phoned by people out here who start with, "I'm calling from poolside." Just like Hollywood. Money doesn't roar out here – it bellows at the top of its voice . . .'

They drove on and Tweed suddenly leaned forward in his seat. Swinging round yet another curve, the highway began to descend. Below them in the distance was a giant bridge with an immense rainbow-shaped arch just below the highway which crossed it. He called out to Paula, sitting in the back next to Marler.

'There's the famous Bixby Bridge. If I remember correctly it's over two hundred and fifty feet above the creek which flows out under it into the ocean.'

'I've seen lots of photos of it,' Paula replied. 'Exciting to actually cross it . . .'

The highway dropped and dropped, Newman skilfully swung the car round more curves, then the road was level. As they crossed the vast structure the wheels were thumping.

'They've put struts of some material across the road over this bridge,' Newman explained, 'to slow down motorists . . .'

They drove on and the scenery grew more hypnotic. Paula kept turning her gaze from the ranges of hills sweeping down to the Pacific to the coast of rugged capes, the sea throwing up surf as it hit great rocks. She checked the map, remembering she was supposed to be navigator.

223

'We're approaching Big Sur,' Tweed warned.

'Mrs Benyon's house, The Apex, is marked as being close to it. What's that old house perched above the ocean on our right? Looks triangular. Could that be it? Alvarez has marked it as somewhere near here,' said Paula.

'And what's that huge crazy mansion of black stone near the top of the mountain on the other side?' Newman asked.

'I'd say that's Black Ridge,' Tweed said grimly.

'That's really weird,' commented Paula. 'All on its own and with a black stone wall which appears to run all the way round it.'

'Mullion Towers in California,' Newman commented.

'And look at the Gothic chimneys and then that enormous picture window on the first floor. It's a caricature of architecture,' Paula exclaimed.

'What isn't round here?' Marler drawled.

'I think this is The Apex, Bob,' Paula called out quickly. 'Yes, it is. Rather a crude wooden sign at the entrance to the drive.'

'Take us up that mountain slope,' Tweed ordered. 'I wonder what Mrs Benyon will have to tell me?'

20

Tweed pressed the bell beside the strange front door, pointed out to Paula the peculiar cabbalistic signs on the paving stones which formed the terrace. 'We've got a real nutter here,' he said to himself. He had decided to bring Paula, who might help to reassure the occupant.

Pressing the doorbell caused cathedral-like bells to peal continuously inside the house. While he waited Paula took a pair of small field glasses from her shoulder bag. She focused them on a large ship motionless about half a mile off the coast.

'Take a look,' she invited.

'The *Baja California V*,' said Tweed, reading the name of the vessel. 'Looks like some sort of large dredger.'

From the far side of the door he heard three locks being opened, followed by the removal of two chains. He lifted his eyebrows at Paula and the door swung inwards. Framed in it was the grossest woman he had ever met. Small, her grey hair tied back in an old-fashioned bun, she was immensely fat, in her early seventies he guessed, and wore a purple dress which had a high collar and draped to her ankles. A jewelled brooch with a strange sign held her collar together.

She had heavy jowls and above a strong nose two dark eyes peered at him. He detected intelligence in them. In each hand she was carrying a walking stick.

'My name is Tweed. I'm English.' He took a chance. 'I've reason to believe your son, Ethan, is in danger.'

'Come in, both of you. I've just made some lemon tea. And I am British. You look like a high-ranking policeman.'

'This is Paula,' Tweed introduced her. 'My assistant.'

He ignored her reference to his being a policeman. The idea seemed to please her. They waited in a curving hall while she relocked the door and refastened the chains.

'My stepson, Vincent Moloch, has somehow obtained a key to my door,' she explained. 'I had a locksmith come from Carmel to secure the door against him. Follow me,' she commanded.

They walked behind her as she proceeded, tapping her sticks. In a large sitting room she sagged into a thronelike chair. With her sticks she indicated two chairs which Tweed and Paula occupied. On a table by her side was a silver pot and one Meissen cup.

'If you would like tea,' she suggested to Paula, 'perhaps you would fetch cups from the kitchen . . .'

'Thank you, but not for me,' Tweed said hastily.

'And I'm not thirsty,' Paula added.

'While I remember,' Tweed said easily, 'that big ship out at sea, the *Baja California* . . .'

'Never been near Baja,' Mrs Benyon snapped. 'It belongs to Vincent. One of his evil schemes.'

'Evil, Mrs Benyon?'

'All his schemes are evil. The ship is supposed to be bringing up core samples from the ocean bed. Something to do with testing the age of California. Fiddlesticks! I don't know what it's doing but it won't be what he says it's there for.'

'How long has it been there?' Paula enquired.

'Over a month, my dear. I had a terrible shock once, in the middle of the night. Heard a great thump. I got out of bed and a small tidal wave was rushing ashore. Yet the ocean was calm as a lake. I saw it by moonlight.'

'Some kind of underwater upheaval?' Tweed suggested.

'Why did you say Ethan was in danger?' she demanded, ignoring his comment.

'Because I have been told VB is a dangerous man.'

'He is!' Her manner became animated. 'He thinks I know too much – and I do. He put guards round my house to keep me in here as a prisoner, but Ethan persuaded him to remove them, bless his heart. It's good to talk to English people again.'

'You said he *thinks* you know too much?'

'I do. I paid the guard master, a nasty piece of work called Luis Martinez, several hundred dollars to let me see inside Black Ridge. I know the routine over there and the rest were all away at a meeting in the AMBECO building in San Francisco.'

'So what did you find out?' Tweed asked as she paused for breath – she talked so quickly.

'First, that chain of so-called observatories he has erected along the mountains are fakes. I got inside the one behind Black Ridge and the so-called telescope is nothing more than an empty barrel – looks like the real thing but has no lenses.'

'Curious,' Tweed remarked.

'He has one real big telescope in the observatory down the coast which he shows astronomers over.'

'Then what is it all about?' Paula enquired.

'Something sinister – and poor Ethan has been forced to use his genius to work on it. Martinez was drunk and is boastful. He took me down an elevator deep underground. There is a tunnel they have dug under the mountains. I saw a lot of Ethan's sort of equipment down there. Charts to record earthquake tremors. Vincent believes he can predict the next earthquake. So many machines in the tunnel I don't know what they do. All evil, evil – and Ethan forced to work on them.'

'Have you told anyone else this?' Tweed asked.

'Not a living soul. Vincent has brought up so many important Americans I might speak to the wrong man. But you are British. I trust the British. Do you know, you're the first Englishman I've talked to in years? In Carmel they have the Anglo-Pacific Club, that's for the Brits.' She corrected herself, 'I hate that word they use out here. I never joined that club,' she went racing on, 'I didn't like the members. All British people who fled their own country and settled here because the climate is good, the living is easy. Why do you keep looking round my room?' she suddenly demanded.

'I was admiring your furniture. You have turned it into a real home.'

Which was not true. Tweed had been examining the

room for any sign of monitoring devices. So far as he could see there weren't any.

'I took a lot of trouble over making it comfortable,' Mrs Benyon replied, and she smirked.

'This Anglo-Pacific Club you mentioned. Who runs it?'

'A Brigadier Grenville. Comes here for the winter but he is the leading light. Half the members give themselves airs and graces, give themselves fake titles you won't find in the reference books back home. Lady this and Lady that. My foot! I hear from an old friend that now Vanity Richmond flaunts herself at their parties.'

'Who is Vanity Richmond?' Tweed enquired innocently.

'Vincent's latest fancy piece. Supposed to be his personal assistant. She has quarters up at Black Ridge. British, too.'

Mrs Benyon was showing signs of tiring. Tweed stood up, said they had an urgent appointment so he hoped she would excuse them.

'Pity, I could have talked to you all day. You will come back and see me?'

'Of course. Mrs Benyon, maybe it would be best if you didn't let your stepson, Vincent, know we've been here.'

'Won't say one damned word to that man.'

'And, if it's not presumptuous, I'd like to pay you a fee for your time. May I?'

'If you insist.'

Paula also had stood up as Tweed moved away from Mrs Benyon's chair a few paces while he brought out a sheaf of one-hundred-dollar bills. He was clumsy, dropped five on the floor which scattered over a Persian rug.

Mrs Benyon leapt out of her chair, bent down to

retrieve the money. Then, with her sticks still perched against the chair, she sank back into it.

'I can walk just a few steps without my sticks,' she felt obliged to explain. 'Now I'll suffer for hours. Any sudden movement shakes me up.'

'You are all right?' Paula asked, leaning over her.

'Yes, my dear. I'll just rest awhile.' She looked at Tweed. 'I much prefer your assistant to Vincent's Vanity. Yours is a real lady.'

'Thank you,' said Paula.

'Curious name, Vanity,' Tweed remarked.

'Oh, her real name is Vanessa. She got the nickname Vanity over here because she thinks so much of herself.'

'I don't think we can get out of the front door,' Tweed reminded her.

'Of course. Just let me get to my feet.'

She made a great performance of slowly standing up, using the sticks. Paula, playing along with the act, took her by the arm. As the front door eventually closed on them while they walked along the terrace Tweed heaved a sigh of relief.

'I don't like her. Greedy,' Paula said.

'I like the information she gave us.' He looked out to sea where the giant so-called dredger ship was in the same position. Using Paula's glasses, he quickly scanned the vessel, then handed them back to her.

'I don't like the look of the *Baja*,' he said. 'I don't like the look of it one bit . . .'

Outside at the top of the drive Newman had stood waiting patiently by the Merc., leaving the engine running for a quick getaway. In the rear seat Marler had lowered a window a few inches, had poked the sniperscope out, resting on the edge of the glass. He was looking up at Black Ridge.

'Bob,' he called out. 'Use your field glasses. We're under observation. First floor of Black Ridge, immediately to the left of the picture window.'

Newman focused the glasses looped round his neck. The window came up close. His grip on the glasses tightened. He was staring straight at Joel Brand, who was looking back at him through his own binoculars. Newman dropped his glasses and began to whistle.

Inside Black Ridge, Brand left the window, ran along a corridor, opened the door to a room. Two tough men in windbreakers sat reading girlie magazines. Each also wore shabby denims. Brand gave them precise orders.

'Pancho, Antonio, there's a blue Merc., parked at the top of Mrs Benyon's drive. My bet is it will sooner or later return to Carmel. I don't want it to get there. Use the two juggernauts which brought in explosives for the *Baja*. Got it?'

'On Highway One, simple,' Antonio answered. 'Accidents will happen. We're on our way.'

'There's a big bonus for both of you,' Brand called after them as they hurried from the room.

Returning to the window where he had looked at The Apex, Brand smiled unpleasantly. It was fortunate Moloch had earlier taken off in the chopper on one of his frequent flights to the AMBECO building. Brand had an idea VB would not have approved of his decision. No reason he should ever know about it. He waved through the window to the tiny figure which stood with his back to him.

'Goodbye, Mr Newman.'

From his high viewing point Newman saw two huge juggernauts crawling down the drive from Black Ridge.

The automatic gates opened for them and they trundled off towards Carmel. He glanced at Marler, who nodded.

Earlier, when about to turn up the drive to The Apex, Newman had waved a hand to Butler behind him, indicating he should drive on. Butler, behind the wheel of the BMW, had understood at once. Instead of following Newman up the drive he had proceeded along Highway One a short distance to where a sandstone gulch reared upon either side of the road. Performing an illegal U-turn, he parked the car inside the gulch, where it was invisible to any watcher up at Black Ridge. Then he waited, chatting to Nield by his side.

Tweed emerged with Paula to find Newman looking grim. He asked him what was the matter.

'Nothing.' Newman grinned. 'Just awestruck by the scenery. Back to Carmel and Spanish Bay?'

'Yes. We can get lunch at the hotel.' Tweed glanced up at Black Ridge, not convinced by Newman's sudden return to his normal cheerful self. 'I'll tell you on the way what we learned from Mrs Benyon. The visit was invaluable . . .'

'Brigadier Grenville?' Newman queried some time later. 'He seems to have promoted himself – if it's the same chap. It has to be, come to think of it. That cricket-playing lad I talked to at the pub near Constantine said Grenville spent his winters in Monterey. Can't be two Grenvilles – both with a military title. Where does he fit in to what's going on our here?'

'That,' said Tweed, 'is what we're going to find out. And I don't suppose you noticed that ship anchored about half a mile out beyond The Apex.'

'You suppose wrong. I had plenty of time to wander round the side of the terrace. I had a look at it with my field glasses. Something odd – unrecognizable – about the structures on the foredeck. Interesting that the *Baja* belongs to Moloch. Reminds me of the strange canvas-covered equipment aboard the *Venetia* off Falmouth.'

'You mean the equipment looked the same on both vessels?'

'No, it didn't. On the surface the *Baja* looks like the standard type of dredger – but not when you check it as I did. What the heck is going on?'

'Maybe Mr Moloch could tell us,' called out Paula from the back seat, where she sat alongside Marler.

'I'm probably the last person in the world he'd want to meet,' replied Tweed in the front passenger seat.

Newman checked his rear-view mirror. The BMW was following them some distance away. They had left Bixby Bridge behind and had climbed high up some time before. The Pacific was now to their left, beyond the other side of the highway. Newman had his hands lightly holding the wheel as they approached a particularly sharp curve with no barrier on the ocean side. He had only to travel a strange route once to be able to recall every twist and turn on the way back.

'What a contrast to San Francisco,' Paula remarked. 'It is so peaceful out here.'

'Let's hope it stays that way,' said Newman.

'That's right,' she shot back at him, 'spoil my enjoyment. I think this is one of the most wonderful parts of the world I've ever seen.'

'It's pretty unique in its grandeur,' Newman agreed.

They were approaching the steep bend, high above the sea. Newman was halfway round when he saw the juggernaut coming – on the wrong side of the highway. On *his* side. A frightful head-on collision seemed inevitable. The massive vehicle would crush the Merc. Tweed showed no reaction. In the back Marler gripped the Armalite. By his side Paula clenched her hands, unable to take her eyes off the advancing colossus.

At the last moment Newman swung his wheel hard

over, taking the car into the other lane. The juggernaut missed them by inches. Then Newman saw another juggernaut coming – again on the wrong side of the road. They'd planned back-up. Behind the wheel Antonio grinned in anticipation. He began to swing his juggernaut to the right to intercept Newman. At that moment Newman rammed his foot full down on the accelerator. The Merc. shot forward like a rocket. It raced past the turning juggernaut. Again there were inches to spare. Antonio had swung his wheel to an extreme angle. The weight of the juggernaut carried him forward. His grin vanished. He saw the cliff edge looming as he desperately tried to turn the wheel back. Too late. Carried forward by its own momentum the juggernaut drove through a hedge and Antonio had a brief glimpse of the three-hundred-foot drop before him. The vehicle toppled over the brink, fell like a propelled missile, dropped vertically three hundred feet, hit the rocks below. The petrol tank exploded. Flames engulfed the cab, a searing spire of flames. The vehicle was smashed, the cab break- ing away, catapulting into the ocean where a large wave broke, spilling surf over the funeral pyre, quenching some of the fire. Then the only sound was the next wave breaking.

21

The moment Newman reached a lay-by he pulled in, parked and pressed a button on the black box. The aerial elevated above the Merc. the spider's web of wires spread out. Grasping the microphone hidden under the dash- board, he sent his message.

'Newman here. Emergency. Two juggernauts tried to smash us up. Well north of Bixby Bridge. One vehicle went over the cliff. The first one now heading south along Highway One. Juggernaut hauled by separate cab attached to it. We are waiting in lay-by on Highway One. Over . . .'

'Message received. Understood. I'm on my way. Stay in the lay-by. Out.'

The distinctive voice of Alvarez had come over very clearly. Tweed turned to look at Paula.

'How are you?'

'Just fine,' she managed. 'I knew Bob would get us out of it. He's great in a tight spot.'

'I agree,' Tweed replied. 'A brilliant manoeuvre, Bob.'

'Compliments will get you nowhere . . .'

He got out of the car to smoke a cigarette and Marler, carrying his Armalite, joined him. Paula, aware of tension in her legs, also left the car. They waited awhile and then a chopper circled overhead, landed on the highway, let out a passenger, took off and settled on a nearby hillside. Alvarez ran to the car.

'You guys all OK?'

'We're very OK,' Tweed assured him through the lowered window.

'I've got news. Due to your information we set up a roadblock south of here. The juggernaut tried to smash its way through. A policeman shot the driver dead. A Mexican. Name of Pancho Corona. We think he was an illegal and was heading for the Mexican border.'

Paula had walked across to greet Alvarez and thank him for his quick arrival. He smiled at her, said it was all in a day's work – another English phrase.

'What are those men doing?' she asked.

A police truck carrying men with ropes looped over their shoulders had just passed in the direction of their attack. Alvarez shrugged.

'They are specially trained. They will go down the cliff with the aid of the ropes to where the other juggernaut crashed into the sea. I saw the wreckage from the air. It is nothing.'

'You seem to be very well organized,' she commented.

'We do our best. Now, you have all had a bad time. I think you need lunch. I will show you the way to a scenic restaurant. It is dramatic.' He looked out to sea. 'Black clouds. The weather is changing. Rocky Point could be quite dramatic. Can this gentleman travel in the BMW, your escort car?'

'This gentleman can,' Marler told him.

'Then I will travel with you in the Mercedes and show you the way. To Rocky Point . . .'

At Black Ridge, staring out of the window, Brand had seen Pancho's juggernaut hurtling along the highway and past towards the south. He guessed that something had gone wrong. He hurried to the room which contained the staff records.

Pancho Corona was not an illegal, but he felt it wise to destroy all evidence that he had been employed at Black Ridge. Extracting the file containing Corona's details, he shredded the sheets inside and hurried back to his own office. From a safe he took a packet of cocaine. He was not a user of drugs but he kept a quantity to plant on enemies. Then a quick anonymous call to the police destroyed his target.

He had put on a pair of surgical gloves before picking up the packet from the safe. No fingerprints. Still hurrying – VB might return at any time – he ran down a staircase leading to the back of the mansion. Outside was a huge garage where the juggernauts had been parked. He casually threw the packet into a corner and strolled back to his office. Now he had a story ready to tell VB about the missing vehicles.

In the restaurant at Rocky Point, Alvarez led them to a table by a huge picture window. Paula looked round at the lavish and modernistic way the restaurant was furnished and decorated.

'This is very impressive,' she remarked.

Tweed insisted he joined them for at least a drink after he had refused lunch. Alvarez explained as he sat down next to Paula.

'You recall when I asked Newman to pause? Then I waved to my chopper perched on the hillside and it took off?'

'Yes, I did wonder what all that was about.'

'The chopper followed your cars and landed on the hill near here. After my drink I'll board it and fly to the roadblock. I prefer to see to everything myself. That way it goes good.' He lifted his glass. 'Cheers! Welcome to California – although I would have hoped it would have been a more peaceful visit.' He downed his drink. 'Now, if you will excuse me . . .'

He had just gone when a distinguished-looking man in a cream linen suit entered. Newman grinned, stood up, called out, 'Good to see you again, Brigadier Grenville.'

Grenville was badly shaken. Hard as he tried he couldn't disguise his discomfort. Newman went over to him, hand outheld.

'It's a small world, to coin a phrase.' He grinned. 'Come and join us.'

'Well . . .'

Newman, still grinning, took him by the arm, guided him over to Tweed's table. He made introductions as Grenville sat down and smiled at everyone. He had made a quick recovery, Tweed thought.

'And, of course, you know Paula,' Newman concluded, sitting down. 'You danced with her the other side of the pond.'

'You're a long way from Porth Navas, Colonel – excuse me – Brigadier,' Paula teased him.

'The locals started calling me Brigadier, so I just let it go,' Grenville explained with a hint of embarrassment.

'And who are the locals?' Paula asked.

'Oh, quite a few Brits have emigrated to the Monterey Peninsula. The climate and all that. Someone had to take the initiative,' he went on with growing confidence, 'so I have founded the Anglo-Pacific Club. You're all welcome to join in. No membership fee. Just have to be British. We have get-togethers in the evening, dancing, too. You'd adorn the company,' he said, looking directly at Paula.

'Thank you.'

'What do the Americans think of your club?' Tweed enquired.

'You're Tweed.'

'That's what they call me, so I suppose I must be,' he replied with a twinkle in his eyes.

'What do the Yanks think? That we're a bunch of snobs. I don't mind. Keeps out some pretty unpleasant people.'

'What sort of people?'

'You're a direct chap. More like an American.'

'What sort of people?'

Paula had the impression Tweed had decided he wasn't putting up with any nonsense from fake brigadiers. Grenville flushed.

'There you go again. Well, the area is floating with

aggressive millionaires and their even more aggressive bejewelled wives. Not the sort of people you'd invite to your club back home.'

'How did they make their money?'

'Oh, in all sorts of industries. They're a rough lot when it comes to business. Maybe they have to be.' He stared at Tweed. 'Now, sir, it's my turn. What do you do?'

'I'm Chief Claims Investigator for an insurance company.'

'Really?' Grenville seemed impressed. 'You must see a lot of the seamy side of life.'

'And the crooked side,' Tweed responded, staring back at Grenville.

'Imagine you do.'

Grenville had paused before he made this response. On the surface it seemed to Newman Grenville couldn't quite make out Tweed, who had a steely look.

Another man walked rapidly into the restaurant, wearing a beige linen suit. Then he stopped as though he'd walked into a wall. Newman jumped up, went over to him as he was turning to leave the restaurant.

'Well, well, if it isn't Maurice. The clan is gathering. I insist you join us.'

He used the same tactic as he had with Grenville, taking Maurice Prendergast by the arm, guiding him to the table. Again Newman was grinning.

'Brigadier, you must remember Maurice – he escorted Paula to your dance in Cornwall. And, Maurice, you had a brief acquaintance with Paula?'

'Nice to see you again, Paula,' Maurice said in a cold voice.

'And to see you,' she replied with a brief smile.

'Hello, Maurice,' said Tweed. 'Do sit down and join the happy party.'

He studied Prendergast. He appeared to have changed since he had met Maurice at his house, The Ark, in Porth Navas. Though he was six feet tall, his strong, clean-shaven face looked haggard. His fair hair was a mess, hadn't been brushed. The humorous smile was gone. His movements, previously slow and deliberate, were jerky.

'Hello, Tweed,' he replied dully.

'Do sit down. How about a drink?' Tweed suggested cheerfully.

'A large brandy.'

He sagged into the chair Newman had hauled over for him. As he put his elbows on the table for support, Paula contrasted him with Grenville. The so-called brigadier was his normal confident self. He pulled at his neat grey moustache as he glanced at Maurice, who was downing the drink Newman had ordered for him.

'Like another,' Maurice said, slurring his words.

Newman ordered another large brandy. The service at Rocky Point was first-rate. The second drink was served instantly. Maurice drank half of it, stared at Paula.

'What are you doing in this bloody lair of runaways?'

'Now, Maurice,' Grenville chided him in a stiff voice. 'No bad language in front of a lady.'

'If you say so.'

'I think we'd better have lunch,' said Tweed, still cheerful as he closed the menu. 'I know what I want.'

The rest of them ordered. Except for Maurice. Marler, who had not said a word since he sat down, was watching Maurice. Paula was also studying Maurice without appearing to do so.

The waiter stood by Maurice, waiting for his order. Maurice glanced up at him.

'I'm not hungry.'

'Better eat something,' Marler suggested.

'Who asked you?' Maurice demanded.

'No one did. Just a thought. People usually eat at lunch.'

'I'm not people.'

Maurice stared at Marler, who gazed back at him. Maurice was the first one to drop his eyes. He spoke to the waiter, who was leaving.

'Come back a moment.' He glanced at Newman. 'I could do with another large brandy.'

Newman looked across the table at Tweed, who nodded his agreement. Maurice glanced at Newman.

'You have to check with the boss?' he sneered.

'Frequently.' Newman smiled and ordered another brandy. 'I have the odd brandy myself. After lunch with coffee.'

'Maurice,' Grenville said grimly, 'I wouldn't if I were you.'

'But you're not me, are you? You're the flaming brigadier.'

'I'm just that.' Grenville laughed. 'A pretty good description. I'm sure the Americans would agree.'

The tension at the table was beginning to get to Paula. She gazed down through the large picture window at the scene immediately below. The view was vertiginous – staring down at the ocean, which had become rough. Great waves exploded against huge jagged rocks, erupted into geysers of surf flung high into the air. Water surged into narrow rocky channels, then submerged the defiles round them. She could see why this was called Rocky Point. There's another cauldron, she thought, recalling Tweed's words. The sight disturbed her. Maurice drank his third brandy.

'Gotta go, folks,' he announced, imitating American speech.

He stood up, rested his hands on the table. Newman was by his side immediately. He took hold of Maurice round the waist, guided him up two large steps, was taking him towards the exit when Maurice protested.

'Take your hands off me. I can make it.'

'Certainly you can,' Newman assured him, not letting go.

At that moment Butler and Nield, who had tactfully slipped into the bar for a sandwich lunch, appeared. Newman nodded his head for them to come forward.

'See this gentleman to his car. He's not feeling well. Harry, drive him home, wherever that may be.'

'Got a dog kennel of an apartment in Carmel,' Maurice mumbled. 'I can drive . . .'

'So can I,' said the sturdy Butler. He took hold of Maurice, relieving Newman of his burden. 'I'll see him home. There are patrol cars along Highway One.'

Butler easily manoeuvred Maurice out of the restaurant. As they disappeared Pete Nield wandered over to Newman and splayed his hands in a gesture of resignation.

'That same chap was in the bar before he came in here. He downed a couple of large brandies one after the other.'

'Harry will get him safely home. Want to come and join us?'

'I'll wait outside in the BMW . . .'

Grenville was speaking to everyone as Newman resumed his seat. His manner was apologetic.

'Can't understand what's got into Maurice. Never seen him like that before. Would have thrown him out of the club if he'd behaved like that. Will do if it happens there.'

'You've never seen him drink too much?' Tweed queried. 'Is that what you're saying?'

'Up to a point.' He pulled at his moustache, glanced towards Paula, who was gazing down through the window. 'He knocks it back a bit, but who doesn't, eh?

241

By the by, we're having a bit of a shindig at the club HQ this evening. Why not come along, all of you? Here's a card giving the details. You'll be most welcome.' He looked at Marler. 'You don't say a lot, sir.'

'Sometimes I find it more interesting listening,' Marler drawled.

Paula took all this in automatically as she gazed down at the seething ocean. She was convinced Maurice had only pretended to be drunk. An immense wave crashed into the tip of the cape which was Rocky Point. It seemed to symbolize the heaving cauldron of California.

22

They were leaving the restaurant when Newman excused himself and went towards the entrance to the bar. Paula glanced in that direction and stiffened. A familiar and attractive woman was greeting him warmly. Dressed in a pale green trouser suit, Vanity Richmond looked her usual glamorous self.

'Look who we have here,' Newman said as he brought her over to them. 'Again it's a small world.'

'Hello, everyone.' Vanity had a roguish smile as Newman introduced her to Paula. 'I remember you,' she said. 'You had a table to yourself at Nansidwell back in Cornwall. We never got a chance to talk.'

'You both have now,' Newman commented cheer-fully.

Tweed merely nodded when they shook hands, saying nothing. Paula was observing Vanity, her long, well-shaped nose, the greenish eyes which seemed to notice everything, the good figure. Her full red lips were smiling constantly and she seemed delighted at meeting them.

'Where are you off to?' Newman enquired.

'Spanish Bay. The hotel on the coast outside Monterey. I'm staying there, as I did during my last visit,' she said as she looked at Paula. 'Maybe this time we could get together? Last time you seemed abstracted.'

'Last time I had a somewhat grisly experience,' Paula said, looking directly at Vanity, who had thrown back her mane of blazing red hair from the side of her face. 'I dragged a dead woman out of the sea.'

'So it was you who found her? How horrible. I read about one of two twin sisters being found – and the other washed ashore in Cornwall. Must have shaken you up . . .'

'You two can chat in my car,' Newman suggested.

'I've got my Audi parked outside . . .'

'Let me borrow your keys and I'll drive it back for you,' Marler suggested.

'I'm also staying again at Spanish Bay,' Paula told Vanity.

It seemed to Paula this was a good opportunity to get to know more about Vanity. She'd also noticed with amusement that Newman never stopped smiling. Vanity thanked Marler, gave him her keys and a warm smile as she gazed straight at him.

On their way back along the highway the dark clouds had disappeared and it was a glorious sunny afternoon. Paula sat in the back with Vanity and they chatted away animatedly. In the front, Tweed, sitting beside Newman, remained silent.

Behind Newman followed the Audi, driven by Marler – and a distance behind him Butler was driving the BMW with Maurice beside him and Pete Nield in the back. Tweed wondered what had caused their delay in departing.

* * *

243

Maurice had felt ill before he climbed into the BMW back at Rocky Point. Butler had accompanied him to the toilet and looked after him. Now, as they drove along Highway One he was surprised by Maurice's swift recovery.

'Sorry to put you to this inconvenience, old chap,' Maurice said to Butler. 'But you were right. Don't often make a fool of myself like that, but I'm worried.'

'Worried?' Butler glanced at him. 'What's on your mind?'

'The situation here – in California and at the Anglo-Pacific Club.'

'Something odd about the situation?' Butler enquired.

'Very. Can't make it out. I've got a premonition of a terrible disaster.'

'What kind of disaster?' Butler asked casually.

'Don't know. There's tension among certain people I know. Can't give you any names.'

'Very informative,' Butler commented. 'Why not?'

'Because I want to be sure I've pinpointed the right people.'

Sounds like Tweed, Nield was thinking in the rear of the car. Gives us a glimpse and then drops the curtain.

'We're nearly at Carmel,' Maurice warned Butler. 'You turn off the highway in a minute. If I could guide you . . .'

'Do that.'

'I'm here – on Junipero,' Maurice said after a few minutes. 'If you could pull in here.'

'I'll come with you,' Butler said firmly. 'See you safely in your dog kennel.'

'No need . . .'

Butler ignored the suggestion, got out with Maurice, walked alongside him into a small complex courtyard, cobbled and with hanging baskets. Maurice pointed to an iron staircase.

'I'm living up there now.'

'Now?' queried Butler.

'Just moved in. Place became vacant suddenly. The rent is reasonable – a murder took place here and the police have just gone away. That's why the rent is cheap. Most people don't like the idea of staying somewhere where something like that has happened. The landlord wanted quick occupation.'

'I'll see you up the staircase. Who was murdered?'

'A private investigator called Linda Standish. I'm not at all worried about ghosts walking. And thank you for seeing me home.'

'All in a day's work . . .'

Arriving at Spanish Bay, Paula was surprised to discover the hotel had given her the same spacious apartment she had occupied on her previous visit. The organization of top hotels in the States was quite something.

Tweed, whose luggage had been taken to another apartment, came in at her invitation and Paula beckoned to Vanity to join them and inspect her quarters. The two women were examining the complex while Tweed fiddled with the large picture window, slid it back and stepped out onto a terrace with a table and chairs. He sank into a chair.

'This apartment is swell – I mean super,' enthused Vanity as they went into the bathroom. 'I'm trying not to pick up Americanisms. Look at that jacuzzi, and the shower stall. This is great.'

'Care for a drink?' Paula suggested.

She investigated the large minibar in the living room, brought out a bottle of Chardonnay, held it up to show Vanity.

'Any good?'

'Very good. One glass will do me.' She wandered out through the open window where Tweed was sitting. 'Fancy a glass of wine, Mr Tweed?'

'No, thank you.'

He resumed the brooding look Paula knew so well, staring at a line of pine trees. Then he got up, wandered along a path crossing the grass. He soon had a panoramic view of the Pacific beyond trim, rolling golf links. The flat roofs of golf carts moved along a lower level, looking as though they were floating by themselves. The calm Pacific was a startling blue. He could see why people would be hypnotized by the sheer beauty of the scene.

'Tweed refused a drink,' Vanity announced merrily as she rejoined Paula. 'Doesn't seem very sociable.'

'He's probably working on an insurance problem,' Paula told her. 'He's got terrific powers of concentration.'

'And I thought it was me. Cheers!'

They sat down on a couch by a fireplace with a large gas-operated log fire which was unlit. Vanity looked round the living room.

'This place oozes comfort. It's so relaxing.'

'Not bad,' Paula agreed. 'You know what I do for a living, so give – how do you earn your daily crust of bread?'

'Like you, I'm a personal assistant. My boss is tough and very successful. You've heard of Vincent Bernard Moloch?'

'The quiet billionaire? You work for him?'

'Yes. And I earn my daily crust like you do, I imagine. Vincent is a workaholic. Makes the average American go-getter look like an idler. I'm at his beck and call both day and night. Luckily I can get by with very little sleep.'

'Does sound a tough job. What does it involve?'

'Keeping his daily paperwork and appointments in order.' She laughed. 'Keeping him in order. I don't know much about what he does. Very secretive, VB is. Always working on some new project.'

'Got one on the go at the moment, has he?'

'Yes. Something which seems to take up a lot of his

246

time. I haven't a clue what it is. There's a borderline I don't cross. The salary is enormous, so I'm careful not to put a foot wrong.' She finished her drink, checked her watch. 'Hope you don't mind. I must fly. Maybe we could have dinner together this evening? I'll call you.'

She looked up as Tweed returned, leaving the sliding window open. It was hot outside. He nodded to Vanity as she got up, held out her hand.

'Sorry that we couldn't talk together. I have to go.'

'Another time, perhaps,' Tweed replied.

'You weren't very amiable with her,' Paula chided him after Vanity had left. 'She's admitted to me she works for Moloch.'

'She's smart. Now we're here she'd know we'd find that out. I'm going along to my room to unpack.'

'You look tired. I'll come and help.'

They were walking along the wide carpeted corridor when a man came round the corner. Brigadier Arbuthnot Grenville stopped, surprised as he tweaked his moustache.

'You people staying here?'

'For a short time,' Tweed said quickly.

'Don't know whether you read my invitation card. We've taken over the Bay Club here for the dance tonight. Good that you are on the spot. See you 2000 hours. Sharp. Do you know whether Maurice got home safely?' he enquired as though not really interested.

'Yes, I gather he did,' Tweed assured him.

'Don't do anything I wouldn't,' Grenville said with a broad smile, looking at Paula. 'That gives you all the latitude in the world . . .'

Tweed was sitting down in his own apartment, his brow furrowed in thought. Paula swiftly unpacked everything. Then she insisted on showing him where everything was.

He had just thanked her when the phone rang. Paula automatically picked it up.

'Could you please repeat that?' she requested. 'Then I'll see if Mr Tweed is available. Thank you.'

She turned to Tweed, her hand over the mouthpiece while she spoke.

'It's Hoarse Voice. Monica told me about him.'

'I'll take it.'

Tweed suddenly was alert, took the phone from her, gave his name and listened for several minutes without speaking. The conversation closed when Tweed spoke for the first time.

'Thank you. I'm grateful – very – for that data.'

'That was the mysterious Waltz,' Paula commented. 'Monica swore me to secrecy when I took a call from him and I was alone in the office at Park Crescent. He refused to say a word when I told him he must have got a wrong number. Later Monica warned me about the caller she had nicknamed Hoarse Voice. Sounds as though he smokes a lot.'

'Maybe.' Tweed paused. 'I've just been warned that time is running out. Whatever project VB is working on should soon be ready for launching. We may have arrived too late.'

Paula called Room Service, ordered coffee. She could sense that Tweed was very worried, which was unlike him. When the coffee arrived she poured two cups, sat in a chair close to him, started talking.

'How did you know Maurice had arrived home safely? When you told Grenville?'

'Butler and Nield arrived soon after us. They're upstairs in two smaller rooms. I saw Harry give me a thumbs-up sign. That meant he had delivered the drunken package.'

'If Maurice was drunk.'

'Why do you say that?'

'It struck me he was putting on a very clever act. Possibly for Grenville's benefit.'

'An interesting thought.'

'Oh, come on. What do you think of Grenville – of Maurice?'

'I think Grenville is deliberately acting out a caricature of the stiff-necked military type. Probably goes down well with the Anglo-Pacific Club lot.'

'So two of them are not what they seem? Grenville and Maurice.'

'No one out here is what they seem. Same applied to Cornwall.'

'Well, what about Vanity Richmond?'

'On the surface she appears to be working hard at a big job. She spends money on expensive clothes. She appears to have a soft spot for Newman. That's all I can make out about her.'

'*On the surface,*' Paula repeated. 'She *appears* ... she *appears*. You sound very dubious about her. How did you know she's working hard at a big job?'

'Because I listened from outside the window. My job is to gather data on everyone who could be suspect.'

'And everyone is suspect,' Paula probed.

'Guilty until proved innocent. Remember that list of suspects you winkled out from the top of the filing cabinet in Linda Standish's apartment. Moloch, Joel Brand, Luis Martinez, Byron Landis and Vanity Richmond. Alvarez told me Martinez is guard master at Black Ridge.'

'Well, at least Grenville and Maurice weren't on the list.'

'A curious omission,' Tweed observed.

'What does that mean?'

'What I said. Now I want you to accompany me to

Newman's Merc., parked out of sight of the hotel. The two of us together will look less conspicuous. I have something very important to do. Call Bob in his room next to mine and ask him to go to the car immediately. I have to make swift contact with Langley.'

They found Newman had arrived in the car park. He was standing by the Merc., its front door open. He had even taken the precaution of summoning Butler and Nield, who were strolling round at a distance to make sure they were alone at this remote spot beyond the hotel. The aerial on the car was elevated.

'I need to get into secret touch with Washington,' Tweed explained. 'Can it be done? It has to be one hundred per cent safe.'

'Easily. Alvarez explained to me how to do it. If he's near a patrol car a special signal will alert him, unless you don't want him to hear. He carries a device which he can attach to any police radio – it scrambles the message so far as the outside world is concerned.'

'Let's get on with it quickly. Show me how – and I have to be alone . . .'

Newman waited until Tweed was sitting in the front passenger seat, then leaned in, pressed a certain combination of buttons on the black box, handed the microphone to Tweed, shut the door and walked away with Paula.

'Cord here,' the familiar voice said. 'Is that you, Tweed?'

'Tweed here. I have information that two juggernauts which are no longer at Black Ridge were both carrying explosives. I—'

'Jesus!' Dillon burst out. 'Are you sure?'

'My informant is exceptionally reliable. The juggernauts are usually parked in a hidden garage behind the

mansion – but one was been stopped by a roadblock
south of Big Sur, the other crashed over the cliff into the
ocean.'

'Alvarez is now listening in. Alvarez, investigate
urgently. Tweed, we are checking an unauthorized explosion which took place in the Nevada desert. One of the
abandoned silos which housed missiles was used. We
can't identify the explosive. It's something new.'

'How powerful?' Tweed asked.

'Brace yourself. Washington is crazy with fear. The
new unknown explosive has the force of ten hydrogen
bombs.'

23

For several minutes Tweed sat motionless in the car when
Cord Dillon had gone off the line. Even from a distance
Paula could see how grim his expression was. She made
a move to go towards the car. Newman stopped her.

'When he's ready he'll join us.'

'I've never seen him look so grim.'

'Leave him alone. He's taking a major decision.'

'He's sitting so still . . .'

As soon as she had spoken Tweed lowered the
window, beckoned to them. His whole attitude had
changed, had become ferociously active.

'First, Bob, I want to talk to Alvarez urgently. Second,
I want you to drive me to the nearest public phone.
Third,' he looked at Marler, who had appeared out of
nowhere, carrying a golf bag which Tweed guessed
contained the Armalite. 'Third, I want maximum protection. I'm sure Moloch knows now where I am. Paula, get
in the back.'

'I'll drive the BMW,' Marler decided, 'and take Butler

251

and Nield with me. I'll be close behind you. Don't be surprised if I suddenly overtake you if I see trouble ahead . . .'

Newman was already behind the wheel of his Merc. He drove up the long winding drive away from Spanish Bay. In the back Paula checked the action of her .32 Browning. Tweed was holding the microphone in his hand.

'Alvarez here . . .'

'Tweed speaking. Where are you?'

'Still at the roadblock just south of Big Sur . . .'

'Stay there until you hear from me – if you can . . .'

'I can.'

'Not possible, I imagine, to get scuba divers who could look under the hull of that ship, the *Baja*, offshore?'

'They'll be here in thirty minutes. From police HQ in Monterey. Will do . . .'

'Thank you.'

Paula was surprised. Never before had she known Tweed to ask for maximum protection. She knew him well enough to realize he was not bothered about himself – he was worried about what he had to do. The momentum was building up.

'I need to phone Professor Weatherby, the seismologist, at his Holland Park home,' Tweed explained tersely.

A few minutes later Newman parked close to a remote phone box. Tweed was out of the car almost before it stopped moving. He ran to the box, began to call Weatherby.

Outside Marler had jumped out of his car to join Newman, followed by Butler and Nield. Marler looked round at the dense pine forests closing in on all sides.

'Not the safest spot,' he observed. 'Harry, Pete, take up positions at the edge of the forest. Stay out of sight and have your weapons ready. Regard any vehicle approaching us as potentially hostile, but be careful – we don't want to shoot up any innocent travellers.'

Newman took up his own position close to the phone box, his Smith & Wesson revolver in his hand by his side. Paula joined him. She found the heavy silence of the forest disturbing. Inside the box Tweed had got through to Weatherby.

'Tweed here. I know it's midnight in London. Hope I didn't get you up.'

'I am up, will be for hours. You sound serious.'

'Can you explain to me – in simple language, please – if it would be possible to trigger an earthquake under the sea off the California coast? Area Carmel–Big Sur?'

'Triggered? Well, recent research has detected movement under the Pacific in that area. You have to understand there are immense tectonic plates, as we call them – vast slabs of the ocean bed – which can grind up against each other. Or even against the coast. It's an event which is highly unlikely.'

'If it happened,' Tweed pressed, 'what would cause it?'

'I suppose a gigantic upheaval underwater could shift a tectonic plate.' He paused. 'I didn't tell you, but Ethan Benyon was working on one such theory, which I find too advanced. Found it in the files he forgot to take with him.'

'A gigantic underwater upheaval,' Tweed repeated. 'Assume it happened. What would be the result if the plate did hit the coast?'

'It would have the power to force its way under the coast. Nature's power is awesome. The result? A catastrophe. But, Tweed, this is so unlikely.'

'Thank you, Weatherby. You've been an enormous help.'

'Don't see how. Where are you now?'

253

'California. Must go.'

Tweed ran back to the car. Newman was in the driving seat as he sat down. He told Newman briefly the content of his conversation, then asked to be put through to Alvarez again.

'Tweed here. I definitely believe the *Baja*'s hull should be thoroughly investigated.'

'It's OK. Scuba divers are on their way, plus a small launch on a trailer.'

'Can I have a word with him?' Newman asked quickly.

Tweed handed him the microphone. Newman identified himself.

'Alvarez, could you wait till I arrive? Be there thirty to forty minutes.'

'I'll see you, Newman . . .'

Driving back to the hotel, Newman had Paula and Marler, who had jumped in at the last moment, in the back. Butler, with Nield by his side, followed in the BMW. As they pulled in to the car park Butler jumped out, came up to Tweed who was climbing out.

'Pete and I are staying with you. No argument. We've been known to disobey orders.'

'You certainly have,' Tweed agreed. 'Thank you.'

'Time to disembark, Paula,' Newman said.

'Time to get moving. I'm coming with you. You'll have to throw me out of the car.'

'And you'd put up a good fight if I tried it. Marler?'

'I'm comfortable where I am.'

Newman sighed, drove off for his destination. Big Sur.

At Black Ridge Grenville left the mansion, walked down the long drive to where his car was waiting at the entrance. In the front passenger seat was Maurice Prendergast.

'I invited Moloch to the dance. He said he'd be delighted to come.'

'I'm astounded.'

'Poor chap doesn't have much social life,' Grenville remarked as he got behind the wheel.

'Poor chap!' Maurice sneered. 'He's a billionaire.'

'Money doesn't always buy happiness. Often the very reverse.'

'He can always cry all the way to the bank, to use a rather hackneyed phrase.'

'Come to think of it,' Grenville recalled as he drove along Highway One towards Carmel, 'he showed most interest when I told him the names of some of the other guests, including Tweed and Paula Grey.'

'Was that the real reason you visited Moloch? You were there a long time.'

'What other reason would I have?' Grenville demanded stiffly.

Neither of them was aware that a figure at a first-floor window had watched Grenville leaving. Byron Landis only left his viewing place as Grenville's car disappeared.

Newman arrived in his car to find that Alvarez had hidden his cars and a trailer vehicle in the gulch Butler had used when Tweed and Paula had visited Mrs Benyon. Instinctively he had glanced up at The Apex as they passed the weird house. The curtain in one window twitched. Mrs Benyon was keeping an eye on developments.

'We have planned it carefully,' Alvarez informed Newman and his companions as soon as they left their car. 'The launch is in the water out of sight of the *Baja* – and out of sight of Black Ridge. The scuba divers, three of them, are on board.'

'I'd like to come with you,' Newman suggested.

'Of course you can. Why else did I wait?'

'I'm coming, too,' said Paula. 'Newman needs someone to hold his hand.'

As she spoke with a smile she extracted a grenade from inside her shoulder bag and slipped it behind her back into Newman's hand. He still played cricket occasionally and was, like Tweed, an ace bowler.

'I may as well tag along,' said Marler.

Alvarez stared at him. Marler looked straight back into the dark eyes. Alvarez, impressed by the calm, easy way Marler held himself, nodded and led the way off the highway down a steep grassy bank to a concealed cove with a small beach. A large launch was tethered to a makeshift landing stage.

Aboard, three frogmen in full gear gazed at the newcomers from behind goggles. One carried an underwater camera. Newman wondered if they were some kind of special service. He boarded the launch, the grenade in a pocket of the lightweight jacket he was wearing. Paula, Marler and Alvarez stepped on the deck and a policeman ashore untethered the rope as Alvarez started the engine, took the wheel.

Rounding a point, they saw the *Baja* starboard-on to the launch. The sea was calm – calm enough even for Tweed, Paula thought. At the stern of the huge dredger a big powerboat was moored. As they came closer Alvarez picked up a loudhailer to give the warning 'Police . . .'

He never had a chance to speak. Men from the dredger had dropped into the powerboat. Its engine started with a roar and it headed towards them at increasing speed. Paula recognized the large man behind the wheel. Joel Brand. This was going to be a repeat performance of the attempt to run down the dinghy on the faraway Helford River in Cornwall.

The powerboat soared towards them with increasing momentum, its prow lifted out of the water. It was big enough to slice the launch in two. Alvarez swung the wheel, but so did Brand, heading straight for them at terrifying speed. Newman took out the explosive grenade, removed the pin, counted seconds, hurled it. The grenade landed inside the powerboat towards its stern.

Paula saw Brand, wearing a woolly cap, which concealed his hair, dive overboard, abandoning the wheel, abandoning the other men aboard. He began to swim towards the shore with the ease and strength of a practised swimmer. The grenade exploded.

There was a dull *crump!* followed almost immediately by a shattering roar as the fuel tank went up. Flames engulfed the powerboat in seconds. A section of the stern rocketed skywards, trailing a flame like a meteor, then fell back into the Pacific where it hissed before vanishing below the surface.

'Proceed with the mission,' Alvarez ordered.

He guided the launch round the wreckage floating on the surface. They were close to the *Baja* when he ordered the frogmen overboard. They disappeared below the sea, heading for the underwater section of the hull. Paula had taken out her small pair of field glasses, was scanning the deck of the dredger.

'That's funny,' she reported. 'Doesn't seem to be anyone aboard.'

'They're all staying below deck,' Alvarez told her.

'Looks like a ghost ship,' she commented.

'More than ghosts aboard that hulk,' he replied. He looked at his watch. 'Should take them a maximum of five minutes to complete the check . . .'

They cruised slowly up and down along the starboard side and still no one appeared. Worse still, after ten minutes the frogmen had not surfaced. Alvarez looked worried, guided the launch away from the dredger's prow and round to its port side. He was just in time to catch a glimpse of a figure in a wetsuit disappearing up a ladder and onto the deck.

'Was that one of your men?' Paula asked. 'He was carrying what seemed like a farmer's prong.'

'Not one of mine,' Alvarez said with a grimace.

'And I think he carried one of those electric prongs divers use to ward off marauding underwater life,' warned Newman.

Paula was leaning over the side, grabbing hold of a floating object. It was the camera one of the frogmen had carried. She handed it to Alvarez. He looked at it, then at Newman.

'More and more sinister. These special cameras are expensive. If a frogman loses its grip on one it floats to the surface. So what happened to the man holding it?'

'He was electrocuted – like the others,' Newman said quietly. 'Like the other two. They have an underwater defence team, which means there's something under the hull they don't want us to see. The bodies should float to the surface.'

'No, they won't,' said Alvarez. 'There's a strong current here below the surface. The bodies could be carried miles away, maybe never recovered.'

'Let's board the ship,' Marler suggested. 'We're armed.'

'Can't do that,' Alvarez told him. 'We have no authority. No evidence.'

'What about that powerboat that tried to run us down?' Paula insisted.

'What about it? I noticed all the wreckage had vanished. No evidence,' he repeated.

'There's the camera,' Paula went on. 'Could Tweed look at copies of any pictures it took?'

'Have them delivered to him today.'

It was a depressed group which headed back for the hidden cove and no one spoke until it had landed. Alvarez acted at once. He handed the camera, which he had placed inside a strong plastic bag, now sealed, to a police officer standing by a patrol car.

'Get this to the photographic laboratory in Monterey fast. I want original prints and three copies last night . . .'

Paula watched the patrol car take off at high speed, siren shrieking, lights flashing. It reminded her of the nightmare drive from the airport to San Francisco when they had arrived.

'That was Joel Brand who swam ashore,' she said, refusing to give up.

'You could swear to that in court?' Alvarez asked. 'A positive identification?'

'Well, no. He was wearing that woolly cap which concealed his hair. I recognized his movements.'

'His movements?' Alvarez shook his head. 'Any shyster attorney could cut you to ribbons in the witness box.'

'Well, didn't anyone see him coming out of the sea?' demanded Paula, turning to a policeman standing by his patrol car. 'He must have crossed the highway to reach Black Ridge. He'd be soaked to the skin.'

'Sorry,' the policeman answered, 'but our attention was focused on waiting for you folks to come back.'

'No evidence,' Alvarez repeated for the third time. 'All in a day's . . .' He stopped. 'No it isn't. I hate losing one man. Now we've lost three. Newman, you'd better get back to Spanish Bay. I'll get those photos – if any – to Tweed.'

24

At Black Ridge in Moloch's office Vanity had heard the sound of the explosion. She jumped up, ran to the window, was just in time to see the powerboat going up in flames. She told Moloch, seated behind his desk, what she had seen.

'Defective engine, I suppose.' Moloch was absorbed in his work. 'Come back, I want to talk to you.'

'What about?' she asked as she sat facing him.

'I'm thinking of handing over some of the key accounts for you to check. You know about figures, don't you?'

'I worked in an accountant's office in London before you hired me. I think I could cope. But won't Byron be resentful?'

'These are key accounts handled by Joel.'

'Doesn't the same objection apply? I don't want to make an enemy of him.'

'I decide who handles what. There are people here who seem to forget I built up AMBECO with my own sweat and energy. Incidentally, I'm going to Grenville's party at the Anglo-Pacific Club tonight. I'd be happy for you to join me. I can take you in the Lincoln Continental.'

'Travelling in luxury,' she teased him. 'But why are you going to this party? Not like you at all. To appear in public.'

'Grenville told me among the guests will be a man called Tweed. I'd like to get to know him.' He smiled drily. 'If I'm escorting you the whole place will be abuzz. The idea amuses me.'

'I'll have to change, have a shower. What time do you want me to be ready?'

'How long do you need?'

'Thirty minutes.'

'Most women would need a couple of hours. The party starts at eight o'clock. Allow three-quarters of an hour to reach Spanish Bay. Half an hour for you to get ready. We'll leave 7.15 p.m. precisely.'

Inwardly Vanity smiled to herself. VB was always so precise about timing. Which was probably one of the secrets of his amazing success. He never wasted a minute.

'I'll be happy to come with you,' she said. 'Time you got out more into the outside world. You lock yourself away too much.'

His pale eyes looked at her. Besides her ability at her work, one of her great attractions to Moloch was the way she never hesitated to talk back to him. He hated staff who fawned. He smiled cynically.

'The outside world? California is a sewer. But I'm sure we'll have an enjoyable evening.'

Newman had just parked the car back at Spanish Bay when a red light started flashing. After making sure no one was in sight, he pressed the button which elevated the aerial. He knew it was Washington. He reached for the microphone.

'Newman here.'

'Cord speaking. How is life in California?'

'Sunny,' Newman replied quickly. He wasn't sure whether Tweed would want him to report the tragedy near Big Sur. 'Can I help?'

'If Tweed is available I need to speak to him urgently.'

'Hold on. He'll be here in a couple of minutes . . .'

He asked Paula to fetch Tweed. The moment he had elevated the aerial Marler had left the car, gesturing to Butler and Nield to fan out. The three men took up observation positions. The car was hidden from the hotel by a high wall and was parked in a rarely used section.

More quickly than he'd expected he saw in his mirror Tweed running to the car with Paula close behind. She took up a position a distance from the car indicated by Marler. Newman handed the microphone to Tweed, left the car.

'Tweed here.'

'This is a very secure line,' Dillon began. 'I assume no one else can hear us at your end . . .'

'Correct.'

'What I have to tell you is top secret. We managed to insert an agent inside VB's armaments factory in Des Moines. A most delicate operation. He's still there.'

'Understood,' Tweed assured him.

'The agent has reported Moloch has perfected an explosive of enormous power. Ten times the power of a hydrogen bomb – as I mentioned earlier. He smuggled out a small sample.'

'Raid the plant,' Tweed said immediately.

'We can't. VB's under government contract to produce the most powerful explosive he can. He hasn't told us he has succeeded. The explosive is called Xenobium. He tested it at that old silo in the Nevada desert.'

'How do you know that?'

'We compared traces of the Nevada explosive with the sample smuggled out of the Des Moines plant. They match.'

'I still don't see why you can't check Des Moines.'

'Because Moloch's accumulated so much political power on the Hill. If we did raid he'd say he'd just perfected it. He would then retaliate by using his political muscle to make sure the existing President lost the coming election. Our hands are tied behind our backs.'

'Xenobium, you said?'

'That's what the stuff's called. Sends shivers down my spine.'

'Doesn't exactly make my day, to paraphrase Clint Eastwood.'

'Tweed, are you getting anywhere?'

For the first time in their long relationship Tweed detected a note of desperation in the American's voice. He replied carefully.

'Pieces of the jigsaw fall into my lap every day. I think I am close to the whole picture. I need to meet Vincent Bernard Moloch. I have to be sure of his motive. We'll keep in touch . . .'

He had a cheerful expression when he left the car. More cheerful, Paula thought, than she'd seen him look for several days.

Moloch chatted away amusingly to Vanity as he drove his cream limo along the highway towards Carmel. He wore a smart dinner jacket and his manner was animated.

'When you met Tweed what was your impression of him?' he asked suddenly.

'Formidable,' she replied promptly.

'I think he must be to hold down the job he does. I want you to introduce me to him. Not as soon as we arrive but later in the evening.'

'I'll do that,' she promised.

'The idea is not for me to go round chatting to other guests,' he warned. 'I'd like a table to myself – just for the two of us.'

'I'll arrange that with Grenville as soon as we arrive.'

'The point is,' he explained, driving expertly, his headlights flashing round the curves, 'I want to observe who is there. I can't rely on anyone else to spot what I'm looking for.'

'Understood,' said Vanity.

What's he up to now? she was wondering. He's got some idea in that complex brain of his. Maybe I'll detect what it is after we've been there awhile.

Tweed was late leaving for the party. The photographs from Alvarez had been delivered by a plainclothes detective who showed him identity.

A handwritten note from Alvarez informed him that the scuba diver with the camera had obviously reached the seabed before disappearing. The photos showed, he had assumed, the sealed core hole the dredger had made when penetrating the floor of the Pacific.

'Make anything of these pics?' Tweed asked Paula.

She examined them using a magnifying glass. Shaking her head, she returned the photos.

'I can't make it out. It looks as though a giant round plate of some material has been used to close the hole.'

'In his note Alvarez says his experts estimate it is six feet in diameter. Beyond that they're stuck. Get Newman in here. I want to talk to Cord Dillon . . .'

Fifteen minutes later he had told Dillon he needed to send the photos to an address in London as fast as possible, that the photos could be the key to the whole mystery. Dillon asked him to hold on. Tweed sat in the Merc. with the aerial elevated. Newman had posted his team at strategic positions round the car. Tweed noticed that Butler and Nield wore new business suits, and called over Newman.

'Why are Harry and Pete dressed to go out on the town?'

'Because they're coming with us to the party. No argument, please. A crowd is just the place to shoot down a target.'

He left the car as Dillon came back on the line. His answer startled Tweed.

'We can't wire these photos. The detail is too important. Give the photos to Alvarez, who is driving to where you are. Should arrive in ten minutes. Give him the package with the address on it. A very new, fast aircraft will be waiting at Monterey airport to fly them to London. A car will be waiting at Heathrow to rush them to the Holland Park address. Will be in touch. Oh, ETA about seven hours from now . . .'

He was off the line before Tweed could thank him. Calling over to Paula, Tweed told her what was happening, to pack the photos and address them to Professor Weatherby. As she dashed off he beckoned to Newman.

'Drive me to that public phone box again. I have to call Weatherby.'

Marler slid into the back seat just before the car took off. Tweed ran to the phone box the moment the car stopped and Marler ran after him, then waited in the shadows. Above them was a star-studded night. Newman wondered why the constellations looked so much clearer in California. Lack of smog in this area, he assumed.

'Weatherby? Tweed here . . .' He explained the new development. The seismologist listened without saying anything until Tweed had finished.

'Very interesting,' he responded. 'Of course, I know a bit about this technique of sinking a special rotating tube to extract a core from the earth deep down, or from the seabed. But I'm not an expert. Luckily I happened to have a John Palister on the line a few minutes ago. He's an old friend, an insomniac, and is coming over for a drink with me in the wee small hours. He's a world expert on drilling cores. When will the photos reach me?'

'They'll shortly be leaving Monterey airport. I calculate they will reach you in about seven hours' time.'

'Seven hours? How are they coming? By rocket?'

'I've got government cooperation. They must be using one of their incredible new supersonic aircraft.'

'Right. I'll get John to stay until they arrive. He'll know what those photos mean. I'll give you a call. But where are you?'

'Spanish Bay. A hotel outside Carmel . . .'

Tweed gave him the number, warned him to wrap up what he had to say since the call would be coming via a hotel operator. Emerging from the phone box, he took a deep breath of chill night air. They drove back to Spanish Bay, picked up Paula, who was wearing a short coat and drove the short distance to where the party was being held. Butler and Nield followed them on foot.

'Now I wonder what this is really all about?' Tweed mused.

The party was in full swing by the time they arrived. Grenville met them at the door, in an evening suit with a scarlet cummerbund. He greeted them warmly, kissing Paula on the cheek.

'More of you than I expected,' he commented, looking at Marler with Butler and Nield behind him.

'We've come to help with serving the guests,' Marler drawled.

Tweed made brief introductions, scanning the large roomful of guests over Grenville's shoulder. At a corner table sat a small neat man, his dark hair brushed back over his high forehead. With him sat Vanity Richmond. Newman, catching Tweed's gaze, whispered to him as Grenville ushered his guests to a large table at the edge of the dance floor.

'That's Moloch. I took a picture of him once, had my camera snatched out of my hands by his bodyguards.'

Tweed followed Paula, who was being escorted to the

table by a buoyant Grenville. He noticed Maurice at a table by himself, emptying a glass with a morose look. Sitting down between Paula and Newman with Marler opposite while Butler and Nield occupied each end, Tweed surveyed the room. It seemed to him Moloch was doing the same thing.

The company was made up of mostly elderly and middle-aged men and women. He sensed an atmosphere of forced gaiety. There was a lot of drinking going on. Younger couples were dancing on the floor in the middle looking bored. A hand fell on his shoulder. Turning, he looked up into the lined face of a white-haired man.

'You're new,' the man said. 'Not come to live out here, I hope?'

'Why?'

'Look around you.' He had a perfect upper-crust English accent. 'They're all miserable, like me. They've come out here for the climate, left their friends at home behind, left their lives behind.'

'Then why don't they go back?' Tweed asked.

'Too late. They've lost touch with their friends, have sold up their homes in Britain. It's cheaper to live out here and they couldn't afford to return. They hanker after old things – the pubs, the villages, even London. It's not the same out here. Don't do it.'

'Thank you for your advice,' said Tweed.

'Sounds tragic,' Paula whispered.

'Probably is. Vanity appears to be coming this way.'

Smiling cheerfully, she addressed Tweed, who simply nodded.

'Mr Moloch would be honoured if you would join him for a few minutes. He's at the table I've just left, the one in the corner.'

'Then why doesn't he come over here?' demanded Paula.

'He would like a few quiet words.' She smiled again

at Paula, not losing her poise. 'The music is rather loud over here.'

Tweed glanced at the four youngsters perched on a platform, hammering out rock-and-roll. He nodded again, stood up and edged his way between the tables. Vanity sat down next to Paula in the chair Tweed had vacated. Grenville came up, a smoking cigar in his hand.

'Everyone having the time of their lives?' he asked, his voice hoarse. He waved the cigar. 'Smoke too many of these things. Still, you can't give up everything. Start with cigars and you find you've gone off drink . . .'

Moloch stood up courteously as Tweed arrived, invited him to sit in Vanity's chair. He resumed his own seat after swinging it round so he could look straight at Tweed, who gazed back into the pale clever eyes.

'I've wanted to meet you, Tweed.'

'Why?'

'Vanity described you as formidable.'

'Depends on the circumstances.'

'I suppose it would. Do you expect to be staying at Spanish Bay for long?'

'As long as it takes.'

Moloch paused. He lifted his glass. He was drinking orange juice so far as Tweed could make out. He put the glass down.

'Can I offer you a drink?'

'Thank you, but I have one at my own table.'

'Are you enjoying the party?' Moloch enquired.

'Not much.'

'Neither am I. I'm going to leave in a minute. Grenville would insist I came. Mr Tweed, we could talk more frankly if you'd be kind enough to visit me at Black Ridge, my home over here near Big Sur. I find the noise distracting.'

'I'll be glad to come and see you.'

'Good. What about eleven o'clock tomorrow morning?

268

There are gates at the entrance. I'll have them open so you can drive straight in.'

'Thank you. Eleven tomorrow morning. Please excuse me – I have friends waiting for me . . .'

Tweed noticed that Butler was standing against the wall a few yards away, looking at the dancers. Not a man to take any chances, Harry Butler. Tweed returned to his table in time to hear Vanity saying something to Paula.

'We could go into Carmel together. I know the best shops. A lot of them are selling junk. I'll give you a ring.'

'That would be nice,' Paula said without enthusiasm.

'Sorry I pinched your chair, Mr Tweed,' Vanity said, standing up and giving him a beaming smile.

'That's all right.'

Vanity hurried back to Moloch who was standing up prior to going. They left together and Moloch moved quickly to avoid Grenville who was heading his way. Then they were gone.

Tweed left soon afterwards, glancing again at Maurice, who was downing another glass of wine. He looked more morose than ever. Am I wrong, Tweed thought – he had noticed earlier that Moloch was staring straight at Maurice.

On the way back the short distance in the car Tweed told Newman about his appointment with Moloch. Newman's reaction was swift.

'Are you mad? Once inside Black Ridge you may never leave the place alive.'

'I'm going,' Tweed replied. 'I must get inside that man's mind. Time is running out . . .'

25

It was almost dawn when Tweed was woken by the phone ringing. Instantly alert, he sat up, grabbed the phone.

'Hello?'

'Tweed? Weatherby here. I have John Palister here with me. I'll do the talking – because of what you said. Palister has examined the photos. There's something peculiar going on. He has never seen a hole six feet in diameter. It doesn't go with the sort of operation you described.'

'Why not?'

'Because he has never come across so large an instrument of the sort which you said had been used. This is not the sort of cavity you could excavate with existing equipment as he knows it.'

'Has he a theory to explain it?'

'Only a bizarre one. That a special new instrument was used to make the hole and bury something huge. Sounds crazy.'

'Yes, it does,' Tweed agreed, for the benefit of anyone who might be listening to the call. 'We can dismiss that out of hand, I'm sure. Please thank Palister for his help. And thank you.'

'What's going on out there?' a worried Weatherby asked.

'I've no idea. Thank you so much for calling . . .'

Tweed got out of bed, stripped off his pyjamas and went to the shower stall. Towelling himself, shaving, then dressing he replayed the conversation in his mind.

Dismiss that out of hand? It was the last thing he was going to do. Clearly a massive drill of unprecedented proportions had been invented. He recalled AMBECO – M standing for machine tools. They would have all the facilities to create a giant drill which was undoubtedly aboard the *Baja*. Another piece of the jigsaw had slotted into place – he recalled his recent conversation with Cord Dillon. A catastrophe was imminent.

Tweed slid open one of the large glass doors he had unlocked. He wandered out from the living room onto the terrace and across the grass. He wanted to see dawn rise over the mountains, to get his thoughts in order. He was now thinking of a conversation he'd had with Weatherby earlier about tectonic plates.

'Early bird,' a voice behind him said. 'Up to see the dawn,' Paula went on.

He swung round, saw she was dressed in a turtle-necked sweater and a dark trouser suit. She tucked her arm in his, smiling. As they walked towards the main terrace overlooking the links and the sea he asked her the question.

'Did you use the precaution I asked Alvarez to supply you with when he called after we'd got back from the party?'

In reply she glanced around. Then she rolled down the turtleneck below her neck, waited while Tweed looked at her, then rolled it up again.

'Good,' said Tweed. 'Did you notice Joel Brand last night at the bar which served the party?'

'Yes. Looking very smart, wearing a duck suit.'

'Quack, quack,' said Tweed. 'That poor sister of Linda Standish's washed ashore in Cornwall knew what she was talking about.'

'I don't. You last said those words when we saw Byron Landis had a duck-waddle.'

'So I did. Look at the view. Magnificent.'

A new day was dawning, the sun, still invisible, rising behind them. It coloured the ocean with weird light, a mix of rainbowlike tints. They stood watching it as the colours changed and the ocean glowed.

'I can understand why people come to live here,' Paula said. 'Pity they don't just visit it instead of settling down here. Then they're trapped. An evil paradise.'

'There's a lot of misguided evil here,' Tweed replied. 'Or so I suspect.'

'Misguided?'

'Just a thought.'

It was eight o'clock in the morning when Joel Brand burst into Moloch's office at Black Ridge. Moloch made him wait, checking a sheaf of papers which he eventually inserted into a file. Only then did he look up.

'What is it, Joel?'

'We have to do something drastic which will throw Tweed off balance. I think he's getting too close.'

'I doubt it. What do you propose?'

'Haven't worked it out yet. Something to shake those friggin' glasses off his nose.'

'I thought you were due to fly to the AMBECO building this morning. Time you departed and got on with your work.'

Without a word Brand left the room and walked rapidly along to where Byron Landis was working. He slammed the door behind him as the accountant looked up from his desk.

Moloch heaved a sigh of relief. He'd been careful not to tell him Tweed was visiting him later in the morning. Joel was getting out of control.

He stood by the window later when he had polished off a mountain of work. At precisely eleven o'clock he saw a BMW drive in through the open gates and up the steep drive. Moloch appreciated punctuality. He sat behind his desk, waiting for Tweed to be shown up. He was surprised his visitor had come alone.

'Mr Tweed, welcome to Black Ridge. Please do take a seat, and what can I get you to drink?'

'Nothing at the moment, thank you. What did you want to talk to me about?'

'You've probably heard some wild tales about me. I thought I ought to set the record straight. I came here from Ghent in Belgium with great hopes. I met a man who had invented a new form of microchip – more advanced than anything on the market. I backed him with money borrowed from a bank, built a plant, went into production. That microchip was so revolutionary it sold like wildfire. I paid the bank back the loan. I was prospering – because I'd worked night and day to get my company off the ground. Then the opposition struck.'

'The opposition?' Tweed enquired.

'Five of my biggest competitors up in Silicon Valley combined to ruin me. First, they produced a microchip similar to mine – but sufficiently different so I couldn't take them to court. They undercut me by fifty per cent – far more than I could do to fight them. They were making huge losses but they had the money to stand them. That, Tweed, was just the beginning.'

Moloch sipped tea which had been brought in by Vanity Richmond. This time Tweed accepted tea himself. He had been watching Moloch as the words poured out. In his office, his host radiated a dynamism he hadn't noticed at Grenville's party: he seemed to exude energy and determination. His shrewd pale eyes stared at Tweed's as he continued.

'The next move my competitors made was to sabotage my trucks carrying supplies to customers. Brake fluid was tampered with. Three drivers died. Six more trucks exploded and four more drivers died. I had trouble finding good drivers who would work for me – the word got around that I wasn't a safe employer. I'll never forgive them for the lives they took. Finally, a bomb exploded inside my plant – seriously injuring ten key workers. My losses in profits mounted and I was ruined. But it was the loss of lives which changed me. I learned one thing.'

'What was that?'

'How to win in America.'

'How do you do that?'

'By being tougher than the competition. I borrowed money again from a bank. That took some fast talking. I rebuilt my plant, but this time it had the most sophisticated protection systems. I hired tough men like Joel Brand to run a security system, to hit back at the opposition. I gave orders . . .'

He paused as Vanity returned with tea for Tweed. She smiled at him.

'I liked your assistant, Paula. Makes a change to have a nice English friend.'

'I'm sure it must do,' Tweed said briefly.

'I gave orders,' Moloch continued, after Vanity had left, 'to send in saboteur teams to the opposition's plants. They had strict orders to overpower any guards without hurting them. Tear gas was used. Then they entered the plants and sabotaged key machinery, holding up production. I'm being very frank with you.'

'You certainly are,' Tweed agreed.

'Visitors from Britain make the mistake of thinking they're coming to a larger version of their own country. They couldn't be more mistaken. Especially where business is concerned. And American society – especially in California and New York – is unstable. I keep meeting women who've got married four, five, six times. They think marriage is a pastime, not a permanent relationship. This is an alien land with alien customs and ethics.'

'Things aren't too good back in Britain,' Tweed observed.

'You're right. But the rise of a great leader is overdue – someone who will clean up the mess, laying the emphasis on self-discipline, order and stability. It will come. Over here it may have gone too far. The drug epidemic started in California.'

'It's arrived in Britain,' Tweed reminded him.

'I know. Another thing about American business and politics. Corruption here is a way of life. It's gone so deep many Americans don't regard it as corruption – it's just business, Tweed. I found out that to succeed I had to get down into the pit with the hyenas. I didn't like it, still don't. But this is a jungle and the toughest fighter wins. When the bank I'd borrowed money from called in the loan at what they thought was an awkward time, I paid it back. Then I bought the bank. They hadn't realized how powerful I had become. Which sounds immodest. But this is America. Then I branched out into armaments – because that gave me a grip on the government. I hired top men from other companies in the industry, stole them by offering huge salaries. It paid off. They produced armaments more advanced than any other company – and I got government contracts. Can you tell now how I built up AMBECO?'

'I'm beginning to get the idea. Why keep on expanding? You must have enough money to last you a dozen lifetimes.'

'Because work is my only pleasure. I was married once. My wife was killed in a motor accident. Now I just have girl friends . . .'

'Seven of which have been murdered, so I heard.'

'That's true.' Moloch looked concerned. 'Why should they be a target? I don't know. I hired a private investigator to track down the killer, known as The Accountant . . .'

He paused as Byron Landis entered the office with a sheaf of files under his arm. He excused the interruption, put the files on VB's desk.

'The latest figures,' the bald man said, blinking at Tweed through his glasses.

'Give them to Vanity to check,' Moloch ordered.

'Vanity?' A resentful look crossed Landis's face. 'Why her?'

'Because I say so. Now take the files and leave us alone.'

Landis retreated with the files, his expression venomous as he closed the door. Moloch shrugged.

'Another problem. Rivalry among top members of the staff.'

'Have you a deputy?' Tweed asked.

'I mentioned him. Joel Brand. He's flown to the AMBECO building in San Francisco. You must visit that with me. It's a weird shape, but it impresses the Americans. That's the name of the game over here – to impress Americans. As you'll have noticed, I only have a small office. What was I saying when Landis barged in? I remember – that private investigator I hired, a nice woman called Linda Standish, was also murdered by The Accountant. That fiend has to be tracked down. I'd shoot him.'

He jumped up from behind his desk as a lean olive-skinned man came in. Moloch stared at him.

'This is Luis Martinez, the guard master. He works under Joel Brand. What is it, Martinez? I'm busy.'

Martinez studied Tweed, who stared back without any expression. He didn't like the look of the man. Martinez grinned at Tweed, showing his flashing teeth, then turned to Moloch.

'I'm going into town to interview a new recruit.'

'Why not interview him here?'

'If he's any good he'd ask for more money if he saw this place first.'

'He probably knows about it anyway. Still, it's your job.'

Martinez left after another glance at Tweed. Moloch picked up his visitor's tray, went towards the door.

'I'd like you to see where I meet an American businessman I need to impress . . .'

Tweed followed him out of the room, along a corridor and down some steps when Moloch had opened double doors. He looked round as Moloch placed the tray on a solid marble slab. The room was vast, had curved walls of marble, a huge picture window overlooking the drive and the Pacific beyond. Green leather button-backed couches were spread along the walls and a marble statue in a pool gushed water down into an oval pool.

Tweed sat down on a couch by the slab where Moloch had placed the tray. He stared up at a huge crystal glass chandelier. Moloch sat beside him, gestured.

'A load of hooey, but millionaires have been impressed out of their socks. I find it vulgar.'

'Must have cost a mint of money,' Tweed ventured.

'All put down to promotion. Landis is a strange man but he's good at tax rebates. You find it impressive, Tweed?'

'Maybe a bit overdone.'

'A whole lot overdone. But I had a wealthy businessman who wanted to photograph the whole room so he could reproduce it in his home. I told him he hadn't the money. He ended up signing a contract I had ready for him. Crude, I know, but we're in California.'

Tweed looked at Moloch and realized he was expressing his real feelings. He remembered the modest office his host worked in. Moloch looked at him.

'Maybe you shouldn't have come here. You might never be seen again,' he teased.

'Look out of that window,' Tweed suggested.

Moloch stood up, stared down to the highway by the entrance gates. A Mercedes was parked with Newman behind the wheel. The aerial on the roof was elevated.

'If I'm not out of here in one hour the Marines arrive,' Tweed remarked.

'Formidable, Vanity said you were. I can see why now. And I gained that impression when you were listening to me in my office.' He had just returned to the couch when a lean-faced man with his hair all over the place rushed in.

'What is it, Ethan?' Moloch snapped. 'I have a guest.'

'There's been a technical hitch.'

'Fix it. Just a minute. Our guest might be interested in your chart recorders. Unlock the chamber door and we'll be with you . . .'

He jumped up a minute later, escorted Tweed up the marble steps and along the wide corridor. A steel door hung open and Moloch warned Tweed to watch the staircase. Beyond the door a steel spiral staircase twisted its way down into a large room. On tables screwed to the floor stood machines with rolls of graph paper. Tweed followed Moloch and stared as a needle traced a fairly regular line across the paper. The needle jumped up suddenly, then dropped, creating a steep triangle. Ethan, who seemed to take a liking to Tweed, pointed to it.

'A small earthquake tremor,' he explained. 'I use an advanced form of the VAN system. We have stations all along the coast both north and south of here. A series of really steep reactions like that, much larger, indicate a major earthquake is imminent. We—'

'I don't think our guest wants to hear a lot of technical jargon,' Moloch interrupted him.

'What is that huge steel door over there?' Tweed asked.

'A safe.'

'A safe?' echoed Ethan, sounding puzzled.

'Where I keep a lot of money,' Moloch whispered to Tweed. 'For bribes. Now we'd better go . . .'

'And I'd better take leave of your hospitality,' Tweed said as they reached the hall. 'Thank you for a most interesting conversation.'

As he walked down the drive towards Newman's car – the gates had opened – Tweed was a worried man. He'd found the chart recorders sinister. But now he knew Moloch's terrible motive.

26

Vanity drove down the drive from Black Ridge as Tweed walked towards the exit. She pulled up alongside him, smiling as usual.

'Mr Tweed, can I give you a lift somewhere? I'm off to meet Paula in Carmel.'

'Thank you, but I have transport.'

'So long as you have wheels, as the Yanks say.'

She drove off and Tweed climbed into the front passenger seat beside Newman, who had retracted the aerial as soon as he saw Tweed coming.

'She certainly moves,' Newman remarked, nodding towards where Vanity was swinging at speed round a bend and up a hill before disappearing. 'Like a whippet. Get anywhere with VB?'

'Drive me to Spanish Bay.'

Newman started the engine, drove off, realizing he was going to get nothing out of Tweed. In the back Marler, hunched up on the floor behind the front seats with his Armalite, waited until they were out of sight of Black Ridge before settling in the rear seat.

Behind them the BMW appeared, driven by Butler,

who had collected it from outside Moloch's house. Nield sat alongside him. Tweed realized that the whole team had been watching over him. All the way along the highway he sat without saying a word, thinking of his recent experience. Nothing in his expression gave away the anxiety he was feeling.

'Go through Carmel,' he said suddenly. 'Drive around it. I want to get thoroughly familiar with it. Go up and down the streets and avenues.'

'Something wrong?' Newman enquired.

'I just have a sixth sense something unpleasant is going to happen . . .'

It was brilliantly sunny when they began. Newman drove along the avenues which climbed up from the sea, turned along the streets which intersected the avenues. The attractive town was laid out very precisely, its pavements lined with shops and restaurants.

'There's Paula with Vanity,' Newman said.

As they cruised past slowly Paula turned her head, waved a hand and smiled at them. Tweed told Newman to drive on.

'Still got that feeling something unpleasant is going to happen?' Newman asked.

'More than ever . . .'

'What a glorious peaceful day,' Paula said to Vanity as they strolled along, stopping every now and again to look in shop windows.

'It's wonderful,' Vanity agreed. 'We're on Junipero now, near the top of the town. Here's my Audi. Would you mind if I slipped off for half an hour to see a friend? She's had a bad time of it – lost her husband to another woman. I don't think you'd find the conversation entertaining.'

'Meet you on that far corner. Then we can have coffee together . . .'

Paula was not sorry to have time to herself. She had recognized Junipero and was close to the courtyard where Linda Standish had been murdered. She wanted to see if she could get inside the apartment Linda had occupied in case she could find something else the police had missed.

From a sunny street where locals were walking and chatting she turned into the narrow entrance to the courtyard, stepping into a different world. The sun had gone, a disturbing silence filled the deserted courtyard and her heels echoed on the cobbles.

There was no breeze and the hanging baskets of flowers were motionless. She walked on into the main courtyard, turning a corner. When she looked back the streets of Carmel had vanished. She paused, gazed at the shops on the ground floor and they all had 'Closed' notices. The memory of Linda's horrible death hung over the place like a sinister shadow. Clearly business was temporarily at a standstill.

She looked up at the apartments above the shops. No sign of life anywhere. The silence, the lack of people, of movement gave her a creepy feeling. Why on earth had she come here? It had been purely on a whim. Then she stared at the iron staircase leading up to Linda's apartment. The door was slightly open.

Gritting her teeth, she opened her shoulder bag, gripped the butt of her Browning nestling in its special pocket. Then slowly, step by step, she began to ascend the staircase.

She wished she'd worn loafers. On the metal treads the soles of her shoes made a noise. She paused again, took off her shoes, held them in her left hand, crept silently up the remaining treads. The police had obviously abandoned the place – the tapes across the bottom of the staircase had been removed. There were no longer any signs of the macabre event which had taken place inside the apartment.

'Anyone at home,' she called out, standing by the open door.

She didn't want to walk in on Anderson, the detective who had been there when she had visited the apartment with Tweed. If startled, he might draw a gun on her. There was no response. Only an uncanny silence. She eased the door open with her foot.

In the gloom – the curtains were half-closed – the room looked just as she had last seen it. The empty desk with the chair pulled back gave her a weird sensation. Linda Standish had lived and worked here for heaven knew how long. She walked in, put on her shoes, held her automatic in her right hand, looked all round. The door to the toilet was closed.

She approached it cautiously, turned the handle, tried to push it open but it stuck. She remembered Anderson had used his shoulder to push open the door when she was last there. She stood surveying the room, trying to imagine any other hiding place Standish might have used to hide a vital document. She couldn't see anywhere she had missed.

With a certain trepidation she sat down in Standish's chair behind her desk, pulled it in. She had a hope that from this angle she might see a fresh hiding place. Her mood was not helped by the fact that the police had left the IRS tax returns Standish had been working on scattered across the desk. They were soiled with fingerprint powder. They never clean up properly, she thought, but she had had the same experience in Britain.

She noticed the faint bloodstains which still covered the desk in different places. Opening the top right-hand drawer she found it empty. The police had taken away the gun Standish had never had a chance to use.

'There has to be something here they overlooked,' she said to herself. 'Why didn't they send a policeman to check the place? Maybe they did.'

The silence in the room was stifling. She felt cut off from the outside world. But she was determined to stick it out, to stay until she was sure there was nothing more she could find. Then she noticed the camp bed, folded and standing against a dark corner. Beside it was a pile of blankets and a folded sheet. Had an American version of a squatter taken over the place?

She opened all the other drawers in the desk and found them full of notebooks which appeared to concern previous cases Standish had worked on. Paula skim-read each one, hoping that she might find something which would give her a clue as to why Standish had been killed.

Behind her the handle of the toilet door began to revolve. It was turned with great care from the inside. The freshly oiled door opened a few inches. The handle was released with the same slow care. A hooded figure in loafers emerged as Paula crouched over a notebook, rejected it and selected another. The figure made no sound, the feet clad in loafers. The gloved hands held a garrotte.

Paula was still crouched over the notebook when, too late, she was aware of another presence in the room. Two hands whipped the garrotte over her head, pulled it tight round her throat. The pressure increased. For a few seconds Paula was in shock.

The wire had immediately cut through the turtleneck of her jumper. Then it met the fine-mesh collar of chain metal Alvarez had supplied at Tweed's urgent request. Even so, it began to affect her breathing. She snatched the Browning out of her shoulder bag, still slung from her shoulder. Resting the barrel on her right shoulder, she pulled the trigger, firing at random. The bullet missed the hooded figure but the pressure on her neck relaxed as the garrotte was dropped to the floor.

The assassin stepped back, took hold of her chair, tipped her over sideways. Falling, Paula always subconsciously went limp. She took the force of the fall on her shoulder, but still held on to the gun as she heard soft footsteps running for the door leading to the outside staircase.

Forcing herself upright, she took a deep breath to counter shock. Then, gun in hand, she ran to and down the staircase. Her attacker had disappeared. She ran on towards the exit from the courtyard, held the gun behind her back as she was confronted by a coachload of tourists who had just disembarked, crowding the pavement. She pushed her way through them, looked up and down the street. The only people she could see were normal couples, strolling in the sun.

Concealing the gun inside the shoulder bag she had thrust back into position, she ran to the nearest corner, stood looking down an avenue. More couples, some stopping to gaze into shop windows. She waited, breathing heavily. No one seemed to notice the ragged tear across her turtleneck. Then she saw a familiar Mercedes approaching. She stood in the road, waved it down.

Tweed was out of the car almost before it had stopped. He noticed the tear immediately.

'What happened? Are you all right?'

'I'm OK. Could I get into the car?'

Like Newman, Marler had jumped out of the back of the car. Tweed helped her into the rear seat, joined her. Peeling down the damaged turtleneck, he carefully unfastened the zip at one side of her neck. All he could see were faint imprints where the chain mail collar had pressed against her neck. Again he asked her if she was all right.

'I'm OK,' she repeated and then told him what had happened. 'My throat's a bit sore but apart from that all is well.'

Newman had returned to his seat behind the wheel. Marler sat beside him. Tweed's reaction surprised them both.

'Drive me to the nearest phone booth . . .

'Take Paula into that restaurant, both of you,' he ordered as the car stopped. 'Get her plenty of still water – no alcohol.'

He leapt from the car, dived inside the phone booth. He pressed numbers from his memory of a phone he had seen on Moloch's desk. The rough voice of a guard answered the call.

'I wish to speak urgently to Luis Martinez,' Tweed snapped.

'He's gone into Carmel to interview someone.'

'Then I'll speak to Byron Landis.'

'Gone to a lunch, also in Carmel. Say, who is this?'

'A close friend of VB. Obstruct me and you've lost your job. Put me on to Joel Brand.'

'He flew to the AMBECO building earlier this morning.'

'Then put me on to Mr Moloch.'

'He's not here. Look, buddy . . .'

He was talking into air. Tweed had put down the phone to join the others in the restaurant. Any of the people he had asked for could have been involved in the attempt on Paula's life. When he sat down opposite her he was surprised how normal she seemed. She was polishing off an omelette and drinking the strong American coffee. He waited until she used a napkin to wipe her lips.

'How are you feeling now?'

'Perfectly all right. Incidentally, when The Accountant – it has to be the person who tried to kill me – bent over me from behind I caught a whiff of an aroma I thought could be perfume. As you know, I have a good sense of smell. I was not able to identify it but I'd recognize it if I whiffed it again.'

'I see.' He looked at Newman. 'Where is Marler?'

'I sent him back to the Standish flat. Oh, here he is. Did you find anything, Marler?'

'Only the weapon – whoever tried to attack Paula dropped something I have inside a sample bag I took from the car.' He held up a large plastic carrier. 'I bought something from a shop to disguise it. Inside here is a garrotte – with two wooden handles at either end of the infernal wire. I think there's blood on the wire – it could be the garrotte used to murder the Standish woman. There's also old blood on one of the wooden handles – probably used to inscribe the letters AC on her.'

'We'll hand it to Alvarez,' Tweed decided. 'His technicians will be able to check whether it's Linda Standish's blood.'

'I have to go,' said Paula, standing up. 'Vanity will be wondering where I have got to. I arranged to meet her.'

'Not by yourself,' Tweed warned.

'It would look peculiar if I turned up with a bodyguard,' she protested.

'She'll never see the bodyguard,' Marler informed her as he also stood up. 'But I'll be close to you . . .'

Vanity was not waiting on the corner where they had arranged to meet. Paula began to wander down into the town, peering in every shop. She already knew from Vanity that she had a passion for shopping.

She was passing a perfumery when she saw Vanity inside. A saleswoman was showing her a new perfume. As Paula watched, the saleswoman sprayed a small quantity of perfume and Vanity sniffed at it. She smiled warmly as she saw Paula entering the shop.

'Sorry I wasn't on the corner. I waited a while and then had a look at the shops down here. What do you think of this? It's a new perfume called Paramour. At least the name's enticing.'

'A bit strong, isn't it?' Paula suggested.

'I think you're right. Not quite me,' she said to the saleswoman. 'I'm in a rush. Come back another day.'

As they walked out Vanity chattered on in her engaging manner. Paula was very thoughtful as they continued to explore the shops. The spray of Paramour had effectively masked whatever perfume Vanity normally used.

27

Vanity had gone inside an antique shop and Paula was looking in the window of another shop when Marler approached her, appearing out of nowhere. He stood a few feet from her and lit a king-size, then spoke quietly.

'Get back to Spanish Bay immediately. A Yellow Cab I've called will arrive any minute. Ah, here it is. Tell Vanity you've just realized you're late for a meeting with Tweed.'

'Trouble?'

'Yes. We're being followed. Don't let Vanity take you back in her Audi. Tweed, Newman, Butler and Nield have gone to Spanish Bay in the Merc. I've borrowed the BMW.'

'Didn't see you.'

'Didn't intend you to. Go and tell the driver of the cab you'll be with him in a minute. Then go in that shop and make your apologies to Vanity . . .'

He turned, had gone before Paula could say anything else. From inside an alley he watched until she was safely inside the cab. Then he ran to the BMW parked among other cars higher up the street.

As he took off he glanced in his rear-view mirror. The grey Chrysler which had been tracking Paula moved faster, overtook Marler, followed the Yellow Cab which had Paula as a passenger. When, later, the cab took the road towards Spanish Bay the Chrysler gave up, soon turning on a route which would take it back to Highway One. Luis Martinez was behind the wheel.

'Thickhead,' Marler said to himself. 'You were so busy following the girl you never dreamt I was on your tail . . .'

There was more traffic on Highway One. Marler kept one vehicle between himself and Martinez, whose appearance had been described to him by Tweed. The Chrysler kept up a good speed along the magnificent coastal road. Marler presumed Martinez was returning to Black Ridge but he never relied on assumptions.

The wisdom of this attitude was proved later when Martinez suddenly swung left off the highway and vanished. Marler slowed down, glanced up the side road where Martinez had disappeared. *Palo Eldorado*, a signpost proclaimed. He continued driving along the highway until he reached a safe place to make a totally illegal U-turn.

He glanced up Palo Eldorado again as he paused. Narrow, the side road was shrouded in trees on both sides and mounted the hillside before going out of sight at a bend. Marler also noticed that near the exit from the side road, oil slicks smeared the road surface. He wondered whether this was where the two juggernauts had waited before attempting to push them over the cliff. Worth mentioning to Tweed.

In the living room of his apartment at Spanish Bay Tweed was holding a battle conference. Present were Newman and Nield. Outside in the corridor Butler strolled up and down to make sure they were not overheard. When Paula arrived Tweed began again.

'Time we summed up the present position. What we do next.'

'Track down this bastard, The Accountant?' Newman suggested.

'No! Moloch remains the main target. And we must find out definitely what he is planning. I don't think we have much time left.'

'What did you think of him when you were at Black Ridge?' Paula asked.

'He has a first-rate brain, tremendous drive and the most persuasive personality – especially when he is being frank, which he was with me. I want you to look at these maps.'

He spread out on a table a detailed map of California and the map with zigzag lines given to him by Professor Weatherby. He waited while his team gathered round and looked at the maps, comparing one with the other. Tweed's index finger stabbed down on an area in northern California.

'That's Silicon Valley.'

'The main zigzag line runs right through it,' Paula observed.

'Exactly. Let me tell you what Moloch told me . . .'

They listened while he recalled every word of his conversation at Black Ridge. When he had finished he gave his own reaction.

'This man came to America with high hopes. He worked like a Trojan to build up his first plant. With the new microchip he was a great success. Then five top firms in Silicon Valley combine to smash him. They use every dirty trick in the book, as you'll have gathered. They ruin him. Before that I'd say he was a decent, hard-working man who honestly built up his own company. It all turns to ashes. What more could turn him into an embittered man – determined to destroy those who destroyed him? With the help of Ethan Benyon, a genius in his field, he plans to wipe out Silicon Valley wholesale.'

'But how?' Paula asked.

'By triggering an earthquake along the San Moreno fault – and that, as you observed, Paula, runs straight through Silicon Valley.'

'But is it possible?' Newman asked. 'To do that?'

'A month ago I'd have said no. Now I'm not so sure. Science is advancing by leaps and bounds in so many fields. So why not in seismology? When a man like Professor Weatherby is worried about what Ethan is working on, then so am I.'

'Sounds so unlikely,' Pete Nield commented, fingering his moustache. 'But there was a time when landing on the moon would have seemed a pipe dream.'

'So how do we go about finding out?' Newman asked.

'We explore every avenue . . .'

He had just spoken when Marler walked in. He had heard what Tweed had just said.

'One avenue I suggest we explore now is Palo Eldorado. For two reasons . . .'

Tweed agreed immediately that they should check the mysterious road. Paula pressed to be allowed to join them and he decided it might be safer if she was with them. It was mid-afternoon when they were driving along Highway One. Paula sat in the front of the Merc. beside Newman while Tweed and Marler occupied the back seats.

Behind them Butler and Nield followed in the BMW. Marler had warned them all to have their weapons ready when they reached their destination. He hadn't liked the look of the strange side road.

The Pacific was not living up to its name. As they drove further and further from Carmel great waves rolled in and broke against the jagged capes which spread away along the coast. A strong wind was blowing offshore and storm clouds were building up.

'You're close to it,' Marler called out to Newman. 'Next turning on your left. You're on it before you realize it.'

Away from the scenic wonders of the highway Newman turned into a strange world. On the tarred road near the exit he saw the dried-out oil slicks Marler had noticed. He thought Marler had been right – that this was where the two juggernauts had waited in ambush.

As soon as they entered the road they were hemmed in on both sides with a dense screen of redwood and eucalyptus trees. In a gap a strange house was built on the slope, three floors, each stepped one above the other. They turned a corner and the highway was gone. They were driving through a dark tunnel where foliage from the trees arched over the winding road.

'Look at those weird places,' Paula called out.

To their left, where a slope rose steeply, were several tumbledown shacks which had an abandoned look. There was even an ancient stone fireplace among the trees. It had a chimney but the rest of the building had gone. More shacks, scattered at random and different levels, appeared amid the trees. Here and there old wooden bridges spanned stream beds. Paula thought she saw movement behind the shacks, shabby figures in bedraggled clothes, one carrying firewood.

'We've left civilization behind, I suspect,' joked Tweed.

He glanced at Paula in front of him. She looked recovered from her ordeal at the Standish apartment. As they climbed higher under the tunnel of trees Paula saw moss-covered walls, huge motionless ferns. The wind off the ocean had no chance of penetrating this wild place. This was a side of California the tourist never saw.

'And just look at that,' Paula called out again.

They had rounded a bend, still climbing, when she saw a small bus sagging to one side under the trees. Without wheels, its sides were smeared with psychedelic signs. More shacks came into view and crude fences made of bark, tilting over and covered with green from damp. Other figures lurched across the slope, dressed like scarecrows, and there was a lot of scrub oak, stunted, miserable versions of oak trees.

A propane gas cylinder perched on wooden struts stood on the slope – presumably for heating and cooking. Again shacks were piled up the slope, some with sagging balconies. Newman gestured upwards where overhead power cables were slung from ancient posts alongside the road.

'People live here,' he said with a note of wonderment.

'I think they're drop-outs,' Tweed commented. 'Relics of the hippies in the nineteen-sixties. They're the debris of so-called Californian civilization. We've gone back a good thirty years.' His voice sharpened. 'Look to the right, Bob.'

Parked up a track was a modern cream Jaguar. A uniformed driver with a peaked cap was slumped behind the wheel, so fast asleep he never noticed the two cars passing. Tweed spoke again, this time sharply.

'Stop, Bob. Switch off the engine. Look to your right.'

Paula was already looking. The trees were now giant sequoias, mighty trunks soaring up towards the invisible sky. Under them, on a level area halfway up the slope, a figure familiar to Tweed was dancing with a girl as a ghetto-blaster spewed out rock-and-roll.

The man was stripped to the waist, wore only a pair of denims and loafers. Without touching the girl, he was dancing back and forth, waving his arms, his hair all over the place. The girl had dark greasy hair, wore a shabby dress and tights with holes in them. Neither seemed to have heard the cars coming.

'That's Ethan Benyon,' Tweed said grimly.

'One way to get your kicks,' Marler drawled.

As they watched, Ethan approached more closely to the girl, his hands reaching out to clutch her. She retreated up the slope, picked up a heavy branch as he came after her. Using the branch as a weapon, she hit him across the ribs. Ethan froze, then let out a chilling scream which went on and on.

'Drive,' Tweed ordered. 'Find a turning place and get out of this Dante's Inferno . . .'

He said nothing else until Newman had turned back on to Highway One. Paula took a deep breath of sea air through the window she had opened. The total silence inside Palo Eldorado had got on her nerves – until she heard the scream.

'That was Ethan Benyon,' Tweed said again. 'A genius, Moloch called him. No doubt he is in his own field of science. But he's as mad as a hatter. Not a comforting thought . . .'

The hammer blow fell when they returned to Spanish Bay. In the car park Tweed said he wanted to get in touch with Cord Dillon. He told Paula, Newman and Marler to stay in the car. Butler and Nield had just returned in the BMW. Newman waved to them to act as lookouts, then pressed buttons on the black box. Tweed automatically reached for the microphone.

'Is that you, Cord?'

'Speaking. Recognize your voice, Tweed.'

'It's time we took action. Urgently. I'd like Alvarez to send more frogmen down to the sealed hole under the *Baja*. They can be armed this time. I want to know whether there's some kind of wireless transmitter attached to the plate sealing the hole. It really is urgent . . .'

'Sorry, Tweed, I can't do that. The special unit which went down has already lost three men.'

'They weren't armed,' Tweed persisted. 'It's a vital act.'

'No can do. Tweed, I have bad news for you. I've been ordered not to harass our friend in any way. Powerful senators have visited the President in the White House. They threatened to veto any future bills he wants passing. You know who has put the pressure on them. I was called to the Oval Office myself, told to leave the target strictly alone. I felt like ignoring the order, but then I'd immediately be replaced. So where would that get us?'

'What about Alvarez?'

'One of my best men. I've recalled him to Langley.'

'What you're saying is we get no more cooperation from you,' Tweed said forcefully. 'Even though I'm sure a national disaster is imminent?'

'You've concrete evidence for that statement?'

'It's inside Black Ridge, I'm sure, and on the seabed, under the *Baja*.'

'Storm into Black Ridge? Risk more lives on the seabed? I can't do it. I have a wife and children to think of. I'd be had for gross dereliction of duty. I told you. I had to go to the White House. Urgent summons. Read the riot act.'

'We're on our own, then? Is that what you're saying?'

'Sure is. And my best advice is for all of you to get out of the US of A pretty damned fast.'

'I understand your position,' Tweed said more quietly.

'Just run. Run like hell. While you're still alive . . .'

28

Tweed held a second battle conference in his suite at Spanish Bay. Everyone was present except Butler, who was patrolling the corridor outside. With his hands clasped behind his back, Tweed, standing, faced the others, who were sitting down. For Nield's sake he recalled what Dillon had said.

'We're on our own,' he concluded.

'We've been there before,' Nield commented in his cultured voice. 'Sometimes it's better that way. Then we have total secrecy. Don't see how that affects the situation.'

'Thank you, Pete.' Tweed looked at Paula. 'I think we had better put you on the first flight home.'

She stood up, her nostrils flaring. Under her elegant dark brows her eyes glared. She stood with her hands on her hips.

'You want to try it? Carrying me aboard a flight kicking and screaming that I'm being kidnapped?'

'I gather I have no option.' Tweed smiled drily. 'You will be staying.'

'You're too damned right I'll be staying.'

She sat down, her face flushed with indignation.

Crossing her legs, she stared at Tweed, who began speaking again.

'You have to understand, all of you, we're in a hostile land. No help from anyone.'

'Been there. So we're there again. So what?' asked Nield.

There was a knock on the door. It was opened by Butler and Alvarez walked in. He flashed a smile at Paula, sat down on the couch next to her.

'We've heard from Langley . . .' Tweed began.

'So have I,' Alvarez replied. 'I thought about it, then I just called Cord again. Told him to stuff his job where the monkey put the nuts.' He glanced at Paula. 'Sorry, but it is good English?'

'Perfect,' she assured him.

'I've resigned,' Alvarez went on. 'Moloch may be able to put pressure on Washington, but he can't put it on me. You folks need someone who knows the territory. I know it like the back of my hand. Let's say I've put myself on temporary assignment to you. I presume you're going on with this?'

'We are.'

'I guessed you would. I handed in my gun to police HQ in Monterey, told them I didn't care how they got it to Langley. Then I went out and bought myself another gun. With a permit. I'm at your disposal.'

'We're all very grateful . . .' Tweed began again.

'None of that stuff.' Alvarez held up a hand, smiled again. 'I smell great danger. I happen to think enough of my country to stay in the act. So what has been happening?'

Tweed explained their visit to Palo Eldorado. Told Alvarez what they had seen. He frowned.

'Took a chance going up there. Not the most dangerous place in California, but risky. Ethan Benyon sounds like a crazy.'

He is. And I'm sure he's a key figure in VB's operation.'

'I've just worked something out,' Paula intervened. 'Moloch invited you to Black Ridge to weigh you up. "Formidable" was how Vanity described you. She probably passed that on to him – and when he saw you he agreed with her assessment. His next move was to pressure the politicians he's bought. I had wondered why he wanted to see you. He's scared of you.'

'I suppose you could be right,' Tweed said dubiously. 'I had a call from Vanity just before you all came in here. She wants to meet me at a place called The Ridge, a restaurant and hotel up the Carmel Valley. 12.30 p.m. tomorrow.'

'We'll all come with you,' Newman said.

'He isn't going to let pass a chance to meet Vanity again,' said Paula, introducing a lighter note deliberately.

'We don't know this place,' Newman warned.

'I do,' said Alvarez. 'A top restaurant. Run by a nice guy. I think I ought to come, too. I know how to get there.'

'You would be welcome to join us for dinner this evening,' Tweed suggested. 'Unless being seen with us would put you in danger.'

Alvarez laughed. 'I'm going to be seen with you a whole lot. What the hell do I care? I'm a civilian now. I accept the invitation with thanks. Where would you like to go?'

'I've heard that there's a very good restaurant in Carmel called Anton & Michel. After today, I feel like a really good meal. Grenville told me about it.'

'You'll get it there,' Alvarez assured him. 'If it's OK by you guys I'll make a reservation for all of us. Time?'

'8 p.m.,' Tweed said promptly. 'Takes Paula an hour to tart herself up.'

'It does not,' she rapped back.

'Don't forget Butler,' Nield suggested to Alvarez.

'How could I forget a tough guy like that?'

He was going to the phone when Tweed asked him to wait a moment. He looked round at everybody.

'I think I should tell you I'm convinced Moloch has a spy, identity unknown, outside his immediate organization. We can trust no one.'

'I never do,' replied Alvarez and smiled again at Paula who smiled back warmly. 'One other thing before I make the call,' Alvarez warned. 'I don't know why Vanity Richmond has asked you to lunch, Tweed. We'd better watch that one . . .'

'Did you invite Tweed to lunch at The Ridge in Carmel Valley?' Joel Brand asked Vanity.

Working late in her office at Black Ridge, Vanity looked up in surprise. She had thought Brand was going in to Carmel for dinner.

'Yes, I did. You said VB wanted me to assess Tweed to confirm his own opinion.'

'So Tweed will be there at 12.30 p.m.?'

'I imagine so. He agreed to have lunch with me.'

'Thank you.' Brand gave her a big smile. 'Don't work too late. It will spoil your beauty sleep.'

'That would be a tragedy,' she said sarcastically.

When he had gone she tried for the third time to call Moloch at the AMBECO building in San Francisco. Once again he was engaged on another call. She decided to give up checking Brand's instruction. Later, her not calling VB again was to have momentous consequences for several people.

A very satisfied Brand soon left the building, climbed into his Citroën to drive to Carmel through the evening dark. He was not only aggressive but also very thorough. He knew that VB would not have approved of what he had planned, but he was Chief of Security.

Brand was not convinced that the fact that VB had caused all official support to be withdrawn from him in Washington was going to compel Tweed to leave the country. Better to make sure he was no longer a menace.

In an emergency, experience had taught him, when springing one trap on a target, it was best to have a back-up – in case the first trap failed. Still, with a bit of luck Tweed would not survive the next few hours.

Anton & Michel was hidden away in another of Carmel's many courtyards. But this one, once you were inside, was far more open than the courtyard where Linda Standish had been murdered. Paula was relieved by the different atmosphere.

It was called Court of the Fountains. As they turned a corner she saw why. In a large open space was an oblong pool full of water. Fountains, spurting water, were illuminated. The whole place gave her a relaxed feeling. Great tall windows lined the outside of the restaurant – long slabs of glass which gave those with window tables a close view of the fountains and the pool.

'This is lovely,' she said to Alvarez.

'It's great,' he replied.

After parking the cars Alvarez had remained behind for a short time, looking up and down the street, empty at this evening hour. Then he had hustled ahead, alongside Paula, and was the first to enter the restaurant after a quick excuse to Paula. Following him, she saw his swift glance round the restaurant, checking every table.

'Looks OK,' he said to Tweed who had caught them up.

They were shown to a large table by the window. The

whole team was there. Newman, Marler, Butler and Nield. Paula sat by the window, opposite Tweed. She noticed Alvarez took the end chair furthest away from the window, presumably so he could scan any newcomers.

The restaurant was almost full and many of the guests had by now reached an advanced stage of their meal. The interior was luxurious and comfortable at the same time. Paula leaned towards Tweed.

'This is a marvellous place. The decor is perfect. And it's got this wonderful view of the fountains. What more could we want?'

'A menu,' said Marler.

A moment later the head waiter appeared, handed out a menu to each guest. Paula noticed Alvarez merely glanced at his, then he was casually gazing round again. She leaned again towards Tweed, keeping her voice low.

'Why is Alvarez on edge?'

'Well . . .' Tweed hesitated, then decided he'd better tell her the truth. 'He says we were followed here from the moment we had left the exit from Spanish Bay.'

'I've just lost my appetite.'

'Would you sooner I hadn't told you?'

'No. I like to know what's going on.'

'That's what I thought. Now, decide what you want. Choose something good.'

Paula gradually relaxed as she consumed an excellent meal, drank a little wine. Newman seemed to be in a good mood and cracked jokes with her, but she knew he was capable of appearing without a care in the world when inwardly he was worried. Tweed drank orange juice and she noticed Alvarez also avoided taking any wine.

'You know,' she said as coffee was served, 'the Americans are wonderful at creating original and high-class restaurants. This place is a good example of their skill in that field.'

'I agree,' said Tweed.

'Everything here is just right,' she went on.

'Perfect.'

Paula was aware that the conversation was stilted, that they were making an effort to appear to be enjoying themselves. Marler smoked more king-sizes than was usual. Butler and Nield joined in the conversation but only Nield had a light-hearted way of talking.

'Paula,' he called out, 'spoil yourself. Have a liqueur with your coffee. That should get the corpuscles running around in circles.'

'It would probably get me running round in circles.'

'That I'd like to see,' Nield continued. 'We could dance the samba, create a sensation. People at other tables seem to be taking life far too seriously. The idea of going out for a meal is to enjoy yourself. And you're looking particularly ravishing tonight.'

'Thank you, Pete. You're dangerous. In a minute I'll order a Grand Marnier.'

'I'll order it for you now . . .'

'I said in a minute.'

She liked Pete Nield. He was good-looking, always calm in a critical situation. He gave the impression of really finding life a great entertainment.

'Glad you think I'm dangerous,' he chaffed her. 'I'm told women can't resist a man who has a reputation for being dangerous. You know why?'

'Tell me.' She laughed. 'You sound like an expert in that way of life.'

'They are attracted to dangerous men because . . .' he leaned forward '. . . they believe they can tame them. They are a challenge. Few women can resist a challenge.'

'If you say so.' She laughed again. 'Are you challenging me, Pete?'

'Don't take him on, Paula,' Newman joked. 'Behind that suave manner is a very experienced Casanova . . .'

Paula was laughing again when a shadowy figure appeared in the courtyard. It wore a wide-brimmed slouch hat pulled down over the forehead, large dark glasses, a scarf wrapped round the lower part of the face, a short trenchcoat and denims.

At first sight there was nothing strange about the garb – it was very chilly outside and Paula had worn her fur coat. Shuffling along at a rapid pace, the figure approached the window. Paula froze in mid-laugh. The invisible eyes behind the dark glasses stared at her. Then both hands were raised and she saw they were clutching a circular object the size of a large soup plate. The figure thrust the object against the glass and it remained there, like a turtle poised at right angles to the ground.

Only Alvarez had noticed her sudden change of expression. He saw the turtle clinging to the window as the figure began to leave the courtyard, its shadow enormous in the illumination from the fountains. He jumped up, kicking his chair back, shouted at the top of his voice.

'*On the floor, everybody. It's a bomb!*'

Having delivered his warning he dived out of the restaurant into the courtyard. He heard footsteps running away but all his attention was concentrated on the turtle. Grasping it with both strong nimble hands, he prised its suckers off the glass, threw it into the pool, dropped flat.

The detonation was deafening. Large fragments of the pool's floor were hurled into the air. One slab crashed close to Alvarez's head, but he was unhurt. Gallons of water burst out, headed skywards, then fell like a huge waterfall. The windows of Anton & Michel were splashed with water which poured down the outside of the glass like heavy rain, but the glass stayed intact.

Inside the restaurant Paula had dived under the table with the others. Panic gripped the restaurant, which had been shaken by the blast. Women screamed, men pushed each other out of the way to find space under tables. Plates of food littered the floor, red wine like blood stained the tablecloths.

Outside, Alvarez had jumped to his feet. He was soaked to the skin, but a mild discomfort like that did not affect in the slightest his abundant energy, his endless determination. With his Walther concealed by his side, he ran like the wind after the strange figure which had appeared like an apparition outside the window.

Reaching the exit, he was just in time to see a Chrysler's rear end disappearing round a corner at speed. He swore. Then he ran back to the restaurant. Time to get Tweed & Co. out of the place before the police arrived.

Tweed had already foreseen the importance of a swift departure. The bill was on the table and he quickly dropped several one-hundred-dollar bills on the plate, which included a generous twenty per cent tip. No waste of time with a credit card, no risk of his being traced through its use.

The team had crawled out from under the table very quickly. The only injury was a bruised left elbow Marler had sustained as he dived for cover. Alvarez ushered them out as confusion still gripped the restaurant.

They hurried to the exit from the courtyard. Paula's last memory of the grim experience was seeing a damaged fountain still spurting water against the restaurant window, which masked their flight.

Reaching the parked cars, they piled inside. Overhead was a starry night and there were no pedestrians on the street. They were driven out of Carmel at normal speed and then on to Spanish Bay.

Tweed, in need of company, asked Paula to come

with him to his apartment after thanking Alvarez for saving them. The ex-CIA man shrugged as though it was nothing, told Tweed his room number and left them.

29

The truth was Tweed had felt depressed even before the bomb detonated. He had been careful to conceal his feelings from the others. It was the job of the man at the top to maintain morale.

Now his mood was one of cold, controlled rage. He paced back and forth in the spacious living room while Paula lit the gas log fire. It ignited at once, creating warmth and a cheerful blaze. Then she opened the curtains the staff had closed earlier, opened them a fraction to check the locks. Outside, walking slowly on the wide grass verge, illuminated briefly by a lamp, was Nield. She threw him a kiss, closed the curtain again. Presumably Butler would take over the night-watch later.

Next she went to the extensively stocked minibar, chose a bottle of Chardonnay, then a miniature of Grand Marnier. Without asking, she poured Tweed a glass of wine and, for herself, a small glass of the liqueur. She only spoke after settling down on a couch near the fire.

'The wine is for you,' she told him. 'I think it might help you think, relax.'

'Thank you.'

He was still pacing with slow, deliberate steps, a certain expression on his face. She sipped at her Grand Marnier.

'If I get tiddly you can help me back to my room,' she joked.

As she had hoped, the glass of wine persuaded Tweed

to stop pacing. He sat down in an armchair opposite her, drank a little, put down the glass, stared at her.

'They think they've seen us off,' he growled.

'With the bomb, you mean?'

'No. I mean Moloch and his staff. I'm referring to the pressure Moloch put on Washington. As to the bomb, I'd be surprised if he knew about it.'

'What makes you say that?'

'My assessment of his character. The fact that the electronics plant blown up in the Thames Valley back home was carefully planned to avoid casualties. That was undoubtedly his work. It was an American competitor who was the target.'

'You said they think they've seen us off,' she reminded him.

'Yes. Moloch is wily and cunning. He's had to be to survive in this jungle of American business. We're going to also be wily. In the morning I want you to go to the reservation desk. Tell them to book six seats on a flight from San Francisco to London. Open tickets to be used at any time. In our names. Include Alvarez. Don't be discreet. Raise your voice a bit. Then ask them to hold our rooms here, explain you'll warn them if and when we have to depart.'

'We're leaving?'

'We're staying,' Tweed growled.

'It's a smokescreen.'

'Precisely. I'm sure Moloch has a watcher permanently in the hotel, a guest or guests to check our moves. He'll think we have decided to give up.'

'But we haven't.'

'No, not by a long chalk,' he said more quietly. 'We're now going on the offensive at every opportunity against Moloch and all his works. We're in hostile territory. No more help from Washington. So we'll play tough. Very tough.'

It was the bomb which had supercharged Tweed. The thought of it exploding next to Paula had enraged him. He was going to fight back – with gloves off. His mind was now filled with ice-cold ruthlessness. This was America. So he'd play it in the American way.

'That lunch with Vanity Richmond tomorrow could be a trap,' she reflected.

'It probably is. So we walk into it and wipe out the trappers.'

'You think Vanity knows that it is a trap?'

'Maybe, maybe not.'

He dismissed this possibility with a wave of his hand as being of no importance. Then he sipped more wine. She had never seen him more alert.

'I think Moloch has an innocent-seeming person, apparently outside his organization, as a spy. I can sniff him, but so far I can't identify him. It wouldn't surprise me if whoever it may be is also linked with Cornwall.'

'That narrows the field.'

'Not enough. From now on. There are several people now out here who were in Cornwall when we were.'

'Including Vanity Richmond, who is a she.'

'Including Vanity,' he agreed. 'So the watchword is trust no one, suspect everyone. I shall warn the others about this separately in the morning. A remarkable man, Vincent Bernard Moloch. A network in Cornwall, another here in California.'

'What about The Accountant?' she asked.

'That killer must be hunted down – located first – then he, or she, must be eliminated.'

Paula stared at him. She had never heard him speak like this before. But having escaped death by inches at the hands of the assassin she agreed with Tweed's attitude. The murder toll – including many women – had been too great, the method used too grisly.

'Another anxiety,' Tweed explained, 'is Ethan Benyon. You saw how he was behaving in Palo Eldorado.'

'Maybe he was on drugs,' she suggested.

'I don't think so. There's something wrong inside that clever head. And his finger is on the trigger.'

'The trigger of what?'

Tweed recalled for her his visit to see Moloch. He described how he had been shown the chamber below Black Ridge, how Ethan had described some of his work with great enthusiasm, his eyes glowing, until Moloch had veered him off the subject.

'Moloch said that steel door in the wall of the chamber was a safe,' Tweed continued. 'I'm sure it wasn't. In a bank vault a door that size swings open on hinges – this one had runners on the floor. The kind of door which leads to an elevator. I think the elevator leads to something under the earth's surface. If Dillon had agreed to our storming Black Ridge – or had done the job himself – we'd have found out what the secret of Black Ridge is. Because I'm convinced there is one – a very diabolical secret.'

'Well, that avenue is closed to us. Seems all avenues of approach are closed to us now Washington has shut down on us. I think . . .'

She never did say what she was thinking. The phone rang, she picked it up, answered, then handed it to Tweed, one hand over the mouthpiece.

'It's Hoarse Voice again.'

'Tweed here.'

He listened without speaking, thanked the caller, put down the phone. He leaned back in his chair, picked up his glass, drank a little more wine. His eyes were gleaming.

'Don't forget to make those BA bookings on the plane home in the morning. Open bookings. Choose a time when the lobby is crowded.'

'You've already told me. I hadn't forgotten.' When he didn't speak for a short time she asked, 'Who is Hoarse Voice? Or shouldn't I ask?'

'You shouldn't ask. The caller gave me a message, a warning. "Don't go to McGee's Landing in the Ventana wilderness." Just that.'

'I've never heard of the place.'

'Neither have I. That is, the exact location. But when I was last here an American told me about the area. It's very wild and dangerous, I gather.'

'And if we get invited out there?'

'We'll go.' Tweed couldn't keep still. He stood up, began pacing again. 'We'll face whatever is waiting for us. From now on this is war . . .'

In the morning Paula was up early, despite only a few hours' sleep. After showering, taking only minutes to put on make-up, dressing, she went along to the spacious lobby and stopped at the reservations desk. They directed her to the concierge desk opposite. The lobby was crowded with people going to breakfast, sitting chatting on couches. An arm encircled her waist. She froze. Surely not another attempt on her life in such a public place? Her right hand dropped to her shoulder bag.

'Hope I didn't startle you, Paula,' a cheerful voice said. Grenville's. She turned round.

'As a matter of fact, you did.'

'Sorry, and all that. Thought we might have a bit of breakfast together. You're looking like the cat's whiskers. A dream come true.'

'Thank you. For the invitation. And the compliment. But I have to dash off somewhere.'

'Bad luck, for me. That chap Tweed keeps you on the

go, I suspect. Really ought to relax now and again, you know. I won't detain you.'

Paula was staring at him. Grenville could be very charming. Since arriving in California he seemed to have developed a very likeable personality. If she hadn't had a job to do she'd almost have been tempted to accept his invitation – to find out more about what he was really like. She was heading for the concierge desk when Grenville returned, grinning.

'Our friend Maurice never learns. He's over there behind that plump lady drinking coffee.'

'Why shouldn't he?' Paula enquired.

'I just saw him emptying something from a hip flask into his coffee. Brandy would be my bet. Maurice starts early in the day. Sorry, I'm intruding on you again. I'll shove off.'

Paula went to the desk, asked in a clear voice for the air tickets to be booked. She made a great palaver about it, asking the girl behind the counter several questions. Then she turned to head back for her room to order breakfast from Room Service. Only way to avoid Grenville.

The first person she saw as she was crossing the lobby was Vanity. Dressed to kill, she greeted Paula warmly. Paula wondered how long she had been in the lobby.

'Isn't it the most wonderful day?' Vanity began with her warm smile. 'I went out onto the terrace. There isn't a cloud in the duck-egg blue sky. Sea's like the proverbial millpond. Still, I mustn't hold you up. You look as though you are in your usual rush.'

Paula smiled, turned to go, almost ran into Newman, who was looking very buoyant. Smartly clad, he wore beige trousers with a knife-edged crease and a blue-and-white check sports shirt. Smiling at Paula, he then took hold of Vanity with his hands on her shoulders, kissed her on both cheeks.

'Sorry if I've held you up for breakfast,' he said.

'Yes, you have. And you have a starving woman on your hands.'

'We'll soon attend to that. See you, Paula . . .'

She watched them walking together to Roy's, the restaurant. Paula felt a twinge of uneasiness. Newman seemed enchanted by Vanity. Was he going overboard? Well, it's his affair, literally, she thought. I just hope he hasn't lost his normal detached judgement.

She went back to report to Tweed what she had seen and heard in the lobby.

Within thirty minutes of Paula booking the open air tickets Moloch had been informed of her action by phone. He told Joel Brand who had just entered his office.

'So the whole lot appear to be ready to take off for home,' he remarked.

'Don't believe it,' Brand replied curtly.

He was wearing a lumberjack's outfit, minus the tool belt. On his feet were a pair of tough leather boots with metal studs in the toecaps.

'Why not?' Moloch enquired, staring at his deputy.

'They're trying to bluff us. You said yourself Tweed struck you as a man who never gives up.'

'I did. But now he finds himself in an impossible position since I persuaded Washington to withdraw all support. He has no authority in America. No status. He has obviously realized this. Hence the booking of air tickets back to Britain.'

'I still don't believe it.'

'You're beginning to bore me.' Moloch's eyes gazed at Brand's. 'Why are you dressed like that? You know I like my staff to wear proper clothes on duty.'

'I ain't on duty,' Brand responded insolently. 'This is

one of my rare days off. You agreed I could take a day when I felt I needed it. I feel I need it. Mind if I borrow the chopper? I'm goin' fishing. You said you'd be here all day.'

'Use the chopper. Try shark fishing. You might have an accident.'

Moloch was already back at examining his papers. Brand was pleased with himself. He had stage-managed that well. Made VB so irked he was glad to be rid of him. With his back to Moloch, he smirked. His chief couldn't handle Tweed. Brand knew he could. Permanently.

'Any of several people could have been eavesdropping on me when I ordered those tickets,' Paula reported to Tweed in his living room. 'Grenville was there, so was Maurice – although according to Grenville he'd already started drinking brandy at that hour. Then Vanity was hanging around behind me.'

'But according to what you told me a moment ago the lobby was full of people. It could have been someone else we don't know about.'

Tweed was examining a map as he spoke. He asked Paula to join him as he pointed to the map.

'There is Carmel Valley. As you'll see it runs a long way inland. Alvarez came in while you were away. That cross shows the hotel called Robles Del Rio Lodge. The Ridge – the restaurant where we're meeting Vanity for lunch – is part of the hotel. Down here' – he pointed to a second cross Alvarez had drawn – 'is a small airfield for light aircraft near what they call the Village, as you'll see.'

'The road along Carmel Valley then continues for miles – to a place called Greenfield. Seems to be in the middle of nowhere.'

'It is. Approaching Greenfield the road is close to the notorious Ventana wilderness. That's where the Rednecks prowl.'

'Rednecks?'

'Alvarez will explain them to you. He's very good on the early history of America – which throws a light on California today. Had your breakfast?'

'No. Grenville wanted me to join him but I evaded the invitation.'

'Then what are you waiting for? Order it from Room Service for both of us here. I feel like the full English.'

Paula was surprised by Tweed's robust attitude. He seemed to be looking forward to the prospect of what lay ahead of them. He was even humming to himself. She paused before picking up the phone.

'I have a feeling this trip up the Carmel Valley could be dangerous.'

'Possibly. Which is why, after we've finished breakfast, everyone is assembling in Marler's room. I've put him in charge of the whole operation. He will be handing out certain equipment.'

'Bob Newman is usually in charge.'

'I know. But he's had a lot to cope with.'

'You're worried his mind might not be totally concentrated on the job? That he's so carried away by Vanity he might make a mistake? An infatuated man doesn't think straight.'

'Bob is thinking more clearly than you obviously realize. I just feel it is time Marler played a greater role. He's a cool man in an emergency.'

'You think there will be one, then? An emergency?'

'I sincerely hope so. It's time we confronted the thugs and gave them a taste of their own medicine.'

312

30

It was another glorious sunny day as they drove towards the entrance to the Carmel Valley. It was also very warm. At Tweed's suggestion Paula was seated in the rear of the Cadillac alongside Alvarez, who had attended Marler's conference.

In the front Newman was behind the wheel with Tweed next to him. Behind them Marler drove the BMW. In the front passenger seat sat Nield, smoking a cigarette, looking out with interest at the countryside. Butler, carrying a canvas holdall looped by a strap over his back, occupied the rear. Inside the holdall, with other equipment, was a Heckler and Koch MP5 9mm sub-machine-gun. It had been handed to him by Marler during the conference in his room.

'Where on earth did you get that?' Paula had asked.

'Don't ask embarrassing questions,' Marler had reproved her with a glance at Alvarez. 'It has a firepower of six hundred and fifty rounds a minute. Standard weapon used by the SAS back home . . .'

The others were also carrying canvas holdalls – including Nield, Marler, Newman and Alvarez. Paula's shoulder bag was bulging. The only passenger not carrying any weapon was Tweed. He had rarely been known to carry a gun, although he was a crack shot.

'That building down there on your right is Mission Ranch,' Alvarez told Paula. 'A very nice restaurant with a superb view over the estuary of the Carmel River and the hills beyond, to say nothing of its ocean view. We might call there for a drink on the way back.'

If we ever get back, Paula thought, but kept the idea to herself.

313

Warm as it had been during the drive to the Carmel Valley, the heat became subtropical when Newman turned off the main road along the entrance to the valley. The further they drove along a well-surfaced wide road the more the temperature climbed. Paula remarked on it.

'That's true,' Alvarez agreed. 'The reason is the valley is cut off from ocean breezes. It is like a funnel. The sun beats down on it, builds up the heat for which there is no escape.'

'No escape is right,' replied Paula, mopping perspiration off her forehead. 'Yet there are some pretty luxurious-looking properties high up.'

'The higher up you are, the cooler you are. And with a good view we are talking of properties worth a million dollars, maybe two or three.'

'This part of California seems loaded with dollars,' she commented.

'It is. People who have made it come here because of the climate and the magnificent scenery. Here you have it all.'

'Including contentment?'

'Ah!' Alvarez let out his infectious laugh. 'Who is content in America? There is always a restlessness, a seeking of a new sensation. Maybe a new wife, a new lady friend. Women are infected with the same disease, always looking for something new, someone new. I believe the trouble is that America is not a country, as in Europe, it is a continent. The sheer scale dwarfs people, so they scuttle around like ants.'

Paula fell silent. She was watching the endless new views which appeared as Newman kept driving round bends, opening up a fresh panorama. On both sides high rolling hills folded behind each other and she had distant views of the valley which seemed to plunge into the interior for ever. Then she remembered what she was going to ask him.

'What are Rednecks?'

'Rednecks,' replied Alvarez gravely, 'are primitive people. You leave behind the California of the tourist posters. They are very tough, carry shotguns – and don't hesitate to use them on strangers. They live in and on the edge of the Ventana wilderness. They are usually big men with thick red necks. Hence the name. Best if we don't meet up with them. But they are a long way down the valley from where we are lunching. Oh, here we are. Newman, be ready to turn right up a winding road. Off the highway.'

Following the instructions, Newman turned, began to climb a steep winding narrow road. The road carried them higher and higher past open hill country. Gone were the wayside hamlets, the turn-offs to general stores and other shops Paula had seen at intervals on the valley road.

Just when she wondered where their destination was they swung round another steep slope and she saw Vanity's Audi parked below a flight of white stone steps. A wooden sign suspended from a post proclaimed *Robles Del Rio Lodge*. At the top of the steps a large trellis of wood framed the entrance to a terrace beyond.

Newman was parking the car with the BMW pulling up behind him when Vanity appeared, running down the steps. She wore a summery white sleeveless dress which emphasized her blazing mane of red hair. Round her waist was a wide leather belt with a gold buckle.

'Welcome, all of you.'

She was smiling constantly. Newman held out his hand, grinning as he kissed her on one cheek. The scene amused Paula. She realized he didn't want a great display of public affection. Vanity turned to Paula, hugged her, and Paula caught a whiff of faint perfume, quite different from the aroma she had experienced when The Accountant attempted to garrotte her.

315

'I've booked Table Four,' Vanity said to Tweed. 'I've had it enlarged. It gives us the most terrific view while we enjoy lunch. But first you will all want drinks. The heat is exceptional today.'

'It would be,' Tweed replied in a mocking tone as she gazed at him. 'It knew we were coming.'

After greeting the others, Vanity folded her arm inside Tweed's, escorted him up the steps with Paula by her side. At the top Paula paused, gazing in admiration at a large oblong swimming pool to their right. She thought she had never seen water so intensely sapphire.

'They have swimming outfits you can borrow,' Vanity told her. 'You could have a dip after lunch.'

Alvarez had a wary expression as he surveyed the place. He took an especial interest in several people sitting by the pool. One slim girl in a swimsuit and a robe had the most amazing legs he had ever seen. She was surrounded by three men and he wondered who the lucky one was – if any of them. She caught his gaze and smiled. He gave her a little wave with his hand.

The proprietor, a good-looking man with a warm extrovert manner, greeted them.

'Lunch is ready to be served only when you are ready to be served. Do look around the place. A waiter is here to provide drinks . . .'

Paula was standing at the inner edge of the terrace where she could look at the view, which was vertiginous. Far below she could see a hamlet called the Village. Nearby was an airfield. A light aircraft took off, climbed into the sky like a dragonfly, vanishing over the summits of pyramid-shaped hills. Then a chopper appeared out of nowhere, dropped, landed on the airfield.

'What have we here?'

Alvarez was suddenly beside her. He produced a pair of field glasses, focused them as the helicopter stopped on the runway.

'Bring Tweed over here. Quietly and quickly,' he requested.

Tweed left the others strolling round the pool, was alongside Alvarez in no time as Paula followed on his heels.

'Trouble?' he enquired.

'I fear so. See those men disembarking from that chopper? The big man is Joel Brand.'

He handed the glasses to Tweed who studied the men alighting from the machine. They all carried golf bags. As he watched, a second chopper dropped out of the sky, landed, disembarking more men. He handed the glasses back to Alvarez.

'The guard master at Black Ridge, Luis Martinez, has left the second chopper,' Alvarez reported. 'More golf bags. You know what that means?'

'Spot of bother?' drawled a fresh voice.

Marler had strolled over to them from the pool. He held a glass of wine in his hand. Alvarez quickly explained what they had observed. He handed the glasses to Marler, who perched his wine on a nearby table then glued the field glasses to his eyes.

'They're all piling into two vehicles,' he remarked. 'A Chrysler and a four-wheel job. Like a Land-Rover. Now what would they want with that? They're off now. Driving at speed up the valley. Intriguing.'

He handed the field glasses back to Alvarez, rescued his glass of wine.

'You know,' he remarked, 'this American wine is really very good.'

'You saw the golf bags?' Alvarez said grimly.

'Of course. Usual method of carrying concealed weapons. Used it myself in the past. Rather effective in this neck of the woods. Just a bunch of chaps off to play a game or two of golf. Merges rather well into the landscape.'

Even though she knew Marler well, Paula was impressed with his off-hand manner. He was probably the coolest person present.

'It does not augur well for us,' insisted Alvarez.

'No.' Marler appeared to agree. 'It doesn't – the fact we haven't had lunch and it must be waiting for us now. You really should throw away that orange juice, Tweed. Do try a glass of wine . . .'

Paula was glad that Newman had gone inside, presumably to chat up Vanity. It meant that Vanity had not overheard their conversation, that she had not observed the landing of the choppers – and had not seen that they had observed the arrival of hostile forces.

The enlarged Table Four was the best one in the restaurant. By now they had the place to themselves. From her chair Paula could see straight down a section of the valley and across it – where range upon range of hills rolled away like a giant frozen sea.

As they ate an excellent lunch she saw Newman staring at Tweed. He had caught on that something had happened and was wondering what it was. Which showed her he was not completely under the spell of Vanity. Paula drank more wine as Marler, chatting and joking, refilled her glass.

Tweed was quiet. He joined in the conversation enough so he would not appear to be disturbed. Near the end of the meal Vanity reached inside her handbag, brought out a long white envelope, handed it to Tweed.

'I was asked to give you this,' she explained.

'By whom?' Tweed enquired amiably.

'Byron Landis. He said he had been told it was important.'

'Who told him that?'

'You sound just like a detective.' She chuckled. 'I'm sure you would have made a very good one.'

Tweed balanced the long white envelope in his hand. It was expensive paper. He turned it over and found it carried a red seal. Embossed in the seal were the letters VB. He opened it, holding it close so no one else could see its contents. The message was typed on flock paper. No address at the top.

I need to meet you urgently and secretly. At McGee's Landing. Please do not fail me.

The letter ended with the initials VB in handwriting. He looked up at Vanity. There was a sudden silence round the table. Nothing in his expression had given a clue to his reaction. He was still amiable when he spoke to her again.

'You didn't answer my question, I believe. I asked you who told Byron Landis it was important?'

'He didn't say. I didn't see any point in asking him. I saw VB's seal on the back, so I presumed it was VB who had told him.'

'Are you familiar with VB's signature?'

'Of course. I've seen it frequently.'

Tweed folded the letter so only the written initials were visible. He held it close to her, not releasing the sheet of paper.

'Would you say those were his genuine initials?'

Vanity studied the shortened signature. For once she looked quite serious and took her time before replying.

'They look genuine,' she said eventually.

'Not so difficult to forge, though. Does he often sign his communications with only his initials? That is, with the initials of his first two names?'

'All the time,' she answered promptly.

'Thank you.'

She was reaching for the bill when Tweed took hold of it. She looked surprised, put out of countenance.

'This is my treat.'

'Thank you for your generous offer. But I will be paying this bill. Incidentally, if you don't think it impolite I'd like to remain here a little longer. It's the sort of place I wouldn't mind staying at. I think I'll ask to see some of the bedrooms. Would you mind driving back by yourself?'

Vanity stared at him with a look Paula found difficult to interpret. She's not best pleased, she thought. Then Vanity recovered her poise, tossed her head.

'If you insist. Come to think of it I've a pile of work waiting for me.'

Newman stood up to escort her out. He had an annoyed expression. They heard the Audi start up and Newman returned, sat down.

'Have another glass of wine, Bob,' Tweed said genially.

'You didn't treat her very nicely, did you?'

'By taking the bill off her?'

'And by telling her to shove off – because that's what it amounted to.'

'Calm down, Bob. Another glass of wine will make you feel better.'

'I think I need another glass to get over that incident . . .'

Tweed seemed in no hurry to leave. He asked the proprietor to show him several rooms. Paula accompanied them. The bedrooms were beautifully furnished. No expense had been spared to make guests with money comfortable and at home.

'You've created a wonderful hotel,' Tweed remarked, holding a second glass of wine. 'If you'd let me have the brochure and tariff? This is just the sort of retreat I would like to visit when I need some relaxation . . .'

Relaxation? Paula could hardly believe her ears. She could never remember Tweed having a holiday. They went outside and found Marler with the other members

320

of the team by the pool. Marler had been talking to Butler on his own. Now he switched his attention to Nield who sat by himself in a chair. Paula had the impression Marler was instructing them. Then Marler gestured to Tweed and Paula. Earlier Tweed had spoken privately to Marler.

'What have you been up to?' Paula asked.

'I shall be driving the Merc.,' Marler informed her. 'Alvarez will be by my side. You will travel in the back with Tweed. Newman will follow us, driving the BMW with Butler and Nield as passengers. I shall drive the lead car.'

'What is all this in aid of?' Paula persisted.

'We're off to McGee's Landing. Alvarez will identify the place for us – when we ultimately get there. Now, Paula, this is what you have to do when we leave the cars . . .'

She listened with growing excitement. Marler's orders were very precise, as though he had foreseen every possibility. He then told Tweed what to do. Tweed nodded his approval.

'You might tell me where we are going,' Paula demanded.

'Probably to somewhere beyond McGee's Landing. I gather from Alvarez the road from there to distant Greenfield passes through some pretty wild and lonely country. Redneck territory.'

31

They drove down the steep winding hill to the valley road. But this time, instead of turning left back towards Carmel, Marler turned right, heading even further and deeper into the valley. Paula asked Tweed to show her the letter Vanity had delivered. She read it, frowned.

'There's no time given for this so-called appointment.'

'I noticed that myself,' Tweed replied.

'Why have we left so late? You seemed to be wasting time at the Lodge deliberately. It will soon be dusk, then dark.'

'Marler's idea, which I agree with. Messrs Brand and his cohorts will have been waiting for hours, wondering whether we're coming. Waiting gets on people's nerves. My aim is to demoralize them before we meet.'

'You really think we are going to meet them?'

'I'm sure of it. So are Alvarez and Marler. They have laid a careful trap. Incidentally, Alvarez isn't too happy with our confronting them. Newman has recovered his poise and can't wait to get there. Ditto with Marler.'

'Ditto,' Marler called out.

'From the plans you've laid,' Paula commented, 'and the armoury you've issued, you appear to be expecting something fairly violent.'

'Possibly the most ferocious firefight we've been engaged in so far,' Marler replied. 'Object of the exercise – to hit Moloch for six, to wipe out as many of his troops as possible. Should be fun.'

Paula didn't reply. She was looking out of the window as they passed isolated homesteads perched by the roadside. Lights were on inside the windows and a deep purple dusk was falling over the valley. At the same time the heat of the day was evaporating and night's chill was descending. On both sides the hills seemed to be closing in on them.

'How much further?' she called out to Marler.

'Quite a distance,' Alvarez replied to her. It was the first time he had spoken. 'This isn't Highway One. We're going very deep into uncharted territory. No patrol cars roam this area. Too dangerous.'

Very reassuring, Paula thought. Alvarez means we've

left civilization behind. Tweed seemed to read her mind.

'Lack of patrol cars is an advantage,' he remarked. 'There will be no witnesses to what happens.'

'Who wants witnesses?' she said with forced flippancy.

The road was now level, on the floor of the valley, twisting and turning round bend after bend. Marler had some while back turned on his headlights. In the beams she saw feeble hedges lining the road, bleak fields beyond. No sign of life anywhere. They had left behind even the odd isolated homestead. They were in the wilderness.

'Won't they see us coming with your headlights on?' she warned Marler.

'Probably. But I can't drive along this road without them. We're not stopping when we reach McGee's Landing. I want to approach that place on foot from the far side. Surprise, I think Napoleon said, is the great element in warfare. Something which meant that.'

Paula reached down into her shoulder bag, rearranged what Marler had given her. She would need a certain weapon the moment trouble started. She forced herself to relax, leaning back against her seat. Tweed put out a hand, squeezed her arm, sensing the tension inside her.

'That bomb against the window at Anton & Michel changed your whole attitude,' she whispered.

'Yes. I decided that instead of us being the sitting ducks we had to go over to the attack. Are you all right?'

'You know I will be when it starts . . .'

The moon was not yet up, which was a factor Marler had counted on. Looking sideways, across Tweed to her right, Paula saw huge gulches between one hill fold and another. The intense blue of the starry night sky created blue V-shapes which she had never seen before. There was something peaceful in the atmosphere which she found comforting.

'McGee's Landing coming up,' Alvarez called out. 'On our right.'

Marler slowed down, dimmed his headlights. A short way back from the road was a huddled collection of one-storey wooden cabins, each joined to the next. Lights shone in all the windows but there was no sign of a single human being.

'The local boozing joint,' Alvarez explained. 'Although the Rednecks distil their own foul brand of hooch. With that inside them they go stark raving mad . . .'

Marler drove on round yet another bend, still slowly, leaning forward in his seat. Then he suddenly turned his lights full on for a few seconds. In the brief glare Paula saw a sign. FALLING ROCK NEXT SIX MILES. He dimmed his lights again.

'The scenery is changing,' Tweed remarked.

The Merc. was creeping along now. To their right Paula gazed at distant black mountains with streaks of what appeared to be snow on their summits. A short distance to their left were sheer cliffs of layered sandstone. The view was grim, bleak and desolate.

Marler suddenly turned his lights on full power. Ahead on either side were old tree trunks, bare of leaves, dripping moss like the tears of death. Tweed leaned forward like Marler. In the blaze of his headlights an immense yellow machine blocked the road. Paula stared at it.

Its engine was chugging away as Marler switched off the motor. A big man with black hair, wearing a blue check shirt, denims and boots was feeding sections of pine foliage into the machine. Paula sucked in her breath and spoke seconds before Alvarez.

'That big man is Joel Brand.'

'And that machine is a chipper,' said Alvarez. 'If we hadn't stopped we'd have had a dense rain of powdered wood spewed over the car, blinding us.'

'Which was probably the idea,' Marler said. 'This is it.'

He waved a hand up and down twice out of the window he had lowered, signalling a warning to Newman in the BMW. Then he started the motor, drove forward and swung left off the road through a hedge, speeding up towards the looming sandstone cliffs.

As he had started to turn off Paula had seen strange heavily built men holding shotguns coming towards them from the field to their right. Newman had followed Marler, was close behind him as the Merc. pulled up at the foot of the vertical cliffs.

'It starts now!' shouted Marler and he dived out of the car.

Paula, Tweed and Alvarez left the car swiftly, remembering Marler's instructions back at Robles Del Rio. Paula dropped to the ground, making herself the smallest possible target. She reached into her shoulder bag, produced the vital object, laid it beside her. The timing had to be perfect. Then she hauled out the Browning, gripped it in both hands, remained very still behind a mound of arid grass.

The rest of the team were following Marler's earlier orders. They were fanning out, crouching as they ran. She saw Butler, holding the sub-machine-gun, way over to her right. Marler was standing, protected by a dead tree trunk dripping more hideous moss, Armalite in his hands.

Alvarez was over to her far left, crouched by a huge sandstone boulder. Newman was leaning into a cleft in the cliff face, his satchel slung over his shoulder. Tweed hugged the ground, close to Paula. From the floor of the car he had grabbed a rocket launcher, now pressed against his shoulder. Nield had slipped into another cleft in the cliff. They were all spread out, making a difficult and wide target. Then Paula saw the men advancing towards them.

Six Rednecks were out in front, carrying their shot-guns and grinning. Behind them was a second file – Brand's thugs, attempting to use the Rednecks as a screen. More men were climbing off the chipper. Tweed aimed carefully, fired the rocket launcher. The missile exploded against the chipper, blowing it to pieces. Then all hell broke loose.

The Rednecks began firing at random. A sandstone boulder fell, landed close to Paula. She looked up and backwards. High up on the cliff rim another much larger boulder teetered. Brand had positioned a man on top of the cliff. Marler calmly turned round, back to the trunk, aimed with his sniperscope. The man on the cliff rim fell, arms spread out, emitting a chilling scream. He hit the ground and the great boulder he had been propelling over the edge fell, dropped on top of the sprawled figure which had set it in motion, crushing him.

There was a sudden chatter of Butler's sub-machine-gun, fired over the heads of the Rednecks. They panicked. One fired his shotgun, hit nothing as his companions began to flee. Confusion. This was the moment. Paula grabbed the smoke bomb, hurled it to land among the running Rednecks. Newman shot down one Redneck who burst through the spreading smoke cloud which obscured the Rednecks. Paula heard shots being fired by Brand's men at random. The smoke drifted away and the ground was littered with the corpses of the Rednecks – shot accidentally by Brand's thugs.

The sub-machine-gun chattered again as Brand's men

began to run away. Five of them fell, riddled with bullets. Luis Martinez rushed forward, his revolver aimed at Paula. She fired first, her target his legs. At the same moment Nield fired, his Walther aimed at the same target's chest. He crashed forward, lay very still.

There was a sudden oppressive silence. A big man in the distance, running, had reached the road. He disappeared behind the wrecked chipper. She heard a car's engine starting up, driving off towards Greenfield. Joel Brand had escaped.

Tweed was the first to walk back to the Merc. He sat inside the back. As he had walked he had looked down at the dead men. Simple men who had not learned to live the normal life others lived. He felt depressed at the scale of the slaughter – but he knew it had been necessary.

He pulled himself together when Paula arrived. As she sat beside him he put an arm round her shoulders. He spoke quietly.

'It was them or us. They were grinning when they advanced towards us. Don't forget that.'

'If this is America I don't want to come back,' she said.

'This is only a part of America – the backwoods. People work hard here to better themselves. It's just not a European system, a European atmosphere. At least, not Western Europe.'

'You're right. I made a bad generalization.' She managed a smile. 'I'm all right, Tweed. It goes with the territory. What's our next move?'

'Our next move,' said Alvarez, who had just returned and had heard her, 'is to drive straight back to Mission Ranch. It will still be open – and it is a unique experience, in the best sense of the phrase.'

32

Paula was relieved to leave the valley. They parked outside Mission Ranch, which was still busy with customers. The moon had risen and Alvarez led them through the main dining room out onto a large terrace. The view almost took Paula's breath away.

Tables were laid on the terrace and Alvarez, taking Paula's arm, led them to a table at the very edge. The night chill made her shiver, then she sat down and wondered why it seemed so warm.

'It's almost hot out here,' she said. 'Gloriously warm.'

'Look up at the heater,' Alvarez said as the others joined them. 'The warmth comes from there.'

She looked up at a metal object shaped like a hat, perched on top of a tall column. It was glowing with warmth which radiated over the table. She felt more comfortable already, more relaxed.

'It's a gas-powered heater,' Alvarez explained. 'It's mobile and you can see more of them ready for use over there – stacked against the wall.'

'What a clever idea,' Newman remarked.

'This is just one instance of where the Americans score,' Tweed said.

While they waited for the wine they had ordered Paula stared at the view. Below them was a grassy plain which had a marshy look. Alvarez explained it was part of the estuary of the River Carmel where it flowed into the sea. Beyond it, silhouetted in the moonlight, steep rounded hills rose up like small mountains. Over to her right was a glimpse of the Pacific. The ocean was calm, a sheet of blue moonlit water which was so still it resembled ice.

'Come over and join us, Harry,' Tweed called out to Butler.

'Thought I'd better stay back there and keep an eye open.'

'No need here,' Alvarez assured him. 'Sit with us.'

Butler settled into a chair, but Paula noticed that when more people came out onto the terrace he checked them. Butler was always on duty.

'Well, we dumped the bits and pieces,' Marler recalled.

He was referring to the fact that he had paused on the way back to throw the rocket launcher down a deep crevasse. That was after he had carefully wiped it free of Tweed's fingerprints. All the smoke bombs they had carried had followed the launcher down into the crevasse. Alvarez leaned over to whisper to Tweed.

'I saw other Rednecks creeping towards the battlefield when we were leaving. They will make the corpses disappear – and get rid of all the relics of the chipper. You see, they won't want anyone to find evidence of what happened. Drugs are grown in that area. The last thing they want is to attract the attention of the police – if someone reported what they had found.'

'That's a relief.'

'Food!' Marler called out. 'We are in urgent need of food.'

A waiter appeared immediately. They gave their orders and sipped their drinks. Paula sat enjoying the changing colours of the superb view. Newman pulled his chair close to Tweed's. No one else was near them but he kept his voice low.

'What is our next move?'

'We've severely reduced the force at Brand's command,' Tweed began. 'Now we can turn our attention to dealing with The Accountant. Also, we must locate the spy I'm convinced VB has outside his permanent

329

organization. Someone who was present in Cornwall, who is now present here.'

'We can start working on that in the morning.'

'I need to know quickly who it is. There are three possible suspects. Grenville, Maurice – and Vanity Richmond.' He looked at Newman. 'I hope you agree.'

'I do agree,' Newman replied. 'Vanity is inside AMBECO, but she was also in Cornwall. There is something about her which worries me, but I can't put my finger on it.'

'Stay close to her. Everyone makes a slip sooner or later. Then I must see Moloch one more time. I want to confirm if he knows about the blood spilt beyond McGee's Landing.'

'He'll deny it, anyway.'

'If he's guilty and denies it I'll know he's lying. I also want to have one more interview with Mrs Benyon. I think she knows more than she's told me so far.'

'Both interviews – assuming you get one with VB – will have to be set up so you have plenty of protection.'

'I suppose you're right,' replied Tweed without enthusiasm.

'I gather we have to move fast.'

'Very fast. Ethan Benyon continues to worry me. I have the feeling that if it comes to the crunch he'll go his own way regardless. That is regardless of Moloch or anyone else. I suspect he's unbalanced.'

'Which is why you want to talk to Mrs Benyon again?' Newman suggested.

'Yes, it is. Whether she'll throw any light on his previous history I'm not sure. I'll have to gain her confidence – not an easy thing to do.'

Paula prodded Tweed. 'When are you going to eat your meal? We may have this marvellous heating device above us but they served five minutes ago.'

'They did?' Tweed asked, staring at the plate before him.

'The evidence is before you,' she joked.

'Women always want you to eat food piping hot,' grumbled Tweed.

'Just get on with it,' Paula told him.

They were completely relaxed after consuming an appetizing meal. Paula drank more wine than was her normal habit but remained sober. She noticed that Tweed seemed self-absorbed, left the others to do the talking, joking among themselves. She nudged him as they were finishing their coffee.

'A penny for them,' she said quietly.

'Sorry. I haven't been a very good dining companion.'

'That doesn't matter. Where did that devious mind of your wander off to?'

'Moloch, of course. I'm wondering whether to drive down the coast to Black Ridge, to tell him what happened at McGee's Landing, see his reaction.'

'Not on your own, you aren't.' She turned to Newman, kept her voice low. 'Tweed is thinking of visiting Black Ridge at this time of night.'

'Must be out of his mind.'

'I heard that.' Tweed leaned across Paula. 'I'm sure he's a man who works well into the night. His mood might be different.'

'Then I'll drive you and Paula there . . .'

There were four people in the Merc. when it moved down the coast road. Newman had signalled to Marler, told him what Tweed proposed, and Marler had said he would join the party. 'I feel like a night out,' he had informed Tweed. Newman drove with Tweed beside him.

A fierce wind blew off the ocean, hammering the side of the car. Huge waves rolled in, broke against isolated brutal rocks projecting from the ocean like fragmented capes. The wild sea surged in below them, creating a permanent belt of creamy surf and spectacular geysers as the ocean smashed into cliffs, elevating churning water high into the air like bomb bursts.

'It's turmoil down there,' Paula observed. 'Incidentally,' she said to Tweed, 'what do you expect to achieve when we do get there?'

'I'm going to ask him, among other things, if I could have a word with the guard master, Luis Martinez, about the seven girlfriends who had disappeared – with three already found dead.'

'But Martinez himself is dead.'

'Precisely,' replied Tweed.

There was turmoil inside Black Ridge. Moloch, freshly shaved and in a neat new suit, ready for a night's work, had returned by chopper from his day at the AMBECO building. Joel Brand was waiting for him in his office as Moloch took off his overcoat.

'Trouble? As soon as I get back?' Moloch demanded, seeing the expression on his deputy's face.

'Big trouble. Martinez has disappeared. So have half a million dollars from the safe.'

'I see.' Moloch settled himself behind his desk. 'You think the two events are linked?'

'They have to be.'

'Well, let's analyse the situation.' He counted on his fingers. 'Four people have access to the safe, know the combination. Yourself, Martinez, Byron Landis and myself. Since I know I'm not guilty that leaves three suspects.'

'Why the hell include me?' exploded Brand. 'I am the one who has reported the theft to you.'

'And so often, as the police will tell you, it is the one who discovers a major theft – or the body, when a murder has been committed – who is responsible.'

'I'm not standing for this!' Brand shouted.

'No, you're not. You're sitting down,' Moloch replied mildly. 'Please remain seated.'

He pressed a button on a compact intercom perched on his desk.

'Byron, come to my office at once. Which means now.'

'I'll chuck the friggin' job in,' raged Brand.

'No, you won't. I pay you too much. In any case, no one ever resigns from AMBECO. They are fired – without a reference.'

'I have reported it to you,' Brand insisted.

'Now you're repeating yourself. Who has replaced Martinez as guard master?'

'Hogan,' Brand said bleakly.

Moloch again pressed a button on the intercom. A rough voice answered.

'Hogan,' Moloch said, 'I want you in my office immediately.'

In no time at all the door opened and a short heavily built man with wide shoulders and a large head, covered with red hair, appeared. His whole manner exuded aggressiveness but he addressed Moloch respectfully.

'Is there a problem, Chief?'

'I want the whole place sealed off. No one leaves or enters without my express permission until further notice. Double the guard force.'

'Yes, Chief. The only problem is Ethan left the building an hour ago in his car.'

'Why didn't you stop him? Did he say where he was going?'

For the first time Moloch was furious. But he had schooled himself to conceal his feelings. Lose your temper and you lose control.

'How could I stop him?' Hogan pleaded. He spread his large strangler's hands. 'Ethan is Head of the Technical Division, Head of the Armaments Division at Des Moines.'

'You have a point,' Moloch agreed. 'Anything else?'

'Somehow his mother bypassed the operator here and got through to him. I don't know what she said but he just took off – to go and see her at The Apex.'

Moloch threw up both hands in a gesture of irked resignation.

'I spend one day in San Francisco and everything begins to fall to pieces. Hogan, do as I told you, but when Ethan returns let him in, of course. Warn me immediately he does get back.'

As Hogan left, his stocky legs moving like pistons, Landis came in. The bald-headed man held a bulging file under his arm – as he always did to demonstrate his industry. Moloch thought he looked nervous. Landis adjusted his glasses twice before hauling up a chair at his chief's request. Moloch stared hard at the accountant, who adjusted his glasses once more. An air of tension gripped the room.

'Byron,' Moloch began, 'did you know half a million dollars has been stolen from the safe to which you hold the combination?'

'Half a million?' Landis stuttered. 'You mean in cash or bonds?'

'You didn't specify, Joel,' Moloch remarked, looking at Brand.

'Half a million in one-hundred-dollar bills. No bonds.'

'How do you explain it, Byron?' Moloch asked genially.

'I can't. They were there early this morning. I noticed

the stacks of bills when I went to the safe for confidential files. And I was, as always, careful to close the safe.'

'Did you see Martinez in that room?'

'Yes. He came in as I was leaving. I thought nothing of it. He uses the other safe in that room for his weapons.'

Brand leaned back in his chair, which creaked under his weight. He was smiling as though glad someone else had confirmed what he had said.

'Take that smirk off your face, Joel,' Moloch said in a cold voice.

'Where would Martinez head for, assuming he has taken the money, which is pure speculation?'

'Mexico would be my guess,' Brand said offhandedly.

'You can both go,' Moloch said suddenly. 'Just don't attempt to leave the building. No, wait a minute, Joel.' He went on speaking when Landis had left. 'Joel, you have handled many millions of dollars, bribing senators and other key figures in Washington. The same applies to MPs and Cabinet Ministers in London who are in my pocket. Were you never tempted to cream a few thousand off the top before you handed over the money?'

'If I wanted more money I'd ask for it,' Brand flashed back at him. 'Don't forget I know enough to put you behind bars in either Washington or London for the rest of your life.'

'I wish you hadn't said that, Joel.'

'I apologize without reservation,' Brand said quickly. He leaned forward. 'You and I have worked together for years – we have been through bad times and good times. Always I have stood by your side. Naturally I resented your insinuations.'

'Erase them from your mind,' Moloch replied after a long pause. 'What you've said is true. Now leave me alone to think.'

After Brand had left his office Moloch stood up, went to the window which looked down on the raging sea. It reflected his mood. He made up his mind, went back to his desk, unlocked a drawer, took out a file marked Standish.

'Now what was the name of Linda Standish's partner at their San Francisco office?' he said to himself. 'Ah, here it is. Ed Keller—'

He pressed buttons on his phone. He didn't think he would be lucky. Few worked like he did and already it was evening.

'Keller here. Who is it?'

'Vincent Bernard Moloch speaking. You're still at your office.'

'Pretty big workload, sir.'

'Mr Keller—'

'Ed will do.'

'Ed, could you do me a great favour? A serious crime has been committed here today. Could you possibly drive down at once to see me at Black Ridge?'

'The answer is in the affirmative.'

'When might you arrive?'

'Let's see. A two-hour drive from here to the Monterey–Carmel area. I move behind the wheel. Then thirty minutes, say, to get to Black Ridge. If I start now.'

'Start now, please . . .'

33

The trip to Black Ridge didn't turn out as expected – it was very grim. They were approaching Big Sur when headlights began flashing behind them. Paula tensed, grabbed the Browning out of her shoulder bag. Newman slowed down, drove with one hand on the wheel as he hauled the Smith & Wesson out of its holster. It was at this moment that Marler called out.

'Don't panic. It's the BMW – ours. I think Alvarez is behind the wheel. Here he comes . . .'

Defying all the stringent rules about not overtaking on the coast road, Alvarez drove slowly past, waving to Newman to park in a lay-by ahead. Allowing Newman to pull in first, he dropped back, parking behind the Merc. He jumped out and spoke as Newman lowered his window.

'I was thinking about what you planned back at Mission Ranch. Decided to follow you. Butler and Nield are with me. This is a bad time of night to go near Black Ridge – well after dark. No traffic about. No one to witness what happens to you. May I travel with you?'

'Full house,' Paula called out.

'Maybe Marler would take over driving the BMW, staying close behind us. Then I could occupy his seat.'

'My pleasure,' Marler assured him, getting out. 'I'm always bored as a passenger. Prefer to drive . . .'

In a couple of minutes they were off again, the BMW driven forty feet or so behind the Merc. Alvarez made his apologies to Tweed.

'I hope you don't regard this as an intrusion, but I do know this area. By night as well as by day. Incidentally, the police back in Monterey are checking the juggernaut stopped by the roadblock – checking it for any trace of explosives. Trouble is I won't get the report. Not officially, anyway.'

'But unofficially?' queried Tweed.

'I may get a tip off. Later.'

'And we welcome your support,' Tweed told him.

They were approaching Black Ridge when from his rear seat Alvarez leaned forward. Searchlights were swivelling over the grounds behind the closed gates. Paula sensed something had disturbed him. He squinted, shielded his eyes against the lights, then stiffened.

'Drive on past, Newman,' he said urgently. 'Don't

even slow down. Just keep on driving down the highway. They're on full alert. The grounds crawling with armed guards, savage dogs. Something has happened.'

Newman obeyed his request, kept up the speed. Behind him Marler followed, also keeping moving. As they passed, Paula saw a large man directing the heavy force of guards, waving his arms. Joel Brand. In the back Alvarez heaved a high of relief.

'That mob looks trigger-happy. I wouldn't mess with them.'

They drove on and moonlight glowed on the savage sea. As they approached a great massif of rock projecting into the ocean, Alvarez touched Paula's arm. The massif reminded her of a small Gibraltar and a narrow road ran off the highway, then spiralled up the massif. A light like a great glowing eye on its summit flashed on and off.

'That is Big Sur Point,' Alvarez told her. 'As you see, it has a lighthouse on top. A very prominent landmark.'

'It's impressive,' Paula agreed.

They had driven further when Paula frowned, staring out of the window with her first-rate eyesight. She leaned closer to the window, gazing out to sea where the rollers swept in like an invading army. Then she was certain.

'Alvarez, there's a body coming in. Look! It just crested a wave-top. Keep watching. It's in a deep trough. There it is again. I'm sure I'm right.'

'I do believe you are,' Alvarez said slowly. 'It's coming in to Pfeiffer Beach. Newman, slow down, we'll come to a narrow road off to the right. You only go a short distance and there's a parking area. We leave the cars there and walk the rest of the way. It's supposed to be closed at sunset but we'll forget about that.'

They turned off the highway. Alvarez reached down, picked up off the floor a large canvas bag he had brought, looped it over his shoulder. They had parked when Paula asked Alvarez, 'What have you got inside that bag? Weapons?'

'Yes, and something more macabre. Not that I think we'll need it. The corpse will be smashed to pieces against the offshore stacks.'

'Stacks?'

'You'll see. I have a powerful torch. We'll need it.'

Butler stayed with the cars while Alvarez led the way on foot, flanked on one side by Tweed and on the other by Paula. His torch illuminated the path running under a canopy of cypress trees overhead. To their left was a dried-up riverbed. Alvarez illuminated it briefly with his torch.

'That's Pfeiffer Creek. Runs down from Sycamore Canyon on the far side of the highway.'

He had to hurry. Tweed was taking great strides, keeping up a cracking pace. Paula thought that had they not seen what was coming in, it would have seemed an enchanted glade. They reached the beach suddenly. No more cypresses. Only soft sand, difficult to trudge across. Alvarez switched off his torch because moonlight was illuminating an amazing scene and Paula gasped inwardly.

Just beyond the tide mark, massive rocks sheered up out of the sea, rocks which were pierced by large arches through which the violent ocean pounded in, broke on the beach. A fierce wind almost blew them off their feet. Tweed, coat flapping round him, pointed. Paula felt a chill which had nothing to do with the icy wind hurtling against Pfeiffer Beach, throwing up the soft sand like a dust storm.

A tall wave, cruising in, carried on its crest the body she had seen from the car. The crest soared on inside the arch, carrying its dead passenger, narrowly missing the rock faces on either side. The bizarre sight reached its climax as the wave plunged through the opening, crashed against the shore, throwing its corpse onto the beach.

Alvarez ran forward, a handkerchief tied round his nose and mouth, gesturing to Newman to adopt the same precautions as he threw him a pair of surgical gloves. He was already wearing gloves himself. Together, they hauled the waterlogged body higher up the beach. It seemed to Newman it weighed a ton, although the man they had dragged out of reach of the hungry sea was slim. Alvarez shone his torch on the face of the man who lay on his back. Paula gasped inwardly. It was the body of Luis Martinez.

'Stay back!' Tweed shouted at Paula. 'There could be infection.'

Out of his large canvas holdall Alvarez produced a roll of cloth which he spread out. It was a body bag. Between them, Newman and Alvarez laid the corpse inside the body bag, which Alvarez, immediately and with care, zipped up. It was a difficult task and Newman was breathing heavily as he followed Alvarez's example, taking off the gloves, throwing them into the sea. The two men thoroughly washed their hands at the edge of the water then took off the makeshift handkerchief masks and threw them after the gloves.

Alvarez walked over to where Tweed waited with Paula and Marler. He also was breathing heavily.

'That is Martinez, guard master at Black Ridge, the man shot by Nield and you, Paula. Give me your hand-guns,' he went on as Nield joined them. 'Someone later used a shotgun on him but Ballistics might still identify your bullets.'

When they handed over their weapons Alvarez walked back to the water's edge and hurled each weapon a great distance past one of the island rocks. By the time he returned Marler had handed Paula a spare Browning, a Smith & Wesson to Nield – weapons he extracted from his own large holdall. He also gave them spare ammo.

'You did a lot of shopping in San Francisco,' Paula yelled above the wind.

'Spent a lot of money.' Marler grinned. 'Never know when spares will come in useful!'

'The water is very deep where your weapons dropped,' Alvarez told them. 'Now we have to carry that body bag to the cars, put it in one of the trunks. It will be hard work . . .'

They had a terrible job transporting the body bag. Tweed and Newman had hold of the front end while Alvarez and Nield grasped the back. They had to trudge slowly through the soft sand with the wind battering their backs as it increased in fury, whipping up more sand particles in their faces.

The going was easier when they reached the path beneath the cypresses but the bag seemed to get heavier and heavier. At one point Alvarez called a halt to give everyone a break from their hideous task. Paula, who had borrowed the torch from Alvarez, had led the way, shining the beam along the narrow twisting path.

They resumed their task. As they came in sight Butler saw what was happening. He had the boot opened up and the four carriers eased it inside. With a sigh of relief Newman hammered the boot shut.

'How in God's name did a man shot near McGee's Landing get into the sea?' he wondered aloud.

'I guess Brand came back for the body later, found a shotgun someone had left, emptied it into the body – heaven knows why. Then he must have had a bedroll – something – and used it to heave it into the trunk of his own car. He probably passed us at Mission Ranch while we were eating outside,' Alvarez suggested.

'But why?' Paula asked.

'Probably because he didn't want any evidence found about what happened near McGee's Landing. So he brings the body along the coast road, dumps it over a cliff. His bad luck was in not realizing the current would bring it in to Pfeiffer Beach.' He smiled. 'Plus the sharp eyes of Paula.'

'So what do we do with it now?'

'We deliver it to VB,' Tweed said. 'I don't think he will be best pleased. I suspect Mr Joel Brand has been going into business on his own.'

The atmosphere at Black Ridge had quietened down. The searchlights were still revolving slowly over the grounds, but there was no sign of the small horde of guards they had seen earlier. Despite Newman's protests, Tweed insisted on getting out of the parked Merc. by the closed gates. He walked up to the speakphone built into one of the pillars, pressed the button.

'Who is it?'

Surprised, Tweed recognized Moloch's distinctive quiet voice.

'Tweed here. We have a body of one of your men here. Dragged out of the ocean. I think you ought to see it.'

'The gates are opening. Drive in. I'll meet you on the terrace.'

Tweed climbed back in the Merc. beside Newman. The automatic gates were already opening. As they drove in Marler, behind the wheel of the BMW, followed a short distance, then parked by the right-hand gate so it couldn't be closed, providing an escape route.

'I can see why VB has succeeded even in the tough free-for-all which is American business,' Tweed mused. 'He can take an instant decision.'

'What are you doing?' Paula wanted to know.

'Divide and conquer.'

'All right. Be cryptic.'

The searchlights had been adjusted, so Newman was able to proceed up the drive without their glare in his eyes. Moloch, dressed in black tie and a dinner jacket, waited for them under a lantern on the steps. He greeted them with a smile.

'Welcome, Tweed. Your visits here are becoming a habit, I hope. Please come inside. It's chilly out here. And who is the very attractive young lady?'

'My assistant, Paula Grey.'

'I admire your taste.' He shook her hand. 'Can I poach you from Tweed? As *my* personal assistant. Vanity has handed in her notice.'

'Before we go in,' Tweed suggested, 'I think you should have a brief look at the contents of our boot.'

Newman was already standing at the rear of the car. Pressing a button, the lid elevated. Using another pair of surgical gloves Alvarez had given him, he unzipped the top of the body bag, stood well back.

'Not too close,' he warned.

The lantern on the terrace shone directly on Martinez's dead face. It had a puffy ghoulish look but was still recognizable. Moloch walked forward, stood by Newman. His expression was grim. He stepped back.

'Where did you find him?'

'Floating in to Pfeiffer Beach,' replied Alvarez. 'He hasn't been in the ocean all that long otherwise you wouldn't know who it was.'

Newman zipped up the bag, closed the boot quickly, took off his gloves. Fountains were gushing on the terrace. He went to one of them, dropped the gloves in the water, washed his hands.

'We'd better go inside,' Moloch said in a calm voice. 'Your present is a trifle macabre. This is my birthday, hence my dressing up – something which bores me. Ah, let me introduce you to my deputy, Joel Brand.'

Brand had appeared, also in black tie and dinner jacket. Paula was surprised at how smart he looked. He gazed straight at her, smiling.

'Just what was missing from the party. A desirable woman.'

'Good evening, Bastard,' Paula replied.

Brand threw back his large head, his shaggy black hair falling over his collar. He grinned and Paula detected a certain magnetism. An unsophisticated woman would find him endearing, she thought.

'I like a lady with guts,' Brand told her.

'That will be enough, Joel,' Moloch said in an icy tone. He looked back to where Newman had climbed back in the car behind the wheel. 'Surely you will join us? I am not going to put a bomb under your car.'

'I know someone else who might.' Newman stared hard at Brand. 'Thank you, but I'll stay right here.'

Moloch nodded, then led the way into the vast and luxurious room he had shown Tweed. The marble blocks were decorated with crystal vases full of varied flowers. Moloch waved a hand.

'That is the staff's idea. A shocking waste of money. Now do sit down. Champagne for everyone?'

Paula perched on the edge of a couch where she could easily reach her new Browning. She accepted a glass. Tweed asked for orange juice. As Moloch served drinks she looked round at the crowded room. Byron Landis, looking nervous was also perched on the edge of a couch. She counted twenty members of the staff, a mix of men and women, all dressed for the party. Light music drifted across the marble room. Then the atmosphere changed dramatically.

'Champagne, Joel,' Moloch said, holding out a glass.

Brand reached for the glass with one large hand, but Moloch held on to it. Puzzled, Brand stared at his chief. The whole room had noticed, the babble of conversation vanished in a deep silence, punctuated only by the music.

'Joel, Martinez has returned. He's outside in the trunk of a car. In a body bag.'

A swift mix of expressions crowded Brand's face. Amazement. Disbelief. Fear. Then he recovered his balance, speaking in a strong voice.

'I don't understand.'

'I thought you might. He was dragged out of the ocean close to Pfeiffer Beach.'

'You mean he committed suicide?' Brand suggested.

'No, I don't. He's been riddled with a shotgun. Not a pretty sight. What's the matter, Joel? Don't you like champagne? You look as though you need a glass.'

Moloch pressed the glass forward. Paula noticed Brand grasped the glass with a steady hand. He was shaken but he had nerve – the dangerous nerve of a man without feeling. Moloch turned away as his deputy drank.

'You know,' he said, sitting next to Tweed, 'one of my problems is with staff – especially those at the top. There is always rivalry – one trying to stab the other in the back. Or maybe they use a garrotte.'

Paula was watching Landis. She saw his hand tighten on his glass so strongly she thought the glass would shatter. Moloch raised his own glass, toasting the whole room.

'This is my birthday party. There isn't enough noise. Enjoy yourselves.'

The babble broke out again, but now Paula detected a false note, as though everyone was anxious to obey the order. Turning to Tweed, Moloch lowered his voice.

'You should see my empire. Come with me. Paula,

you also are invited. And your friend. I didn't catch your name.'

'Alvarez,' said Alvarez stiffly.

Paula was amazed at the grotesque series of events. First, by the iron-nerved way Moloch had reacted to the sight of Martinez's body. Second, by the strange atmosphere of the birthday party. Above all, by Moloch's ruthless confrontation of Joel Brand in public.

As they walked along a corridor a small, tough and stocky man with a large head appeared from a doorway. He had a gun inside a holster hanging from a wide belt round his thick waist.

'This is Hogan, now appointed guard master,' Moloch explained. 'Excuse me a moment while I have a word with him.'

Despite his taking Hogan aside and speaking in a low tone Paula, with her acute hearing, heard every word.

'There is a Merc. parked outside. Ignore the man at the wheel. Take two men, open the trunk and remove the body bag inside. Deposit it in the large fridge inside one of the garages. Then lock the garage and keep the key yourself.'

Paula was watching Tweed. Only because she knew him so well was she able to detect a sense of relief. Tweed felt a load had been taken off his shoulders. He had hoped this was what would happen – before leaving the car he had ordered Newman not to interfere if Moloch's men took away the body bag. He had taken a tremendous gamble back at the exit from Pfeiffer Beach – when he had told his team to transport the corpse to Black Ridge. The gamble had paid off.

'Sorry about that. I'll lead the way. What you are going to see was Vanity's idea. I think it's arrogant, but it does impress American businessmen. In here.' Moloch led them into a room which was not his normal office.

The walls were covered with maps. One of the States. Another of South America. The third of Europe. The last of Asia. On each one were large circles indicating where Moloch had plants.

Tweed stared at the maps. Moloch's empire was vaster than he had realized, greater than the data Monica had unearthed. The sheer world sweep of AMBECO was frightening.

'You cover a fair amount of territory,' Tweed remarked.

'The largest conglomerate in the world,' Moloch replied. 'I am not impressed by its size, but one fight led to another.'

'Where is Vanity, incidentally?' Paula asked.

'I have no idea. Perhaps, like me, she doesn't like parties. Now I want to introduce you to someone.'

He showed them inside his small office where a tall, good-looking American was making notes, checking a sheaf of papers. He stood up as soon as Moloch entered.

'This is Ed Keller,' said Moloch. 'He is the partner in the late Linda Standish's private investigation agency. He came here to look into the disappearance of Luis Martinez. Ed, this is Tweed, a top insurance claims investigator.'

'I've heard of you,' Keller said as he shook hands. 'When Linda visited London you were very kind to her.'

'I hope so. I suppose you are also investigating the disappearance of Mr Moloch's women assistants who are still missing?'

'Never give up. Especially as I'm also determined to track down The Accountant – he murdered my partner. Seems he moves like a ghost.'

'He'll find himself in the wrong place at the wrong

time,' Tweed assured the American. 'Now, we really must leave. And thank you for your hospitality, Mr Moloch.'

The strains of dance music filtered into the hall, striking Paula as uncanny when she recalled recent events. A dance of death? Outside, when Moloch had ushered them out and closed the door, Paula saw Vanity sitting next to Newman in the car. She was amused because they swiftly disentangled themselves from an embrace. Newman jumped out, went round to open the door for Vanity to leave.

'The removal men arrived just before Vanity found me here,' he called out to Tweed.

'Removal men?' Vanity queried.

'Furniture,' Newman replied.

'I ought to get back to the party now,' Vanity commented and said good night to everyone.

As they drove down the slope they saw the right-hand gate was still open, blocked by the BMW. Newman continued on to the highway, followed by Marler, turning in the direction of Carmel.

'Three thugs removed the body bag,' Newman reported. 'Never said a word. What's the idea?'

'It was rather a desperate decision I took,' Tweed explained, 'but it worked wonderfully. My aim was to get the top people at each other's throats. Angry men make the wrong move. A form of psychological warfare. Now, what have we up there?'

Parked outside the terrace of The Apex was a car. Mrs Benyon had a visitor. This was the second unexpected twist of the night. Tweed told Newman to drive up the slope to The Apex.

34

Tweed's dangerous gamble had succeeded beyond his most hopeful expectations. Moloch returned to his office the moment his guests, including Keller, had left, summoned Brand, Landis and Hogan. He was behind his desk as they came in together.

'Don't sit down!' he shouted at them. 'Stand up and stand still.'

'Something wrong—' Brand began.

'Shut your big trap! Martinez's body is in the large fridge in a locked garage. Hogan, give me the key.'

Nervously, Hogan trudged forward, laid the key on the desk.

'Now go back and stand where you were,' Moloch barked.

'Isn't it dangerous to keep a body on the—' Brand began again.

'It's dangerous to open your stupid mouth. Don't do it again or you're finished,' Moloch raged.

'Excuse me, but I don't know why I am here,' Landis ventured.

'You're here because one of you murdered Martinez with a shotgun, then walked off with half a million dollars.'

'Shotgun?' Hogan sounded puzzled.

'A shotgun, you ham-fisted cretin. I've checked the roster. All of you were absent from Black Ridge this afternoon.' His voice became an alarming purr. 'Did someone play truant while I was away in San Francisco?'

'I went into Carmel to meet a girl,' Landis mumbled.

'A call girl, I presume?' Moloch sneered. 'Her name?'

'Lola.'

'It would be. Give me her address. I'll have Keller check that out.'

'I was her last customer.' Landis adjusted his black tie, a nervous gesture Moloch noted. 'She'd borrowed a flat on Junipero from another girl. When I left she was off to San Francisco. She said the money was better there.'

'How very convenient. Her last name?'

'Never knew it,' Landis mumbled.

'May I ask a question?' Brand suggested quietly.

'If it's relevant. It had better be.'

'You mentioned the loss of half a million dollars . . .'

'I wondered which of you would be the first one to pick up on that. Taken from the safe. You gave the combination to Hogan when he was appointed guard master?'

'Yes, I did,' Brand said eagerly.

Hogan looked at him. His face was a picture of uncontrolled hate.

'So, all three of you could have opened the safe,' Moloch said fiercely. 'Now I wonder which one of you is now half a million dollars richer?'

'May I ask you, who is this Keller?' Brand asked in the same quiet voice.

'He's the man who is going to investigate all three of you inside out and upside-down.'

'I don't like that,' protested Brand.

'So what are you going to do about it?' Moloch purred. 'And where were you this afternoon?'

'I went fishing.'

'Gone fishing!' Moloch's tone was like a whiplash. 'Catch anything?'

'No. The wind blew up.'

'Anyone with you who can confirm your thin story?'

'I went alone. I always do.'

'What about you, Landis? Meet anyone during your kicks trip?'

'No, I didn't. Not anyone I can remember.'

'And what happened to you, Mr Hogan?' Moloch demanded.

'I drove up Palo Eldorado. I was looking for that girl Ethan sees. I was going to warn her off.'

'How very noble of you. See anyone who can confirm that?'

'Don't see anyone up Palo Eldorado. The hippies hide when they see you coming.'

'Great!' Moloch threw up his hands. 'So not one of you has an alibi. You're all suspect.' He leaned forward. 'Well, you might like to know why Martinez is having a freezing time in the fridge. I'm bringing in a Medical Examiner to check exactly how he died.'

'But that's dangerous—' Brand began again.

'Dangerous for one of you. The ME I'll use is in my pocket. May take a few days before I get his report. Now, all of you – get the hell out of here. Get on with your jobs.'

When he was alone in his office Moloch stood up, stared out of the window down at the coast where the Pacific roared. It suited his mood. The three key men at the summit of his organization would be disturbed, but he'd had no option. At this vital moment when the coming operation was soon to be launched chaos reigned.

Then he remembered that Ethan was missing. Why on earth had he disobeyed orders and gone to see his mother?

Tweed got out of the car as Newman turned off the engine. It was parked just below the terrace running round The Apex. He asked Newman and Alvarez to stay with the car while he visited Mrs Benyon with Paula.

Then he heard above the howl of the wind and through a ventilator by the front door the scream of a voice. It sounded like a soul in the torment of hell.

'I'll kill you! I said I would. I'll kill you, you hideous creature. I'll kill California!'

Tweed pounced on the iron knocker, hammering it down with great force. He glanced at Paula. She took out her automatic, held it by the barrel, slammed at the ventilator with the butt. There was a sudden silence as the wind dropped briefly.

They heard someone on the far side of the door releasing chains, unlocking several locks. The door opened slowly and Paula slipped her automatic inside her shoulder bag when she saw who it was. Ethan stood framed in the doorway, illuminated by an inside light.

His eyes were almost staring out of his head. His tie was loose, his hair all over the place. He gazed at them and then smiled strangely, pointing a finger at Tweed.

'I know you. I showed you the upper chamber at Black Ridge. You were interested in my chart recorders. Yes, I know you.'

'May we come in, please?' Tweed suggested. 'It's rather cold out here.'

'My mother awaits you. Damn her to hell.'

He pushed past them, ran round the corner. As they entered they heard his car engine starting up. Paula closed the door on the elements as Tweed walked into the living room. Just as on his previous visit Mrs Benyon sat upright in her thronelike chair.

'Good evening, Mr Tweed. And Paula. Please do sit down. I expect you heard my son. He's a little upset. There's a party up at Black Ridge. Vincent's birthday. May he never see another.'

'Not very charitable,' Tweed replied. 'And we did hear your son. A little upset? He sounded to be in a manic rage.'

'I don't like the word manic.'

'Mrs Benyon,' Tweed said gently, 'this is important. Has Ethan ever needed medical attention? Has he ever had what they call a nervous breakdown? Doesn't he need help?'

'Oh, no!' She hammered the stick in her right hand. 'Not one of those places. Not again. That's why he hates me.'

'Not again? Then there has been trouble in the past?'

'You are British. I would not tell this to an American. They gabble.' She paused. 'When he was working for a Professor Weatherby back home Ethan was obsessive. He thought he had discovered some new theory in seismology. He didn't let Weatherby know what he was doing. He began behaving strangely. He would shout at me at the top of his voice. He even did it to strangers in the street. They thought he was going to attack them. They reported him to the police. I had to do something.'

'Yes, I understand.' Tweed's voice was persuasive, sympathetic. 'What did you do?'

'A special doctor saw him. He coaxed me into signing a piece of paper. Ethan was taken away for treatment. That was after he had left Weatherby. Ethan has never forgiven me. In a few months he recovered. But he has never forgiven me,' she repeated. 'That is why he hates me.'

'Must be difficult for you,' Paula suggested.

'He goes into a trance of rage. The only way I can bring him out of it is to hit him with my stick. Vincent doesn't understand. He came in once when I struck Ethan with both my sticks. Vincent tore the sticks out of my grasp, broke them, threw them on that fire. Luckily I had spare sticks.'

Oh, come on, Paula thought. You can walk as well as I can. You're just trying to intimidate VB. Sounds as though it doesn't work.

'I could talk to Vincent,' Tweed suggested while Paula

was thinking, 'but certain events have taken place recently at Black Ridge which would make this the wrong moment. What did Ethan mean when he screamed, "I'll kill California"?'

'I've no idea. Just his bad temper. He doesn't like the Americans. Says they're too brash for his liking.'

'Yet he works for one.'

'No, he doesn't. Moloch is a Belgian. He's kept his Belgian citizenship. Ethan prefers Europeans.'

'Is he rather shy?' Tweed asked.

'Always has been. His whole mind is devoted to seismology and to breaking through new frontiers in his field.'

Tweed sat silent for a short time, deep in thought. Paula knew he was taking a decision. He spoke suddenly.

'You are British, Mrs Benyon.'

'Yes. And proud of it. I lived in Cheltenham before I came out here when Ethan was offered this huge job by VB.'

'I would advise you to be ready to go home at a moment's notice. To transfer all your assets to a bank in Cheltenham. Would you consider doing that?'

'Yes, I'd like to go home,' she said instantly. 'I have faced the fact I can't do anything more for Ethan. And his latest threat was the last straw.'

'I repeat,' Tweed emphasized, 'be ready to leave at a moment's notice. Pack up now as far as you can. Don't forget to transfer your assets back to Britain in the morning. Just hold on to enough to keep you going for a few days.'

'When should I go, then?'

'When I phone you. I will use the code word Angelo so you know it is me talking. Mention this to no one. And I think perhaps we should go now.'

'Thank you, Mr Tweed.' She held out her hand. 'It has

taken a load off my mind – talking to you. If I may say so you are a very kind man.'

'I don't know about that.' Tweed smiled at her. 'But one thing is for sure – I am a very realistic man. Your phone number is . . .' He gave her a number. 'I noticed it on the phone in the hall.'

'You have a remarkable memory.'

'Just a knack for remembering figures.' Tweed winked at her. 'Don't get up – we can see ourselves out . . .'

'What was all that about?' Paula asked.

They were sitting in the back of the Merc. Tweed didn't reply. He was staring out of the window at the wild coast below as they moved along Highway One – back towards Carmel. Behind them Marler followed in the BMW with Butler and Nield. After a while Tweed spoke.

'Alvarez, do you think it would still be possible to contact Cord Dillon?'

'I don't know. You mean if we elevated the aerial?'

'Yes. But only when we get back to Spanish Bay.'

'We could try,' Alvarez said in a dubious tone. 'I suppose it would depend on what you wanted. All back-up for us has been withdrawn.'

'This would be to request the ultimate support,' Tweed said grimly.

He didn't elaborate. Paula glanced at him and he was sunk in thought again. The storm coming off the Pacific was increasing in fury. It began to rain heavily. Great sweeping curtains of rain flooded the windscreen and Newman slowed. The wipers were full on. *Whip-whap-whip-whap* . . . They passed again through steep sandstone gulches with walls rising vertically on either side. They were furrowed vertically where previous storms had cut into them. Tweed began to hum a popular song.

'You sound surprisingly cheerful now,' Paula observed.

'I am. I have just made up my mind what to do. I'm going to set a trap for The Accountant.'

'How are you going to do that?'

'By providing bait which will be irresistible.'

'What bait?'

Again he made no attempt to elaborate. Rain was streaming down the windscreen like a waterfall, the wipers were finding it difficult to cope. Newman leaned forward, straining to check where he was. It was only because he had driven along Highway One several times that he knew what was coming next. They passed several cars parked illegally, headlights full on – drivers who had felt unable to cope any longer.

Rivers poured across the road, the Merc.'s wheels sent up great gushes of spray. How Newman was able to continue driving was beyond Paula. Alvarez kept stroking his hand over his dark hair, a nervous gesture. Paula's hands were clenched together in her lap. Only Tweed seemed indifferent to the appalling weather conditions.

'We're approaching Carmel,' Newman said eventually. 'It gets a bit wet here, doesn't it?'

The storm withdrew as swiftly as it had blown up. They were just about to pass Mission Ranch when Tweed tapped Newman on the shoulder.

'Slow to a crawl. There are still lights in Mission Ranch. They must have kept the place open because of the storm. See that car just leaving ahead? Grenville is behind the wheel. Follow him.'

Inside the Standish apartment he had rented cheaply – due to the murder, well-publicized – of the previous occupant, Maurice prepared to leave to keep his rendez-vous. His lean face was freshly shaven, he wore a smart two-piece suit, and the last thing he did after putting on a trenchcoat, was to pull an object from the inside of his sleeping bag and thrust it into his pocket.

'I'd make a good hippie,' he said to himself, 'but not in the outfit I'm wearing.'

Inside the metal cabinets where Linda Standish had kept her files on previous cases he had found a blank space. All the files had been carted off to police head-quarters. Linda had also used the cabinet to store a few clothes. Maurice had found a rail and on one side several good clothes hung from it. On the other were the worn second-hand clothes he'd picked up from a local thrift shop.

He checked his watch again. He would be in good time for his rendezvous with the man who would be coming to meet him. He thanked Heaven the rain had stopped as he left the apartment and walked down the staircase and into the damp night.

'Can't I persuade you to stay?' Moloch asked Vanity in his office. 'If it's a question of money . . .'

'It isn't – not now.' She smiled at him as she sat in the chair facing his desk. 'I've accepted a very lucrative job in New York. I've signed a contract.'

'Contracts can be broken,' Moloch persisted. 'I can break any contract.'

'But I can't.' She smiled again. 'You've found me trustworthy. If I broke my word to my new employer then how could you go on trusting me?'

'Which company?'

'I can't tell you that. Secrecy is part of the contract.' She smiled again. 'I'll be here a bit longer. That gives you time to find a replacement.'

'I'll double your pay.'

Vanity shook her red mane, smiled again. 'No can do. And if you're worried I'll break any confidences between us, I won't. Keeping the faith is part of my way of life. And now, if you don't mind, I'm tired and I'd like to get some sleep.'

When she had gone VB spent a long time staring out of his window, watching the great explosions of surf as the ocean broke against the rocks. Out at sea the *Baja*, large as she was, heaved and tossed under the impact of the storm. He shuddered, went out into the corridor.

From the direction of the marble room where the party was still in progress, he saw Ethan coming towards him. The boffin glared at him, walked past without a word. There had been a fanatical look in his staring eyes which worried Moloch. His whole world seemed to be crumbling.

Going back to his office, he took a trenchcoat from a hook behind the door, put it on quickly, then hurried to the rear of Black Ridge where a Sikorsky chopper waited. A roster of pilots was permanently on duty so he could take off at any time. The pilot dropped to the ground inside the hangar.

'Any instructions, Chief?'

'Yes. Very important. The machine must be kept fully fuelled for take-off at any hour. A pilot must be on duty here round the clock. I'm sending guards to keep everyone else away from the machine. Check the roster now – inform the other pilots . . .'

Inside the building he met Hogan, swaggering along a corridor. Hogan noticed VB's pale face looked even paler than usual.

'Make sure a team of guards is on duty at the hangar where the Sikorsky is waiting. Twenty-four hours a day. There's a bonus if you do a real job.'

He hurried back to his office, closed the door, tore off the trenchcoat, hung it from the hook, ran to his desk.

Opening a deep locked drawer, he took out a radio-phone. Within minutes he was instructing the pilot of his Lear jet, standing in an outer area at San Francisco International.

'Ben. Ready the jet for a flight to London. Polar route, of course. Stand by for my arrival at any moment.'

35

Grenville seemed so intent on driving to his destination he didn't notice the Merc. following him with dipped lights. There was other traffic about – men and women going home after waiting for the storm to abate – which helped Newman to hide his presence.

'Where is he going?' Paula asked as Grenville entered Carmel.

'That's what we want to find out,' Tweed replied. 'Perhaps he was delayed by the storm. He seems in a hurry to get to wherever he is going.'

'Maybe he's going to the police station on the corner of Junipero and 4th,' Alvarez said sardonically.

'I doubt that,' replied Tweed.

'Well, that's where we are. On Junipero.'

Newman was crawling. He suddenly turned down 5th Avenue, parked just beyond the corner. Tweed and Alvarez were out of the car instantly, followed by Paula. They peered round the corner.

'That's Maurice he's meeting. All tarted up,' Paula exclaimed.

Alvarez had produced a pair of night glasses from his holdall. He focused them, then whistled softly.

'I'm damn sure Maurice just handed Grenville a packet. My guess is the packet contains cocaine. Now Maurice is getting into Grenville's car.'

They ran back to the Merc., told Newman what was happening. He drove back round the corner after making a U-turn, just in time to see Grenville's car disappearing down a turning past the next block. He followed. They then found they were touring the blocks of Carmel, constantly turning in a different direction. After five minutes Grenville parked outside the entrance to a courtyard. Both men left the car, vanished inside the yard.

'Only one place they can have gone at this time of night,' Alvarez commented. 'I know that courtyard. Papa's.'

'Who on earth is Papa?' asked Paula.

'Only the biggest drug dealer on the West Coast. The police have never been able to get anything on him.'

'Does it tell us anything?' she persisted.

'It tells me who the go-between is,' Tweed commented.

'Go-between?' queried Paula.

'Back to Spanish Bay,' Tweed ordered. 'It's vital I get in touch with Cord Dillon.'

They parked in the usual place behind the hotel. Newman was pressing buttons, after elevating the aerial. With not much hope, Tweed grasped the microphone.

'Tweed here. Anyone out there?'

'Only me,' Dillon's voice answered. 'What the hell is it?'

'We're planning to leave California in a hurry,' Tweed said, speaking rapidly. 'It could be within the next few days. That's pretty near a certainty.'

'Glad to hear it. I told you to go home.'

'Cord, it will be an emergency exit. I need transport for an unknown number of passengers. An aircraft to take us fast to San Francisco International. The pick-up to be somewhere between Spanish Bay and Big Sur. Precise details of where we are at the last moment.'

'A Chinook,' Dillon replied promptly. 'Day or night-time pick-up?'

'Could be either.'

Alvarez reached for the microphone, took a firm hold on it. His voice was calm, positive.

'Cord, Alvarez here. When pick-up point is known tell your pilot I'll signal – if it's night – with four flashes, brief interval, four more flashes and so on. If it's daytime, I'll wave my handgun round and round over the top of my head.'

'Got it,' Dillon replied. 'The Chinook will arrive Monterey airport within hours, then wait. I have one in your area. Understood?'

'Understood. Thank you.'

'I've heard of a Chinook,' Paula said when Alvarez had placed the microphone back on its hook. 'What exactly is it?'

'Helicopter. Big job. Can carry forty troops. Funny shape. We're in business, Tweed.'

'He didn't ask why you weren't back in Washington,' commented Paula.

'No, he didn't.'

Back in his apartment, Tweed told Paula to check with the concierge that their earlier bookings for a flight to London were being reconfirmed day to day.

'Also add the names Mrs Benyon, Alvarez, and Julie Davenport.'

'Who is this Julie Davenport?'

'My secret weapon. Remember, in the States Julie is sometimes the shortened version of Julian.'

'And I'm not supposed to ask who Julian is?'

'That's right. Also book a seat for Peregrine Hamilton.'

'If you say so. I think I'll do it now. I noticed when we

came in the lobby was deserted except for a few staff. No one will be there to eavesdrop on me—'

She broke off, on the point of leaving the apartment, when the phone rang. She picked it up, listened, handed it to Tweed.

'It's Hoarse Voice,' she whispered.

'Tweed here.'

He listened, then gestured for Paula to wait. Paula saw him frown, then he listened again. It was quite a few minutes before he put down the phone.

'Yes,' he said, 'do as I suggested.'

'So we are getting out of California?'

'Soon. If we survive. I should send you home now.'

'You know my answer to that. I'm going along to the lobby.'

As she hurried along the corridor the words echoed in her mind. *If we survive.*

On her way to breakfast the following morning Paula met Vanity. She thought the normally exuberant Vanity Richmond looked preoccupied.

'Good morning, Vanity,' she said. 'Another lovely day. What are you doing here? I thought you slept at Black Ridge.'

'I do, but I couldn't do that – sleep, I mean. So I got up early and decided to come here for breakfast.'

'Let's have it together.'

'Great idea.'

'I hear you're leaving your job with Moloch,' Paula said casually as they sat down at a table in Roy's. 'I'd have thought it would be difficult to get a bigger job than the one you have.'

'Not really. In any case, I feel it's time to have a change. Wanderlust you'd call it, I suppose.'

'Admit it,' Paula teased her, 'you're just a natural career girl.'

For the first time Vanity smiled. They chatted for a while and then Vanity said she had to go to the powder room but she would be back. Left on her own Paula's mind moved into high gear. What was going on?

There was something ominous in the way Tweed had made arrangements for a sudden departure at short notice. Why were the next few days so important? Who were the extra passengers Tweed had asked her to book seats for on the flight home? Why did they need a helicopter to reach San Francisco? And what was the 'bait' Tweed proposed using to trap The Accountant? Paula did not feel at all happy about what was happening.

The odd thing was she had sensed a similar unease in Vanity's attitude. It was as though some sinister unidentified menace was hanging over them. Vanity came back after quite an absence. She picked up her shoulder bag off her chair.

'Sorry, Paula. I've had a call to return to Black Ridge at once. I suppose His Lordship has another mountain of work he wants me to attend to yesterday. Please do excuse me.'

When she had gone Paula got up from the breakfast table. If Vanity had gone to the powder room, why hadn't she taken her shoulder bag?

She was crossing the lobby when Grenville appeared from nowhere. He took her by the arm, was at his most charming.

'You go with the morning and the weather. Bright and beautiful.'

'Thank you.' She noticed he had pouches of fatigue under his eyes, but he still carried himself erect and had his normal air of self-confidence and bounce. 'What are you doing today?' she asked.

'Trying to find Maurice. He's disappeared. Blighter owes me a large sum of money. Shouldn't have granted him the loan – he'll just spend it on drink. Awful thing to say about a fellow countryman, but you must have noticed. Everyone else has.'

'He struck me as being very sober when I met him once in Cornwall.'

She was watching Grenville as she spoke. He looked thoughtful. Then he guided her to a couch. Settling himself, he glanced at her.

'Funny rumour going round about Tweed. Heard it at breakfast. Chap told me Tweed was going to the flat where that Standish woman was murdered. Thinks he can find some evidence the police overlooked, I suppose.'

'Who told you that?' Paula asked quickly.

'Don't know the chap from Adam. An Englishman. Not one of my people at the club I run.'

'When is he going there?' Paula demanded.

'Hold on, old girl. You sound like The Thatcher in one of her wilder moods. The answer is I've no idea. Whole thing sounded barmy to me. Then another chap, Dawlish, who attends Anglo-Pacific do's, told me the same thing. Place seems abuzz with the rumour. Off already?'

'I've just remembered a phone call I've got to make. A friend . . .'

Almost in a panic, which she forced herself to quell, Paula hurried to Tweed's room. She pressed the bell repeatedly, got no response. Running along the corridor, she pushed open a heavy door leading to the lawn and the terraces outside rooms. No one was about as she continued running to the outside of Tweed's room.

She stopped on his patio, peered inside the living

room. No sign of Tweed. She hammered on the window with her clenched fist. Maybe he was taking a bath. Pressing her face against the glass, she saw the door leading into the bathroom from the entrance to the living room was open. He would never have left it open if he was taking a bath or a shower.

She ran back to her own room. She had left the windows open to let in fresh air. Slipping inside, she tore into the bedroom, went down on her hands and knees, tore free the pouch containing spare ammo she had Sellotaped to the underside of the bed.

She went out the direct way, through her bathroom, then stopped. The large circular mirror about five inches in diameter, which she used occasionally when applying make-up for a special occasion, was gone. It was the type which folded down into a compact disc. What the hell was going on?

Then she remembered she'd noticed the window she'd left open was closed more than she had left it. Someone had come into the room from the outside. To pinch a make-up mirror? She knew something strange was happening but couldn't work out what it was.

Restless, she left her apartment, hurried out of the hotel in search of Newman. She reached the lobby doors leading to the outside world just in time to see Grenville pulling away in his car. In the distance she saw Vanity's car disappearing round a bend, exceeding the speed limit inside the hotel's grounds. Where was everyone going?

Moving swiftly, she walked along the arcade of shops leading to the car park where Newman left the Merc. Butler was sitting behind the wheel. He got out, gave a rare smile.

'You're off too, then?'

'Who else has left?'

'Well, Vanity just took off like a rocket. Then Grenville drove after her, at a more sedate pace.'

'I know that. I saw them going. Where is Newman?'

'Taking a shower. He told me to stay here to watch over the car. Apparently Tweed told him last night nothing was happening this morning, so he could sleep in. He told Marler the same thing. All quiet on the Western Front.'

'Is it? Has anyone else left? Where is the BMW?'

'Oh, Tweed took that. I offered to go with him as back-up but he said he was only going to interview someone in Carmel, that it would be better if he was on his own . . .'

'When did he leave?'

'Must be half an hour ago. Funny thing was he took one of my Walthers with him. Said maybe that would make me feel better about not going with him.'

'Oh, my God!'

I'm going to set a trap for The Accountant . . . By providing bait which will be irresistible.

With horror she recalled Tweed's words the previous evening. Then she realized the significance of the rumours Grenville had told her about. Tweed had spread them. He had probably phoned Black Ridge anonymously, giving someone the same rumour. It would be all over Black Ridge – large company staffs were always gossip shops. It hit her like a blow in the stomach. *Tweed* himself was setting himself up as the bait inside the Standish apartment. And he had decided to take on this dangerous job all on his own.

36

Tweed sat at the desk where Linda Standish had died. He had brought with him a sheaf of Spanish Bay note-paper. On the sheets, now scattered over the bloodstained desk, were various meaningless figures he had scribbled at random. On one sheet was a list of suspects.

In front of him, partly concealed by one of the sheets, was the make-up mirror he had borrowed from Paula's apartment. From Paula's description of her horrific experience when The Accountant had attempted to garrotte her, he had realized the murderer must have crept out from the toilet behind him. The non-magnifying side of the mirror was now angled so he could partly see behind himself.

The right-hand drawer beside him was half open. Under a sheet of notepaper was the Walther he had obtained from Butler.

Prior to settling himself behind the desk, he had wandered round the block, noting the cars parked by the kerb. He had seen Maurice emerging from the exit to the courtyard. Maurice had paused, went back inside as though to fetch something he had forgotten. He was smartly dressed in a lightweight business suit.

Tweed had continued strolling round the block to give Maurice time to leave the apartment. In his pocket Tweed had a bunch of skeleton keys given to him by Marler on a previous occasion.

Earlier, well before leaving Spanish Bay, he had used the phone to call several people who had been at Grenville's Anglo-Pacific party. He had told them he had heard that Tweed was visiting the Standish apartment during the morning. He had also made an anonymous call to Black Ridge, giving Hogan, who had answered the phone, the same message. Since most of the British residents were bored a lot of the time, he had no doubt they would chatter about what he had told them.

Satisfied that he had given Maurice sufficient time to depart, he had entered the courtyard, climbed the iron staircase.

The fourth skeleton key had opened the door to the

apartment. Entering cautiously, he had observed Maurice's sleeping bag spread out against one wall. Leaving the front door open a few inches, he had explored the room. It had a fusty smell.

When he opened the tall metal cabinet he had seen how Maurice had two wardrobes. One of old shabby clothes, the other of smart suits. He had smiled to himself, closed the door again. When he tried to open the door to the toilet it was firmly jammed shut. He remembered the difficult job Detective Anderson had had, pushing his whole weight against it to gain access.

It was then that he had settled himself in the chair behind the desk, had started his swift scribbling. Buried deep inside the courtyard, Tweed could hear no sound of traffic, no sound at all. The heavy silence which would have disturbed most people had no effect on him.

He had deliberately told none of his team what he intended. Any sign of guards watching the yard – even from a distance – could scare off The Accountant. After sitting there motionless there had been a brief incident, but he had dealt with it in his usual calm way. He began scribbling more useless figures on one of the sheets. An immobile figure might well arouse suspicion if The Accountant decided to visit him.

Tweed was iron-nerved. The fact that he had set himself up as a target for an assassin who had never been caught caused him no anxiety. And his patience was infinite. The only sound he heard was of footsteps walking across the cobbled yard below the staircase. He waited for the footsteps to mount the staircase, but they receded. The locals probably used the yard as a shortcut.

Several times he dropped his hand inside the open drawer to make sure he could grab the Walther quickly. The movement became practised. It was all a question now of whether his rumours had reached the right person.

He glanced at his list of suspects. He was convinced

that among the list of names was that of the assassin. But he was uncertain which name was that of the killer who called himself – or herself – The Accountant.

Tweed had taken one other precaution before entering the apartment. While strolling round the block he had observed down a side street a curious shop sign – one of many in Carmel, a town of quaint and complex character. The symbol was of a large wooden pipe, curved downwards rather like a Sherlock Holmes pipe.

Walking into the tiny shop, he had bought a tin of cigars. Outside, he had emptied the cigars into a litter bin. He had then prised off the lid, kept it and thrown the rest of the tin into the bin.

Tweed always carried gloves in his trenchcoat pocket. Inside the apartment he had taken out one glove, inserted the lid of the tin box inside the glove so it rested on the palm of his hand. He now wore the glove on his left hand. He had recalled how only the chain-mail necklace round Paula's throat had saved her from being garrotted. The tin lid was a poor substitute for chain-mail, but it was better than nothing. He had rested his left hand in his lap – his ungloved right hand was needed for the Walther.

Time passed. Nothing happened. Tweed continued to wait.

At Tweed's suggestion, Newman had slept late. When he eventually woke he had a shower, shaved at leisure, dressed and went along the corridor towards Roy's for breakfast.

To his astonishment he saw Butler sitting on a couch in the lobby. Seating himself beside him he spoke in a low voice.

'I thought you were guarding the Merc.'

'I was. Tweed came out, drove off by himself in the

369

BMW. Later, Paula appeared. When I told her about Tweed she took the car and she drove off. By herself.'

'By herself!' Newman almost went ballistic. 'Why didn't you go with her? Are you out of your mind?'

'She insisted on going by herself. Try arguing with Paula when she has made up her mind. Oh, Tweed borrowed a Walther off me.'

'A Walther? This gets worse and worse. Where was Tweed off to? And where was Paula going in the Merc.?'

'No idea. Neither of them said. I thought it peculiar, but arguing with Tweed or Paula when they've decided to do something is a waste of breath.'

'Let me get this clear,' Newman snapped. 'First Tweed drives off in the BMW – after getting a Walther from you. Then Paula arrives, takes the Merc. and she drives off somewhere unknown. Have I got it?'

'You have. There was nothing I could do,' Butler protested.

'And you've no idea where either of them was going to? So they left separately?'

'That's what happened.'

Newman sat stunned with anxiety, trying to decide what to do. An English woman he had talked with briefly at Grenville's party stopped to have a word with him. He stood up.

'Have you heard the rumours? Most odd, I thought.'

'What rumours?' he asked politely.

'Your boss, Tweed, has gone off to visit the Standish apartment where that poor woman detective was murdered. A lot of people are gossiping about it. Seems a little ghoulish, if you don't mind my saying so.'

'I wonder if you could do me a great favour,' Newman said quickly. 'Have you a car I could borrow for a short trip? Mine has broken down. It's a question of a friend being taken ill suddenly.'

'Of course. Come with me. I have a Cadillac in the car park. Here are the keys. Not too seriously ill, I hope.'

'I won't know till I get there.'

The English woman wasted no time. Walking briskly, she escorted Newman to her cream Cadillac. He thanked her as he was unlocking the door, climbing behind the wheel.

He took off at speed the moment he had left the car park. It sounded like madness. Tweed, he felt sure now, was inside the Standish apartment. Keeping within the speed limit, remembering that other drivers' lives were at stake, he raced as best he could for Junipero. He didn't realize he was too late.

Tweed was scribbling more figures on a sheet to keep himself alert when he saw the toilet door open behind him in the mirror. A hooded figure emerged, holding a garrotte. Tweed was reaching for the open drawer when the hooded figure's right foot slammed into the drawer. Tweed snatched his hand out of the way just in time before his fingers were broken.

He tried to push his chair back with a violent lurch, but the assassin had both feet against the back legs of the chair. Tweed was trapped. He jerked his gloved hand up to his neck. A second later the garrotte swept over his head, pressed against his glove, ripped through the cloth, came up against the metal lid.

Tweed used the gloved hand to force the garrotte away from his neck. Then he felt the wire touch the other side of his neck where there was no protection. His head was going to be severed from his body.

The bulky bedroll against the wall came to life. Paula slid out of it. Lying on the floor she raised her Browning. She fired one random bullet. It startled the assassin who leapt back, giving her an open target. She pressed the trigger again and again. The magazine held nine rounds. The hooded figure staggered back towards the door. She was amazed at how hard her target was to kill. It was still stumbling back towards the half-open door as she continued shooting, emptying the magazine as it reached the top of the staircase.

Outside Newman was nearly at the top of the staircase when be saw the figure begin to fall over backwards down it. He grabbed it round the waist, heaved it up and back inside the room. It was a dead weight. He pushed it forward and the corpse slammed down on the floor, one hand fixed to the garrotte. Closing the door, Newman reached down.

Tweed was on his feet, using his gloved hand to screw up the papers which he rammed into his pocket. The mirror went into the other pocket, then he turned round, the Walther in his hand.

'Who is it?' Paula asked, breathless.

Newman carefully took hold of the hood. The figure was sprawled on its side. Pulling off the woolly hood – with slits for the eyes – Newman exposed the face. The face of Byron Landis.

37

'Byron Landis!' Paula exclaimed. 'How strange. He called himself The Accountant and he is one.'

'A neat piece of bluff,' Tweed commented. 'He thought that as he was an accountant no one would dream he'd use the phrase he did to describe himself.'

'So you were sensible,' Newman said. 'I thought you'd set yourself up as a target without protection.'

'You're wrong,' Tweed told him. 'I did come here on

my own – I was worried any sign of back-up would frighten off the assassin. Then Paula turned up on her own, wearing loafers, as you see. So she made no sound as she entered the apartment. I saw her in the mirror, put my finger to my lips so she wouldn't speak. I had an idea the killer might be hiding in the loo. Then I gestured for her to leave. She shook her head, saw the sleeping bag, got inside it and waited. I couldn't argue with her, as I wanted to. The Accountant – *if* he was in the loo – would have heard. Paula just saved my life.'

'So the quiet, unassuming Landis was the serial killer,' Newman replied.

'He was a sadist – I think he enjoyed killing people in the hideous way he did. But professional assassins are always well paid for their dirty work. Before we get out of here – which we should do quickly – check his pockets, Bob.'

'Tampering with the evidence,' Paula joked nervously.

It had been a nerve-racking time for her – waiting inside the sleeping bag. Her ordeal had ended when she pulled herself swiftly out and began shooting at Landis. It startled her how many bullets it took to kill him, but she knew that once she started firing, Tweed – her main anxiety – was safe. Now she felt cool and in command of herself.

'What have we here?' Newman said partly to himself. 'And here . . .'

Out of each breast pocket of Landis's jacket he extracted a fat envelope. He flicked open the unsealed flap, showed the contents to Tweed and Paula. A thick sheaf of banknotes. Putting on his gloves – he had dropped out the metal plate – Tweed riffled through the one-hundred-dollar bills.

'I'd say there is twenty-five thousand dollars here. Now let's see the other one.' Again he riffled through banknotes. 'Another twenty-five thousand would be my guess. Landis was paid fifty thousand for taking a life. The question is who was the paymaster?'

Tweed used his gloved hands to rub the outside of the envelopes vigorously, destroying any fingerprints Newman might have left. Then he bent down and inserted the envelopes back inside the corpse's pockets. Straightening up, he looked down at the body.

'Well, there's all the evidence the police need. And he's holding the garrotte. I'll make yet another anonymous call – this time to Detective Anderson. But only when we're well clear of this place and I can use a public phone.'

Newman drove the English woman's Cadillac he had parked on a nearby corner, behind their own parked Merc. and the BMW. They stopped many blocks away when Tweed pulled up outside a call booth.

First, he phoned Anderson, speaking through a silk handkerchief, breaking the call when Anderson demanded his name. Then he called Black Ridge. Again it was Moloch who came on the line, which suggested to Tweed something had happened and Moloch was monitoring every call.

'You know my voice. Don't mention my name,' Tweed rapped out quickly. 'I have serious news for you. The Accountant is dead as a doornail, shot by someone. Want to know who he was?'

'Yes,' replied Moloch, who never wasted a word.

'Your accountant, Byron Landis. He had fifty thousand dollars in his pocket – to kill someone. Now who in your organization has that kind of money? Apart from yourself. And the police have been informed. I'm sure you'll be receiving a call from Detective Anderson.'

He broke the connection before Moloch could reply. Inside the booth he took out the tin lid he had dropped out of his glove. Again he used the glove to wipe it – this time clean of his own fingerprints. Leaving the booth, he dropped the lid inside a nearby litter bin.

The three cars arrived back at Spanish Bay with an interval between their being parked. Newman went in search of the English woman.

'Give Marler your Browning to get rid of,' Tweed advised Paula. He smiled drily. 'I'm sure he'll have a replacement to give you. Marler always looks after you so well.'

'You made two calls from that booth,' Paula told him.

'The second was to Moloch. Reporting the identity of The Accountant, the fact that he was dead. The only fact I omitted was the location of the body. Now Moloch can't arrange for its swift removal. Also I told him that I'd informed Anderson, that he could expect a call from the detective.'

'What was the idea of that?'

'Just something to rattle his nerve. Throw the enemy off balance and he may get confused.'

Moloch was further disturbed by Tweed's message. He took immediate action. Putting in a call to a certain powerful official in Sacramento, the state capital, he was blunt and forceful.

'Jeff? VB here. Get moving on this one. A Detective Anderson, presumably stationed in Carmel, is about to cause me trouble. He's working on the Standish murder. If you want to stay on the payroll, have him taken off the case. In his place put some moron who stumbles over his own feet. Got it?'

'I'll take action immediately. Is there a bonus in it for me?'

'Jeff, you received a large payment from Joel recently. You gave a receipt, made out to Joel, as you have done in the past. And you were photographed from a building opposite as you took the pay-off. Would you like the photograph – and all previous receipts – to be sent to the *San Francisco Chronicle*?'

'Sorry, I'll get on it now . . .'

Moloch slammed down the phone. Byron Landis? Now he had yet another major problem on his mind. For the first time in his life Vincent Bernard Moloch was beginning to feel overwhelmed.

Ethan opened the heavy door in the corridor at Black Ridge, the door leading to the underground chamber Moloch had shown Tweed. Closing it on the other side, he ran down the iron staircase into the chamber.

His face was beginning to look cadaverous, brought about by the mental tension he was labouring under. There was no one else in the vaulted chamber as he checked a machine he had not shown Tweed. It was an advanced strong-motion seismograph. The starter, pendulum and timing circuits were located on the left, the recording drum and the film on the right.

He ran his hand through his hair, dishevelled even more than usual as nervous excitement gripped him. The drum was recording steeper vertical jumps, forecasting a major quake along the San Moreno fault. From experience he knew it might be a while before the earthquake struck.

Going to the door, which Moloch had described as a safe, he produced a key, unlocked it, slid it sideways, revealing a large metal cargo elevator. Stepping inside, he pressed the button which locked it so no one could follow him, then pressed another button. The elevator began to descend into the bowels of the earth.

'Get on with it! Get on with it!' Ethan fumed aloud.

It always irritated him the time it took for the elevator

to reach its destination. He stood chewing the nails of his left hand with impatience, his strange eyes glowing. When the elevator eventually stopped he pressed another button. The rear side opened and fluorescent lights in the roof of the tunnel automatically illuminated.

Ethan left the elevator, stepped aboard a powerful engine which was linked to a series of flatcars behind it. Starting the motor, he travelled along the single rail laid at the base of the tunnel, which had curved walls. This was one quality he would grant the Americans – with any form of construction they were experts and worked like beavers.

There were similar tunnels beneath each of the fake observatories AMBECO's Engineering Division had constructed along the coast of California. All were linked to the tunnel Ethan was now travelling along in the small cargo train. He stopped the engine as he neared the end of the tunnel, got out and entered a small room excavated from the side of the wall.

At the end of the room was a huge aperture, filled with an obscene black object like the nose of a massive shell. It was, in fact, a Xenobium bomb.

Ethan ran across, stroked the nose of the immense bomb. He began speaking to himself although there was no audience to hear him.

'You're going to work for me, my little baby. *Soon! Soon!! Soon!!!*'

His voice had risen to a shriek which echoed weirdly along the tomblike tunnel. He then checked the charter-recorder, a less sophisticated device than the master machine in the upper chamber. With delight he observed it was recording the same steep vertical jumps as its master.

'It's coming,' he exulted. 'I'll kill Mother. I'll kill California . . .'

He returned by the same route, reversing the cargo

train which had carried sections of the bomb to its resting place. Technicians from Des Moines had assembled the sections into the completed bomb under his supervision.

Reaching the corridor at Black Ridge, he ran to his office, locked the door and opened the secret safe he had had installed while VB was in Britain. Inside were two levers let into the rear wall, connected to the master system. One lever detonated the series of Xenobium bombs hidden below the observatories along the coast. The other lever set in motion the Xenobium bomb buried deep in the Pacific seabed below the *Baja*.

Both systems had a five-minute delay once the levers were pulled. Giving Ethan five minutes to run and board the chopper always waiting in the hangar behind Black Ridge. It was his escape system.

He touched each lever, gently, lovingly, closed the safe, shut the panel which concealed it. Then he did a little dance round his office, trembling with joy.

38

In his living room at Spanish Bay Tweed was examining once more the map Ethan Benyon had drawn showing the route of the San Moreno fault. Seated on another couch Paula and Newman watched him, exchanged occasional glances with each other.

'Are we waiting for something to happen?' Newman asked eventually.

'We're waiting for someone to arrive. We have eliminated The Accountant, now I want to identify the spy I'm convinced VB has here – just as he had the same person in Cornwall.'

'How do I come into this?' enquired Marler, standing by the window. 'Do I twist his arm?'

'No. You close the curtains when I tell you to. We have to build up an atmosphere of terror to unnerve the two people I shall be grilling.'

'No good asking him who they are,' Paula commented drily.

'If both accept my invitation they will arrive separately,' Tweed told her. 'One hour apart. Both, I suspect, have an avid desire for money. I offered each one ten thousand dollars.'

He folded the map quickly as someone pressed the bell outside. He nodded to Newman to let the visitor come in.

'Incidentally,' Tweed said quickly, 'you can all join in the grilling if you see an opportunity I've missed.'

Newman unlocked the door, stood aside and Maurice Prendergast walked in. So far as Paula could tell he was stone-cold sober. Wearing a smart blue chalk-striped business suit, he looked around in surprise as Newman locked the door behind him.

'I thought this meeting, Tweed, was going to be just between the two of us.'

'Do sit down, Maurice. I like my friends to be present when we are having a pleasant chat. Something to drink?'

'Sparkling water would be acceptable. Look, Tweed, before we start talking I'd like to see the colour of your money.'

Fishing behind a cushion, Tweed produced a fat envelope, opened it, showed Maurice the wad of one-hundred-dollar bills it held.

'Ten thousand dollars there,' Tweed said in a grim voice. 'I know you'll take my word for it.'

He thrust the envelope back behind the cushion while Newman raided the minibar, poured a glass of water, plonked it on the table in front of Maurice, who had sat down facing Tweed.

'Too much light in here,' Tweed remarked. 'All this

glaring sunshine. A bit like it was in Cornwall, don't you think, Maurice?'

Marler closed the curtains and stood in front of them with his arms folded. Maurice frowned, stared round, caught Paula's bleak expression.

'What the hell is going on?' Maurice demanded in his gentleman-like voice.

'You're about to earn ten thousand dollars. Or are you so flush with money from your secret work that a mere ten thousand doesn't interest you?'

'What secret work?'

'Here and in Cornwall. You tell me.'

Maurice lifted a finger, eased it round his collar as though it was uncomfortable. He looked back at Paula again, who continued to gaze at him bleakly.

'What the bloody hell are you on about?' he demanded.

'I'm on about the fact that Vincent Bernard Moloch built up a network of informers in that cosy little community down in Cornwall. That he's repeated the exercise here. Very odd to find you spending time here when you only have a pension to live on. Unless, of course, you have a far more lucrative source of income.'

'And where would I get that from?'

'From Moloch, of course. And it's interesting, Maurice,' Tweed hammered on, 'that most of the time, even at this hour, you appear to be drinking. Yet this morning you turn up here as sober as a judge. Thought you'd better have your wits about you? Was that it?'

'It's my business if I like the odd drink . . .'

'The odd drink!' Paula burst out. 'You've been sozzled up to your eyebrows every day – until today. You drink like a fish.'

'Didn't expect that from you, Paula.'

'Are you trying to kid us up you don't knock back drink like it was the water you're drinking now?'

Maurice was drinking from the glass Newman had supplied, when Paula asked the question. He spluttered, dripping water down his front. Newman took a napkin, started dabbing him dry. Maurice snatched the napkin out of his hand.

'Easy now,' Newman warned as he refilled another glass and replaced the one Maurice had been using.

'I've had enough of this.'

Maurice started to get up. Newman's hand clapped down hard on his shoulder, forcing him back into his seat.

'I'm just beginning,' Tweed told him. 'What about Porth Navas? Where were you when that poor devil Adrian Penkastle was stabbed to death?'

'How do I know?'

'If you don't, who does? And how were you able to afford the air fare here? What are you living on? Or should I ask who are you living off?'

'That's my business. You make me sound like a pimp.'

'Are you a pimp, then?' Marler asked casually.

'I'll break your friggin' neck,' Maurice raged.

'It's been tried before,' Marler replied. 'So far with little success. You haven't answered Tweed's question. Where do you get the money from?'

'I save up to come over here, to get away from winter back home. I live in that claustrophobic Porth Navas because the rent is cheap. If you must know. I'd like to go now – begging your permission, Mr Tweed,' he said sarcastically.

'Maurice, here is your fee. Of course you can go.'

Prendergast stared in disbelief at the envelope Tweed was handing to him. He took it cautiously, as though expecting it to be snatched from his grasp. Then he stood up, looked directly at Tweed.

'I didn't know you went in for this sort of interrogation.'

'It's an emergency, Maurice,' Tweed said quietly. 'Thank you for coming.'

'Thank you for nothing . . .'

When he had gone Tweed sat back on the couch. He made a dismissive gesture with one hand.

'Now we shall see.'

'See what?' Paula queried. 'We didn't seem to get much out of him.'

'Wait. Maurice is shaken, in a furious temper. I think he'll drive off. Butler will follow him. If Maurice goes to a phone we'll know he's phoning his master. At Black Ridge.'

Butler was expert at tailing a suspect without his target knowing he was being followed. Behind the wheel of the BMW he followed Maurice Prendergast away from Spanish Bay and into Carmel. En route Prendergast passed several public call booths, stopped at none of them.

Inside Carmel he drove up a steep avenue towards the top of the town. Parking near The Pine Inn hotel, he checked his watch, then hurried along a side street. Butler cruised slowly after him, saw Prendergast enter a small restaurant. Little Swiss Café.

Butler drove past slowly, glanced inside, gripped the wheel in surprise. Prendergast was sitting at a window table. Facing him was Vanity Richmond. Already they seemed engaged in a lively conversation. Prendergast was smiling while Vanity laughed.

Driving back to the nearest phone booth he could remember, Butler called Tweed, reported to him.

'So it doesn't look as though Maurice is your spy inside Moloch's camp,' Newman decided.

Tweed had just told them what Butler had seen and

said. There was a silence as Tweed mulled over what he had heard. Paula was the first to break the silence.

'What Butler told us doesn't prove Maurice innocent,' she protested. 'Instead of using a phone he could have passed on his information to Vanity. After all, she is still VB's personal assistant. She could drive back to Black Ridge and inform VB about Maurice's interrogation. Maurice could just have realized he was being followed.'

Tweed didn't react. He still seemed to be trying to solve a difficult problem. The phone rang about an hour later. Grenville had still not appeared for his appointment. Paula took the call.

'It's Hoarse Voice again,' she said.

Tweed took the phone, listened, asked the caller to repeat something. Then he put down the phone, looking serious.

'Have any of you heard of Moss Landing?' he enquired.

'It's not like McGee's Landing, I hope,' responded Paula.

'No. It's rather a weird place on the coast. It lies north of Monterey on the way to Santa Cruz. It's the kind of place you pass driving to San Francisco which you never notice ... I remember it well the last time I was over here.'

'So you noticed it,' Marler commented.

'It's my job to notice things other people miss. It's a bit off-side from the main highway. It's also a port for certain shipping coming in from the Pacific.'

'So what's significant about Moss Landing?' Paula wanted to know.

'I've just heard that there's another huge dredger – similar to the *Baja* – operating offshore. I think we ought to go and take a look.'

'What about Grenville?' Newman asked. 'You were going to question him when he arrives.'

'He's very late.' Tweed checked his watch. 'I don't think he's coming.'

'Isn't that in itself suspicious?' Paula suggested.

'Maybe. Now, I think we'll all go to Moss Landing. We don't know what might be waiting for us . . .'

After finishing her full English breakfast at the Little Swiss Café, saying goodbye to Maurice, Vanity drove back along the coast road to Black Ridge. At one stage she patted her stomach. She'd eaten two fried eggs, the very appetizing American streaky bacon and potatoes, all washed down with strong coffee.

Well, she thought, you may be putting on weight but this is the moment to keep up your strength.

She didn't have to use the speakphone at the entrance to announce her arrival. Brand had seen her coming, had opened the gates. He was waiting for her on the terrace as she parked.

'VB wants to see you. Now. Yesterday.'

'You mean immediately?' she asked sweetly and swept past him.

He glowered viciously, but by then she had disappeared inside the mansion. Moloch was waiting for her in his office. He invited her to sit down, asked if she'd like come coffee.

'Thank you, but I'm awash with it. I gather you wanted to see me. Brand displayed his usual good manners.'

'Brand doesn't know the meaning of the word manners. Vanity, this is very confidential.'

He had shared many confidences with her. For years he had regarded the right woman as far more trustworthy than any man. A high-ranking male always had his eye on Moloch's job, was capable of the most elaborate intrigue. There had been many abrupt sackings the moment a man close to him stepped over the line.

'Understood,' was all Vanity said.

'America is a cesspit. Society over here, as I've explained to you before, has collapsed. In private life – as in public – anything goes. I've had enough of the place – its lack of any ethics or morals. Which is why I've been transferring my assets secretly to the East.'

'Not to Russia, I hope.'

'Of course not. No, to Asia, to the Middle East. The moderate element in the Muslim world still reveres the family, can still keep to a business deal, once concluded. I'd like you to come with me – in the same capacity you have here. But with a large increase in salary.'

'That's very generous of you.' Vanity paused. 'When were you thinking of leaving for the Middle East?'

'You know me.' He smiled. 'Once I've made up my mind I get on with it. I may leave any day now. First stop, Britain.'

'May I sleep on it?' she suggested. 'I do have that new job in New York waiting for me. And I've signed the draft contract.'

'Draft?' Moloch smiled again. 'You mean you haven't yet signed the final contract?'

'That's the position.'

'If they kick up I'll buy them out. Everyone is for sale.'

'I'm not.'

'I didn't mean you,' he said hastily. 'I was referring to the potential new employer in New York. If he wants compensation because you've changed your mind I'll pay him off.'

Inwardly Vanity was amused. Nothing stopped VB when he wanted something. It was like trying to stand in the path of a tornado.

'I'd still like to sleep on it,' she insisted.

'Do that. I'll triple your present salary.'

'Thank you.' She stood up. 'Now I have a pile of work I need to get through . . .'

While they were talking Ethan walked into Joel Brand's office. He hadn't bothered to knock and this irritated Brand. He thought everyone – except VB – should knock before they entered his room. But he was too smart to protest. Ethan, he sneered to himself, was VB's little pet.

'What is it?' he rasped.

'Moss Landing. You still have guards on the water-front there checking for suspicious intruders, I assume.'

'You assume wrongly. I had a team up there for weeks and no one suspect ever appeared. So I withdrew them.'

'Withdrew them!' Ethan began to get excited, his voice was shrill. 'Are you mad?'

Brand made a supreme effort to control himself. If anyone was stark raving crazy it was Ethan Benyon. Out of sight below the edge of his desk he clenched his huge fists. Ethan went on yelling at him.

'The other dredger, the *Kebir*, is working off Moss Landing! The work it is doing is vital to the interests of AMBECO. It must not be interfered with. Haven't you heard about the three frogmen who tried to sabotage the *Baja*?'

'They were dealt with – as you doubtless know,' Brand replied in an ice-cold voice.

'Supposing the same thing happens at Moss Landing? Then the *Kebir* will be successfully sabotaged. The work of years will be destroyed. You've disobeyed orders!' he screamed.

Brand remained seated. He knew if he got to his feet he would hit Ethan. No one had ever spoken to him like this before. The real trouble was he was short of man-power – the battle at McGee's Landing had reduced his security force.

'I'll send a fresh team up there this morning,' he said.

'Then why are you sitting with your great backside in that chair? Send the team north immediately, tell them to break speed limits to get there. Do something, you ugly hulk!'

Fortunately, for Ethan's sake, he stormed out of the room. Brand was steaming with rage, but he wanted to counter the danger that Ethan would complain to VB. He pressed a switch on his intercom.

'Hogan, assemble a tough, armed team now. Have them ready in five minutes – sooner if possible.'

'Will do,' said Hogan quickly. 'It will weaken the security on Black Ridge if—'

'Just do it, for God's sake. Get to Moss Landing.'

'I could use the chopper to go on ahead.'

'No, you can't. VB has impounded that for his own personal accommodation. Use wheels. When you get there, stay there. As soon as you arrive, trawl the whole of Moss Landing. If you see any suspicious characters, get rid of them. The ocean is close enough. I want your team at Moss Landing in half an hour.'

'Half an hour? There are patrol cars.'

'I said thirty minutes. You know where the patrol cars are. So slow down when you have to, then take off like Concorde again. Why are you still on this intercom?'

From Spanish Bay the Merc. led the way, driven by Newman with Tweed alongside him. In the rear sat Paula and Alvarez, who had insisted on coming with them.

Behind them Marler drove the BMW with Butler and Nield as his passengers. All of them except Tweed carried large satchels. It was Marler who had overridden Tweed, saying they must have a variety of weapons, that they didn't know what they were walking into.

'You look worried,' Paula called out to Tweed.

'I am. Moss Landing is well north of Big Sur, where the *Baja* has been working. The two vessels are covering a huge stretch of coastline. I suspect Moloch's operation is on an even vaster scale than I had imagined. Can't we go any faster, Bob?'

'We can. I can drive at eighty, we get stopped by a patrol car, then we never do reach Moss Landing. I'll leave the worrying to you if you'll leave the driving to me.'

'Bob is doing his best,' Paula commented as they drove onto Highway One, turning north.

'Yes, he is,' Tweed admitted. 'It's just that the news came as a shock. We'll get there when we get there.'

'Marler told me he'd checked Moss Landing on the map,' Paula went on. 'When we arrive he'll peel off in another direction. He's planned a kind of pincer movement on the area.'

'Sounds good strategy,' Newman remarked and concentrated on his driving.

'I wonder what happened to Grenville,' Paula mused aloud. 'We did wait another hour for him.'

'He'll turn up,' said Alvarez, 'alive – or dead.'

On this sombre note they continued north. Once Monterey, with its pine forests, hilly roads and panoramic views, is left behind the journey along Highway One becomes boring. Paula made a comment to this effect.

As they passed a sign post to Castroville, vast fields, like plains, spread away to their right almost for ever. There was a distant view of hills, vague silhouettes just below a bank of inland clouds. Sunshine blazed down on the two cars, making the interiors uncomfortable.

In the distance ahead of them loomed a huge concrete structure with a tall chimney. It did not add to the beauty of the landscape.

'That's a power station,' Alvarez called out. 'And here

we come. To Moss Landing. Turn left just ahead, Newman.'

Paula peered out of the window and thought she'd never seen a more derelict-looking, shabby collection of buildings: mainly one-storey, and made of wood. After turning off the highway the road had narrowed, its surface left something to be desired, and Newman had slowed to a crawl. Behind him the BMW disappeared down another turning.

'Isn't it charming,' Paula said.

They passed a large cabinlike structure with the invitation *Phil's Fish Shop – for a cold beer.* Beyond were rundown antique shops and the arid ground was littered with broken old rowboats, discarded tyres and other unwanted rubbish.

'In America,' Paula commented, 'they don't take away their junk. They just dump it on the nearest vacant lot. Travelling once from New York to Boston by train I saw expensive houses with flat lawns. Then a steep slope covered with rubbish the owners had just thrown over the edge. What a strange place America is.'

'A friend of mine in New York,' Newman said, 'a third generation American he was, and very intelligent, explained to me that the crowd of immigrants who once flooded through Ellis Island were the people who couldn't make it in Europe. If they had, why would they have emigrated? So, he said, the immigrants had only one thought in mind. How to make money. Ever since the dollar has been their symbol, the more of them the better. Now, what have we here?'

To their right a large freighter was berthed. Its hull was rusted but men were working on it. Further along the wharf was a large fishing vessel. Paula could now see the exit to the ocean.

'Despite its scruffy appearance,' Tweed commented,

'Moss Landing is a working port. It's tucked away, so anyone up to no good would find it a good place to use as a base. Bob, pull up by the harbour exit, then loan me your field glasses . . .'

They were now deep inside what seemed to Paula to be an enormous junkyard. Not exactly a tourist attraction. As the car parked at the edge of the wharf she saw what had caught Tweed's attention. About half a mile offshore was a giant dredger, the duplicate of the *Baja*.

Alighting from the Merc., Tweed focused his glasses on the ship. He scanned it from stern to bow.

'That's called the *Kebir*,' he informed everyone. 'Bob, there's some equipment on deck – big stuff concealed under canvas. Does it remind you of the *Baja*?'

'It does,' Newman agreed, after using the glasses Tweed handed to him. 'In every respect. So much so that if the name wasn't different I'd have said it was the *Baja*.'

'You folks are way off limits,' a growly voice shouted.

They swung round. Hogan was standing a few yards away, holding an automatic rifle. Perched behind derelict cars Paula saw more men, all with weapons.

39

'This is a public wharf,' Newman shouted back. 'Have you a permit for that rifle?'

He had seen something the others had not. A slim figure was creeping up behind Hogan, crouching low as he dodged from one wrecked car to another. Newman kept trying to hold Hogan's attention.

'Don't need no permit for this little killer,' Hogan shouted back, giving a croaking laugh as he raised the rifle, aiming it at Paula. She froze. 'Anybody makes the wrong move and she'll need a new body,' Hogan went on. 'Got a pretty nice body . . .'

Pete Nield reached him, his Walther gripped by the barrel. He brought it down on the back of Hogan's large head. The stocky man fell forward and Nield fell on top of him. Hard as he had struck, Nield's blow had not knocked out the tough Hogan.

He twisted sideways, his hands clutching Nield's throat. He swung him sideways, closer to the edge of the steep drop over the brink of the wharf. The slim Nield was in trouble. Newman dashed forward and bullets began to ricochet close to him.

'Get your friggin' heads down or I'll blow them off!'

Butler's voice. Perched on top of a rickety water tower with an iron ladder up its side, he swivelled his submachine-gun. A rain of bullets swept over the heads of Hogan's men. They ducked. No more bullets were fired at Newman for the moment.

Hogan had Nield, gasping for breath, at the brink of the drop when Newman fell on him. He grasped Hogan's hair, hauled him back as he released his grip on Nield, who slithered away from the edge. Pulling Hogan's hair with a fierce tug, Newman suddenly slammed it down on the concrete rim of the wharf with all his strength. Hogan's body convulsed, slid sideways, went over the brink and hit the water with a wild splash. As he peered over, Newman saw the body drifting away. The tide had started to go out.

Butler's gun ceased firing as he ran out of ammunition. The only sound, briefly, was the distant grinding buzz of men with power tools working on the freighter, effectively muffling all sounds of the life-and-death struggle now taking place.

One of Hogan's men stood up quickly, hurled

something at the foot of the water tower where Butler was perched, ramming a fresh mag. into his weapon. The grenade exploded, tearing a gaping hole in the tower which began to collapse. Butler ran down the leaning ladder like a squirrel. He had just reached the ground when the whole tower toppled away from him.

Newman was running towards Paula, pointing towards the satchel he had dropped. Flat on the filthy ground, she slithered towards it swiftly, plunged her hand inside, came out with the hand holding a grenade. Tweed was crouched behind a bollard, holding the Walther Marler had slipped into his pocket just before they left Spanish Bay.

'Paula, Bob, *get down!*' he ordered.

Paula hugged the ground even closer as Newman flopped beside her. Between them lay the satchel Paula had grabbed hold of. In the doorless doorway of a single-decker coach, red with rust, one of Hogan's men was taking a careful aim with an automatic rifle at both Paula and Newman.

First shot gets him or they're dead, Tweed thought.

He held the Walther in both hands, took careful aim, then pulled the trigger. The man aboard the wrecked coach stood quite still, an expression of disbelief on his face as a dark red stain on his shirt blossomed. Then he fell forward, head first, into a mess of scrap metal. It made a jangling sound as his dead body disturbed it.

Both Paula and Newman had a grenade in their hands as more of Hogan's men, screened by sheets of scrap metal, began firing nonstop. They each lobbed their grenades at the same moment. The two flying objects arced in midair, dropped behind the screen, detonated. The shooting ceased abruptly.

'Any more for the Skylark?' an upper-crust voice called out.

From behind his bollard Tweed saw Marler standing

inside the huge barrel of what remained of the water tower. It gave him a commanding view of the entire area, even though the height was much lower than it had been when Butler had opened fire. Two more of Hogan's men, crouched behind a large ugly square of metal – the remains of a car which had been through a crusher – reacted.

They stood up on either side of the square block, rifles swinging to aim. Marler shot each one of them using his sniperscope. He waited, his gaze covering every point of the compass. No one else appeared.

'I think that's the end of the party,' he called out.

They drove slowly past the freighter. The workmen were still intent on using their power tools, which made a deafening sound close up. None of them looked up – time was money in their pockets.

Before leaving, they had had to help a hobbling Butler inside the BMW. He had injured his knee when the ladder up the water tower had crumbled. Paula insisted on examining the knee, used a first-aid kit to disinfect and bandage it.

'Lot of fuss about nothing,' the sturdy Butler had grumbled.

'Just keep quiet and rest it,' Paula had reprimanded him.

They continued to drive slowly as they left the mess which was Moss Landing. Turning onto the highway, Newman accelerated, with Marler following suit behind him. Tweed was anxious to get clear of the battlefield before a patrol car appeared.

'That was quite something,' said Paula and let out a sigh. 'Do you think they were waiting for us – or does Moloch keep the place under heavy surveillance as a matter of course?'

'We'll never know,' Tweed replied. 'The main thing is we all survived. America is an eventful country.'

'Well, at least it's peaceful on the highway,' Paula replied. 'And I'd better stop thinking that way. Every time I do something horrendous happens. I could do without any more events.'

It was not a characteristic Paula remark. Tweed was careful not to look back at her. Was the strain telling on his team? His worry was increased by her next remark.

'You said,' she began cheerfully, 'that Moss Landing wasn't like McGee's Landing. Remember?'

Tweed said nothing. He knew when it was best to keep quiet. Napoleon had once said that in war morale was to the material as three to one. Something close to that. Perhaps it's my fault, he was thinking. I've been brooding too much recently. I must pay more attention to keeping up morale.

'Well, we have again reduced the strength of the security forces at Moloch's disposal,' he pointed out.

'Very considerably,' Newman agreed. 'He must be very short of manpower now. Maybe the only solution is for us to storm Black Ridge, find out what's really going on inside that place.'

'Under no circumstances,' snapped Tweed. 'He'd immediately inform the police. We'd be arrested and no longer free to do anything.'

'Tweed's right,' said Alvarez, speaking for the first time. 'I suspect he may have one or two top men in his pocket. That we don't do. By the way, I was able to get a buddy to sneak out a copy of the report on the examination of the juggernaut stopped at the roadblock. The time when the driver was killed in the shoot-out.'

'Did it reveal anything?' Tweed asked.

'Yes. Traces of a new incredibly powerful explosive

394

called Xenobium. The scraping samples were sent to Washington – experts there came up with the findings.'

'I thought you'd lost all touch with Washington,' Paula commented.

'Even when I'm sent to Siberia' – Alvarez grinned at her – 'I have buddies who will do me favours. Advantage of being with the CIA a long time.'

'What are they doing about that?' demanded Tweed.

'Sweet nothing. Moloch is manufacturing explosives for the government at his Des Moines plant. Checkmate. Oh, maybe I ought to confess – they say it's good for the soul.'

'Confess to what?' Paula was curious.

'Back at Moss Landing I saw a couple of hostiles with guns creeping up on Marler from behind him. They weren't too professional. They moved close together. I came up behind them, shot them in the head, shoved the remnants into the ocean. Don't tell Marler. Why make a big deal out of it?'

This is typical of Alvarez, Paula thought. A naturally modest man, he didn't want to have Marler thanking him.

'There's no doubt, then,' Tweed persisted, 'that the juggernaut had traces of Xenobium – which suggests it had been used to transport a large quantity of the explosive from Des Moines to Black Ridge?'

'No doubt at all,' Alvarez told him.

'Our trip to Moss Landing was worthwhile in more ways than one,' Tweed said in a positive tone. 'We now know there is a second so-called drilling dredger much further north. The twin of the *Baja*.'

Inwardly his heart had dropped at Alvarez's confirmation about Xenobium. He had little doubt the *Kebir*, like the *Baja*, had drilled a giant hole in the seabed, had then inserted and capped a massive bomb. A much larger area of the Californian coast than he had realized was bracketed by potentially enormous explosions.

'Bob,' he said, 'when you spot a quiet public phone box stop the car. I have an urgent call to make.'

At Black Ridge Ethan could hardly contain his joy and excitement. On his personal radio-telephone – which bypassed the main switchboard – he had heard from the skipper of the *Kebir*. The short call had given him the code word which confirmed everything was now operational.

That meant the bomb had not only been buried and capped – but also that the radio transmitter, on top of the bomb and linked to its interior, was in position. Ethan did a little dance, skipping a few steps, then he unlocked the wall safe. Inside, between the two levers, were two switches. One was already depressed, so the radio-transmitter below the *Baja* on the seabed was operational.

Slowly, Ethan pressed down the second switch. He was almost in a state of ecstasy. He stroked each lever before locking the safe, closing the wall panel which concealed it. Now he only had to wait for the foreshocks predicting an earthquake to increase and he'd pull the levers. There would be a five-minute delay before the signal was transmitted to both bombs. The result? Immediate detonation.

Leaving his office, he hurried to the door which led to the upper chamber. He had constantly to check the recorders, to see when the sinister sharp upturns of the needle on the strong-motion seismograph shot up much higher. As he descended in the elevator he spoke aloud, gleefully.

'Goodbye, Mother . . .'

*   *   *

The following morning after breakfast Tweed was strolling with Paula across the golf links down towards a quiet endless Pacific. They were passing down the same boardwalk Paula had used when she saw a woman floating in under the moonlight. It gave her an odd feeling. Tweed pointed towards the ocean.

'Strange to think that crossing those thousands of miles of sea the first land you would come to would be Japan.'

'I find the thought a little intimidating,' she replied. 'I have been wondering whether Newman was right – that our last resort is to storm Black Ridge.'

'Wouldn't work. I've seen the steel door which leads to the chamber housing the chart recorders. And I told you about the solid steel door in a wall of the chamber, the one which I'm sure leads to an elevator. That will be locked. By the time we reached the chamber – assuming we ever did – the police would have arrived in force. I noticed in Moloch's office his door is very heavy with a strong lock on it. At the first sign we were attacking the place he'd lock himself in and call the police.'

Over to their left in the distance a forest was vaguely silhouetted. The illusion was caused by a dense veil of mist which had drifted in from the ocean. The scene was so beautiful Paula found it hard to realize the terrors they had experienced in this apparent paradise. She looked to her right.

A few hundred yards away Newman was walking with Vanity. She had hold of his arm and they seemed deep in conversation.

'Bob,' Vanity was saying, 'I'm leaving AMBECO.'

'You are?' Newman couldn't conceal his surprise, his alarm. 'Where are you off to?'

'Maybe New York. I've had the offer of a big job there.'

'That means I won't see you again.'

'Does it?'

'I could fly to see you in New York,' he said quickly, encouraged by her response.

'It might be fun. Just the two of us.'

'It would be,' he said with enthusiasm. 'When are you going? I have some unfinished business to clear up with Tweed.'

'I also have to clear up some work for VB. Why don't we keep in touch with each other's movements?'

'Why don't we?'

They had almost reached the ocean and could hear the surge of the surf swishing on the beach, when Tweed swung on his heel, took Paula by the arm, began to stride back up the boardwalk.

'What's happening?' asked Paula.

'We can't wait and wonder any longer. We have to take action. I need to phone Weatherby. I'll have to risk going through the hotel switchboard.'

Paula was accustomed to Tweed's methods. After returning from Moss Landing the previous day he had spent most of his time sitting in his living room, staring into space. She could almost hear the wheels of his brain turning at high speed. At one moment he had picked up a packet of cigarettes Newman had left on the table. Lighting one, he had taken short puffs. Tweed had hardly ever been known to smoke.

He had had all his meals sent in by Room Service. Paula had stayed with him, knowing he was deeply troubled. It had been late when she retired to her own room to go to bed. Tweed had phoned her that morning, had suggested they had breakfast in Roy's. After that, he had said he'd like a walk down to the beach.

Now he was striding up the boardwalk at such a pace

398

she had to hurry to keep up. In the distance she saw Newman watching. He had noticed the speed with which Tweed was returning to the hotel.

'It's strange,' she said, 'looking around at all the golfers travelling around in their carts, playing on the links as though everything was normal. And you have a look on your face which suggests the world is coming to an end.'

'Maybe this part of it is about to do just that . . .'

Inside his living room he perched on the edge of a couch, pressed buttons on the phone, recalling Weatherby's number from memory. The door bell rang, Paula answered it, and Newman entered. He called back to Vanity in the corridor. 'I'll see you in a few minutes in the lobby.'

'Is that you, Weatherby? Nine o'clock in the morning here, so I reckon it's five in the afternoon there.'

'It is. You sound as though it's something urgent.'

'Sorry to bore you – going over the same ground again. Operator, this is a bad line . . .' Tweed waited for a voice to reply, for a click which would tell him someone had been listening in. Nothing happened. 'Weatherby, this call is going through a hotel switchboard. I think it's all right but we won't take any chances. I'm talking about Mr Xenobium, an explosive character. You're with me?'

'I am.'

'If two of him were on the seabed out here – at widely separated points – and he blew his top, could they shift the plate?'

'The tectonic plate? Shove it inwards?'

'Exactly.'

'They'd have to be of a magnitude I've not come across.'

'More than ten times the power of Mr Hydrogen.'

'Each gentleman?'

'Yes.'

'That's a frightening amount of power. And yet, I'd have thought it unlikely the plate would move.'

'Even with Ethan directing the scenario?'

For the first time in the high-speed conversation there was a long pause. Tweed waited. Then Weatherby came back on the line.

'If Ethan is controlling the project I'd be very worried. He might manage it. Especially if a real quake was imminent.'

'Thank you.'

Tweed put down the phone. He looked at Newman and asked his question.

'What did that poor Standish twin say to you when you hauled her out of the water at that cove below Nansidwell?'

'Water was coming out of her mouth. She had trouble speaking. But I caught what she said. "Quack. Quack."'

'What she was trying to say was, "Quake. Quake." She was trying to warn you about an earthquake.'

'Well, I'll be damned.'

'Let's hope all of us aren't. Now I must call Mrs Benyon. I don't think we have much time left.'

Tweed pressed more buttons, again recalling the number from memory.

'Mrs Benyon? This is Tweed. Angelo, to use the code word we agreed so you know it's me speaking.'

'You have a very distinctive voice, Mr Tweed. I'd have known it was you,' she replied in a vigorous tone.

'We are visiting Black Ridge. Can you pack in one hour? Good. We'll pick you up about one hour from now.'

'I'm already packed. I was moving back to my old house – to get away from Black Ridge.'

'Stay where you are. We'll call for you. Lock all doors. Let no one except myself in. Excuse me, I'm in a rush.'

Tweed stood up, clenched his hands. He looked at Newman again.

'Have you packed ready for instant departure? Have you told the others to do the same thing when I called you late last night?'

'Yes to both questions. What's this nonsense about going to Black Ridge? You turned down the idea of storming the place.'

'I'm going to see Moloch. I want to make one last effort – to persuade him to lock up Ethan Benyon. Paula, you can come with me.'

'I'll drive,' Newman said. 'What's the betting Alvarez appears like magic?'

40

When Tweed led the way Alvarez was sitting in the lobby, appearing to read a newspaper. Vanity was walking back and forth, a mobile phone in her hand. Newman went up to her.

'We're on our way to Black Ridge.'

'So am I. I was waiting to tell you. VB called me and told me to drive there like the wind.'

'We'll travel in convoy. I'll be out in front.'

'Bet I overtake you.'

'Don't.' He gripped her arm. 'Trust me. Don't do that. Stay on my tail.'

'Well don't blame me if I bang your bloody tail!'

She tossed her red mane, then caught sight of Paula. She realized Paula had overheard what she'd said and smiled.

'Bob and I do have our fights. Just now and again.'

'Good for you.'

Tweed was already outside the lobby, heading for

where the Merc. was parked. Newman ran past him with Alvarez at his heels. Vanity, fleet of foot, shot past them, dived into her car, dropped the mobile phone on the seat beside her. Newman reached in, grabbed the phone.

'What the hell—' Vanity began.

'I need a mobile to make an urgent call on the way,' Newman lied. 'If a call comes through for you I'll wave you down. So stay behind me, please.'

'Please? That's better.'

Newman drove away from Spanish Bay with Tweed, Paula and Alavarez; behind Vanity's car he saw the BMW following. Marler was at the wheel with Butler and Nield in the back. Trust Marler not to miss a trick. They made good progress along Highway One. It was another wonderful day, the sun glowing down out of a duck-egg blue sky. There was a pleasant breeze off the ocean which helped to cool the atmosphere.

Paula had been intrigued by the skilful way Newman had relieved Vanity of her mobile phone. Despite the obvious growing relationship between them, Newman's brain was still in high gear. He had taken the mobile to avoid any risk of Vanity reporting to VB their imminent arrival.

They were more than halfway to Black Ridge when they saw the endless queue of cars, almost bumper to bumper, stationary ahead. Newman swore inwardly. He got out as a State trooper strolled past the queue.

'What's the problem, officer?' he asked.

'The problem, Brit.,' said the trooper, six feet tall and built like a quarterback, chewing gum, 'is you're not going any place for a long time. Now, move the jalopy as far off the highway as you can get it.'

'Why?'

'Maybe because I say so. Maybe because there's been a multiple pile-up blocking the highway. Maybe because we're waiting for lift trucks to pick up the mess, clear the highway. Wouldn't you say that was a good enough reason?'

'Certainly I would,' Newman agreed amiably.

No point in tangling with the law at this stage. He told the others what had happened.

'It's going to delay us badly,' Alvarez remarked.

'We'll get there eventually,' replied Tweed.

He seemed the coolest person in the car. He had long ago learned that when you couldn't do anything you relaxed. Newman walked back to Vanity who had been joined by Marler, explained the situation.

'We could be here for hours,' Vanity told him. 'Isn't it fortunate I'm well organized? I'm always ready for a breakdown in a remote place. In the trunk is a cool bag with a hamper. Food, wine and coffee. Tell me, Bob, does Tweed prefer strong coffee or decaffeinated?'

'Strong,' Newman replied automatically. 'You think we'll be here long?'

'Long enough to clean out my cool bag when everyone has had their rations. These multiples take some clearing up . . .'

In his office at Black Ridge Moloch was working like a beaver. He was shredding documents which should never see the light of day.

He had to check every sheet in case there was something he had to keep. It was a laborious job but one only he could do – some of the data was dangerous. As usual, Joel Brand entered without knocking. Moloch put a blank sheet on top of the pile he was working on.

'What is it? I am very busy.'

'Vanity hasn't turned up. I thought you asked her to get over here fast.'

'I did. I hope she hasn't had an accident.'

'She might have,' Brand said maliciously, 'there's been

a multiple pile-up back along the highway towards Carmel.'

'I'll try and get her on the mobile. Haven't you anything to do with the time I pay you so much for?'

Opening a drawer, he took out his own mobile, pressed buttons. In the modern world it seemed he was always pressing buttons. The phone call worked, but there was a pause after he'd spoken before Vanity came on the line.

'Sorry for the delay. The one answering you. And for the delay in getting there,' Vanity's voice came over clearly. 'There's a multiple pile-up on the highway. It's going to take hours to clear. I'll get there as soon as I can. I'm OK.'

'That's all that matters. I'm shredding. Just get here when you can . . .'

Vanity handed back the mobile Newman had rushed to her. In her other hand she was holding a sandwich.

'You seem to want the phone more than I do. And that's all we needed.'

She was referring to the fact that American mechanical efficiency seemed to be taking a day off. A huge break-down vehicle, which had arrived to help remove the smashed-up cars blocking the highway, had itself broken down. This meant calling more help to remove the breakdown truck before work could start on clearing the cars involved in the pile-up. Ambulances had arrived from the opposite direction, had taken away casualties and several fatalities.

'This could go on for ever,' Paula fumed.

Her patience was not helped by the fact that Tweed had fallen fast asleep. They had cleaned out Vanity's hamper, had drunk all her coffee before there were signs of movement. By now it was mid-afternoon.

Gradually the queue of cars ahead of them spread out, many breaking the speed limit in their annoyance, once clear of the State troopers. Newman increased speed.

Eventually, with the traffic now thin, they saw the strange Gothic towers of Black Ridge come into view. Tweed was peering out of his side of the car, told Newman to slow down as they came close to The Apex.

Mrs Benyon was standing on the terrace, staring down at the highway. She'd had the sense, Tweed noted, to leave her luggage out of sight. He leaned out of the window, waved to her. Then he made a U-turn gesture, hoping she'd grasp that they would be coming back for her. She waved back to acknowledge that she'd understood him.

When he had woken up to eat, Tweed had made several cheerful comments. This was to disguise the grim foreboding he had felt after talking to Professor Weatherby. His apparent buoyant mood had not been helped when he had overheard Vanity telling Newman that Moloch was busy shredding documents. This suggested to him VB was on the point of departure.

As they approached the closed gates of Black Ridge Vanity saucily slipped ahead of Newman. Using her monitor, she opened the gates and drove up the slope with Newman following. Behind them Marler slowed, stopped his car close to the right-hand gate to prevent its closing. You never knew when an escape route would be needed.

Arriving at the heavy front-door, Tweed pressed the large bell. Alvarez was alongside him when the door was opened, framing an unpleasant-looking man in a camouflage suit. His bruiser-like face surveyed them without enthusiasm.

'Who the hell are you?'

'CIA,' Alvarez said, brandishing a folder. 'Here to

keep an appointment with VB. No need to inform him. He's waiting for us.'

'I'll let him know first.'

Camouflage Suit turned his back on them, raised his hand to lift a wall phone. Alvarez took three swift steps forward, holding his Walther by the barrel. He brought down the butt on the back of Camouflage Suit's head. The thug sagged to the floor.

'He'll be out for half an hour,' Alvarez said as though it was normal routine.

'I thought you'd handed in your resignation,' Paula said as Tweed led the way down the corridor.

'I forgot to hand in my credentials,' Alvarez replied and grinned at her.

Tweed reached the door to Moloch's office. He tried the handle. The door was locked. On the wall was a phone.

Tweed took hold of the phone, lifted it off the wall grip. He heard Moloch's voice.

'Who is it?'

'Tweed. I have to speak to you urgently about Ethan.'

'I'm too busy. Go away. You should have made an appointment.'

There was a click as Moloch broke the connection. Newman had joined the group as Tweed opened a door on the opposite side of the corridor. Inside, behind a large desk, sat Joel Brand. He began opening a drawer.

'How did you get in?' he barked.

'Don't do it,' said Newman, pointing his Smith & Wesson. 'If you have a gun in the drawer, leave it there. And don't come out in the corridor. I have a bullet waiting for you. Oh, you won't be needing that phone.'

Walking in, he grabbed the phone off the desk, ripped out the cord connecting it to a plug in the wall. He gave the intercom the same treatment.

'Don't forget the bullet,' he warned, backing out of the room and closing the door.

Tweed was already opening another door on the same side of the corridor as Moloch's. Inside a tidy office Ethan sat behind his own desk, drinking a cup of coffee. His hair was neatly brushed, he wore a good suit, he smiled pleasantly, stood up when he saw Paula.

'Can I do something for you gentlemen?' he enquired in a very English voice.

Tweed stared hard at him. The transformation in Ethan's personality and appearance was startling. He looked round the room. It was just another office.

'You are Mr Tweed,' Ethan went on. 'I'm sorry if my manners weren't all they should have been when we last met. Fact is I'd had too much to drink. My own fault. I rarely touch alcohol.'

'I was looking for Mr Moloch,' Tweed said.

'First door on your left as you go out. This side of the corridor. Not the opposite side. That's the office where we keep our pet bear, Joel Brand. My apologies again.'

Tweed closed the door, followed by Newman, who had also peered round Ethan's office. Walking further down the corridor, Tweed tried to open the great metal door leading to the chamber. It was locked, immovable. None of them realized that while inside Ethan's office they had been within yards of the controls inside the concealed safe in the wall.

41

Tweed stood outside the closed door to Ethan's office while he looked up and down the empty corridor – empty except for the unconscious guard slumped on the floor in the distance. Newman stirred restlessly.

'Something wrong?'

'The atmosphere here,' Tweed said. 'No sign of guards outside. We've only seen one inside – he's on the floor. This is the headquarters of AMBECO, largest conglomerate in the world. Today it reminds me of a ghost mansion from which most of the inhabitants have fled.'

'Or are dead,' Newman reminded him.

'Moloch has locked himself away . . .'

He stopped speaking as a door opened and Brand walked into the corridor. Newman aimed his revolver at the big man. Brand grinned, raised both hands, went on grinning.

'The war's over – or didn't you know? You're looking particularly attractive this afternoon, Miss Grey, if I may say so.'

He smiled, and the smile had no lecherous undertone. His words had been polite, had even sounded sincere. Paula stared at him. This was a different Brand and once again she could see how he would be attractive to women.

'Thank you,' she replied quietly. 'Why has everything changed here?'

'I honestly don't know. But I have the feeling AMBECO has at last come to the end of the line. The golden days have gone with the wind. May sound corny, but that's how it seems to me. Newman, I've met some tough fighters in my time, but you take the prize. That must have been quite something – out at Moss Landing.'

'Where?' Newman rapped back. 'Never heard of the place.'

'Good reply.' Brand grinned again, lowered his hands, kept them to his side, palms outwards. 'Tweed, a long time ago – at least it seems like that – I advised VB to let me finish you off. He refused. I think I was right, if you don't mind my saying so. You've outwitted, outmanoeuvred us every time. I think I'm going to have to look for another job. I suspect VB is clearing out of the States. He's always hated the place. At least I've saved money – have half a million dollars to get by on.'

'You have a lot of dead men on your conscience,' Tweed replied.

'So' – Brand spread his hands – 'it goes with the territory, I guess. This is America. I once knew a guy who told me what it was all about, an American. Way back, in the early days, there was a drive to the West, towards this coast. It was every man for himself. A guy got in your way, you shot him – before he shot you. Something of those wild times linger. It's what makes the Yanks rougher than the Europeans. I did say rougher – *not* tougher. They crumble under pressure.' He grinned again. 'We've crumbled under pressure from you.'

'You said VB was clearing out,' Tweed reminded him. 'Where to?'

'The rumour is he's headed for the Middle East. He has Arab pals out there, another fortune in their banks. He's moving on.'

'I think we'd better do the same thing,' Tweed said firmly.

Brand walked ahead of them. Newman was close behind him, still holding his revolver, ignoring the fact that Tweed had shaken his head. Next to Brand's office a door was open. Tweed heard the sound of a teleprinter chattering away. He stood in the open doorway.

'Hello there,' said Vanity, seated behind her desk.

She had a computer and a fax machine on her desk. Reaching out, she took hold of a handful of paper spewed out by the teleprinter, waved it at him.

'No news is good news,' she said with a smile. 'This

is junk. I'm clearing my desk.' She looked over Tweed's shoulder at Newman. 'I'm like you that way, Bob. When I've started a job I finish it.'

'You're leaving here, then?' Tweed asked.

'I guess so. Take care.'

Brand escorted them to the front door, then left them to go back to his office. He never looked at the guard, still unconscious on the floor. Tweed was the last to get into the car. For a few moments he stood on the terrace, looking up towards the battlements of the mock Gothic edifice. He had a strange expression on his face, Paula noticed.

'Ethan seemed a changed man, too,' Paula commented as Newman drove them down towards the open gate.

'He looked to be putting on an act to me,' Alvarez remarked.

'I found his manner even more sinister than when we saw him dancing with that girl up at Palo Eldorado,' Tweed replied. 'It was most disturbing.'

'Funny atmosphere in the whole place,' Paula said.

'It reminded me of a ticking bomb,' Tweed responded.

Leaving Black Ridge, both cars were driven a short distance along the highway, then swung off up the slope to The Apex at Tweed's request. He got out of the car and Mrs Benyon appeared, without sticks and carrying a suitcase in each hand.

'Am I glad to see you,' she said to Tweed.

They put her luggage in the boot of the BMW. Then Tweed and Newman helped her manoeuvre her bulk into the front passenger seat. She chuckled, looking at Tweed.

'Either the seat is too small or I'm too big. The latter is the problem, I'm sure. Thank you for not forgetting me.'

Tweed thought she too was a changed person. She

looked content, almost happy, relieved. Quite obviously she couldn't wait to leave California. He supposed she had had too many years of strain and stress over Ethan. There came a point when you could take no more anxiety. You just wanted to be free of it.

He got into the front passenger seat of the Merc. Newman was obviously anxious to move off. He sat tapping his hands on the wheel, glanced behind at Paula and Alvarez, looked at Tweed.

'I suppose we are ready to push off?'

'We're ready now. We've done all we can at Black Ridge. The time has come to look after ourselves.'

'Thank Heaven for that,' Paula called out.

Newman drove down the slope, turned left along the highway, rammed his foot down, keeping an eye open for patrol cars. Behind them Marler followed, driving the BMW. In the back sat Butler and Nield.

'The temperature's dropping,' Tweed observed. 'Strange the way it plummets about four in the afternoon.'

'It will soon be dusk,' Newman said. 'I'd like to get back before dark.'

'We were delayed for hours by that pile-up,' Tweed reminded him. 'I have to call Monica. It's ages since I last spoke to her. She may have news.'

'I was going to drive straight back to Spanish Bay,' snapped Newman. 'I suppose you could make your call from Mission Ranch.'

'Too public,' Tweed replied. 'Take us into Carmel to that phone booth I've used before.'

'You could phone her from Spanish Bay,' Paula suggested.

'I need a safe phone. I'll use a booth in Carmel.'

He had detected irritation in both Newman and Paula. The atmosphere at Black Ridge had affected them all. Looking out of the window he saw menacing storm clouds drifting in from the Pacific. The sky was clearer further out and the sun, a giant red disc, was sinking close to the horizon. Like Paula behind him, he went on watching a sight which tourists from all over the world found hypnotic. The lower rim of the sun reached the horizon, began to drop behind it. He was surprised how swiftly the sun sank, disappeared, like a huge coin dropping into the slot of tomorrow. But would there be a tomorrow?

Shortly afterwards they passed Mission Ranch below them. A crowd of people were gathered, gazing at the fireglow where the sun had vanished. Newman never gave them a glance, driving on at the maximum speed limit within Carmel. Then he pulled in to the kerb.

'There's your phone booth. You've got what you wanted.'

Tweed dived out of the car. The deep purple of dusk had faded as night fell. Couples were walking into restaurants. Inside the booth he called Park Crescent, so far away.

'Tweed here, Monica.'

'Oh, thank Heaven. I thought something had happened to you. I've been calling Spanish Bay for hours.'

'Why?'

'Is this a safe phone? Are you calling from the—'

'It's a safe phone. What's the problem?'

'I thought you ought to know. My contact at Lloyd's told me the *Venetia* is still standing off Falmouth harbour. The skipper has informed the Harbour Master it will be leaving within forty-eight hours. Destination, a cruise in the eastern Mediterranean. I think it will be heading for Beirut. There's a conference of top sheiks meeting there in a fortnight's time. All the billionaires.'

'Thank you. That's significant.'

'Don't go. There's more. Someone has twisted an arm high up here. Jim Corcoran, Security Chief at Heathrow, has been ordered to make special arrangements to receive a Lear jet tomorrow afternoon. The VIP aboard will be Vincent Bernard Moloch.'

'Thanks again. That is significant. See you shortly, Monica. We will soon be on our way back.'

I hope, he thought as he left the booth. More couples were strolling round the tree-lined streets of Carmel. He was crossing the pavement to the car when he felt he was walking on quicksand. It was the first tremor.

42

Tweed stood very still. He looked quickly up and down the street. The few couples in sight had also stopped. One man put his arm round his companion's waist to reassure her. The long loaded pause continued. The ground was now stable. There was no fresh movement. The people in the street who had frozen, like a still from a film, began to move again.

Hurrying to the car, Tweed got inside next to Newman. Paula's voice was calm with only a hint of tension.

'What on earth happened?'

'California is in the earthquake belt,' Tweed replied. 'So I imagine that was not a unique experience.' He kept the urgency out of his voice. 'Bob, let's get back to Spanish Bay.' He went on speaking as the car began moving again. 'Monica reported that Moloch is expected at Heathrow tomorrow in his Lear jet. The *Venetia* is still waiting off Falmouth. Its new destination – when it sails – is still the eastern Mediterranean.'

He glanced at Newman, who caught the brief

expression on his face. Without commenting Newman increased speed gradually. Once outside Carmel he rammed his foot down. Paula's tone was steady as she spoke.

'That means Moloch is leaving the States – maybe for good. I wonder why?'

'He's decided to find fresh pastures for his activities, I feel sure,' Tweed replied casually. 'So there's really no point in our staying here any longer. Alvarez, we're ready to leave. Paula has seats booked for us on the next flight out of San Francisco International. When we get back could you try and summon up the Chinook to fly us there?'

'Sure thing. Guess I'll come with you, see you safely home.'

'That would be a good idea.'

There was a strange atmosphere inside the car as it entered the grounds of Spanish Bay. No one spoke and the silence had an awkward character – no one wished to express the fear they were feeling. No one wished to speak in case they said the wrong thing. As they approached the car park Tweed laid an arm along the back of Newman's seat, leaned close and whispered something. Newman merely nodded to show he'd understood. The Merc. pulled up in the usual place. While Tweed was getting out of the car Newman released his seatbelt, pressed a button to elevate the aerial with the spider's web of wires. He was pressing more buttons as Alvarez slipped out, got into the front passenger seat, grasped the microphone. Tweed leaned into the car.

'Everyone assembles in my apartment with their luggage.'

He was praying Alvarez would contact Cord Dillon as he walked quickly back to the BMW, which had pulled up behind them. He opened the front door, smiled at Mrs Benyon.

'I want you to come with me. I'll carry your things.'
Then he gestured to Marler and the other two men.
'Assemble in my apartment in two minutes from now.
With suitcases.'

Butler, despite his injured knee, was heaving out
Mrs Benyon's two suitcases from the boot. He shook his
head when Tweed attempted to relieve him of his
burden.

'Take care of the lady,' he said firmly.

Strains of dance music drifted out from somewhere
on the chilly air. The sound struck Paula as odd, like the
last dance before a great battle. As she walked to the
hotel entrance she heard Alvarez speaking in a staccato
voice. He had got through to Cord Dillon.

She saw Tweed pausing at the entrance. He was
looking back up the drive into the distance. She had the
distinct impression he was expecting someone to arrive,
hoping that they would. Then he hurried inside on his
way to his apartment, moving with swift steps.

Shortly afterwards she was the first to enter Tweed's
apartment. He had slid aside the glass windows, was
holding his own suitcase. He always travelled light. Mrs
Benyon sat on a couch.

'What about the hotel bill?' Paula asked.

'I paid that before we left for Black Ridge. Paid it to
include tomorrow night, but warned them we might have
to leave early.'

Newman came in, followed by the others. Alvarez
was the last to arrive. He gestured towards the window
Tweed had slid open.

'We go out there. The Chinook is on its way. It will
land on one of the greens on the golf course. I know
which one. Let's get moving. I need to be out there to
signal with my flash when it comes in.'

'I'll be out there shortly,' Tweed said. 'I'm waiting at
the front.'

415

'Don't wait all night,' Alvarez warned. 'The Chinook pilot won't.'

At Black Ridge Ethan was inside the upper chamber, his eyes glued to the strong-motion recorder. The vertical markings were still jumping at irregular intervals, but so far there was nothing dramatic. He stood, staring down, fingertips in his mouth as he gnawed at them.

He couldn't keep still. He kept moving round the chamber, then hurrying back to the seismograph. The regular foreshocks convinced him San Moreno was about to erupt. Why was it all taking so long? He had bitten his nails down to the quick.

'Come on! Come on!' he said aloud.

He was working himself up into a frenzy. Rushing over to a table, he poured himself more coffee from a thermos into a plastic cup, swallowed it. In his haste he almost choked. He walked back to the seismograph with his eyes closed. He opened them, stared like a man hypnotized.

Very steep markings had jumped way above their predecessors. Steeper even than he'd expected. He flung the cup across the chamber, spilling coffee over the floor. He flew up the ladder, opened the heavy door leading into the corridor. It was deserted. Then a door opened and Joel Brand came out.

'It's coming now!' Ethan shrieked at him.

'What is?' growled Brand.

'The greatest earthquake in the history of the world. *My* earthquake . . .'

Brand grabbed the revolver from the holster by his side. He aimed, fired. The bullet travelled harmlessly down the empty corridor. Ethan had slipped inside his office, had double-locked the door from the inside. He heard Brand turning the handle furiously, then the handle stopped turning.

Ethan had already opened the panel, inserted his key in the wall safe, exposed the interior. His hands were damp with perspiration. He rubbed them on the backs of his trousers, gazed at the two levers. Taking a deep breath, he took hold of each lever with one hand, pulled them down with a mighty jerk. The system was operative. He had five minutes to board the waiting chopper.

Opening his office door, after taking an automatic from a drawer in his desk, he peered out. The corridor was deserted. Where could Brand have gone? With the automatic trembling in his right hand he ran along the route which would take him to the hangar. The moment he emerged into the cold night air he heard the beat-beat of the helicopter's rotors. It had come out of the hangar, was lifting off.

'Wait for me!' Ethan screamed.

Inside the passenger section Moloch looked down, saw Ethan waving his arms madly. He sighed as the machine gained height. He never wanted to see Ethan Benyon again. Mad as a hatter, he thought. Why did I ever not realize it earlier? All the signs were there. Because I didn't want to recognize it.

On the ground Ethan was beside himself with terror. He ran back inside the house, hurtled along the corridor to the front entrance where cars were parked. Arriving outside he saw Brand about to get behind the wheel of Moloch's Lincoln Continental.

'The swine,' Brand snarled.

'Who?' asked Ethan, hardly knowing what he was saying.

'VB. He slammed the door of the chopper in my face and it took off. Where the hell do you think you're going?'

'Take me with you,' Ethan pleaded.

Brand rammed his elbow into Ethan's ribs as he attempted to open another door. Ethan staggered back, collapsed on the ground. By the time he stumbled to his feet the Lincoln was driving at top speed down the slope, headlights blazing as it passed through the open gates, turned right onto Highway One.

Brand drove at manic speed, roared past the drive leading up to The Apex. He never gave a thought to Mrs Benyon, intent only on reaching San Francisco in record time. By his side on the passenger seat was an automatic rifle. If he met a patrol car he'd gun down anyone who tried to stop him.

His huge muscular frame was tense. He felt the ground under the car shudder, pressed his foot down further. Then he heard the horrendous explosion. Glancing out to sea his eyes opened wide. The ocean seemed to be lifting. He saw the *Baja* tossed high into the air as though it were a rowboat. The Xenobium bomb beneath it had detonated. The vessel turned turtle in midair, plunged back downwards into the incredibly high mountain of water hurled up by the explosion. It disappeared but Brand kept his nerve as the highway climbed steeply, swinging round dangerous bends without slowing down.

He was passing Point Sur when the huge massif split in two, creating a canyon through which the ocean surged in a Niagara of water. The lighthouse toppled down inside the canyon, vanished under the water. The sea was now flooding across the highway but Brand didn't slow – he drove through, sending up great gushes of spray which blinded his windscreen. He turned the wipers full on, saw a bend just in time.

Ahead, along a straight stretch of highway, he saw that a crack was splitting open the road. It was only a few inches wide when he drove over it. In his rear-view mirror he glimpsed the crack widen to a crevasse. Under the Lincoln the ground was shuddering again. He kept the huge stretch limo moving. He was approaching the Bixby Bridge.

One of the wonders of American engineering, the most often photographed Bixby Bridge was opened for traffic after completion in November 1932. The central arch, over the creek running into the Pacific two hundred and fifty feet beneath it, was a span more than two hundred and fifty feet long. Driving over it cars went thump thump as they crossed the strips of material laid across it to slow down traffic.

So far Brand had seen no other cars from the moment he had left Black Ridge. Glancing up the mountainside to his right, he gazed in trepidation as a millionaire's modernistic house simply slid down the slope, breaking up as it continued to slide. Inside other fabulous properties the lights suddenly went out as powerlines were fractured. The moon was rising as Brand's teeth were bared in a rictus-like smile.

He took the bridge at full tilt, ignoring the slow-down strips. He was almost halfway across when the arch began to climb into the air. Gripping the wheel of the Lincoln Continental with all his strength, he drove up the mounting arch, reached the summit, saw a split appearing right across the arch. The Lincoln leapt over the gap, started descending the far side. In a trance of terror, Brand felt the entire structure heaving sideways and seawards. The Lincoln swivelled out of the right-hand lane into the left.

Brand threw up a useless arm across his head in horror as the whole bridge continued to tilt, then collapsed. He had no time to take his foot off the accelerator as the stretch limo shot over the rails, now at a much lower angle. The Lincoln was a rocket in flight. It hammered into the cliffs on the Carmel side like a shell from a gun, the petrol tank exploded, flames engulfed it from end to end. The relics fell into the boiling ocean below. Where the great Bixby Bridge had once stood there was only a wide gap, the broken structure swallowed up by the Pacific far beneath what had, for so many years, been a marvel of Highway One.

On the golf links near Spanish Bay, a short time before Ethan had pulled the levers, the Chinook, a large ugly helicopter with a box-like stern, landed on the green where Alvarez had signalled with his torch. Everyone was aboard except for Newman, who stood at the foot of the ladder, staring anxiously back at the hotel for a sight of Tweed.

'Can't wait much longer,' the co-pilot shouted down from above.

'You *are* waiting for a VIP,' Alvarez said, standing beside the co-pilot, flourishing his CIA credentials.

'A few minutes more. No longer . . .'

Outside the lobby in front of the hotel Tweed was enduring the most nerve-racking wait he could remember. Then he saw two men hurrying towards him from the direction of the club. Grenville with Maurice Prendergast.

'Some minor crisis?' Grenville enquired calmly. 'We saw your lot arriving, rushing about like frightened rabbits.'

'Some rabbits,' Tweed snapped. 'Both of you go out the back way by Roy's. Board the chopper you'll see waiting on the links. A major earthquake is due.'

'A major crisis, then,' Grenville responded.

He stubbed the cigar he had been smoking, followed Maurice who had already started running into the lobby. Tweed walked up and down, counting his paces to concentrate his mind. Then he stopped. An Audi, driven at high speed, jerked to a stop a few feet away from him. Vanity Richmond jumped out, holding a suitcase.

'I caught your signal when you stood in my doorway – smoothing down your hair. Got trapped behind a juggernaut crawling along the highway. Ages before I dared overtake.'

'You're here. That's the main thing. Come on.'

Taking her by one hand, he ran with her into the lobby and out of the door next to Roy's. From the terrace they could see the lights of the big Chinook. Grenville and Maurice were already mounting the ladder.

'Hurry up!' Newman shouted at them.

'What the hell do you think we're doing?' Vanity snapped back at him.

She flew up the ladder, followed by Tweed and Newman. The co-pilot hauled up the aluminium ladder, slammed the door shut.

Tweed stood at the doorway to the pilot's control area. The rotors were already whirling, faster and faster. He had to shout.

'What is happening at San Francisco International? A major earthquake is coming.'

'A special flight has been laid on. There have been shocks in San Francisco,' the pilot shouted back. 'Washington has arranged the flight. We have time to spare.'

Alvarez put his mouth close to Tweed's ear, kept his voice down.

'For Washington read Cord Dillon . . .'

The Chinook was lifting off, higher and higher, then it began its flight north, over the ocean. Entering the main cabin Tweed had the impression the Chinook had been furnished for top brass. Rows of comfortable double seats lined both port and starboard with a central aisle, occupied the fuselage. Vanity was sitting next to Newman, who waved cheerily. Tweed chose a seat by himself on the starboard side next to a window. It gave him a view of the coast.

They had passed Monterey and he estimated they must be close to Moss Landing when, looking down, he saw in the moonlight the *Kebir*, twin dredger with the *Baja*. As he watched, a tremendous explosion shook the Chinook. The helicopter bucked, but the pilot had it under control within seconds. Paula had moved forward, seated herself beside Tweed just before the explosion.

'What on earth was that?' she asked.

'The second Xenobium bomb detonating. Ethan's work. Look down.'

She leaned over him, stared. The *Kebir* had keeled over, was wallowing in a turmoil of surf and raging water. As she watched it sank, as though sucked down by some enormous force. A tidal wave appeared, more like a mountain than a wave. It drove forward to the coast, inundated it, continued inland across the flatlands until she could no longer see it. She sat down, let out her breath.

'It looks like a cauldron down there.'

'It is a cauldron. Lord knows what's happening to the south of us . . .'

The San Moreno earthquake, combined with the detonation of the Xenobium bombs, produced the colossal reaction Professor Weatherby had eventually feared. The tectonic plate off California was shifted under the coast. The results were catastrophic.

Starting just north of Los Angeles, a gigantic chasm opened up in the Earth's surface. In certain areas it ran inland, in others it destroyed the coast for ever. LA itself did not escape the devastation. Several buildings constructed of two wings at right angles to each other split apart. Shudderings from the ground travelled up the buildings, increased in ferocity as they reached the tops. The buildings broke in two, one wing going one way, the other in a different direction. Cars parked in the streets were flattened like sardine cans. Because they were office buildings and it was after working hours casualties were light.

Not so in homes on the edge of the sprawling city. People inside concrete structures were crushed. Further away pictures were shaken off walls, ornaments crashed off mantelpieces, doors broke loose from their hinges. All this was nothing compared with what happened when the chasm opened from Santa Barbara north to San Francisco.

After being knocked to the ground by Brand at Black Ridge, Ethan was terrified by what he had released. He ran round the back of the mansion, started to climb the hills looming above, despite the height at which the mansion stood. He had reason to be scared out of his wits – he knew what was coming.

The ocean gathered itself up into one of the most feared products of a major earthquake – a tsunami, the Japanese term for a mighty tidal wave. Scrambling up the slope, he paused for breath, looked back and screamed. A wave higher than Black Ridge, a monster in the moonlight, green with a curl of surf at its summit, rolled majestically forward. At that moment Ethan felt the ground trembling under his feet. Looking down, he saw a huge chasm ripping the slope asunder. The monster wave slammed against the hillslope, struck him in the back, toppled him into the chasm. Millions of tons of ocean flooded down into the chasm. Ethan was drowned.

When it eventually receded the wave took half the coast with it. A landslide shifted the Gothic mansion of Black Ridge, clawed it down the slope as it broke up into a thousand pieces. Other three-million-dollar houses were sliced off the slope, carrying their inhabitants down into the depths of the ocean. The whole landscape in the Big Sur area was transformed into a series of ugly island crags.

The chasm continued ripping north, devouring forests, hamlets, highways in the most terrible rampage in the history of man. Ethan had tampered with Nature, had paid the penalty – but so did many others. The earthquake registered 8.9 on the Richter scale. Later, casualties were estimated at 150,000.

Tweed realized they were in trouble as the Chinook began its descent on San Francisco International Airport. The pilot landed his machine close to a waiting Boeing 747. The plane was surrounded by State troopers holding guns.

'People are panicking trying to board our plane,' he warned Paula.

'Poor devils.'

'Let's just hope we can reach the aircraft.'

'You'll have to force your way through two files of troopers,' reported the co-pilot who had entered the cabin. 'Just keep shoving until you're inside the 747.'

'I must look after Mrs Benyon,' Tweed said.

'I'll help you,' Paula insisted. 'It's chaos out there.'

It was worse than that, Tweed thought, glancing out of the window. He stiffened. In the distance he saw the lights of a Lear jet moving down a runway. As it passed near an overhead glare light he read the huge letters painted on the fuselage. AMBECO. The jet took off, climbing rapidly as it gained height. Vincent Bernard Moloch was leaving America.

43

There is nothing more frightening than a panic-stricken mob stampeding out of sheer terror. As they left the Chinook, climbing down the ladder, the sound of the rotors whirling ceased. It was replaced by another sound. The howl and yells of the vast crowd fighting to board the Boeing. It was every man – and woman – for themselves. The thin veneer of civilization had vanished – the mob was like a mass of savages, pressing against the two lines of armed State troopers forming a narrow aisle leading to the British Airways plane.

'Follow me!' shouted Alvarez.

He led the way, flourishing his CIA folder in the faces of the troopers. Behind him came Mrs Benyon, clutching only one of her suitcases. Tweed had hold of one of her arms, Paula gripped the other. Mrs Benyon was remarkably calm. She used her bulk to press her way forward after Alvarez between the backs of troopers struggling to hold back the seething crowd, holding their automatic rifles in both hands, parallel to the ground, to act as a makeshift barrier.

One American woman, her face contorted with fury, broke through behind Alvarez. A trooper hoisted his weapon to hit her with the butt. Paula grabbed his arm with her free hand.

'Don't! Please don't hit her.'

Her voice carried. At that moment the ground under the airport had shuddered briefly, silencing the crowd for a short time. The trooper looked surprised, then heaved the intruding woman back with his body. She yelled at Paula.

'Friggin' Brit. You'll get away. You're OK!'

Paula felt guilty because what the woman had screamed at her was true. If they ever reached the Boeing she would get away while the woman would be left behind. Tweed sensed her reaction.

'Concentrate on getting Mrs Benyon to safety,' he rapped out.

The struggle to reach the aircraft went on. At times Alvarez was able to walk a few yards along a clear aisle as Tweed and Paula hurried Mrs Benyon after him. Then the protecting line would give way and Alvarez had to wait as the troopers fought to clear the way. Then he would press forward as control was – briefly – regained. The mob began baying in rising unison.

'Kill the troopers! Kill the troopers! Kill them!'

This is turning very ugly, Tweed thought, but he kept the reaction to himself as the nightmare movement forward continued. Paula saw one woman among the crowd in tears. A tall handsome Negro next to her, obviously a stranger, put one arm round her and she buried her face in his large chest. The Negro saw Paula's expression. He waved to her with his free arm, grinned. Paula wanted to burst into tears herself. Then a fresh horror occurred.

A white man, with a bony, skull-like head, had produced a knife. He was stabbing people at random, forcing his way forward to where the troopers stood. Several of his victims collapsed. He was close to the Negro, who turned round, saw what he was doing. He clenched a huge fist, using his free arm, smashed it against the jaw of the man with the knife. The attacker slumped out of sight, was trampled underfoot.

'Oh, my God!' she let out.

'Keep moving,' ordered Tweed.

The file of troopers, originally forming a straight line to the waiting aircraft, were now bent into a conga-like formation, but still stood shoulder to shoulder. Glancing back, Paula saw Newman close behind, gripping Vanity's arm as he pushed her forward. Her face was twisted in an expression of strain. Lord, I'll bet I'm looking like that, thought Paula. Newman grinned at her, motioned her to keep moving.

Quite suddenly, Paula was aware of something huge looming above them. It was the Boeing. They had almost reached the plane. Ahead she saw troopers desperately attempting to keep the mob back from the mobile staircase alongside the fuselage. Mrs Benyon gave her bulk an extra heave to force their way through between the backs of troopers.

'Be careful on the steps,' Tweed shouted in her ear.

Mrs Benyon reached the foot of the mobile staircase. She mounted them rapidly, one hand still clutching her suitcase, the other holding on to a rail. Paula followed, careful not to look down. Tweed did look down as he climbed the steps. He estimated there must be forty troopers, half on one side, half on the other, keeping the mobile staircase in place.

Suddenly Paula found herself inside the aircraft, guided to First Class by the female purser who had managed to greet her with a smile. Only then did she realize she was still holding the ticket Tweed had handed her aboard the Chinook, that the purser had checked it swiftly before leading the way. Exhausted, she sank into the aisle seat, determined not to look out of the window. Tweed took the window seat, stared out.

The seething, frightened mob seemed to hem in the plane, but then he observed a fresh line of troopers, holding back the huge crowd of people desperate to board. A woman sat in the aisle seat opposite Paula, several feet away since in First Class the aisle was spacious. The purser was examining her ticket.

'You are Hiram Bellenger? Hiram is a man's name.'

'I'm Hiram.'

A tall heavily built man had slipped aboard and stood by the purser. He smiled broadly.

'This is my sister. She's taking my seat. I insisted. I can catch the next flight tomorrow. Let me have the ticket.'

Pulling it from the purser's hand, he took out a fountain pen, crossed out his Christian name, leaving only the letter 'H'. He handed back the ticket to the purser.

'Her name is Harriet, so now everything is in order. I guess I'd better leave now.' He caught Paula's expression, patted his large bulk. 'Don't look like that, lady. I'll have a few beers in the city, then, as I just said, catch a flight tomorrow. With my bulk aboard the plane would be overloaded.' He smiled again, squeezed Paula's shoulder. 'Safe flight . . .'

Then he was gone and again Paula had trouble controlling her emotions. Tomorrow's flight? Would there be a tomorrow for Hiram? She felt sick. Tweed grasped her hand.

'The bad and the very good. We've seen them all today.' He looked back. 'Mrs Benyon has fallen asleep. Everyone else is with us. Bob, Marler, Nield, Butler – and Alvarez.'

'I don't understand the number of times Alvarez has got away with waving his CIA folder.'

'I'll explain later. And Vanity is seated next to Bob. She looks washed out, but she's chatting to Newman.'

'I don't understand why you were so anxious to wait for her back at Spanish Bay.'

'I'll explain later.'

All the passengers were aboard. Tweed secretly wondered how on earth the plane would ever take off. Peering out of the window he saw American organization in a crisis at its best. The pilot had ordered the cabin crew over the tannoy to lock the doors, take their seats. The jet engines were humming, rising to a crescendo.

'They're clearing a path for us,' Tweed informed Paula as he pressed his face close to the window.

'How are they doing that? They'll never get us through the crowd.'

'They are doing it . . .'

Alongside and ahead of the aircraft motorized open cargo trolleys carried troopers with their rifles. As the pilot edged the huge machine forward the trolley-loads of troopers were driving aside the mob, which was shaking fists, shouting abuse.

Two men in the mob, crazed with fear and rage, ran ahead of the moving aircraft, lay down in its path. At the risk of their lives four troopers dived off the lead trolley, ran ahead, grabbed hold of the prone men, dragged them out of the way. Inwardly, Tweed heaved a sigh of relief. Then he felt the shudder of the second tremor coming.

A slitlike crack appeared across the runway. Tweed compelled himself to show no reaction for fear of upsetting Paula. She had also felt the movement.

'What was that?' she asked.

'The pilot testing his brakes,' Tweed said quickly.

In the moonlight he could see the crack. Were they heading for total disaster at the last moment? The pilot increased speed, sped over the crack before it widened. The plane was roaring down the runway and then Tweed felt it lift off, become airborne. He squeezed Paula's hand.

'We've taken off.'

'Thank Heaven. I'm drained of emotion.'

'I'm sure we all are.'

Climbing steeply, the aircraft curved over towards the ocean. The manoeuvre gave Tweed a bird's-eye view of the magnificent city of San Francisco. As he gazed down he blinked. The cone-shaped AMBECO building was moving. The huge rollers it had been erected on to make it earthquake proof differed in design from those beneath the TransAmerica building. The giant cone began to spin slowly, then it keeled over, toppling slowly before the entire structure collapsed.

The plane continued its great curving sweep, climbing all the time, giving Tweed a view of the Golden Gate Bridge. The most famous bridge in the world was shaking from side to side. Awestruck, Tweed watched as a gap appeared in its centre and the highway crossing it fell into the moonlit waters below, sending up a massive splash. There had been no traffic on the bridge. It vanished from view as the aircraft went on gaining altitude, eventually levelling out at thirty-five thousand feet as it headed Polar Route for Heathrow.

44

Flying over the Canadian North-West Territories, the Lear jet sped onward through the night. In the luxurious passenger cabin Moloch sat alongside his new British personal assistant, Heather Lang. He had summoned her from her job at the Des Moines explosives plant to fly to San Francisco aboard another of his jets. She had been waiting for him in the cabin when he had landed from Black Ridge aboard the helicopter. After delivering her, the second jet had immediately returned to Des Moines.

'When we get to Heathrow,' Moloch was explaining, 'we fly by Brymon Airways to Newquay in Cornwall. A car will be waiting to drive us from there to Mullion Towers.'

'Your headquarters in Britain,' she had replied. 'Is that our new base?'

Heather Lang, in her thirties, was an attractive brunette who had drive and competence. She wore a pale grey power suit over a white blouse. The suit showed off her good figure, had a short skirt revealing her long shapely legs. She had a Roman nose under blue eyes and good bone structure, tapering to a determined chin. She was a woman of great ambition.

'No,' Moloch replied to her question. 'Soon we board my floating palace, the *Venetia*, lying off Falmouth. Then we sail for Beirut in the Lebanon. I have an exotic house high up in the Lebanon mountains. It is cool up there the whole year round.'

'It sounds exciting,' Heather replied.

'I am transferring my whole operation to the Middle East,' Moloch went on, after a swift glance at her. He was amused to see she was impressed by the description he had just given her – language he rarely used. 'Incidentally,' he went on casually, 'I am doubling your salary.'

'That's very generous of you, VB. Thank you.'

Yes, it was generous, he was thinking. But it was worth it. You bought loyalty in the crazy world which was emerging. He gave her the file he had been glancing through as he spoke. The name on the front had been erased earlier by his felt-tip pen – the name Ethan Benyon.

'Shred that for me now, please.'

The teleprinter, recording a bulletin from Reuters beamed to the jet by satellite, had spewed out a reel of paper. When she had finished shredding papers which meant nothing to her, she detached the Reuters report, brought it to Moloch.

He read it quickly. More news about the great San Moreno earthquake. An item caught his attention and he smiled to himself.

Among the devastated plants destroyed in Silicon Valley,

California, were fifteen of the world's most advanced electronic companies . . .

He checked the names and saw that the list included the five competitors who had combined to destroy his first business venture in the States years before. It gave him great satisfaction to read their names a second time.

Also it meant that, with the two extra companies he had just bought up in the Thames Valley, he had three key companies which could almost monopolize the world supply of advanced microchips and other advanced equipment. His assistant sat beside him again. They had both recently eaten the excellent meal supplied by the chef included in the crew. He laid a hand on her knee.

'If you are loyal to me – completely loyal – you could go a long way and earn a great deal of money.'

She glanced at him without a hint of enticement on her pale face. He removed his hand.

'I'm only interested in hard work,' she replied.

'Then go and tell the radio op. to send a message to Heathrow. First, book two seats on the Brymon Airways flight to Newquay. One-way tickets. Then tell the pilot when we arrive at Heathrow he is to wait for two passengers he will fly to Newquay when they arrive from San Francisco. A Colonel Grenville and a Maurice Prendergast.'

'They are officials in the company?' she enquired.

'One of them establishes counter-espionage networks for me.'

'That sounds exciting.'

'It's a job like any other . . .'

Tweed had returned to his seat aboard the British Airways plane forging its way through the night. He sat down as a steward began pulling out tables for a meal. Paula had just suppressed a yawn.

'I don't know whether I can eat a thing after what we've experienced.'

'Try something,' Tweed urged. 'Otherwise you'll suddenly feel hungry in the middle of the night.'

'I'll make the effort.'

'Incidentally, when I went to the loo I peered into Club Class. Both Grenville and Maurice are occupying separate seats. They came aboard, of course, under the assumed names you booked tickets under.'

'You make it sound as though they're important.'

'One of three people aboard this aircraft is the spy Moloch uses to set up watcher networks. It has to be someone, as I mentioned before, who was in Cornwall and then arrived in California.' He glanced back. 'Newman and Vanity seem to be getting on well together.'

'They have done for some time. How are you going to detect this spy?'

'By having all the suspects followed when we have landed at Heathrow. I'm sure Moloch will want to use the same person again. We must stop that . . .'

He paused when he saw that on the TV screen Paula had erected there was a news flash, beamed in, he presumed, by satellite. Besides the spoken commentary in an American voice, there were graphic pictures of the devastation caused by the earthquake. Paula leaned forward.

'Surely that was Big Sur? It's split into two islands – the sea now runs in between them. The lighthouse has gone.'

'Point Sur,' Tweed corrected her. 'Lord, the whole coastline has been smashed up.'

'And look! Black Ridge was on that hillside. It has just disappeared. I wonder if Moloch was inside it?'

'VB is flying ahead of us in his Lear jet.'

'Now he tells me.'

'I saw the jet taking off from San Francisco airport. Quite a while before we took to the air . . .'

He paused as the purser arrived with a sealed envelope which she handed to him.

'This radio message just came in for you, Mr Tweed.'

He thanked her, opened the envelope, unfolded the sheet inside, read it quickly and grunted with satisfaction. He handed it to Paula. She read it and looked at him.

VB expected arrive here by jet this afternoon. Two tickets booked Newquay. The Blimp and the Morris travelling on to Newquay by jet. Cheltenham interception. Monica.

'Which, translated,' Tweed said in a low voice, 'means that VB is going straight on to Cornwall soon after he arrives. I don't know who is accompanying him. Also Grenville and Maurice will be transported to Cornwall aboard Moloch's jet. The second message from the Lear jet ahead of us was intercepted by GCHQ at Cheltenham. At long last the authorities are waking up to the fact that VB is a deadly menace.'

'That's what I gathered. Monica, as usual, has been clever in her wording. Does it affect our movements?'

Tweed didn't reply. A steward had just brought them their first course. He looked at the two mini-bottles of opened champagne which were untouched.

'Did you want something more to drink?'

'What we have will do very nicely. For the moment,' Tweed replied.

He poured Paula's bottle into her glass on the chair rest, then poured his own, much to Paula's surprise.

'You hardly ever drink.'

'It's been tension almost from the time we set foot in sunny California. Time to relax.'

They clinked glasses and Tweed drank a whole glassful, then refilled both glasses. Paula looked at him.

'You're going it a bit. For you, I mean.'

'We'll get another couple of bottles. I've heard this stuff does you good.'

'Great idea. We arrive tiddly at Heathrow. Best way to pass a night flight. I'm ravenous,' she said, sipping the chicken soup.

'What did I tell you?'

He glanced over his shoulder, as he had done a few minutes earlier.

'Vanity and Bob are knocking back the champers as though there's no tomorrow.'

'Not so long ago in California I thought there wouldn't be one. Look at the TV now. Silicon Valley has been obliterated.'

'Which was the object of Moloch's titanic exercise. I'm sure he's congratulating himself now – regardless of the casualties. I think his character has undergone a transformation.'

'How do you mean?'

'I think he has had to fight so hard and for so long in America that the iron has entered his soul, as they used to say. And he now has so much power he can only go on to do one thing. To accumulate more power. And he can do it. Through the Arab connection.'

'Those pictures we saw are grim,' Newman remarked.

'The ones we saw on your little TV set?' Vanity queried.

'Those pictures. And all the horror was caused by the ambition of one man – Moloch.'

'He has a remarkable brain,' she said. 'While working for him I never ceased to be astonished at the speed with which he would take a major decision. It was a unique experience to work for such a man.'

'Sounds as though you admire him,' Newman commented.

'I admire his brain. That doesn't mean I admire the man. Stop twisting my words.'

'I wasn't aware I was twisting anything,' snapped Newman.

'You're like a bear with a sore head.'

'Maybe it's the company I keep,' he fired back.

'Change the company, then,' Vanity snapped.

'I might just do that.' He glanced at her. 'I'd have thought that with a good meal inside you you'd be in a better temper.'

'Nothing wrong with my temper. You keep provoking me.'

'Not intentionally. Perhaps it's all in your mind.'

'It would be in *my* mind, of course. Why do they have to pull the shutters down over the windows? I like to see out.'

'Nothing to see. It's night-time.'

Vanity rammed up the shutter with great force. She peered down into the darkness.

'I can see lights. A small cluster. We're passing over southern Greenland.'

'No one lives in Greenland.'

'Yes they do. I think it's Godthaab. That's on the Polar Route. Next we'll pass over the southern tip of Iceland.'

'Not a bad place to take a holiday. It's very unusual.'

'I think I will take a holiday when we get back. On my own. I rather fancy going back to Cornwall . . .'

Grenville was sitting bolt upright in his seat. He didn't believe in slouching in public, even when going to sleep. In the seat behind him Maurice Prendergast had stretched out his comfortable chair so it formed a makeshift bed. He had a blanket over him and was just nodding off when a steward shook him gently by the arm.

436

'Mr Prendergast? Sorry to disturb you. A message has come in for you via the radio operator.'

'Really? Can't imagine who knows I'm aboard this flight.'

He shook himself awake, took the sealed envelope handed to him by the steward. Opening it, he read the message.

My Lear jet will be waiting for you at Heathrow. You are invited to join me at Mullion Towers, Cornwall. Please tell Col. Grenville the invitation is extended to him. I look forward to your company. VB.

Maurice roused himself, stood up, looked along the Club Class. Everyone appeared to be fast asleep in the dimmed lights. He'd had to switch on his own personal light to read the message.

He was going to tap Grenville on the shoulder, but from the motionless posture of the figure in front of him he decided Grenville must be fast asleep. He didn't fancy waking the often choleric colonel too abruptly. He walked to the side of the seat, gazed down. Grenville opened his eyes.

'What is it, man? At this hour?'

'Message for you. It's for me, too. Was addressed to me, as you'll see. Here it is.'

Grenville took the sheet of paper, read it slowly, frowned. He looked up at Maurice with a distasteful expression.

'What's all this about?'

'Don't ask me.'

'I just did. And keep your voice down. People are sleeping.'

'So I have observed. I suppose it's an easy way to get back to Cornwall. Can't imagine why Moloch has bothered.'

'Neither can I.'

Both men regarded each other with mistrust as Grenville handed back the sheet of paper.

45

Arriving at Heathrow, Tweed headed straight for the office of Jim Corcoran, Security Chief. Its occupant looked up from his desk when Tweed walked in, closed the door.

'I smell trouble. For myself,' Corcoran greeted him.

Corcoran gestured to a chair, shook hands as Tweed remained standing.

'It's an emergency. Two men, Grenville and Prendergast, are boarding Vincent Bernard Moloch's private jet. I want take-off of that jet delayed a few hours. Technical hitch – whatever.'

'This time you're asking too much.' Corcoran spread his hands in resignation. 'I'd help you if I could but Moloch draws a lot of water these days.'

'Can I use your phone? I want to speak to Howard.'

'Be my guest . . .'

Tweed got through to Monica who immediately transferred him to Howard, the pompous Director of the SIS. Tersely, Tweed explained the problem. Howard asked for Corcoran to be put on the line.

'Howard here, Jim, old boy. Long time no see. I've just got back from a session with the PM. Yes, the PM himself. He wants total surveillance on Mr Moloch. You therefore have my authority – and by implication the PM's – to delay that jet, as Tweed has requested. Vital you assist us.'

'I'll do it, then . . .'

Later, Tweed had explained what had happened to Paula as they sat in the back of Newman's Merc., retrieved from Long Stay parking where he had left it prior to their departure for California. Behind them Marler drove his own car with Butler and Nield as passengers.

'So,' Paula commented, 'once again when the chips are down Howard turned up trumps – to mix metaphors.'

'It's significant,' Tweed told her 'There's obviously been a dramatic sea change in the PM's attitude towards Moloch.'

'We could have done with his backing earlier,' Paula commented. 'By the way, what has happened to Vanity? She disappeared pretty smartly after we disembarked.'

'Vanity,' Newman called out, 'decided she wanted a holiday – on her own, as she put it. It was pretty stressful while we were in California.'

'A holiday where?' Paula wanted to know.

'Cornwall.'

'How is she getting there?'

'In her own car. Like us, she left hers at Heathrow when she flew to California.'

Newman lapsed into silence as he drove well outside London. Paula pursed her lips. It was clear Vanity and Newman were no longer on the best of terms. They must have had a fight aboard the plane. She frowned, turned to Tweed.

'Strange how everyone is rushing back to Cornwall. Moloch has returned there. We know from Monica that Grenville and Maurice are on their way – by courtesy of VB's private jet.' She lowered her voice. 'And now Vanity is also on her way to where it all started. Your three suspects, one of which may be Moloch's spy, the person who sets up his networks.'

'I had noticed that,' Tweed said drily.

'Moloch's spy is important, I should have thought,' she prodded.

'Very. Has to be apprehended at all costs. But who is it?'

It was the beginning of September. The two cars made good time, crossing the border into Cornwall, and Paula noticed the leaves were beginning to change colour. Green was being replaced by a mix of red, gold and orange.

Autumn was on the way – under a clear blue sky with the sun glowing as brilliantly as anything they had seen in California. It was still warm. Paula gave a sigh of pleasure.

'It's good to be home again. California may be a scenic marvel but there's nothing to beat Britain for the change of seasons.'

'California *was* a scenic marvel,' Tweed corrected her. 'Now it's a shattered coast.' He held up the newspaper he had been glancing at. 'Look at these pictures of Carmel.'

'They're more like photos I've seen of the devastation during the Second World War bombing. Isn't that the street where you made calls from a public booth?'

'Yes, it is. Half the buildings – art galleries, restaurants, shops – are rubble. Monterey escaped any damage. The San Moreno fault zigzagged inland after levelling Carmel. "The greatest earthquake in history" is how the papers are describing it. Moloch has a lot to answer for.'

He looked up. Newman was driving along a dual carriageway and a car was overtaking them like the wind. Behind the wheel Vanity waved saucily to them and roared on ahead.

'She's pushing it a bit,' Paula remarked.

'She has to get there first,' Newman said and again lapsed into silence.

'Where are we staying, by the way?' Paula asked Tweed.

'At Nansidwell again. It provides a good view of the waters off Falmouth. I got Monica to book us all rooms while I was in Jim Corcoran's office.'

'Literally back to where it all started. Well, at least we saw Mrs Benyon safely off to Cheltenham in that car waiting for her. I think she was so relieved to be back on British soil. I wonder who arranged to have the car waiting for her?'

'I did,' Tweed replied. 'During the night aboard the plane when you dropped off to sleep I sent a message to Monica. The least I could do for her.'

'What happened to Alvarez? I never had time to thank him for all his help.'

'I did that. He asked me to give you his affectionate regards. He was in a hurry to catch the next flight back to the States.'

'I still don't understand the role he played.'

'Tell you about that later. We have two major tasks ahead—' He broke off to call out to Newman. 'Don't forget we're calling in at Truro on the way. We have to hire cars for Butler and Nield. I want everybody mobile for what lies ahead of us.'

'What exactly does lie ahead of us?' Paula asked.

'First, to locate Moloch's spy. Second, and far more important, to prevent Moloch from ever leaving Britain, no matter what means have to be used. I'm really worried about what he could do. His conglomerate has invented the Xenobium bomb – with more than ten times the power of a hydrogen bomb, Cord Dillon said. Supposing he is in a position to sell the details of its make-up and construction to certain hostile Arab countries? They could destroy the Western world.'

'What a terrifying thought.'

'The only alternative is to destroy Moloch.'

* * *

At Newquay airport, an airfield in the middle of nowhere, VB and his new assistant, Heather Lang, transferred themselves and their luggage to a waiting chauffeur-driven Rolls-Royce.

Before settling back beside her, Moloch closed the glass partition between them and the chauffeur to provide privacy. As the car drove off sedately for Mullion Towers Moloch rested on his lap the briefcase attached to one wrist by a locked handcuff. Heather glanced at it.

'I suppose I shouldn't ask, but you keep that close to you as though it contains a fortune.'

'A great fortune,' he replied with a bleak smile, 'but not in banknotes or jewels. Rather in sheafs of stuffy papers.'

She didn't press him any further. She had already realized her boss would tell her only what he wanted her to know so she could do her job properly. One of Heather's many talents was to keep her nose out of matters which did not concern her.

Yes, a great fortune, Moloch was thinking as the Rolls drove on through arid countryside. Like travelling through a stony desert. Inside the briefcase were the formulae, the details of the constructions of the Xenobium bomb. He had no doubt that the leaders of certain Arab countries would pay millions for the information.

Always meticulous in planning, Moloch had phoned Heather before she had left the Des Moines plant. He had ordered her to shred a whole batch of documents in a certain file labelled Project Eclipse. Now all details of how to construct a Xenobium bomb had been destroyed – nothing was left to give the Americans a clue as to how to set about building such a bomb. The only data in the world was inside the briefcase on his lap.

'Not my idea of Cornwall,' Heather remarked, staring out of the window.

'Oh, the tourist attraction is the beaches and the coves

442

enclosed inside magnificent cliffs on the coast. That's where holidaymakers flock. This is the real Cornwall. When we get to Mullion Towers I want you to transmit this message via the radio operator on duty to the skipper of the *Venetia*.'

As he was speaking Moloch scribbled a cryptic message on a pad. The meaning would be clear to the skipper but to no one else. He handed her the message, then closed his eyes and fell asleep. It was by taking brief catnaps that he could work through the nights.

I wonder what it could contain? Heather thought as she folded the message, slipped it inside her wallet.

She was looking at the briefcase nestling in her boss's lap. From what he had said, little though it had been, she had the impression that its contents were worth millions. It never crossed her mind that the data could herald the end of the world.

46

It was evening when Newman drove his Merc. down the sloping entrance to Nansidwell and parked in front of the country hotel in exactly the same place he had parked when they were last there. It seemed a decade ago to Paula.

'The place looks just the same,' she said, then stared at another vehicle. 'Isn't that Vanity's car?'

'It is,' Newman said without enthusiasm. 'And don't blame me. I didn't know we were staying here until you told us on the way down, Tweed.'

'I don't see why anyone should be surprised,' Tweed replied.

Other cars came down the drive, parked. Marler was behind the wheel of one, Butler another and Nield a third. They had successfully hired extra transport in Truro. One of the staff came out, told them the proprietor was away on business, but greeted them with equal warmth. Everyone found they had been allotted the same rooms as on their previous visit.

Later, walking down the staircase behind Newman for dinner, Paula saw Vanity, wearing a snug gold dress with a high collar, sitting on the banquette opposite the compact bar. Jumping up, Vanity grasped Newman's right arm, her full red lips smiling.

'I waited for you, Bob. They have the same table for us.'

'Isn't that just dandy,' Newman replied.

'I love the warmth with which a man greets an old friend,' said Vanity, addressing her remark to Paula.

'Maybe he's jet-lagged,' Paula responded without a smile.

'A bottle of good wine should oil the works. It will most certainly oil mine,' the irrepressible Vanity shot back, still smiling. 'Come on, you old curmudgeon,' she said to Newman.

They were entering the dining room when Newman saw Tweed outside on the terrace. He had a pair of field glasses glued to his eyes and was gazing fixedly out to sea. Newman escorted Vanity to their table, excused himself, then joined Tweed.

There was an autumn chill in the evening air which reminded Newman of California. For a long minute Tweed said nothing, then handed him the glasses.

'I've been studying the *Venetia*. Lit up like a cruise ship again. I'm trying to identify those large objects on the fore and aft decks covered with canvas.'

'Could be anything,' Newman replied as he scanned the vessel. 'No sign yet that it's on the verge of departure.'

'You've seen the helicopter on the helipad?'

'Yes. A Sikorsky. Big job. But the *Venetia* is a big ship. Must have cost a few million.'

'I think it's waiting for a VIP to board it. Oh, look. A chopper has arrived, is circling over the vessel. I suspect the PM has at long last pressed a few buttons.'

'It will be from Culdrose near the Lizard. As you probably know the RAF has a big training airfield there for chopper pilots.'

As he watched the helicopter, lights winking to port and starboard, continued to circle high above the *Venetia*. Newman grunted.

'I think it's photographing the *Venetia* from all angles. Maybe it is also trying to identify those mysterious objects on deck.'

As he spoke the chopper flew away inland. Newman lowered the glasses, handed them to Tweed. They wandered back into the entrance hall on their way to the dining room.

'I'd better get back to Vanity before she starts kicking up,' Newman mused.

'You appear to have a firecracker on your hands,' Tweed observed with amusement.

Earlier he had told everyone in Truro they no longer needed to keep up the pretence they didn't know each other. When he entered the dining room Newman saw two guests seated at separate tables. He clapped a hand on Grenville's shoulder.

'It's a small world, to coin a phrase, Brigadier.'

'Colonel,' Grenville snapped, startled. 'And as a journalist I'd expect more original language.'

'Waiting for someone? Or something to happen, Colonel?'

Newman moved on before Grenville could reply. The ex-officer looked rattled, disturbed by Newman's unexpected intervention, Tweed noticed.

'Well, if it isn't Maurice,' said Newman with a broad grin. 'A long way from the Standish murder apartment, aren't we?'

'Do you have to bring that up? And do keep your voice down. Half the dining room is listening.'

'Yes, it has gone quiet, hasn't it? Enjoy your trip down in Vincent Bernard Moloch's jet? I expect you did – having the Brigadier ... beg his pardon, the Colonel – with you.'

'Why don't you just shove off – and enjoy your dinner with your licentious girl friend.'

'Maurice.' Newman bent down, put an arm round Maurice's shoulder. 'If you don't wash out your mouth with soap and water I'll close it for you with my fist. Now get on with your meal and I hope it chokes you.'

He removed his arm, still smiling. A silence you could hear gripped the dining room. Grenville, who had heard every word, was paying undue attention to the pattern on his plate. Newman strolled over to his table, sat down facing Vanity, still smiling.

'Time a bottle was opened. Ah, here is the wine list.'

'I've never seen you like that before,' she whispered.

'Stick around. The show has just started,' Newman said in a loud voice.

Tweed sat down at Paula's table, facing her. In another corner Marler sat by himself, an amused expression on his face as he lit a king-size. Muted conversation began again but people kept casting glances at Newman. Grenville and Maurice were also aware they had become centres of interest. Both men looked uncomfortable and were careful not to look round the dining room.

'What was all that about?' Paula asked in a low voice.

'Newman doing his own thing, improvising brilliantly on the spur of the moment. He's shaken the nerve of two of my suspects.'

'And he's dining with the third one.'

'That's right,' Tweed said cheerfully.

Most of the thirty or so guests were drinking coffee in one of the two lounges when Tweed strolled out of the exit into the courtyard with Marler. He then led him round to the terrace to a point where they could stand with the now empty dining room behind them.

He gave Marler special and very detailed instructions, then handed him the field glasses. Marler focused them on the *Venetia*, nodded, handed back the glasses.

'I think you're right,' he said.

'Pity you hadn't got the Armalite.'

'But I have,' Marler assured him 'When we parked our cars in Long Stay at Heathrow I chose a quiet slot. Then I dismantled the Armalite, crawled under the car and attached it to the underside of the chassis with medical tape. At this moment it's resting snugly in the boot of my car parked not thirty feet from where we're standing.'

'It's too late tonight to make arrangements.'

'Dear boy, it's never too late. I have a wad of fifty-pound notes in my back pocket. I'll try the Marina Club down by the harbour first. May be a trifle late to bed. A red pennant at the stern of the craft will enable you to identify me.'

'I'm guessing,' Tweed warned him.

'And in the past you've shown yourself to be a good guesser.'

Marler was getting into his car when Paula, in search of Tweed, saw him. Curious as to where he could be off to at this time of night she went over to him.

'And where might you be off to?'

'Goin' fishin'.'

* * *

Paula was just disappearing round the corner to the terrace as Marler zoomed off when she heard someone coming out of the hotel. Pressing herself against the wall, she watched. Grenville hurried across the courtyard, got into his car, backed it and proceeded slowly up the drive. Seconds later Butler, who had dined with Nield, ran out, dived behind the wheel of his car, drove off.

Wearing her short fur coat, Paula pulled out a pair of kid gloves, was putting them on before joining Tweed on the terrace when Maurice came out, went to his car, started up the engine and in turn disappeared. 'What the hell is going on?' she said to herself.

She turned to go, heard the door to the lounges open yet again. Nield ran out, slipped inside his car and vanished up the drive. Her head was spinning as she walked up to Tweed, told him what she had just seen.

'It was like something out of a film,' she ended.

'Which means Butler and Nield are on top form, despite enjoying a good bottle of wine between them.'

'On top form to do what?'

'To carry out my orders. Butler is shadowing Grenville and Nield is shadowing Maurice. It's logical to presume that now Moloch is back the spy will contact him at Mullion Towers. Some time tonight we'll know who the spy is.'

'Vanity's car has disappeared from the yard,' Paula reported.

'I see,' said Tweed grimly.

When they arrived at Mullion Towers Moloch and Heather were greeted by a short, squat woman with grey hair and fierce-looking eyes. Her mouth above her squarish jaw was a thin line. At the front entrance she gave Heather a brief hostile stare, then her mouth cracked into what Heather presumed must be a smile.

'This is Mrs Drayton, the housekeeper,' Moloch explained. 'Drayton, meet my new assistant, Heather Lang.'

'You'll want your coffee, sir,' Drayton said, ignoring the new assistant.

'In my office, please. We have a lot of work to do. The radio op. is on duty?'

'Carson is always on duty.'

Leading the way, Moloch ran swiftly up a wide curving staircase from the spacious entrance hall to the first floor landing. He pointed to a door.

'That's the powder room if you'd like to use it. My office is the one with green baize cloth on the outside . . .'

Seating himself behind his desk in the small room – Drayton had already switched on all the lights – he opened a file. The windows were uncurtained. Moloch felt shut in if they were closed after dark. He had unlocked the handcuff attached to his briefcase, had perched the briefcase by the side of his chair when Heather walked in.

'I'm ready for work.'

'First, I'm expecting a visitor later this evening. When they arrive I'll want to see them privately. You can go to the communications room, two doors along on the opposite side of the corridor. Wait there until I ask you to come back. You can get to know the radio op., Carson. Unlike Drayton, he's good-humoured.'

'I don't think Drayton likes me. Not that it matters.'

'She's never liked any of my assistants. Some elderly ladies like to think they're running the show, but Drayton is very reliable. Take no notice of her.'

'That shouldn't be difficult.'

As he spoke Moloch had been scribbling a message on a radio pad. He handed it to Heather.

'You can read it. Then take it to Carson for transmission to the *Venetia*.'

Not expected to sail for two weeks. Keep the system running. All hands to remain on board. No shore leave. VB.

'So we shall be here for quite a while,' Heather observed.

'On the contrary, we will be sailing very shortly. That message means the opposite of what it says. The skipper will understand. I expect the signal to be intercepted by GCHQ at Cheltenham.'

'GCHQ?'

'The government signals station. It listens in to all radio transmission. Now we're in Britain I have to assume all our radio messages are recorded by that outfit.'

'I'll take it along now . . .'

Waiting until she had gone, Moloch pressed buttons on his phone. He was calling Nansidwell. When one of the staff answered he asked to speak to one of the guests urgently, giving a name. When the guest came to the phone Moloch's order was brief.

'Get over to my HQ here when you safely can tonight.'

He put down the phone, stood up and stared out of a window into the night. There was a different atmosphere about Mullion Towers and it bothered him. He had never liked Joel Brand but he had always felt secure with Brand in charge of security. Now there were no guards left.

Normally, Brand would have brought a large team of men back with him. They had all been wiped out in California. It gave him an eerie sensation to be alone in the large mansion with only Mrs Drayton and Heather.

The thought crossed his mind that he could have summoned a team from the *Venetia*. He rejected the idea. It was vital that everyone aboard remained on the ship. Any sign of men coming ashore, making their way to Mullion Towers, might draw attention to him.

He went to a large cupboard, opened the doors. Inside

were various clothes, including some outlandish ones. He put on a check peaked cap, then a shabby old raincoat. Looking at himself in a mirror he was surprised at the transformation in his appearance. At that moment Heather returned.

'Oh, I'm sorry,' she began, 'I was looking for—'

Then she stopped, staring at the figure in the peaked cap who was gazing back at her.

'VB! I scarcely recognized you.'

'You've said the right thing. The opposition may be out there. Instead of riding in the Rolls to the harbour we shall use the old Ford Escort in the garage. I would like you to drive it when we leave. Take only one case – you can buy what you like when we reach Beirut.'

'How do we reach the ship from the waterfront?'

'A large launch will be waiting to take us out to the *Venetia*. We go aboard as inconspicuously as possible when the time comes.'

While talking, Moloch divested himself of the raincoat and cap, putting them back into the cupboard. He was glad to observe that Heather accepted this strange development as just part of her job. She was probably the coolest of all the assistants he had hired. Moloch had a shrewd eye for a highly competent woman who, in return for a big salary, would give him loyalty.

'It sounds like good organization to me,' Heather commented. 'And Mrs Drayton has informed me dinner is ready. She said she hoped we wouldn't wait all night when she'd taken the trouble to cook a hot meal.'

'Then let's not wait. The message was sent off by Carson?'

'He sent it as soon as I handed it to him.'

As Moloch descended the curving staircase he found the unnatural silence disturbing. Up to now there would have been guards to greet him respectfully, some of them acting as servants. His footsteps, and those of Heather following him, echoed as he started to cross the wood-block floor of the entrance hall.

Feeling rather stupid, he checked the locks and chains on the heavy front door. What was there to worry about? But for years, once he left his office Moloch had been surrounded with staff, many of them armed. He crossed the hall, entered the large panelled dining room, sat down at one end of the long dining table. He noticed Heather's place was laid at the far end.

'Come and sit next to me,' he told her.

'Does that mean I have to change the seating arrangement?' barked Mrs Drayton who had just come into the room carrying a tureen.

'It does,' Moloch snapped.

'If you'd told me to start with it would have saved time. Is this the way you want me to serve meals in future?'

'It is.'

No point in telling Drayton that this was probably the last meal he would ever eat at Mullion Towers. He must remember to leave her an envelope with money and a note saying her services would no longer be required. He wondered how much Brand used to pay her.

By his side against his chair rested the briefcase he had brought down with him from his office. He only felt safe with it close to him – it was his passport to untold riches in the Middle East.

Heather sensed his unease in the large dining room. She chatted to him, made him join in the conversation. There was a strange atmosphere in the house, she was thinking, but she took care not to refer to it. Why did she feel she was participating in the Last Supper?

They had just finished the meal, were drinking coffee, when the doorbell rang. Drayton, who had just poured more coffee, was about to hurry to the front door when Moloch spoke.

'That will be a visitor I'm expecting. I'll answer the door. You clear up in here. Heather has to send a message from the radio room.'

47

Tweed had become so restless at Nansidwell that Paula had persuaded him to talk to her in her room away from the guests in the lounge who were chattering like magpies about nothing.

The first thing he did when they had entered the room was to go over to the window. Again he focused his glasses on the *Venetia* and the surrounding waters. Paula joined him by his side, placed her hand over the lenses.

'Enough is enough. Sit down in that armchair. I asked the head waiter downstairs to bring us up more coffee.'

'Thank you.'

'Now.' She perched on the arm of his chair. 'I've rarely seen you so on edge. What's it all about?'

'When did Vanity go off in her car?'

'I've no idea. It must have been after dinner. I noticed her car was gone when I told you before.'

'Where is Newman?'

'Again, I've no idea. He may have gone for a walk.'

'Without telling me? That's not like him. I saw his Merc. is still parked outside.'

'Is that all that's worrying you?' she asked softly.

'No. Moloch has to be stopped from leaving the country. I don't care how we achieve that. Look, I have to call Howard. No one does the right thing when I'm absent.'

At that moment the waiter arrived with more coffee. He poured for both of them. It seemed to Tweed that he was taking for ever to perform this simple function, although actually he was simply providing them with the normal excellent service they had experienced at the hotel.

Tweed reached for the phone as soon as they were alone. He got through to Monica, who immediately transferred him to Howard. Tweed thought it significant that Howard was still at Park Crescent at this late hour. Normally he went off to his club for a drink in the evenings.

'Tweed here. Look, Howard, something drastic has to be done—'

'Is this a safe line?' Howard interrupted. 'Where are you calling from?'

'From where we're staying. Nansidwell Country Hotel. Surely Monica has informed you.'

'Yes, she has. Then I can't discuss anything with you.'

'Why the hell not?'

'Call me from a public phone box.'

'Oh, didn't you know? I carry them around with me in my coat pocket!'

Paula watched as Tweed replaced the phone with such care she knew only will-power had prevented him from slamming it down. She edged his cup of coffee closer to him.

'What happened?'

'The pompous fool clammed up on me.'

'Then it had to be something he could only talk to you about on a safe line. You're the one who is usually so careful about security.'

'You're right, of course,' Tweed agreed, then sipped coffee.

'We could drive to that phone box in Mawnan Smith,' she suggested.

'It may be too late then.' The significance of what she had just said suddenly struck him. 'We haven't any transport.'

'Yes, we have. Newman gave me a spare key to the Merc. a long time ago. In case of emergency.'

'This *is* an emergency . . .'

'He jumped up out of the chair. From his pocket he produced a 7.65mm Walther automatic, a mag. He rammed the mag. into the butt. Paula stared at him.

'Where did you get that?'

'Marler gave it to me. He knows a man outside Truro who can supply handguns – for a price and no questions asked.'

'Marler seems to know illegal weapon suppliers in the most unexpected places all over the world.'

'Part of his job. We must get moving. Give me the key to the Merc.'

'Get moving to Mawnan Smith?' she asked as she delved into her shoulder bag, handed him the key.

'No time for that. You know the way to Mullion Towers – you went with Newman on the raid he launched against the place when we were last here. Can you find it in the dark?'

'Yes, I can.'

'Then get us there. Fast.'

Moloch received his visitor in his office. He took from a locked drawer an envelope, lifted the flap to show the contents. A wad of fifty-pound notes.

'There's forty of them – two thousand pounds. It's only an advance. The chauffeur-driven Rolls outside will take you to Newquay airport in the morning. Catch the first flight from Heathrow which will land you in Beirut. By going on your own no one will associate you with me. I want you to set up a new network of informers. Most Arabs love money. Haggle with promising recruits – they expect that. Contact me at my house in the Lebanon mountains. Everyone knows where it is. You did well here and in California. Do equally well in the Lebanon.'

The visitor checked the number of banknotes, put them in a bag. Moloch made one more remark.

'You probably noticed there was a Tourist air ticket to Beirut. People who travel Tourist are regarded as of no importance. Someone may be watching at Beirut airport.'

The visitor left the room. Both had been standing up when Moloch had handed over the banknotes. He went to the uncurtained window, peered out into the night. Had he been unwise to carry out that transaction with the curtains open?

He went to the side window, peered out again. Who would be about in this isolated spot in the dark? The answer was no one. Moloch clasped both hands together, squeezed them tightly. He had recovered his steel nerve.

Paula navigated for Tweed. The headlights were undimmed as he drove the Merc. across lonely and desolate countryside. Although she had a map in her lap, she rarely referred to it. Even at night she could recall the tortuous route Newman had followed on the afternoon of the raid on Mullion Towers.

'Pretty grim out here, isn't it?' Tweed remarked. 'No sign of civilization.'

'We left that behind when we passed through Mawnan Smith. You could have stopped and used the phone box.'

'No time left for that. I think Moloch could be leaving in the early hours. We've met him. He didn't get to the top of the world by wasting time. At least I have a second string to my fiddle.'

'Who is that?'

'Where do I go here?'

'Turn off to the left. I was just going to tell you. We are close to Stithians Dam.'

'What's that?'

'The end of the world.'

At Mullion Towers Heather had ventured into the large kitchen after checking to make sure Drayton was not about. Inside a cupboard she found a hamper basket. She had just taken it out when Drayton returned.

'What you doin' in my kitchen?' she growled. 'Get out.'

'Mr Moloch wants me to pack a hamper.' Heather smiled at the grim face. 'We need a decent amount of ham sandwiches, apple pie, if available, cutlery, and some fruitcake. I'll get a bottle of wine from the cellar. Oh, and a thermos of hot coffee would come in useful.'

'Would it now? Sure you wouldn't like some caviar? And before you walk off with that hamper I only takes me orders from Mr Moloch himself.'

'Mr Moloch, *himself*, instructed me to ask you to make up the hamper. He's a busy man. We don't want to upset him, do we?'

'You takin' over as housekeeper here?'

'I couldn't possibly do the job half as well as you do. I noticed how well the antique furniture is polished. You make a lovely job of keeping this place nice.'

'Flattery, just cheap flattery . . .'

But Heather saw Drayton taking out a loaf of bread from the large fridge as she left to fetch a bottle from the cellar. Moloch had made no request to her for a hamper but she foresaw a long wait for the launch by the dockside. Although he had said a launch would be waiting she suspected it would need to cross the water from the *Venetia*. His departure was so secretive that she couldn't imagine the presence of a launch by the dockside.

The stone steps down into the cellar were badly worn. She couldn't find the light switch so she used the torch she always kept in her shoulder bag. She found two bottles she thought Moloch would approve of, one white, one red. She was holding on to both of them, had almost reached the top of the steps when she slipped. Both bottles of wine left her hands, she grabbed for the single rail as her body swung through an angle of a hundred and eighty degrees, then sagged as her left leg gave way. When she tried to get up a spasm of pain wrenched at her.

'Drayton!' she called out. 'Drayton! The wine cellar . . .'

'What have you done to yourself?'

It was Moloch's voice. He switched on the light, checked her leg, told her to remain still while he called a doctor. In fifteen minutes Dr Brasenose arrived. He wasn't keen on night calls but the inducement of a fee of two hundred pounds in cash brought him quickly.

'I've bandaged her up,' he told Moloch later, looking at the couch where he had carried his patient. 'She has a fracture – not compound, I'm glad to say. But she needs rest and attention in a private hospital. I can arrange that now.'

'How long for?' asked Heather, white-faced.

'Two weeks at least. Can't be sure until we see how you progress.'

'I have to go abroad.'

'Only when you have completely recovered.'

'Reluctantly, I agree,' decided Moloch. 'When you're fit you can come out and join me.' He frowned to stop her mentioning the destination. 'The Rolls will drive you to Heathrow. I'll arrange for a First Class ticket for your flight from there. Now, Brasenose, arrange for her to be taken at once to the private hospital.'

Moloch regretted he wouldn't have her company on his trip, but he had acted decisively as he always did.

'Don't worry,' he assured her. 'I can drive myself when I depart for London.'

As she had in the past, Heather marvelled again at Moloch's command of himself, his quick thinking when he had given a false destination.

Checking his watch, Moloch left the room. Hurrying upstairs he changed into the shabby raincoat and the check peaked cap. He glanced again in the mirror to check his appearance.

You look just like a common seaman, he said to himself. If there's a net you'll slip through it like a small fish.

48

Tweed swung slowly round a corner and the narrow road sloped down. He braked, stared in surprise at what lay below.

'What is that thing?'

'That's Stithians Dam. Quite a big one, with a steep drop.'

'The lake – I suppose it must be a reservoir – it's holding back is pretty huge. Again, there's no one about. Not one house since that hamlet we left behind.'

'That,' Paula said, 'was Stithians. What there is of it. And from here you can see – silhouetted against the moonlight on top of that razor-edged ridge – is Mullion Towers.'

'We'd better get on . . .' Tweed paused. 'Look, there's a car coming up towards us.'

'It's Butler's car. I think he has someone with him in the front passenger seat.'

'We'll go and meet him,' Tweed decided.

He drove down the slope, flashing his headlights. Butler's car had stopped, just above the slope leading down to the dam. When Tweed arrived, he stopped, jumped out of the Merc. and went over to the other car. Beside Butler sat Grenville as Butler pointed a Walther at him.

'Why are you holding a gun on him?' Tweed asked.

Grenville was sitting very erect, a savage look on his face. Butler gestured towards him with his head, still holding the gun.

'Here's your spy – or rather, Moloch's spy. I followed him to Mullion Towers. I've got a video camera with me. It has some interesting pictures of Grenville meeting Moloch in a first-floor room. Moloch is handing him a bundle – and I do mean a bundle – of banknotes. I waited outside behind this bastard's car, grabbed him before he could get into it. I searched him. He's got a whole wad of fifty-pound notes in an envelope inside his pocket. Plus a one-way Tourist ticket to Beirut.'

'Beirut? That's pretty conclusive evidence,'

'Just take a look. Come on, Corporal, give.'

Butler, still suffering from the after-effects of jet lag, tried to do two things at once. To extract the envelope, which he succeeded in doing, handing it to Tweed – and to keep his gun trained on his prisoner. Grenville moved with astonishing speed. He grabbed the Walther out of Butler's hand, flung open the door on his side, dived out of the car, dropped the Walther in his haste.

He began to run away from the two cars, down the slope towards the tall dam. Tweed ran down the slope after him, stuffing the envelope in his pocket. He continued running as Paula took off after him, wishing to Heaven she had her Browning.

Grenville reached a low, locked gate leading to the narrow pathway along the top of the dam. He swung over the gate, ran along the pathway with the dense dark reservoir to his right, the steep curving wall of the dam to his left. Tweed was gaining on him when Grenville looked round. At that moment Tweed's foot caught in a rabbit hole. He sprawled on the arid grass face down, winded by his fall. Grenville reached down into his right-hand sock, emerged with his hand holding a small gun.

Standing up, he aimed it point-blank at Tweed's prone body. Paula sucked in her breath in fright. Grenville did not have to be a crack shot to kill Tweed, and he was a military man. He took his time, getting his aim perfect. A shot rang out and Paula felt a chill from head to toe. Then she gazed in disbelief.

Grenville had dropped the gun, was pressing both hands to his chest as he slowly fell forward over the guard rail. His body plunged straight down the side of the dam – over a one-hundred-foot drop. He hit the curving side of the dam halfway down, causing his body to bounce outwards. In the silence of the night there was a loud splash as the body fell into the water at the foot of the dam, vanished under the water's surface.

Looking back up the slope, Paula saw Butler lowering the Walther he had rescued from the grass. It had been a long-distance shot, but she remembered Butler was a marksman with a handgun, that at the training centre in Surrey Butler had come out top in handgun practice.

Tweed climbed back up the slope, joined Paula. Together they went up to Butler, who was looking haggard.

'Thank you is all I can say,' Tweed told him. 'Otherwise I'd have been dead meat.'

'My turn to apologize. I checked him for weapons, but overlooked his socks.'

'And I think Moloch may have left Mullion Towers for his ship,' Paula told them. 'Just before I took off down that slope I saw the headlights of a car below Mullion

Towers. I think it was taking a different route to Falmouth.'

'In that case, back to Nansidwell. I'll drive,' said Tweed.

During their drive through the night Paula examined the contents of the envelope Tweed had handed her. She whistled.

'Grenville had a lot of money. And here's the ticket to Beirut Harry mentioned.'

'Conclusive evidence, as I said. And Grenville was in Cornwall and in California – to set up and run networks for Moloch. My guess is Moloch had instructed him to organize a similar network of informers in the Lebanon. I think the MoD may now open up and tell me his record – when they've seen Butler's video.'

'The Ministry of Defence was evasive, I remember you said. That was before we left Britain. But it looks as though Moloch is going to get clear away.'

'He might. Then again, he might not.'

'I don't see what there is now to stop him.'

'Fate might intervene.'

'You don't usually rely on fate.'

'No, I don't, do I?'

There were still a few people having a quiet drink in the lounges at Nansidwell. After parking the car, Tweed strode briskly on to the terrace. Once more he gazed seaward through his field glasses, focusing them on the *Venetia* and the waters round the vessel.

'Anything happening?' Paula asked.

'No change. I'll probably be up all night watching the ship. You'd better get to bed. It has been rather a full day.'

'I'm not sleepy any more. And I feel hungry again. I could just devour a chocolate sundae. Why don't we watch from my room? It's more comfortable up there.'

'Good idea. So long as I'm not disturbing your beauty sleep.'

They had just walked back to the courtyard when Vanity's car appeared down the drive and parked. She was driving and Newman was sitting alongside her. She was giggling as she got out.

'What have you two been up to – I mean the part you can tell us about?' enquired Tweed.

'We've had such fun,' Vanity said, throwing her arms round him and giving him a great big hug. 'I like you.'

'You're supposed to like me,' Newman retorted. 'We found a most intriguing and obliging pub.'

'He means I've had too much to drink,' Vanity told them with a wicked grin. 'Actually Bob drove there and back. I just took the wheel at the top of the drive. I hoped I'd bump into you, Tweed. Then you'd think I'd been very wicked.'

'You mean you haven't been?' Paula asked with a look of mock innocence.

'I could do with a Grand Marnier,' Vanity said at the top of her voice as they entered the lounge.

'But what would a Grand Marnier do to you?' Newman suggested.

'Let's find out!'

'It will end up with me carrying you up to bed.'

'Can I give a hand?' called out a jolly, red-faced man with a pronounced Yorkshire accent. 'I'm rather good at helping maidens in distress.'

'This one isn't distressed yet,' Vanity told him. 'And what makes you think I'm any longer a maiden?'

There was a burst of laughter, in which Tweed joined, among the guests seated on couches. Paula, seeing a glass of Grand Marnier sitting at the edge of the bar, strode forward and grabbed it, bringing the glass back into the lounge. As she sat down to sip it while Vanity glared at her in pretended fury, Paula saw Maurice with an empty champagne glass in front of him. Nield was sitting in the other lounge, grinning.

'Maurice, you've got an empty glass,' Paula said as she went over to him. She drank half her Grand Marnier, then tipped the rest into his glass. 'Bottoms up, down the hatch—'

'And all that jazz,' Vanity added merrily. 'Look what I've found perched on the bar.' She held up a glass of Grand Marnier. 'There's a magician hiding behind that bar.'

'I am going to have to carry you up those stairs,' said Newman, and sighed loudly. 'The things I do for England.'

'Had we better get up to my room so you can watch that ship?' Paula whispered to Tweed in a very sober voice.

'Good idea. We get VB before dawn or not at all.'

'Want me to come?' Newman asked in a quiet, serious tone.

'I told you to look after Vanity,' Tweed replied with assumed sternness.

'I don't understand where Vanity comes into all this,' Paula said as they mounted the staircase.

'If she comes into it at all.'

'Oh, we're back to playing hard to get . . .'

Moloch, wearing the shabby raincoat and the peaked cap, was close to the waterfront of Falmouth. At that hour the town, hemmed into its valley, was deserted. He drove the Ford Escort slowly along Market Street, then stopped once again to make sure he was not being followed. He had done this half a dozen times during his journey from

Mullion Towers. By his side on the passenger seat was the briefcase, complete with chain and handcuff.

As he listened, he heard the most nerve-racking noise break the silence. Peering up out of his window he saw the source of the terrible screeching which got on his nerves. A row of huge seagulls, perched on a gutter above several buildings, was looking down at him as though about to swoop in a concerted attack.

He pursed his thin lips, thinking he'd like to shoot the whole row of birds. After glancing several times in his rear-view mirror, he drove on a short distance, then swung left under an archway down a ramp leading to the water's edge.

Stopping the car, he flashed his headlights four times, then switched them off. Now all he had to do was to wait. The launch which would take him to the *Venetia* was moored a distance out to avoid attracting attention. It would take a little while before it berthed at the bottom of the ramp to take him aboard.

Moloch found the waiting a test of endurance. Normally so active, he hated sitting in the car, unable to do anything. He picked up the briefcase, attached the handcuff to his left wrist, and then there was nothing to do but wait in the exposed position he felt himself to be in.

He wished he had Heather with him. She would have helped him to pass the time. It had been bad luck that she had slipped on the steps of the wine cellar. Anyway, he told himself, that's the last of my bad luck. Out at sea they seemed to be having trouble getting the engine of the launch started. He began to worry that they might never get it moving. That would be a disaster. He was anxious that the *Venetia* should slip away into the open sea while it was still dark. He forced himself to be patient.

*   *   *

In his stationary powerboat, Marler, anchored close in to the shore where he had a wide view of the *Venetia*, sat with a fishing rod held in both hands. Unlike Moloch, he could wait for hours without fretting.

Much earlier, he had driven down to the Marina Hotel at the edge of the harbour, a large white building on two levels with a staircase leading up to the restaurant. Parking his car, he had mounted the staircase, wearing oilskins he had purchased from a nearby shop selling fishing tackle. He had also purchased a rod and other equipment a fisherman needed. Hoping no one would notice, he had left his golf bag in the cloakroom, accepting a ticket.

'I'm willing to pay good money to hire a powerboat,' he had mentioned at the bar with a glass of beer in front of him.

'Might try Ned. The big man further along the bar. But he'll charge you. All depends on whether he likes the look of you,' the barman had informed him.

Marler had decided to talk in his normal upper-crust voice. This might give Ned confidence that he could afford to pay whatever price was asked.

'The barman said you were Ned,' Marler had begun, placing his glass of beer on the counter. 'I'm looking for a powerboat to hire.'

'Cost you – just supposin' I decided to oblige you. What you be wanting a powerboat for?'

'I'm an international photographer. I've been commissioned by *Time* magazine to take pics of the Cornish coast at night. The moon is up, so this would be an ideal time.'

'I've heard of *Time* magazine. Anyone who works for them makes a packet.'

'I survive.'

'You won't get one anywhere else at this time of night. And I'm relaxing. Shop's closed, so to speak.'

466

'What would it cost to open it up?'

Ned, who towered over Marler, gave him another look, took a drink of his own beer, then named an exorbitant price.

'That includes a deposit?'

'That's extra.'

Ned named another outrageous price. Marler nodded, drank a little more of the beer he hated. He pretended to be considering the amount.

'I'll need identification and references, too,' Ned added.

Marler reached into his pocket, brought out a wad of banknotes, counted them, pushed them along the bar.

'There are your references.'

He was thinking he could almost buy the powerboat for the amount Ned was asking. He waited while Ned carefully checked the money. He waited again while Ned finished his glass of beer. Never hurry locals in Cornwall.

'Because you looks like a gentleman I'll do you a favour, let you have the powerboat until dusk tomorrow. Follow me.'

The large sum of money had vanished inside Ned's worn sleeveless leather jacket. Which is how Marler came to be sitting in the powerboat hour after hour, his fishing rod gripped in both hands. The golf bag lay out of sight on the deck. The funny thing was Marler had no interest in either fishing or playing golf.

49

Tweed was peering through his field glasses again from the window in Paula's room. He had drunk two cups of coffee, had left a refill untouched. Paula felt she would like to confiscate the binoculars.

'Probably nothing will happen tonight – or rather this morning. It's well after midnight.'

'If you want to get some sleep that's all right by me,' Tweed said amiably. 'I'll go down on to the terrace.'

'I'm not the least bit sleepy. I wonder how Newman and Vanity are getting on.'

'You shouldn't ask questions like that.'

He had just spoken when there was a tapping on the door. Unlocking it, Paula found Newman outside, invited him in.

'Come in and join the party. The night watch goes on.'

Newman grinned and walked over to stand next to Tweed. He took the glasses handed to him, examined the *Venetia* from stern to bow.

'I'd say that something is happening,' Newman commented.

'What's going on?' Paula called out as she dashed over.

'Look for yourself. There's a lot of crew moving about on deck. At this hour I find that unusual, prophetic.'

'They do seem very active,' she agreed, focusing the glasses. 'Almost as though they're getting ready to set sail.'

'We need a better vantage point,' Tweed decided. 'Bob, I'd like you to drive me back along the coast so you can park under that big hotel facing seaward. We'll have to be quick.'

'Wait for me,' said Paula, putting on her fur coat. 'It will be chilly down there on the front.'

Unlocking the front door to the exit from Nansidwell was like solving a cipher. Newman was fiddling with the bolt when Paula pushed him aside.

'Let me do it. I watched the proprietor locking up when we were last here. He showed me how to get out.'

In no time at all she had the door open. They ran to Newman's car. Tweed sat next to him as Paula dived into the back. Newman revved up before backing and turning up the drive.

'You'll have woken up everyone in the place,' Paula scolded him.

'We all sleep too much,' he replied.

Tweed sat in silence while they were driven down the hill and past the marshes on their left. In a few minutes they were moving along the front. Newman parked below the large hotel Tweed had mentioned.

'You see,' Tweed told them as they stood on the pavement above the sea, 'we have a ringside view.'

Paula inwardly agreed he was right. They were gazing out across a sea as calm as the proverbial millpond and the centrepiece was the great yacht, ablaze with lights.

'I'm waiting for a launch to leave that ship to pick up Moloch from the harbour,' Tweed remarked. 'Unless we've missed that while we were driving here from Nansidwell.'

'I doubt if we've missed anything,' Paula told him, 'considering the speed with which Bob drove us down here. He seemed to think he was competing in the Grand Prix.'

'I did that once,' Newman replied. 'Came in eighth. You have to practise at anything if you're going to come out tops. Look at the way Marler goes down to the firing range in Surrey at every opportunity.'

'By the way, where is Marler?' Paula enquired.

'Mooching around somewhere, I imagine,' Tweed said.

'Mooching around under your instructions, I'm sure.'

Like Tweed, Marler was also expecting some kind of launch to leave the *Venetia* to pick up Moloch, assuming he was sailing from Falmouth that night.

Anticipating that it would be a cold job, Marler wore several woollen pullovers under his suit and oilskins. By now his gloved hands were freezing. To keep his fingers agile, he made a point of taking off his gloves at intervals and wrapping his hands round one of the coffee flasks he had brought with him. Then he would drink some of the hot coffee.

As he did so he studied the decks of the *Venetia*. Like Newman, he had observed the constant activity. To keep his presence secret he had resisted the temptation to use his monocular glass. For all he knew, men with powerful binoculars on board were scanning the shore for any sign that they were being watched.

He doubted whether they could see him, tucked away as he was under the lee of the outer harbour. Behind him rose a row of whitewashed houses with grey tiled roofs. There were no lights on in any of the houses at that time of night.

Occasionally he would slip inside the control cabin, where he had earlier closed the curtains. He sat by a small gap he'd left between them, smoking a king-size while he watched. Then he returned to the outside world and his fishing rod.

How would I try to sneak aboard that ship if I were Moloch? he mused. The best bet, he decided, was to take out a large craft filled with a party of hired revellers. In this way Moloch could conceal himself among the crowd.

Holding the fishing rod, he settled down to wait. So many men would eventually have found such a vigil getting on their nerves. Not so Marler, accustomed to his own company. Patiently, he waited.

Someone else, not two miles away from where Marler waited, was having more trouble controlling his impatience. Seated in the Ford Escort, he kept the engine running to maintain some degree of warmth inside the car. Moloch had an urgent desire to get out, to walk up and down the ramp, but he forced himself to resist.

What infuriated him was the time the men aboard the launch were taking to get the engine to start. If Brand had been aboard, he reflected, he'd have got it started at once – because Brand would have checked the engine beforehand, would even have had a second launch in reserve.

'I'm the richest man in the world,' he said to himself, 'and here I am, parked in an old car in the cold, unable to do anything but sit and stare.'

He wished he had brought Heather Lang's hamper with him, but in his haste to leave Mullion Towers he had forgotten about its existence. He felt hungry when he recalled seeing Drayton cutting ham sandwiches in the kitchen while the doctor examined Heather. He was also beginning to feel very thirsty – and not a damned thing inside the car to drink.

He comforted himself by clasping the briefcase nestling in his lap. Inside was the equivalent of many times the value of the Crown jewels. And still he had to wait for the launch to start moving. Already it was the longest night he could remember.

I'll sack the man in charge of that launch, he thought viciously. Put him ashore without any money at some place like Naples.

Earlier he'd had the radio on, turned low, but had then decided it might give away his presence. Reluctantly he had turned it off. The only sound then was the gentle splash of the sea swishing at the bottom of the ramp. It did nothing to curb his growing impatience.

'No sign yet of Moloch going aboard,' said Newman, standing on the front. 'Unless he's already aboard. It

471

could have happened while we were driving from Nansidwell.'

'I don't think so,' said Tweed. 'If that was the case the vessel would have started moving by now.'

Paula was walking up and down the front, stamping her frozen feet to get the circulation moving again. Her gloved hands were inside the pockets of her fur coat. There was no one else about. Since arriving they had seen no traffic pass along the road behind them.

Newman started banging his gloved hands together, his field glasses looped round his neck. It was surprising how cold it was at that hour. He put it down to the fact that they were standing on the edge of the motionless sea.

And, he said to himself, the real trouble is we were in California just long enough to get used to the heat.

Only Tweed seemed unaffected by the waiting, by the cold. He stood in his raincoat quite still, like a Buddha contemplating eternity. It reminded him of the old days when he was in hostile territory in a foreign land, waiting in the night for a certain figure to emerge from a building.

'Sooner or later it will happen,' he said as Paula returned. 'And when it does I expect all hell to break loose.'

'It would make a change,' Paula commented.

'Wait until you experience it,' Tweed warned. 'It could be a little too dramatic for your liking . . .'

50

Moloch could hardly believe it. The launch was proceeding to the ramp, its engine chugging over happily. He flashed his lights again, turned off the motor, left the car. Standing at the top of the ramp he glanced round. No one else was in sight. He pulled his cap down further over his high forehead, marched down to the water's edge, his briefcase in his right hand, the cuff attached to his wrist.

The launch edged its way in, paused close to the ramp so that Moloch could step aboard. Brushing aside a helping hand, Moloch sat down on a seat near the stern. He looked up from under the peaked cap. There were only two other men aboard.

'Morton, are you in charge of this fiasco?'

'Yes, sir. I wouldn't call it a fiasco. Had a bit of trouble getting the engine to fire.'

So, later, it would be Morton who was put ashore at Naples without a penny in his pocket. He'd find he was marooned in a tough city.

'Why only two to crew this launch?' Moloch demanded.

'Orders were we had to make sure we were not conspicuous, sir.'

'Can the other crewman handle this launch?'

They were already moving towards the exit from the harbour and the open sea. The launch was not moving with any speed, but this at least Moloch approved of. A craft rushing back to the *Venetia* might have attracted attention.

'No, he can't,' Morton replied as he handled the wheel, guiding it past the huge repair dock. 'This is Gunner. He's called that because he handles one of those special weapons we have aboard under canvas.'

'I see.'

Moloch did see. It meant that if anything had happened to Morton his mate, Gunner, would have been useless handling the launch. Brilliant organization! Once again he found himself missing Joel Brand. Now, huddled in his seat, he was gazing round to see if anyone was observing their departure. The harbour had a sinister stillness. Even a large freighter at anchor was showing no sign of movement. The scene reminded Moloch of a frozen tableau. Only port and starboard lights indicated this was a real harbour.

'Is the skipper ready to sail?' he asked.

'Has been for several hours. Once you're aboard we can sail the seven seas. I don't even know our destination.'

'Then the skipper has kept his mouth shut. Any sign of the ship being watched?'

'None at all, sir. At this time of night most folk are in their beds. Frankly, begging your pardon, I wish I was.'

Moloch kept a retort which sprang to his mind to himself. He needed this cretin to get him safely aboard. By now the launch had reached the exit and the *Venetia* came into view. It seemed to Moloch further out than he had expected. Which was probably a good thing – it meant the ship could sail into the open sea more swiftly.

He watched the huge vessel coming closer and closer. As the launch drew near, a staircase was slung over the starboard side to receive its master. In the moonlight it looked to be the most beautiful vessel in the world. As the launch bumped alongside the landing stage Morton warned his passenger to wait until the launch was securely moored.

As if I'd take a chance now, Moloch said to himself.

He reached up to adjust his cap which was tight round his head. The skipper, a Greek, was waiting to help Moloch on to the platform at the foot of the steps.

'Welcome aboard, sir. We are ready to sail when you give the order. The Harbour Master has been informed of our destination.'

'Good.'

Moloch stepped on to the platform, aided by the skipper. He had reached the top of the staircase when he decided he could stand wearing the tight cap no longer.

Reaching up with his left hand, he took hold of it, tossed it into the water. Then he hurried to his stateroom. The moment he entered the luxurious apartment he tore off the shabby raincoat, threw it into a valuable Ali Baba pot which served as a trash bin.

Now, for the first time in hours, he felt safe. But until the vessel sailed he kept the briefcase chained to his wrist. On an antique table, laid with a fine lace cloth, was an array of the finest drinks. The engines were humming, causing a faint vibration, as the skipper entered the room.

'A double Scotch, sir? With ice?'

'Just straight. No ice, no water.'

He was glad to get away from the iniquitous American habit of serving drinks with icebergs. They had, of course, no idea that it killed the taste of the drink.

'Thank you,' he said to the skipper. 'Pity you couldn't join me.'

'Never on duty, sir. There is the menu. A waitress, very good-looking, will come to take your order when you press the bell. Now, if you'll excuse me, I must hurry to the bridge.'

Aboard his powerboat, Marler had watched with interest then with growing disappointment as the launch came into view, headed for the *Venetia*. Through his monocular glass he had studied the three men inside the craft. At the stern was huddled an obvious working man, wearing a scruffy raincoat and an old peaked cap. Presumably a member of the crew being taken aboard.

Later, still watching through the monocular, he frowned as he saw the staircase lowered over the side of the big yacht. A stocky man in a blue blazer and a nautical cap was descending the staircase to receive the new arrival. To Marler he had all the appearance of being the skipper.

Why all the ceremony? he said to himself.

But for this incident, he might have lowered his glass. Instead, he continued to focus it on the launch's arrival at the platform. He followed the ascent of the crew member up the staircase, then stood very still. Through the glass he saw the cap being thrown over the side, exposing the face of the man who had worn it, the high forehead, the pale face.

He had a flashback to Grenville's party in California, to the time when he had stayed in the background, watching Moloch sitting at a corner table. He gave a low whistle.

'That was clever, chum. You damned near got away with it.'

'Vincent Bernard Moloch has just boarded the *Venetia*,' Tweed reported to his companions as he held the field glasses glued to his eyes. 'He arrived dressed as a workman, but then got overconfident at the last minute. He threw his cap overboard and I had a clear view of him.'

'He's going to get away,' Paula protested. 'I can hear the very faint hum of the engines starting up.'

'We'll just have to go after him in Beirut,' Newman responded.

'Not a healthy place these days, the Lebanon,' Tweed warned.

'Then, as Paula said, he's slipped through our clutches. Bet he never returns to Britain.'

'No, he won't,' Tweed agreed. 'He'll make the Thames Valley the new Silicon Valley of the world – which will give him even more power.'

'It's so frustrating,' Paula snapped. 'After all the risks we took in California.'

'And over here,' Newman reminded her.

'So evil triumphs,' Paula groaned. 'I feel so helpless –
just standing here and watching him sail away.'

'Unless, of course,' Tweed remarked, the glasses still
pressed against his eyes, 'my secret weapon works . . .'

Inside the control cabin of the powerboat Marler had
started up the engine. He was careful not to make any
dramatic dash towards the *Venetia*, which would have
attracted attention immediately.

Instead he manoeuvred the powerboat out into the
open sea slowly, chugging along at a sedate pace. At that
moment he had a bit of luck. Another powerboat, driven
by a young man who had two girls on board, came racing
round Rosemullion Point, tearing towards the harbour,
close to the *Venetia*.

The girls aboard were waving bottles, clad only in
skimpy swimsuits despite the cold. As they were passing
the yacht they threw the empty champagne bottles
against the hull. One of them waved her fingers in a
suggestive gesture at members of the crew peering over
the rails.

'Stoned out of their skulls,' Marler said to himself.

But he took advantage of the diversion to edge his
powerboat closer to the yacht. He was still careful to keep
his distance. His approach had so far gone unnoticed –
the crew were too interested in the girls aboard the racing
powerboat, now zigzagging across the water, leaving
behind a snake of ruffled surf.

Marler cut his engine out. Leaning down, he extracted
from the golf bag the Armalite rifle it had concealed.
Attaching the sniperscope, he then inserted an explosive
bullet into the weapon, laid it along a banquette, and
waited.

* * *

'That ship is escaping,' Paula said bitterly. 'You can see it's on the move. Moloch has made it. Nothing can stop him now.'

'Listen,' said Tweed.

The silence of the night was broken by the beat-beat of aircraft engines. Three helicopters appeared from an inland direction. One by one they swooped low over the retreating vessel, so low they were barely above the level of the complex radar system perched on top of the mast above the bridge.

'The crew is removing the canvas covers from those mysterious objects on the decks,' Tweed reported, holding the glasses to his eyes. 'Oh, my Lord, they have ground-to-air missile launchers.'

Appalled, he watched as two of the helicopters returned to buzz the vessel again. One was diving low over the sea when they all heard a sinister *whoosh*! A missile had been fired off the deck, it struck the incoming helicopter. The machine turned sideways, nose-dived into the sea. Paula watched with growing horror as the second helicopter tried to take evasive action. There was a second *whoosh!* The helicopter turned over sideways, its main rotor blown to pieces, then it soared downwards, hit the water with a tremendous splash, vanished under the sea.

'Moloch has gone mad,' Newman burst out.

Paula was watching the third helicopter, further away. It had time to turn away, heading out to sea before it curved and disappeared inland. There was a sense of deep shock as Tweed and his companions watched the *Venetia* getting up speed. Newman was the first to break the silence.

'Those were choppers from Culdrose, the RAF training base for trainee pilots. Culdrose is an airfield beyond Constantine – it's near the top of the Lizard.'

'See that powerboat with the red pennant at its stern?' Tweed said. 'It has Marler on board.'

'What on earth can he do?' Paula asked vehemently. 'Not a thing. I notice he's keeping his distance from the *Venetia*. Thank Heaven for that. Let's hope he keeps away.'

'So that was what Howard was keeping from me on the phone,' Tweed said quietly. 'The MoD had ordered helicopters to buzz the ship. They didn't know it was heavily armed with missile launchers. It's a tragedy. Young pilots uselessly slaughtered so that man can build up even more power.'

'I can hear a different kind of aircraft coming,' Paula told them. 'Its engine sounds so different from those of the choppers . . .'

She stopped speaking as an advanced supersonic warplane appeared from high up in the sky. Tweed guessed it had been standing by, had been summoned by the third chopper which had escaped. Moving with incredible speed the new plane suddenly started to descend from a great height. Tweed caught sight of it for a brief moment in his glasses.

'It's armed with missiles—' he began.

He stopped speaking as they all heard a more high-pitched *whoosh!* A missile from the supersonic plane landed in the water, no more than fifty yards from the bow of the *Venetia*. Exploding, it erupted a huge column of water near the ship.

'A deliberate miss, that one,' Tweed said. 'What they used to call a shot across its bows . . .'

Inside his stateroom aboard the vessel Moloch had seen the missile land close to the *Venetia*. He jumped up from the table so suddenly he upset his meal. With the briefcase dangling from his wrist, he ran out and up a companionway on to the deck where a Sikorsky rested on its helipad. Climbing the ladder, he leapt through the doorway the co-pilot had opened when he saw him coming.

'Get me off this vessel *now!*' he shouted. 'You have extra fuel tanks so you can reach France. Roscoff is your destination. We'll radio ahead for a car to pick me up. But for God's sake get this thing into the air!'

Marler had stood in the stern of his powerboat, watching everything that had happened through his monocular glass. He had even seen Moloch scrambling up the ladder with the briefcase chained to his wrist. Time to take a hand in the proceedings.

He opened up the throttle and the powerboat surged forward, only slowing down, then stopping when he was much closer to the hull of the *Venetia*. The skipper of the luxury yacht, scared witless by the missile which had landed just ahead of his bows, slowed the engines, then stopped the ship.

Marler calmly picked up his Armalite, went towards the stern, perched the barrel of the rifle on the top of the cabin, looked through his sniperscope. The rotors on the Sikorsky were whirling madly. It suddenly took off, climbing vertically up from the helipad.

Marler elevated his rifle. The crosshairs closed on one of the extra fuel tanks. The Sikorsky was hovering for a few seconds, prior to flying off out over the sea. Marler pressed the trigger. The explosive bullet burst inside the fuel tank.

There was a terrific explosion, heard onshore. Fire engulfed the Sikorsky, turned it into a fireball. It fell as it had risen. Vertically onto the deck close to a missile which had not been fired. There was a second even more tremendous detonation. The Sikorsky vanished inside the scorching flames which soared up the full length of the vessel. The exploding missile had torn a huge hole in its starboard side. The *Venetia* was transformed into an even more gigantic fireball from stem to stern. Slowly, it heeled over to starboard. There was a terrible hissing, boiling sound and then the ship sank, vanishing altogether.

Epilogue

At Park Crescent everyone was present except for Vanity, who was waiting in Newman's car by the kerb outside the front door.

'I've had a long chat with Vanity,' Tweed explained. 'She said she'd prefer to wait outside. She's really a very modest lady. And she is a lady. That story about how she had prowled the States, living with one rich man after another, was only a cover story. It gave her charisma to become Moloch's assistant. Cord Dillon cooperated fully. He was responsible for her apparently not having any real identity. Cord and I decided that was the best way to protect her.'

'Protect her?' queried Paula.

'Yes. She is actually one of the bravest undercover agents I have ever dealt with. Her father was English, her mother French. Which is how she came to work for counter-espionage in Paris. I borrowed her because she was least likely to be known in America. She was Hoarse Voice.'

'You mean,' Monica said in a tone of amazement, 'that you had infiltrated her inside Moloch's organization?'

'I, with Cord's help, did exactly that. Which explains why, whenever I met her, I ignored her, appeared to dislike her. More cover for her. And Cord arranged, unofficially, for Alvarez to continue helping us. Vanity warned me, among many other things, about the Xenobium bomb.'

'Now happily, I assume, non-existent,' Marler drawled.

'That's right. You told me Moloch carried aboard the Sikorsky a briefcase chained to his wrist. I'm sure that contained the know-how for making the bomb.'

'What about Grenville?' Paula asked. 'Why was the Ministry of Defence so close-mouthed about him?'

'My contact there at last agreed to be frank. Grenville was a major in the Channel Regiment. He was thrown out quietly for embezzling large sums of money. The Army never did like its dirty linen being washed in public – or even in private.'

'And the mysterious Maurice?' Paula persisted.

'He was unofficially on leave. Actually his job was to find out what Moloch was up to. He's returning to his old job with them.'

'He's asked me out to dinner.'

'I should accept,' Newman said with a smile.

'I'll think about it. I wonder how Mrs Benyon is getting on?'

'She's settling down in Cheltenham very quickly,' Tweed said. 'I had a long chat with her on the phone. She's rejoined a bridge club and several charities she belonged to long ago. I gathered she was very relieved to be back in Britain.'

'Then that about wraps it up,' said Butler, speaking for the first time.

'Not quite. Vanity gave me a list of MPs, et cetera in this country who accepted payments from Moloch, plus another list of senators in the States who accepted even larger sums. I sent it on to Cord. They'll all have to answer some pretty awkward questions. And Cord has found evidence that Joel Brand murdered all Moloch's missing women assistants.'

'But what will happen to AMBECO?' Newman wanted to know.

'I've heard moves are afoot to break up the whole conglomerate. It will probably be sold off bit by bit to other firms. No one will get a big slice of it. Both Washington and London have had enough of too much power in the hands of one huge organization.'

'I'd better get off,' Newman said, standing up. 'Otherwise Vanity will start kicking up.'

'Don't forget her real name is Vanessa,' Tweed warned. 'She was the one who invented Vanity – to build up the false image of herself she had created. And her other name is Julie. So make your choice. Taking her out to dinner?'

'Yes. I know rather a nice restaurant in Paris . . .'

He was followed out by Marler, Butler and Nield. Paula and Monica remained behind their desks.

'So everything is cleared up in the end,' remarked Paula.

'Everything except the catastrophic ravages of the earthquake.' Tweed was glancing at more pictures of the disaster in a newspaper. 'It will take a long time before what Ethan Benyon caused to happen in his madness becomes only a distant memory.'